The Faces

Of Hector

Book 13

Of The Warrior Series
By

Sandra J Yearman

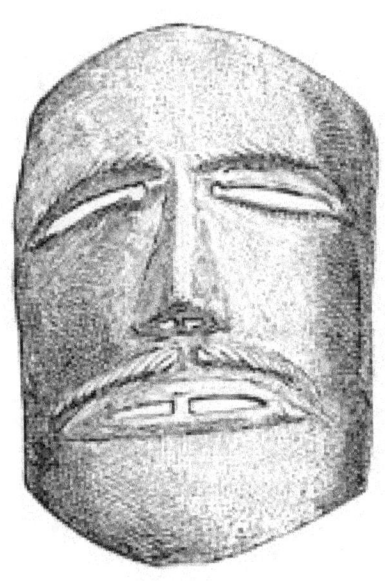

Seraphim Publishing LLC

We Will Bring Light To All The Dark Places

Registered trademark-Sandra J Yearman

Seraphim Publishing
438 Water St
Cambridge, WI 53523
sandrajyearman@gmail.com

Library of Congress Catalog Number: 2017900866

ISBN: 978-0-9984057-1-1

First Edition

About The Author

Sandra J Yearman is a native of Wisconsin, where she currently resides. She graduated from the University of Wisconsin with a Bachelor of Arts degree in Journalism. Sandra was a member of the United States Army Reserves for over twenty years. She retired from the Dane County Sheriff's Office in Madison Wisconsin as a sergeant.

Sandra is a cancer survivor and it is on this journey that she says she found her voice and began to write. She established Seraphim Publishing LLC in 2008. Sandra has spent decades supporting and working with rescued domestic animals.

Books written by Sandra:

Novels

Brother Kings
The Scroll And The Sword
Song Of The Second Son
The Faces Of The Damned
A Single Lion Roars
Stand Before The Children
Tyrants, Dictators And Kings

Politicians And Kings
Armada Of The Dead
The Eyes Below
Illusions And War
Prophesies And War
The Faces Of Hector

Poetry

A Gathering Of Angels
I AM Who You Seek
A Celebration Of Angels
The Time Of Angels Is At Hand
The Warrior On Bended Knees
Celebration of God
On His Wings
The Voice Of An Angel
If I Had Wings
Souls On Fire
As Angels Hover Over
From The Mist The Angels Came
You Are The Song
Be Still
Walking With Angels
When Angels Smile
Angel Dreams
An Angel's Touch
Dancing With Angels

This book is dedicated to those who are trying to save our world.

Contents

Contents

Contents

Chapter I
The Letter

"I love my wife," Noah said as he and Tessa were cuddled under the blankets kissing in the early morning hours.

"And I love my husband," she said then giggled. "That is fun to say. Although I still have to get used to it."

"Tessa, I know we agreed to wait until Othnial returned before we got married. But if you get pregnant before that, I think we should have someone else marry us."

"It really doesn't matter to me when we get married. We can wait for him."

"No, I think I will have a back-up plan."

Tessa laughed loudly. "I don't know why that sounds so funny."

"Last night Rosa said she wanted to give us an engagement party but it would be after Gideon's. While I think that is nice, she asked me a dozen questions that I couldn't answer. You're going to have to talk with her."

"Noah, with everything that has been going on I haven't given one thought to the actual ceremony. Besides, if what we suspect is true, she may not be in the mood to throw a big celebration."

Sudfad had received the letter that identified the person behind Michael's assassination. The man was a Grand Master named Radnor. Sudfad had not spoken with anyone in his household about this information because he wanted to process it first. A regular man he could declare war on but a Grand Master, Sudfad had no idea how to even find him.

Mathas' morning meeting started an hour earlier than usual at the request of Claudius. Dominic's and Turner's teams had moved out of the castle and back into the house they shared.

The team members entered the King's castle as one large group. Seth, Jasmine, Tessa and Noah immediately separated from the rest and walked into the office where Olin and Elexas were already working. Both of these young people now had chambers in the castle.

"Did you find out anything new?" asked Jasmine.

"Last night we went through both of the wedding books which I have to say Elexas enjoyed much more than I did," said Olin and grinned. "Everything looked normal but we noticed that Otto and Ruthie were on both guest lists, which I suppose would be expected. But there were also lists of who gave what gifts; I suppose so they could write thank you notes." As Olin spoke Elexas showed the others the lists.

"Uncle Otto gave Mathas and Rosa a silver tea set which included a huge basket of exotic teas. I have to wonder if there could have been something added to the teas. Especially if Rosa and Mathas weren't used to drinking them they might not notice a change in the flavor."

"Then he gives Josef a large amount of money and Isabella a necklace. Ok, I don't get invited to a lot of weddings but do these seem like unusual gifts?" asked Olin. "To me it sounds like he could be paying Josef off and there is no description of the necklace."

"They are unusual gifts," said Tessa. "Olin, last night Noah and I were talking. He was here when they were interrogating Isabella. They gave her the truth potion and Gideon put her into a trance. Noah says that the right questions have to be asked with both of these procedures. So my question is, could the Master erase some of her memories?"

"Yes, he is very powerful. And apparently the Sanuri is an old friend of this family. The Master would know that the Sanuri has special powers and take precautions."

"She was only thirteen when Juleta was born which means she was eleven or twelve if she helped in some plot against Rosa's first baby. Is it possible she didn't know what she was doing?" Noah asked.

"Of course," said Olin. "So far, we haven't found anything that indicates Isabella wanted to become a witch or dark lord. In fact, Elexas found a couple of entries in her diaries where she says she is afraid of someone because of their magics, but who knows if that is even the truth. Juleta on the other hand seemed driven to find out everything she could about dark magics."

"We need to ask Rosa and Mathas some questions," said Elexas. "But we don't want to give anything away yet."

"I know," said Tessa. "I just feel so bad for them."

Claudius started off Mathas' meeting. "I am sorry to wake everyone up so early but last night the men who have been watching the house of Hector's parents found a body in the back. The house sits on the shore of the ocean and the body was on the shoreline although the person, it was a man's body, was killed on land. We know that because the sand was soaked with blood."

"We have no idea who the man is but he is dressed like a hired killer. After finding the body, our men walked up to the house and found the back door had been kicked in. They went into the house and found the cook dead on the kitchen floor and another man dead on the front stairway. The house had been ransacked. We have no idea of what they were looking for. I am having my men search the place then I will leave a note for Hector after this meeting."

"We were planning on going to Zorta after the weddings but now I will need to hear what Hector has to say. In the meantime, Sorren, Edward, Kate and Edward's team are planning on leaving for Zorta immediately after the wedding ceremonies. They are going to look into businesses in that area. Edward is posing as an investor."

"As you know we have no idea if King Fahra was involved with Juleta or the Insidiae. While he has never taken aggressive action against another kingdom he certainly seems to have a lot of criminals and members of the Insidiae doing business in his kingdom."

"So that is another thing our team is going to be looking into. They may be in Zorta for a while."

Claudius sat down and Matthew stood up. "Turner has not heard from Abbott, so later today we are going to Castor. I have made arrangements for two platoons of soldiers to be there also but they will not be wearing their uniforms. We don't want the Ruala warriors to be seen traveling with us so Gad, Hadu and Bryce will be leaving for Castor right after this meeting."

Rosa entered the room while Matthew was speaking. When he finished she marched to the front of the room and handed Mathas an envelope. "Read this then let me explain before you start yelling," she said in an uncharacteristically defiant manner.

"Rosa, what is going on?" asked Mathas.

"Dear, please just read the letter."

The group sat in silence and watched as Mathas' face turned red from anger as he read the long letter. "I assume that since you gave this to me here that you want the group to be aware of it?" he asked Rosa through clenched teeth.

"I think they have to be," she said. "Do you want to tell them or should I?"

"Oh, let me," Mathas said sarcastically. "This is a letter to Hector. Rosa does chastise him for the man he has become but then she tells him of all the pain that Juleta brought us. She wants him to tell his parents that they have a grandchild." Mathas paused to control himself. "This I would go along with but she also tells Hector that he is Sarah's father and if he wants to see her that Rosa will make the arrangements." Mathas handed the letter to Claudius and everyone could see that the King's hands were shaking.

"Rosa, what the hell are you thinking?" asked Mathas.

"Now it is my turn to explain and please let me say my piece," said Rosa. "I have thought long and hard about everything that Claudius told us about his meeting with Hector."

"I know that Hector is a monster and that our daughter may be directly responsible for that. I also know that Sarah and his parents seem to be the weakness in his armor."

"I am talking to him as a mother and I am the only person in this group who can reach out to him in such a manner. No one ever tried to reach out to Juleta and maybe if someone had; well, some things could have been different."

"Mother, surely you don't think that you can change him?" asked Matthew.

"No but perhaps I can connect with him on some level and if that doesn't bring a change in him then maybe it will benefit us in the long run."

Noah quickly stood up before anyone could speak. "Rosa, you can't do this, at least not yet..."

"Noah, no!" Tessa said loudly. Now everyone in the room turned and looked at Noah and Tessa who were sitting with Dominic's team, Ryan, Olin and Elexas.

"Alright, what is going on?" demanded Mathas.

No one spoke but Jasmine, Seth, Tessa, Ryan, Olin and Elexas all looked at each other guiltily, which everyone in the room saw. Noah was still standing and now the rest of this group stood with him.

"Noah, why did you say that?" asked Rosa.

"We are following some leads," Noah said. "And they could take us to some terrible places. We don't want to say anything until we have proof because what we would say would hurt you."

"Please don't make us tell yet," said Tessa. "Perhaps it will be nothing."

"Does it involve Hector?" asked Mathas as part of him did not want to hear about this information.

"We don't know yet," said Noah. "But if our suspicions are true it could put some of you in more danger. Tessa is right. Please let us return to our work and tell you if we discover facts."

13

"I don't like the sound of this at all," said Claudius.

"Claudius it is really bad," said Ryan. "At least our suspicions are. Really, no one wants to hear about this. If we find out that these things are true we will tell all of you immediately."

"Tell us," said Mathas.

"No," said Tessa. "It will break your hearts and if it is not true we have given you pain for no reason. Please, let us go back to work and try to figure this out."

"You found something in the things I gave you, didn't you?" asked Rosa. No one responded to her question.

"Rosa, what did you give them?" asked Mathas.

"My personal letters and the books of our family and weddings. I thought they could find something and I believe they have."

"I hate to defy you, Mathas," said Noah. "Let us tell Claudius and see what he thinks. I promise you this information will hurt both you and Rosa and if it isn't true, why would we want to do that to you?"

Mathas looked at Rosa then at Claudius. "Noah, tell me can Rosa ask that Clarence and Catherine be told they are grandparents?" asked Mathas.

"Yes," said Noah.

"Rosa, write another letter to Hector and include only that information and tell him that I also agree to that," Mathas said. "Claudius and Matthew, I want you to leave with Noah's group now and hear what they have to say. Then return to me."

When everyone had gathered in Sudfad's study for the morning meeting he stood up and walked in front of his desk. "I received a letter last night that is both disturbing and in a way a relief. I probably should have shown it to my family but I needed to digest it first."

"There are many things in this letter that are rather unbelievable. Please let me tell you the background because that is necessary to tell you about the specific section that affects us. There are many different things that come together here."

"Noah, Tessa and Angus were in a hotel restaurant in Langer when Hector sat down at their table. He told them he wanted to make a deal and almost immediately the Angel Adam started talking to Tessa and showing her images, which apparently he hadn't done before; that is to show her images. Hector wanted to talk to Mathas or Claudius and Adam said to get Claudius and his sons."

"Adam also showed Tessa that Hector was in a great deal of danger and that she and Noah should protect him until he had a chance to speak with Claudius."

"Protect him!" yelled Raul. "Isn't he supposed to be really powerful?"

"Son, please. I am getting to all of that. Hector had a room in that hotel and Adam told Tessa to get him into that room immediately. Angus rode to get Claudius. While interesting the next page isn't important so you can all read it later. When Claudius, Stephan and Thaos walk into the room Thaos punches Hector who falls but makes no attempt to fight."

"Hector tells them that Samael is blocking his transformation into a demon for various reasons. Hector is suffering from the side effects of Juleta's magics and he is weakening; which apparently is why he wants to become a demon. He said he saw the battles in Ganz and saw Miranda. He asked Claudius to ask this Angel to protect his parents and little Sarah. It turns out that he knew about her all along and was watching over her."

"He gave Thaos a pile of papers which contained all of the bounties that Juleta had put on the ruling families. It also contained bounties on team members including Madeline, Javier and Turner's group. Hector had cancelled all of these bounties. Hector said he couldn't cancel the bounties that Andrac had on Madeline and Javier because Andrac wants the information that they stole from Hector in Port Friada instead of money."

"That information involves ongoing experiments with the Second Sons and I will cover that section later. Now this is the part that concerns our family: When Samael put out the information about his Gefrey Games he had a list of what he wanted as entrance fees. Among many other things were The Seven Sons and The Keepers of The Scrolls. Now remember that."

"Ahriman, for those of you who don't know, was a powerful demon and had suspicions of who we were, which we all knew. He owned the souls of Emeric, Banaka, Karzman and Teivel. After Ahriman was taken to the Abyss, Samael conquered that demon world. Samael was a long time enemy of Ahriman's and apparently some in the hell worlds thought that Samael had something to do with Ahriman's demise."

"When Michael, Raul, Simon and Matthew killed Teivel, Samael became convinced that Michael was one of The Seven Sons as did others. Now that you have all of those connections we move on."

"There were thirteen Grand Masters in Opots out of that group, Emeric and Banaka only had one friend and his name is Radnor. He hired the assassins from Salszar to kill Michael as revenge for the deaths of Teivel, Emeric and Banaka and as a way to strike back at Samael."

"Samael took Michael's death as a personal insult and has put out the word that he wants the person behind it. So all the beings that would be hunting us have now been searching for who was behind the attacks. Hector discovered it was Radnor and told Samael. Hector wanted to get on Samael's good side again which he did although Samael is still blocking his transformation. Hector said that while it is impossible for us to find a Grand Master, it is not for Samael. So the attacks will be avenged."

"There is a great deal more in this letter which we must discuss, but we do have a clearer picture of the threats against all of us." Sudfad paused. "Honestly, in a way I am relieved to finally know who killed our son, but in the same breath I am now fearful of attacks against my other sons."

"How do we know that Hector was telling the truth?" asked Simon.

"The Angel Adam said he was," said Sudfad. "Perhaps we should take a break before we go into the rest of the letter." Sudfad could see that all of the women in his family were crying.

Chapter II
The Investigation

Claudius and Matthew followed Noah and his small group into the office. Seth shut the door behind them. The walls were covered with various types of charts and timelines. Olin grabbed two large sheets of paper that were hidden between a wall and a small sofa. He unrolled them on the long table. Jasmine and Elexas got small items and placed them on the corners of the papers to keep them from rolling back up.

"Rosa brought the group a huge pile of personal items. There must have been a hundred letters in a pouch as well as books she was putting together for the family. She put together a book of things as she planned her and Mathas' wedding and started another one for Isabella," explained Noah.

"These books are really fancy with lots of drawings so she said they took her a long time to work on. She said before she finished Isabella's that Isabella had changed and Rosa lost interest in working so hard to give her a gift. Then Rosa forgot about them. Ryan why don't you take it from here."

"You know we have been making charts and timelines of everything because we have been finding so many discrepancies," Ryan said. "And a lot of the discrepancies are between what Isabella wrote in her diaries and other accounts, including interviews."

"Matthew, I know you haven't had time to come in here since you returned but that bedroom on the left is nothing but shelves that are filled with baskets of papers and books that we have gone through. There is just so much information that we had to make the charts to keep things straight."

"We all read the additional diaries that Isabella had hidden in banks. Everyone noticed a huge change in her personality and writing from before she got married to three weeks after she was married. It was like an entirely different person was writing in those books. So we have been concentrating on what could have happened to her during those three weeks. That is what Fahron is looking into too."

"So Tessa, Jasmine and Elexas are reading all of Rosa's letters. Most of which were written when we had those big wars and all the women were home alone. The letters between Rosa and Renya are really emotional and those women told each other everything. That is how we learned that Rosa and Mathas had a baby boy a year before Juleta was born. He died almost immediately of unknown causes."

"I didn't know that," said Matthew.

"It's true," Claudius said.

"Rosa says that she had a healthy pregnancy until the last few weeks. She got sick and doesn't remember much except for constant nightmares about demons," Ryan said. "Tessa was reading that letter and when she told us that part Olin got scared and I am going to let him tell you why."

"Prince Matthew, I used to be a dark lord and I come from a family of witches, warlocks and dark lords. Since I can remember I have heard stories about people having to pay debts with the lives of new born babies, especially sons. Have you been getting letters about everything we have been learning here?"

"Yes," Matthew said softly.

"The Master was part of the original plot of the Second Sons. King Sharonne of Stordt was the person where the line of the evil seed started and he had to pay with the lives of five newborn sons, of course he was getting money and power for this. But it would have been the Master who would have demanded that payment."

"And you think that happened to my brother?" Matthew gasped as the color drained from his face.

"Let me finish please," said Olin. "From the people here we learned that the demons and dark lords have been trying to figure out who The Seven Sons and The Keepers of the Scrolls were for centuries. And some of them suspected your families."

"Then we have all of this information about Juleta. Without going into detail, she was scaring the shit out of people and doing strange things when she was a very little kid."

"People aren't born dark lords, you have to work at it like a college degree. Otto sold Joanna's and Jack's souls when they were babies. They were normal kids who had to work really hard to become powerful. It sounds like Juleta was born with a dark soul. She would have needed a teacher and manuscripts to learn enough to scare people and how and when did that happen when she was a kid?"

"We found out that Uncle Otto requested an audience with Juleta when she was thirteen. An audience! Uncle Otto; are you kidding me; he was so arrogant. The only being he bowed to was the Master. None of this has been making sense. Unless, the Master or someone else put into place a plot to curse this family that is suspected of being the people of prophesy. The Master could easily do it but he would need someone on the inside to bring him things like some of Rosa's hair. Isabella was living here at the time."

"I need to sit down," Matthew said. Noah poured several glasses of whiskey and passed them around.

"So with the information I just told you, all of us in here started really looking at all of this information differently. For the Master or whoever to work these kind of magics he would have started before the first baby was born. So the first son dies mysteriously and the second child is like a demon incarnate," Olin said.

"These timelines on the table are what we are working on. We had been concentrating on Isabella and the time frame of her marriage, now we went back to before Rosa and Mathas had their first baby."

"Claudius, you fought in those wars and they sounded horrible. It sounds like everyone who wasn't fighting was doing something to help. Mathas seemed to be at his castle more than you and Fahron but he was still gone a lot too."

"Now, this information we got from letters and diaries: Isabella was young and already jealous of her older sisters so it sounds like she latched onto Rosa in the beginning. But with the war and other things Rosa didn't have as much time for Isabella."

"In fact, Rosa writes that she feels guilty because sometimes she doesn't see Isabella for days at a time."

"Then Isabella starts to write about her anger towards Rosa for ignoring her. All of you know of Isabella being an insecure person but she was also very angry. She writes about leaving the castle for days at a time then getting pissed because no one even noticed that she was gone."

"She writes about meeting a group of traveling people, she called them gypsies. She thought they were exciting. She would stay with their group and drink and dance and she had her first sexual encounter with them. She wrote about getting so drunk that she would wake up and not remember the night before."

"These people told her she had to pay to become one of them and she says she would come back to the castle and steal things, bags of things and give them to these people. Renya and Tasha were already gone and for some reason Isabella wasn't as angry at Mathas as the others; so she stole a lot of things from Rosa. Jewelry, clothes, a silver comb and a silver hairbrush among other things. She lists what she stole but she doesn't say if the people she called gypsies requested these specific items."

"Then she writes that she wakes up after getting drunk with her friends and the entire gypsy camp is gone. She is lying on the ground on a blanket. This made her feel even more betrayed and she is really angry for a long time. Jasmine do you want to talk about what you found?"

"Well, we know that Isabella started going to the orgies right after she was married and that she took Juleta to them. We also know that both Isabella and Juleta had sex with the same men and women and both became very involved with Joanna. But we thought that started after Isabella was married. Now, Isabella doesn't write a word about being friends with Joanna prior to that but Rosa writes several times how happy she is that Isabella finally seems to have a friend. That she is spending a lot of time with Joanna Franks."

"Matthew, I don't know if you have read any of the diaries they found in the banks but Isabella goes into so much detail about every little thing, like her meals that it was driving all of us nuts."

"So why wouldn't a lonely teenage girl write that she had a friend? Rosa said they spent a lot of time going shopping and eating in restaurants. Isabella doesn't write a single word about any of that."

"Olin forgot to tell you," said Seth. "That spells or plots or whatever can be made so they happen at all different times. So say something happened to Isabella when she was with those gypsies, which by the way was before the first baby was born; the spell could affect her later in life."

"We have found so much contradicted information between Isabella's diaries and other sources that we believe the diaries, at least later in her teens might have been written with the purpose of someone finding them. But we don't know who or why."

"Let me stop you here," said Claudius. "I just want to make sure that I am following your lines of thought. Are all of you thinking that Juleta was planted into this family to destroy it and maybe Sudfad's?"

"Yes," said Tessa. "And we think that Isabella helped. But she may not have really understood what she was doing at first. And from what I have heard, it sounds like Juleta was trying to destroy her family."

"We keep uncovering little things," said Ryan. "For example. Olin just found the guest and gift lists from Mathas' and Isabella's weddings. Otto and Ruthie attended both. Otto gave Mathas and Rosa a silver tea set and a huge basket of exotic teas. Olin said something could have easily been put into those teas. Then Otto gives Josef a bunch of money, five large bags of gold coins to be exact and gives Isabella a necklace that is not described. Does it sound like he may have been paying off Josef? And that necklace that Olin had was the brand of the Master and he didn't even know it."

"Noah, hand me that bottle of whiskey," Claudius said. "I need to think about this for a moment." He poured more whiskey into his glass and gulped it down. "Did you find more big things?"

"No," said Noah, "But we only discovered this the day Matthew came home. So everything we learned has been in the last three days. We have a lot more work to do."

"Claudius, it would really help if we could ask Rosa some questions but none of us want to tell her about this," said Elexas.

"I agree, I don't think we should tell her yet," said Claudius. "What do you think Matthew?"

"I don't want to tell either of them at all."

"But this is who we are going to tell," said Claudius. "I will send Stephan and Thaos home to get Bella and you tell her what you told us. I am sure that she can answer a lot of your questions. Bella was in a carriage accident and lost a baby she was carrying. She and Rosa took a lot of comfort in each other. But we need to tell Fahron because his investigation could actually be part of this."

"Claudius, can we pull all of these people out of their other duties and have them just concentrate on this for now?" asked Matthew. "Then I think we tell Father that we are forming a group just to research these leads. You will be the head person. I will be on it too. I would like to bring Angelina or Shara in since they are healers, after what Ryan said about those teas."

"Sorren will be going to Zorta with Edward but let's bring him in. He may know a lot about what happened during that time frame. I would like Stephan and Thaos in on this too because they know everyone who is involved but should we since they have their weddings coming up?"

"They've already done their preparations," Claudius said. "Now the women have taken over. I agree with everyone you have suggested. I think both Angelina and Shara should join us. The only thing I can't decide is if we should say anything to Mathas."

"Please don't," said Matthew. "The voice in my head is telling me this is probably all true but he was so hurt by both Juleta and Isabella. Let's wait until we know more."

Claudius looked at the young people standing before him. "You do know that Mathas is not used to being told no. I think the looks on your faces made him fearful of what you would say. It took guts for all of you to do what you did. And you were right. It is not the time to tell them of this. You also are doing a great job on all of this. I will reward you."

"I think we would just all like to find out that none of this is true," said Tessa. "They are such nice people and they have already been through so much. Matthew if you haven't read these letters you should, some of them made us cry."

"I need to change the subject a second, before you leave," Olin said. "Claudius, you know my father sent me here to kill Sam Endleson. I haven't been in contact with him since. I handle the family finances and those books are at my mother's house. What do you want me to do?"

"Well, I guess first you need to tell me what you want," asked Claudius.

"I want to stay here and work with all of you. Don't laugh but you are more of a family than I've ever had. I need to let Mother know something and Father may need more money soon. I was wondering if some of you want to go to my mothers' house or come home with me and look at the books and I don't know... I could bring everything here and work on them. Mother doesn't want to do it and she doesn't know about Father's accounts."

"Olin, let me talk this over with the others," said Claudius. "We may have some people going there soon. We told Ruthie that you were alive and what you did. She said you could live with her and Matilda."

"I want to stay here."

"I don't think it is safe for him to go there alone," said Noah.

"I agree," said Claudius. "Olin, don't write to anyone until I get back to you on this."

"Before we go back in the meeting," Matthew said. "Noah, just how involved is Hector in all of this?"

24

"Honestly, we don't know yet but everything we read he is mentioned in. He ran around with all of those people and as powerful as he is, it is not safe for Rosa to be near him. If Juleta was involved in a plot he might finish her work."

Mathas was speaking when Claudius and the others returned to the meeting. Claudius and Matthew walked to the front of the room.

"Well," said Mathas in a demanding tone

"It is exactly as they said," Claudius explained. "They are following up on some information. What they have uncovered so far is serious. So serious that Matthew and I are forming a group just to follow these leads. We have chosen specific people because of what they can bring to the table. Sorren you, Shara and Angelina need to hear about this and Shara will need to bring all of her papers on old medicines and magics."

"Thaos and Stephan, you both leave now and bring Bella back, then the three of you need to be briefed. I need to find Fahron also."

"We will be pulling that group out of the regular research and they will just concentrate on these leads. Dominic, you and Turner will oversee the other research. We will have to put the groups in separate offices."

"We should tell Dominic then," said Noah. "In case they come across something we can use."

"I agree," said Claudius. "Don't any of you think that we are keeping you out of this for reasons other than this needs to be worked on in a small group. When we release the findings all of you will understand why."

"Claudius, I need to be briefed," said Mathas.

"No Father, really if any of this is true," Matthew paused. "This is like having a nightmare. You don't want to share it unless you have to."

"Well, I for one will not be able to concentrate after this," said Mathas. "Everyone has things on their plates. I will leave you to your work." Mathas stood up and walked out of the room and Matthew followed him. It was obvious to all that the King was furious.

Stephan and Thaos brought both Shara and Bella to Mathas' castle. Fahron and Angelina had already returned to the castle. Matthew and Claudius rounded up everyone else who was supposed to be a part of this secret group and took them to the office. Ryan and the others repeated everything they had previously said to Claudius and Matthew.

"This just keeps getting more horrible," said Bella. "I understand why everyone else is here but why me?"

"There are questions that the group has and they don't want to ask Rosa. I thought perhaps you could give them some answers," said Claudius. "Mathas is irate but neither Matthew nor I think he should be told anything at this point."

"I agree," said Fahron. "Bella, if you can't answer the questions we can get Isadore. All of you were so close during that time."

"Actually I think all of you did the right thing," said Shara. "What mother wants to even think something like this could happen. But just so I am clear, you don't think that Isabella sold her soul at any time?"

"If she did it would certainly explain the change in her behavior," said Olin. "But wouldn't your Angels have told you?"

"And the Sanuri looked into her mind," Fahron said.

"Olin did say that the Master is powerful enough to erase some of her memories so that could have happened," said Seth.

"Once again everyone is talking about Isabella like she is a victim," Angelina said. "Personally, I don't think she ever was a victim of any kind and I would not be surprised if we find out she was directly involved with a lot of this."

"What do you need us to do?" asked Sorren.

"First thing, this group has a small list of questions to ask all of you. A lot are concerning the time frame of the wars. And others are about when Isabella was younger," Claudius said.

"Then we still have a mountain of information to go through. Bella, I would like you to go over the things that Rosa brought. Fahron if you want to get Isadore that might really help."

"I'll get her and brief her on the way," Fahron said. "Then I am going to all of the banks and see if Josef had any accounts."

"Angelina, of course you can read any or all of this but we would like you to look up any information on old medicines and magics that could possibly be used for something like this."

"Sure but wasn't Olin a dark lord?"

"I was a lousy one. I never did any of the work," said Olin. "But I will help you if you have books here."

"Ok, I have heard about babies lives being taken for debts," said Thaos. "I never knew if any of it was true. But let's just say all of this is true. You said that Rosa said Juleta was angry since she could walk. Is it a possibility the kid was replaced?"

"Yes," Angelina said. "But wouldn't you think the Angels would have told us?"

"We can ask them," said Tessa.

"You're kind of new at talking to them," Sorren said. "They usually want us to work things out before we call them. I will bet you anything that if we called them now they would listen to what we have and tell us to go back to work."

"Sorren is right," said Claudius. "I need to go and leave a note for Hector about the break-in at his parent's home. I'll be back right after that."

27

Chapter III
Collaboration

Sudfad gave a long break to the people in his meeting, many of whom were upset after hearing the details of Michael's assassination. He passed the letter around the room and asked staff to bring glasses of wine and whiskey into the room. It was the first time that Nyla, Saran and their friends were allowed to drink wine in Sudfad's home. When everyone had a glass, Sudfad said a toast to Michael. Many other's also said toasts which led to stories. Talking about Michael helped to heal the pain for his friends and family.

After an hour Corsa was handed the letter to read. When she got to the third page she stood up. "Excuse me a moment," she said loudly. "For those of you who weren't in Langer, I don't know if you know this detail. At the time of the attack, Matthew, Angelina, Shara, Erebus and a lot of soldiers were standing with Michael, Javier and Edward yet the assassins only shot at those three men. What Hector said about Radnor makes sense for Michael but why were Javier and Edward attacked also? Do people think they are The Seven Sons?"

"That is a damn good question," said Simon. "I didn't know that. When everyone is done, I want to read that letter again."

"I agree," said Sudfad. "When everyone feels up to it, there is still a lot that we need to discuss with that letter. The two subjects that I want to make sure we discuss this morning are the bounties on Madeline and Javier and the experimentations of the Second Sons. I don't know what Miranda is planning but personally I don't want Archetenus and Jared going to Marba."

Claudius was a man who stood out in any crowd. He towered over others and he was as solid and muscular as he was tall. He carried himself with the confidence and bearing of a military commander. His presence spoke volumes. Never in his life did Claudius have to tell people he was tough, they took one look at him and they knew.

He walked into the Lady's Slipper Tavern midmorning. Lots of men wearing blue bandanas were sitting at the tables and they all stared at him as he walked up to the bar.

"I have a note that Hector is going to want to read right away," Claudius said loudly to the bartender who glanced at a man sitting at a table behind Claudius.

"You must be the leader since everyone is looking at you," Claudius said as he walked up to Clev. "Are you Clev?"

"How do you know my name?"

"I do my homework," Claudius said. "Do you know who I am?" Clev nodded and Claudius handed him the envelope. "Hector needs to see this. If you don't believe me read the damn thing yourself. I don't care but I don't know if he will." Claudius stood at the table while Clev read the note.

"Claudius, I am sure he is going to want to talk to you. Have a seat. Sam get Claudius a drink," Clev said and walked out of the tavern.

Claudius sat down at the table and looked at the men sitting with him. "I like the bandanas better than those hats you had," Claudius said and several of the men grinned.

"We do too," said the man sitting across from Claudius.

Clev walked back into the tavern. "Claudius, come with me," Clev said and grabbed a bottle of whiskey off the bar. The men walked out of the tavern and into the hotel next door. They walked up several flights of stairs and Clev opened the door to room 317.

"You look like hell," Claudius said to Hector as he walked into the parlor of the chambers. "Is that from fighting or Juleta's curse?"

"Mostly fighting," Hector said as Clev filled three glasses with whiskey. "So tell me what happened."

"I told you that your words kind of haunted me so I decided to have men watch your parent's house. We figured others were watching it too, if nothing else your men."

"So I had my men standing in the shadows. Last night the lights went out around ten, which seems to be about the time that housekeeper and her husband go to bed."

"None of my men saw anything suspicious until this morning when one of them is walking along the shoreline and sees a dead man next to the water but directly behind the house."

"My soldier ran up to the house and saw that the back door had been kicked open. The housekeeper was dead on the kitchen floor and her husband was half down the front steps. The place had been all torn up. I have no idea what they were looking for. The housekeeper and her husband both had their throats cut but there weren't any other marks. And they were both in their night clothes. There wasn't any demon writing or anything on the walls."

"The guy on the beach had a couple of knife wounds. He looked like a hired fighter but none of my men recognized him. Other than all the blood, the sand in that area had been wiped clean so I think whoever did it came by boat. My men are still guarding the house and bodies because I thought you might want to see them."

"Clev can go with you," Hector said.

"I have another letter for you. I figured your head guy would need to read the one I wrote. I wasn't sure you wanted him to read this one." Claudius took an envelope out of his shirt pocket and handed it to Hector. "It's from Rosa."

"Do you know what she wrote?"

"I didn't read it but she told me and I have more to tell you when you are done."

Claudius watched Hector's face as he read the letter. Hector never looked angry and for a brief moment Claudius thought he looked sad. The letter was several pages long; when he was done reading Hector said, "I didn't tell them to protect Sarah not to make them suffer."

"I think we all realize that which leads me to something else. Rosa and Mathas are fighting over the other things she wanted to write to you." Claudius leaned back in his chair and stared at Hector.

"I don't know if you are a part of Juleta's plot to destroy her family and I hope not. She has caused them enough pain. Sarah brought life back to them."

"Hector, they don't know that I am telling you this. After I told Rosa that you had been watching over your daughter, I think she thought you had turned good. She wants to offer for you to visit Sarah. Of course since you were part of Juleta's plot to murder Margarit, you can understand our concern. Rosa doesn't believe that any parent should be separated from their child. You know Rosa, she is not naïve but family is very important to her."

"Hector if they decide to set up these visitations, I will have people there and if you so much as scare Rosa I will tear you apart."

"I would expect nothing less. Honestly I don't know if I could afford to even do that. I can't let anything weaken me now."

"I wondered about that."

"But know too that Juleta played everything close to the vest. I kidnapped Margarit but I was told she wanted to lure Mathas there for a battle. I didn't know until afterwards that she was going to sacrifice the kid. I'm not saying I am innocent of anything. She always had her agendas and I had mine."

"I can't believe Mathas would let me visit but if he did, we would have to find some place neutral. You do know that every beast in the continent is watching your homes. A lot of demons saw that Angel on the shoreline when the armada attacked and that reinforces their suspicions that some of you are The Seven Sons."

Claudius didn't say anything. Both men were aware that they were trying to read each other. "Now that armada, I was involved with that. Damn, I lost an entire army. Your Angels have anything to do with that?" Hector asked and Claudius smiled.

"Hector, you really look bad. Can I get you something? Our healers are powerful but they pray to The Great Ruler and that probably isn't going to help you the way you want."

"Guess I should have taken Stephan up on his offer," Hector said and both he and Claudius laughed.

"You used to play with my son. You stayed at our home. Your family has more money than they know what to do with. You were always popular. Hector, I don't know why you are doing all of this and I am not asking you to tell me. But take it from someone who has seen way too much death. Life is short. For all your power and money you live in the shadows. You always have to look over your shoulder and you don't look well. You can change that."

"You sound like my father. Claudius, you certainly aren't a naïve man. Sometimes you can't stop things, you have to see them through. I am not a victim in any of this and don't think that I am."

"I never have. I just don't understand your choices. So changing the subject, do you want to send a note back to Rosa?"

"Not today but tell her I will think about this."

"Stephan and Thaos are having a second wedding ceremony for their wives in four days. We planned to leave after that to go to Zorta. But I am telling you now Clarence and Catherine can't move into that house the way it looks. So think about what you want and let me know." Claudius stood up to leave.

"I owe you."

"Hector, I have a question and the answer would be a great payment."

"Let me hear the question first," Hector said with a grin.

"What was Juleta?"

"What do you mean? She was a dark lord."

Claudius wanted an answer to the question as much as he wanted to see Hector's reaction. "Rosa suddenly becomes sick two weeks before she delivers her first child. During those two weeks she dreams about demons. The boy is born and dies immediately. A year later Juleta is born. As soon as she could walk she was scaring others."

"She was a powerful dark lord as a child. How can that be? Was the first child some kind of payment so a demon could take over Juleta's body?"

"Well from the looks on both of your faces what I said can't be too crazy. If my suspicions are right and you didn't know about that, what does that mean for you? And what does it mean for Mathas' family?"

"Claudius what you said, do you know it to be true?"

"Yes."

"Claudius sit back down. Clev you can stay. I honestly didn't know any of that. But if it is true let me tell you what you are dealing with. Only the most powerful demons can possess the magics to do what you are suggesting. And I am talking about the Old Ones."

"Could the Master?"

"Yes. I really can't believe how much you know. In very old and dark magics a life is required to produce a life. So if something took over Juleta's body after she was born, and that is when it would have happened, yes a life would have been required. Also there are some who believe that taking a babies' life gives them the youth and extends their own lives."

"And I assume the Master is one of those?"

"Yes. Claudius he is more powerful than most demons. Don't mess with him."

"Too late for that son. Hector, I know you are a very smart man and I can see the wheels turning in your head. You and Clev both looked scared for a moment. What aren't you telling me?"

"Let's say that something took over Juleta when she was born. Whoever was responsible would do their homework and know that the Sanuri is often in that home. So how the hell would they disguise a demon? Seriously. There are a lot of really bad things in these worlds besides demons. I don't know what she was but I shared a lot with her in many ways."

"Whatever I said to her probably went to her benefactor which could really work against me. But it is Sarah that I am worried about. Let me look into this. Clev knows that we have a truce for family matters but my other men don't. If I send anyone to you it will be him."

Claudius nodded and he and Clev walked out of the chambers.

"Got a horse close by?" asked Claudius.

"Yeah, in front of the tavern," said Clev. "But I want to get a couple of my boys."

"Clev, I have to assume that your boys were watching that place too. Did they see anything?"

"They saw less than what your men did."

"So you are thinking that something is blocking you guys? I don't understand all this magic crap. But if something created a block would it only work for certain people?"

"Yeah," Clev said solemnly.

"Well that makes a hell of a lot more sense," Claudius said. "Get your men. I'll wait here."

Claudius, Clev and two of his men rode through the streets of Langer. Clev started to laugh. "I'll bet there are some who are shitting their pants seeing us together."

Claudius grinned. "I know you can't tell me a lot and I'm not asking except for when it comes to protecting Clarence and Catherine. If there are specific threats, are you going to let me know?"

Clev didn't say anything for a few moments. "You're right, it is not my place to give you information. But in this instance, I think Hector will let you know. Right now anyone could be a threat. He has a lot of enemies."

"If that is the case then do you want a wall built around their house and soldiers? Once you look at this place, I can't imagine you are going to have them move in there, unless you have a crew really clean it out. And if you want a different house are you going to let them pick it out? Son, I'm not asking you for any secrets but I do need more information."

"I understand and I'm not being a dick. I just can't give you those answers right now. Let me look at the house and I will talk to him and get back to you."

They rode in silence for the next few minutes until they arrived at the house. The soldiers stationed there recognized Hector's men but none of them said a word. Claudius, Clev and the others dismounted. "My men aren't going to attack you," Claudius said as they walked around the house and towards the shoreline. "At least not this day," he added with a grin. They could see the body on the beach and a soldier standing near it.

"Check it out," Clev said to his men.

When Claudius and Clev were alone Clev said, "When he told me he was going to ask you to do this, I told him never in a million years. I will say I am surprised."

"Clarence and Catherine are innocents caught up in all of this, as is Sarah. Honestly, I was shocked that he asked us. Personally, I think that says a lot for him. And before we reach our men I am saying something just to you. I was against Rosa's idea of letting him see Sarah. But seeing the way he looks. Clev do you have kids?"

"None that I know of," he said with a grin.

"It's none of my business what he is going through and I'm not asking questions. But he might want to consider holding his daughter one more time before... well you know what I am saying."

35

"We don't recognize him boss," said one of Clev's men. "And his pockets are empty except for a few coins." Clev looked at Claudius.

"We searched him too and that is all we found. Any idea who he works for? Is it you?"

"No."

"Well, you can't tell me those two old people inside killed him. And why would whoever did this kill one of their own? My men didn't do this. If you've got multiple groups threatening them, we need to deal with this."

"We're thinking the same thing," Clev said and all four men turned and walked to the back door of the house. Clev examined the broken door for a moment then they entered the kitchen where another soldier was standing guard over a body.

"Do you know their names?" asked Claudius. "Because we should let the families know."

"I don't but I will get that for you."

The four men walked through the large house. Claudius noticed that Hector's men were examining the walls.

"Are you thinking there is invisible writing?" Claudius asked and Clev grinned. "The whole place got it bad but this room got it the worst." Claudius said and opened the door to a bedroom. "Now, I know this was Hector's room when he was a kid because our families were friends. Unless something was taken, there isn't a damn thing in here that says this was his room so who the hell would know that?"

"Really look this room over," Clev said to his men then motioned for Claudius to go into the hallway. "Who would know this? I mean who were his friends in those days?"

"Fahron's, Mathas' and my family and Otto's that I know of. Of course I can't speak for Otto's people but none of the rest of us had anything to do with this. Now, Hector was a popular and good looking kid so I would assume he brought people home."

Claudius looked at Clev for a moment then said. "I am going to give you a bit of information. How much do you know about what happened to Otto?"

"We know you were investigating him then the whole damn city blows up," Clev said with a grin. "We weren't sad to see him go. But he was really powerful; you couldn't have destroyed him by yourself."

"I want to make a deal of sorts," said Claudius. "I know we are on opposite sides of the fence on just about everything. But a hell of a lot of innocent people got hurt by Otto. I can give you information about Jack. The Master changed his appearance and I am assuming he is an enemy of yours."

"What do you want?"

"Information about innocent people getting hurt. We moved all of those poor bastards who were living under the city. War should be fought between soldiers not the weak and families. I'm asking for a little integrity on your side. I am sure we will have plenty of chances to exchange information in the future."

"Claudius, I hope we are never in the position where we have to kill each other because I like you. I can tell you this. It wasn't us who had anything to do with those sacrifices. Not all beings require sacrifices. But the Master is big into that. When you are watching people who worship demons they will increase the sacrifices if they are scared shitless or they want something really bad. The numbers of people that Otto was grabbing would lead me to believe he was scared and that is part of the reason we are here."

"Fair enough. First, we interrogated his men and they said he got really scared of something a couple of months ago but no one seems to know why. And for Jack; a mob lynched Andre and was chasing Jack down when the ground seemed to swallow him up. It actually did and to get out he made a lot of promises to the Master. He has black hair now, black eyes and his right hand and arm were a demon's. The Angels warned us that when he comes back it will be with a vengeance."

37

"I believe we can do business," Clev said. "I will have my men guard this place so your soldiers can go. And you are right about the house. I will tell Hector every single thing we have discussed. You still want us leaving you information at the Excelsor Hotel?"

"Yes. But it does seem like your men and my teams all recognize each other. If something is urgent just go up to one of them."

"Yeah, those damn Rualas are hard to miss," Clev said and grinned. "You can take your soldiers now. I'll leave my two here and get some more."

After Claudius released his soldiers from the house he rode to Ryan's shop. Artis was helping some customers in the front of the store. Claudius walked into the back and motioned for Ralph to come with him. They both sat at the front table and drank coffee until Artis was done.

"I need to talk to both of you," Claudius said.

"Is anything wrong? Is Ryan alright?" asked Artis.

"No it's nothing like that, have a seat. I don't know how much Ryan has told you but he is helping us on some big projects," Claudius said. "He's not going to be around the shop for a while."

"We'll take care of things; don't you worry," said Ralph.

"Well, that is what I wanted to talk to you about. The two of you are damn near family now and you watch this place like it's your own. Want to be managers? Of course that will mean a big pay raise." Claudius laughed at the stunned looks on the faces of the men.

"Sure, I mean we would be honored," said Artis. "I think we are both in shock."

"Good. Here is some of your pay," Claudius said and handed each man a small pouch of gold coins. "Bella is still doing the books and she told me you have to be running short on supplies." "Order what you want, you don't need our permission just give her the receipts."

"What do you want us to do with the money?" asked Artis. "The last couple of days we've given it to your family when they set up the tables. But that is a lot of cash for them to carry and it means we have to leave it in that box all night. We don't have a safe here. Ryan usually took it home."

"I'll send someone from the family to get it before close on the days that Ryan isn't here. I'll tell the guys in back that you are their bosses now. Think there will be any problems?"

"No, the only guy we ever had problems with was that Ted," said Artis. "Did you ever find him?"

"No and I forgot about that. If he would come in here, you tell the soldiers patrolling the streets. In fact, tell them if you ever have any problems in here. Let's go back and make the announcement."

Chapter IV
Sisters of Tameric

As Claudius was riding back to Mathas' castle he heard Miranda's voice in his ear. "Do you think it was wise to make a deal with Clev?"

"I know, I am not sure about that. But I thought they probably hear things before we do and if I can save a life that would be good. But in the future I will ask you what information I should give them."

"Actually, you did more than you realize. Hector and Clev trust no one but each other but they both like and respect you. They know where you stand and you know where they do. While both of them are murderous monsters they are feeling a sense of relief dealing with you. It would benefit you to play on that."

"Clarence and Catherine truly are victims of their son's choices and they do need protection."

"Got any ideas?"

"Well since you ask," Miranda said and Claudius grinned. "You need to get them out of Zorta. Ask Mathas to let them stay in one of the cottages on the royal grounds. They will be physically safe."

"Hector did not want to show weakness in front of you but Rosa's letter touched his heart. He will tell his parents about Sarah. Clarence and Catherine share the same nightmare that Mathas and Rosa do. They were all good parents and their children chose to become monsters. Neither couple has been able to really open up about their feelings and fears but with them all living on the same property they will talk and heal."

"You know I have been waiting to talk to you about Juleta. I wanted to be better prepared first and in a way I am afraid to hear the truth."

"Do you want to hear it now?"

"Yes."

"First, the children who work for you have done well. If you have not realized it Olin is looking at you as a father figure and wants to please you. Do you know why he and Elexas are working so hard and doing so well even though they still don't feel that they fit in?"

"Because we protect them?"

"Because you saw them."

"I don't understand what you mean."

"Claudius, you have always had a presence that draws attention but there are many in your world who feel invisible. They believe that no one cares about them because no one notices them. Just like the homeless who Gideon would walk past without seeing."

"Elexas and Olin have made poor choices their entire lives and the choices they made were usually based on their need for recognition. I am not talking about honors. I am talking about people recognizing that they are alive. You and your teams gave faces to the faceless and by that simple act you have changed them and the courses of their lives. Tell the others, in fact I wish you could tell your entire world."

"That was the good news. Olin was right about the first son of Rosa and Mathas being a debt but the Master was not behind that crime. And Hector was right that there are many monsters in the worlds besides demons. You should stop your horse because this will take a few minutes."

"First, you need to understand that there are locations in the worlds where people believe there is more power. Why they believe this is unimportant right now but Langer and Port Friada are two such places. So they draw people who would find ways to harness that power and use it."

"Is that why there are so many dark lords in Port Friada?"

"Yes. Now the reason you haven't seen as many in Langer is because your city has been controlled by two powerful forces."

"One was Otto's empire and the other an ancient order called the Sisters of Tameric. Tell me where have you heard that word before?"

"Tameric is the name of the hell worlds in Nunc, that was the map on Michael's back. And Karzman was from a village named Tameric. Are they related?"

"In a way. Women have been victimized in your world since the beginning of time. Many have turned to magics as they falsely believe this is the only way they can get enough power to protect themselves. Thousands of years ago a small group of women fled to the Tombs of Mercha in Lentz to hide among the dead. People were superstitious in those days so the women believed they would not be followed to a graveyard."

"These women had been brutalize in horrible ways. They did not run to the tombs as a group but as frightened individuals. And they all believed they would die among the dead."

"These women met and took comfort from each other. There were thirteen and they gave each other strength. They taught each other skills and soon the group was hunting, fishing and building shelters. One day a father and his two daughters came upon this group of women."

"The man was Emon and his daughters were Tahira and Mab, they were three of the Grand Masters of Opots. They violated those women's bodies and souls. While some could say that Emeric and Banaka were the founders of the Insidiae, Emon and his daughters were the founders of the Sisters of Tameric."

"This organization is worldwide. The Insidiae was created for power and greed. The Sisters of Tameric was created for power and revenge. The sisters themselves are not human nor are they demons. They are a unique race, they carry the blood of humans, Grand Masters and demons because Emon, Tahira and Mab gave them to the Old Ones. They are vicious and cunning."

"This group is not just women as the name would lead you to believe but it is the women of the group who have the bloodline. It was such a group that posed as a small group of gypsies and befriended Isabella."

"They knew who she was. They defiled her but she was more than a willing subject and she joined their group. That was her big secret. That organization didn't worry about The Seven Sons or The Keepers of the Scrolls, they wanted this kingdom for several reasons. The first for its power, the second the geographical advantages and the third because it was the area of their origin."

"You are a military commander and are well aware that groups seek to obtain the resources of other lands. Yet all of you have been so caught up with the prophesies and attacks that you have lost sight of that. There are groups who would desire Lentz for reasons that have nothing to do with the prophesies."

"But back to Isabella. She was the first princess to join their group and they had big plans for her. But part of the plans were for her to live a chaste life until they sent her the husband of their choosing. Isabella did not want that. Even as a child she had great passions and dark desires so she bartered with the group. She promised them Rosa's and Mathas' first child so that the second could become a vessel for the Sisterhood."

"Isabella knew full well what she had done and watched Juleta with horror. Isabella didn't know what kind of a monster Juleta would grow into. And what was Juleta? Hatred and revenge."

"But the Sisterhood was not happy with Isabella. They were not used to being told no, especially by a spoiled child. They cursed her and told her they would still send her a husband but he would bring her to ruin. The curse they put upon her was to greatly exaggerate her desires and passions."

"Her needs, fears and other characteristics were so exaggerated that she often felt as if she was going crazy. And that is why many of you have wondered if she was really two people. But of course we could have cleansed her of all that if she would have prayed."

"The children of these two monsters are untouched by the darkness of their mothers. It was no accident that Selen delivered Sarah. Selen prayed constantly and we answered her prayers."

"I suppose the one good thing you could say about Isabella's curse was that her desire for motherhood was also exaggerated so she protected her children even from herself."

"Your group has already figured out that Juleta and Isabella acted in ways to repel others; these are the secrets they were hiding. And before you ask, do you know that Matthew is the first member of his family to really believe in The Great Ruler and not just do lip service? Think about that when you wonder why we did not stop some of these things."

"The Sisterhood is such an old and secretive organization that many do not know of them. Otto's father was told about them by the Master. The Master and the Sisterhood do not get a long and he will demand their members as sacrifices whenever he can. And Otto did sacrifice some of the members. When he found this out, that is what filled him with fear."

"But, we can't forget Isabella's husband in all of this. Josef was not sent to her by the Sisterhood, in fact, no man was. But Josef was on Otto's payroll to keep him informed of Isabella and Juleta because Otto knew the details of their connection with the Sisterhood. Josef committed no crimes and was always loyal to his King and kingdom. He is a good father."

"Fahron will find the money trail. It is always your choice but you asked me earlier if I had ideas, my idea would be to get information from him and not punish him. He did have feelings for Isabella and some would say that was punishment enough. Otto told Josef that he was afraid that Juleta had done something to Isabella and that is why he wanted her watched."

"When we started this conversation you told me you wanted to save innocent lives and asked if I had ideas. Is that still the case?"

"Miranda, I understand you have rules you have to go by but can you and I agree right now that what I said will always be the case? It might save us some time."

"You have not only made a pact with a devil but a pact with an Angel today. Not many can say that. I have given you all of this information for several reasons. No matter how brilliant your people are they would have wasted months trying to find it and their resources could be put to better use."

"I would suggest that you focus on the Second Son experiments and Andrac. You have established a rapport with Hector and Clev. Tomorrow you tell them what I told you about the Sisterhood, Juleta, Isabella and Otto. This information will have more significance to Hector than you will understand. In return you want information about the Second Sons and Andrac. Hector does not support either and will not be compromised telling you."

"You are a brilliant man and a good negotiator; you will know when you need an ace up your sleeve and I will give you that ace. Hector doesn't want to be a demon but he believes that is the only way to escape the curses of Juleta's magics. But they do not come from the transformations, they come from her connection with the Sisterhood. He will know what to do with that information."

"Why are you helping him?"

"For the same reason I helped Archetenus only instead of me appearing to him you will give him my words. It is up to you whether you tell him the reason. I am giving you a great deal of responsibility here. Will you accept it?"

"Of course I will..."

"Before you ask that question I want to finish. The Sisterhood will seek revenge. Otto is already gone so they will go after Jack. But it will take Jack, the Sisterhood and Hector a long time to figure out the information I am giving you. And during that time many, many innocent people would be killed. If Hector chooses to attack or negotiate with the Sisterhood that is his choice but the innocents will no longer be in the crossfire."

"And let's go back to Josef. His crime is not telling Mathas about Otto's alleged fears; punish him for that. But since he never really understood what was going on with his wife, he doesn't realize how important some of the information is that he has. Use him as an ally. Trust me, you will need all you can get in the future. And that goes back to Hector. While you represent two different worlds you have many of the same enemies."

"Miranda, of course I will do whatever you want but Hector is such a monster. Why am I speaking your words? Wouldn't they have more impact from you?"

"Claudius, you are a faithful man who has always believed in The Great Ruler. Speaking with an Angel is part of who you are now. Hector would never listen to me and his fears would drive him deeper into the darkness. You are a man of his world. A man of battle and integrity. A man who he knows speaks the truth. He will listen to you."

"Rosa said it perfectly. He may not change his ways but don't you think having some kind of a connection to us is better than none at all? Perhaps he changes just one choice but by that decision many are saved. If you don't think it is worth the effort that is your choice."

When Claudius returned to the castle he walked directly into the office that Noah's group was working in. "Stop everything," Claudius said. "I just spoke to Miranda and she gave me the answers we've been looking for because she said you would not have found them and we need to put you on something else. Please gather everyone and I will do a briefing but I have to talk to Mathas and Rosa first. Bella, Isadore I will need you in there. Is Fahron here?"

"He's in the other office talking to Dominic," Seth said. "I will get him."

"Wait a moment. All of you should know that Miranda said you were brilliant to figure out what you have. I would really take that compliment," Claudius said.

"Ryan, I hope you don't get mad but I stopped at your shop and made Artis and Ralph mangers. I increased their pay. The place was packed and they were running out of supplies so they will put an order in. Are you mad? I did this to take some of the burden off from you."

"No and I've been worrying about the place. Thanks, this really helps."

"Of course, you are still the boss and they know that," Claudius said to Ryan then turned to Stephan and Thaos.

"While Ryan is working here, we need to send someone to the shop at the end of the day to get the money. I didn't realize how much that was at times."

"No problem," said Stephan. "So are you going to tell us about Hector?"

"In the briefing. The bastard looks like he is dying. Where is Matthew?"

"Castor with Turner's crew," said Thaos.

Fahron, Isadore and Bella sat with Mathas and Rosa as Claudius told them everything that Miranda had said. These three couples had been close friends most of their lives. They held each other up during the worst of times and Mathas and Rosa now needed that support.

Claudius left nothing out; he told them every word the Angel said. "I have called a meeting to tell everyone else. Mathas stay here with Rosa. When Matthew returns do you want to tell him or have me?"

"I don't know yet," said Mathas in a hoarse whisper.

"I know you have a great deal to work through but I will meet with Hector tomorrow. If you have decided to let Clarence and Catherine live in a cottage, let me know."

"Of course they can," said Rosa. "Miranda is right; it might be nice to talk with them."

"Mathas, if you want to take a couple of days off we can handle things," said Fahron.

"I might. I feel like my head is spinning. Fahron the entire thing with Josef is in your hands. And Claudius you have Hector. Is Sorren still planning on going to Zorta?"

"Yes, unless you need him here," said Fahron.

"No, have him go. Can you assign someone to do whatever needs to be done to the cottage?"

"Isadore and I can do that," said Bella. "Claudius was everything broken in that house?"

"No."

"Ask Hector what we should get for his parents. I am sure they would feel comforted with something from home," said Bella.

"Actually, write him a note," Claudius said. "He really responded to Rosa's. Perhaps we can slowly work through that wall."

Fahron and Claudius met with the team members in the Great Hall. It did not go unnoticed that Mathas was absent. The people in the room sat spellbound as Claudius told of the information discovered by Olin and the others, the meeting with Hector and the words of Miranda.

When Claudius finished, Fahron spoke about his investigation which now hit a dead end because Josef was Fahron's prime suspect for giving Isabella military information. "Angus, I would like you to work with me on this," said Fahron. "We need to have him questioned. I don't know if I should have him brought here."

"Are you going to punish him?" asked Stephan with a grin. "Because I like what Miranda said that being married to Isabella was punishment enough."

Fahron chuckled. "I don't know yet."

"Well, if you do punish him, you will probably need to bring him here," Stephan continued. "Or I am sure that Angus trusts someone in the Guardians to question him. And the priests are going to Malga, some of the Patronus could do it. That's a long trip if we don't have to make it." Fahron nodded but did not speak.

"Ryan, you, Olin and Elexas get all the charts and stuff that you made and put them up in here so everyone can see them," Claudius said. As soon as the three young people left he spoke to the group. "Miranda wanted me to tell you something."

"She said that Olin and Elexas are doing so well and are so dedicated because we saw them. I didn't know what she meant and she said there are a lot of people, like those two who feel invisible. They feel like no one cares about them because no one sees them. She said just recognizing them as people made the difference and that is something she wants us all to remember."

"Boy, that is really sad," said Tessa.

"She said that most of the crap they did was to get attention," Claudius said and shook his head. "Never in a million years would I have thought of something like that."

Chapter V
Hector

Claudius didn't know why he had difficulty sleeping but every time he dozed off he woke up with the feeling that someone had called his name. He finally got out of bed and went to his study. He did a couple hours of paperwork then dressed. He left a note for Bella and rode towards Langer. After twenty minutes of riding he said, "Miranda are you making me feel like this?"

"Next time you should ask before you leave the house," her voice said. She did not appear to him. "Are you going to see Hector?"

"Yes."

"Good, now listen to me carefully. Turn around and go to the Village of Tyger. I've already awaken Sorren and Shara and they know you are coming. Take them to Hector so Shara can help him. She knows what to do. He is so weakened that curses are attacking him and he knows it."

"Before you ask, yes I am helping him because like with Archetenus if Hector dies a worse being will take his place. That is why Samael has blocked his transformation. Juleta paid a fortune to get her revenge. Samael already has another demon lined up to take his body."

"I wish you would have told me this before," Claudius said with frustration.

"Next time you will know to ask."

It was ten miles to the Village of Tyger, then a two hour ride to the City of Langer. The Lady's Slipper Tavern stayed open all night. It was barely dawn when Claudius walked inside. He didn't see Clev but he saw one of the men he had spoken to the previous day.

"Get Clev, I need to talk to him at once. It's a matter of... just get him now!"

"How do I know you are telling me the truth?"

50

"Well, I guess if I'm not they will tell you to kill me. Now!"

The hired killer jumped out of his seat and returned a few minutes later with Clev. Sorren and Shara were standing on the walkway. Claudius met Clev before he entered the tavern.

"Clev, if you are ever going to believe me, now is the damn time. I know what is wrong with Hector. And these people will help." Clev looked at Sorren and Shara.

"I'm a healer. Take us to him," Shara said.

"He got considerably worse last night didn't he?" asked Claudius.

"Yeah, how do you know?"

"I will tell you everything but he needs Shara now!"

The four people ran inside of the hotel and up the stairs to Hector's chambers. He was lying in bed and moaning. "Hector," Claudius said loudly. "An Angel told me what is happening to you. It's a combination of the Sisters of Tameric and Juleta. She cut a deal with Samael and when you die, he has another demon ready to take your body and apparently he's a hell of a lot more dangerous than you are so the Angel sent us here to help you. I'll explain everything but we can't waste time here, son."

Hector was trying to focus his eyes as he stared at the people in his room. "Ok," he said weakly.

"Clev, I need some hot water," Shara said and took off her shawl. "All of you can stay in the room." As Shara spoke she took the contents out of a large carrying case and placed them on a small table. "I need a cup," she said.

Sorren brought her one and she poured liquid from several vials into it then prayed over it. "Help him to sit up so he can drink this," Shara said and Sorren lifted Hector's shoulders. She poured the liquid down his throat then tore his shirt open. His chest was covered with blisters. As she sprinkled a mixture on his blisters, Clev entered the room with a coffee pot filled with hot water.

"What are those blisters from?" he asked.

"Hector is so weak that curses are attacking him," Shara said. "Clev, you can stay in here but you must do as I say and some of it may sound unbelievable."

Shara took the pot of hot water and mixed it with several powders. She prayed after she added each ingredient. She swung around and looked at the men so quickly that Clev jumped.

"Because he is a dark lord and wants to be, I can't use some of my normal medicines on him. Do you see those movements under the skin on his arms?" Sorren, Claudius and Clev all walked close to the bed. "Those are demon snakes. I will need one of you to hold his head up so I can pour this down him then the other two pull your swords because those snakes are going to jump out of his body."

"You have to cut their heads off," Sorren said as he helped Hector to sit up. Shara poured the mixture down his throat. Hector started to moan. Screams were heard as the curses were being broken. Sorren placed Hector's head on the pillow then pulled his sword out of its sheath.

"Shit!" yelled Clev as they watched the snakes moving in Hector's body. The screams became louder and louder then a snake lunged at Claudius, who destroyed it. Snake after snake jumped out of Hector's body as they tried to escape the tonic. Fifteen minutes later there were twenty dead snakes on the floor.

"How could that many be in him?" asked Clev.

"I'll bet that was one of Juleta's curses," Sorren said. "I'm throwing these damn things in the hearth."

A dark cloud started to form over Hector. Shara threw some blessed water on it and the cloud disappeared. "Roll him over so I can see his back," she said.

The four people worked on Hector for over an hour. "He will be sleeping for a while," Shara said and sat down at the table in the parlor. She was exhausted. Clev brought a bottle of whiskey and four glasses to the table.

"Shara, you want one?" he asked.

"Normally I don't drink whiskey but I will take one now."

"Clev do you want me to tell you everything now or wait until he wakes up?" asked Claudius. "I'll tell you now you won't believe some of it."

"Hell, I wouldn't have believed all those snakes could be in him," Clev said and looked at Shara. "Any idea when he might wake up?"

"At least an hour," she said wearily. "But he is going to need medicine. If I write things down can you give it to him?"

"Sure, but you are really going to have to explain things. I'm certainly not a healer."

Suddenly Shara jumped up. "Clev where do you get your food?"

"The kitchen downstairs. Why?"

"Don't eat it, none of you can. Miranda just showed me someone poisoning the food. Sorren, he can't stay here."

"Clev, we don't believe in what Hector or you do but we are trying to save his life. Let's just put our cards on the table and say that none of us trust each other," said Sorren. "We can take him to our village; that way Shara can watch over him. But I don't want your whole damn army there. And if any of you commit any crimes you will wish you had demon snakes in you. So what do you say?"

"Right now I have to trust you. Let me get some men and we can move him in a boca. I'll be right back."

Before Clev could open the door there was a knock and one of his men barged in. "Boss, Neil and Big Al are dead. They were eating breakfast downstairs. I think they were poisoned."

53

"Make sure none of the other men eat here. Then go in that kitchen and find out who did this. I'm moving the boss," Clev said and ran out of the chambers.

"Is everyone coming after him now because he is so weak or is something else going on?" asked Sorren.

"I don't know but I have a really bad feeling," Claudius said then walked onto the balcony and looked at the sky. Soon he saw Enrops. He motioned to them. "Go to Mathas' castle and tell him that we are trying to save Hector's life so he doesn't turn into a worse monster. We are taking him to Sorren's village but we expect to be attacked."

The Enrops left and Claudius looked at the street below. Nothing looked out of the ordinary. The streets were bustling with activity. The sun was up and all of the businesses were open. Claudius heard a commotion and looked down to see one of Hector's men being thrown out of the Lady's Slipper. Stephan walked out of that tavern and onto the street.

"Boys, we're up here," Claudius yelled. "Come on up." He didn't want to yell out the room number.

Sorren walked down to the lobby and led Stephan and Thaos to the chambers. "So this is like Archetenus all over?" asked Stephan when he walked into Hector's bedroom.

"Close," Claudius said. "I sent Enrops to Mathas' castle. We might need some help."

Clev stopped as he entered the chambers and saw Thaos and Stephan. "We're here to help," Thaos said. "But we did bang up a few of your boys trying to find Claudius."

"Six of my men have been poisoned," Clev said. "I will pay you well for the help. I have a boca in front."

"We don't want any pay," Claudius said. "But since Samael wants Hector to die, I wouldn't be surprised if we have a fight on our hands."

"Give me a few minutes to pack some stuff," Clev said.

54

"Did you tell him?" Stephan asked Claudius.

"Not yet, we were working on Hector. Demon snakes were jumping out of him," Claudius said as he looked at the street below.

"Clev, I don't know how many men you've got here but I'm not seeing a lot. Don't get pissed but I sent a note to our teams saying we might need help. I've got a really bad feeling."

Shara made a bed in the back of the boca while some of Hector's men carried him out of the hotel. "I'll ride in back with him," she said.

"Bet you never thought we would be fighting on the same side," Stephan said to Clev with a sarcastic grin. Clev nodded at him and they started out.

Claudius and Clev rode in the lead. Thaos and Stephan rode directly behind the boca. Sorren rode beside it. Two of Hector's men were in the front seat of the boca and another twenty were spread out around it. All of the men had been told to watch for any signs of attack.

The ride through the streets of the city was uneventful. But as soon as they left the city limits the air became thick. "We've got company," Clev yelled.

"Miranda, touch us!" yelled Sorren.

"Oh, I am going to do better than that," she said. Suddenly Miranda and Adam appeared in the roadway. Hector's men screamed as they were blinded by the light reflecting off the armor of the Angels. "Hector! Clev! In front of us now!"

Sorren quickly dismounted and went to the back of the boca to help Hector who was awake and trying to get up. "Come here son," Sorren said. "Don't keep them waiting."

"You better do as she says," Claudius said to Clev. "I wouldn't want to piss her off."

Clev slid off his horse. He was crying and had no idea why. He staggered as he walked towards the Angels. Then he got on his knees.

Stephan dismounted and helped Sorren get Hector out of the boca. Both men were helping him walk. Hector stopped, frozen with fear when he saw the Angels.

"Before us!" demanded Miranda. "You seduce and dance with demons and you are afraid of Angels now?"

"I can do this," Hector said to Sorren and Stephan. The men let go of his arms. It took all of the strength that he had but Hector walked to Adam and Miranda. He was so gripped with fear that he couldn't breathe. His heart was pounding so loudly that he couldn't hear. He did not speak. He walked to the Angels and fell to his knees.

"The area as far as you can see is filled with Samael's armies. He sent them because he wants you dead. Your master wants you dead. Do you remember Claudius telling you why we are helping you?" asked Miranda.

"Yes," Hector said in a whisper.

"Your men are filled with fear; those who feed on hatred and chaos. The others are not. In fact, they are prepared to fight. Does that tell you anything?" Answer me!"

"That you are stronger than Samael?"

"That The Great Ruler is. Hector these men are risking their lives to protect you; their enemy. They deserve some answers. Tell them why you are on this path? Why you would give up all that is good in this world for darkness. Tell them!"

"Power," Hector whispered.

"They did not hear you!"

"Power," Hector said in a louder voice but choked on his words.

"You defile children, kill and rape. You spread your poison and fear in this world and you mock The Great Ruler for power! Well my little demon; today you are being given a gift. You will see the false gods you worship for what they are."

Sorren and Stephan were still on foot, Thaos and Claudius were on horseback and they all moved towards the Angels. "Miranda, touch us and we will fight at your side," said Sorren.

"You should take him to your village," said Adam. "The entire route is filled with demons."

"Are there enough for all of us?" Sorren asked with a grin and thrust his sword into the ground.

"You are stuck with us," Stephan said and grinned.

Adam and Miranda both smiled. "Hector, you are seeing two miracles today," Adam said. "Look at the others."

Hector and Clev fearfully turned around. "They are glowing. I have seen that before," gasped Hector. "What is that?"

"Faith," Adam said as the cloaks fell away and exposed the armies of Samael which filled the skies and the land. From the distance was heard the war cries of the Ruala warriors. Sorren screamed a war cry and ran to his horse.

The boca and the people on the roadway were completely surrounded by demons. Hector and his men were filled with fear but they pulled their swords.

"Why aren't they moving?" asked Claudius.

"Fear," said Adam. "Samael can't see us but he sees four glowing humans and he stops his armies. Your false god isn't as powerful as you think Hector. And now what Samael fears; all the worlds will bear witness to." Adam and Miranda turned and struck their swords together. Hector's men fell from their horses by the vibrations of millions of voices who would witness the battle.

"Samael release your minions!" yelled Adam. "Surely the powerful demon does not fear us."

"Angel, we will fight with you," said Hector.

"You have not earned that right. Your soul is black," Miranda said. "You were once studying to become a priest of The Great Ruler. You know what to do but all of Heaven can hear your thoughts and see inside of that cold heart of yours."

Miranda turned and faced the demons. "Samael, we are waiting!" yelled Adam.

The screams of the powerful demon were heard by his armies and transmitted to the worlds. The screams were so piercing that some of Hector's men were bleeding from their noses and ears.

The battle began.

Twenty minutes earlier three Enrops flew into the Great Hall of Mathas' castle. The birds flew frantically around the room and screamed. Fahron was leading the morning meeting. "What are you saying?" he yelled to the birds who now flew directly to him.

"The Angel Miranda sent Claudius, Shara and Sorren to help Hector. If he dies he will turn into a worse monster. They are going to take him to Sorren's village but Samael has his armies everywhere. Miranda and Adam helped us to get here." All of the warriors jumped out of their seats.

"Wait! Wait!" yelled Dominic. "We can't fight those demons unless we ask the Angels to touch us with holiness. Miranda, Adam please touch us and we will fight with you."

Most of the people in the room now started to glow. Fahron and Angus did not. "Ask them!" yelled Fennel. "You won't be able to hurt the demons without them."

Both men hesitated. "Miranda, Adam please touch me with holiness," Fahron said in a low voice and instantly became dizzy as the holy energy flowed through him.

Angus stared at Fahron, then he yelled loudly, "Angels touch me!" Angus yelled a war cry as he felt the energy. The group ran out of the room.

Seth and Lawrence weren't able to fight yet because of their injuries from a battle with the Hutas. Noah started to run out of the hall then turned back and kissed Tessa. He left without saying a word.

"What just happened?" asked Olin.

"Some demons you can kill and some you can't. Samael always sends the ones you can't," Lawrence explained. "If the Angels touch us with holy energy we can kill the demons. We still have to fight them but we are equal."

"Lawrence where are you going?" asked Deborah.

"We can't ride out to battle but we can still protect the Royal Family." Lawrence said as he and Seth stood up.

"I'm coming with you but I need a sword," said Elexas.

"So do I," said Tessa.

"Do you know how to use one?" Lawrence asked then laughed at the disgusted look that Tessa gave him.

"One of these days I am going to slap you," Tessa said to Lawrence then laughed.

"Ryan and Olin take care of Deborah," said Lawrence.

Claudius, Sorren, Thaos and Stephan knew that Miranda and Adam did not need them to defeat that army. The men fought because of honor and because of love. They would not stand by and watch the Angels fight. Each man had sworn a covenant and they would not break it for all of the beasts in hell.

When Adam and Miranda allowed Samael to see them, they also made him aware that they were transmitting the battle to all of the worlds. The last time they did that all of Samael's enemies attacked him as they believed him to be weak. Samael was holding his own against the other demon armies but his pride was greatly wounded. He would not let that happen again.

He watched as two tiny groups of humans and Rualas fought with the armies that terrorized the universe. "How dare they stand up to me! Me!" Their arrogance enraged him. The demons in Samael's hell domain fled in terror as their master's temper tantrum exploded.

"What is happening now?" yelled Thaos as the demons stopped fighting.

At first the demons appeared to be withdrawing but they were merely backing up to make room for their master. A black, thick cloud started to form in front of the Angels.

"He's here," gasped Hector. "Samael is here!"

The team members from the castle who were fighting stopped too as they didn't understand what was happening. "We need to go forward," yelled Dominic and led the charge. They trampled the demons in their path.

Thaos was the first to hear Hector's words. "It's Samael! It's Samael!" yelled Thaos and ran towards the Angels. Hector cringed in fear. Sorren, Claudius and Stephan also ran towards the Angels but suddenly all four men were frozen in their steps.

"This is Adam's fight," Miranda said loudly. "He had to watch that abomination rape a world. Now, he comes here to this tiny planet, where the humans do not bow before monsters."

"Samael, these human warriors would fight you but I have stopped them to spare you the humiliation," said Miranda loudly. Bolts of lightning appeared in the dark cloud. Miranda smiled and said. "Sorren tell him what you are thinking."

"Just show yourself and stop the damn games. You aren't impressing anyone," Sorren yelled with contempt. The earth shook. Lightning hit the ground and screams from hell were deafening.

"No Shara!" Clev yelled and tried to grab her as she ran past him and Hector. The Angels did not stop her movement. She ran to Adam who was still wearing the guise of a human. She motioned for him to bend down and she whispered into his ear. Miranda smiled warmly as Adam looked emotional.

"Yes My Lady," Adam said and quickly spun around. A sword appeared in his hand and it glowed with splendor.

"Samael fight me or I will let the humans have you," taunted Adam.

The dark cloud started to take form and the legions of demons knelt before their master. As he took shape, Samael presented himself as a Talmuth, then a Rogett, then a Huta. He was flaunting the souls that he owned. He presented faces of demons and humans and lastly he presented the face of Hector and laughed.

"Not anymore!" Hector yelled and weakly walked towards the demon. "I am a monster but I am not your monster anymore! I denounce you. You have no power over me."

Suddenly Claudius, Sorren, Thaos and Stephan could move again and they all walked up to Hector, who was having difficulty standing.

"You are such a disappointment," Samael said in a condescending tone. "Too bad your wife isn't here to see you standing between the two who she really loved."

"Hey don't insult us buddy," Stephan yelled and all the men laughed. Miranda allowed the windows to open and everyone on the battlefield now heard the voices of the millions of beings who were watching the humans ridicule Samael.

"Your victims are watching you Samael. Are you going to fight?" asked Adam.

Samael screamed again and engulfed Adam with thick darkness. Claudius and the men started to run forward. "No!" said Miranda. "He was waited long for this day."

The dark cloud around the combatants prevented the men from seeing but they could hear the sounds of battle. A battle that Adam had wanted for centuries. The powerful Angel could have defeated Samael quickly but he wanted to savor the moment. The worlds watched as these two ancient beings fought for the souls of mankind.

Suddenly Samael screamed as the dark cloud was dissolved by a brilliant white light. The men weren't sure if Adam had changed form or if the light prevented them from seeing him. But it appeared that a white lightning bolt shot upwards dragging the King of Demons through the skies.

Dominic and those he led had arrived at the battleground in time to see this spectacle. The warriors now clapped, yelled and screamed war cries.

Miranda looked upward and even though she was speaking to beings that understood countless languages they understood her simple words. "Samael has been destroyed!" Screams and cries were heard through the open windows. Beings from countless worlds celebrated the defeat of the monster who terrorized them.

Samael was greatly hated by his peers and no one mourned his loss. The moment that Adam started to ascend into the sky with Samael other demons were conspiring for his territories.

The demon Sorphat left the Kingdom of Stordt and returned to Samael's hell world as he would fight to become king there. He dragged Toni into hell with him.

The legions of demons in the skies and on the land disappeared and Hector collapsed on the ground.

Chapter VI
Looking for Answers

Madeline knocked on the door to Sudfad's study before she entered the room. "I am sorry to interrupt," she said excitedly. "Javier, Tessa and Noah are engaged and they want me to be in the wedding." She walked towards her brother and handed him a letter. He smiled.

"What is wrong?" asked Madeline as she saw the somber looks on the faces of Sudfad, Raul and Simon.

"We just received a message from Enrops," Sudfad said. "The Angel Adam defeated Samael and locked him in the Abyss. Enrops are suddenly appearing everywhere with the news."

"Well, that is wonderful," said Madeline. "Why do you look concerned?"

"We don't have the whole story yet," said Simon. "But the reason Adam fought Samael is because Samael was attacking Claudius, Sorren, Shara, Thaos and Stephan because they were trying to keep Hector alive. Apparently Julcta paid Samael a fortune to have a really bad demon takeover Hector's body. All the Enrops know is that Hector denounced Samael, which shocked us all then he collapsed. We don't know if he died or if that demon will take over."

"And we don't know if Samael got Radnor," Raul said.

"Certainly this new demon can't be as bad as Samael and if he is, the Angels will defeat him too," Madeline said. "Actually this news makes me feel really safe because if Adam could defeat Samael, he can protect us from Andrac and Gilder."

"Changing the subject," Javier said to Madeline. "I assume you read this entire letter?"

"Yes, I thought you should discuss it with Sudfad," Madeline said. "I will leave you to work."

Madeline turned to leave but turned back to the men. "Sudfad, Tessa is like our sister. Would you and Renya mind if I held a little engagement party for them?"

Sudfad, Raul and Simon all grinned. "Mother is lost if she isn't planning something," said Simon. "Just make sure she doesn't take everything over."

"Actually, something like that might be really good for her now," Sudfad said.

"Madeline, you should know that your idea of a small party and Mother's may be two very different things," Raul said and grinned. Madeline laughed and left the room.

"All of you need to read this letter," Javier said. "Tessa is talking about research they are doing into Juleta and Isabella and it is not good."

Sudfad had not yet received the letter from Fahron that told of Miranda's words to Claudius. Tessa's letter was the first Sudfad's family was hearing about the plot responsible for the murder of the first son of Mathas and Rosa."

"Is he dead?" yelled Claudius.

"No," replied Thaos as he knelt near Hector. "Miranda is he turning into that demon now?"

"He is still the demon he ever was but that other one is not taking over his body. But he will need your help to heal. He denounced Samael but he is still Hector. Don't forget that."

"Why did he pass out?" Clev asked as he now knelt beside Hector too.

"Because of the connection that was severed when Samael was destroyed," said Miranda.

"Why didn't you pass out?" Stephan asked Clev.

"He didn't own me," Clev said.

"So you're just like that normally?" Stephan asked sarcastically and Clev laughed.

Shara was examining Hector as the men talked. "We need to get him into the boca. He is very weak. I am sure there are still curses sent to attack him."

"You're going to keep taking care of him?" asked Thaos.

"Yes," said Shara. "Unless Miranda tells me not to."

"You will be helping him more than you know," Miranda said. "As you did my brother."

"Yeah, what did you say to him?" asked Sorren.

"I told Adam that we all loved him. Then I told him to kill that monster."

All of the team members on the battlefield escorted Sorren's group to the Village of Tyger. They didn't believe that Samael's demons would come after Hector again but he had many other enemies. No one wanted those who were protecting Hector to be hurt.

"So what does this mean for all of you now?" Claudius asked Clev.

"You mean Samael gone? Don't really know. But maybe now would be a good time to tell me what you wanted to earlier."

"That might be something better explained when we are alone," Claudius said. "Once we get to the village, I'll ask Shara if she can wake Hector up."

Clev nodded. "You are the strangest people. You hate us yet you would have died to protect us."

"Oh hell," said Sorren with a grin. "We just can't pass up a good fight."

Renya was pleased when Madeline asked her to help plan an engagement party for Tessa and Noah.

"Let's get Vitomas and Annabelle and all go into the city," Renya said. "A day out might do us all some good. You know dear, Dominic's men are as close as brothers. I think their love for each other is the only thing that kept them alive; they had such horrible lives. We should send them invitations so they come too and Turner and his men for Tessa."

Madeline smiled. "I think they would like that. And I would very much like to hear about the freedom fighters of Ryed. I know that Noah must be special to have stolen Tessa's heart. She is very beautiful and men are always chasing her."

"Well, I am looking forward to meeting her. She sounds very spunky."

"Oh Renya, you have no idea," Madeline said and laughed.

Corsa was not avoiding her new family but ever since she read the letter explaining Radnor's part in the murder of Michael and the attacks on Javier and Edward, she was on a mission. She almost lost her husband once and refused to let him be a target again, only she didn't understand who wanted him dead or why.

Corsa had borrowed many journals from Gabriel to read and this morning she accompanied Archetenus and Jared to Erebus' library.

"Gala, I have to say you are looking pretty at home here," Jared said kiddingly when she let them into Erebus' house. Gala blushed and the men laughed.

"Hey, Erebus is a good guy," said Archetenus. "Delilah thinks you two make a good couple."

"Oh you two," Gala said and put her hands in the air. "You just like to embarrass me."

"I am telling the truth," Archetenus said and laughed again.

"Gala, I hope that you don't mind that I came along today," said Corsa. "I am trying to find some reason why Javier and Edward were attacked."

"You are always welcome here," said Gala. "In fact, that is why I am staying here so I can let you into the library."

"Sure," teased Jared and laughed again when Gala blushed.

"I am sure these two fools told you that the books are safe but personally I wouldn't push it. If you think something isn't right call to Ruth right away," Gala said to Corsa.

"Did you hear that? She called us fools," Jared said and laughed again.

"Are you really going to spend the day with these two?" Gala asked and Corsa laughed. Gala unlocked the door to the library. "I just baked a pie. I'll be back. Do you want coffee or milk?"

"Both," said Archetenus. "Sounds good."

"I can't believe how big this is," Corsa said with awe as she walked through the library.

"There are side rooms full of books too," said Archetenus. "And not all of them are unpacked. If you find anything on the Second Sons let us know. What exactly are you looking for?"

"I am not sure," Corsa said as she suddenly felt overwhelmed.

Matthew, Turner, Bart, Louis and Garvis had arrived in Castor the previous evening. Matthew got them all rooms in the same hotel. After they settled in, they had dinner then went in and out of many taverns looking for Abbott and his team.

Thirty soldiers from Langer arrived in Castor in small groups prior to the arrival of Matthew and Turner's team. All of these men were wearing civilian clothing and half of them were staying in the same hotel as Matthew.

Castor was a seaport city. It was open all night to service the hundreds of ships and thousands of sailors who arrived daily. It did not boast anything as notorious as the Catacombs but it was a city filled with taverns and some were very dangerous places.

Like Turner's group before they joined the teams, Abbott's group had a clandestine meeting place. Castor also had tunnels under the city. These were originally built hundreds of years earlier for defense.

"I don't like the looks of this," Turner said as he led his friends into the underground office of Abbott's team. It was a small cave that was filled with furniture which was now overturned and thrown around. "See if there are any files in here," Turner said as he picked up a chair.

"I found some blood," Louis said as he picked up pieces of a broken chair. "Someone got hit with this."

They searched the cave without finding anything of interest besides the blood. Then they searched the tunnels. It took almost an hour before Garvis discovered some symbols on a tunnel wall.

"This is Quinn's symbol," Garvis explained to Matthew. "See that split in it; that means he is wounded. And those lines mean intruders. He must have been alone when he was attacked."

"We'll keep searching the tunnels," Turner said.

"Your symbols are ingenious," said Matthew. "Our teams should develop something like that."

"You have so many members; that would be a lot of symbols to memorize," Bart said. "Unless you only used them on small missions."

"Quiet," said Turner in a low voice. "I heard something." Turner's group was carrying lit torches but they were small and cast limited light.

"This way," said Turner and led the group straight then to the left. They found a man lying on the ground, Turner rolled the man onto his back.

"He's not one of ours," said Louis.

"What happened to you?" asked Turner as he helped the man to sit up.

"Not rightly sure," said the man as he rubbed the swollen area on the back of his head. "Some of us stay down here. We have a little place down this tunnel. The last two nights all these strange guys have been running through here. Hey, why are you down here?"

"We're looking for some friends," Turner said. "They had a sort of room near the beginning of these tunnels, near the docks."

"Yeah, I know who you're talking about. Nice enough fellas. Don't know why they would have meetings down here though cuz they always dress real nice. Someone busted up their place."

"Did you see who did it?" Turner asked.

"No, but it's probably those same guys. They roughed up our place yesterday then just now I was going home and they run past me and knocked me into the wall."

"What did they look like?"

"I don't know, regular guys. Regular mean guys."

"Which way did they go?"

"Straight ahead towards our place."

"We'll get you home," Turner said and helped the man to his feet. "What is your name?"

"Conway but everyone calls me Connie."

"Well, Connie let's see where you live."

Matthew took Turner's torch as he helped Connie to walk. "Do you want to go to a physician?" Matthew asked.

"Naw. I'll live," Connie said. "Hell!"

"Connie stay here," said Turner as they all heard the sounds of fighting.

69

Matthew ran forward first and the others followed. Within moments they entered a medium sized cavern that had been turned into a shelter for some of the homeless of the city. Half a dozen thugs were attacking people.

"Try someone who can defend themselves," Matthew yelled and hit a man with one of the torches, the man's hair quickly caught on fire and he started to scream. Turner and his crew wasted no time in attacking the other hired killers.

Turner, Louis, Garvis and Bart were tough men and good fighters. The thugs were taken by surprise, they fought well but not good enough.

"What are you doing down here?" yelled Matthew as he threw one of the men against a stone wall.

"Screw you!"

"I can set you on fire too. Now start talking."

"We don't have a fight with you."

"No, you just pick on people who can't defend themselves. I am Prince Matthew and these are the people of my kingdom so I would say you do have a fight with me."

"Prince Matthew," some of the people whispered.

"I'll hang you in the streets," Matthew threatened. "Start talking."

"Matthew let us work on them," said Turner. "We have ways of getting information that no one can resist."

"Hell Kane, I'm telling them," yelled one of the men who was tied up. "Some guy in the Piccadilly Tavern paid us good money to find some guys down here. But these ain't them."

"Who were you supposed to find?" demanded Turner.

"Some guys wearing suits who have meetings down here. But we ain't seen them. Just these guys here and they don't know nutin."

"Did you tear that office apart?" Turner asked.

"No, we found it like that yesterday. We think someone beat us to the money."

"What do you mean?"

"We each got a bag of coins now and get another when we bring those guys back to the Piccadilly."

"And what is the name of the guy at the Piccadilly?"

"He didn't give it but you can't miss him. Big with marks all over like something blew up in his face."

"Well, we're going for a walk," Turner said.

"He'll kill us if you take us in there."

"Pity about that," Turner sneered.

All of the thugs were tied up except for the one who had caught on fire. He had run out of the cavern screaming.

"Wait," Matthew said to Turner then addressed the people in the cavern. "We have business to take care of here. Tomorrow morning, an hour after sunrise you come to the Gates Way Hotel. I will buy you all breakfast and we will talk." The people smiled and whispered among themselves.

"The Piccadilly isn't far," Matthew said to Turner's crew as they pushed the criminals out of the tunnels.

"We can save you a lot of trouble if you tell us why you were sent for those guys," Bart said to the prisoners.

"He didn't tell us," said Kane. "And we didn't ask. And you guys might just get your asses kicked in there."

"We might," said Matthew.

Matthew and his group exited the tunnels where they had entered them; near the docks. Some of Matthew's soldiers were standing near the entrance. "Get some more, we are probably going to have a fight on our hands," Matthew said to one of the soldiers. "We're going to the Piccadilly."

The Piccadilly was in a seedy area of the city but it was by no means the most dangerous tavern in that area. The soldiers from Langer were keeping an eye on Matthew and Turner, so they were spread along the streets. They now formed a group that stormed into the Piccadilly. Ten soldiers burst through the back door as their comrades burst through the front.

Some of the patrons jumped and they all stopped what they were doing when it appeared that the tavern was under siege.

"I'm Prince Matthew and I need to talk to the man who sent these crooks after my friends. Our fight isn't with the rest of you, of course unless you want it to be."

The men in the tavern were tough and they were drunk, they started to look at each other and Matthew knew there would be fighting.

"You're not welcomed here, prince or no prince," spat one of the men and a soldier hit him over the head with a whiskey bottle.

The Horn of Shana was blown by the soldiers coming from Fort Castor. The men in the tavern heard it and understood the significance.

"Yeah, I may have forgotten to tell you about that," Matthew said. "You can all end up in the dungeons or go on with your night; it's your choice."

As Matthew was talking, some of the soldiers were searching the building.

"Well, look at what we found hiding in the kitchen like a rat," said one of the soldiers as he and another pushed a large man into the main room of the tavern. The man had marks and scars all over him.

A company of soldiers from Fort Castor surrounded the tavern. The Captain in charge entered through the front door. "The one's tied up were attacking innocent citizens. Hang them all in the streets and put signs on them with their crimes," Matthew ordered. The Captain turned and called more of his men into the tavern.

"Any of the rest of you want to join your friends?" Matthew asked challengingly and all of the men in the tavern stayed in their seats.

"Wait, you can't do this," yelled one of the thugs. Matthew didn't respond. "We might have information to trade."

"I'm listening," said Matthew.

"Well, we sure can't tell you here."

"Take them to the dungeons instead," Matthew told the Captain. "And this one comes with us."

Soldiers from Fort Castor stayed in the tavern as Matthew and Turner's team left with the man who had hired the thugs. As soon as they walked out of the building Garvis pushed the man into an alley.

Turner and Bart pinned the man against the side of a building while Matthew searched his pockets. Matthew threw the man's weapons on the ground. He pulled five small pouches of gold out of the man's jacket pockets but Matthew didn't find anything else.

"Who did you send those men after?" Matthew asked.

"I'm not telling you shit!"

"Matthew move," Turner said and motioned to Louis who pulled a knife from his belt and grabbed the right hand of the big man. Louis inserted the tip of the knife under the man's thumb nail and the man screamed in pain. "We can keep doing this all night," Turner said. "So talk."

"In my right boot. The paper is in my right boot," said the man as he was crying from the pain. Louis grabbed the man's leg and pulled his boot off while Turner and Bart held him.

"What is your name?" asked Turner.

"Rudy."

"Well Rudy, you made a fine choice."

"There is a bounty on them," Louis said as he read the paper.

"Where did you get this?" asked Turner. The man didn't answer. "You've got nine more fingers before we start on the toes."

"The Wax Vixen. It's a tavern but a nice, kinda fancy one. There's a guy that sits in there day and night playing cards. His name is Steele and he dresses real fancy. He was handing them out."

"When was this?"

"Two nights ago."

"Has anyone collected?"

"Not that I know of. I wouldn't have paid those morons if they had."

"What else do you have to tell us?" asked Louis and grabbed the man's hand.

"Steele doesn't own the tavern but he and his men took it over. The place is filled with professionals."

"And?" asked Louis.

"That's it." Louis pulled out his knife. "Ok, Ok. There's rumors that Steele's girl is a witch. I've never seen him with her but I did see the back room once and the walls are covered with strange writings and blood."

"Were there any altars in there?" asked Matthew.

"What do you mean?"

"A place where they sacrifice people."

"Hell no! I went back there because I thought there was a card game. There's the same furniture there always was; card tables. There's just that shit on the walls."

"Give him to the soldiers," Matthew said to Turner. Then he said in a lower voice. "Miranda what are we going into?"

"That writing is not living. It is intended as an intimidation ploy and it works. Steele is a criminal that you need to remove from this city but your friends are not with him. And they are not going to be safe for long where they are."

"Will you tell me?"

"What should you be asking?"

"Will you help us?"

"Yes. Andrac set the bounties and there are more than humans hunting those Elods. The Masthead Hotel, room 515 and hurry."

"Captain Flores all the prisoners go to the dungeons but we need to get to the Masthead Hotel right away and prepare for a fight," Matthew said.

Chapter VII
Rescued

The Masthead Hotel was on the far north side of the city whereas the Piccadilly was on the south side. Matthew and his men mounted their horses and raced through the streets of Castor. Matthew yelled Miranda's words to Turner. The men searched the streets with their eyes as they rode. They were looking for Andrac's monsters.

"Quinn is bleeding again," yelled Baird as they hid in a hotel room. "Damn, we need some supplies."

"Tear up those sheets," said Abbott as he watched the streets from one of the hotel windows. "No one is leaving here now."

"If we live through this bullshit, I'm joining up with Turner," said Spencer angrily. He was peering out of one of the side windows. "We should have left days ago."

"Don't bitch at me," said Abbott. "I said that right away. You're the ones who couldn't make up your damn minds. Maybe the only thing we've got going for us is that I haven't contacted him yet and I said I would. He'll come looking for us. I know him that well."

"Just what are those demons going to look like?" Matthew yelled.

"Almost anything," yelled Bart. "If Andrac is smart he will give them human faces."

"Great," said Matthew under his breath.

Citizens jumped out of the way of the racing horses. Matthew told Captain Flores to have the Horn of Shana blown so people would know to get out of the streets.

"Shut up!" snapped Abbott. "Do you hear that?"

"That horn?" asked Watkin. "That's the soldiers."

"And they work for the King and so do the teams. We need to get to them," Abbott said.

"That sound is getting louder," said Spencer. "Don't leave the room until we see them."

"Shit! I can't believe it," yelled Cabot. "Turner and the guys are with them. They're stopping in front."

Abbott ran to the front window of the hotel room and opened it. "Turner, we're up here and there are demons inside."

"Miranda!" yelled Matthew as he dismounted and ran into the hotel lobby.

Guests and employees jumped and stared as Matthew, Turner's team and soldiers ran into the lobby and up the stairs.

"What is going on?" yelled the desk clerk. "What is going on?" No one took the time to tell him.

The men were running up five flights of winding stairs. They didn't stop to talk to anyone. Matthew was in the lead and stopped so abruptly when he reached the landing of the fifth floor that Turner ran into him. "Stop!" Matthew yelled.

Only the men in front of the group could see what Matthew was looking at. Miranda was standing on the fifth floor facing a pack of what appeared to be demon dogs.

"I am sending you home to your master," Miranda said to the demons who did not approach her. "He will understand my message."

Andrac was in his workroom as he called it but it was really a huge prison where he did experiments on Elods and creatures. The pack of dogs appeared in front of him but immediately they turned back into the Elods they were before he violated them. Screams and cries not only filled his prison but all of Inferus as the monsters were turned back into Elods and the chains fell from the prison doors.

"No!" screamed Andrac as he found himself locked inside of one of his cells.

The men who had been turned into demon dogs gathered around the cage. "The Angel said you would understand her message," said one of the men.

"Let's burn him alive!" yelled another. "Gather wood."

"Wait," said the first man. "Angel, what would you have us do?"

"Holy Shit! Abbott you changed," yelled Spencer.

Abbott ran to a mirror and started to cry. "Someone removed the curse. I'm an Elod again."

"Let us in," yelled Turner and Cabot ran to the door and unlocked it.

"Boy, are we glad to see you guys," said Spencer. "Did you see those demon dogs?"

"The Angel Miranda got rid of them," said Matthew.

"She must have remove the curse," said Abbott who could not stop crying. "How do I thank her?"

"All of the Angels can always hear you," said Matthew. "What curse?"

"Andrac had turned him into a type of demon too," said Turner.

"We really need to get Quinn to a physician," Baird said anxiously."

Matthew was standing in the doorway and turned and yelled, "We need a physician in here right away. If they don't want to come because of the time tell him I will pay triple."

"Pack your things and we're taking you to our hotel then tomorrow you're coming to Langer," Matthew said to Abbott's men. "We're not forcing you to join our cause but it isn't safe for you here. Some guy named Steele is handing out bounty sheets on all of you."

"We need to deal with him," said Turner as he was kneeling near Quinn.

"Captain Flores will be raiding that place tonight" said Matthew.

"Turner, I'm joining your crew," said Abbott.

"I think we all are," said Spencer. "Screw this. Andrac put those bounties on us just like you said."

"Make way! Make way!" yelled a soldier as he was leading a physician up the stairs.

Matthew moved into the hallway and Abbott followed him. "Prince Matthew will you help me to thank that Angel?"

Matthew took Abbott's arm and led him to a different area of the hallway. "The Angel's name is Miranda. And they don't always appear but she can hear whatever you say. Turner said that all of you are raised to be afraid and to hate everything. The Angels are good, you don't have to be afraid of them. Abbott, do you know that we saved the Credo and they live in Wetpr? I'm telling you because you are all free men now. You can have whatever lives you want."

"Never in my life did I dare to dream of being a free man. I have to tell the others. But first how do I talk to the Angel?"

"Just like you are talking to me. Just say what is in your heart."

"Angel Miranda, thank you so much for taking that curse from me. I didn't want to be a monster. I don't know why you did this but it was the most wonderful act ever. I am in your debt. Please let me know how I can repay you for your kindness." Abbott started to sob.

"I believe she heard you." Matthew said then realized that the soldiers standing in the hallway were watching and listening to Abbott. "Let's go back into the room," Matthew said and led Abbott by the arm.

"He will live but he has lost a lot of blood," the physician was saying when Matthew entered the room.

"Can he travel in the back of a boca?" asked Matthew. "Just to Langer."

"He should stay in bed one maybe two days and then possibly you can put him into a boca."

"We need to get him out of here now. Can we move him to another hotel?"

"It will be dangerous."

"What is your name?"

"Kincaid."

"Doctor Kincaid. I will pay you very well if you come with us to the Gates Way Hotel and watch him for a while."

"Very well, but he cannot ride a horse and the men will have to be careful moving him down the stairs."

It took almost an hour to get Quinn into a bed at the Gates Way Hotel. All of Abbott's men wanted to stay in one set of chambers although Matthew had previously paid for several rooms. So Matthew told some of the soldiers to stay in the extra rooms.

After everyone was settled in, Matthew ordered food and bottles of whiskey and wine to be brought to the rooms. Turner's crew decided to eat in the chambers that Abbott's men were in and they asked Matthew to join them.

"Prince Matthew will you tell them what you told me?" asked Abbott.

"I don't know how much you know about us," Matthew said. "But, my father King Mathas and my uncle King Sudfad of Wetpr are leading the fight against demons and dark lords. We have highly trained teams of warriors like you besides our armies. If any of you want to work with us you are hired and we will protect you but you need to know that we serve The Great Ruler and it was one of His Angels who got rid of those demon dogs and helped Abbott."

"And it was our people who helped the Credo to escape. They have their own community in Wetpr and are doing very well. All of you are free men now. If you want to live with the Credo I am sure they would welcome you."

"How did you do such a thing?" asked Cabot suspiciously. "How did you enter Inferus?"

"Honestly, I was not with that team but the Angel Miranda who helped you tonight and the Angel Adam got the people in and out," said Matthew. "You don't have to make any decisions tonight."

"Is it true that Javier and Madeline are alive?" asked Spencer.

"Yes but the assassins who killed Prince Michael used a variety of poisons on their arrows and Javier and the third man who was attacked, his name is Edward, barely survived. They are being cared for in King Sudfad's castle."

"Did you know that Madeline was engaged to Prince Michael and that she and Javier work for King Sudfad? They may be leading their own teams after they both heal. Turner and his men want to work with them but in the meantime they are temporarily assigned to another team."

"We work with the men who were the freedom fighters of Ryed," said Turner and everyone heard the pride in his voice. "We have all become family and I never in a million years would have imagined that."

"If you guys decide to work with us," Matthew explained. "We will assign you with Turner's men until we find out what Javier and Madeline are going to do. But we have a number of other teams also. In fact, two others are in Lentz now and the rest in Wetpr. They travel around like you do."

"We'll tell you all about it," Garvis said to Abbott's men. "But they are all great people and we get paid well. But they work as hard as we do so sometimes we are working around the clock. But all of you are used to that."

"You've sold me," said Spencer. "But just out of curiosity what is the community that the Credo have?"

"King Sudfad gave them a great deal of land," Matthew said. "They are building homes, farms and businesses. Sudfad has schools on the royal grounds because so many of our children were being stalked. The schools are protected so all of the Elod children are going there and some of the Elods are teaching. There is also a college."

"Does anyone else feel like they are dreaming?" asked Spencer.

"The Abuckto and sorcerers have long arms," said Cabot. "This is not over."

The men who had been transformed from demon dogs walked to the Temple of the Abuckto. All along their route they told everyone they met how the Angel Miranda had saved them and had imprisoned Andrac. Other people who also had been returned to the bodies they were born with, flocked to these men for they had no idea what had happened to them. By time this group reached the temple they numbered in the thousands.

The spokesman was named Rod and he hand been one of the demon dogs. When they reached the temple Rod yelled, "We were your monsters and an Angel of The Great Ruler saved us. Come out and look upon us!"

The members of the Abuckto walked out of the temple and faced the people. "What did you say?" demanded Baruk, the leader of the Abuckto.

"The Angel Miranda who saved the Credo has lifted your curses upon us. She has imprisoned Andrac," yelled Rod. "She told us to pray to The Great Ruler and to ask Him to send us Angels."

"Your blasphemy will be punished," Baruk yelled and started to raise his arms.

"Great Ruler we need Angels!" yelled Rod and soon everyone in the crowd was yelling the same words. Suddenly the yelling stopped and the crowd looked in awe at five spectacular Angels who were standing behind the Abuckto, blocking their retreat into the temple.

When the crowd started to fall to their knees the members of the Abuckto spun around and gasped. Some drew their swords.

Miranda, Daniel, Ruth, Adam and Cyril stood on the top steps of the temple and their light was blinding.

"Your weapons are useless against us," said Adam. "The Abuckto were once the shamans and priests of your people. They taught the word of The Great Ruler. But you have desecrated Him and everything He stands for. You steal and mutilate His creations so that you will feel powerful. Today the people of Inferus will find out that you and the sorcerers are nothing but hatred and greed. You have no power!"

"Only The Great Ruler is all powerful," Cyril yelled to the crowd. "And that is why the Abuckto forbid you to know of Him. Today we give you your world back. Pray to The Great Ruler to make wise choices. Do not follow the paths of the Abuckto."

The members of the Abuckto were terrified. "What are you going to do with us?" asked Baruk.

"What do you think you deserve?" asked Ruth. "We could turn you into monsters but you are already abominations. Should we ask the people, who you have terrorized for centuries, what your fates should be?"

"No, don't do that," Baruk said.

"Rod, come up here," called Miranda.

Rod was kneeling and now stood and slowly walked up the stone steps. He was not fearful but overwhelmed by the presence of the Angels. He knelt again once he was directly in front of the holy messengers.

"Rod stand and tell your followers what we spoke of," Miranda said.

Rod lost his fear and yelled with great enthusiasm. "The Credo called to the Angels and they took them from Inferus. The Credo live now in the world above. They have homes and businesses and churches. I asked if we could go there too."

"Rod stay where you are," said Daniel and walked forward. And as he walked the people suddenly realized that Benedict was walking with him. They gasped, some clapped but most stared in wonder.

"Benedict, if these people would like to join you in the world above would you help them?" Daniel asked.

Benedict walked a couple of steps closer to the crowd. "I am sorry but this is very emotional for me. I led a secret life here. I was bred to be a member of the Abuckto but my heart belonged to The Great Ruler and I was the leader of the Credo. I thought that I was a faithful man but it was my daughter Anka who called to the Angel Miranda. No one else had ever called the Angels or the Spirit of The Great Ruler into Inferus before."

"Because of the faith and courage of my daughter we were rescued and can now worship without persecution. King Sudfad of Wetpr has given us so much land. Beautiful, rich land and we are building a community. You are welcome to join us but do not bring this darkness with you."

"The choice is yours," said Daniel. "You may remain in Inferus or we will transport you to Benedict's community. Gather your families. You do not have to bring much; you will be provided for. We will wait here for you to return."

The crowd dispersed and people ran to tell their friends and families but the Angels had amplified all of the voices and everyone in Inferus heard the words being said. Gilder and other sorcerers also heard the words and they hid in fear, waiting for the Angels to leave.

Anka saw her father disappear from their home with the Angel Daniel. She ran to the spot where they stood and screamed for Miranda.

"Father," Anka yelled and ran to Benedict when she materialized on the temple steps. She was crying hysterically.

"Why have you brought her here?" Benedict asked Miranda.

84

"Tell her why we are here," Miranda said.

"The Angels are saving everyone," Benedict said emotionally. "We are bringing them home."

Anka now ran to Miranda and hugged her legs. "Miranda are you leaving the bad people here?"

"Yes child. We've healed the people who they turned into monsters," Miranda said.

"You can't leave the animals because they are tortured too," cried Anka. "Please save them." Miranda did not speak. "Miranda please, they look like monsters too but that is because of the sorcerers. Can't you make them look like they are supposed to? There is a lot of room in the world above. Isn't there room for all of us?"

Miranda smiled then looked at the Abuckto. "You hypocrites! You say you represent what is holy but you have spent your lives terrorizing everything in this world. You spread your hatred until it is a plague. You want ultimate power! You want to be gods! Well, let's see how much power you have when there is nothing left to victimize!"

Sudfad's family was gathering around the breakfast table when the ground shook so violently that people had to hold onto things to keep from falling.

"Are we being attacked?" yelled Raul.

"Jared wake up!" screamed Zoya as a picture fell from the wall in their bedroom. He jumped out of bed and grabbed a sword. "We need to get to the castle," Zoya said and quickly dressed.

The World of Nunc shook as the passageways to Inferus were sealed. The Abuckto, the sorcerers and those who chose to stay with them screamed with rage and cursed the Angels and The Great Ruler.

The Elods who suddenly appeared in the Elod community in Wetpr laughed and cried. Many fell to the ground and kissed it.

"You are not Credo but it is The Great Ruler who saved all of us," Benedict announced. "We will give thanks to Him for being delivered from hell."

Chapter VIII
The Announcement

As with the downfall of Samael, the Angels instantly sent Enrops into Wetpr and Lentz with the announcement that the Elods had been rescued from the Kingdom of Inferus and the passageways were destroyed.

Dominic and his team were running out of their house; prepared for battle when they received the message. Mathas too, believed he was under attack when Enrops flew into the castle with the announcement.

Claudius, his sons and daughters, Gideon and Ashley were traveling to Langer when they received the information.

"Something is wrong," said Thaos.

"What do you mean?" asked Ashley. "This is wonderful news."

"The Angels defeated Samael yesterday and the powers of Inferus today," Thaos said. "Something is going on."

Madeline started to cry when she heard the news. Sudfad told all of the men in his family to saddle up as they were going to the Elod community.

"We want to come too," said Nyla.

"No, I don't want any of you leaving this castle until we understand what is happening," Sudfad said.

Gabriel's household was sitting down for breakfast when the earth started to shake. Those who were not comforting scared babies and children ran to other rooms to grab weapons.

"Everyone come back to the dining room now!" yelled Natasha. "Boys get everyone then you can play with the Enrops," she said to the children.

"The Angels rescued the Elods and creatures of Inferus and brought them to Benedict's community," said one of the Enrops, when everyone had gathered in the dining room of Gabriel's home. "The Abuckto and sorcerers are still there but all of the passageways have been destroyed."

Gabriel and Raphael looked at each other solemnly for they were the only ones who truly understood the meaning of the actions.

"Raphael this is wonderful," said Vivian. "Why do you look like that?"

"This is exactly like Ryed. The Angels cleared our way so we could concentrate on much worse things," Raphael said.

"You know Sudfad will go to the Elod community," Gabriel said. "We should leave now too."

Matthew received the announcement from the Enrops and pounded on the door to Turner's chambers first. Turner was awake because of the shaking of the earth. "Get your men and meet me in Abbott's chambers; you are never going to believe what has happened," Matthew said and ran down the hallway.

Alex, Kent and George had been told about Inferus prior to this morning. As everyone they were shocked by the news. But these three brothers were also surprised that they were riding with Sudfad as representatives of the Royal Family. They understood why Javier was riding with the King and Princes but these three Nordes warriors had not really felt like members of Sudfad's family until this very moment. Although they did not speak, the pride was evident on all of their faces.

"Seriously, tell us again," said Bart. "I am so shocked I don't think my brain is working."

"I don't know all of the details yet," said Matthew with a huge grin as he looked at the emotional faces of the Elods in the room.

All of these men were hardened warriors and they all looked as if they would cry. "All I know is that Miranda turned all of your people who had been turned into monsters back to themselves. And the men who had been turned into those devil dogs led your people to the Temple of the Abuckto then apparently they all called for Angels and a bunch of Angels came. They gave the people a choice and everyone who wanted to leave was transported to Wetpr to that community I told you about."

"And the Enrops I spoke with didn't know how Anka or Benedict got in Inferus but Anka begged the Angels to save the creatures so they wouldn't be tortured anymore, so it sounds like they are in Wetpr too. Then the Angels locked the Abuckto and sorcerers in Inferus. I hope none of you planned to go back because all the passages are destroyed."

"We really are free men," Louis said as tears ran down his face. "We are really free."

The Ruala team members from Gabriel's house flew ahead and told Sudfad that others from the household were riding to the Elod community too. Sudfad slowed down so his friends could catch up with them. Emeral and Maxwell were with this group and they were overwhelmed to witness not only a world changing event but a miracle.

Sudfad led this combined group down the main street of the Elod community and the Credo cheered and applauded. The Elods who had just arrived from Inferus had no idea who Sudfad and the others were but when the Credo told them, they too cheered.

Sudfad rode up to Benedict, dismounted and the two men embraced. "This is King Sudfad of Wetpr," Benedict yelled to the crowd. "His people came to Inferus to help us escape and every one of them was wounded trying to save us. We lived in his castle and he treated us as family. He has given us this land and everything we have needed to start new lives. This is a very different world than we had been told. This is a very good world."

Although it was early, Matthew ordered the finest wine in the hotel to be brought to the room of Abbott's team. The men drank toasts to their freedom and to the end of a nightmare that had lasted for centuries.

Most of these men had sat in stunned silence until Matthew started the toasts. Now they laughed and cried. Garvis and Spencer jumped up and danced around the parlor as others clapped to the music only they could hear. They never realized before how good freedom sounded.

As Benedict made introductions, the newly arrived Elods eagerly sought to shake the hands of the people of this new world.

Raul picked Anka up and set her on his shoulders. "We heard that you were responsible for saving all of the animals," Raul said. "Boy, the kids at the castle are going to love you." Anka smiled brightly.

"Mother are you alright?" asked Calen and put his arm around Emeral.

"This is history in the making," she said. "Our world will never be the same after this morning. Do you realize that?"

After the introductions, Benedict called Rod to come forward. The huge crowd became quiet as he explained how he had been abducted and turned into a demon. Then he told them how Andrac had sent a pack of demon dogs to Castor to kill Abbott and his team.

"We were breaking their door down when we felt this, I don't even know how to explain it; a warmth. We turned and saw the most beautiful Angel. Of course we didn't understand what she was but it was like she was talking to us in our minds. Her name is Miranda and we felt healed just being in her presence. She told us a group of men were coming to save Abbott's team and in that instant the men appeared behind her."

"Then she said, so the others could hear too, that she was sending us back to our master and he would understand her message." Rod became emotional as he spoke.

"We appeared in Andrac's prison and as soon as he saw us the curses were lifted and we were people again and he was locked in a cell. We heard the chains falling from all of the cells except for his. And everyone...she removed the curses from everyone." He paused to compose himself. "We wanted to kill Andrac but I asked the beautiful Angel what she wanted us to do."

"She told us to go to the Temple of the Abuckto and not to be afraid. She said to call to The Great Ruler and ask Him to send Angels to Inferus. And she told us to gather everyone and to tell them her words. We did what she said and five Angels appeared on the steps of the temple and saved us all."

Gabriel and Raphael walked up to Raul, Simon and Javier who were standing together. Raul saw the looks on their faces and took Anka off his shoulders. "Why don't you tell your new friends about the Learning Center and find out if they want to go," Raul said.

In the meantime, Javier motioned for Kent, George and Alex to join them. "When we were going to Ryed to destroy Teivel and the Grand Masters the Angels cleared the way for us. We believe they are doing it again," Gabriel said.

"What do you mean?" asked Alex.

"They destroy Samael and stop the Gefrey Games and in the same twenty-four hours they close the passages to Inferus. This is unheard of."

"Why would they do that, I mean clear the way?" asked George.

"Because we can only concentrate on so many enemies at one time. I think they want us to focus on something really bad," said Raphael. "And my guess is the Master and the experiments."

One of the soldiers knocked on the door to the chambers' of Abbott's team. "My Lord, all those people are downstairs now and the hotel staff doesn't look happy."

"I forgot about them," Matthew said and quickly left the chambers. As soon as he got to the first floor, the hotel manager ran up to him and said disapprovingly.

"My Lord, these people said that you are buying their breakfast."

"I am. Fix them a feast," Matthew said and grinned at the disgusted look on the manager's face. Then he walked past him and into the dining room, which at this time of the morning was filled only with the homeless.

"I am Prince Matthew and I want to thank all of you for coming. I don't know if you have heard that in Langer we have provided shelters and food for the homeless while we are building them a neighborhood. I will do the same here but I will need your help. I will be in Castor for two days, I would like some of you to volunteer to be on a committee to help me and I will pay you for your services."

"What kind of help do you need?" asked a man.

"To begin with I will need the numbers of families in need. And the ages and numbers of children so we can start a school. Then I want a list of names and skills. In Langer we are setting many people up in their own businesses. And if any of you want to move to Langer where we already have these projects in motion I will need a list of those people so I can provide enough transportation. You don't have to make any decisions now."

One man stood up and humbly took his hat off. "My Lord, what kind of shelters do you have set up in Langer?"

"Understand this was kind of a spur of the moment thing. But we are building barracks for our new navy when we discovered many people who were living under the city. We moved them to the barracks and established a huge kitchen nearby. Their neighborhood will be on the same land because many of them have trades that we need to hire to support our navy."

"Can you tell us about this neighborhood?" asked a woman.

"We showed them the land and told them to tell us what they wanted. They drew up plans for a business area and homes. Of course some of the businesses will be in the homes. Some wanted farms, so those plots are on the outskirts of the neighborhood. We have a temporary school set up while we build a real one and we are building offices for physicians."

"Admiral Gideon is responsible for all of this so I am sorry that I don't have more details for you. I was on an assignment when he organized most of this. But I can tell you that the kingdom is paying for everything. And understand that we aren't forcing this on anyone; it is your choice."

"Since you already have this started," asked a man. "Would there be enough room if some of us wanted to go there?"

"Father has assigned an army of carpenters to work on this project and all of the people who were homeless have skills and they are working on their new homes too. Actually, I couldn't believe how fast the neighborhood is going up when I first saw it."

"In case you don't know. We are starting a navy and eventually will have thousands of sailors so think of all the services we will need for them. We will need absolutely everything. Seamstresses to make the uniforms. Cobblers for the shoes. Black smiths, carpenters and the list goes on. They are also building a general store in that neighborhood."

"As I said, I will be here for two days and if any of you want to return with me, you can see the works for yourselves." The room filled with excited chatter. "But I would like some of you to meet with me after breakfast just so I have people to go to. The only person I know by name is Connie."

Connie stood up. "I am a barber by trade. The Hutas drove me out of Ganz. Think those sailors will need haircuts?" he asked with a grin.

"Connie, you just volunteered to make a list of the skills and businesses we need to build," said Matthew. "We need more teachers too; are there any in this group?" Two women and a man raised their hands. "Please stand up. What are your names?"

"I am Oliver," said the man. "And this is Myrtle and Violet."

"I am not forcing you to move to Langer but we sure could use you. Can I ask the three of you to get me the ages and numbers of children? And lists of supplies?"

Turner walked into the dining room and handed Matthew a cup of coffee. "You want me to start lining up bocas?" he asked loudly.

"How many people are thinking of coming to Langer with us?" Matthew asked then laughed as it appeared that most of the people raised their hands. "I need a volunteer to get the numbers here then give them to Turner so he can setup the transportation."

After the meeting, Matthew sent messages to his father, Gideon and Dominic. He told of the rescue of Abbott and his team. Of Miranda transforming Abbott and the demon dogs. Matthew explained that Quinn was injured and they would be delayed in returning but when they did they would be bringing Abbott's crew to join Dominic's team and bocas full of homeless people who wanted to live in the neighborhood Gideon was building.

Mathas' morning meeting started out with the topic of Inferus. Thaos and Stephan also realized that the Angels were possibly helping to reduce the number of adversaries so the teams could focus on a big mission. These two men told the group about their experiences on the mission in Ryed.

Next, Claudius stood up and explained the events with Hector and Samael from the previous day. "Sorren isn't going to be attending any meetings while Hector and his men are in the village, which is understandable."

"I will ride out there later with any messages."

Angelina stood up. "I'm not sure I like my mother taking care of that animal."

"That is exactly what Ingr and Nikki said this morning," said Thaos. "Don't you girls ride out there and stir things up."

Angelina stared at Thaos for a moment then smiled, "Us?" she said sweetly.

"We're in trouble now," Stephan said and laughed.

"To get back to Hector," Claudius said. "After we got him into a bed in the village, Shara woke him. She gave him some kind of tea and he was pretty alert. I told him and Clev every damn word that Miranda told me and for the first time I saw that boy look shocked."

"First, he was shocked that Miranda was helping him but in hindsight I think she knew Samael would make an appearance but I didn't tell him that."

"Then he was shocked about the whole thing with Juleta and the Sisters of Tameric. He knew of the group but he couldn't believe that Juleta could fool him so. Now mind you, Hector hasn't changed his ways; he is just too damn sick to do anything. But he is beholding to us and so is Clev. They wanted to pay us and of course we didn't take the money. Both men have said about a dozen times that they owe us. I guess we will see if they come through. I did tell them that Miranda said we have some of the same enemies."

"Mathas, I told him that you offered a cottage to his parents for the time being and he liked that idea. Bella wanted me to ask him what they should get out of that house but there was just too damn much going on. So she sent a note today."

"Claudius, I am riding out with you," said Angelina. "I don't trust those men in our village."

"Well, besides the fact that your people out number them and are better trained," Claudius said and grinned. "I heard Clev tell his men that if any of them violated Sorren's rules that he would kill them himself. But you are welcome to ride along."

"I think a few of us will join you," said Dominic. "Changing the subject, where are Angus and Fahron?"

"They are both looking into Josef's accounts and other things. Then they are going to write up a list of questions and have some of the Guardians interrogate him," Mathas said. "Now I have a question. Are some of you still planning on going to Salar soon?"

"Yes," said Noah.

"Rosa and Margarit are going to be traveling with you. It turns out that Hannah and the head of the medical school developed a program just for Margarit. She can start her studies towards becoming a physician and if she decides she doesn't like it, she is still young enough to study other things."

"But, I have to warn you Margarit hasn't slept or stopped talking since she found out about this. And I have to tell you that I am very proud of the girl. When are you leaving?"

"That depends on us," said Ryan. "I don't know if Claudius told you that he made Artis and Ralph managers at the shop so I could spend more time here."

"Do you need more help?" asked Mathas.

"No, but there is just so much stuff," Ryan explained. "I would suggest we build a library just for our work. Right now we are trying to organize everything. Rosa had all these shelves put into the office and they are already full. We will need more."

"Stephan are the carpenters far enough along on that new office that we can start moving these people up there?" asked Mathas.

Stephan stood up and addressed the group. "I don't think any of you have seen what we are doing. We started out tearing the walls down between a few chambers. Then every time Mathas or Father would go up there we would make changes. Basically we have an entire wing of the castle now."

"I've had carpenters working around the clock. After the meeting let's go up there and look around. If you want to start moving stuff up there we can."

"Do we need that much room?" asked Ryan.

"Well, we are leaving some sleeping chambers up there too. A lot of you have been working all night on this project and catching naps when you can," Stephan explained.

When Sudfad rode out to meet the newly rescued Elods he brought maps with him. After the initial introductions, he spread the maps out and showed Benedict and the others the additional miles of land he was giving them.

"This all rich land," Sudfad said. "The only caution is this area here. That is the border where the Kingdom of Stordt starts. The only way you can tell is it is usually lined with border guards. The last few kings have been demons so I would highly suggest you stay clear of that area."

Sudfad and Raul returned to the castle and got the rest of the family members to bring to the Elod community for introductions. Gabriel and Raphael returned to their home for the same purpose.

The newly arrived Elods were both surprised and confused to see Madeline and Javier with the Royal Family. Many people were so frightened by them that Sudfad and Benedict addressed the crowd together to explain the presence of these two people.

Simon sent soldiers into Salar to buy bocas full of food and supplies. That evening a huge feast was held at the Elod community. The Royal Family and Gabriel's household were honored guests.

While the adults had to overcome their fears in this new world, the children almost immediately became friends. The children from both Sudfad's and Gabriel's household brought toys and taught their new friends how to play with them.

In the coming days many members of the Royal Family of Wetpr as well as soldiers worked around the clock at the Elod community building homes for the newly arrived refugees.

Chapter IX
Allies

After Stephan showed the teams their new office space he and Thaos rode into Langer to check on Selen. She had been feeling like she was being watched for several months so Thaos stationed soldiers at her home.

With the money that Juleta left her, Selen bought a house in the City of Langer. It was considerably larger than the cottage she had lived in in Zorta. Hilgra shared the house with her. It had a beautiful yard and a large garden which both women tended.

Hilgra owned a magic shop in the Catacombs and Selen worked for Gideon and Ashley. She managed the Adam's Homes they were building in Langer. Selen had a lot of people who worked under her and although she had never been a manger before, she loved the job and the people loved her.

As soon as Claudius' family first learned that Hector was in Langer, Thaos had soldiers escorting Selen everywhere. At her request the men wore civilian clothing. He also increased the number of soldiers who guarded her home. This assignment was coveted by the soldiers as both Selen and Hilgra cooked for the men.

Thaos and Stephan walked into one of the Adam's Homes and were immediately greeted by six children. "Hold out your hands," said Stephan as he handed them candy.

"You're spoiling them," Selen said with a big smile. "I am surprised you found me. I am checking on the supplies in all of the houses today."

"We may have handed out candy at a few others," Thaos said and grinned. "We already checked your place and its fine. Has anything suspicious happened?"

"Just this," said one of the soldiers. "As soon as we got here the next door neighbor said some woman asked if Selen worked at their house and they told her, she worked here. The woman asked if they would give this to Selen."

As the soldier spoke he took a coin out of his pocket and handed it to Stephan. "I've never seen anything like that," the soldier said. "And Selen didn't want to touch it."

Thaos looked at the gold coin which appeared to be very old. "I have no idea what this is," he said and handed it to Stephan. "Did the neighbor describe the woman?"

"It's Mister Harper and he is half blind. All he could say is she seemed nice and looked normal, whatever that means."

"Thaos, I don't want that," said Selen.

"We're going to Sorren's village after this," Thaos said. "We'll ask Hector about it."

"Has he mentioned me?" Selen asked fearfully.

"No, but the guy is half dead and has been fighting for his life against both enemies and curses," Stephan said. "He was in really bad shape yesterday. We're hoping he can talk a little today."

"I kind of feel sorry for him," said Selen.

"Don't; he is still the monster he ever was," said Stephan. "But hopefully some good will come out of this besides keeping a worse demon from coming to this world."

When Claudius, Angelina and some of Dominic's team arrived at the house where Hector was staying, Nikki and Ingr were already inside. They as well as Angelina were wearing their warrior's outfits instead of their normal dress, which was meant to let Hector know their intentions.

"Why doesn't this surprise me?" Claudius said sarcastically as his group walked into Hector's bedroom. Hector was sitting up in bed. Shara and Clev were also in the room.

"I've been getting my chops beat by the prettiest girls in Langer," Hector said weakly and smiled.

Shara laughed. "The girls are setting these two straight."

"Which is why I am here too," said Angelina and pushed through the people until she was standing next to Hector's bed. "Shara is my mother. If either of you do anything to even scare her I will cut your balls off."

"I really don't doubt that," said Hector with a grin. "But your folks and Claudius' family have saved me a hundred times over. Trust me, I won't be behind hurting any of them. And if anyone else does I will take care of them."

Angelina rolled her eyes and Hector and Clev laughed. "He's already put word out that all of you are under his protection," said Clev. "I sent the guys out this morning."

"All of you have such a reputation that I don't know if it will help but I have a reputation too," said Hector. "I haven't changed but I always keep my promises and pay my debts."

"Miranda is he telling the truth?" Ingr asked loudly. "She says you are. So I have a few questions. Did you really stop all of the bounties on our families?"

"Yes and I will make sure no more are put on you."

"I don't understand you at all," said Nikki. "It sounds like you really love Sarah but you steal children and sell them to monsters. How can you do that? What would you do if someone did that to your child?"

"I believe you destroyed that part of my operation," Hector said.

"We just busted up that one auction," said Claudius. "And the girls are right, that was pretty damn disgusting."

"Well you did more than that. All those buyers that lived after fighting with you, were burned at the stakes by Amundsen. And the priests from Leven are taking in all the kids. I wasn't the only one in that business and as far as I know it has stopped in Ganz."

"Miranda was that the only place he had that?" Ingr asked. No one else heard Miranda's voice. "Will you curse him if he ever does that again?" Ingr didn't say another word but looked at Hector and smiled.

Claudius roared with laughter. "Now that is an approach I didn't think of. Hector, I came here to talk about a couple of things and we can send these people out if you want. First, do you remember what I told you yesterday?"

"Every word and they can stay."

"Did anyone tell you about what happened in Inferus this morning?"

"Yes. Sorren called to your birds and they told him a lot of the details. Can't say I am sorry to hear about any of that. Andrac always made my skin crawl."

Claudius stared at Hector for a moment before he spoke again because he was trying to decide if he wanted to give Hector some information. Both Hector and Claudius were shrewd men who calculated every word they said to each other.

"That is two major plays by the Angels in two days. The last time they did something like that was to clear our path for another matter. Any idea what could be worse than Samael and Andrac?"

"Have you ever heard of the Originator?" Claudius nodded. "He is the original demon and from what I heard he makes the Old Ones look like pussies. The Master is like his head lieutenant in this world and you've been messing with him."

"Interesting," Claudius said and Hector grinned.

"Claudius, you guys are committing suicide but I got to tell you, I admire your guts," Hector said.

"We heard that the Originator had a couple of doorways into this world but the Angels closed them up. What prevents him from creating more?" asked Claudius.

"That is a hell of a good question. Ingr don't roll your eyes at me girl. Ask Miranda if I am lying. I really don't know but after seeing your Angels I would imagine they have a lot to do with it. Or maybe it's something with the old magics. Those magics aren't anything like the magics used today."

"What do you mean?"

"Today's magics are like words. The original magics were like living things. Like little demons themselves and they are very dangerous and very powerful," Hector said. "But, you do know that the Originator has a foothold in pretty much every world. So he's not hurting for victims."

"What are you two doing here?" Stephan asked Ingr and Nikki when he and Thaos entered the room.

"They've been asking the Angels to curse me," Hector said and winked at Stephan.

"Do Angels even do that?" Stephan asked Ingr and she only smiled at him. "Hector, I would say you are in deep shit." Hector and Stephan laughed.

"We've got a couple of questions for you and would appreciate a straight answer," Thaos said. "Are you the one who's been watching Selen?"

"No. But my men told me she was being guarded so I thought something was up. She is a decent person, who took care of my baby. You don't think it was Juleta do you?"

"Well, something is scaring the hell out of her. And today a woman left this at some other people's home and asked that they give it to her. Any idea what it is?" Thaos handed Hector the coin as he spoke.

"This is bad," Hector said seriously. "This is the calling card of the Sisters of Tameric." He handed the coin to Clev. "I wonder if they want information about Juleta." Suddenly Hector's eyes widened. "Shit, I hope they aren't looking for information about Sarah. Damn it! Clev have our boys watch her too."

"She thinks you're after her so that would only scare her more," said Thaos. "We'll take care of her. So why would they target Selen?"

"I don't know other than information but I don't know what that damn pact was that Isabella agreed to or what Juleta may have promised them. All I know is some of their members were in Langer, which I thought was strange since they tend to shun places with a lot of people. Don't ask me why."

"Anyways some of Otto's guys grabbed them and they were sacrificed to the Master. That order and the Master hate each other so that is probably a war in the making. Now I wonder if they were in Langer because of Selen."

"Their members can look like anything. They don't all look like warriors like your people. You could think you are talking to some sweet little grannie and she could kill you."

"So you weren't the one who was having her followed and leaving things on her doorsteps in Cadia?"

"No. I knew she was there and that she had gone to the monastery but the Sanuri had already taken Sarah. What did they leave on her steps?"

"Flowers with a note that someone wanted to talk to her," Thaos said.

"Yeah, flowers aren't my style," said Hector. "Shara any idea of how long you are going to have to put up with me?"

"A couple of weeks. I am still giving you medicine to fight against the curses. You have to regain your strength."

"Well, when can I get out of bed?"

"I was going to start walking you today but trust me you are considerably weaker than you feel. I'm giving you all kinds of nutrients and that is helping. If you don't believe me, Clev can describe the snakes that came out of you. Your body was not made to share it with things that large. I'm still not sure of all the damage they may have done."

"Boss, she's telling the truth. I just shit when those things started jumping out of you. All three of us were fighting them. I can't believe you lived through that."

"I can't just lie around," Hector said. "I need to get back to work."

"What? You don't think there is enough crime without you?" Nikki asked sarcastically.

"Thaos, does she bust your chops as much as mine?" asked Hector with a grin.

"You know it. She keeps me in line."

"No, I want to do some research."

"Hector, we will heal you but you will not do black magics here," scolded Shara.

"I'm not that kind of dark lord," Hector said and laughed. "I do research the same way you do but I probably have different contacts. Shara, could I have some paper and a pen?" Shara took the items from a dresser drawer and handed them to Hector. He talked to the group as he wrote.

"Your Angel was right, we do have the same enemies, at least right now. Otto and I always competed for territory but that is the fun part of all of this. But he did some crap and tried to set me up for it. That was part of the reason we were watching him. See he knows how far my reach is so if he is trying to set me up that tells me he has something big going on."

"Then that damn Sisterhood is here. Clev told me what you said about Jack and I appreciate the information. I don't know if you realize how big Otto's operation is. I am going to grab some of it and that should bring Jack out of the shadows. The Sisterhood is looking for him so that should bring them out of the shadows too."

"Right now, I think we can all agree that we need to find out more about both organizations." As Hector spoke he wrote short notes on several pieces of paper and started to pile them on the bed.

"This may be a rare moment in time when we are working together so I suggest we make the best of it. You can read these notes before Clev handles them."

"In addition to contacting those people, I want the boys in the Catacombs and on the streets. I want them focused on Jack and the Sisterhood," Hector said to Clev. Then he looked at Claudius who was reading the notes. "My men will get the information that I am asking from those people one way or another. But only Clev has the authority to barter. In the realm I work in, paying people off works the best because they all have prices."

"The things I am asking for are reading materials but I won't lie, some may have strong magics attached to them. I assume your Angels are watching over you, so hell; just ask them to disable the magics. They are like protections for the manuscripts. Honesty, I may be too weak to do it even if you trusted me enough."

"But I am also sending my men into the streets to find out information the old fashion way. If you want to send some of your men with mine for this, I have no problem with that. And the Sisterhood uses powerful old magics. You better have more than a few soldiers watching over Selen." Thaos quickly left the room.

"Hell, I forgot this," Claudius said and took an envelope out of his shirt pocket and handed it to Hector. "It's from Bella. She and Isadore are fixing up the home for your parents and they have some questions."

"I am sure she will bust your chops a little too," Stephan said and grinned.

"I wouldn't expect anything less," Hector said then read the letter. When he finished he handed it to Clev. "Claudius, she wants to know what Mother wants from the house. I have no idea. She and Isadore can go to the house whenever they want. Clev will make sure they are protected since we still don't know who broke in. But this is very nice of her."

"Claudius, we'll go with her to the house," Ingr said. Claudius nodded.

"Hector, is it a possibility that the Sisterhood was here for reason's other than revenge against Otto?" asked Claudius. "Because when you said about the pact that Isabella made and possibly Juleta, my blood ran cold."

"Yes. I tend to have my men watching our most formidable opponents; I don't underestimate them. You probably know this but the members of the Insidiae basically worship money. That is how you talk to them. Money and power. But the Sisterhood is all about hatred and revenge. They started out as a group of women who had been victims of something and they made a pact of revenge."

"Who did they make the pact with?" asked Claudius.

"Grand Masters and Old Ones. They were big into Ahriman when he was around. So you can't buy them off. And you know what Juleta was like, I can't believe I didn't see it. She was an example of how their hatred has manifested over the years. I will tell you a secret, most demons can be bought but not these gals. And they are bad enough to war with the Master, so that should tell you a lot there."

Hector stopped talking for a moment. "Wait a minute. Stephan why did they leave that coin with the neighbors?"

"I don't..."

"Miranda said to tell him," Ingr said.

Both Stephan and Hector smiled.

"She said to tell him the whole story," Ingr added. "Or do you want me to?"

"I think I better; you girls really want a piece of him," Stephan said and chuckled.

"After we broke up your ring of baby rapers, a lot of the people in our group adopted the kids, including us and Gideon. We were told that your men deliberately left one of the cages open so some kids would escape because you knew we would run into a trap to rescue them."

"Well, the Angel Adam, he's the one who defeated Samael carried those kids to the monastery. Gideon and Ashley adopted the two boys."

"Gideon, wanted to thank Adam so he is building those Adam's Homes as safe places for children. They're building them in Wetpr too. Selen is the manager of them here and was in one of the homes when the neighbors brought that coin over."

"The reason Miranda wanted you to tell me that is so I understand that the Angels must have protected those places with holiness. That's why the Sisterhood can't go near them. Selen would be safer staying in those homes."

"And just so you know. I did set up that trap but it wasn't to kill you. I wanted to negotiate the kids for those books you got of Juleta's. Talk about a plan going wrong," Hector said and laughed then he got a strange look on his face.

"I just thought of something," he said and wrote another note which he handed to Claudius to read. "I am not sure that manuscript even exists. I have only heard rumors about it and it will cost me but it might help us understand more about Isabella and Juleta. Now that I know those two crazy bitches were involved with the Sisterhood, well their craziness may be linked to that."

"I've got to ask," said Stephan. "Did you really love Juleta?"

"No but she offered me what I wanted. I just didn't realize the price," Hector said then grinned again. "Girls, stop with the eye rolls will ya. I'm good but I make mistakes too. I am just determined to learn from them."

"When we were first negotiating our relationship it was a business arrangement. I became her head lieutenant and agreed to play along with some of her schemes. Yes, we had sex but I'll tell you that lasted a few weeks then she made me into Thaos and I almost killed her."

"Why did you let her touch you?" asked Stephan. "You had to know she was insane."

"Stephan, you and I have always been alike in a lot of ways. We love to fight and be challenged but don't anyone touch our families and friends. That's why Juleta went after your family because it was the only way to hurt you. Well, a lot of people were going after mine. But Father and Mother don't know about a lot of it so don't tell them. So I faked my death and changed my looks. Besides, if she could really pull that off not only would we make lots of money but we…"

"Would have more power," said Claudius.

"Yes."

"Before you go any farther," Claudius said. "We suspect that she killed people and replaced them with her clones or whatever you want to call them."

"Now, Claudius that information will cost you."

"Most of the books we got from her were ledgers that had symbols instead of names," Claudius said to the surprise of everyone in the room. "We had a lot of people review them and it looks like a hell of a lot of people died so she could steal their power and give it to you. And the spell books; the Angels disabled before they let us touch them so considering what you said about old magics they might be useless for you."

"Damn you guys are good," Hector said. "The only thing you got wrong is that she didn't give me all of that power, if she did do you think I would look like this now. She tried to absorb it and it almost killed her. No person can hold that much power inside of them. What I have been trying to figure out is what she did with it. All of you look really confused. From now on when you think about powerful dark magics think of them as living things, like creatures. She took them from people and put them some place."

"This is going to sound really stupid," said Angelina. "But if we think of them like that, well, do they need to be kept under certain conditions or cared for in some way?"

"That is not a stupid question at all. I have heard that you too are a powerful healer so I suppose you and Shara read those ledgers. Can you tell me a little of what you saw?"

"I can't believe this but Miranda said I can," said Angelina. "They were basically really long charts. Every person had a symbol to identify them. We found that same symbol written on the pages of the spell books but then she was...ok, think of them as recipes. She was changing the ingredients by adding different herbs and potions but she didn't write why she was doing this. She also didn't write the size and weight of the person which would determine the dosage amounts. But from what we read most of the people died no matter what she did."

"I am going to have to think about that but...I am trying to think of a good way to explain what you were reading," Hector said. "Let's go back to what Shara and Clev said about those snakes in me. Let's say those snakes were dark magics, the real magics not the amateur kind. Shara said a body wasn't created to hold something that large. So the snake jumps out and now there is not only a hole in the body but as Shara said, what was damaged? Now the snake is on the floor, instead of cutting the head off you want to harness it, what do you do?" He paused. "You all look horrified."

"Hector, you just gave us an entirely different view on things we have been trying to figure out," said Shara. "And we have friends..."

"I know about your friends and now you understand what they went through. Erebus is legendary. Using the scenario I gave you he was filled with snakes but he did it all on his own. He worked hard and never sold his soul. Then there is Olin who is as opposite as he can be. Clev was watching Tessa chase him through the streets." Both Clev and Hector laughed.

"Since she seems to speak with Angels all of the time I assume she called to them but honestly she could have taken him on her own," Hector continued. "The Master gave Otto quotas and that is the only reason that Otto gave that kid some powers. He is much better off with you but know that there are bounties on him already; the Master and Jack."

"And Hilgra. I've been watching her because she seems to be the healthiest of any of us. Is that because of your Angels or your medicines?"

"The Angels," said Angelina. "We haven't figured out a medicine that works. But Miranda said that some of your side effects were caused by the Sisterhood too. What exactly does that mean? Are there cures?"

"I really don't know. It could actually be worse. I have never studied medicine and was hoping you may have made some breakthroughs," said Hector.

"Hector, we used a variety of medicines," explained Shara. "With the old medicines in particular we ask The Great Ruler to work through us. That is why it was difficult for me to help you because if I would have given you the full doses, the holy energy would have either killed you or changed you."

"I am really surprised you didn't do it then."

"Miranda helped me. You see you still have freedom of choice. I shouldn't be making those choices for you." Both Hector and Clev stared at Shara then looked at each other then back at her.

"I am going to change the subject here," said Claudius. "Because you look so weak Hector that I don't know how much more you can talk. You were telling us about your contract with Juleta."

"Basically that is what it was. She hired me to run her operations. But I was also screwing the boss which was alright for a while. Once I agreed to everything and we finalized the contract she suddenly acted like I agreed to marry her."

"But, I don't think she loved me because I don't think she was capable of loving anyone. She only wanted to possess them. But I did see some kind of a change after she had Sarah. But that didn't last long. The thing I could never figure out is how she got the baby into a monastery. Unless Lazo took Sarah inside. Juleta was so dark that she couldn't go into a place like that."

"Juleta left some letters for me and Thaos. She wanted us to kill you and she would stop the bounties on our families," said Stephan. "She made it sound like you didn't know anything about the baby."

"She lied. Selen didn't know it but I was in the castle while she was delivering the baby. Juleta told me when she was going to have her. I think she thought Sarah would bring us back together. I swear Juleta imagined this relationship between us." Hector laughed. "Just like she did with you and Thaos. You know before I got into this dark lord thing, when we were kids she used to talk about you being her boyfriend. She said you wanted to keep the relationship a secret because of your families. Even then I didn't believe her."

"And that reminds me," Hector said with a smile. "Me and the boys were riding to her castle that day all of you attacked it. I was so disgusted with her I thought 'let her get what she deserves', so we left. But what the hell were those blue birds you were riding? We just sat there for a while and watched you. The damndest thing I ever saw."

"They are Blue Hengers," said Angelina. "They are the ancient war birds of the Heavens. They can kill Talmuth."

"I'll tell you that was the best battle I was ever in," Stephan said.

"Boss, I'm going to get started on these notes," said Clev. "I'll send one of the guys in."

"We'll guard him," Angelina said and all the men in the room smiled.

"I might be afraid of that," Clev said and grinned.

"I'll be alright," Hector said to Clev. "You girls want to play some cards?"

"Do you cheat?" asked Nikki.

"Hell ya," Hector said and laughed then he looked at Stephan. "Why don't you go with Clev as a sign of good faith? Don't you two kill each other now."

"I'll get some things from the hotel," Clev said and he and Stephan walked out of the house. Stephan stood back while Clev handed out assignments to his men. Clev saddled his horse and the two headed to Langer. After a few moments Clev said, "I probably shouldn't be saying this but I think he is enjoying being around all of you. It's like he is back to his old self."

"You been with him long?" asked Stephan.

"Yeah, I was part of his original crew. Hell, I'd have to count now how many years that's been."

"Well, I probably shouldn't be saying this either but for all the power and money you guys have; your lives seem kind of shitty. When was the last time you danced with a girl or went out for a drink without having to worry about getting killed? I mean I like to fight as much as the next guy, maybe more, but I still enjoy life."

"You aren't getting an argument from me," Clev said and grinned. "We are all basically enemies and who knows if we will have to kill each other someday but the last couple of days kind of seem like the old days. I had forgotten what they were like."

"I am half tempted to say something but I will get skinned alive," Stephan said and chuckled. "In three days Thaos and I are having second wedding ceremonies for the girls. I'm half tempted to invite you so you can see what a normal life is again. The problem is we've got a lot of kids and some we rescued from you. And then there is Margarit."

"Neither he or I were at that camp so the kids wouldn't recognize us, except for Margarit. But he won't be in any shape by then. But I would be half tempted to go," Clev said with a grin.

Chapter X
Mercy

When Thaos and Stephan entered Hector's small bedroom, Dominic and his team walked outside of the house. After Clev, Thaos and Stephan left, Dominic peeked his head into Hector's room and asked, "Shara, do you need us for anything? We left because it was getting too crowded."

"Actually, I could use a couple of you. I need to get Hector up to walk a little. But I need to examine him first. Angelina, I want you to help me. The rest of you should step out for a few moments."

"They can stay," Hector said. "I don't care."

"You're naked under these blankets," Shara said.

"I'm not shy," Hector said and laughed. "Yep, there go the eye rolls again."

Shara sat down on the side of Hector's bed. "Hector, I am a healer. It is not a title, it is who I am. And I will help you unless the Angels tell me not to. But I will be honest, I don't know the difference between the symptoms I am seeing from the curses and what could be caused by Juleta's magics. Do you know what all of the side effects are?"

"No. I have some of her books too. And one of them sounds like a continuation of the charts that Angelina talked about. It tells about side effects."

"It would really help me to help you if I could see at least a few pages of that book."

"I will have Clev get it but it's not in Langer so it will take a few days."

"Good," Shara said and held out her hands towards Hector. "Squeeze my hands as hard as you can. You won't hurt me." Hector did as she asked. "Do you remember me having you do this in that hotel room?"

"No."

"That day your right hand was considerably weaker than your left. Now they are both equally weak, which is expected. I think your right arm was being affected by the curses. Did you notice that it was a strange color?"

"Yes," Hector said in almost a whisper.

"It looks much better now."

"Hector, can I feel your strength, so I know where you are?" asked Angelina. After he squeezed her hands, Angelina examined his.

"Those demon snakes," Shara explained. "We have dealt with them before but only with the Second Sons. In each case the man did not know he had a tattoo of the Mark of Satan on the back of his head. The snakes came out of those tattoos and left horrible wounds. I have been so busy just trying to keep you alive that I haven't really examined your tattoos and I would like Angelina to help me. Is that alright?"

"Yes." The people in the room could hear the fear in Hector's voice.

"Angelina and Hector, I want to show you something. The snakes that were jumping out of Hector were coming out of his arms and stomach."

"And his leg too," said Claudius.

"Look at this," Shara said and pulled the blanket down far enough to expose a large bruise on Hector's stomach. "There aren't any wounds and I don't know if that is good or bad."

Angelina touched one of the bruises. "Does that hurt?" she asked.

"I hardly felt you touching me."

Angelina and Shara looked at each other and Angelina pressed hard on the bruise. "Did that feel any different?"

"That I felt."

Without turning around Shara said to Nikki and Ingr, "Girls stand at the foot of the bed and lift the blankets to his knees. I want you to softly touch his feet and legs. Hector, I am doing this so we can tell if you have lost sensations. We've been seeing that with some of the poisons being used on our people. Hector, I want you to just look at me and not at the girls."

Nikki pulled the blankets back and both girls looked at each other then at Claudius and Dominic but no one spoke. Angelina saw the looks on their faces then looked at Hector's feet. "I can do that," she said.

"No, we'll do it," said Ingr.

"Damn girl!" yelled Hector and jumped. "Did you stab me?"

"No, honestly I barely touched you with my finger," Ingr said. "Hector have you seen your feet?"

"No," he said fearfully.

"Before you look, they do look better than they did yesterday." Shara said and stood up. Nikki pulled the blankets off Hector so he could see his feet which were swollen many times larger than normal and were a variety of colors. Hector's eyes grew wide but he didn't speak. "Is this from Juleta's magics?" Shara asked.

"I don't know. I assumed every time I felt sick or something happened to me that it was from the transformation."

"We've seen something like that before," said Dominic and he and Fennel walked to the foot of the bed and squatted down so they could look at Hector's feet. "Hector when Ingr touched you did it burn?"

"Yeah and hurt like hell."

"In the swamps of Ryed there are a lot of poisonous snakes. One is called a yellow head and when it bites you, you have the same symptoms but how can that be?"

"Actually that gives us a lot to work with," Shara said happily. "Can you stay with Hector while Angelina and I make some medicines?"

"Sure. In Ryed we would make a poultice from ground nuberry nuts, flour and ..." Dominic was interrupted by Ingr.

"Just go with them. We'll watch Hector," she said.

"I know you are weak but you really look like you could use a whiskey," Claudius said to Hector and walked out of the room.

Ingr and Nikki sat on the bed on either side of Hector. "If it is poison from that snake, could Juleta make it attack you with magics?" asked Nikki. "Or did someone poison you while you were in Langer? We heard about what happened to some of your men."

"I don't know," said Hector. Claudius walked into the room and handed Hector a cup of whiskey. "Thanks, I need this."

"Claudius, the men who were poisoned at the hotel, did they have reactions like this?" asked Ingr.

"I never saw them, we were just trying to get Hector out," Claudius said to Ingr then he looked at Hector. "Think any of your guys know?"

"You can ask them," Hector said. "But I think this group came out with us. They may not have seen the bodies either." Claudius left the room again to speak with Hector's men.

"I suppose we can play cards while we wait," Ingr said as a way to cheer Hector up. "I'll get some." She left the room.

"Ingr get Shara," yelled Nikki as Hector's eyes rolled back and he started to convulse. Nikki was alone in the room with him. "Miranda, I don't know what to do here," she yelled as she held Hector to keep him from flailing out of the bed. "Miranda, what should I do?"

"What do you think?" asked Miranda.

"I can't believe I am doing this," Nikki said. "Great Ruler will you help him? Will you show us what to do to help him?"

Shara and Angelina ran into the room and pushed Nikki away from Hector. She walked to the foot of the bed and said in a low voice.

"Miranda, he is a monster. I don't even know if I should have prayed for him."

"Your lesson for the day," Miranda's voice said in Nikki's ear. "It never hurts to pray for someone, no matter what they are like."

Turner and Matthew rode to Fort Castor to speak with Captain Flores and to interrogate the men who had beaten the homeless people.

"I lost nine men in the Wax Vixen," Flores said angrily. "The place was filled with professionals and it was one hell of a fight. We killed a lot and the rest are in the dungeons. Steele got away in the chaos. I found out where he lives and searched his place. I've got soldiers watching it. You want to interrogate some of those guys?"

"Yes," said Matthew. "You are welcome to join us. I'd like to see if they have any information before you hang them."

Claudius ran back into Hector's room when Shara, Angelina and Ingr ran past him. "Claudius help us hold him," said Shara. Dominic and Fennel now ran into the room. Dominic was carrying a large bowl.

"Hold his legs still and I will put the poultice on his feet," Angelina said.

"His teeth are clenched," Shara said. "Claudius, as soon as he relaxes, I need you to lift his head so I can pour some tonic into him."

"Angelina, I will help you," said Ingr. Both women covered Hector's feet with the poultice as Dominic and Fennel tried to hold his legs still.

"My heart isn't in this so it is your call," Nikki said. "Great Ruler help them."

"You know that was a better prayer than you thought," said Cyril as he appeared in the room. "Nikki, you do know that others suffer from the same maladies as Hector. If you can find cures, you will be helping many more than him." Everyone in the room heard his words.

Nikki and Ingr had not yet met Cyril and were shocked at his appearance. "Everyone this is the Angel Cyril," said Claudius. "And we would appreciate any help you can give us."

Cyril walked to the head of the bed and placed his hand on Hector's forehead. Hector instantly stopped seizing. Claudius lifted his head and Shara poured tonic down his throat. "He cannot hear us." Cyril said. "Because he trusts you, he will give you some more of Juleta's ledgers. Shara and Angelina this is a time for you to rise above her contempt for him and think of him as a practice patient."

"There will be a war between the Sisterhood and the Master and you will see many of these things again. You will also be horrified to find out how many more people Juleta practiced on than you know of. Many are suffering and you can help them. But it will require both faith and a great deal of hard work on your parts. I would suggest that you do not tell Hector about the book that Risha gave you but use it in your research. Someday you may realize what a gift that book is."

Shara reached out and gently touched Cyril's clothing. "What is there about you that seems so familiar?"

"You have connected with me many times. You said it yourself. Being a healer is not a title for you. It is a calling. You look upon this man who is the worst monster who you have ever met and you did it with the heart of a healer. You have shown him Mercy. People seldom realize how planting small seeds can grow into gardens someday but they can. Isn't that worth a try?"

"Are you an Angel of healers?" asked Angelina.

"You could say that."

"Then will you help us?" asked Shara. "I will do the work but I may not know the questions to ask. Will you offer suggestions?"

Cyril smiled. "First, I would suggest that you take one of the extra cottages that Sorren built for the wedding ceremonies and turn it into a work room. You will need many more herbs than you have now. A garden next to that cottage would greatly benefit you."

"Have Hilgra help you. She is very knowledgeable in unusual plants. She came from a long line of healers and combining that with the magics she used to have she knows a great deal of information."

"Dominic and Fennel, in your life of horror you were exposed to many things not seen in other areas of this world like the yellow head snake. That is because of the evil in Ryed. Some of those monsters were created by magics. Someone from your team should work with Shara and Angelina when they can. Your experience will help them."

"I will," said Fennel. "I have always been interested in medicines."

"Juleta was a vessel for the Sisters of Tameric like Roch was for the Insidiae. While both of these monsters thought they were strong and independent, their masters had more influence over them than they realized. I tell you this because Juleta's attempts to make corrections in her magics are connected to the Sisterhood."

"Those notes that Hector sent out. He is paying a fortune for manuscripts. All of you need to read them for many reasons. Hector has many choices to make in his life. Shara stop feeling guilty that you are feeding a monster. They are his choices to make. You have made your choice and that is to show Mercy and to be an honorable healer. While it may be difficult for you to understand now. All of you will benefit from these experiences."

"Earlier Miranda told Nikki that it is always beneficial to pray for someone no matter what they are like. You do not bow before darkness but I will tell you that showing Mercy especially to your enemies is a blessing far beyond your comprehension. Shara, you said you would heal him unless we told you to stop. We are not telling you to stop. We are telling you to use this experience to its fullest."

After Cyril left, Dominic and Fennel rode to the Catacombs to tell Hilgra what the Angel said. Nikki and Ingr found Sorren on the training field and told him. The three then, picked out a cottage. Ingr and Nikki cleaned the inside while Sorren got a group of men to clear an area for a garden and build a fence.

While Thaos was riding into Langer, he asked Miranda how he could best protect Selen from the Sisterhood. Now he met with Selen in her home. She started to cry when he told her about the Sisterhood and the coin.

"We had this all wrong," said Thaos. "Hector knows you took care of Sarah and he wants to protect you for your kindness. I believe that few things have meaning for him but his child is one. Selen, I will continue to have soldiers guard you but if you really need help, Miranda said you have to call to them. She said you have the faith but that you don't feel worthy."

"Heck, if they help someone like me, they sure will help a good person like you."

"Thaos, you are a good person. I saw that in you from the beginning."

"Then you saw more than I did."

"Am I a danger to the children?"

"No, they are protected. Apparently the reason that woman couldn't leave the coin at the Adam's Home is because the Angels have blessed them."

"What I don't understand is why they want to talk to me? You know Thaos, maybe I should. I don't want to be afraid the rest of my life."

"Ok, stop there. If anyone is going to talk to them it will be me. At least until we figure out what is going on."

"Alright but we should tell Hilgra too."

"I am going to the Catacombs after I get you back to work."

"What are you two doing here?" Thaos asked Stephan and Clev as he ran into them on the main street of the Catacombs.

"I can ask you the same," said Stephen with a grin.

"I want to warn Hilgra about the Sisterhood," Thaos said then he looked at Clev. "You probably already know this but she lives with Selen."

"We'll go with you," Clev said. "Those women think that we are after them and we aren't. If they get into trouble they can go to our guys for help too. Don't look at me like that Thaos, we're professionals. Let's put it this way, if we want someone, we get them; period."

"Alright," Thaos said. "I did tell Selen it wasn't Hector who has been after her."

"Then let's go for a drink, I'm buying," said Stephan. "We've been in some of the skankiest places I've ever seen."

"What the hell have you been doing?" Thaos asked.

"The boss wants a bunch of manuscripts, they are rare and expensive so we are putting out the word," Clev said then looked at Stephan and grinned. "He's just touchy because this toothless whore wanted him." Thaos laughed loudly.

"I've still got shivers going down my spine," Stephan said sarcastically.

Hilgra was dusting items on shelves when the three men walked into her shop. Her eyes widened when she recognized Clev. "It's alright," Stephan said. "Can we talk for a few minutes?"

"Sure," Hilgra said. "Follow me." She led the men behind some thick curtains, into a small kitchen. "Would you like some coffee?"

"Sounds good," said Thaos.

"All of you?"

Thaos looked at Clev and Stephan who nodded. "Yeah and don't be afraid. Hector and his men aren't after you. We had that wrong."

The men noticed that Hilgra's hands were shaking as she handed them each a cup of coffee. "Have a seat," she said and set a cake and plates on the table.

"Hell, if we knew you served treats we would come in more often," Stephan said kiddingly.

"Well, you know you are always welcome here. But seeing Clev is making me nervous. Why are the three of you together?"

"You know how Selen has been feeling like someone is watching her?" Thaos asked but didn't wait for Hilgra to respond. "Well, someone has been but it isn't Hector's men. A member of the Sisters of Tameric left a coin for her this morning. Apparently it is their calling card."

"Oh my god, they are monsters. What do they want with Selen?"

"We are just guessing but probably information about Juleta," Thaos said then looked at Stephan and Clev. "Selen suggested that she should talk to them so she doesn't have to live in fear. I told her I would."

"That might not be wise," said Clev. "They seem to hate men." Then he paused. "You know we might be able to use this to our advantage. Let me talk to Hector before you do anything."

"All of you wait right here," Hilgra said and quickly left the kitchen. She returned several minutes later with a stack of books. "Take these and read them. They are histories of groups. Now none of these books is totally about the Sisterhood but there are sections on them."

"Thanks, how much are they?" asked Stephan.

"For all you have done for me, nothing."

"We're paying you," Stephan said and placed a small bag of gold coins on the table.

"Hector said the Sisterhood can't come into places that are holy," Thaos said. "I am increasing the guards for both of you but you will have to call to the Angels too."

"Hilgra, my men will help you too," said Clev. "Like I told these guys, if we wanted you we would have you. We mean you no harm."

"Well, that makes me feel better."

"This is the coin that was left for Selen," Thaos said and handed it to Hilgra. Have you ever seen one before?"

"Yes and hand me that really thick brown book. It has drawings of these," Hilgra continued to talk as she looked through the book. "The Sisterhood is big in Stordt, don't ask me why. Here," Hilgra said and turned the book so the men could see the pages.

"Like most groups they tend to intimidate people," Hilgra said. "From what I have read they used to kill men, castrate them and hang them in public places. They would put one of these coins in the men's mouths. After a while all they had to do was drop a few coins and they got what they wanted."

"See these symbols, the flame with the sword stands for the Sisterhood. The group of thirteen eyes represents the original Old Ones in this world. And that sign there. The smaller eyes in the upside down triangle represents the Grand Masters. So this coin tells who they are aligned with. I heard the women who started the group were real victims and probably aligned with the Old Ones and Grand Masters for protection."

"Hilgra, do you have more books that explain symbols?" asked Stephan.

"Yes, quit a few."

"I'm buying them all. The group in Wetpr has been pulling out their hair trying to figure some of this out."

"Have some more cake while I get them."

"Damn, I never thought to see if Hilgra had stuff to help us," Stephan said. "Talk about missing the obvious."

Hilgra returned several minutes later with four more books. "You aren't going to like what I say, but Nikki and Ingr might have a lot better chance of getting information than you guys."

"You're right we don't like it," said Thaos.

"Hey, those two practically pinned me and Hector to the wall. They can handle themselves," Clev said and grinned.

"You aren't married are you?" asked Thaos.

"No," Clev said. "It's kind of hard in this line of work."

"I know exactly what you mean. I couldn't afford to have feelings for anyone until I got out. But let me tell you things really change. Then you start having babies and you worry about things you never paid attention to before," Thaos said. "Ask Stephan. I think he is worse than me."

"Hilgra don't tell our wives I said this," Stephan said with a big smile. "I'm half tempted to invite these two to our weddings just so they can remember what a normal life is."

"The only problem would be Margarit," Thaos said then looked at Clev. "She had nightmares for almost a year after you guys stole her."

"I told Stephan that Hector and I never went to that compound where the kids were in Ganz so they wouldn't recognize us; so we won't scare them. Actually I would come but Hector won't be in any shape to even get out of bed."

"After you left, Hector said he was going to use those kids to negotiate for Juleta's books," Stephan said to Thaos.

"That's the truth," said Clev. "But the guy running the operations got greedy and set up the auction. You killed him, if you hadn't we would have. That whole damn thing backfired. After that Amundsen covered the kingdom with our wanted posters."

"I was one of those kids," Thaos said. "You aren't getting my sympathy."

"Yeah, we read about that in the paper," said Clev. "Between those stories, the priests at that monastery and Amundsen, everyone's businesses are shut down in Ganz."

"Can't say that I am sorry," said Thaos. "There's a lot better ways you guys can make money." As Thaos spoke his body stiffened and everyone could hear the anger in his voice.

"Thaos, I am not going to say anything one way or the other," said Clev. "I don't want to fight with you."

"And no one is fighting in my shop," Hilgra said. "And I am changing the subject. I got a letter from Erebus. Did you know that he and the Sanuri are traveling to Ryed?"

"Yeah," said Stephan.

"He said they have had a really strange trip. They are still in Stordt and for the first time they didn't see any border guards or anyone else. Of course they haven't really gone into the cities or villages but he said they haven't met one single person on the roads. He said they both feel like they are being watched. I am worried about them."

"I'm sure they are being watched," said Clev. "Do they know about the wars going on in Ryed? That's not the place to be these days."

"The Angels told them to go," Stephan said.

"Why?" asked Clev.

"You know if we knew we probably wouldn't tell you," Stephan said and laughed. "But that is kind of how the Angels operate, they tell you to do something then it's a surprise when you get there."

"I hear people in the shop," Hilgra said and stood up. She walked into the front of the store and returned a few moments later with Dominic and Fennel. "I'll make some more coffee," Hilgra said as they sat down with the other men.

126

"Why are you guys here?" asked Stephan.

"We've got a lot to tell all of you. And Clev don't run off or anything until we are done," said Dominic.

"Is Hector alright?" Clev asked anxiously.

"He is now but all of you need to hear this. The short version is that right after you left, Shara wanted to walk Hector so Fennel and I were going to help her. She examines him first and had some concerns. Then she asks the girls to touch his feet and legs to see if he has feeling in them. His feet were really swollen and different colors. We've seen that before. A bite from the yellow head snake will do that."

"We go with Shara and Angelina to make a poultice then he starts going into seizures. Long story short, Nikki prayed. I am not sure what she said but Cyril showed up. Turns out he is an Angel of healing or healers. He stopped the seizures so Shara could give Hector tonics."

"Now this is the part that concerns all of you, Hilgra can you put that down and come to the table? Cyril said that a lot of what Hector is suffering from is from Juleta's connection with the Sisterhood instead of side effects from his transformation. Cyril said that there will be a war between the Master and the Sisterhood and we will see a lot more of these symptoms in people."

"Cyril said that since Shara showed Mercy to her enemy that he would help find cures. Hilgra, he wants you and Fennel to work with Shara and Angelina. They are setting up a cottage just for this work and Sorren is having a garden space made because they will need rare plants and apparently that is your specialty."

"Clev, Hector has to give Shara some of the pages of that ledger that tells what the side effects are so she can work on medicines to cure them. But they can be cured. It will be a lot of work on their part."

"He said too, that some of the manuscripts that Hector is buying will have information," said Fennel.

"But he can be cured?" Clev asked.

"Yes, but how long probably depends on how hard everyone works," Dominic said. "But as soon as Cyril left, Ingr, Nikki and Sorren started working on the cottage."

"Does Hector know this?" asked Clev.

"He wasn't awake when we left," said Fennel. "So Hilgra will you help?"

"Yes, but are you saying that we can find cures to the side effects of Juleta's medicines?"

"Yes."

"I need to hire someone to watch the shop or I am going to have to close it so I can help," said Hilgra. "This is so wonderful. I've been so afraid of what could happen to me."

"I might know someone," said Clev. "She's like you a healer and a witch. Her name is Annie and she works in Cadia. That's where I have to go to get the ledgers."

"Does she have brown curly hair?" asked Hilgra. "And works in a shop near the ocean?"

"Same gal. She's nice; I am sure you two would get along."

Thaos and Stephan looked at each other and smiled. "Should we tell him?" asked Stephan.

"We've got a team leaving for Zorta tomorrow," said Thaos. "I'm sure you could ride with them. With all of the demons after you it might be safer."

"Do I even want to ask why they are going there?" Clev said.

"Probably not," said Thaos then he paused. "Now, come to think of it, Hector said that he and Otto were rivals. We're trying to track down all of the money that Otto funneled to Juleta."

"How do you know he did?" asked Clev.

"We took all of the paperwork from his home, office and safety boxes," said Stephan.

"Talk to Hector about that before your team leaves."

"Are you telling us that he didn't know about that?" asked Thaos.

"Just talk to him."

"Is anyone going to the village now?" asked Hilgra. "Because I will close up and go with you."

"We are," said Dominic.

"I think we all are," said Thaos.

Chapter XI
Honor and Shame

"You scared the hell out of us son," Claudius said when Hector awoke.

"What happened?" he asked and sat up. As soon as Hector moved he became incredibly dizzy and grabbed his head.

"I've got a lot to tell you. Think you are clear headed enough to listen?"

"I don't know," Hector said. "My head is pounding. Maybe some coffee will help."

"Stay here; I'll get Shara."

"I don't think I could get out of bed if I wanted to," said Hector and tried to smile.

Matthew, Turner and Flores got little information from the men they interrogated other than normal criminal activities in the city. They learned even less about the bounties that Andrac put on Abbott's team other than the man named Steele was handing out the posters. Steele had disappeared. Flores had soldiers watching both Steele's hotel room and the Wax Vixen, where he ran his business. The problem for Matthew was that no one could really tell them what Steele's business was so Matthew feared that a man like Shanksaw was operating in his kingdom.

Matthew had previously told Captain Flores to hang the men who had attacked the homeless. These thugs knew their fates and were making many promises to escape the noose. Matthew consented to letting the men go with the stipulation that they get information on Steele and give it to Captain Flores.

As far as Matthew was concerned, the members of both Turner's and Abbott's teams were not working while in Castor. Other than helping Abbotts's men pack their belongings for the move to Langer, these men had little to do.

They decided to help with the group of homeless people who would also be moving to Langer. Matthew gave the team members money and they bought bocas, horses and supplies for the journey. They got lists of names, ages of children, labor skills and other important information that Matthew requested.

Although the trip to Langer was not a long journey, Matthew was concerned about Quinn and hired a healer to travel with the group. Matthew was anxious to return home since he was going to be in Stephan's and Thaos' wedding ceremonies.

Since most of Claudius' family was spending the day in Sorren's village because of Hector, their children who were attending warrior's training were allowed to spend the day also.

When Claudius left to find Shara, Hector was alone in his room for the first time.

"Is he dead?" asked Marty. "He sure looks dead."

Hector smiled and opened his eyes. "I sure feel dead." He said and looked at nine children who were gathered around his bed holding knives. "Are you going to stab me?" He asked with amusement.

Cassidy stepped forward, unaware that Claudius, Shara and Angelina had entered the small house. Shara was going to speak but Claudius motioned for her to be quiet. The adults watched the children through the open doorway.

"If we have to," Cassidy said. "Margarit wanted to come and look at you and we came to protect her."

Amy and Margarit had been holding hands and now Amy walked closer to the bed and yelled, "You stole our friends. You're a bad man. And how come you look like my papa?"

Hector pulled himself to a sitting position. "Are you Thaos' girl?"

"He's my second papa. He and Uncle Stephan saved Sally, April and me from a bad man like you," Amy said defiantly. "How come you look like him?"

"Juleta made him look like Thaos," Margarit said.

"How?" asked Logan.

"With her magics," Margarit said and all of the children stared at Hector.

"I did steal Margarit and I shouldn't have. Margarit, I am sorry. Juleta wanted me to get you but I honestly didn't know what her plans were. But who else did I steal?"

"Marty and Logan," Cassidy said angrily. "You put them in a cage."

"Who are Marty and Logan?" asked Hector.

Sorren's son Peter stepped forward and said, "They are." And nodded at the two younger boys. "My father said you had all kinds of kids in cages. You don't put people in cages!"

"Is there a way I can make it up to all of you?" Hector asked.

"Stop stealing kids!" Marty yelled.

"I'm out of that business; besides Ingr told the Angels to curse me if I ever did it again. But I do apologize to you. Tell me your names."

Amy's curiosity was stronger than her fear and she walked closer to Hector and touched his face. "My papa is more handsome," she said and Hector laughed loudly.

"She's Amy," said Sorren's oldest son. "Thaos and Nikki adopted her. That's Margarit. Those two girls are Sally and April and Fahron and Isadore adopted them. That is Cassidy and Claudius and Bella adopted him. Marty and Logan were adopted by Gideon and Ashley. This is my brother Peter, I am Nathaniel and we are the sons of Sorren and Shara," he said proudly.

"Well, it's nice to meet all of you. I am Hector. Why do you all have knives?"

"We're in warrior's training," Cassidy said proudly.

"Do you learn how to use those knives in that training?" Hector asked.

132

"We learn all kinds of things like tracking and living in the woods," Amy said with obvious pride.

Cassidy took a step closer to the bed. "We learn a bunch of other things too. We learn about being good warriors. We learn about honor," as Cassidy spoke his voice got louder and he moved closer to the bed. "We learn that warriors fight each other; they don't hurt kids and people who can't defend themselves. You aren't a warrior are you?"

Shara put her hand over her mouth to keep from making a sound and Claudius was overwhelmed with pride at hearing Cassidy's words.

"Wow," Hector said. "I don't know what to say to that."

"Uncle Stephan said you used to be a nice man but you changed," Marty said. "How come you changed?"

Hector didn't answer the question. Margarit walked close to the bed and said angrily, "I had nightmares for a really long time after you stole me. You scared me."

"I am sorry Margarit." Hector said sincerely. "Why did you want to see me?"

"I don't know, I just did," Margarit said as her anger diminished. "But you don't look so scary anymore. What's wrong with you?"

"Witches sent curses on him," said Peter.

"Actually, Juleta did," Hector said.

"Why?" asked Margarit.

"Because I went against her."

"But she is dead," Margarit said.

"But her curses aren't," Hector said. "Why are you so curious?"

"I am going to Wetpr to learn to be a physician," Margarit said proudly.

"Good for you," said Hector.

"Sally and I are healers," said April.

"The rest of us are kids," Marty said and Claudius, Angelina and Shara tried hard not to laugh.

"Can we see your feet?" Peter asked excitedly.

"Sure but don't touch them because they hurt like hell," Hector said with a grin.

Peter pulled back the blankets and all of the children ran to the foot of the bed. "Oh yuck!" yelled Marty then started to laugh.

"What caused that?" asked Sally.

"The curses. I'm not a healer so I can't explain a lot," said Hector.

Thaos, Dominic, Stephan, Clev, Hilgra and Fennel walked into the house. "What are you doing?" asked Stephan and the children stopped talking and looked into the parlor.

"We're listening to our children," Claudius said with a big smile. "And I couldn't be prouder of any of them."

"Grandpa are we in trouble?" asked Amy.

"Not with me," Claudius said and all of the adults squeezed into the bedroom.

"I thought your wives busted my chops," Hector said to Thaos and Stephan. "Your kids are a whole lot worse."

"Really," Thaos said with a grin. "You kids can put those knives away now."

"He let us look at his feet," Marty said and giggled.

"Clev, some of these kids are from the compound in Ganz," Hector said. "And you know Margarit. Some of the other kids were stolen too but not by us. We owe them. Send one of the boys into town to buy them something."

"I'll talk to the guy about that," Angelina said. "Let me know who you send."

"Boss, we've got some stuff to tell you and it probably shouldn't be in front of the kids," said Clev.

"You kids can come back and visit me later," said Hector. "And bring a checker board."

"Ok," said Peter and the children left the room.

"So what was that all about?" asked Stephan.

"They just faced their nightmares," Hector said.

After meeting with Hector, Stephan and Thaos took Clev to meet with Angus and Edward. Although the meeting was heated at times, after an hour they agreed it would be mutually beneficial to travel to Cadia together. Clev was going to take twenty men. Angus' and Edward's complete teams were going which numbered over twice as many warriors.

Sorren canceled his plans to go to Cadia because he did not want to leave his village with Hector and his men in it. There hadn't been any problems with Hector's men and Hector promised that there would not be. But both men realized it would be an opportune time for Hector's enemies to attack because of his weakened condition.

It was almost dark when Claudius and the members of his family who had been at Sorren's village arrived home. Gideon and Ashley were already in the castle. Ingr ran into the parlor before anyone else entered the castle. "Do you all have drinks?" she asked quickly. "Good because you are going to need them."

"Ingr what on earth..." Bella did not finish her question because Amy, Cassidy, Logan and Marty ran into the parlor with their arms filled with packages. Thaos, Stephan, Claudius and Nikki followed the children and they too had their arms filled with packages.

"Where did you get all of this?" Ashley asked her sons as they kissed her.

"Hector bought it for us," Amy said.

"What!" said Bella loudly.

"We made him feel bad because we yelled at him," Marty said and laughed. "Do you want some candy we have bags of it."

"We want to hear about Hector," Gideon said sternly.

"Let me start off," said Claudius as he started pouring drinks. "We can fill in the details later but Hector's condition got considerably worse. I was watching him and left for a couple of minutes to get Shara and Angelina. During those minutes our crew, Fahron's girls, Sorren's boys and Margarit sneaked into Hector's room with their knives drawn."

"This just gets worse," gasped Bella and took a sip of her wine.

"Actually it was great," said Claudius. "Shara, Angelina and I entered immediately after the kids but they didn't realize it. They told him the things that we've all been wanting to. I don't think he ever sees the faces of his victims or has them demanding answers. He apologized several times. And he talked with them nicely. He knew they came into his room to face their fears."

"I was so proud of all of them," Claudius said. "And when they were done none of them were afraid anymore. Our Cassidy called him out. Tell Bella what you said."

"He asked why we all had knives and we told him from our warrior's training. Then he asked us about that and Amy was telling him," Cassidy paused and looked embarrassed.

"Son, you have nothing to be embarrassed about," said Claudius.

"I told him that we learn about honor and how to be good warriors and that warriors fight each other and they don't hurt kids and people who can't defend themselves. Then I said, 'you aren't a warrior are you'."

"Did he get mad?" asked Bella.

"No," said Claudius. "He turned even whiter and just stared at the boy. But they all had enough to say to him." Claudius chuckled. "Amy kept asking him why he looked like Thaos then she walked up to him and touched his face and said that her papa was more handsome."

"That's my girl," Thaos said with a big smile.

"And after little Marty got done yelling at him to not steal kids anymore he said that Uncle Stephan said Hector used to be a nice guy but changed. Then Marty asked him why he changed. Ok kids you can tell them the rest," Claudius said and chuckled again.

"Why did you even go in there?" asked Ashley.

"Margarit wanted to look at him and we all went to protect her," said Logan. "She really yelled at him too. Then he let us look at his feet." All of the kids laughed loudly.

"Juleta cursed his feet and they are really big and different colors," Marty said as he laughed.

"I think there is a lot that we need to be filled in on here," said Bella. "So when did he get you the toys?"

"He said he owed us and gave one of his men and Angelina a bunch of money and told them to spend all of it on us," Cassidy said. "And he told us to come back and visit him and play checkers so we did."

"Honestly, I am not sure if I am more mad or shocked by all of this," said Bella. "He sounds like he has two different personalities. Is he insane?"

"He might be," Stephan said. "But I spent the day with Clev and we talked a lot. He said that Hector likes being with us and it's the first time in a long time that he is acting like his old self."

"Kids why don't you take your new toys into the toy room while we talk," Stephan said. After the children left the room he continued. "Clev was part of Hector's original crew and they got together when they were pretty young."

"They started robbing things for the adventure and they sounded like they had some good times. Like all of the rest of his men, Clev said that Hector really changed because of Juleta. Now, Clev didn't come right out and say this part but a couple of times he made it sound like they got into something that was way over their heads and there was no turning back."

"So then I gave Clev shit about stealing the kids and he got really defensive and said that at least Hector comes right out and says he's a criminal. Clev said that is a big business and most of the big shots are people like Otto who appear to be pillars of their communities and churches."

"Now the thing that I found interesting is listening to Clev talk about their businesses and that is how they look at it. Father was right, Hector doesn't ever see his victims; he sees his money ledgers. Personally I think it is great that the kids gave him hell. And after talking to Clev, who wasn't complaining but just talking, their lives sound pretty crappy. I asked him when was the last time he danced with a girl or went out for a drink without worrying about getting killed and he couldn't remember."

"Tell them the rest," Thaos said with a huge grin.

Stephan laughed, "You are going to get me killed."

"Stephan what happened?" asked Ingr sternly.

"Nothing, I just told Clev I was tempted to invite him and Hector to our weddings so they could remember what a normal life was again. But I told him that you would skin me alive."

"What did he say?" asked Nikki.

"That Hector is too weak, which he is and Clev isn't coming but would like to," said Stephan. "So am I sleeping in the barn tonight?"

"No, I would be really mad if the kids hadn't gone after him," Ingr said. "Nikki and I have been yelling at him too. And he doesn't even get mad. In fact, he acts like he is glad to have the company. I'm starting to feel sorry for him but I know I can't."

"Bella, are you alright?" asked Ashley.

"No. Hector used to stay here with Stephan. They were playmates and I just couldn't understand how he could turn into such a monster. I know he is but I need to see him for myself. Claudius tomorrow morning I am going to visit him."

"Claudius, we'll go with her," said Nikki.

"I may want to speak with him alone for a little while girls. I am a mother and someone who used to take care of him; I am curious to see how he responds."

The group leaving for Cadia decided to wait to depart until after Mathas' morning meeting. Claudius was asked to speak first as both Mathas and Fahron were disturbed that their daughters brought home gifts from Hector.

"Shara, Angelina and I were there and the children were incredible. When I get done telling you what they did and how they handled themselves all of you will be proud of them too. I realized listening to our children that Hector represented their fears and nightmares. They decided to face those fears and they did it with the honor of young warriors," Claudius said.

As Claudius spoke, Rosa entered the Great Hall and sat down. She too wanted to hear about the encounter. After Claudius finished speaking she quickly left the room.

"We'll be out here if you need us," Nikki said as Bella walked into Hector's bedroom and closed the door.

Hector heard Nikki's words and opened his eyes and his surprise was evident on his face. "Bella, I never expected to see you," he said and sat up.

Bella was carrying a basket which she set on a small table. "Wait, I'll help you," she said and piled some pillows behind his back.

"What smells so good?" Bella didn't answer his question but took a plate of freshly baked sweet rolls out of the basket and handed it to him.

139

"Bella, I can't remember the last time I had sweet rolls," he said with excitement.

"I didn't know how you drink your coffee so this is black, if that is alright." As she spoke Bella took a canning jar out of the basket that was filled with coffee and poured some into the cup on the table.

"Have some with me."

"No, I just ate," Bella said and sat down on the side of the bed. "You are reminding me of when you were a boy. You always loved those rolls." Hector heard the sadness in her voice.

"Bella, I'm not that boy anymore."

"I guess I needed to see that for myself. You know I did know that you changed your appearance but it is still a shock. You were such a handsome boy why did you do that?" Then she smiled. "I didn't mean you aren't handsome now."

"Juleta went after your family to hurt Stephan and Thaos. Others were doing that to me. I finally faked my death and shortly afterwards Juleta offered me a new look. I guess I should have asked more questions," he said jokingly but then quickly changed his demeanor. "Bella, my parents don't know about most of the threats against them so please don't say anything."

"I won't." Bella smiled at how quickly Hector was eating the sweet rolls. "You have been the talk of my household for days and I have to admit that sometimes they sound like they are talking about two different people. Who really are you these days?"

"I wish I had a good answer for you."

"Oh you can do better than that. From what I hear you rule an enormous empire and yet you sit before me as the boy I used to take care of."

"I do rule an empire and I enjoy much of what I do but coming back has made me miss a lot of my former life. Actually Clev and I were talking last night. We kind of forgot what our former lives were like. Now Bella don't give me that look, you aren't going to reform me."

"I'd like to spank you if I could," she said and laughed.

"As weak as I am, you probably could," he said and grinned.

"Hector, I am not asking you to reform but I have a question for you and I am asking for an honest answer." He looked at her without speaking. "Stephan is no fool but he can't let go of the friend he used to know. He and Thaos are having a second wedding ceremony for the girls day after tomorrow. As soon as I open that door the girls are going to invite you for Stephan's sake."

Hector looked shocked. "I am no fool either," Bella continued. "And we have been blessed with a house filled with children and grandchildren. Hector, I have no problem with you coming but you look me in the eye and you tell me if you will be a threat to anyone in our home."

"Bella, I promise you that I wouldn't hurt anyone in your family but you have to understand I live and work in a very different world. Everyone is trying to kill off their rivals to say nothing about my enemies. I cannot guarantee that trouble won't follow me. I am shocked by this and I appreciate it but I can't even get out of bed by myself."

"Shara, Sorren and Angelina will be there. You haven't seen Matthew because he has been on a mission but he will be there too. If you really want to come we can figure something out."

There was a bold knock on the door. "Bella is in there," Nikki said loudly.

"The boss needs to hear this," said Clev and opened the door.

"I heard, what is it?" asked Hector with a serious demeanor.

"It's your daughter," said Rosa as she pushed past Clev and walked into the room carrying a beautiful three year old girl with brown eyes and long black curly hair. Ingr and Nikki smiled as they stood behind Rosa.

Bella too smiled and took the plate and cup out of Hector's hands. He couldn't speak he just stared at his daughter. Rosa walked to the bed and handed Sarah to him. "We adopted her and had no intention of telling her about her life but, well, I guess the rest depends upon you," Rosa said.

"She is so beautiful," he said in awe. "Clev look how beautiful she is."

"I see that boss," Clev said and smiled.

Sarah stared at Hector then touched his hair. "What is your name?" she asked then giggled. Hector looked at Rosa.

"You can tell her," said Rosa.

"My name is Hector," he said and hugged the little girl.

"Does Mathas know you are here?" asked Bella.

"No," said Rosa. "I was sitting in the meeting listening to Claudius talk about our children meeting with Hector yesterday and I decided it was time he met his daughter."

"Hector, we are not making the same mistakes with her that we did with Juleta," Rosa continued. "The Sanuri has assured us that there is no evil in her and if we suspect anything we will take her to him."

Hector nodded, he couldn't stop staring at Sarah.

Chapter XII
Stopping One

Mathas was not aware that Rosa had taken Sarah to visit Hector. He was leading discussions about the numerous letters that he had received from Matthew. Not only did Matthew talk about Abbott's team and the need to set up facilities for the homeless in Castor but also his fears that the man named Steele could be another version of Shanksaw. These discussions led to the idea of forming another team to work in that city.

The monster in Hector took a back seat as he played with his daughter. He was surprised at how much love he felt for the child he had rarely seen. He wore his emotions on his sleeve and seeing this Nikki and Ingr felt comfortable to invite him and Clev to their wedding ceremony.

This invitation led to a serious discussion. "Boss, I don't like the idea of leaving you here with Sorren, Shara and me gone. I know you need those documents but could we send Keith?"

Hector looked at the women in the room and explained. "Keith is Clev's head lieutenant in a matter of speaking. But he does not have most of the knowledge or power that Clev does and he knows nothing about the truce between our families or about Sarah."

"Boss, you know there is more than that," said Clev. "I wouldn't feel comfortable having him around these people and well...that's...well... you know what I am saying."

"What are you saying?" demanded Bella. "It's my family and friends you are talking about."

"Clev likes all of you and if you haven't noticed with the way he treats me, he is very protective of those he likes. Let's just say Keith isn't as sophisticated as us," Hector said and both he and Clev laughed loudly. "And that is saying a lot."

"Would he be here then if Clev goes to Cadia?" asked Ingr. "Because he doesn't sound like someone we want around our babies."

"And that is what Clev was getting at," Hector said. "But I am in no condition to go to a party."

"Now that you bring it up, I'm not sure it is a good idea to leave you here either," said Bella. "Besides the threat of attack what if you have more medical problems? Our home is only ten miles away. Do you think you could ride in a boca that far? I can fix up a chambers for you and if you feel up to it you can join the celebration."

"Boss, I'm not just saying this because I want to go," Clev said with a grin. "But, I think that is the best plan."

"And what will people think when they see me there?" asked Hector.

"This wedding is just for close friends and family," said Bella. "You probably already know everyone there. Our team members will be there and of course Fahron and Mathas. If you don't want to deal with them you can just stay in the chambers."

"Let me think about that," Hector said then turned to Rosa. "Rosa, I would like to talk with you and Mathas. I want to give you money to raise Sarah."

"We don't need the money and you know that," Rosa said in a scolding tone which surprised everyone. "Hector, you listen to me and you listen good. We lost our daughter and we would have done anything to have prevented that. I can see the love in your eyes when you look at Sarah. You have a chance to be in her life. You don't have to be a criminal for money. You already had plenty of money. Is whatever you are doing worth losing a child? Take it from me that is a pain you can never forget and you actually have the ability to do something about it."

"Do you want this precious child to find out her father is a monster? Hector, I could just shake you," Rosa said angrily. "I promise you there will be a day when you look back and regret the choices you have made."

144

Rosa was a gentle person who rarely got angry. Everyone in the room stared at her since her face and voice betrayed her emotions.

"Mathas and I have been quarreling about letting you see Sarah. He is trying to protect her not punish you. I am going back and tell him what I have done. I wanted to see for myself how you responded to her. I would agree to allow you to come and visit and I will try and talk Mathas into it but Hector you have to give some too. And handing out money like it is candy isn't going to do it."

Rosa paused for a moment as she composed herself. "There is one more thing that I want to say to you. I feel like I never really knew Juleta and perhaps I have never really known you. But it sounds like she was instrumental into turning you into a monster like her. If there is any truth in that; I am truly sorry. We should have stopped her before she brought so much pain into this world."

Mathas' morning meeting was long. It was decided that Mathas would write to Gabriel and request that one of the teams be assigned to work in Castor. The ruling members would pay all wages and expenses and provide a house for the team. After a great deal of discussion Angus stood up and volunteered his team for the assignment which pleased everyone in the room. Angus said that he too would write to Gabriel and King Sudfad.

The meeting was about to end when the doors to the Great Hall opened and Rosa, Bella and Clev walked inside. Claudius was talking and stopped and stared at the three. "Is something wrong?"

"Well that certainly depends on many things," said Bella. "May we address your group?"

"Now I know something is wrong," said Stephan only half kiddingly.

"I will start," said Bella with such a voice of authority that many in the room smiled. "For those of you who may not know, this gentleman is Clev."

145

"He is Hector's head lieutenant. Rosa, Isadore and I took care of Hector when he was a boy because he was a playmate of our children. For days he has been the topic of conversation in my home and honestly it sounded to me like my family was talking about two different people. So this morning I visited him to see for myself."

"While I expected the worst, I believe my experience was with Archer; that is the name he had when he lived among us. I asked him direct questions and believed the answer's he gave me."

"Ingr, Nikki and I have invited him to our home for the wedding ceremonies. Initially we did this because Stephan still has a place in his heart for his old friend. But as we all spoke, Clev brought up some very real concerns."

"Sorren as well as Clev and Hector have been concerned that there will be attacks on the village so that Hector's enemies can take advantage of his weakened condition. Then there are the concerns if he has another medical crisis and Shara and Angelina are gone."

"Some of you are looking at me like you are wondering why I am presenting this to the group. Well, the morning got complicated..."

"Bella, before you continue," said Thaos. "Where are Nikki and Ingr?"

"They are guarding Hector," Bella said. "Now Rosa has something to say."

"Mathas, you are going to be very angry with me. But after listening to Claudius this morning I took Sarah to see Hector. I knew that Bella and the girls were there." Mathas glared angrily at his wife. "Mathas, I had to see for myself. He looked at her with such love and as Bella said, he seemed more like Archer than the monster we call Hector. I said a few words to him."

"She yelled at him," Bella said with a smile.

"He is a fool to give up contact with his child and I told him that. He wanted to speak with you because he wants to give us money to support her. Well, that set me off. I am not going into all that I said to him but I spoke my mind. I told him that nothing was worth losing a child and that I would try to talk you into allowing him to visit her periodically but that he had to give up something too. As he started to speak, well Clev needs to explain the rest."

"I know I am the last person you are going to believe but the Queen's words really affected my boss. For all that he is and all that you think he is he does have feelings and he does care about people. May I approach you, My Lord?"

"Yes," Mathas said warily.

"As you may know he cannot get out of bed or he would be here himself. He is not hiding from you." Clev walked to the King and handed him a piece of paper. "There is much more for me to tell you after you read that."

"Hector said that as a sign of good faith that he is not our enemy that he is turning over a list of documents and books to us," Mathas told the group.

"Mathas, perhaps I should talk with Clev since you are so angry," said Claudius. "May we see that note?"

"My Lord, Hector and I are both criminals, we won't lie about that," said Clev. "But you have to know that he would never do anything to hurt Sarah and honestly he has changed so much being back here with all of you. I wish he could stay like this. But we live in a different world and that brings me to the next things."

"I am Hector's head lieutenant as well as his childhood friend. Under me is a man named Keith. He assumes some of my duties when I am on other assignments but basically he is an enforcer. This is a room of warriors so I don't believe that I have to explain what that means."

"As you know I had planned to go to Cadia with your teams this morning. I did not feel good about leaving Hector in his condition nor did I feel good about..."

"Just say it," said Bella. "Both Clev and Hector thought that Keith was too much of an animal to be around any of us. So now you know what we were all thinking at the time."

"Hector and I were discussing if we should have Keith go with the teams. I don't know if you understand that all of the things that Hector is giving you are locked up in Cadia. He and I are the only two who know the locations. As we are discussing this, Hector gets this," Clev said and handed a note to Claudius who was standing next to him.

"Who is this from?" asked Claudius.

"One of our men in Cadia," said Clev.

Claudius handed the note to Mathas. "It says that Keith and fifty of his men were found near the border between Zorta and Lentz. All of the men were dead but there wasn't a mark on them."

"Ingr called to one of your Angels who said they were not responsible," Clev said. "Which means a powerful demon was or the Master. I don't know if the Sisterhood could pull something like this off. Everything we are telling you, we already told Sorren because we don't want to put his village at risk."

"I have been authorized to bring up several suggestions for your consideration. First, we don't want to put any of you in danger but as you know, Hector can't even walk yet. We will move someplace else if you have some suggestions."

"Did you tell that to Sorren?" asked Mathas.

"Yes and he said we insulted him," said Clev. "We don't understand how your Angels work or even what they are about but we do understand that they are powerful and they seem to protect you."

"Hector is willing to give you the locations of these items so you can get them yourselves but he will only give it to people he knows he can trust. Which in this case would be Claudius, Stephan, Thaos, Sorren or Matthew. King Mathas, he just knows that you would not be the one going for these items."

"Before any of you consider agreeing to this, you have to understand it is going to be dangerous. Hector is giving you these items, whether you get them now or at another time is up to you."

"Clev, I think you will understand when I ask this," said Fahron. "But do we even know if any of this is true?"

"Ingr called to Miranda but it was Adam who answered her and I think Hector and Clev were the only ones in the room who couldn't hear his words," said Bella and looked at Clev. All this secrecy is driving me crazy," she said with disgust. "We already told Clev and Hector what Adam said but Hector thought it would change your choices. Hector's men are being killed all over by his enemies."

"He will be receiving more notices in the next few days. They know he is weakened and that I didn't really understand; something about feeling power but they don't know the facts so there are a lot of stories going around."

"Adam and Miranda are blocking them from finding him in the village and Sorren was told that. Hector knows the items that he is giving you are important but...this part we didn't tell you Clev. They will be even more important for us than Hector realizes."

"We asked Adam if we could bring Hector to the castle for the weddings and he said that was our choice. Then Nikki asked if the Angels would keep blocking Hector and Clev and Adam said they would. Now, as I look around the room I want to address the looks I see on all of your faces, especially my family."

"Boys, the girls invited him for Stephan. While he may be your enemy now he once was a very close friend. And anyone who has seen him knows he is too weak to be a danger to anyone. I had to help the boy sit up in bed." Bella now swung around and faced the King.

"Mathas, what Rosa did was an act of Mercy not betrayal certainly you can understand that and if you can't perhaps it is time you visited your son-in-law."

"Now, I have not gone on any of your missions but you tell me one person in here who hasn't said that when the Angel's say or do something there is always so much more to it. So you don't understand why they seem to be protecting Hector. Is it for us to understand? I certainly am not condoning his life now but if the Angels are protecting him there has to be a very good reason. So stop looking angry and just do what they want."

Claudius smiled and put his arm around Bella and kissed her on the cheek. "I think it's time we promoted Mother to a military officer," Stephan said kiddingly.

Fahron followed Mathas into his study. The King was too angry to speak to anyone so he ended the meeting and left the Great Hall. Mathas poured two large glasses of whiskey and handed one his friend.

"Fahron, I don't know what is happening to me. I am not a man prone to anger but...I don't know how to explain it. I can run a kingdom but I can't control anything in my own family."

"Your family has never needed to be controlled and that is not the issue here," Fahron said.

"What do you mean?"

"Mathas, we have been friends since I can remember and we are more alike than we probably care to admit. You feel like you failed. You think you should have protected Juleta and Isabella from themselves and then protected everyone they hurt. You are and have always been a good man and father. But you cannot make choices for other people."

"You are mad at Rosa because you want to protect her and Sarah. I felt the same way for a long time because of Timothy. I will tell you I really don't know what to think about any of this with Hector but I believe that Bella is right."

"There is so much we always don't seem to understand about the Angels but later we always learn there was a really good reason for what they did or what they asked us to do."

"I am going to the village to visit Hector for myself, you are welcome to come with me or I can deliver a message if you like." Mathas didn't respond and Fahron paused for a moment. "You do know why Rosa and Bella are doing this don't you?"

"Doing what?" Mathas asked angrily.

"Trying to connect with Hector?"

"It is beyond me."

"Isadore was with them a couple of days ago and Bella called to Miranda. All the women were and still are concerned for, well everyone. You know none of our wives are fools, they know how dangerous Hector is. Miranda told them that there was still some humanity in Hector but he was quickly losing it to the darkness. They asked Miranda a bunch of questions without getting any real answers, you know how that can be."

"Then Bella said to Miranda that she felt there was something the Angel wanted to say or she wouldn't have come. Miranda said that the women were asking the wrong questions. She said they wanted orders and Miranda was not going to tell them what to do and then she said 'What would it hurt to make a monster remember what it is like to be human again? Perhaps he would enjoy it enough to fight for it. Or perhaps it would change just one choice in his life and that choice might be very significant."

"Well, why the hell wouldn't they tell me that?"

"Would you have listened to them? Even hearing that you would never have allowed Rosa to meet with him. And yet she may possibly have made the biggest connection."

"Do Claudius and the others know what Miranda said?"

"I really don't think so. I think the woman were going to try it their way first."

"If they haven't left, have Claudius and the boys come in here will you?"

"Do our wives know too?" asked Thaos after Fahron repeated the story about the encounter between Bella, Rosa, Isadore and Miranda.

"They have to. They invited him to our weddings. I'll bet they have known since the beginning," said Stephan. "Nothing personal Mathas but I can understand them not telling you but why not us?"

"Have I been that bad?" asked Mathas.

"You've been walking around like you want to punch someone," Claudius said. "And we all understand that this is very different for you than for us. But for whatever Hector is, he didn't make Juleta what she was. You...we all need to remember that."

"Isadore will be here soon and we are taking Benny out to visit with Otis' family. We plan to visit Hector too."

There was a knock on the door and Thaos opened it. "I am just the messenger so don't anyone yell at me," Tessa said and smiled. "Fahron, your wife and son are here and they are in the parlor with Bella and Rosa."

"Tessa come in here a second and close the door," said Stephan.

"Am I in trouble?" she asked and laughed.

"Actually we need a woman's prospective on something," Stephan said. Tessa laughed again. "I am serious. And you need to be honest with us."

"I already don't like this," she said.

"Short story," Thaos said. "Our wives, all of them, spoke with Miranda about their concerns about Hector. She wouldn't tell them what to do but she said he was losing his humanity quickly then she asked them what it would hurt to make him remember what being human was like again. She said he might just want to fight for it or it could affect a significant choice someday."

"That makes a lot of sense to me," Tessa said.

"But they went behind our backs to connect with him. They didn't tell any of us," said Mathas.

"What is your question for me? I don't understand," said Tessa.

"Why do you think they wouldn't tell us?" asked Stephan.

"Seriously are you really asking me this? Is this some kind of trap or something?"

"No, we are serious," said Stephan but grinned.

"There isn't a woman working with us who would have told any of you that. First, you are all such protector types you either wouldn't let your wives do what needed to be done. And I will repeat that, what needed to be done. Or you would have limited what they were doing. And they have the advantage of connecting with him in a way that none of you can."

"Now you tell me Claudius, if you tried to connect with him on an emotional level would he believe that? Would he trust you? The problem here isn't that they didn't tell you, it's that you don't give them enough credit. You need to trust your wives more. Ok, now that I said my piece am I fired or anything?"

"No," said Mathas and smiled. "But don't be surprised if we pull you in here again to explain things."

"Great," she said sarcastically and the men laughed.

"But since you are all smiling for a moment. I am sure you all have invitations but Renya and Madeline are throwing an engagement party for Noah and me. Madeline wanted something small but it sounds like it is going to be a lot bigger than she expected."

All of the men laughed. "Renya has a very different idea of what small means," Mathas said.

"They would like Dominic's and Turner's teams there too since they are basically Noah's and my family but I don't know what that means for your work. And Mathas, I probably shouldn't be the one to ask but these classes that Hannah arranged for Margarit. They may have turned into more than we thought."

"It sounded like you wanted us to take Rosa and Margarit there and pick up the learning materials but these may be actual classes she attends. If so, do you want us to stay and bring them back?"

"This may be perfect," Mathas said. "I can send the family to Wetpr while we workout all of this with Hector."

"Mathas, I don't mean to be disrespectful but did you listen to anything I said?" asked Tessa. "You need to talk this over with Rosa because she might be needed here. You both are filled with guilt that you couldn't have stopped all the wrongs that Juleta did. Don't you see that is what Rosa is trying to do now? Even stopping one is worth the effort."

Chapter XIII
The Deal

Turner's and Abbott's teams took over the preparations to move the two hundred and twenty-three homeless people from Castor to Langer. Matthew was now free to focus on other matters.

When Captain Josef married Isabella and became a member of the Royal Family, Mathas gave him the command of Fort Castor. Josef was a well-liked and respected commander. Josef resigned from his position and divorced Isabella when he learned of her betrayal of their marriage and their kingdom. Almost immediately after his resignation he returned to his parent's home in the Kingdom of Puntd, where he had previously sent his children.

Captain Marshall worked with Josef and had been given temporary command over the fort when Josef left. All Marshall was told was that the King was working on new assignments for his officers. Josef's resignation and hasty departure from the Kingdom of Lentz ignited a barrage of rumors and wild speculations.

On this morning Matthew met with Captain Marshall and told him the true story about Josef's departure. Against Mathas' wishes, Matthew was open about many of the sorted details concerning Josef and Isabella.

"Josef was and I hope still is my good friend," Marshall said. "All of this just makes me damn sick."

"Understandably we don't want all of these details made public," Matthew said. "But there are several reasons that I shared this information with you. Father will soon be announcing that General Benson will be taking over command of this fort. At that time it is our hope that you will accept a new position. It will come with a promotion but...well let me explain it first."

"The more that we uncover the more the ruling families fear that there have been numerous breaches of our security."

"We know that Isabella was part of that but we haven't yet determined to what extent and we haven't figured out how she obtained such sensitive information. None of us want to believe that Josef was involved but honestly there are just so many unknowns at this point."

"You know this fort and the men serving here. We need you to audit the books before Benson takes over. But the positon we are offering you is a lead investigator to determine what information was compromised and how to prevent such acts of treason from happening again. While we believe you have what it takes for such a position, you will have to decide if your friendship with Josef will prohibit you from acting impartially."

"Matthew, thousands of our people were killed in that armada attack. I would give my right arm to find the traitors. I am honored and excited about this position but you do pose a good question. May I have the night to think about it? I don't want to accept such a position if I don't think I can be at the top of my game."

"Understandably and I commend your honesty. There are a few other things we need to discuss, then I want to take you on a tour of the site for the new naval yard and the land I just purchased for building a neighborhood for the homeless."

After the meeting with Captain Marshall, Matthew was feeling that he had accomplished his goals and was content to travel home the following morning. But as he was riding out of the fort he received word about a large group of bodies that were found west of Fort Castor and the River Shey near the Village of Pasot.

After the deadly armada attack and the destruction of Usman's small empire in the northern lands, the Kingdom of Lentz was undergoing many changes. The Angel Miranda had warned King Mathas that his kingdom was a doorway into the continent for invaders.

In the weeks and months that followed these two major events, Mathas, Fahron, Sorren and Claudius met with their generals and remodeled the defense system of the kingdom.

In addition to an extensive hospital system that was being built throughout the kingdom, Commanding Admiral Gideon had received approval to build three naval yards. One in Langer, one in Castor and the third near the Village of Silth, which was north of the City of Langer. Two more naval yards were being considered. One would be on the far northeastern coastline near the Village of Florence and the fifth would be on the northern border of the kingdom near the City of Stoba.

Two more forts were going to be built in the areas north of Langer which had previously been the lands of the Valdore Tribe and the Neutral Zone. Since Chief Sorren was now a ruling member of the kingdom he approved a third fort to be built on his lands.

Two well respected men, General Hatus and General Tamour had been reassigned to oversee the construction of the forts. These men had previously been on an assignment for King Sudfad where they investigated members of the Insidiae who had infiltrated the Military of Wetpr.

During this assignment these two seasoned generals learned of terrorist groups for the first time. King Mathas felt that the experience these men gained working in Wetpr would benefit them in upgrading the defenses of Lentz.

Many of these projects where still in the planning stages and the men in charge of them were searching for people to build and man these new facilities.

General Fahron's primary duties were in the defense of the kingdom. He and Admiral Gideon had sent posters to every kingdom in Opots. These posters listed all of the jobs available in the military and navy as well as civilian jobs. Because of these posters people were coming to the Kingdom of Lentz in droves.

Matthew had already received the letters containing the information from the morning meeting. He knew that Hector's men were being killed and expected this latest discovery of bodies to also be Hector's men.

Turner rode out to the site with Matthew and Captain Marshall; all three men were surprised at what they found. Sergeant Wicksom quickly approached the three men. "My Lord, it was a caravan of families and they were all butchered by Hutas."

"Hutas! Are you sure?" asked Matthew.

"See for yourselves," said Wicksom. "There are a few bodies of the savages here too."

"My Lord, I will be increasing patrols in all of the areas," Captain Marshall said. "I wonder what is bringing those devils this far north."

"I am going to request an escort tomorrow," said Matthew. "We just have so many women and children who will be traveling with us."

Claudius, Thaos, Bella, Clev, Stephan, Isadore, Benny and Fahron traveled as a group to the Village of Tyger. Mathas was not yet ready to speak with Hector.

"Well, this is a surprise," Stephan said when the group walked into Hector's small bedroom. Hector was sitting up in bed. Ingr, Nikki, Angelina, Hilgra and Shara were also sitting on the bed and they were all reading books and eating cookies. "Here we were worried that you girls would kill him."

Ingr jumped off the bed and kissed Stephan. "Actually, we are all doing research together. Nikki and I brought all of the books that you bought from Hilgra with us. Some of this information was new to Hector and he has been explaining stuff to us that we didn't understand."

"I know, who would have ever thought," Hector said with a grin. "But I will say it's been a long time since I had this many women on my bed and we were just reading." Angelina punched Hector's arm and the other's laughed.

"Hector do you remember Fahron and Isadore?" asked Claudius.

"Certainly," Hector said and extended his hand to shake hands with Fahron.

"This is Benny, we recently adopted him," Fahron said. "He was one of the children that Deckor was holding captive."

"I had nothing to do with that," Hector said defensively. "Why was he holding them as captives?"

"We were hoping you could tell us," said Fahron. "They were in cages deep in the ground."

"Now that is interesting," Hector said. "Can I look at the boy? I won't hurt him."

Fahron set Benny on the bed and Hector handed the boy a cookie. "He doesn't talk much," Fahron explained. "Some of the children that were rescued belonged to families in the city but not all of the children were claimed."

"Benny can you show me your arms?" Hector asked. "I'll give you another cookie." The boy did not speak but pulled up his shirt sleeves and showed his arms to Hector. "Benny do you remember when you got that tattoo?"

"Tattoo," said Bella with surprise.

"Yes, he has a small one on his right arm," Isadore said.

Benny nodded his head. "Was it before you were put on a ship?" Hector asked. Benny nodded again. "Were your parents with you?" Benny shook his head from side to side as Hector handed him another cookie. Benny do you remember anything from that trip?"

"It was scary," Benny said and started to cry. Isadore picked him up and hugged him tightly.

159

"Selling children is a big business," Hector said. "I know that none of you like hearing that but it is the world we live in. A cute little guy like that; Deckor could have made a lot of money off. So why didn't he sell the kids? I knew Deckor well and he was all about money and ego. And putting the children underground is extreme."

"When children are stolen from other continents the sailors often tattoo them. I am willing to bet that some of those kids had rich and or powerful families and Deckor was afraid that the children would be traced back to him."

"So what are you saying?" asked Nikki.

"Benny could be a prince or the son of a warlord. Honesty, I have never heard of anyone hiding the children underground like that. Were there guards?"

"We weren't there," said Thaos. "But there was a small army guarding those kids."

"Now this is just thinking out loud," Hector said. "Deckor always had so many irons in the fire that he didn't like making a lot of waves because he had a lot to lose if he was exposed in any area. I'll bet he bought some of those kids with the idea of selling them and then found out who some of their families were and stashed the kids until he felt it was safe."

"Can you tell from the tattoo what continent he was from?" asked Fahron.

"No, the tattoos are so the ship's captains can claim them as property. That tattoo is the one that Deckor's ships used."

"All of this makes me feel even worse," said Isadore. "We certainly don't want to..." she stopped talking and looked at Benny.

"We did come out here to just visit you too," Fahron said as he tried to change the subject. "Mathas isn't ready yet. He knows you aren't responsible for what Juleta turned into but...well you know how protective he is and it is tearing him apart that he couldn't protect Juleta and Isabella from themselves."

160

"I am sure he is irate with Rosa for bringing Sarah out here with me and my men," Hector said. "I hope he isn't too hard on her. It was a wonderful thing that she did."

"Well, you will get your chance to see him," Stephan said. "We are bringing you to the castle when Sorren and Shara come. Mother will fix up a large chambers with several rooms unless Clev wants his own."

"No, I will stay with him," Clev said.

"You can stay in the chambers or we can bring you to the celebration if you feel up to it," said Stephan.

"His clothes are full of blood," said Ingr. "He needs some clean things. Clev is there anything in that hotel room?"

"Yeah, but nothing fancy if that is what you mean?"

"I was just thinking clean," said Ingr. "The wedding isn't going to be formal but we can certainly pick up some things for you two to wear, if you want."

"Are you serious?" asked Hector.

"Sure. If you want something fancy, Ashely has the nicest men's clothing. But there won't be time to tailor anything," Ingr said. "Write down a list and your sizes if you know them."

"Can you hand me a piece of paper and a pen?" Hector asked. "Actually can I have a couple of pieces of paper? Have your men left for Cadia yet?"

"They postponed it," Claudius said. "After Clev told us about the documents you are giving us, they didn't want to start out until we spoke with you. Then they thought if they were postponing it for one day it might as well be a couple so they could come to the wedding."

"Good, so are any of you going with them?" Hector asked as he continued to write.

"Thaos and I are," said Stephan.

161

"What no honeymoon?" Hector asked with a smirk.

"Every day is like a honeymoon," Stephan said and grinned.

"I don't know whether to punch him or kiss him," Ingr said kiddingly.

Hector handed a piece of paper to Clev, "Here, write your sizes on this. It's time we got some new things."

"Do we need all of this?" Clev asked.

"Just write down your sizes," Hector said. "I am going to need more paper." Shara left the room and returned moments later with several more sheets of paper. Hector wrote for several minutes without speaking. After he finished writing on both sides of one large piece of paper he handed it to Stephan.

"You two read that now and tell me if there is anything you don't understand. Those are the locations of the items I am giving you. As you can see they are in safety boxes but, now pay attention Stephan." Stephan laughed and looked up from his reading. "The items that have stars by them are ones that you are going to have to call your Angels to break the spells. The spells are on the locks not the items themselves."

"Read that thoroughly because when you get there you need to know what you are doing. The boxes are under different names. I will write letters giving you permission to go into those boxes and Clev will give you the keys."

"It's going to take me a little while to write all of those letters. They should be put into envelopes. Clev said you are going to Cadia to track down the money that Otto gave to Juleta. Why?"

"We are still trying to figure out what she was doing," said Fahron. "She has been a constant threat to so many of the people here."

"There are reasons I am asking this. Are you looking for things in particular?" Hector asked.

At that moment Claudius heard Miranda's voice in his head saying, "Now you use the card up your sleeve."

"I may be telling you more than I should but you are showing us good faith," said Claudius. "We are going to try and stop the Master and the experiments of the Second Sons. Now, we heard that you and Juleta were trying to create an army with the transformations. Are we stepping on your toes?"

"That was Juleta and Deckor. Ok, I am going to put my cards on the table because I am taking advantage of us working together. Juleta was into the strange things like the transformations and the ancient curses. I am more a regular criminal. I am into things that make me money. Several of you have pointed out that I don't need the money and you are right. You might say it is the challenge of the hunt for me, if that makes sense."

"I like the logistics of figuring out everyone's moves if you know what I am saying. Juleta got me into the Insidiae so she would have a powerful backer because they really hated her. I don't mind most of that organization because it's about money. There's a lot of really normal people in that group then there are people like Juleta, Deckor and Meekos and his sister. And yes, I heard about your teams going after Roch. I hated him, wish I could have been there."

"I have gotten more into the magics as I am trying to figure out all of the crap she did to me."

"We heard that she made a lot of promises to investors and now they want you to pay up," said Thaos. "If that is true, how do they want you to pay?"

"Actually I was just getting to that. And I have to say it's amazing all of the crap you guys know. Is it hard work or the Angel's telling you?"

"Mostly hard work," said Thaos. "But you aren't answering the question."

"As I told you originally Juleta and I had a business arrangement. Thaos, she wanted you to be her head lieutenant then Lazo started telling her that you were leaving all the time because you had a girl stashed away."

"I knew it was a lie because my men saw you helping that old man and his grandson but it was my way into the position. I didn't tell her about that family nor did I tell her you had a girl. I kind of made myself available."

"I knew she was a little crazy because I would see her at Otto's orgies. You know Isabella brought me to my first one then she and Juleta got into a fight over me. Funnier than hell. But I am getting off the subject. When I started doing jobs for her, it was meeting long enough to get an assignment then bringing her the goods and getting paid. And I will tell you she seemed pretty damn normal all of the time."

"As I got to know her from the business end I realized that she was brilliant. She could look at something in ways that normal people couldn't and you must know by now how she liked to strategize. I was actually impressed with her in the beginning. She was always a heartless, ruthless bitch but Stephan, you are what set her over the edge and I am serious. And now that I know she was basically created by the Sisterhood that could have been an intentional trigger."

"You know how paranoid she was, well when she found out about Ingr something really snapped in her and she just kept getting worse. She trusted me more than the rest of you but she didn't completely trust me."

"And there is a reason I am going into all of this. After she made me look like Thaos, I almost killed her. She had to stop me with magics. And that was the end of our honeymoon. Sometimes she hated me then she would act like we had this loving relationship, which we never did. It was sex and business nothing more; until she got pregnant."

"She used that to try and get me to come back to her. Honestly I didn't want a kid, especially with her. Until I held Sarah. You guys don't have to believe me but that baby stole my heart."

"So, because I was so pissed at her transforming me, she stopped telling me anything about that part of her operations. She made promises to get investors and yes some of them have been coming after me, unfortunately most of them don't want their money back. They want the product that she promised. And that was a surprise to me because she promised them different things. And some of it sounded so crazy."

"You know she could change people's faces but then she was experimenting with their body sizes like with that Zane you grabbed in Cadia. He was an old man and she made his body look young. But she was experimenting with changing people's heights and with animals. I didn't find out until recently that she had talked to Andrac on several occasions about creating armies of demons. You know he turns his own people into demons. Juleta was telling him that she found a way to create life from scratch."

"What people want are her books and ledgers of her work. I know there were ledgers of the transformations like me and Hilgra but I don't know if all the other stuff she was promising was hot air or if she was really doing experiments. And she got involved in the Second Son thing to try and get on the good side of the Master but I bet he knew she was a product of the Sisterhood."

"So what is all of this getting to? Ask your Angels. I have no intention of doing experiments. Personally, I like hiring regular men instead of creating them. But all of Juleta's investors are either enemies of mine or rivals. So this is what I am proposing."

"If you can find any of her work, I will tell you who the investors were and I am sure they are your enemies too. You know if they are purchasing armies of demons they plan to use them against somebody. Then I would think we could pull a fast one on them like screwing with the paperwork or something. Or you can have those books but I need to get those guys off my back."

"I know that Otto bought her some ships. They bear the same symbol as mine which I assume you know. They are docked in Cadia and were basically used for slaving"

"Where would she sell slaves?" asked Claudius.

"Dark lords. Dieter must have used hundreds of them to build his underground tunnels. You don't think that most of them pay for labor do you? There are five ships and they are docked near the Lazy J Tavern. If he gave her money for more than that I don't know about it and I want to. Even though I inherited her organization she kept a lot of secrets from me and planted a lot of traps."

"Can I interrupt for a moment?" asked Hilgra. "Hector do your ships do regular transports like merchandise?"

He laughed, "Most of them, why?"

"Because as soon as we get those documents we will find out what plants we need and some of them may be very rare."

"Whatever you need for medicines you let me know and I will make sure you have it. And before I finish with my proposition for you, here this is your wedding presents." Hector handed Thao a piece of paper.

"So this is a surprise?" asked Thaos.

"It's a good surprise," Hector said. "Now back to my proposition, as far as I can see it is a win, win for us to work together on some of this. I know you and your friends are suspected of being The Seven Sons and The Keepers of the Scrolls and honestly a lot of people and demons know that too. And a lot of them don't give a shit except that they are afraid you will find out about their activities and stop them. You are kind of regarded as the law if you didn't know that."

"If you can get me information, I can give you information about people and groups you might not even know are after you." Stephan was starting to speak but Hector said, "Let me finish. You told me what that Angel said about finding cures for the curses on me. I will give Shara and your group all the stuff I have on those transformations but I want you to work on curing me. And if by chance you can figure out how to make me look like my old self again, I will pay you a fortune. Do we have a deal?"

"Yes," said Claudius. "I just realized that you are probably going to be here for a while. Are you going to stay in the village or buy a place?"

"Clev and I just started talking about that."

"Well, you know the Angels are blocking you so your enemies can't find you here. That may change if you move out of the village so we may need to talk about that later. I am bringing this up not only for your own safety but the safety of others."

"I understand that, what I don't understand is why your Angels would help me."

"Maybe some of the information you give us will help us stop something much worse than you," said Claudius. "What was the story on Zane? Did he ever exist?"

"Yeah, he's a real guy. But he doesn't look like the Zane you found. That poor bastard was a set-up. She knew that if you survived her curses you would come looking for her so she planted him and if you didn't come, well he would have died anyways. She must have made three or four guys who looked like him so you might run into another copy again. And if you do, know that he is probably a set-up too."

"The real Zane is an old guy. He is a warlock and lives in Ganz. She thought of him as kind of a mentor. Since you mention him, he probably can give you some answers."

"So then why haven't you talked to him?" asked Thaos.

"Talk to him, hell I've tried to kill him. It isn't that easy. He does this thing where he can disappear; don't ask me how. But I do know that Juleta paid him a lot of money to put curses on me. So if you run into him, be careful."

"So why the big build up about him?" asked Stephan.

"To throw her family off. Haven't you connected the dots yet? She was trying to create armies of monsters. Part of it was for power and profit but you know who she was going to attack first don't you? She was determined to have the throne of Lentz."

Chapter XIV
The Day before the Weddings

Honey, I need to move my arm; it's asleep," Noah said as he awoke in the early morning hours.

Tessa did not open her eyes but smiled. "Well, I certainly hope that is the only thing that fell asleep," she said then giggled.

Noah laughed and they kissed passionately.

Both Angus' team and Edward's team were staying at Mathas' castle. The two leaders got up early so they could discuss their upcoming mission in Cadia. Claudius had met with them the previous afternoon and told them the information that Hector had given him. Claudius had not told Hector that the teams also planned to investigate King Fahra of Zorta. They did not know if he too was a terrorist or just gave harbor to such.

Sudfad and Renya habitually got up early and had coffee on the balcony of their chambers. They liked to watch the sunrise and have a few moments of peace before the day began. Sudfad was taking his first sip of coffee when a small flock of Enrops landed on the balcony railing.

The letters he received were focused on Hector. This was the first in-depth information that he had received about Hector's condition, cooperation and the words of Miranda, Adam and Cyril. Sudfad gave the letters to Renya to read.

"I am calling a family meeting before the big one," he said. "This might have more significance for us than we realize."

Everyone in Claudius' household rose early this morning because the wedding ceremonies were scheduled for the following morning. The men laughed when they found their wives congregated in the main kitchen reviewing their lists.

"So what are you planning?" asked Thaos as he poured himself a cup of coffee.

"Ingr and I are getting a boca and going into Langer with all of you. We're going to work with Ashley and get the things that Hector and Clev want and there are a couple of other things being altered. Then we are taking the clothing to the village and going back to Langer to buy all of the things on Bella's list."

Stephan grabbed one of the lists and wrote the name of a jewelry store on it. "All of you girls should go there and pick up your gifts," he said with a big grin. "It saves us a trip."

"Oh you boys," Bella said in a scolding tone but smiled.

"Bella what are you doing today?" Claudius asked then laughed at how flustered she suddenly looked.

"The weddings are early in the morning, so we might have guests coming tonight. I am preparing everything for the ceremonies as well as chambers. And while I am talking about that, you might want to decide if you want to bring Hector here tonight instead of in the morning. He will take longer at everything."

"That means that Shara or Angelina should stay here too," said Claudius. "I will...actually all three of us don't need to be at the meeting. Do one of you boys want to go with the girls today?"

"I will," said Thaos. "I don't know Hector and Clev as well as Stephan does; I should spend more time with them. But let me drop the kids off at training first."

"Well, let's think about this," said Stephan. "If we are taking the kids to training let's just talk to Shara, Sorren and Hector. Then we can tell Mother what their plans are when we come back here for the girls."

The adults in Sudfad's family met in the dining room before breakfast and read the letters from Lentz. When everyone had finished Sudfad asked, "Madeline and Javier what do you think?"

169

"You are the only ones in this room who have met Hector. Does any of this make sense to you?"

"What surprises probably all of us is the part the Angels have played," said Javier. "But as Claudius said in his letter they always have good reasons for what they do."

"I don't know Hector," said Annabelle but look at how much time Miranda spent with Archetenus so he wouldn't turn into a powerful demon, maybe that is what they are doing here."

"I have no doubt," said Javier. "But after Claudius said that Miranda told him to have a card up his sleeve, I know there has to be more to this."

"When were these letters written?" asked Corsa.

"Two days ago," said Raul. "The Angels didn't help the Enrops get here."

"Shara is an incredible healer, it will be interesting to see what she finds. I wish I was working with her."

"You can go home and study with her," said Javier. "You could go back with Noah, Tessa and the others."

"I'm not leaving you," she said.

"I love us being together," said Javier. "But this could be an opportunity of a lifetime for you. You are such a dedicated healer. At least think about it."

"If you decide to go back at least one of us will go with you," said Alex. "And I agree with Javier."

"Well, I will think about it," Corsa said.

"Getting back to the letters," said Madeline. "You know that Miranda set Samael up with this. Which I think is wonderful so that is one very positive thing. Then stopping Hector from turning into more of a monster is another. Do you really think there is more?"

"It's hard to explain," said Raul and picked up an apple from the large fruit bowl on the table. "No matter how many different ways we could figure out how to look at this, the Angels always see more. And things that we would never consider. Personally, I think we will all be surprised before this is over."

"They aren't carrying knives this time," Thaos said jokingly as Cassidy, Amy, Logan and Marty ran into Hector's room ahead of Stephan and Thaos.

Hector was sitting up and he and Clev were reading some of Hilgra's books. "Grandma wants to know if you are coming to stay with us tonight," Amy said loudly.

"Are you going to live with us?" asked Logan.

"No," said Hector. "Just come to the weddings. Do you want us to come tonight?"

"Now kids don't repeat this," said Stephan then laughed because he knew they would. "But the women are crazy getting everything ready today. And since the ceremony is pretty early in the morning Mother is telling people they can come tonight. She thought it might be easier for you to come too instead of hurrying in the morning. But we have to talk to Shara and Sorren first. We can certainly take you home with us but we want a healer on hand."

"It doesn't matter to me," said Hector. "Whatever works the best for all of you."

"We'll be out later to get the kids and the girls are buying your clothes so they will be out this morning yet. Just let us know what you decide," said Stephan.

"We all get to be in the wedding," said Amy excitedly. "So Grandma said we have to be careful and not get hurt today." All the children laughed.

"So you know one of them will," Thaos said and grinned.

"If you kids get done with training before they come back, visit me," Hector said. "We can play some checkers."

"Ok," said Cassidy.

"Have you read these books yet?" Hector asked.

"Kids, why don't you go to the training field," said Stephan.

Hector waited until the children left before he spoke. "The books talk about all different groups including the Master. If what we are reading is true, after the original members of the Sisterhood aligned with the Grand Masters and the Old Ones they started to practice dark magics. Now, remember they started out as a really small group of women who were severely victimized. Which tells me they weren't warriors and some of them were probably injured."

"It doesn't say it in the books but I am assuming they turned to magics for protection and retribution. As word got around about the group, others, many others, joined them. It sounds like it was the only way for these women to be safe. A powerful healer named Naomi joined the group. She was an elder woman and under her they combined the magics and the medicines."

"This says she developed horrible plagues to send upon their enemies. But she never did. Several books make reference to the creation of plagues but don't explain about what happened. And they don't mention her notes or recipes but they do say she experimented on captives."

"Now what I question is what stopped them from unleashing those plagues. Those women have sworn oaths of revenge. I am telling you for a fact that something stopped them. I just don't know what."

"Is Hilgra coming back out here today?" Hector asked.

"I assume so," said Thaos.

"I don't know where she is getting these books from but they are very good. I want to buy what she has."

"She has a lot," said Stephan. "I mean an entire room full. Maybe we should buy more too."

"Well, these are your books that we are reading now," said Hector.

"Are you thinking there is some connection between that elder woman and Juleta?" asked Thaos. "It was just the tone of your voice when you talked about it."

"I don't know, just a bad feeling. Here read these two pages for yourself and tell me if you don't see some similarities."

Matthew led the caravan from Castor to Langer. They started out two hours after dawn. Captain Flores led the military escort of two hundred soldiers. The excitement of the families who were moving to Langer was contagious. Everyone was happy and Matthew allowed one of his soldiers to lead the group in songs.

Sudfad started his morning meeting at the usual time. Before it ended he received three more letters from the ruling members of Lentz and Madeline received a very long letter from Tessa. All of these correspondence helped the group to build a better picture of what was going on in Langer and with Hector. By the end of the meeting all of the people realized that Hector probably had information that would be vital for the mission that Archetenus and Jared were to work.

It was shortly after noon when Ingr, Nikki, Stephan and Thaos walked into Hector's bedroom. Each person was carrying an armload of packages. "The girls may have gotten a little carried away," Stephan said with a grin. "What's the matter?"

Hector picked up two notes that were on the small table next to his bed and handed them to Stephan. "That's almost two hundred men that I have lost in the last few days," Hector said angrily.

"I asked Sorren if I could bring some more of my men out here. Since there haven't been any problems, he approved so Clev just returned with them now."

"So after you improve are you going to keep staying here?" asked Nikki as she was taking clothing out of the packages.

"I don't know but at least my feet are improving from that medicine that Dominic and Fennel made. I could actually walk this morning. Of course I can't get far," Hector said and grinned.

"It doesn't sound like you are in the mood for this but do you want to try some of these things on?" asked Ingr. "At least the clothing you are planning on wearing tomorrow because Nikki's mother will tailor them for you."

"I've got to tell you that I appreciate everything you are doing. I'm not used to it," Hector said.

"Well that is just damn sad," Ingr said kiddingly to Hector. "Stephan help him put these on."

"Welcome to the party," Thaos said jokingly to Clev. "You're next."

Clev grinned as he saw Stephan helping Hector to stand while Ingr and Nikki were inspecting his clothes. "Is this all clothes for us?" Clev asked as he looked at the piles of clothing on all of the furniture.

"Honestly, we weren't sure if you really knew your sizes," said Nikki so we bought different sizes. We'll return what doesn't fit."

"Now you know what it's like to be married," Stephan said with a grin.

"I'm not changing in front of the girls," said Clev. "What do you want me to try on first?"

"Hector!" yelled Sorren as he marched into the house.

"Is there a problem?" asked Ingr.

Hector smiled and shook his head from side to side to indicate no. "Sorren, I may be a criminal but I am not a freeloader," Hector yelled as Sorren entered the room. "You won't take money so we will pay with supplies. You can have the bocas and horses too."

"That's a hell of a lot of food son," Sorren said as his anger diminished.

"Sorren, you are housing us, feeding us and protecting us. That is worth more than those supplies. I told Clev to get everything but whiskey. I don't want my boys drinking out here in case they start to act like fools. Clev is coming to Stephan's with me. That big guy with the red and gray mustache is named Showers. He will take care of things while we are gone and he knows the rules. But if there are any problems, I want to hear about them right away."

"Angelina organized a couple of competitions on the training field," Sorren said. "She was afraid of your boys getting bored."

"Hope your guys aren't sore losers," Thaos said and chuckled. "These warriors start practicing their skills when they are kids."

"Showers will keep them in line," Clev said as Ingr handed him a stack of folded clothes. "He's a mean son of a bitch. Oh, sorry ladies, I shouldn't have said that."

"You will be sorry if you don't get into those clothes," Ingr said jokingly.

"Yes My Lady," Clev said and laughed. He walked into the parlor.

"He won't change in front of the girls," Thaos said to Sorren.

"Interesting," Sorren said. "Normally my brother Hugo is in charge when I am gone but he is coming with us. Grant will be taking my place and he is a tough son of a bitch too," Sorren said with a grin. "Let's introduce our men before we leave."

"Mine fit pretty well," Clev said as he walked back into the room. "You did good."

"Let me see," said Nikki with such a voice of authority that it made Clev grin.

"We got you new boots too," said Ingr." And we bought different sizes. Hector, we also got you moccasins in case the boots hurt too much."

"You girls thought of everything," Hector said and winked at the men. "Sorren, I have a legitimate shipping business. I told the women that if they need anything for the medicines to let me know and I will get it. That really goes for anything here. I want to repay your kindness."

"I really can't think of anything but thanks for the offer," Sorren said. "Actually Shara, Hilgra and Angelina are really excited to learn about different medicines and work on cures. They are acting like kids."

"That makes me happy," Hector said. "I have been trying to decide if I should tell you something since it is water under the bridge now. When I was just doing odd jobs for Juleta, she sent me and the boys to follow Thaos a couple of times. We realized he was spending time in Minges with that old man and that boy who Claudius adopted. You don't have to believe this Thaos but we didn't tell her what you were doing. Mainly because it wasn't her damn business."

"We saw you in a lot of taverns watching Usman's men too. Well, it got to the point that when you would visit those guys we would follow you to Minges then spend time in the taverns. There is one near the fishing docks called the Sunset. I don't know if any of you knew that the bartender worked for Usman. His name is Red. Obviously the place was filled with Nordes warriors all the time who didn't know they had a spy among them."

"Wait, how did you know?" asked Sorren.

"Because Juleta and Deckor were close and he's the one who got Red the job. Deckor was always passing information to Usman."

"Well…Thaos that was the trip when you fixed the roof for that old guy. We just drank and played cards. A really pretty girl from your tribe was sneaking around with one of Usman's boys. The two really looked in love. So you got the picture and we are all in that tavern at the same time. Well, that couple I was talking about were sitting at a table kissing when all of a sudden they jumped out of their seats."

"She runs to the bar and grabs a guy and sticks her knife against his throat. It got our attention. Then she starts yelling at him. Then the guys yell back and the bartender yells. And we realize that the bartender is giving information to some of Usman's men about Angelina. Turns out Usman wanted her bad. That girl heard it and basically attacked the four guys. Her boyfriend goes to help and the bartender hits him over the head with a club."

"We jumped in because those four guys were beating on that girl. We eventually got kicked out. Usman's men dragged the boy away and I wouldn't be surprised if they didn't kill him. That girl really took a beating. It turns out there were more of Usman's men in the place than we thought. We all got our butts whipped. But we got the girl out and brought her here. She wouldn't let us take her to a physician."

"I'm telling you in case Red is still working there because he was the one handing out information."

"He is and I appreciate this," Sorren said. "Was the girl's name Raven?"

"I don't know but she did have black hair. Real pretty girl."

"She's dead now," Sorren said. "But that does help to explain some things."

"Juleta did send demons after my friends," Thaos said.

"Well, she didn't hear anything from us. But she probably had guys watching us watching you. You know how paranoid she was. But you know that Lazo would go back and tell her everything you said."

177

"Figured as much," Thaos said. "But we should probably change the subject." Thaos was looking at Ingr and Nikki and now all of the men did.

"Lazo got into our castle and cut Ingr up really bad with a knife," Nikki said emotionally. "He was going to kill the babies but she wouldn't stop fighting with him. She died but the Sanuri helped her somehow."

"I never heard about any of that," Hector said. "Did you kill him?"

"Father and Sorren were bringing one of the babies to Ingr and found them. Father beat Lazo so bad that he looked like ground meat," Stephan said. "Lazo did that because he hated me; he didn't have enough balls to attack me."

"And you are sure that Juleta didn't have anything to do with that?" asked Hector.

"She was long dead," Stephan said.

"Well, I'm still being attacked by her curses. I am just saying it sure is a possibility. She and Lazo were closer than you may have thought."

"I'll be back," Sorren said. "I'm sending warriors after Red."

"Feel free to take some of my boys with you," said Hector. "Like I said that place was filled with Usman's men. Now I know that war is over but you really don't know how many escaped."

"Let me change and I will go out with you," Clev said to Sorren. "I'll get volunteers but tell them your men are in charge."

Chapter XV
Conflict

Sorren, Shara, Hugo and Greta brought Hector and Clev to the home of Claudius. They arrived late afternoon, thinking they could avoid other guests who might be spending the night at the castle. Hector had requested this because he didn't want anyone to have difficulties because of his presence there.

But Hector could not hide his presence for long. Nikki's mother Gladys and her children were at the castle. She kept going into the chambers to do last minute alterations on the clothing that Hector and Clev bought. All of the children kept running into the chambers to show the men their pets and toys. Bella entered the chambers to chase the children out and brought in a huge tray of delicacies.

"Clev, open that cupboard near the big window," Bella said. "It's filled with whiskeys and wines. There are glasses in there also." Hector was sitting on the sofa in the parlor. "Hector if you need to go to bed just say so. And we know the kids can be a bit much so don't be afraid to tell them you don't want a visit. Now, in each bedroom there is a small cabinet. The top of the cabinet's roll back. There are chocolates, nuts and fruits in them. Everyone is running late today so we won't have dinner for at least another hour."

"Bella, will you sit down and have a drink with us?" Hector asked.

"I would like that," she said. "I'll have red wine."

"The chambers are wonderful," Hector said. "We don't really live very fancy anymore. But you have a lot going on here so don't feel like you have to wait on us. And I really hope that our presence doesn't cause you any problems."

"Can I be frank?" Bella asked.

"I've never known you not to be," Hector said and grinned.

"I don't know if you are going to think this is an insult or not but it's like having the old Archer back. All of us liked the person you used to be. And maybe you really didn't changed that much it's just that you have such a reputation. I am trying to say that we are glad you two are staying here. You used to be so much a part of the family that it somehow seems right to have you here."

Hector grinned and looked at Clev who laughed. "He's laughing because he was just telling me how much I am like my old self again and I was arguing with him about it. But I do appreciate your words."

"I am not trying to reform you," Bella said and laughed. "But I always liked Archer. And I really didn't know what to expect from Hector. But I need to change the subject a moment. We have the cottage almost ready for your parents. It's been painted and we have all new furniture. We are having a patio and garden put in and Isadore and I dug up some of your mother's rose bushes and planted them there."

"We packed up things like pictures, books, knickknacks and we took her good dishes and put them in the cottage. Of course they will probably be eating in the castle but we want to stock up on food and put flowers in there. But we won't do that until we know when they are coming."

"Thank you. Let me pay you."

"Hector, don't insult us. Your parents are our old friends, we want to do this for them. Have you told them yet about Sarah?"

"I was going to wait and do it in person but you heard what Rosa said. So I sent them a letter. I don't know if they have it yet."

"That will give them something positive to think about. Clev sit down here and join us," said Bella. "I want to tell you some things but before I get to that, we have some rules in the house. We rather expect our guests to act like family; that is what we prefer. Now, I know you boys may feel strange but right now you are the only ones who do, so relax and enjoy yourselves."

"But if you see or find out about a problem or threat let us know right away. And that brings me to the next subject. Has anyone told you why Stephan and Thaos are having second wedding ceremonies?"

"No, I thought they were being romantic," Hector said with a grin.

"Well, it is a touchy subject and if they didn't tell you please don't bring it up until after tomorrow. Juleta sent flocks of ravens to attack the weddings of Prince Raul and Prince Simon. She sent armies of demons to our home to kill everyone at Stephan's and Ingr's wedding. We were not prepared and a lot of people died. And if it wouldn't have been for the Sanuri, Stephan and Matthew would have died too."

"Close friends of both Thaos and Nikki were killed and the demons started to eat some of the people. Ingr couldn't think about her own wedding day without sobbing. So Stephan is giving her another. I was very serious when I said if you see or hear anything let us know. Of course we are better prepared but we also have a home filled with children and babies now. I was really proud of the boys when they decided to do this."

"I am sorry she did that to all of you. I didn't know anything about it and if I had I would have stopped it. She was obsessed with Stephan but why did she attack the weddings of the Princes of Wetpr?"

"Well, you know they are family with Mathas and Rosa and now they seem like family with us too. Raul and Simon both married women who had been prisoners of King Roch. They are two of the most beautiful girls you will ever meet and I mean inside and out. But they also survived hell and they, well Stephan said they are smart on the ways of the streets. Vitomas and Annabelle spotted Juleta immediately for what she was when no one else did. Apparently they were gracious but they told her they would be watching her, which angered her."

"Rosa also said that Juleta was jealous because those girls are well thought of and their husbands are so handsome. If there was something else I don't know about it."

"That is interesting," Hector said. "I am not surprised that she was jealous but did you know how hard she was trying to get into the Insidiae? I wonder if she really went there to get information possibly about those girls. I am sure that Roch wanted them back."

"So are you saying that her jealous tirades might have interfered with some kind of plot?" asked Bella.

"Absolutely, Juleta never went to functions like that probably because she would get so jealous. If there wasn't a plot, I wonder if she had feelings for one of the Princes."

"Well, she had never met Simon before and Raul didn't like her and he did not hide his feelings. In fact, he always called her a female version of Roch. If you don't mind I might tell them that. We plan to visit soon."

"I have certainly heard of those people but I don't know them. If you are going there and tell them... let me back up a moment. I do remember hearing about the weddings because they were big news in every kingdom. Juleta was not as strong in those days with her magics. If she wanted to curse them or something she probably stole some of their things to use with the magics. It's up to you if you want to tell them that."

After Bella left the chambers, Clev filled his and Hector's glasses with whiskey. "Boss, I really like these people. I hope we aren't going to get them hurt."

"I know. And believe me I have been thinking about that. But if their Angels are protecting us they sure as hell will protect good people. How would you feel about us getting a place here? I need to stay close to Shara for a while. And with Mother and Father here and Sarah. I just don't know. I don't want to get any of them killed."

"I like it fine here. In fact, I like it better than any place we've been. But what kind of business are you going to set up? They may be your friends but none of them will take any shit. And Boss, I really would prefer not to have to kill any of them."

182

Norge was a giant of a man. He significantly towered over any other man in the Village of Tyger. He was incredibly strong and the scars on his body showed that he was an experienced fighter. He was also Sorren's cousin and godfather of Angelina.

Clev had accompanied Sorren to the training field of the village earlier in the day. Sorren stopped the competitions and repeated Hector's story about Raven and Usman's soldiers; then he asked for volunteers to go to Minges and find Red.

"I demand to lead that group," yelled Norge angrily. "Or I will go by myself."

"It's yours," said Sorren. "Any volunteers line up behind Norge."

"Damn!" said Clev when he saw Norge marching towards him and Sorren. Clev was not easily intimidated but even he took pause when he looked at Norge.

"Listen up!" yelled Clev. "The boss says that any of you who want to join the fight can but Sorren's man is in charge."

Both Sorren and Clev laughed as almost every man and woman on that training field now lined up behind Norge. "Norge pick who you want or take them all," Clev said loudly. "But if they don't follow your rules the boss wants to know."

Norge led the warriors to Minges. They rode hard and fast. For the members of the Nordes Tribe it was personal. Hector told them of a spy who had betrayed them. A spy who endangered their beloved princess. And he told them of enemies who beat one of their warriors in an unfair fight.

Showers led Hector's men. He rode next to Norge and the two of them made an intimidating pair. Hector's men just wanted to fight but they had come to like and respect this group of warriors who were giving them shelter.

Since Showers was a leader he was privileged to more information than the hired fighters. He had not been with Hector the day the Angels defeated Samael but he was told about it. And he was told how a small handful of people were determined to protect Hector and Clev, although they were enemies themselves.

Hector was a powerful force and this was the first time that he had been so incapacitated. Never, had Hector's armies taken shelter or help from others before. Showers knew that Hector felt beholding to the Nordes Tribe. Showers joined the fight not only as a sign of good faith towards the Nordes warriors but to let anyone who was spying on them know that the armies of Hector were not in hiding.

Matthew had driven their caravan hard and the group reached the City of Langer by late afternoon. The families were taken to the barracks at the naval yard where other families helped them get situated and proudly showed them the homes and businesses they were building.

Matthew gave Captain Flores a tour of the area and explained that a similar naval yard and neighborhood would soon be built in the City of Castor. Then Matthew made arrangements for Captain Flores and his troops to spend the night in Langer.

Claudius, Thaos, Stephan, Ashley and Gideon arrived home later than any of them expected. Gideon was ecstatic when they entered the house and handed bouquets of flowers to Bella, Ingr, Shara, Gladys and Nikki. Ashley was already carrying her flowers and laughing at Gideon. "We're celebrating," he announced and walked into the parlor to pour drinks.

"How are things going with Hector?" asked Stephan in a whisper.

"Just fine, honestly it's like he is becoming the old Archer every day," said Bella.

"We can hope," said Claudius. "But don't let your guard down."

When everyone entered the parlor Gideon said, "I have wonderful announcements. All of you are aware of the plans we have for the naval yards. I have been wanting to promote three of my officers to admirals and have them each command a naval yard but I have been so severely short staffed that I haven't been able to pull them out of their assignments."

"And during all of this I have been in constant correspondence with Commanding Admiral Wainburst because both of our navies will be patrolling the same ocean. So it is reasonable to assume we will be working together at times. He has transferred nine hundred men to us to help our navy get up and running. We can expect them within the next few weeks. This is a great leap forward for us."

"I just put over two hundred more people in your barracks," Matthew announced as he stood in the doorway with his family. "We need to get those homes built." Everyone in the parlor had been focused on Gideon and did not hear Matthew and Angelina walk in with their children. All of the people happily greeted each other. Sorren, Shara and Greta each quickly took one of the children before anyone else could hold them.

The group had a toast to the navy and another to Matthew's return. "Is Hector here?" Matthew asked. He too had been a childhood friend of the now notorious criminal.

"Yes, he and Clev are in a chambers just down the hallway and they have been perfect gentlemen," Bella said. "In fact, I had to chase the children out of their chambers so Hector could get some rest. I hope you don't plan to start anything Matthew."

"I'm not going to start any fights at least not now. Angelina has been keeping me up on everything. Honestly, I don't really know what to think."

"Well, I don't know what he is like when he isn't with us," Bella said and smiled. "But except for him telling me that I can't reform him, he's more like the old Archer every day. I understand there is much that needs to be worked out but this night and tomorrow are for our children. Any hostilities can certainly wait."

"Don't worry Bella, I feel the same but I do want to see him," Matthew said.

"The third door on the right before Claudius' study," Bella said.

Matthew and Angelina held hands as they walked to Hector's chambers. "It's Matthew and Angelina," he announced as he knocked on the door. Clev opened the door. Matthew immediately saw Hector sitting on the sofa and the two men stared at each other. Angelina gave her husband a nudge to get him to enter the room.

"I'm not here to start anything," Matthew said. "I just wanted to see you. Boy, you really look like hell."

"Thanks," Hector said with a grin. "Have a drink?"

"Sure and Bella said we are eating in twenty minutes," Matthew said as he and Angelina sat down. Clev handed them drinks. "I'll be honest I don't know what the hell to think. I was in Castor because Andrac put bounties on one of our teams. But everyone has been writing to me. And damn it sounds like you are two different people."

"That's what Bella said too," said Hector then he looked at Clev and laughed. "Clev's telling me that I am turning back to my old self and he likes me better that way. It's strange being back here but it's nice. I'd forgotten about this life."

Matthew didn't say anything for a few moments as he stared at Hector. "Claudius tells me that we called a truce and it seems that everyone is abiding by it except for Father. You know he will be here tomorrow."

"Can you blame him?" Hector asked. "I'll tell you if our situations were reversed I don't know if I would be as generous and kind as all of you have. Did Angelina tell you that Rosa let me visit with Sarah?" Matthew nodded. "She did it behind Mathas' back. I really hope he isn't hard on her. That was a brave and nice thing she did."

"You know I don't think I would have imagined Hector using words like 'kind' and 'nice'. I heard about the kids confronting you. Margarit's not even afraid of you anymore," Matthew said.

"Hell, you think I look bad now you should have seen me that day."

"You know what I mean," said Matthew. "You knew they had to face what scared them most and it was you and men like you. You could have been an ass to them. Why?"

Hector grinned, "Those little shits made me feel guilty as hell and they really busted my chops. But they also had so much courage. They knew what they were doing and saying. And let me tell you that adults wouldn't talk to me like that. They are all going to be fine warriors some day. Which they told me that I'm not because I don't have any honor."

"Did they really say that?" Matthew asked and smiled.

"They sure did," Hector said. "Hell, I didn't know what to say. I mean some of those kids were from the compound in Ganz, they had legitimate complaints."

"I've heard they have been coming to visit you and play checkers. It surprises me that you would do that."

"They are good kids and ask Clev, we both are enjoying the company. We don't live like this."

"Boss ask them," said Clev.

"I don't want to keep putting Sorren and his people out but I need to stay near Shara and Angelina for a while; maybe a long while. So Clev and I have been talking about me getting a place here. The problem is that we don't want any of you to get hurt. We know that for some reason your Angels are helping us now but I can't imagine that will last long. You know my parents are coming back here?"

"In a way that doesn't surprise me," said Matthew. "Where are you thinking of getting a place?"

"Clev and I were just talking about that. Rosa said that she was going to try and talk Mathas into letting me have visits with Sarah. So I might want to stay close."

"I don't think any of us will have a problem with that except you can't be a criminal here. Don't you have any legitimate businesses? And as for being in danger, hell we always are. We might have more people after us than you do."

"Ok, you boys have had your chance to talk, now it's my turn," Angelina said and stood up with a stern look. Clev started laughing so hard that he spit out his whiskey.

"Hector, we are working really hard to help you. And it's not just for you. The Angel Cyril told us that a lot of people are still suffering from Juleta's magics and a lot more will when the Master and the Sisterhood go to war. You are not moving from the village until the Angels tell us because you are a dead man the moment you leave. If you haven't realized it you are our patient and we are learning how to help others while we help you."

"And furthermore," as Angelina spoke she put her hands on her hips which made all of the men grin. "I haven't said a lot to you except for that first day but you seem like a fool to me. You already have all the money in the world. Clev's not even sick and he looks like hell. Why do this to yourselves? Everyone you care about is here. You're getting your old life back. I don't know what you are all about but you really need to get your priorities straight."

"Angelina, I hear what you are saying but you have no idea what..."

"You just stop right there," she said angrily. "Don't give me a story that you can't stop or walk away from whatever you are in. A man as powerful as you can do whatever he wants. And if you need help well look around you. Even the Angels are helping you. There aren't any excuses; you need to make choices and I don't think you want to."

There was a knock at the door but before Clev could open it Sorren peeked his head into the room. He was laughing and said, "Sorry for listening but her voice carries. Bella wants everyone at the dinner table now and she told me to carry Hector if he couldn't make it."

Norge and Showers led their combined armies into the Village of Minges just after dark. Showers had most of his men surround the tavern. People on the streets started to leave because they could see there was going to be trouble. A few of Shower's men entered the tavern and took seats in the back of the huge room.

Norge and Showers walked in together and were followed by the Nordes warriors. Norge recognized Red behind the bar. The tavern was filled with loud drunken men. Norge walked behind the bar and picked Red up and held him in the air. "Quiet!" yelled Showers.

"For those of you who are Nordes we just found out that Red is a spy that Deckor put here to give information to Usman," Norge yelled and threw Red over the bar. Red fell on a table that collapsed under his weight. He jumped up and Showers punched him. Red stumbled backwards and Norge grabbed him again.

"Raven heard Red telling Usman's men how they could capture Angelina. Raven attacked them and a group of Valdore soldiers beat the hell out of her," Norge threw Red into a wall as he spoke. Men were quickly jumping up from their tables to get out of the way.

"If there are any Valdore's hiding in here fight like men or do you only gang up on women?" Norge taunted. And the room burst into a battle scene.

It was clear to everyone seated around the dinner table that Hector and Clev felt out of place.

"Why do you look so uncomfortable?" asked Claudius. "It's not like you haven't eaten here before."

"Don't really know," Hector said.

"He's wounded because Angelina beat him up," Matthew said kiddingly and Sorren and Clev laughed loudly.

189

"Your wives just keep busting my chops," Hector said and grinned.

"I couldn't help but hear," Sorren said. "And she was right, you do need to stay with us for a while. Now, if you want to move to a bigger house and move your things in, that's fine. The place we put you in is close to ours that was the only reason."

"I would like that," said Hector. "But you have to understand that this is the first time anyone has..."

"Taken care of you?" asked Ingr.

"I was going to say helped us out but it's the same," said Hector. "And it is not a comfortable feeling. I don't really understand why all of you are doing this but I certainly don't want to put you into any more danger than you already are."

"Hey, the Angels aren't blocking our enemies," Stephan said sarcastically.

"That you know of," said Hector.

"Point taken," Stephan said.

"I am thinking about getting a place here but you aren't fools you know there are a lot of considerations," Hector said then looked at Matthew and grinned. "And yes I have some legitimate businesses too."

"So if you can't stop yourself from being a crook," Nikki said with a big smile. "Just run the legitimate businesses here. I am sure you have homes in other places too."

"He's always being watched," said Clev. "He would like to be closer to his parents and Sarah but others will find out about them if he stays here."

"We are protecting them," said Claudius. "Son, I don't think any of us have an issue with you living here. But you would have to be more Archer than Hector and you know that. I guess the question is can you live a double life."

190

The trees around the Sunset Tavern were decorated with hanging corpses. A sign was displayed on Red's body detailing his crimes.

Norge did not burn the tavern down because it was not owned by Red. Only the men who were identified as Usman's soldiers were hung but the numbers still surprised Norge who now wondered if more of Usman's men were in the area.

"I know your boss doesn't want your men drinking but how about I buy one round and we head back," said Norge. Showers slapped him on the back and yelled for his men to return to the tavern.

Chapter XVI
The Wedding Gift

Jack Franks had been in hiding since the demise of his father, sister and brother-in-law. Although the Master had greatly altered his appearance, Jack's normally paranoid personality took on new dimensions. He was able to convince some of his father's hired fighters who he was and put them back on the payroll. The problem for Jack was getting access to the family money.

He was irate when he discovered that the ruling members had seized his father's home and bank accounts. But fortunately for Jack, the only accounts that were seized were the ones in Langer. Jack was traveling to Port Friada with a dozen hired fighters. He had men in Langer who were spying on the ruling families and sending Jack any information they learned.

Jack was aware that members of the Sisterhood were in Langer. And he knew that Otto had sacrificed some of their members to the Master. Jack was also aware that Hector and his men had been seen in Langer but suddenly disappeared. This fact disturbed him more than the presence of the Sisterhood because he knew what a formidable force Hector was.

Otto and Hector had become rivals once Hector took over Juleta's empire. Otto had many rivals but Hector had grown up in Langer and knew considerably more about Otto and his family than Otto felt comfortable with. Otto was a shrewd man but he was not a fighter, so instead of direct attacks against Hector he tried several times to frame Hector for actions committed by Otto's men.

Hector was a strategist and was usually prepared for Otto's attacks but as Hector's health became worse he was not able to stay on top of the politics of his criminal life. Otto was in the midst of setting up an elaborate plan to blame Hector for the deaths of the members of the Sisterhood who were sacrificed when he was killed. The plan was never implemented.

Jack was considerably more of a fighter than his father had ever been but he was not as intelligent as his sister or as shrewd as Otto. The three of them all had specific roles they played within their organization. Jack oversaw the 'dirty work' as his father called it and worked directly with the hired fighters to protect his father's interests. Jack was a cold and heartless man but he was not a courageous man. He usually paid others to do what he could not or would not do.

It was as if Claudius' household exploded two hours before sunrise. All of the staff and women were frantically preparing for the wedding ceremonies and guests. The house was filled with excited children running through the hallways with two barking puppies chasing them.

Both Clev and Hector jumped out of their beds as Thaos and Stephan entered their chambers. "Get your asses up!" Stephan yelled. "We're hiding out in here." Stephan was carrying a pot of coffee and Thaos was carrying cups and a bottle of whiskey.

"I think I would rather be fighting Hutas than be out there," Thaos said and started pouring whiskey into the cups.

"Hector do you need help getting out of bed?" asked Stephan as he walked into the bedroom and saw Hector struggling. "Damn, that's what you get for screwing Juleta," Stephan joked and the men laughed. "I still can't believe you did that."

"So what are you hiding from?" asked Clev as he added coffee to his cup of whiskey.

"Boy, you guys must be sound sleepers," Thaos said and opened the door so they could hear the noise. All of the men laughed.

Stephan helped Hector into the parlor. "Bella told us about your first wedding," Hector said. "If I would have known what she was doing I would have stopped her. I hope you realize that."

"Yeah that was an ugly day," Stephan said. "We are better prepared this time."

"I stopped all her bounties on you," Hector said. "So you shouldn't have to worry."

"Hate to sound paranoid but every time we let our guards down some crap happens," said Thaos.

"Sorry I'm late," Matthew said and walked into the room.

"I wasn't sure you would understand the message," Stephan said with a grin and handed him a cup of whiskey and coffee.

"Now that we are all here I have an announcement," Thaos said with a big smile. "This morning Nikki told me she is pregnant again."

"Congratulations," said Stephan. "A toast to Thaos and Nikki."

All the men raised their cups of coffee and said congratulations to Thaos.

"I couldn't even think about having a relationship when I was in the business, so now I am making up for lost time," Thaos said. "You guys should try it."

Both Clev and Hector laughed. "Can't imagine that is going to be for a while," said Hector. "Besides I don't do so well with marriage."

"It's not my business but did you really marry Juleta?" asked Stephan.

Hector looked at Clev who laughed. "It's a little complicated," Hector said. "Could I have another one of your special coffees? This is when I was screwing her and we were in negotiations for me being her head lieutenant. We were drinking and the next thing I know its morning and she's telling me we got married. I didn't believe her at first but she showed me this altar and told me that we exchanged blood and damn if I didn't have a wound on my wrist. And it wasn't long after that, that she turned me into you," Hector said and nodded at Thaos.

"You mean you got married at a demon's altar?" Stephan asked. "What exactly does that mean because knowing her..."

"It means she sold my soul to Abraxas without me realizing it and before you ask, I can hold my booze so I'm thinking she drugged me. You know you can't just say to a demon, 'Hey I was drunk give me my soul back'. Of course, I didn't even realize that at the time. I was pissed at her but we had negotiated a great contract. But like I said a week later I looked like Thaos and tried to kill her."

"I thought Samael owned your soul," said Matthew.

"He bought it from Abraxas. Once your soul is sold it's like being a slave because they just pass you around. They do it to other demons too."

"So you have your soul back now?" asked Matthew. "I find this really confusing."

"I'm not really sure because I don't feel right and it's not all because of the curses," said Hector. "That's why I need to get back to my research."

"Don't get pissed," said Matthew. "But we have been told that if a demon owns you he can see through your eyes and our families are here. Adam, Miranda anyone can we ask a question?"

Hector and Clev both jumped when Adam appeared in the room. They jumped because his presence almost knocked them over. "Shit, why are we smoking?" yelled Clev and jumped out of his chair.

"Someone owns both of you," said Thaos.

"I've never sold my soul to any demon," Clev said fearfully.

"How many times did Samael pull you into his domain?" asked Adam. Both Clev and Hector were greatly intimidated by the Angel and didn't speak. "He couldn't have done that unless he owned you."

Adam's presence became less intense and the skin of Clev and Hector stopped smoking. "But how could he own me without my knowing it?" asked Clev.

"You and Hector are bonded in ways other than friendship," Adam said. "You were not born monsters yet monsters you became. When did the savage in you become uncontrollable?" Both Hector and Clev stared at Adam. "I am not giving you that answer because you have choices to make. But I would suggest that the two of you figure out that answer."

Adam turned to Matthew. "We are protecting all of you. You will not be punished for the Mercy you are showing to these two. But know that they wear many masks."

"Angel why are you helping me?" asked Hector with fear in his voice.

"That is a complicated answer," Adam said. "You relish in spinning webs. You walked into one and never even realized it. For all of your intelligence you are a fool. And you dragged your loyal friend with you and look at what he has become. The two of you do not feel comfortable in this home because you gave up your humanity a long time ago."

"Think of your time here as a lesson in humanity. Hector, you have been so lost in the darkness that you are blinded to so much. You think you are in control but you are a puppet. Take this time to think about who you dance for." Adam disappeared.

"Wait Angel! Is that it?" Hector yelled but Adam did not return.

The weddings were held in the gardens in the back of Claudius' castle. Immediately outside the patio doors of the parlor was a stone courtyard. A stone pathway led from the courtyard through various gardens. The pathway stopped at another stone patio that had fountains and now had a large wooden arbor that was covered with flowers. Beneath the arbor was a small altar that was filled with white flowers and white candles.

High Priest Felix, who was the senior high priest at the Langer Headquarters of the Patronus priests officiated the ceremonies.

Musicians played stringed instruments as the guests took their seats. Cassidy, Marty and Logan were walking people to their seats while Amy and Margarit handed out roses to the women who were attending.

Stephan and Thaos walked to the altar together but stood on opposite sides of the arbor. Matthew and Gideon followed them. Matthew stood next to Stephan and Gideon stood next to Thaos. All these men were wearing their dress uniforms. Ryan was wearing a suit and initially stood behind Matthew but he was to change his positon after the brides were handed to the grooms since he held all of the rings.

Angelina and Ashley walked down the aisle wearing flowing lavender dresses. They held bouquets of different shades of purple flowers.

Claudius walked Nikki down the aisle and Sorren walked Ingr. The young brides were both wearing elegant yet simple dresses of different designs. The dresses were an off white and the material was light and flowing. The dresses were sleeveless and the tiny straps were off the shoulder. Both women wore amethyst and pearl jewelry which their husbands had bought them for the occasion.

The ruling families and the immediate families sat in the front seats. All of the team members who were in Langer attended including Abbott's and Turner's teams. Many of the Patronus priests who were stationed in Langer also attended as did Selen, Hilgra, Elexas and Olin. There were also many members of the Nordes Tribe as well as other guests.

"I thought this was supposed to be small," Clev said as he helped Hector to the ceremony. They deliberately came late so the other guests would be seated first. The two men took seats and looked around at the hundreds of people in attendance.

"It has been a long time since I have been to a wedding," Hector whispered to his friend.

To the relief of all, there were no threats. Claudius' castle was surrounded with soldiers and all of the guests were prepared for an attack but none came. After the two couples said their vows they turned and faced their guests who applauded loudly. The couples laughed at the war cries that were being yelled as they walked back towards the castle.

Mathas walked next, he was carrying Sarah. Rosa walked beside him and was holding Margarit's hand. Hector and Clev were sitting in the last row of chairs. Mathas looked shocked when he saw them. He did not speak but momentarily stopped and stared at the two men. Rosa pushed her husband to get him to continue walking.

The guests were directed by staff to walk through the parlor, into the hallway then into the Great Hall where other musicians were playing. Stephan and Thaos led their brides to the dance floor as soon as they entered the room.

Ryan, Elexas and Olin stayed together as a group. They were curious to see if Mathas and Hector would fight. Both Elexas and Olin were now allowed to attend the morning meetings and had been hearing about Hector but even with the briefings they were shocked to see how bad he looked.

Tessa and Noah were walking around the Great Hall looking at how everything was set up and for the first time they talked about their ceremony which made them both feel overwhelmed. When Bella entered the room, they walked up to her. Noah was going to speak but Tessa blurted out nervously, "Bella can we pay you to help us with our wedding?" Both Bella and Noah laughed at how frightened Tessa sounded.

"Why do you sound so scared?" asked Bella.

"I don't know. I don't think I ever paid attention to what all was involved before," Tessa said.

"I would be honored to help you," Bella said. "What kind of wedding do you want?"

"No idea," Noah said with a grin. "All we know for sure is that we want Othnial to officiate and she wants Madeline in it. We haven't really gotten around to talking about it."

"I will do it on one condition," Bella said. "That you don't pay me."

"That isn't right," said Noah. "We can't imagine all of the work that went into this."

"It is a lot of fun for me and I don't think I will have the opportunity to plan another for some time. Why don't you look around and decide if there are things you like in particular and we can meet next week to start getting some ideas."

The young couple decided to go back outside and look at the way the wedding area was set up before the staff took things down. They walked into the back courtyard through a door in the Great Hall. As they walked around the building they heard voices.

"Are you two fighting?" Noah asked somewhat kiddingly.

"No," said Hector who was still sitting in one of the outdoor chairs.

"Hector, you really don't look good," said Tessa. "Do you want help inside?"

"Neither of you look good," said Noah. "Clev are you sick too?"

"I just heard Adam's voice," Tessa said. "He told me to tell you about Gideon. He does this thing where he can put people into a trance and..." Tessa paused as she listened to the Angel speak. "He can help you remember something." Both Hector and Clev stared at her without speaking.

"Both of you look kind of scared," Tessa said. "It's probably not our business but can we help you?"

"Hector, I am going to tell them," Clev said. "Because I will admit it, I am scared. How can a demon own my soul when I've never sold it?"

"What exactly is this thing that Gideon does?" asked Hector.

"He's done it to me and it didn't hurt," Noah said. "He puts you to sleep but you aren't totally sleeping then he asks you things. In my case I had nightmares about Tessa for a long time before I even met her. Then when we started dating I didn't know why I was so scared for her."

"Hector, I am assuming you are afraid that he will try to get other information from you. He won't. Gideon is a man of integrity. But he usually has more than one person in the room, to take notes. But you don't have to have that. Do you want us to bring Gideon out here and tell you what he does?"

"Now don't laugh," said Tessa. "But after what Clev just said, if Gideon does this he won't be in danger will he? Demons won't jump out of you or anything will they?"

"Under other circumstances I would laugh at that," Hector said. "This morning Matthew, Stephan and Thaos were in our chambers. We were drinking and talking. Stephan was asking me some questions about Juleta but there were things that I couldn't remember. Then we talked about Samael owning my soul. I'm skipping some parts here. They asked me some questions then Matthew called to Adam to see if they were in danger being near me."

"The Angels are protecting all of you. But that Angel told Clev and me that we were owned and that we've been puppets without knowing it. He said we should try to remember when we first became savages. Just so you know, I don't remember selling my soul the first time and Clev never has."

"Noah get Gideon. I'll stay with them," said Tessa.

"I don't want to take him away from the celebration," Hector said.

"Listen buddy," Tessa said. "First, Angel's just don't pop in for visits and secondly, the only time Adam just starts talking to me is when I am with you. If he is saying this, it is important and probably needs to be taken care of soon."

"What do you mean he only talks to you when you are with me?" asked Hector.

"I talk to him all of the time but he usually doesn't talk back. When he appears he talks but like I said they don't just decide to visit. I suspect the two of you are in some really bad trouble that is about to get worse."

"I think I need a drink," Hector said.

"We can wait on that a bit," said Gideon as he, Claudius, Noah and Sorren walked up to Tessa and the men.

"They can tell you the details," Tessa said. "But Adam told them that something owns their souls and they need to figure out when they first became savages," Tessa explained. "And just now Adam talked in my ear and told me to tell them about what you can do, Gideon. Clev said he never sold his soul and Hector doesn't remember the first time he did. Sorry for jumping in," Tessa said to Hector. "But this is unusual and Gideon needs the facts first because this could be dangerous."

"Let's move this into my study," Claudius said. "We need some privacy."

After they entered the study Claudius said, "Boys, we aren't trying to pry into your business or trick you into giving us information but we did hear most of what Tessa said and we agree. If you are going to be controlled by something we would like to deal with it now since you are living with us."

"Tessa and I can leave," Noah said and took her hand.

"You can stay if you want," Hector said. "Especially since the Angel talks to her. It will make more sense if I tell you about our conversation with Stephan, Thaos and Matthew this morning."

After Hector finished explaining about the encounter with Adam, Gideon explained how he learned to put people into trances and how he handles the situations. "If you two agree to do this, I am going to ask Adam for guidance because I don't know if this is dangerous for you or us. Would you have a problem with that?"

"Hector, I am doing it," said Clev. "I have to find out. You can watch me and decide if you want to do it. Gideon, do whatever you need to do."

"Tessa will you go outside and just tell Bella that we are conducting business in here so she makes sure no one disturbs us," Claudius said.

"Clev, we can leave," said Sorren. "But after those damn snakes jumped out of Hector, I'm inclined to stay since we don't really know what we are dealing with."

"That's fine just don't let anything drag me into hell," Clev said nervously as he sat down in the chair that Gideon had prepared. Tessa returned to the room and she and Noah stood with their backs against the door to prevent anyone from entering.

"Adam, I would appreciate any help you can give us here," said Gideon. "And please protect everyone here." Adam did not appear but Gideon heard his voice. "But it is their weddings," Gideon said then paused. "He said Stephan and Thaos should be in here."

"I'll get them," said Noah and quickly left the room.

Noah explained to Thaos and Stephan why Gideon was going to put Clev and Hector into trances. The men entered the room without speaking. Everyone sat down except for Tessa and Noah.

Gideon slowly moved his pocket watch in front of Clev's eyes. Gideon spoke softly and in a few moments Clev's head fell forward. Gideon heard Tessa gasp and looked up. Hector, Thaos and Stephan were all unconscious and their heads had fallen forward.

Adam appeared in the room next to Gideon and said, "You can't go on this journey with them. You won't need to ask questions. The Angel gently touched each of the four men on the sides of their heads. "Do not interfere with them," Adam said to the others in the room. The four men started to move in their chairs and to groan as if they were having nightmares.

202

Clev suddenly screamed, Stephan was clenching his teeth and sweat was pouring down his body. Thaos started to yell at some unseen enemy and Hector collapsed on the floor. The others in the room watched with horror but did not speak as Adam was watching all four men. Hector started to go into convulsions and Tessa ran forward but Noah pulled her back.

Clev too fell out of his chair. "You bitch!" Stephan yelled. Thaos was hanging onto his chair as if something was pulling him away.

"Adam what is going on?" asked Claudius.

"You might say they are reviewing their dark sides because it is in the shadows that they will find the answers they need."

Stephan suddenly jumped out of his chair and landed on the floor on his knees. He shook his head several times then looked at the people in the room as if he didn't recognize them. "Adam is Juleta alive?" he gasped.

"No but she was a vessel of the Sisterhood so in a small way she lives on. Perhaps you can help the others out."

"How?" asked Stephan who now turned and looked at the other three men. Stephan jumped up and grabbed Thaos' arm. "Thaos hang on to me and jump out the door," Stephan yelled. Thaos did a forward roll out of his chair and accidently kicked Stephan in the process.

Stephan ran to Hector, "Clev next," said Adam. Thaos now had his consciousness back and ran to Hector. Both Stephan and Thaos were yelling at these men.

"What's wrong they aren't coming?" yelled Stephan.

"Their demons are pulling them back in," Adam said.

"Well do something," yelled Stephan.

"Adam how do we help them?" Thaos yelled as he was pulling Hector by both of his arms.

Clev and Hector suddenly jumped to their feet; both men were wide-eyed and sweating profusely. It took them a moment to get oriented.

"That attack was imminent but fortunately for you it happened when you had friends to help you out," Adam said to Hector and Clev. "You have thrown so much away in the pursuit of power and money. Now all of you sit down and what do you remember?"

"I was dreaming about Juleta, I mean I think I was dreaming about dreaming about her," Stephan said. "She was screaming that she loved me then...did she curse me?" Adam nodded.

"Thaos what do you remember?" asked Adam.

"I was in the parlor of her castle where she always had those demon statues. She was screaming at me then yelling for demons...actually I don't know."

"We didn't get married at an altar, she served me up," said Hector angrily. "But I don't know to who, I just felt like I was being pulled down a shaft."

"I don't even know what I saw," said Clev fearfully. "Angel what was it?"

"Now it is time for the four of you to understand what you have in common," said Adam.

"Juleta," said Stephan.

"And what else?'" asked Adam.

"Stephan and I grew up in this area but Thaos and Clev didn't," said Hector. No one else spoke for a moment as they were thinking about Adam's question.

"They are all good looking men who have strong personalities and are fighters," Tessa said. "And in a way they are like mirror opposites of each other. I mean in some ways you could see them all being friends but two are good now and two are really bad."

Adam smiled and asked, "Does anyone else want to expand on that thought?"

"The first time we met in that hotel room you showed Tessa something like the mirrored image of me and Hector. Is that the clue?" asked Thaos.

Adam did not answer Thaos' question but asked, "What else do they have in common?"

"They are all strong men," said Noah. "Did Juleta have feelings for Clev too?"

"What kind of men did Juleta fall in love with?" asked Adam.

"Well, it sounds like she slept with anyone but all of these guys are muscular with dark hair and similar traits," said Tessa. "Oh my god! Was she making more of them?"

"I don't know about Clev but the others rejected her," said Sorren.

"I did too," Clev said. "She came on to me after she married Hector. I knew she was just trying to get him jealous and I didn't want any part of it."

"So she cursed us all because we rejected her?" asked Stephan.

"Yes, but I believe you already knew this," said Adam. "What you didn't know was the extent of her hatred. The Sisterhood wanted a powerful player in this world so they tricked Isabella into helping them create a monster. Juleta came into this world as a strong monster who not only turned on her loving parents but the Sisterhood. She considered them weak compared to the other monsters like the Master."

"Hector, she was trying to create in you the perfect husband who would adore her and never betray her. She created an image of herself. She did much more than to change your appearance but you already know that too."

"Clev with all of the darkness in you, you are a man of loyalty and you have remained loyal to your friend no matter what the hardships. But this life is wearing on you too. Do you remember what you heard in your nightmare?"

"Juleta was cursing me and said I followed Hector around like a dog so...," he paused and the color drained from his face. "That is what I saw. She turned me into a demon dog and set me on Hector."

"I saw me fighting with Thaos or maybe it was Hector," said Stephan. "I killed whoever it was."

"Can you just tell us what is going on?" asked Thaos.

"Juleta wanted all of you and hated all of you. She also had opportunity to be near all of you. At some point she drugged each one of you and took some of your hair. She has maintained a connection with you through that," explained Adam.

"She was insane but she was shrewd. She realized she might be defeated and put into motion many types of, I am going to say traps for lack of a better word and like real traps they have triggers. She was delusional and paranoid. She feared that all of you would gang up and ridicule her so she set traps for you to kill each other. What were you doing this morning?"

"Drinking together and ridiculing her," said Stephan. "So that was a trigger? Does that mean we can't talk about her anymore?"

"If I would not have intervened you would have been sucked into those worlds that you briefly experienced," said Adam. "But what did you do?"

"They helped each other," said Claudius.

"So you broke that curse," said Adam. "That was my wedding gift to you."

Chapter XVII
Power

"We all thank you," Hector said to Adam. "But I don't understand why you are helping me and Clev. I understand the others."

"Hector for all of your brilliance you don't understand much," Adam said. "And I am not saying that to be mean. Nor am I done with all of you because you are still more intertwined than you realize."

"Did she sell our souls too?" Thaos asked fearfully.

"I will get to that but first we are going to have a discussion," Adam said. "Hector, what was the reason you gave to Claudius for your choice to get involved with Juleta?"

"Power. She offered me a great deal of power," Hector said suspiciously.

"Your life of crime started out as a game because the poor little rich boy was bored. A game you mistaking thought you could control. You were like Isabella and Juleta more than you realized; now tell me what did you think of them?"

"I loathed them both. They were both crazy and always seeking attention. I never want attention. I don't understand how I am like them."

"Was it attention or acceptance they sought?" asked Adam but he did not wait for Hector to answer the question. "Like you, Isabella wanted excitement and thrills regardless of the consequences. Like you, Juleta wanted power and wealth. But both of these women appeared weak to you because they sold their souls and thus sold their will power and internal strength."

"The irony is that you were a more powerful person when you commanded your own power. You have said that you don't remember selling your soul and that is true."

"But you were also studying to become a priest. You know how to get your soul back, you proved that to us on the battlefield with Samael. But you descended into hell because you thought it would give you the riches you desire in this world."

"You started out wanting power as a game now it is an addiction and that is because on some level you realize you have no real power because you sold it."

"Thaos and Hector, I want you to really look at each other. Thaos you were just a step away from becoming him. And Hector you are but a prayer away from becoming Thaos. No Thaos, no one owns your soul or Stephan's soul because you have made the right choices but all four of you were on the same path."

"All of you wonder why you seem to get along so well when you are enemies. Stephan and Clev, neither of you wanted power but you wanted the thrills. You two should talk and you would realize that when you were at certain crossroads in your lives you made the opposite choices which brought you to where you are this moment."

"Hector, your lesson today is that people who really own their power don't strive for it. In fact, the really powerful people are so content and confident that they sometimes fail to realize what a motivating force power is for others. And if you don't believe me look at some of the others in this room."

"Now to answer all of your questions. Yes, Juleta has more traps but all of you now know that you can call to us and we will help you. Hector your soul is not your own nor is Clev's, but that is a journey you must take."

"What do you mean?" asked Clev.

"You aren't strong enough to fight to get your soul back but The Great Ruler is. Clev, if you don't know how to pray there are many here who can teach you," Adam said. "You both have choices to make. If Hector chooses to continue his descent into hell will you continue to follow him?"

"There is more to this," said Thaos.

"Of course there is," Adam said. "But you need to connect the dots to see the picture. First, Thaos what single act led you to changing your life?"

"When I decided to warn Stephan and Claudius about Juleta."

"She offered you many things. The same things she offered Hector, why didn't you take them?"

"Because she disgusted me and working for her made me even more disgusted with myself. I didn't draw a line in the sand until I thought she was going to steal Ingr."

"Hector, for all of the lip service you give Juleta you have never really gone against her. You are an extension of her and part of you enjoys that and the other part hates yourself. You are a lot of contradictions and you have a lot of choices to make," said Adam.

"Now for a riddle," Adam continued. "Who came first the chicken or the egg?"

"Now wait, we thought you were talking about Isabella and Juleta with that riddle," said Stephan.

"This is a maze you are operating in and none of you asked for clarification. Let's talk about power again. All of you feel victimized because of Juleta's attacks against you and you have all said that she is effective because she knew all of you so well. What is the reverse side of that coin?"

"That we knew her better than anyone else, that if we work together we have the power," said Stephan.

"You said that like it was a question; it is the right answer. The Sanuri always uses an example of a puzzle so if Juleta's plans are a puzzle don't you think that each of you hold a sizeable piece? You have many of the same enemies. Juleta is gone so who is still putting her plans into motion? Is it one person or demon or many?"

"All of you have different agendas and I will not tell you what choices to make in life but I will tell you that you would all benefit from continuing this truce and collaboration you have started, at least for a while. Isn't it ironic that you have to show Mercy to your enemy to save yourselves?"

Adam turned and looked at Tessa. "And for you young lady. You told Hector that I only talk to you when you are with him. I have been talking to you your entire life, you just wouldn't listen to me until you could see me with your eyes. Yet you recognized me and Miranda the moment you saw us and it wasn't just from your mother's drawing. Heaven talks to every person all the time; it is your choice if and when you listen to us."

"That is another lesson for you," Adam said as he turned and looked at Hector and Clev.

Adam disappeared and Stephan said, "I am not ruining another wedding day for Ingr. No one talk about this today!"

"Agreed," said Clev. "I feel like I've just been beaten up."

"I do too," Thaos said.

"Well, we have a home full of guests. We need to get back out there," Claudius said. "And that goes for Hector and Clev too."

Ingr saw the group first as they returned to the Great Hall. She ran up to Stephan and kissed him. "Where have you been?" she asked but before he could answer she asked, "What's wrong?"

"I wasn't feeling well," Hector said. "They took me to the study to sit down for a little while."

"My Lady we need to dance," Stephan said and escorted Ingr to the dance floor.

Thaos was looking through the crowd for Nikki and smiled when he saw her. "Claudius get Bella. Nikki and I have something to tell you. Sorren, you and Shara should be there too. I'm getting Gladys," Thaos said with a grin and disappeared into the crowd.

"Sorren, will you get our wives? I believe we are going to need cigars," Claudius said with a huge smile and left the room.

"You two are welcome to join us at our table," Gideon said to Hector and Clev. "Just don't talk about what happened yet."

Tessa and Noah were already on the dance floor. "You know there is so much more to all of that don't you?" she whispered.

"I know but we aren't talking about it now. Tessa do you know why Stephan and Thaos had these second weddings?"

"No."

"After this dance we will go outside and I'll tell you."

High Priest Bernard was sending daily dispatches to Kings Sudfad, Tobias and Mathas. High Priest Othnial sent daily letters to Gabriel and Dominic, while Padre Thomas and Padre Bartholomew sent daily letters to General Colter at Fort Nora, High Priest Rueben at the Nora Headquarters of the Patronus, High Priest Nicholas at the Philiste Headquarters of the Patronus and High Priest Philetus who was the ranking member of the Patronus at the monastery at Malga.

This division of work was very deliberate. The letter writing was a time consuming task. Not only were these men undertaking an arduous journey but a dangerous one. They had already been attacked by two small war parties of Hutas.

Padre Bartholomew and Padre Thomas had befriended Gala during their stay at Sudfad's castle. She found them eager students of the healing arts. Both priests now used their medical training to help the Patronus priests who were injured in battle.

"You two have been sitting here like a couple of sticks in the mud," Stephan said as he and Elexas walked up to Clev and Hector. "Clev, I promised you a dance with a pretty girl and Elexas volunteered."

"I haven't danced in a while," Clev said apologetically. Elexas laughed and the two walked onto the dance floor.

"I'm in no condition to dance," Hector said almost angrily.

"I didn't ask you," said Stephan sarcastically and sat down at the table. "Are you feeling that bad or aren't you any fun anymore?"

"Both I think," Hector said then grinned. "People have been coming up and talking to us; that surprised me."

"They are good people plus you do know a lot of them. Has Mathas talked to you?"

"No, I don't expect him to."

"Thaos and I were talking and we are all going to be hung over or tired or both tomorrow. But the next day the four of us should get together and talk. We'd like to do that before we leave for Cadia. Which reminds me; are we bringing your parents back with us? Because Thaos and I aren't staying there as long as the teams are."

"I've been trying to figure out when would be the safest time but I don't really know if it makes a difference. They know you are coming and I told them I might not be able to give them an exact date for safety reasons. So they should be packed. Mother is so happy to come home that I suspect she has been packed for a while."

"This is changing the subject but I have kind of a favor to ask," said Stephan. "That kid Olin, you know who he is. He wants to ask you a question but he is afraid to come up to you."

"I've seen him watching me. Any idea what he wants to ask?"

"No. But he never knew that Otto sold his soul to the Master. Of course we fixed that," Stephan said with a grin. "But he's kind of feeling lost and betrayed. And his father is..."

"I know who his father is but is this a setup?"

"What do you mean?"

"You telling me about this kid when Clev and I are in the same situation."

"Actually he does have a question for you and maybe your situations aren't that uncommon in the crowds you run with."

"Yeah, get him," Hector growled.

Stephan didn't leave the table. He looked at Olin and Ryan and whistled loudly and both young men walked up to the table. "This is Ryan and Olin and this is Hector but all of you already know that. Do you want me to leave?"

"No," said Ryan. "In fact, you should stay. We already talked to Claudius about what we want to ask."

"Hector, King Mathas has appointed Ryan, Elexas and me to be in charge of information. The teams keep getting books and papers and things and we kind of put everything together," Olin explained.

"I am going to interrupt for a moment," Stephan said. "Hector, these kids are like little geniuses. Talk about seeing things from different perspectives and they never stop working. Mathas not only gave them the jobs but a wing of the castle because he is so impressed."

"Thanks," Olin said excitedly. "Well, we have so much stuff you can't believe it and some in languages that no one understands. Ingr and Nikki were telling us how all of you have been reading those books and you were explaining a lot to them so we wondered if we could show you some of the things we have and maybe you could explain them to us."

"Of course we have to show Claudius first; the things that we want to show you," Ryan said. "But if you are too sick we will understand."

Hector grinned. "Of all the things that I thought the two of you were going to ask me that definitely wasn't it. Sure."

"How long are you staying with us?" asked Ryan.

"I think until tomorrow or the next day."

"We could ride out to the village," Olin said.

"That's not safe for either of you," said Hector and looked at Stephan.

"I agree," Stephan said. "And Thaos, me and possibly Father are going to Cadia in a couple of days. But we will figure something out for all of you to get together."

"We need to be there," Ryan said. "I don't want to just send things out because there is a lot to talk about."

"I understand," said Stephan. "Let me work on this."

"You two sure seem excited about your work," said Hector to Ryan and Olin.

"It's like trying to put a puzzle together; it's kind of addicting," Ryan said. "And we concentrate on all of the small details that the warriors don't have time to worry about."

"This might work for all of us," said Hector. "Because I've got some mysteries to solve too." Then Hector changed his tone. "Olin it was smart for you to join up with this group. You're a lot better off here."

"I know. It's so strange because in some ways I hardly know them but they feel like my family," Olin said then he laughed. "Of course I never really had one so I don't know what one is supposed to feel like."

"When you are up to it, I'll see if Mathas lets me bring you to their office," said Stephan. "All of the walls are covered with charts and maps. They are the ones who figured out what happened with Isabella and the Sisterhood. Like I said, they are really smart kids."

"There is a lot that I am trying to figure out about all of that too," said Hector. "How did you do it?"

"Can we tell him?" asked Ryan.

"Yeah, between all of you maybe you can fill in some blanks. I have to get back to my bride," said Stephan.

"We should get Elexas," Ryan said.

"Let them have a couple of dances," said Stephan and grinned.

It was nightfall when a small flock of ravens landed in the campsite of Jack Franks. "Are you shitting me?" he repeated over and over as he read the note. "This could be really bad."

"What is it boss?" asked Reid who was Jack's new foreman.

"A bunch of Hector's men were riding with Nordes warriors. They rode into Minges and busted a place up. They hung all of Usman's men who were in there. If those groups are working together this is going to be a hell of a lot harder than I thought. Damn, I need to think this all over again."

The Sanuri and Erebus had been traveling southwest through the Kingdom of Stordt. They expected to arrive in Nora the following day. They were carrying a great many documents for the commanders at Fort Nora. They also carried letters and gifts. But it was the chest of gold coins in the boca that made Erebus nervous. Sudfad was sending it to General Colter for some projects.

"Did you worry about things like this when you had your powers?" the Sanuri asked with a grin and handed Erebus some tobacco for his pipe. They had just finished eating dinner and were sitting near the campfire.

Erebus laughed. "Actually I did. But it's the fact that we haven't had even a hint of trouble that bothers me. My skin has been crawling since we entered this kingdom."

"I will admit it has been an unusual trip," said the Sanuri. "But things in Wetpr and Lentz aren't normal now either. I've started looking forward to our daily letters just to find out what is going on." Both men laughed then the Sanuri abruptly stopped.

"We have company he whispered and set down the book he was holding. "Come out, I know you are there," he yelled into the shadows of the night.

Tina and Charles slowly walked into the ring of light made by the campfire. "Erebus, why don't you fix our friends something to eat," the Sanuri said and stood up. "Come, you are welcome to join us."

Both Erebus and the Sanuri were shocked at the emaciated couple who stood before them. Their clothing were nothing more than filthy rags. They themselves were filthy and they both had wild looks in their eyes which the Sanuri and Erebus noticed immediately.

"Do you remember us?" asked the Sanuri. Charles nodded but did not speak. Erebus quickly took two chairs from the back of the boca and set them near the fire.

"Thank you," Tina said in a whisper as she sat down.

"We saw your fire," Charles said and looked around the campsite.

"That smells good," Tina said to Erebus who was now frying ham and eggs. He looked up at her and realized she was drooling. He put a second frying pan on the fire.

"What are you doing out here?" the Sanuri asked the couple.

"Sorphat left; he took that Nordes girl with him," Charles said in a dazed manner. "We were looking for him. Do you know where he is?"

"I could venture a guess," said the Sanuri. "Did he leave the throne here?"

"I think so," Charles said then stared at Erebus who was handing him a plate of food.

"Take it," said Erebus. "It's safe to eat." Charles looked at Tina who was eating her food so quickly that she was choking.

"Why are you looking for Sorphat?" asked the Sanuri.

216

"I don't remember," Charles said and started to devour his food.

"Who is king now?" asked the Sanuri.

"I don't know," Charles said then he too started choking from eating so quickly. Tina almost threw her empty plate at Erebus who filled it again. He started cooking more food.

"Why is it so quiet here? We haven't seen any soldiers or border guards," asked the Sanuri.

"They're dead," Tina said nonchalantly as she continued to eat. "Sorphat killed the ones who wouldn't follow him."

"Tina can I look into your mind?" asked the Sanuri.

She shrugged her shoulders. "Can I keep eating?"

"Yes," he said. "But I will need you to stand up."

Erebus noticed that Charles was acting agitated and watching the Sanuri closely. The Sanuri had his back to Charles.

Months earlier both Tina and Charles became terrified when the Sanuri asked to look into their minds. Now Tina stood in almost a stupor. She finished eating a second plate of food and Erebus handed her a third as the Sanuri tried to understand what he was seeing in her memories.

"Charles, may I look into your mind?" asked the Sanuri as he turned towards the man.

Charles had his head down and was now shaking it from side to side. He was drooling and kept repeating "No". "Tina we need to leave," he said and both Ruala's dropped their plates and ascended into the night sky.

"Would any Angel care to explain what I saw?" asked the Sanuri.

Miranda appeared. "Sorphat is embroiled in battle over Samael's hell region. He has abandoned this kingdom but not turned it over to anyone else."

"While he has killed many, most of his men are in a sort of stasis. He has a protective bubble, so to speak, over his castle and riches."

"And the citizens?" asked the Sanuri.

"Coincidently posters have appeared announcing numerous jobs in both Lentz and Wetpr. The people can leave because there are no border guards to stop them."

"And Nora?" the Sanuri asked.

"The citizens of Nora now pray to The Great Ruler to protect them," said Miranda. "But all of this might mean a change of plans for both of you." She smiled. "Erebus, I couldn't help but overhear you say that you knew that castle like the back of your hand. There are items in there that would not only help your cause but save many because they would no longer be in the hands of monsters."

"And the bubble?" Erebus asked.

"I thought, I would tag along," said Miranda. "You would be wise to continue to Nora. Colter needs many of the things that you are carrying and he has valuable information for you. Tell him your change of plans. The following morning start your journey to Taperia."

"Did you send Charles and Tina here?" asked Erebus.

"They stopped listening to the voices of Heaven a long time ago. They have no will of their own because they sold it. They have been told repeatedly what they need to do but they refuse. That is not uncommon in your world."

"I have seen people who were incredibly addicted to Shartish act like that," said Erebus. "Is it more than selling their souls?"

"No, just a different type of demon."

Chapter XVIII
Changes

The following morning Mathas' meeting started two hours later to give the party goers more time to sleep. But the ruling members themselves arrived at the usual time because Gideon wanted them to meet the men he was promoting to admiral positions.

The Sanuri and Erebus did not see Charles or Tina again that night, although they both expected to. They got up early and resumed their journey. The Sanuri sent Enrops to tell General Colter the time they expected to arrive at Fort Nora. Then he sent flocks of Enrops to Sudfad and Mathas telling them about their change of plans. The Sanuri included the information about Sorphat, Charles and Tina in the letters.

Many of the wedding guests stayed at Claudius' castle since the wedding celebrations ran late into the night. Mathas and his family had returned to their home and brought Olin and Elexas with them since these two young people were now living in the castle.

Breakfast was being served to the wedding guests in the Great Hall when flocks of Enrops entered the room and started to distribute letters. Hector and Clev were also in the Great Hall when Angelina and Shara walked up to them.

"We just want to tell you something to think about," said Shara. "I just got a letter from one of the team members in Wetpr. She lives there with her husband but she was one of my students and she is a serious and dedicated healer. She knows that we are working on cures for you and has offered to come here and help. Her name is Corsa and Angelina suggested that if you wanted to stay here at the castle that Corsa could stay here also. It is just a suggestion."

"Corsa is beautiful," said Angelina with a sly smile. "But she doesn't take crap from anyone. So don't think you are going to flirt with her or intimidate her. Actually, I think she would be a good person to work with you."

"I haven't done either with any of you," Hector said with indignation. "What makes you think I would act like that with her?"

"Hector, even sick you have a presence about you," said Angelina. "To say nothing about your reputation. You know there's a reason it has just been a few of us taking care of you."

"I am a little insulted. I appreciate what all of you have been doing. I have no intention of compromising the situation."

"As you are starting to feel better you don't want to always follow our directions," Angelina said. "And that is normal and we expect to see more of that behavior. But Hector, we really don't know what we are dealing with so it is important that you do as we ask. If you disobey Corsa she might just tie you to the bed."

"Well, now that brings up a distracting image," Hector said and laughed. "Is she the one who married Javier?"

"Yes," said Shara.

"I am surprised he would let her come here," said Hector.

"He suggested it but besides the medicine she is looking for answers as to why Javier and Edward were also attacked," Shara said and Kate spun around. Kate and Edward were sitting at the next table.

"I heard all of that," said Kate. "When is she coming?"

"She wants to know if we want her here first," said Shara.

"Tell her yes and I'll write to her too," Kate said and looked at Edward. "I may not be going to Cadia."

"I don't know if I want the two of you looking into that," said Edward.

"She and I almost lost our husbands and we lost our baby because of that attack," said Kate. "I think we are the perfect people to investigate it."

"I don't have the answers," said Hector. "But Edward is right; that is a dangerous road. But it is a road worth traveling. The one thing I have realized since I became involved with all of you is that so much of what is happening concerns us all. It is like we are all in the same spider web. I talked with Ryan and Olin for hours last night and I am going to work with them; especially after yesterday."

"What happened yesterday?" asked Angelina.

"We can get into that later," Hector said. "Kate, go to Cadia with Edward. I already have men looking into that attack. And while they found out a great deal about the reason for Michael's murder they didn't find out any information about the other attacks. I will tell them to continue looking into it. But it will take a little time because they are in Salszar."

"You sent your men there?" asked Edward with obvious surprise.

"No, they were already there. My business is expansive," Hector said with a grin.

Most of the people in the room had stopped talking and were listening to the conversations between Hector and the others. Ryan stood up. "Hector, Turner's team found a bunch of symbols in the underground tunnels and we've figured them all out except for two, which are related. Olin thinks they are the marks of the assassins and whoever hired them. If I show you do you think you could tell?"

"If I can't I can find out," said Hector. "Can you draw them?"

"No but we have the drawings in the office. Are you going to be here today or move back to the village?"

"He's staying here today," said Shara. "He needs to get some sleep before he travels again."

221

"We'll bring the drawings here after the meeting," said Edward.

"I only have the one copy so Ingr will need to make another," Ryan said.

"Do you want me to go to the meeting?" asked Ingr.

"We'll come back here," Edward said. "You can draw it then."

"I'm still going to write to Corsa," said Kate. "We can start comparing notes." Edward smiled. "Shara, are you going to tell her to come here?"

"Yes, she will be a great help with our work. She's very bright."

"Since you are looking for cures for me, let me know if she needs anything. Like an escort here," said Hector.

"Some of our people are going to Wetpr for a visit," Angelina said. "She'll come back with them."

"Hector, you need sleep to heal. I would suggest you take a nap after breakfast," Shara said. He grinned and nodded.

Unlike Michael, Javier and Madeline were eager to learn their roles and duties in their new family. Neither this brother nor sister had any desires to sit on the throne; it was having a family that motivated them.

Madeline initially stood back so that Sudfad's household could get to know Javier and see in him what she saw. But now Madeline was becoming more involved with the training. They both attended training with the new ruling members of the kingdom. Sudfad's family as well as Gabriel, Raphael, Maxwell and Joshua were impressed with the enthusiasm, work ethic, knowledge and abilities Javier and Madeline possessed.

This morning Sudfad started out his meeting discussing letters he had received earlier in the morning. "Both groups of Enrops said the Angels assisted them in their journeys and in one case the birds also delivered a message from the Angel Adam. That is the letter we will discuss first. Sudfad read Claudius' letter out loud.

222

Claudius described, in great detail, the episode in his study the previous morning with his sons, Hector, Gideon and Clev. After Sudfad finished the letter he handed it to the group and said, "The message was more for Archetenus and Jared than anyone else. The two of you are not to start your mission until the Angels tell you to do so because there is much information that needs to be uncovered first and now that Hector is helping our teams, that information will be found more quickly."

"The second letter is from the Sanuri and perhaps Joao and Elan should read it in private first."

"If it's about Tina and Charles just tell us," said Joao. "I don't even consider them family anymore."

"Very well," Sudfad said. "As you know both the Sanuri and Erebus have been writing to us about how strange their journey has been through Stordt. Last night Charles and Tina visited them. The couple appeared to be starving. They were filthy and somewhat disoriented. They said they were looking for Sorphat but couldn't remember why."

"Of course the Sanuri and Erebus fed them. Tina allowed the Sanuri to look into her mind but he doesn't understand the shards of memories that he saw. Although Tina was calm, Charles became agitated as the Sanuri was looking in her mind and made Tina fly away with him. As soon as the two left, the Sanuri called to the Angels and Miranda appeared."

"Sorphat took Toni and is fighting for control of what was Samael's hell region. But he has not totally given up the throne to Stordt. In fact, the castle has some kind of protective bubble around it and all of the soldiers are in a type of sleep. Erebus had said earlier that he knew that castle like the back of his hand. Miranda asked him if he would be willing to go into it to retrieve items that would be valuable to our work and items that were dangerous to others."

"The Sanuri and Erebus will meet with General Colter today then travel to Stordt instead of going straight to Ryed. Miranda will assist them in entering that castle. Of course all of you can read this letter too."

"I just decided to bring something up before we discuss these letters. I had previously told everyone that since Javier and Madeline are willing to assume duties that at the end of training we would discuss reassignment of jobs. I hope that you have been thinking about that, so keep that in the back of your minds," said Sudfad.

"With every letter we have received we have been shocked at the involvement between Hector and our teams. And although the Angels keep warning them about him, they also seem to be almost forcing everyone to work together. Now add that thought to the back of your minds."

"Corsa has been doing research with Archetenus and Jared. She has also written to Shara and offered her services as a healer to help with looking for the cures for Hector and others. Corsa, the little that I know you I would expect that you would continue your investigation into the attacks while you are in Langer." She laughed and nodded.

"So this is what I want to open the discussion with. Gabriel and Raphael, we know you were considering offering Javier and Madeline teams before the attacks. Even if they accept I don't think that either of them have healed enough for those roles. And now that they are members of our family they have more roles and responsibilities."

"I am thinking about sending Javier and possibly Madeline to Langer with Corsa. While Stephan and the others knew Hector in his youth, Javier and Madeline knew him as the criminal. I consider Hector a great resource for us and I think that Javier and Madeline could tell if he was lying to our people. But I don't want this to be confrontational or to put either of them in a bad position. It is my understanding that at one time Hector had feelings for Madeline."

"Well, first we should ask them if they are even up for something like that," said Annabelle. "Madeline is still grieving and Javier hasn't healed yet."

"I know," said Sudfad. "It will be several weeks before our friends from Langer come here. Then who knows how long they will stay. I want to give everyone plenty of time to think about all of this."

"I will certainly go," said Javier. "Almost immediately after I told Corsa to go, I decided that I wanted to go with her. But what does this have to do with our training?"

"Instead of running a team fulltime, you could be like Raphael and me," said Gabriel. "You could work here and go on missions as needed. It sounds like Turner's team just fits with everyone and now that Abbott's team has joined them they are fully staffed with well-trained people."

"But we know they all would prefer to work with you and Madeline so the assignment to Dominic's team was temporary. If you want to be on a team fulltime instead of working with us, then this would be a good time for you to start setting things up in Langer."

"And on the flip side of that," Gabriel continued. "If you want to be a part time team member then maybe you can help them get organized."

"Javier and I get letters almost every day from Tessa or one of the others," said Madeline. "Turner's group have basically become family with Dominic's team and that's not just because Tessa and Noah are getting married. At this point my thoughts would be to keep Turner's group on Dominic's team and add Abbott's team to them permanently. And I will go to Langer also. Honestly, I find everything that is going on intriguing."

"Good," said Sudfad. "Do you want to stay at Mathas' castle or I can make other arrangements."

"I think we would rather stay with Dominic's team," said Javier. "They have a mansion so there is plenty of room and it sounds like Mathas is having to deal with a lot since Hector arrived. Madeline and I would only add to his distress."

"And Gabriel, I have already made my decision," said Javier and I believe that Madeline has also. I want to remain here and assume my duties as a member of this family but work on the missions as I am needed. There are several reasons for that," he said with a big smile. "I want to be a part of Sudfad's family. Corsa's brothers are going to college here and I want to be here for them and my bride and I might be expecting our first baby, but we aren't sure yet."

Renya and Madeline stood up and hugged Corsa and Javier while the others applauded. "Javier and I have talked about these opportunities at great length and I have made the same decision," said Madeline. "We have spent our lives playing others and for once we want to experience life as ourselves with a wonderful family."

Mathas' morning meeting started off with Gideon introducing his new admirals. "This afternoon, we are pinning their bars on in front of the troops then we are having a small celebration for everyone at the building behind my office. You are all invited to attend," Gideon explained.

"It is with great pride that I introduce Admiral Moraine who will be responsible for the naval yard in Castor. Next is Admiral Crowley who will be responsible for the naval yard in Langer and thus freeing me up for other duties. And Admiral Brinkman who will be responsible for the naval yard in Silth." Everyone in the room applauded.

"These men have worked diligently with me and know what we want and expect at these naval yards. And with the sailors who are being loaned to us we can get the training up and running as well as preparing the ships and buildings."

"Since this is a new industry here. We are doing business with many companies in Ganz. I will be going down there at some time to purchase more ships. I am telling you now in case any of the teams are going down there."

"After this morning these new Admirals will be attending our meetings when they can but today, well let's say they have personal business to take care of," Gideon said with a grin. "They are all making arrangements for their families to join them here."

There was another round of applause then Claudius joined Gideon in the front of the room. They described what happened the previous morning with Thaos, Stephan, Clev, Hector and the Angel Adam. Then Stephan and Thaos each gave a brief explanation of what they experienced.

"I know I have prejudices in this matter so I want to make sure I am understanding this correctly," said Mathas. "Adam wants us to work together for the time being?"

"Yes," said Claudius.

"I was there too," said Sorren. "And am I the only one here who feels like the Angels are practically throwing us all together?" Sorren did not wait for a response. "Now, my people and I are prepared for the worst but I've got to tell you so far there hasn't been one problem. And Hector bought my village about a year's supply of food for the hospitality. And his men and mine worked well together in Minges."

"I'm not saying that we let our guards down but so far it has not been a bad experience. And he is giving us information for payment."

"And that leads to the next issue," said Stephan. "Come on up here." Ryan, Olin and Elexas walked to the front of the room. "As all of you know, our young geniuses here pretty much work night and day. And they have done more with all of that information in a few weeks than we did in months. But they get stumped too. They spoke with Father and want permission to discuss some of the papers with Hector to see if he can help figure them out."

"Father needs to approve what they show him but as far as I am concerned it is a win, win for us. The problem is getting them all together. It's too dangerous for the kids to ride out to the village by themselves. Shara got a letter from Corsa and she will probably return with us after our visit."

"Corsa could stay at our home and watch Hector or I could bring him to the office once in a while. All of you can discuss these ideas."

"Ryan, tell them about this morning," said Edward.

Ryan looked at Mathas like he expected to get yelled at. "Shara was saying that Corsa is investigating the attacks. So I told Hector about those symbols that Bart saw in the tunnels, the ones we think were made by the assassins. Hector said that if he couldn't recognize them that he would find someone who could because he has men working in Salszar."

"Ryan, you don't have to look at me like that," Mathas said. "I am not going to yell at you."

"Hector has been on his best behavior around us because we are saving his skin. We all know he's not a good person and maybe one day one of us will kill him," said Edward. "But for now I say we take advantage of the situation. If the Angels want us to work together all of you know there has to be a damn good reason. And Mathas for as much as you hate him, he is one of Juleta's victims too."

"I know that a lot of you are afraid to talk about him in front of me. But I certainly don't hate him as much as I hate myself and that is something I am trying to work through," Mathas said. "I also don't want anyone put into danger. I don't understand what the Angels are saying but I am certainly not going to go against them and I do agree with Edward."

"Now having said that, I am not ready to talk to him. Rosa made me realize that I am so filled with anger at Isabella and Juleta that I now get explosive and honestly I am afraid I will take it all out on him. And as bad as he looked yesterday that would probably kill him."

"So this is what I am going to do. Matthew is going to be working closely with Gideon on these naval yards so he will be gone. Claudius, Stephan and Thaos will be going to Cadia. Sorren and Fahron are covering so many additional duties but Sorren can you oversee Hector?"

228

"Sorren, Tessa and I will help you," said Noah. "We're kind of getting to know the guy. And I think he is a little intimidated by her because Adam is always talking to her." Tessa laughed. Sorren looked at Noah and nodded.

"I can do that," said Sorren. "But will you let us bring him into the office here if the situation dictates?"

"I will leave that to you Sorren, but like I said I am not ready to talk to him," said Mathas.

Immediately after the meeting, Stephan, Thaos, Edward, Kate, Olin, Elexas and Ryan rode to Claudius' castle. Stephan knocked on the door to Hector's chambers as he said to the group, "He might be sleeping." But when Stephan heard laughing he opened the door.

"As long as he won't sleep we're studying," said Nikki. Shara, Hilgra, Ingr and Clev were also in the room.

"Well we're joining the party," Stephan said. Clev started bringing more chairs into the parlor and Thaos smiled when he saw the looks that Clev and Elexas were giving each other.

"These are the drawings," Ryan said and handed two sheets of paper to Hector who was sitting on the sofa. Hector sat up straighter and stared at the drawings.

"Tell me again where you found these," Hector said.

"Javier's and Madeline's team joined up with us," said Stephan. "But before that, all of their meeting places were in the tunnels that run under this city. They would make their own marks on the walls to tell each other where they were and they found these."

"Olin, you were right," said Hector. "But this is a little strange. First, remember that anyone who put the hit out on Michael was going against Samael and they would be aware of that. Secondly, I am sure that Edward is suspected of being one of The Seven Sons but I really doubt if Javier is and he is fairly well known. I can't be positive but I think there were two hits put out."

"Can everyone see these? See this sword with those lines wrapped around it. Those lines represent silk scarves; that is the sign for the Warlock Zourlock from Salszar and on either side is a set of double 'R's. The double 'R's is the sign for the Grand Master Radnor who we know put the bounty on Michael."

"But this second one is different. See there is Zourlock's sign but this symbol is different. It's kind of hard to see but there are four "T's inside of each other. The only sign I know of like that belongs to a criminal gang in Ryed. I'll bet you that Dominic knows them. There are four brothers and their last name is Teshmer."

"Never heard of them," said Edward.

"Why do you have such a strange look on your face?" Ingr asked Hector.

"First, you have to understand that Zourlock's assassins are the best and they are very expensive. I mean like an entire fortune expensive. Radnor had the money but as far as I know the Teshmer brothers are really small time. They couldn't afford a bounty like this. And that would be for one man, the price doubles for two."

"And from what I understand Edward and Javier barely know each other so why them? I am wondering if this is a trick but that too is unusual. Assassins are a proud lot, they usually don't disguise these kind of symbols. Think of these as bragging rights."

"Is it possible they shot the wrong men?" asked Kate.

"Zourlock's men are professional's with a worldwide reputation. It would be damn hard to believe they could screw something like that up. And you said they only shot the three men and no one else."

"Hector, they were cloaked," said Kate. "Erebus did some dark magics because no one could see them. The warriors appeared then burst into flames."

"And Erebus had given up his magics so he kind of went crazy and ended up in the World of Illusions," Stephan said.

"First, I have never heard of Zourlock's men hiding," said Hector. "They are bold and cocky and proud of what they do. I am wondering if this was to set Erebus up."

"We did think about that," said Edward. "But it was a fluke that the three of us ran down that street together."

"Do you know if Samael destroyed Radnor?" asked Thaos.

"I heard he was looking for Radnor but nothing more," said Hector. "This first symbol makes perfect sense but this second one doesn't at all. You need to tell Dominic and his boys. Or better yet, bring them here and we can discuss this."

"Another thing that you have to understand is if someone is wealthy and powerful enough to be able to afford Zourlock's assassins they too boast about it."

"And to put someone else's' sign on something like this is not only a death sentence but a black mark against you in the underworlds."

"So you know it was someone who was rich and powerful enough to even contact Zourlock and someone who had access to magics strong enough to hide those men."

"Erebus is on his way to Ryed," said Thaos. "I'm writing him a letter with everything you just said. Got any paper in here?"

When Thaos gave his letter for Erebus to some Enrops he also asked that part of the flock bring Dominic and Fennel back to the castle because Hector had uncovered some information.

Chapter XIX
Teams

The Sanuri and Erebus made better time than they expected. They arrived at Fort Nora midmorning. Generals Colter and Orlan were the two Wetprian commanders assigned to the post which was the only Wetprian fort located in hostile territory. While the kingdom and the Kings of Stordt were hostile the people of Nora were not.

The Sanuri smiled as he and Erebus drove through the gates of the fort which was bustling with activity. Civilians had built beautiful gardens and planted orchards outside of the fort walls. And homes were now built on the land surrounding the fort. This entire area had once been unused land.

"You're early," Colter said as he and Orlan walked up to the boca.

"And you have the prettiest fort I have ever seen," said the Sanuri with a big smile.

"It's all the citizens. They did the same thing at the Patronus Headquarters," said Orlan. "I've never been stationed any place before where the people loved us."

"You saved them all from hell, what do you expect?" asked the Sanuri as he climbed down from the front seat of the boca. "We have a huge chest of money for you. It's going to take more than a couple of men to move it. We've got lots of paperwork and gifts too."

Orlan called a sergeant to the boca and gave him orders to have the chest moved. "What else needs to be brought in?" Orlan asked the Sanuri.

"I'll show them," said Erebus.

"We have women from the city doing the cooking here," Colter said. "They've fixed a meal for you."

After the Sanuri and Erebus handed over all of the items they were delivering they followed the generals into a private dining room in one of the buildings.

The Sanuri waited until the food was served and the servers had left the room before he spoke about the encounter the previous night with Tina, Charles and Miranda. After he finished speaking the generals looked at each other then Orlan spoke.

"Well, that explains a lot. Before we got the message about Samael we were getting reports of fighting among the King's soldiers. Most of what we were hearing was coming from travelers and Enrops. It sounded like Taperia was a war zone. Then it's like everything just stopped. Now mind you, they don't bother us or the City of Nora anymore but we would still see the patrols. We haven't seen any sign of the King's soldiers for, I don't know, close to two weeks."

"So what is it you are going to get from the castle?" asked Colter.

"Don't know yet," said Erebus. "So we don't know if we will be delivering whatever we take then coming back this way because, as you know we were headed for Ryed."

"When the Angel said we have important information for you the only thing that I can think of is the news out of Ryed," Colter said. "You know there is a civil war going on there and for the first time, maybe ever, the people are fighting for their freedoms and they are more than holding their own. In fact, they are doing so well that those two generals who are trying to take over the kingdom are calling in reinforcements."

"And not just hiring more soldiers and demons. Both Generals Goebel and Astar were close with Teivel and they are rivals. It was Astar who attacked the monastery at Rubar or I should say tried to. Sudfad told us what the Angels did. But after that we heard reports that Astar...well I will just say what we heard. We heard he got his ass handed to him by a little old lady so he is the laughing stock of the kingdom. A lot of his soldiers left him and joined Goebel."

"And we heard that Astar looks different now but those stories keep changing. Both those generals are ruthless murderers and now Astar is humiliated, so he hired some guy who is supposed to be a really badass warlock. His name is Malus."

233

"That's not possible," said Erebus. "Malus was my friend and I saw him sucked into a hole by Ahriman. The demon took both him and General Cerephus. That was the rip in time that Ahriman created in those caves near Roch's castle." Erebus was now talking more to himself than to the others.

"Malus was very wealthy and had no family so I gave his castle as well as mine to the Angel Ruth to give to the peasants. Sanuri is it possible that he escaped from hell?"

"More likely he was brought back, if that is the real Malus," the Sanuri said to Erebus then looked at Colter. "So what exactly has this new warlock done?"

"That we don't know. All we've heard is that he is powerful and a monster."

Most of Dominic's team rode out to Claudius' castle after receiving Thaos' message. Hector showed them the symbol with the four "T's and asked about the Teshmer brothers.

"They must have worked their way up if they have a sign," said Dominic sarcastically. "And I agree this doesn't make any sense. Those four men are not the brightest lights in the sky. In fact, it is amazing that any of them are still alive. They are highwaymen and more than once they tried to rob someone and ended up running for their lives. We were going to stop them once but figured they were more dangerous to themselves than others."

"Unless something has really changed they couldn't afford food much less a bounty," said Fennel.

"Did you tell Hector what happened in Ryed?" Lawrence asked Stephan and Thaos.

"Yeah," said Stephan. "And he is convinced those attacks were a setup to get to Erebus."

"Edward had to take Kate out of the room because she was so upset," said Ingr. "So don't really talk about it in front of her."

"From what they've told me," said Hector. "Erebus used his power to channel holy energy that not only attacked the demons in Ryed but demons in the hell regions. I can't believe he is still alive. Your Angels must really be protecting him."

"I have a question," said Noah. "So we think that someone who is rich and powerful used the Teshmer's sign instead of admitting who they really are. But why the Teshmers?"

"Because Erebus is a brilliant man and would have figured that out," said Sorren as he now entered Hector's parlor. Shara told me what you have figured out. You know the Angels sent him and the Sanuri to Ryed. Well, I called to Ruth," Sorren looked at Hector and Clev. "She was the Angel with us in Ryed. All she said was they had a change of plans and we should be getting the letter tomorrow. The fact that she didn't say more than that is suspicious."

"Thaos, I was told that you sent Erebus a note. Anything that wasn't in that note write down now and we will ask the Angels to help the Enrops deliver the letter."

Sorren now looked at Hector, "My wife tells me you won't sleep."

Hector laughed. "You sound like my father."

"You know you need to rest to heal. That's the last I will say on that subject. I don't know if the other's told you that I have been put in charge of you now and I want to make a few changes in the way we have been handling you so I met with Mathas and Rosa after our meeting this morning."

"I'll be honest, I expected you and your men to be pains in my ass but you haven't been at all. I am not sure why, but we all seem to be in a situation where we need each other. So this is what I did. First, your men are moving your things into our largest open house. Showers has them getting your stuff from the hotel. It has four bedrooms, a parlor, a kitchen which we filled with food and a bathing room. Of course Clev's things are being moved in there too. If you want someone else living in the house, let me know."

"These extra houses I had built for guests because we had a wedding that bonded our tribe and the Ruala Tribe and it was big doings. So I moved Showers in a house close to yours and I am letting him assign your men to the other buildings. And there are a few things I want to add to that but I will come back to it."

"Mathas is so pissed he is ready to explode but you're not the one he is mad at. He's obviously mad at Isabella and Juleta and he's beating himself up because he didn't stop them or save them. So the reason I am telling you this is, he will allow you to have visits with Rosa and Sarah but he prefers they take place in the castle. He thinks it is safer than having them travel and we can bring you to the office to work with our people. But he is not ready to speak with you yet."

"Of course if you screw anything up, those privileges will be revoked."

"How often can I see Sarah?" asked Hector who was surprised by the news.

"That is for you and me to work out and you know Rosa; she thinks it is important for you to spend time with your daughter. Do I need to tell you that to be strong enough to travel that far you need to do what Shara and Angelina tell you?" Many in the room now laughed.

"You've convinced me. I am very happy about this Sorren. Thank you," Hector said with sincerity.

"You are helping us too and we appreciate that. Now for your men. Showers can keep them in line but they are getting bored and you are going to be with us for a while. Got any ideas what you want them to do?"

"Clev and I were talking about that."

"I'd suggest you put them back in the Catacombs," said Sorren. "If you haven't guessed we have eyes and ears in there too. And today we heard that Jack Franks has been hiring his old crew back. Apparently he is pissed because we seized all the family fortune but he has money stashed in other areas. He and twelve of his men left for Port Friada a couple of days ago."

"Stephan it's time to get my parents," Hector said and picked up a piece of paper and a pen and started writing a note. "Of course Jack will have spies and you know they will be watching all of you. But my boys know who most of them are." Hector stopped talking and concentrated on his writing. He showed the note to Clev then handed it to Sorren.

"You can read that too," Hector said to Sorren. "Shara wants me to stay here today. Will you give that to Showers? It's the information you just gave me. I am telling him to send the boys after Jack's men and to go back to the Catacombs."

The next morning Angus' team, Edward's team, Thaos, Stephan, Claudius and Clev left for Cadia. Many months earlier when Thaos and Stephan helped Selen escape from Cadia, she had to leave her home and belongings behind. Thaos now carried the key to that house. He had a list of things that Selen wanted and he wanted to search the house to see if the Sisterhood had left any messages for her.

Seventy-five soldiers also traveled with this group but they wore civilian clothing. The plan was for the teams to stay in Cadia and investigate Juleta's holdings in addition to investigating the allegiances of King Fahra. This King gave political shelter to many people who were enemies of the Kingdoms of Lentz and Wetpr. The ruling members of Lentz were questioning Fahra's involvement with these criminals.

Claudius, Thaos and Stephan were going to search Selen's home then get Hector's parents and move them to Langer. Clev was going to help them with the move after he handled some business for Hector.

Since Clev was going to Cadia, Showers took his place with Hector. Showers arrived at Claudius' castle early that morning and helped Sorren and Shara move Hector back to the Village of Tyger.

While no one actually spoke about it, Olin knew there were bounties on him for his betrayal of Otto.

After Dominic's members learned that Mathas had canceled the morning meeting they held their own meeting with Ryan, Olin and Elexas in the office in Mathas' castle.

"Ryan, we didn't want to say a lot yesterday," Dominic said. "But do you realize that the reason none of us want the three of you traveling to the village is that Olin has bounties on him because he went against Otto?"

Both Ryan an Elexas looked shocked, "Did you know this?" Ryan asked Olin who nodded. "Well, why didn't you say anything?"

"I really didn't want to talk about it," Olin said.

"After our meeting with Hector, I talked with Sorren then later with Claudius," said Dominic. "The three of you seem to get along very well with Hector and he is giving us information which I think we all want to take advantage of. We don't know how long Claudius will be gone and although Sorren is in charge of Hector, he is over his head with assignments right now. So, I am going to review the information you want to discuss with him."

"I think I am a little more anxious to get things covered with Hector than the others, so this is what I would like to do. The three of you prepare the things you want to discuss with him. Then I am just going to ask the Angels if there is anything in that pile that they don't think we should let him see. Then our team will take you back and forth to the village."

"I know we have so much stuff in this office to review yet, but do you think you are far enough along that we could take things out to him at least a couple of times a week?"

"That would be great," said Ryan enthusiastically.

"Obviously we aren't going to show him the personal items that Rosa gave you, but I think we should show him Isabella's diaries. What do you think?" asked Dominic.

"That would help us so much," Olin said.

"Elexas, you are being quiet," Dominic said. "If you feel uncomfortable going back to the village you certainly don't have to."

"I'm not sure," Elexas said hesitantly.

"Well you aren't arrested or anything," said Jasmine. "You're working on the team now so you don't have to be embarrassed." Elexas didn't say anything but everyone could see that she looked upset.

"Are you going to be ok?" Fennel asked Elexas. She nodded. Fennel now addressed the group. "You know we still need to get a healer on the team. I forgot about that until Shara was talking about Corsa yesterday. If she comes here maybe she could help us out too, if we need it. Corsa was really good."

Noah looked at Tessa and said, "Corsa is Javier's wife are you two going to be able to get along?"

Tessa blushed deeply. "How do you know?" she stammered.

"Turner happened to mention it," Noah said with a broad grin.

"Oh he did, did he," Tessa said. "I didn't tell you because it was nothing. We never fell in love or anything and it was years ago. We are friends and I am happy for him. But now that you mention it, she might not know so don't tell her. Why are all of you grinning at me? Do you all know?"

"He may have mentioned it during a meeting," Seth said and laughed.

"I am going to kill him," Tessa said angrily. "Why would he even tell that?"

"He wasn't being mean," said Noah. "This is before you and I started seeing each other. Somehow it just came up."

"My dating life just happened to be the topic of conversation at the King's meeting. Is that what you are telling me?" Everyone laughed except for Ryan, Olin and Elexas because they didn't know what the group was talking about.

"Yes," said Jasmine. "I know I'm laughing but I would be mad too."

"So what else did he say?" Tessa asked suspiciously.

"This was before any of us met you and he wanted you working with us," said Lawrence with a grin. "He was telling us how great you are."

"Lawrence don't you lie to me," Tessa said. "I can tell by the way you are grinning there is more." No one said anything, they laughed. "Ok what did he say?"

"That you had a crush on Noah and you kept talking about how cute he was," Jasmine said.

"Well that was true," Tessa said and laughed. "But I don't think that Mathas and the others needed to know that."

"Don't hurt him because he is walking you down the aisle," Noah said as he continued to grin.

"He may not be able to walk," Tessa said adamantly.

"When the group finished laughing Dominic said, "Elexas, when you have a moment I would like to speak with you."

"Am I in trouble?" she asked and looked concerned.

"No," Dominic said.

"He wants to warn you about Clev," said Jasmine.

"I'm not going to tell him anything that I shouldn't," Elexas said.

"I never thought you would," said Dominic. "Elexas, you are one of us now and we watch out for each other. While you are a very bright woman...well, you heard that some demon owns Clev's soul. Do you understand what that means?"

"Not really."

240

"Before he explains," Fennel said. "Any of you are allowed to date whoever you want, that isn't the issue. But it is obvious that Clev is attracted to you and we want you to know all the information in case you decide to have a relationship with him."

"Well, that is a relief," she said.

"First, you heard what Edward said. Hector and all of his men are being on their best behavior. And personally I am surprised at how likeable they are. But when a demon owns that person, well, not only can he manipulate the person to do whatever he wants but he can usually see through that person's eyes," explained Dominic.

"Then why are you showing him our paperwork?" asked Elexas.

"That's why we are running it past the Angels first. Elexas, we know you can certainly take care of yourself. But you could have a wonderful time with him then he suddenly hurts you. Just keep these things in mind," Dominic said.

"Are you mad?" Tessa asked.

"No, I am shocked that any of you care. And if you can't tell I am attracted to him too, but we haven't even kissed. He actually acts shy around me. Of course not as shy as Ryan did," she said kiddingly and laughed.

"Elexas, if I would have met the person I like now, I would have reacted differently," Ryan said.

"Really?"

"Yes. I don't understand why you were always trying to act like someone you aren't but we all like the real you." As Ryan spoke tears came to Elexas' eyes. "I didn't mean to make you cry."

"I am just touched by all of this."

"Clev is really scared that a demon owns him," said Noah. "If he likes you he may be afraid to be around you because he doesn't want to hurt you."

"If you are together and the demon takes over, you are going to have to call to the Angels," Dominic said. "Because even if you can fight him you may not be able to stop him."

"What is bothering you?" the Sanuri asked Erebus as they rode in the boca.

"I told you that Cerephus had hired me to help him set Roch up because he planned to take over the kingdom. Well, after Roch is exposed by The Lion his condition gets worse and we didn't have any idea what was happening to him. Meekos shows up at the castle and tells us about Roch being the vessel for Omnibus and offers us money to take care of him. You see, Meekos didn't know what was happening to Roch either. And he was afraid that if Roch was too weak to be the vessel that he and those other priests would be greatly punished."

"Cerephus wanted to kill Roch before he turned into a powerful demon. I was doing spells to try and find out what has happening to Roch and I was being threatened every time, which is unheard of, so I wrote to my friend Malus and he came to the castle to help."

"One day when Meekos was there, Malus takes us to the cave where the transformation was to take place and there are hell creatures in the cave. Then we realize there is an opening between worlds. We tried to close it but Ahriman pulled Malus and Cerephus into the opening and we never saw them again. I wanted to try and get them out but Meekos convinced me that the same thing would happen to me."

"So you are filled with guilt because you think you are responsible for your friends being killed."

"Yes, I didn't realize that until Colter said Malus' name."

"Why don't you tell me the long version of that story? It may be important."

After a great deal of contemplating, Hector called Showers into his room in the new house and explained the truce that was set up with the people in Langer.

"Boss, I am glad you told me and I know you like to keep things close to the vest. But it is hard for us to protect you if we don't understand everything too. Now honestly, I really like these Nordes warriors. Talk about tough, even the women but they are really good people. But I did wonder why they were helping us. Now after listening to you it sounds like they are protecting us. And you say it's because of their Angels. As damn crazy as that sounds, a lot of things make sense now."

"You know the reason I'm not talking about this is because I want to protect Sarah and my parents," Hector said. "And you know the more people who know something...well... someone will talk."

"Boss, some of us were outside when the Queen brought that little girl in here. She looks just like you used to; we aren't blind. And if we can see that so will others. I had a wife and son once and the Hutas killed them. I know what it is like to love a kid. We'll help you protect her."

Hector stared at Showers for a couple of moments. "Why don't you pour us a couple of drinks and I will tell you the rest of the story."

Chapter XX
Alliances

While the core members of Dominic's team were dealing with Hector, the newer members continued to do research. This was fascinating for them since they were learning about their enemies as well as the histories of the teams.

Mallory was a beautiful Venator with curly blonde hair, green eyes and dimples. Her normally fun loving personality was taking a back seat as she threw herself into doing research. Mallory was a well-trained warrior and confident of her abilities or at least she was until she joined Dominic's team. The more she learned about the roles and accomplishments of her friends who were already team members the more she felt she had to prove herself.

Brock was the only other Venator on that team and he was not as interested in doing the research as he was with learning everything he could about the tribes and training of his teammates. The Clan of Gesmal were somewhat isolated in Ryed and being on the teams exposed these young warriors to many new things. Brock often went to the Village of Tyger to train with the Nordes warriors.

He was a handsome man with a muscular warrior's body, black hair and blue eyes. He was admired by many of the women on the team as well as in the Nordes Tribe. Elexas was very attracted to Brock but she was afraid to get too familiar with any of the team members. While Brock realized he was the object of admiration he was an intense warrior and wanted to prove himself on the teams.

Dominic, Fennel, Seth, Jasmine, Lawrence, Noah and Tessa escorted Ryan, Olin and Elexas to the Village of Tyger later that morning to meet with Hector. The three young people had some of Isabella's diaries as well as other papers, charts and maps to discuss with Hector.

Although Hector was weakened by traveling he was very interested in the items presented to him. He allowed Showers to come into the room as the group was discussing the materials. Dominic's team noticed the intensity with which Hector was reviewing the charts, as if he was memorizing every detail.

"You do really good work," Hector said to Ryan, Olin and Elexas. "And I almost feel guilty asking this but can you make copies of some of these things for me? Since Dominic is going to let us work on more things then we previously thought, I'm thinking about putting up a little office in one of the extra bedrooms here. Then we can work out here too. I am so tired just from traveling from Claudius' place that I can tell I am not going to be able to get to the castle often."

Olin, Ryan and Elexas immediately looked at Dominic with excited anticipation which made him laugh. "Hector, I think you and I are of the same mindset. I don't know how long this truce will last and I would like to take advantage of it. Let's look at that room and perhaps we can fix it up as a workspace."

"My only concern is that you seem as excited about all of this as the kids here and I am concerned that you aren't going to rest. You look a lot worse than yesterday."

"I feel worse and it just frustrates the hell out of me," Hector said. "And I have never been a person to sit still so this goes against my grain."

Jasmine looked at Showers and said sternly, "I don't know if you realize that our healers are having all they can do to keep him alive and if he doesn't start to heal he will die. Everyone has been trying to be nice to him but he needs someone to tie him down." Hector laughed.

"Is that true boss?" asked Showers who looked concerned.

"That's what they tell me," Hector said. "They're waiting for a beautiful healer from Wetpr to come and kick my ass."

"She won't be here for a couple of weeks and you may not be alive by then," Jasmine said. "Shara and Angelina are getting really frustrated with you and none of your men want to go against you," Jasmine continued.

"It is in our best interest to keep you alive so are we going to have to bring team members in to make sure you take care of yourself? You can grin all you want but I am not kidding. Hector, have you looked in a mirror? Maybe that's what we should do is fill this house with mirrors so you can see what we see."

"She stabbed Teivel in the eyes when he was transforming into a demon and got a lot of information from him," Seth said proudly of his wife. "She's a force to be reckoned with."

"I would very much like to hear that story," said Hector.

"Show us the room you want fixed up, get some sleep then I will tell you," said Jasmine. "Hector it's almost like you have a death wish. You can see Sarah now, you have a lot to live for." Hector looked angry as he listened to Jasmine scolding him. "Good, get mad but think about what I am saying."

One of Hector's men walked into the room. "Sorry to interrupt boss but there are two people here who say they are with this team and they have something important to show everyone."

"Bring them in," said Hector.

"Sorry to interrupt your meeting," Brock said as he and Mallory walked into the room. "But we found some things that you should see."

"Hector, Showers this is Mallory and Brock, they are Venatores from the Clan of Gesmal in Ryed and new members to our team," Dominic said.

Jasmine saw the way that Hector was looking at Mallory and laughed. "Hector won't follow the healer's orders so we need babysitters to keep him in line," Jasmine said. "Do you two want the job?"

"What's he supposed to do?" Brock asked as he looked at Hector.

"Basically sleep once in a while," Tessa said.

"So tie him up and drug him," said Mallory. "He shouldn't need a babysitter."

"Do you think you could do that if it needed to be done?" Dominic asked with a huge grin.

"We are Venatores?" she said proudly.

"You've got the job," Dominic said. "You will get double pay. We are going to fix up an office out here so we can all work together."

"It won't take two of us to watch him so can one of us train with the Nordes while the other stays here?" asked Brock.

"As long as you get him to get some sleep," Dominic said to Brock and Mallory. "Hector, how many bedrooms are in this place?"

"Before we go into that," Hector said with a sly smile. "Are you two married?"

"Friends," said Brock and laughed. "She's single if that is what you are asking."

"You've got the jobs," Hector said. "And I will pay."

"The problem with that is everyone who you pay doesn't want to piss you off," said Fennel. "We'll pay their salaries. Do you know how Venatores are trained?"

"Oh yes," Hector said. "They are impressive warriors."

"I don't," said Showers.

"They start training as little children and by time they are older children they hunt groups of demons by themselves," Hector said. "They are notorious warriors. And I am intrigued."

"First, I am not doing this to be your girl buddy," Mallory said. "If my bosses want us to keep you a live we will, so don't think you are paying me to be a date or something."

"Never considered it," Hector said and grinned.

"Yeah, I really believe that," Mallory said sarcastically. "But we are getting off the subject. We need to clear this table so Brock can show you what we have."

As Mallory spoke, Brock opened a leather pouch that he was wearing over his shoulder. As he placed items on the table he explained, "Mallory and I were going through one of the boxes of papers taken from The Rooster when we found this little envelope that looks like a personal letter which was unusual because everything else is clearly business paperwork."

"The letter looks old; it's from Teivel and it's written to Joanna. In it he is talking about Otto coming to Ryed with her and Jack. Teivel tells her over and over again how beautiful she is and that he can't stop thinking about her. He is offering to send her money to visit him. Most of this is flirting but on the very last page he warns her not to tell Otto because of the pact that was made."

"He says he needs Otto to organize the operation and he thinks that Otto will pull out if there is a relationship between Joanna and Teivel. Then he goes on to say that Otto is walking a dangerous line because the other members of the four T's don't particularly like his attitude and insinuations. Then he ends it by saying that he cannot wait for her next letter."

"Then Mallory remembered something she had read in one of Isabella's diaries," Brock handed the letter to Dominic and opened one of the diaries. "Isabella is going on one of her tirades about how pissed she is that Joanna is going on another trip. Isabella is jealous and wondering if Joanna has a secret lover. But this is one of Isabella's early diaries which would mean that Joanna was a young teenager. Do you think her father let her travel alone to Ryed?"

"Then we found this," said Mallory. "In one of Otto's ledgers there are monthly payments to the 4T's. And look how much money. Twenty thousand dollars. How could anyone pay that kind of money every month? We went through all of the money ledgers and found that the payments started ten years ago."

248

"So the four T's can't be those Teshmer brothers. And that is more than the payments that we have seen to the Insidiae. What do you think?"

"First, I think you two did a great job," Dominic said then he looked at Hector and asked, "Any ideas?"

"No and that bothers me because I make it my business to stay on top of everything in my field. So how could an organization exist that long without me hearing about it? And I can't imagine Otto letting Joanna visit Teivel; he was a barbarian." Hector carefully inspected the letter. "Can someone light a candle and bring it here?"

Noah grabbed a candle and lit it with the fire in the hearth. He handed it to Hector. "I am going to show you a trick to see if letters are real and not tricks. Everyone stand behind me." Hector held up the first sheet of paper that the letter was written on then he held the candle behind it. "Can you see that T?" The others stared at a large T that was becoming visible behind the writing. "This letter is real. Let me check the other pages."

The group watched as Hector held each sheet of paper in front of the candle, they saw Teivel's personal mark appear on each page. "Most leaders in the underworlds have some kind of symbol like that, it is put on the paper with magics instead of an actual process," explained Hector.

"Is yours an H?" asked Seth.

"No, it's my sign, the swords and dots," Hector said then paused as he studied the letter. "I can't explain it but I have a really bad feeling about all of this. If I had to take a wild guess I would say that there are Grand Masters involved with this or demons from other worlds. You know that Emeric and Banaka were setting up the demons here to be taken over...they a..." Hector's head fell forward.

"Let's get him to bed," Dominic said. "Before he passes out." Dominic, Fennel, Seth and Noah carried Hector into his bedroom and put him into bed. He was asleep within moments.

"Double pay starts today," Dominic said to Brock and Mallory. "One of you stay with him. We'll get things to start setting up an office and bring your gear back here."

"What do you need me to do?" asked Showers.

"Just so you understand he is in a serious condition," said Dominic. "He needs to start minding the healers. I will take full responsibility if my staff chews his ass."

"Now, why don't you help us figure out where he wants the office and which room Mallory and Brock can have."

"I'll stay but I want to get Shara first," Mallory said and smiled at the way that Elexas was looking at Brock.

"I'll get her," said Jasmine and left the room.

Five hours later Dominic's group returned to Hector's house and started to put together an office in a large bedroom. The men were moving the bed out of the room when they heard Hector yelling for Showers who was carrying one end of the bed. Showers looked at Mallory and laughed. "I don't really want to go in there," he said.

"Mallory, what did you do?" asked Tessa when she saw her friend smiling.

"I'll go in there," Mallory said as Hector continued to yell.

"I can't believe you really did this!" Hector yelled when Mallory walked into the room with Tessa, Jasmine and Showers behind her. These three laughed when they saw him in bed with his right arm tied to the headboard and his left ankle tied to the foot board.

"You have been acting like a child," Mallory said as she sat down on the side of the bed and untied his arm. "That is not all I did. I asked Shara to give you something to sleep. You've been asleep for five hours. Do you feel any better?"

"I will when I get circulation back in my arm," Hector said with a grin.

"Now don't yell at Showers," Mallory continued. "He's here to protect your interests. Brock and I are here to keep you alive." As she spoke Mallory got off the bed and untied his leg. "Do you want to get up because we are putting the office together?"

"If you weren't so damn pretty, I'd be pissed," Hector said then grinned again. "Usually when a woman ties me to the bed its fun."

"I don't understand that and I'm not going to ask," said Mallory as she helped Hector to sit up. "Shara and Angelina are really concerned about you, Hector. Hilgra's been helping them and they are working night and day in that little cottage."

"When Clev returns he will have manuscripts that should help them," Hector said.

"Boss, I was going to untie you but she threatened to tie me up too," Showers said with a huge grin.

"Yeah, I can see how this is going to play out," Hector said as Showers helped him to stand up.

"Are you hungry?" asked Mallory. "I made some stew and biscuits. It's nothing fancy but we need to get more food in here. I think you've been drinking whiskey instead of eating."

"I could eat," said Hector. "Is there enough for the others?"

"Of course. I will go out and get food when Brock watches you."

"I'll send some of the boys out to do some hunting too," Showers said as he helped Hector walk into the room that was being made into an office.

"She really did drug me and tie me to the bed," Hector announced as he walked into the room and everyone roared with laughter. "Then she threatened Showers if he helped me." Hector was laughing too as he spoke.

"If one of you can watch him, I'll get us some food," said Mallory and left the room. Jasmine followed her.

Twenty minutes later Jasmine walked into the office with an armload of dishes. "Since all of the tables are in here, this is where we will eat. Seth can you push them together?"

Tessa and Elexas helped Jasmine and Mallory. The women brought in two huge kettles of stew. Platters of biscuits, butter and honey. A large pot of coffee and a pitcher of milk.

"Don't argue," Mallory said as she set a glass of milk in front of Hector. "Brock, we need to get more food today."

"Do we have enough for breakfast?" Hector asked.

"No," Mallory replied.

"Write a list of what you want and Showers will send some of the boys into town to get it. And don't be afraid to order a lot." As Hector was talking he tasted his stew then hungrily ate several mouthfuls. Then he took a bite of his biscuit. "You're a good cook."

"He says that like it is a surprise," said Mallory sarcastically.

"Mallory and Brock will share the other bedroom," Dominic said to Hector. "We put two smaller beds in there. One can sleep while the other watches you."

"If you need bedding or anything put it on the list," said Hector.

"Dominic, since we are going to be out here," Brock said. "Can you send our pay to our families?"

"I can do that. How much?"

"We don't need much so send most of it home."

Jasmine looked at Hector and Showers who were staring at Brock and explained, "Besides the honor of being on the teams, most of us come from poor families so the money we make we send home. Seth and I are married and everything I make goes to my family here."

"So all of you work like dogs and risk your lives for honor," Hector said and shook his head. "Mallory hand me that damn list."

"Ok, but if all you put on it is whiskey, I'm crossing it off."

Gideon and Matthew had planned a trip to Castor but postponed it when Claudius decided to go to Cadia with his sons. Gideon did not want to leave the women and children in the household, even though he could have asked the teams to stay at the castle. In a short period of time Gideon's and Claudius' families had become as one.

Matthew and Gideon stayed in Langer and worked on future plans for the naval yards. "Matthew, perhaps you should go with me on my next trip to Port Friada. Almost everything we need for the ships we are purchasing from companies there. It would save us a great deal of time and money if we could talk some of those companies into expanding their businesses and come to Langer."

Matthew nodded as he was reviewing one of the charts that Gideon was showing him. "We understood that this was going to be a huge undertaking but it is just so much more than we realized. While we both agree that someone from the ruling families, needs to be a part of this I do go on missions. You need more than just three admirals, you need an entire staff; don't you agree?"

"Most definitely. And I have some ideas in mind. But two of the men who I would fight to get still work for Wainburst. Since he is helping us I don't want to cause hard feelings."

"Do you think they would be interested in coming here?"

"I know they would; I've already spoken with them."

"Is there something Father or I can do to help with all of this? Pay Wainburst or offer something?"

"I have been thinking about that. Wainburst is a fighting man and a good man. We have the same concerns, the same enemies and we may be patrolling the same waters, which is why he is helping us. Perhaps we could draw up a treaty of sorts stating that we will all work together and offer our naval yards and ports to them."

"Say for example one of their ships is damaged, it might save lives if they could dock in Lentz. See where I am going with this?"

"Write up what you are thinking and we will present it to Father."

The group traveling to Cadia wasted little time in their journey. They pushed themselves hard and reached Cadia at midnight of the third day of their trek. It was no accident that they entered the huge city under the cloak of darkness. Before entering the city, the group divided into smaller groups so they would be less conspicuous. Like all port cities in Opots, Cadia was a city that was always open so the streets were filled with people.

The groups met up in South Cadia, then they rode to Hector's compound. Per Hector's orders, Clev was to take the entire group to the compound which was on the southern tip of the city and north of King Fahra's castle. This was the location where Hector's parents were in hiding. The compound was an old mansion on the shore of the Sea of Grevdt. Hector had a huge stone wall built around the home. Although the wall made the property look like a fortress the courtyards and home were beautiful.

Hector had offered the compound to the teams to use but they wanted to get a feel of the city before they decided if that would be their base of operations. Clev rode ahead of the group and met with the hired men standing guard on the wall who then called to their boss.

The man in charge of the compound was called Dagger because he lost his left eye in a knife fight. Hector had been sending regular correspondence to Dagger so he was aware that the group was coming. Clev had sent word to Dagger with the time the group expected to arrive. Now as they rode through the gate towards the mansion, the group could see that the buildings were well-lit and people were active. Clarence and Catherine were standing on the covered front porch and waving to their friends.

Catherine hugged Claudius and Stephan but stared at Thaos. "I don't mean to be rude it is just disturbing to see how much you and Archer look alike," she said.

"I can't imagine what this must be like for you," Thaos said. "I will tell you it shook me too when I first saw him."

Clarence shook hands with the men and everyone entered the front foyer of the mansion where a small army of staff led the people to their chambers.

"We have a feast prepared so everyone come back down after you get your rooms," Clarence said happily.

Introductions were made during the feast as people entered the Great Hall. It was obvious to all that Clarence and Catherine were delighted to have guests. And everyone was excited at meeting the Ruala warriors. Many tables were set up with lavish decorations. There was a head table in the front of the room for the leaders of the group as well as the leaders of Hector's men.

Clev had letters from Hector which he handed to Dagger, Clarence and Catherine. Dagger's letter was instructions for how he should treat the guests.

After things settled down and everyone was seated, Dagger said to Claudius, Edward, Angus and Clev. "I just want to make sure we are all on the same page here. The boss told me that you have business here and that it is his business too. He says that all of you can stay here and that we should back you up if you get into trouble."

"While that is very generous of him, we may not be staying," Edward said. "We plan to basically pull a con and we may need to stay in a hotel, or at least some of us."

Catherine and Clarence were sitting at the same table and Clev glanced at them before speaking. "The boss has been hit hard by the witch's curses and honestly these people are the only reason he is still alive."

"They are looking for information on the witch and I will be getting different manuscripts that hopefully will help the healers who are taking care of him. Sorry Catherine, I didn't mean to make you cry."

"That is one of the awful things about being in hiding; our only child needs us and we can't be there for him," Catherine said emotionally.

"Catherine, our healers are remarkable," said Claudius. "And they are working very hard to help him."

"I'm going to tell them," Clev said and laughed. "You know how stubborn Hector is. Well, he won't do what the healers tell him. He won't sleep and he would rather drink his meals then eat them so one of the leaders named Dominic assigned two of his people to babysit the boss. They are both Venatores and the woman is apparently beautiful and a couple of times she has actually tied him to the bed to make him sleep." Everyone laughed except for Catherine.

"What are Venatores?" she asked meekly.

"Exceptionally well-trained warriors from Ryed," Claudius said. "The look on your face; what did you think they were?"

"Well, now that we know about witches and warlocks and what not, I never know what to expect."

"Catherine, they are good people. They aren't punishing him but they are making him eat his meals and get some sleep," Claudius said. "And I suspect that Hector is going along with it because Mallory is so pretty."

"Clev said that she is Hector's type," Stephan said with a grin. "So that was a planned move on Dominic's part."

Everyone could see how emotional Catherine looked. "We have gifts that I planned to give you later but I think we will give you one now," Claudius said. "Stephan, give them the picture that Ingr drew."

Stephan took a small rolled paper from an inside shirt pocket and handed it to Catherine, "My wife drew this of your granddaughter."

Both Clarence and Catherine were overjoyed to see the picture. "She is so beautiful," said Catherine and showed the drawing to Dagger.

"She looks just like Hector did when he was Archer," Clarence said. "We can't wait to meet her."

"As I said we have lots of gifts and letters and I know that Bella already wrote to you about all of this but she and Isadore have fixed up one of the cottages on the royal grounds for you," Claudius said. "And it looks really nice."

"They even replanted some of your rose bushes and got things from your home and put in there. Now, Mathas and Rosa want you to know that you can live in the castle also, so the choice is yours."

"This all sounds so wonderful," Catherine said. "We just want to go home."

"Do you know about the attack at your house?" Claudius asked and Clarence nodded. "Hector thinks it is too dangerous for you to live there and the place was pretty torn up. But if you really want to, we will station soldiers there."

"We'll have to think about that," Clarence said and put his arm around his wife.

"It's probably not my business but since the boss said we should help you; what are you looking into?" asked Dagger.

"We found documents from a mutual enemy that said he funneled a lot of money to Juleta and it sounds like she has more businesses here than Hector knows of. Hector didn't know about this arrangement and since he and all of us are still victims of her attacks we want to get to the bottom of it," Edward explained.

"Well, there ain't a man here who doesn't hate that witch. Let us know what you need."

"Besides those five ships and the Lazy J Tavern do you know of any other holdings or businesses she had here?" asked Edward.

"Five ships, I think there are a hell of a lot more than five. Oh, sorry Catherine, I shouldn't have swore in front of you," Dagger said. "It was confusing at first because she puts the same symbol on the side that the boss does on his ships so we always thought they were his. Then maybe, I don't know a month ago all of the sailors on one of the ships gets sick. Well, I heard about it and sent some of our men to check it out."

"Well, none of those sailors were our men but they were real sick. So sick that no one wanted to go near them. So my boys say they will get physicians if the crew tells us who they work for."

"They gave us their paperwork but I have it in the barn, we don't want to touch it none. We got them physicians and healers but they all died."

"Did anyone figure out what the sickness was?" asked Thaos.

"No, but we wondered if it was some of the curses that she sent against the boss but why would she do that to her own crew?" asked Dagger.

The next morning the core members of Dominic's team, Elexas, Olin and Ryan arrived at Hector's house early in the morning as was becoming their routine.

Mallory was fixing breakfast when the group entered. "He's awake. Brock and Showers are with him," she said to her friends.

"I need a minute with him," Tessa said and she and Noah walked into the bedroom while the others either went to the kitchen to help Mallory or into the office.

"Hector, we need to talk for a minute," Tessa said.

"Do you need us to leave?" asked Brock.

"He might," said Noah. "We can help him walk."

"This isn't about my parents is it?" Hector asked with concern.

"No and it might be nothing," Tessa said and sat down on the bed next to him. "Javier and Madeline are basically my family and I know you used to have a thing for her a long time ago. They are both coming back here to work with us. I just need to know if you are going to be a threat to them. Hector, you have a strange look on your face what are you...oh my god, do you still like her?"

"I haven't seen Madeline in a long time. She stole my heart then screwed me over."

"Doesn't sound like you are over that," said Noah.

"Why is she coming? I understand why Javier would because his wife will be here."

"I'm just going to be straight with you and I hope you will be with us," Tessa said. "You do know that she was engaged to Prince Michael and it was real love. So his family basically adopted her and Javier because they consider them family. Michael's death hit her hard then she almost lost Javier too, well she has been really emotional."

"All of us send letters back and forth and they know you are working with us. Sudfad asked them if they wanted to come and work here since they know you and could probably tell if you are pulling a fast one on us. She has been intrigued by all of this and volunteered to come. That's the truth so tell me are you going to try and get even with them? And I hope you realize by now they were just doing their jobs."

"No I won't hurt them; I was just shocked. It might be nice to see her again."

"Well, if that is really how you feel then you should try and get better," said Tessa.

"I don't have much of a choice with Mallory and Brock here," Hector said and laughed. "So are they going to be coming out here and working with us?"

"That's the plan," said Noah. "And I don't know if this is going to make a difference with Corsa's care of you but they just found out that she is pregnant."

"Well, I'm certainly not going to hurt the girl," Hector said angrily.

"Not you, maybe the curses but we are just guessing," said Tessa. "If you don't want them here just tell us."

"No, that is fine."

"You don't really sound fine," said Noah.

"It just brought up old memories. I really did care about her."

Chapter XXI
Intruders

The teams in Cadia were up early. After breakfast they split up and rode into the city. Angus' team was going to the government offices to get information about businesses and landholdings. Edward and Kate were disguised as a wealthy couple who were considering opening businesses in the area, both legal and illegal businesses.

Catherine and Clarence were packing their things while Clev was obtaining the long list of manuscripts and other items that Hector wanted.

Claudius had promised to take Hector's parents shopping because they wanted to buy gifts for their granddaughter and others but he, Thaos and Stephan were going to Selen's house first. They brought a small boca which a soldier was driving. As soon as the men approached the house they could see that the front door had been kicked open.

Claudius and Stephan entered through the front door and Thaos and the soldier through the back. There were no intruders in the house which had been ransacked. "Glad we got her out of here," Stephan said. "I wonder what they were looking for."

"Miranda," Claudius said out loud which surprised the soldier since he had no idea who Claudius was talking to. "I have a really bad feeling is that because of you?"

"You are learning," Miranda's voice said and all the men heard it.

Thaos saw how frightened the soldier looked and said, "Miranda is an Angel."

"I need to sit down," the soldier stammered.

"There are many things that Juleta owned and things that others believe she owned that are being sought," said Miranda. "Since Selen was close to Juleta and poses no threat she will be targeted for information. Now, before you ask your questions what do you know about Juleta?"

"She was hateful and vindictive," said Stephan.

"Insecure and always seeking attention," Thaos said. "She was...now wait a minute. I am remembering what Adam told us the other day. She was always seeking power because she didn't feel like she had it because she sold herself."

"I am impressed, you are listening and remembering," Miranda and teasingly. "It is difficult for you to understand the mindset of people in her world which is why it is fortunate in many ways that you and Hector have called a truce. You will need to speak with Clev about this. If you want power what would you do Claudius?"

He didn't speak for several moments, "Other than call to you I don't know. Is this a trick question?"

"You are a powerful person in your own right and calling to us is the right answer. Now imagine yourself always afraid but you don't even understand what you fear. Juleta was a paranoid and untrusting person because of her fears. How would she try to gain power?"

"Demons and spells," said Claudius. "I am sure there are all kinds of things that she thought would help her gain power but I don't have a clue what they might be."

"And that is where Hector and Clev are invaluable; they can give you answers that you cannot find in other places. Selen is innocent. She has no idea what people are searching for and has no information that she has not already given to you. But in your haste to enter the house you did not see the alarms. You will have company soon and they can be killed. But you would be wise to get some answers from them."

No sooner had Miranda finished speaking when three beings entered the house. They wore armor breast plates and bracers. They wore metal helmets with two large protruding horns and metal masks that covered their faces. They carried shields and swords.

Stephan was facing the front door and threw a knife which lodged in the throat of the first intruder. As he went down his partners made sounds that were a combination between grunts and yells and charged. The soldier jumped out of his chair but instantly went into a forward roll. His idea was to get behind one of the intruders but instead he tripped him and the being fell to the floor. He and Thaos jumped on the fallen intruder while Claudius and Stephan fought with the third being.

The fight was not easy because the intruders had incredible strength. The one on the floor quickly threw Thaos and the soldier off from him and got back on his feet. The attacker who was fighting with Claudius and Stephan did not give them an opening to stab him. These monsters were huge but quick on their feet.

Thaos was thrown into a wall near the front door when Clev and a dozen of Hector's men ran into the house. "Keep one a live," yelled Claudius. Even with the reinforcements, the battle did not end quickly but both intruders were overpowered and tied up.

Each intruder was lying on the floor hogtied with multiple swords pointing at him when Stephan pulled off the first helmet. "Damn what are they?" he asked with disgust as the face of the being looked like a massive pile of worms. Thaos pulled the helmet off from the second being.

"Look boss," one of Clev's men yelled. With the helmets removed the beings were shrinking in size and within moments that had dissolved into puddles on the floor.

"What the hell!" yelled Thaos. "Clev do you know what they are?"

"No and that is a bad sign. Those helmets were giving them power so there has to be magics attached to them so be careful."

"Miranda," called Stephan.

"Take their armor to study; the magics are now disabled." Only Stephan heard her voice.

"She said she stopped the magics but we need to take the armor and study it," Stephan said then looked at Clev. "How did you know we needed help?"

"Just had a feeling," he said. "Did you guys tear up this place?"

"No but we triggered an alarm when we came in," Claudius said as he was looking at a breast plate. "Were these demons or something else?"

"I'm not sure of that either," said Clev. "But let's get this crap out of here."

"I promised Selen that I would get some of her things," said Thaos. "Hopefully not everything is broken."

"Have the boys help you," said Clev. "I think we need to get the hell out of here."

Since Dominic's team was coming to Hector's house every morning, Brock and Mallory would take the opportunity to take breaks from his care.

Hector had been fairly quiet during breakfast which was unusual for him. Now as the women were clearing the table he said. "I have kind of an unusual request. It is becoming more apparent to me that I will be here considerably longer than I thought. And Tessa and Noah informed me this morning that Javier, Madeline and Corsa will be joining us. And my parents are coming. Ladies, I have a proposition for you. I would like to make this house a little more like a home."

"While I appreciate the hospitality, it is sparse in here. If I give you money and send some men with you will you buy furnishings and some toys for Sarah? And I want furnishings for all of the rooms. I am sure we could use more dishes and utensils in the kitchen and anything you would like for the office. I will pay you to do this."

"We will do it because it sounds like fun," said Tessa. "Hector, I don't know if we can consider ourselves friends but we are working together."

"You are always offering to pay us and it is kind of insulting. Now, we should get some nice rugs in here, especially for when Sarah comes. Dominic do you mind if we do this today?"

"Be my guest. You deserve a little fun. All of you can go if you want." Dominic laughed when he saw the smiles on the women's faces.

"Seth will you help us measure?" Jasmine asked then she turned to Hector. "Ryan's shop has the nicest furniture in the city do you have a problem with us buying it there?"

"Of course not," said Hector. "Let me get you some money."

"Ryan, you can go too since they will be at your shop," Dominic said.

"Thanks, I have some ideas," said Ryan.

Showers helped Hector walk into his room and they returned with two huge bags of gold coins. "If you need more let me know," said Hector. "And treat yourselves to something."

After the group left Dominic said, "That was nice of you."

"I don't mean to insult any of you but this is very difficult for me," said Hector. "I have always been strong and healthy and giving orders. I guess I don't know how to ask people to do things for me."

With the help of Clev's men Thaos had many of Selen's things packed in the small boca. The armor of the intruders was also put in the boca but the men covered it with blankets. They quickly left the house and returned to the compound.

No one wanted Catherine to learn of the attack so Dagger was brought outside to look at the armor. "I haven't heard of those beasts but I have seen that symbol on the shields. There's a couple of ships in dock with that same mark." The symbol was a fist with blood dripping from it.

"Where exactly are those ships?" asked Claudius.

"Some of my men will go with you," Dagger said.

As the soldiers from Lentz and Dagger's men were saddling up Miranda spoke to Claudius. "And what do you intend to do?"

"Attack those monsters and get information," Claudius said then he paused for a moment. "Is this a trap?"

"Your behavior is always predictable. While others would flee you run into the fire without questioning who set it. You have already fought the monsters. The ships are illusions, doorways you might say."

"Should we destroy them and how? Ok before you say it, will you help us? And who sent them and why?"

"Yes I will help you. You know you have many enemies but you are wondering who knows you are in Cadia."

"Did Hector do this?"

"No as difficult as it is to believe you really are allies now."

"So someone has been waiting for us to return? Do they know about Catherine and Clarence?"

"No, this is one of several traps that are set for you because it is believed that Thaos and Stephan did find some of Juleta's things."

"So what is everyone looking for? Is that the same thing the Sisterhood wants?"

"Well, it's about time someone asked. She hid fortunes of money and she did not acquire it all by theft. She blackmailed many powerful people. People who were glad to hear of her demise but are afraid that she left notes behind. Then there are all of the meticulous notes she took from her experiments and the objects she purchased or stole for power."

"It is time for you to pay as much attention to your enemies as they do to you. This in itself will lead you to many things. The ships have been destroyed."

266

Claudius briefed the leaders about Miranda's words. The group did not go to the docks. Claudius and some of his soldiers took Catherine and Clarence into the city to shop. He did not invite anyone else because he felt that Hector's parents wanted to speak with him alone.

Once they entered a store Clarence said. "We are so appreciative of you coming for us. Everyone is trying to keep things from us but we know something is really bad. Will you tell us?"

"Do you really want the truth?"

"Yes," Clarence said as tears formed in Catherine's eyes.

"Hector is a notorious criminal. He got involved with Juleta for the power and he inherited her organization. He, well they both had a lot of enemies but now that he is weakened by these curses others are coming for him. We are protecting him in ways you can't imagine."

"He is very sick but honestly it is a good thing. My personal feelings are that he got so caught up with being Hector that he forgot who Archer was. Now that he is with all of us, and he has stayed at our home too, well, Bella says there is more of Archer every day."

Clarence and Catherine did not interrupt Claudius as he spoke but their hearts sank a little more with each of his words.

"His fears for your safety are very real so please do as we tell you, at least for now," continued Claudius. "You may not know this but we have often been enemies, I mean Hector and all of us who run the kingdom but we have declared a truce for family reasons and honestly we are all getting along well. I don't understand many of the choices he has made but I like the boy. But you need to be prepared when you see him. He does look bad and he wouldn't take care of himself."

"I recently learned that one of our female team members was scolding him and asked him if he had a death wish. He got mad at her but honestly it was a fair question."

"Rosa is trying to get him to bond with Sarah and hopefully with you there the old Archer can come alive again."

"It is so difficult to believe that our son has done some of the things that we have heard," said Catherine. "Do you know if all of those horrible things are true?"

"Catherine, I don't know about all of them but I can personally attest for some of them and I will not go into that further. I am going to change the subject in a way. There is a great deal that I do not understand about Hector but I have come to believe that being at the top of a criminal empire is a lonely life. Our teams are basically his enemies and he seems to enjoy their company. Of course everyone is being on their best behavior."

"You can't change what he has done but perhaps you can help him remember the life he used to have and make him feel it is worth living again. That is what we have been trying to do."

It was almost noon when Jasmine, Mallory, Tessa and Elexas walked into Hector's house. All of the women were laughing loudly.

"You sound like you're having fun," Dominic said.

"We did," said Jasmine. "And we will tell you all about it but we have to start lunch. Hector, Ryan has the rest of your money."

"I told you to spend it all."

"We have three large bocas full," Elexas said and laughed.

"And since we had money left over we went to the docks and bought seafood, steaks and other treats," Mallory said. "You'll have a feast in about thirty minutes."

"Sounds great," Fennel said and started clearing off the table.

All of the men laughed as Ryan carried a giant basket into the room. The basket was filled with toys and clothing for Sarah. "The girls might have gotten a little carried away," Ryan said and he too was laughing.

He set the basket on the floor by Hector who picked up a little blue dress and held it up for the others to see.

"Sarah is going to love all of you," Hector said and Jasmine marched into the office.

"No Hector, you tell her that is from Daddy," Jasmine said in a scolding tone and Hector grinned.

Tessa had run out to the bocas and was coming back into the house. "Noah, will you bring in that basket of wine. Hector, we bought nice dishes and wine glasses because your parents are coming but we have to wash them all first."

"And when they come we will put flowers in here," said Mallory. The excitement of the women was contagious and all of the men were smiling or laughing.

Two of Hector's men walked into the house. "What do you want unloaded first?" asked one of the men.

"We have to empty the rooms, clean the floors and put the carpets down first," said Tessa. "If you want to start moving Hectors and Shower's things that would be great."

"Me?" said Showers with surprise.

"Just wait until you see what we bought you," Jasmine said excitedly.

"Hector, Shaun and Larry were a lot of help; can they eat with us?" asked Tessa.

"Sure," Hector said and stood up. "Everything can come out of my room but that chest. You won't be able to carry it far."

"Please don't tell us it's full of demon snakes or something," Tessa said kiddingly.

"No, money," Hector said and grinned.

Mallory's mouth fell open. "That huge chest is money?"

"Guess we should have spent more," Tessa said and all of the women laughed again.

Noah carried in a large basket filled with bottles of wine. "Wait until you see all the stuff they bought," he said and laughed.

"No!" said Jasmine. "No peeking, we want to surprise you."

"Do you want some help?" asked Seth as he saw all the women scurrying around in the small kitchen.

"Help Elexas with the shrimp and lobster," Jasmine said.

"If anyone else wants to help we have a bunch of things that need to be cut up," said Mallory.

"I can do that," said Noah. "This all looks great."

Ryan left the house and returned with a large pouch, "Hector, I've got your money but this I paid for," Ryan said. "Since Olin couldn't come with us we got him something."

"What is it?" Olin asked with a huge smile. "A fiddle! Ryan thanks so much."

"Can you play?" asked Lawrence.

"Yeah, but I haven't played in a while. Let me warm up and I will play something for you after lunch."

Ryan handed an empty leather pouch and a pouch with about two hundred dollars in it to Hector. "Did you kids get yourselves something?" Hector asked.

"Honestly we really didn't have time," said Ryan. "I had to get another boca from my shop to carry everything. But I think you will really like it."

"I am sure I will," Hector said. "I'm the only one not working. Want some help?"

"Want to open some bottles of wine?" Tessa asked and carried four to the table.

Thirty minutes later the table was filled with cheeses, breads, fruits, sauces and all manner of seafood. "The first course is ready," Elexas announced throughout the house and to the men working outside.

"This is great," said Fennel.

"Since there are so many steaks to cook it will take a while so just start eating as we bring them to you," Mallory said as Tessa and Jasmine set four plates with steaks on the table.

Noah carried two huge platters of fried potatoes into the room. "I've got to admit this is fun," he said. "The castle is kind of formal for my taste."

"Showers, I don't think I have ever seen you smile this much," said Hector; Shaun and Larry laughed at the look on Shower's face.

"I'll tell you I can't remember ever eating this good," said Showers. "And the company is as good as the food."

"I thought you were supposed to be the mean one," Jasmine said kiddingly as she set a steak in front of him.

"He is," said Larry and grinned.

"Hector when your parents come, they can have our bedroom," Brock said. "Mallory and I can camp outside."

"The hell you are; we will figure something out," Hector said then grinned. "Of course Mallory may not like my first suggestion."

"Shut up Hector," Mallory said and laughed. "He keeps telling me that when a woman ties him up it's supposed to be fun." Everyone at the table now grinned at her.

"Do you know what he is talking about?" asked Dominic.

Mallory looked up from her plate and saw that everyone was looking at her and smiling. "I have a feeling I don't."

"I'll tell her," Elexas said and pulled Mallory into the kitchen.

The group laughed loudly when they heard Mallory say, "What...wait...what?"

Elexas and Mallory laughed too as they returned to the table; Mallory was blushing. "Brock, you tie him up from now on," she said. Brock was taking a drink of wine and spit it out as he laughed and the room exploded with laughter.

By late afternoon, Hector's house had been transformed with beautiful furniture, rich drapes, rugs and bedding. All of the rooms in the house were large except for the kitchen. The parlor now hosted a dining area. There were small desks and bookshelves in all of the bedrooms. Three walls of the office were lined with shelves the fourth wall was saved for hanging charts. The furniture was both practical and considerably more comfortable than the previous furnishings.

Hector was pleased and tried to pay everyone but no one would take his money. After Dominic's team left and Hector and Showers were alone in Hector's bedroom, Showers said seriously, "Boss, I know this truce is temporary but it's gonna be damn hard going back to being enemies with these folks. I really hope you don't order me to kill any of them."

"Now you sound like Clev," Hector said.

Chapter XXII
The Demon Within

Late that evening, Mallory walked into Hector's bedroom with a small tray. "Shara is trying a new tonic for you and I didn't taste it but from the smell I brought you water and whiskey to wash it down," she said and laughed.

Hector was sitting up in bed and reading, "I can actually smell that from here," he said. "I might need the whiskey first to numb my throat."

"I'll be back," she said and set the tray on the small table next to his bed. She returned a few moments later with a bottle of whiskey.

"I know I keep saying it but I really like what you girls did; wish you would let me pay you back."

"I am sure we will think of something. Now drink your medicine and then I have some questions for you."

"Only if I get to ask some too."

"That's fair," Mallory said and laughed as she watched Hector choke down the glass of tonic. He quickly drank the small glass of whiskey then the glass of water. "That bad?"

"Yeah, I hope this stuff works," Hector said then he started to cough. She poured more whiskey into his glass. When he stopped coughing she said, "I have some things to explain before I ask you my questions and I think they are important so just listen before you yell or anything."

"When have I yelled at you?"

"Let's see; every time I tie you up," she said and smiled.

"That's different," he said and grinned. "Trust me if I really yelled at you, you would know it."

"Actually it was your comment today about tying you up that made me think about some things."

"So you are thinking about having sex with me?"

"No you fool and stop grinning. But listen to me. Before we realized there were bounties on Javier, Corsa was trying to figure out what was going on. She was fascinated with Isabella and was trying to imagine how she would think. Now, Corsa had never met Isabella but she was reading everything our teams had on her."

"So at lunch when we were joking around about sex, I started thinking and went back and read some notes. Now tell me if I have anything wrong here. I am trying to get into Juleta's mind. It seems to me that her idea of love is absolute control over another person and if that person doesn't let her control them she feels betrayed."

"You hit it on the head, go on."

"You're the one who said she lost it when she found out that Stephan was in love with Ingr. And look at all the anger she sent at Nikki and Ingr because she was jealous. And she didn't even have relationships with Stephan and Thaos."

"The Angels told us that she was trying to create you to be the perfect husband. She did have a relationship with you, at least sexual and you have a child together. Then she made you her head lieutenant. We know she didn't trust anyone so she must have trusted you, at least more than the rest. I am assuming that she felt like a scorned woman and we have all heard stories about what men and women do when they feel like that."

"I think that she would punish you if you had any kind of a relationship with another woman and punish that woman too. Hector do you remember when the curses first hit you? Is it possible they are triggered by you having sex with someone or feelings for someone? Because if that is a possibility we should look into this before Madeline gets here. You are looking at me like I am crazy but I am serious."

"Not at all, I think you are brilliant and I am amazed at how much you know about me."

"Our teams keep notes and we brief each other every day. We don't know what is happening to you and even the smallest detail might be important."

Mallory suddenly started laughing and turned red. "What are you thinking?" asked Hector.

"I really shouldn't say it."

"Tell me."

"Well, it's not funny but as vindictive as Juleta was I wouldn't be surprised if she cast a spell so your penis would fall off when you had sex with someone else. I am sorry I shouldn't laugh."

"Mallory, I need to get to that book shelf," he said so she would move since she was sitting on the side of the bed.

"I can get what you want."

"Those are all the new books I bought from Hilgra, I don't really know what is over there."

"Hector, you're naked," Mallory scolded as she helped him out of bed.

"I predict there will be a day when you like that," he said and grinned. "And besides now you know it didn't fall off." She laughed and helped him to the bookshelf. "Mallory, what you said would fit right into the ideology of the Sisterhood. You are welcome to stay and help me look through some of these books. When is Brock coming on duty?"

"Not for a couple of hours."

"It seems like you work more hours."

"That's because I do the cooking too. Trust me you don't want him to cook. Everything would taste like that tonic."

As Mallory spoke, Hector chose four books from the shelves. Mallory walked next to him as he returned to bed. She didn't need to help him walk but he was so unsteady she was afraid that he might fall.

"In case you are interested," he said and smiled. "There isn't anything between me and Madeline. I fell for her a long time ago but we didn't date or anything and she used me to get some magic books."

"Well, Tessa and Noah said you seem to have feelings for her and that is your business unless you try to get even or if my theory is right." Mallory paused. "I probably shouldn't tell you this but all of the team members say that both Madeline and Javier are very different people than they expected. You know they were basically slaves to the powers of Inferus. And now that they are free, well everyone really likes them."

"So what are you really saying?"

"I expect the Madeline that is coming here is a different person than the one you fell in love with and that could be good or bad. But either way she is still grieving so even if something were to rekindle between you two, she still has to work through that."

"This is going to sound insulting but I don't mean it that way. For a young girl you are wise. I noticed that in Brock too. Is that part of your training?"

"Actually yes. We learn to read everything, people, nature, demons. And we learn to sense things without using our eyes. If you want, Brock and I can show you some demonstrations sometime."

"I would like that. I find your people fascinating."

"This coming from the guy who spent a fortune trying to turn into a demon. You could probably have fed my village for a year for what you paid for that."

"So you are reminding me that you are a demon hunter," he said and smiled.

"You're pretty smart too," she said sarcastically. "I will help you with those books but I think I will get a glass of wine first. Do you want anything to eat?"

"I'll take another piece of that cake. But before you go what did you want to ask me?"

"Basically, what I already said."

"I can tell there is something else. Just ask it."

"I don't think you want me to."

"Now you have my curiosity up. Mallory just spit it out."

She sat down on the bed and looked angry. "I don't understand you. You have everything, money, family, a good life, good looks, friends and you throw it all away to become an abomination. You keep telling us it is for power that you do these things but I don't think you realize how much power you had. Hector there is something else driving you and maybe it is some of Juleta's insanity."

"You ask about our training. Do you know why Brock and I never leave you alone with our friends? Because we've both seen the beast in your eyes. It's like there is something inside of you and honestly we don't know if you are even aware of it. You have been friendly and nice with all of us. And everyone keeps saying that they like you which is a problem because one of us may have to kill you someday."

"What do you mean you see the beast in my eyes?"

"I am trying to think how to explain it. Think of hearing a sound then looking at a window as something quickly passes it. Hector, your eyes actually change. Ask Brock if you don't believe me. I am not saying this to be mean. Hector for all your power, Brock and I don't know if you are even in control of yourself."

"That's what that Angel said," he said in a hoarse whisper. "Do you see any other changes in me?"

"Sometimes a smell but honestly with all of the stuff that Shara is giving you and putting on you that could be the cause. I am surprised, you look scared and I expected you to get mad."

"When you get your wine will you wake Brock up and bring him in here too?"

Mallory returned to the bedroom with a tray of food, wine and Brock. "I will be honest," Brock said. "I am not sure that I am happy that Mallory told you."

"Well I am and I need both of you to be really honest with me. What exactly do you see?" asked Hector. Brock and Mallory could hear the fear in in voice.

277

"It's like we are talking like now then suddenly your eyes change," Brock said. "They go from round and brown to yellow and narrow. And when that happens we both sense the evil in you."

"I have heard amazing things about how your people train so they can still hunt demons even if they are blinded or wounded. I believe what you are saying, I just can't explain it. But I can tell you that I haven't felt right for some time. And this does scare me since I will be around Sarah and my parents again."

"But weren't you transitioning to become a demon?" asked Mallory.

"Yes, but Samael stopped everything and returned me to my former self. And even if he hadn't, this shouldn't be happening. Have you told Dominic and the others?"

"No because we wanted to watch you more," said Brock. "We were afraid that if that beast inside of you knows we know that something will change."

"I have been a savage man for a long time. Is that what you see?"

"So is Showers and we don't see it in him," said Brock. "That is why one of us is always awake and with you. We didn't know if you even knew about this."

"Have you seen it in Clev?"

"We haven't really been around him but we sent Kate a message to watch for it," Brock said.

"When Dominic and the others get here, tell them. They may have to call to your Angels."

"Well, we can do that. You can too and you know that," said Brock.

"I doubt if they would come if I called."

"Great Ruler send us Angels," Mallory said out loud.

All three people were shocked and overwhelmed when The Lion appeared in the room. The intensity of his presence caused them to cry. "Who are you?" asked Hector fearfully.

"He is the most powerful warrior Angel in the Heavens," said Brock. "This must be really bad."

"Hector, I have been watching you for a long time and I am not pleased with what I have seen. Mallory was right. You had a life that others pray for and you threw it away to become a puppet for demons. They pass you around like that tray of food and you don't even realize it. And all the while you believe you are in control. You are thinking that you have heard my voice before and you are right. We speak to all but you choose to listen to other voices. So my monster, why would you want an Angel here?"

"Is there a beast in side of me?"

"There is more than one. Some you have created and others were planted. And why does this worry you? You are an exceptionally intelligent man who once studied to become a priest for The Great Ruler. You know that you have been feeding your demons. Do you want me here so you can gain more power over your being or because you want to repent?"

Hector did not answer. "As I thought," said The Lion. "I will not help you feed your demons. You have many choices to make." The Lion disappeared.

Hector, Brock and Mallory did not sleep that night; they sat up and talked and did research. An hour before dawn, Mallory started to make breakfast. As soon as she left the room, Hector said, "Brock, if the beast comes out when I have Sarah or I am with my parents I expect you to kill it." Brock nodded.

When Dominic's team arrived in the morning, Brock and Mallory met with them and explained about the beasts within Hector and what The Lion said.

"While I understand your reasoning, this is the last time either of you will withhold information from the team. Do you understand that?" asked Dominic.

"Yes," said Brock. "The only thing I haven't told you yet is he said that if we saw the beast when he was with his family that he expected me to kill him. And that surprised me."

"I think it surprises us all," Dominic said. "Is Showers with him?"

"Yes but we don't know if he knows anything," said Brock. "Hector does want to meet with you."

"Breakfast is ready," said Mallory. "Will someone help me put these platters on the table?"

Dominic, Fennel and Brock walked into Hector's bedroom. "He doesn't know," Hector said and was referring to Showers. "Trying to decide if I should tell him."

"Considering what you asked Brock to do, I would suggest it," Dominic said. "Breakfast is ready so we can discuss if over a meal or not, it is up to you."

"What is going on?" asked Showers when he saw the solemn demeanors of all of the men.

"Believe me, you won't believe it when I tell you. But changing the subject for a moment, did Mallory tell you her theory?"

"I didn't know she had one," said Brock.

"Well, that is why she was in my room to ask me some questions and I think she might be onto something which may be connected to the other thing. Let's talk about that first."

Once everyone was seated at the breakfast table, Hector asked Mallory to repeat everything she had told him the previous night.

"I guess the question is have you been having sex and do the onset of curses correlate to those times?" asked Noah.

"Yes, to the first and I have to figure out the rest," Hector said. "Now we can go into that other thing."

Although the team had already been briefed by Mallory and Brock they sat in silence as the information was repeated.

"I don't understand any of this boss," Showers said. "There is something inside of you?"

"Yeah and I have to figure out what. But I believe it is dangerous, even more dangerous than me. Showers, I told Brock that if that beast came out when I had Sarah or my parents that he should kill me that order goes for you too."

"Boss, I can't do that."

"If I am attacking my family, you can and you will!"

There was silence in the room for several moments then Tessa said out loud, "Adam is that what you were talking about when you showed me a bunch of Hectors?"

"Who is she talking to?" Showers asked.

"An Angel," said Ryan.

"Well, I'll be damned," Showers said.

"He's not answering," said Tessa. "Adam if any of you want to join us you are welcomed to. Because how do we fight this?"

Adam appeared and it was the first time that Olin and Elexas had seen him. Showers and Hector too saw the powerful Angel and they were filled with fear.

"You're Adam," Olin said in awe and got out of his chair and walked up to the Angel. Olin kneeled down. "How can I ever repay you?"

"Stand," Adam said. "Perhaps later you can tell Hector and Showers your story." Adam looked at Hector. "You have not called to me but even with your darkness you understand that you are a danger to so many. Asking Showers to kill your body will not kill the beasts; they are strong within you."

"Is it the beasts inside of him that are killing him?" asked Mallory.

"That question is more complicated than you can imagine," said Adam. "There are two kinds of demons, the ones such as Samael and the ones humans say are within them, like Juleta's rage and hatred. People control who they give their power to. Olin did not want to give his power to the demons anymore and he is now free and we will speak more about that later."

"Hector has both types inside of him and they are all fighting to take control. Right now the human is hanging on by a thread and if it were not for his enemies, those of you who are caring for him and protecting him, he would have already lost the battle. It is his ego that is preventing him from acknowledging this."

"Is that demon that Samael sold him to inside of him?" asked Tessa.

"No. That monster was so strong that the human would have been killed instantly."

"We know there are always many reasons that you have us do things," said Dominic. "And we accept that. And it is obvious that Hector needs to make choices but he isn't so how do we protect others from the beasts inside of him?"

"Hector, you dance with demons and yet you are afraid to speak to me," said Adam. "Did you really hear what Dominic said? You still consider these people your enemies after all they have done for you and they will risk their lives further. Isn't it time you took some responsibility for your life, for your actions?"

Hector did not speak. "Hector enjoys his life of darkness and that is why he doesn't speak. It will swallow him up and he will exist no more yet he hangs onto it like any other addiction," said Adam.

"We cannot make his choices for him," said Dominic. "But we are here for a reason. What is it you want us to do?"

"Just your presence is keeping the demons at bay. You have already reminded Clev and Showers that there is more to life than the nightmares of their existence but you haven't yet gotten through to Hector."

"Life is more complicated than any of you realize. People throw around words like destiny but have no real idea of what that word means. Hector still has a role to play. You might say a journey to take and you are keeping him alive so he can do that. Then when he makes his choices they will be final."

Hector started to go into convulsions. Several people at the table jumped up to help him. "Do not touch him," said Adam. "The demons inside are raging."

A horrendous growl came out of Hector but he was not making the sound. Suddenly a dark cloud flew out of him and directly at Adam who now had his sword drawn. Every one jumped out of their seats. Adam sliced the darkness with his sword and it disappeared. Hector stopped convulsing but he was unconscious.

"When he awakes tell him," said Adam.

"I can't believe that tried to attack you," Olin said.

"That is how strong the demons are inside of him."

"So you want us to continue as we have?" asked Dominic.

"With one exception. Fear is a seed that grows into darkness. You know there are bounties on Olin. It is reasonable to be cautious and protective. But to allow him to become imprisoned by his fears is an entirely different matter. You are priests, teach your people," Adam said then turned to Olin.

"I have come whenever you have called to me. Do you not think I will do it again?"

"I am sorry. I won't forget." Olin said. "Do you want me to tell Hector how you saved me?"

"Tell him but do not expect a change."

Chapter XXIII
I Remember

Because of the attack by the strange creatures, Claudius wanted to stay in Cadia a little longer. He did not want to leave the teams until they had some idea of what they were dealing with in that city. Clev too felt uneasy about leaving although he did not understand why.

Catherine was so thrilled to be going home that she planned extravagant feasts for every meal. At breakfast she announced, "I want to have a special party before we leave. Claudius, do you know what day that will be?"

"Something unexpected came up with our work," Claudius said. He was referring to the attack at Selen's house. Catherine and Clarence had not been told about it. "I had thought about leaving tomorrow but we might be here an extra day or two. Is that a problem?"

"No because it will take me a little while to get things organized. Dagger, I want a list of the men who have been stationed here to watch us."

"What exactly do you want?" Dagger asked.

"Names, I want to get everyone gifts. And yesterday I was so overwhelmed that I only bought for Sarah, I would like to get some gifts for others. Dagger, if you have suggestions for gifts for your men I would appreciate it. Or you are welcome to come along."

"That is very generous of you Catherine. I would like to come along and since you will be buying so much some of the boys will come with us." Dagger did not want to worry Catherine but he was very concerned for her and Clarence's safety.

Dagger and his men were initially insulted when they learned they were assigned to protect Hector's family. The men imagined the worse but Catherine and Clarence quickly changed their attitudes. Hector's parents were kind and gracious to all of the men and treated them as family.

Dagger in particular became very attached to the couple. In a way they became the parents he never had. This notorious group of hired killers treated Catherine and Clarence with care and respect. Claudius and the team members saw that immediately and it surprised them.

After the Angel Adam left, the men carried Hector into his bedroom. Then returned to the dining area to discuss the situation. Showers was visibly shaken. "I've got so damn many questions that I don't know where to start," he stammered. Tessa left the table and returned with a glass of whiskey for him. "Thanks," Showers said and drank the entire glass with one gulp. "All of you act like you see this all the damn time," he said.

"Actually some of us do and there are things that we have to explain to you but ask your questions first," said Dominic.

"Are you really priests?"

"We are all studying to be priests," Dominic said and smiled.

"You all look like professionals, well except for the ladies. And Angels are real and I never thought an Angel would look like a warrior. It's like nothing is what I thought."

"Welcome to our world," said Fennel. "Showers," Fennel now looked at the end of the table. "Ryan, Olin and Elexas you might not know this either. We have found that the behavior of the Angels is like a code. But first you have to understand that while demons demand that a person does things the Angels are very different. The Great Ruler created all of us with freedom of choice and the Angels can't compromise that."

"So they can't come right out and tell us things that will affect the choices that we make. For us that is frustrating a lot because we are trying to figure out a lot of things."

"I am going to interrupt here a moment," Dominic said. "And I apologize to our people that we haven't been good about teaching you some of these things. Angels rarely appear like Adam did so when they do, know there is significance to that."

"Usually we hear them talking in our heads but even that takes a while to learn. They tell us that they and The Great Ruler speak to us all of the time but most of us don't listen."

"The second thing is since we have offered to work on their behalf they appear to us a lot more than they do others but they choose who they appear to. When Olin and Elexas first joined us we could see the Angels but they couldn't. Adam has saved Olin twice now and this is the first time that he has seen him. So Showers before Fennel finishes, you have to understand that one, it was a big deal that Adam appeared and maybe a bigger one that he appeared to you and Hector."

"Excuse me but I'm going to pour another drink," Showers said.

"I'll get it," said Jasmine. "You need to hear this."

"There are different types of demons and I will be honest I don't know all the species," said Fennel. "Our concern is whether they can be killed by us or not. Now you started to cry too when Adam appeared and that is because of his holiness. You know that if we felt it the demons in Hector sure did. And that demon had the balls to attack an Angel. All of this is significant. It is telling us that Hector is in a lot more trouble than at least I thought."

"Well what about me?" Showers asked.

"Do you own your soul?" asked Noah. "Because Clev and Hector both just found out that demons owned theirs and they didn't remember selling them."

"As far as I know I do but...I can't remember the last time I felt this scared. How do I find out?"

"The Angels can tell you," said Tessa. "We can help you talk to them. I never knew they existed until a few months ago and I've been so excited that I talk to them all the time."

"Every time I walk into our room she is talking to Adam," Noah said with a grin. "And its everyday stuff like if she was talking to a friend."

"Well, I figure he can tell me to shut up if I annoy him but we are getting off the subject. Showers the bottom line is that Hector is in a lot of danger and we suspect that you are too since Adam appeared before you."

"Noah and I were present when Adam appeared before Clev and Hector and Adam said that Clev was a loyal friend but asked him if he would follow Hector into hell. You probably should be thinking about the same thing. Whatever you decide is your decision but we will help you if you want it."

"It doesn't surprise me but it does concern me that we haven't even scratched the surface with Hector," Dominic said. "What Adam told us before is that Hector is so controlled by the demons that he can barely make his own choices. We wanted him to remember what it was like to be human again. We don't think he will turn good but perhaps we can help him get enough of his power back to be able to make his own choices."

"But don't you think he has some since he told us to kill him if he hurt his family?" Brock asked.

"What I don't understand is why the hell you are helping any of us," said Showers.

"Now this is something that all of us are learning the hard way," Dominic said. "Whenever the Angels ask us to do something there are always a lot more things involved than we realize. Sometimes they give us an assignment like protecting our enemy and we are all bitching about it and when it is done we see that we saved a lot more than one man."

"Showers, you have a lot of battle experience," said Lawrence. "When you plan an attack you have to think of every possible scenario which is what we do and every single time the Angels saw more than we did. So while Adam hasn't directly told us, we think that Hector is a huge threat to others and he may not even be aware of it."

Not only did Dagger have men shopping with Catherine but many men were in the city watching over her. Claudius and his sons felt free to accompany the teams.

The previous day little had been accomplished. Angus' team did not find any businesses or land holdings under, Juleta's name, Otto's name or any name they thought might be associated with the two. Edward's team had been meeting with people and did not learn any interesting information.

"You know we may be looking at this wrong," Stephan said as he was walking down the main business street with Thaos and his father. A lot of people are interested in Selen because they think she has something. Maybe she does but she doesn't realize it. You know how shrewd Juleta was. We only found the things she wanted us to find."

"Selen did say that whenever Juleta yelled at her that the next day Juleta would give her a gift," Thaos said. "Maybe there is something in those items."

"What did she give her?" asked Claudius.

"I really don't know other than the first gift was a fancy blouse," Thaos said. "But that makes sense. Let's go back and search her house again."

"She wouldn't have hidden anything," said Stephan.

"No, but we didn't pack all of her things. There might be something in there that she didn't even realize."

"You know Juleta would anticipate all of this so if she hid something it would have to appear inconspicuous," said Claudius.

Showers was a tough and fearless man but he now felt overwhelmed. He had many questions for Dominic and the others. As the people talked, Mallory kept leaving the table and checking on Hector.

"I don't know why I am so worried but I am going back in there and sit with him," she announced at the table.

"You didn't get any sleep last night," Jasmine said. "I'll go in there."

"But you can't see the demon in him. Besides I am really awake. I am going to look through those books that he wanted to read."

"Just so you know," Brock said to the group after Mallory left the room. "She told him that all of us like him but that is a problem since we might have to kill him some day."

"Hell, I told him the same damn thing about you guys and he said Clev said the same," said Showers. "We are all supposed to be enemies but I haven't met a bunch of people who I like and respect like all of you in a long time. And I don't just mean the teams, this entire tribe is something."

"I think that is just plain sad," said Tessa. "Who the hell says we have to be enemies? Is it Hector? Really is it him?"

"That's a good question," said Noah. "I think we've thought of each other as enemies for so long that we don't even question it."

Thaos, Claudius and Stephan looked at Selen's house with new eyes. After three hours Stephan poured himself a glass of water and sat down on what was left of the sofa. Claudius and Thaos walked into the room a few minutes later. "Stephan, we screwed up," Thaos said. "Claudius tell him."

"I wasn't with your group but wasn't the story that Juleta sent Selen to Port Friada and when she returned she saw that the castle was destroyed and got scared and came here?"

"Yeah," said Stephan. "So if she was too scared to go into the castle then she didn't take her belongings. Except for what she had on her trip." Stephan paused. "Thaos, did she buy this place furnished?"

"I have no idea, why?"

"You know Selen's style. Everything is frilly and flowers and light blue. Look at these awful paintings. They don't look like anything she would have and not that I am an expert on decorating but they don't go with anything else in the house."

Claudius walked up to one of the six large paintings in the room. All of the paintings were painted with dark colors and had thick dark wooden frames. "This is the lighthouse just north of Langer," Claudius said and took the painting off from the wall.

"Don't take it apart until we call to the Angels," said Thaos. "These colors are so dark you don't really notice the pictures until you are right next to them. This one is her castle. These paintings have to mean something."

"Great, this is our castle," Stephan said. "Miranda or anyone would you join us?"

It was the Angel Ruth who appeared in the room. "Ruth, I am surprised that you came," Stephan said. "But thanks for coming. Are these paintings cursed?"

"No, but they are what you have been searching for. Now I have a question for you. When do you usually see me?"

"When something has to do with Ryed or Michael or Erebus," Claudius said. Ruth didn't say anything. "So these paintings have something to do with one of those three?"

"Selen was sent to Port Friada because Juleta planned to kill her father and sister and didn't want Selen to know about it. Juleta gave her more errands than just to put that package in a safety deposit box. Selen has been so traumatized by the events that she didn't remember to tell you because the errands seemed insignificant to her. She does not look at the world through the eyes of a warrior."

"Juleta asked her to pick up these paintings which were in a store room. Juleta told her that the paintings had great sentimental value to her. Selen also picked up a book at a book store, which Juleta said she ordered. It looks like an ordinary novel but it was sent to her from Teivel. The book is in code and when you get it call to me and I will help you with it. Do not show Hector these items."

"These paintings are so dark because the paint covers things underneath. Take them to Wetpr and have Annabelle work on them."

"She will remove the paint without harming the items underneath but it will take her time to do so. Send her a message so she expects them. She will need to make arrangements for her children."

"What are they?"

"Call to us when Annabelle is done with them."

"Is there anything else we should look for?" asked Thaos.

"Juleta had many schemes; these are but a few. The woman rarely slept because of her insanity and spent all her hours plotting."

"But I am changing the subject now. While you have been searching this home, Tessa called Adam into Hector's house at the village. Because of their training, Brock and Mallory can see the demons inside of Hector. Demons he did not know existed."

"Wait, how could they do that?" asked Stephan.

"His eyes would change when the demons were looking out. They now realize that he is hanging onto his humanity by a mere thread. He is scared but is not considering changing his life. Adam told them what we have not yet told you. Hector has a role to play in this world and all of you are keeping him alive long enough to do that. But he has so little humanity that he is barely capable of making his own choices. That is why Miranda and Adam told you to remind him that humanity is worth fighting for."

"The monster named Showers is terrified and like Clev he has bonded with all of you and doesn't want to consider you enemies. But they take their orders from their boss although it may not actually be him who is giving them."

"Is he too dangerous to be around our teams and families?" asked Stephan.

"Your presence is helping him and your wives as well as your teams know to call to us. And now Showers does too. One of the demons inside of Hector attacked Adam. Do I need to tell you how powerful a demon must be to do such a thing?"

"I am confused," said Stephan. "You mean there are demons like the ones we can see, inside of him?"

"Yes and his personal demons which now take on personas of their own."

"Well how do we get them out of him?"

"Shara and Angelina have been told and they will perform some of the rites of the old medicines which include us. But ultimately the choice is his."

"You wouldn't be going through all of this trouble if it wasn't important," Stephan said. "What do you want us to do?"

"Thaos that could have been you," Ruth said. "If it was, what would you want done?"

"I would want someone to knock some sense into me."

"And when people tried to how did you react?"

"I struck back."

"When did you stop striking back?"

After a short pause Thaos said, "When I met Claudius."

"Claudius to use a term from your world," Ruth said with a smile. "I believe you just drew the short straw."

He nodded. "Considering that; when do you want us to return home?"

"Catherine will have her celebration tomorrow night. While it may seem silly to you, she brings humanity to those men. The morning after would be fine."

"Who sent those monsters after us yesterday?" asked Thaos.

"They were conjured up by Jack. He is aware of the business dealings that his father had with Juleta and he wants to reclaim all of his family money. He will be in Port Friada soon to meet with Andre's family. Your enemies unit."

"How did he know we were coming here?" Stephan asked.

"Because this is where the businesses are but he doesn't know how to find them either."

"Are they hidden somehow?" asked Claudius.

"You are looking in all of the wrong places. Think about it." Ruth said and disappeared.

Hector had not regained consciousness by time Shara, Hugo and Angelina entered his house. Showers and Dominic's team were in the office. Only Mallory was in the bedroom watching Hector.

"Can we help or watch?" asked Jasmine.

"You may watch," Shara said to the group. "So that you can learn but it is important that in no way do you interfere. Showers do you think that you can do that?"

"Honestly all of this scares the hell out of me. I know you are helping him. I won't do anything."

"At times he will look in distress," said Hugo. "And that is because of the demons. We will tell you if we need you to do anything otherwise just watch."

"He hasn't moved a muscle," Mallory said when the group entered the room. "I heard what you said. Since Brock and I can actually see the demon do you want us to assist?"

"For now, stand near the bed with us," said Shara.

The group stood in silence and watched as the three powerful healers took items out of their pouches and prayed over each of them. Hugo lit a strange smelling candle while Angelina chanted and poured blessed water around Hector's body. The entire time Shara was praying over Hector. When Angelina shook blessed water on his body, Hector began to move and to moan. Now all three healers stood over Hector and prayed. Dominic and the other priests joined them.

Hector started to thrash around. Growls and curses were coming from him but he was not conscious. The bed itself started to shake. The candle blew out and even though it was daytime the room became dark.

"Adam," Tessa whispered. "We might need you."

While the others continued to pray, Shara ordered the demons to release Hector.

Hector started to sweat profusely and yell "No." The floor too was shaking. The priests and healers prayed in a mantra while Shara demanded that the demons leave. Hector started to scream. "Great Ruler we need your presence here!" Shara yelled and a wind filled the room as did the screams and curses from hell.

Everyone in the room suddenly felt strange but they didn't understand why. Hector let out a blood curdling scream and the room became light again. The shaking stopped. Hector quickly sat up. He was gasping for air and looked terrified. "I remember," he said. "I remember."

"Don't move son, let us check you over," said Hugo as Hector continued to catch his breath.

"What the hell happened?" Hector asked as he realized the room was filled with people who were staring at him.

"First, take a moment and pay attention to your body," said Shara. "Then tell us how you feel." These words brought fear to Hector who now quickly looked at himself.

"No, how do you feel?" asked Angelina. "Strong, weak, sick that sort of thing. And take a moment. Don't look at everyone, concentrate on yourself. Close your eyes if you have to."

Hector closed his eyes and got his breathing under control. After a few moments he said, "I feel better, I don't really know how but I do. I feel stronger."

"Hector do you remember what we talked about last night?" asked Mallory.

"You mean the beast in me?"

"Well, they kind of started to take you over. We called to an Angel and one of the demons jumped out of you and attacked him. Shara, Hugo and Angelina just did a ritual to get rid of the demons so don't call them back."

The fear was evident on Hector's face as he looked at the faces in the room. "Showers, you look scared shitless was it that bad?"

"It was boss. And personally I don't ever want to see that again. How the hell did those things get in you? And before you answer that, I know you haven't made your mind up about these folks but you can't believe what they have done to save you." It was the first time that Showers ever spoke to Hector in a scolding tone and Hector realized it.

"I'll get him some food," Jasmine said and left the room.

"The looks on all of your faces are scaring me," Hector said and tried to make it sound like he was kidding.

"It should," said Shara. "You are an expert on demons. Do you know how strong one has to be to attack an Angel and that was just one of them in you. That is part of the reason you haven't been healing. Hector, I assume you are going back to your old life but I will tell you with certainty that if you let them take you over again that you will die."

"What do you mean, let that happen to me?" Hector asked.

"Some of those demons were like the ones we can see and fight," said Dominic. "Adam said the rest were your personal demons that you have fed so much that they have taken on their own personalities in a way and don't ask us to explain that."

"Son, I don't really know you," said Hugo. "But I believe you are at a crossroads in your life. I would suggest that you think seriously about your decisions. Now, when you awoke you repeated that you remembered something, what was that?"

Hector closed his eyes and held his head. "Are you in pain?" asked Shara.

"No dizzy, someone write down what I am going to say," as Hector spoke the others could hear the anger in in voice. Tessa got some paper and a pen. "I woke up because I heard screaming and looked around. I was in a basement or cave or something. Isabella was screaming and running out of the room. Otto yelled to Joanna to get her. I looked around and there were altars, lots of altars and all kinds of people were tied to them. I was tied to one and tried to break free but I couldn't. I saw Clev tied to one and yelled to him but he was unconscious."

Hector paused, "We were young. That bastard sold people who were at his orgies. And knowing him it must have been to the Master. Then it was like I was dreaming. I was in a bed and I heard women's voices arguing. One was Juleta." Hector paused again then opened his eyes and looked at that others.

"There were women in the room wearing priest's robes and they were confronting Juleta. They were all yelling. Juleta was saying that she didn't owe them anything and they could not control her life and they were saying that she was betraying them and denying her destiny. One of them called her a traitor because she was making offerings to the Master." Hector closed his eyes again so he could recall his memories.

"One of the women said that Juleta was working with all the enemies of the Sisterhood and would be punished. And she was screaming at them. Then I must have made noise because they all looked at me. And Juleta told them to leave me alone. Then I don't know what happened and the next thing I remember is waking up as Juleta has me tied to an altar, I must have been drugged because everything was so blurry but I saw Clev shackled to a wall."

"Adam, Adam," yelled Tessa. "Does anyone still own his soul?" She stared at the floor in silence and everyone in the room watched her. "I am not sure I understand." Tessa looked at Hector. "Otto did sell you to the Master who still owns your soul. The Sisterhood was mad at Juleta because she wasn't doing what they wanted her to and they thought that you were a distraction so to please them she sold you and Clev to Ahriman. I think she was trying to save both of you from the Sisterhood."

"The Master got mad at Juleta because she knew he owned your soul so he punished her somehow. But the demons that were inside of you had nothing to do with that. He keeps showing me these really old books, do you know what that means?"

"I think so," said Hector. "The old magics are like life forms. You have to protect yourself when coming into contact with them. That's probably how I got those demons."

Tessa stared at the floor again as she listened to Adam. "He is blocking the Master from seeing or hearing everything and has since you denounced Samael. So that means the Master saw you with us and the Angels. But you still have curses on you and they are from Juleta but the Sisterhood is looking for you too because they think you have something they want. Something of Juleta's."

"So the Master is probably on a rampage and I truly don't know what the Sisterhood is after," Hector said.

"Hector, the Master owned my soul too and I asked Adam to help me and he got it back. It didn't hurt or anything. He must be protecting you from the Master now," said Olin.

"Hector, you should know that Adam told us that you had a role to play in this world, a kind of journey to take and the demons had such a hold on you that you couldn't even make your own choices anymore. Apparently you need to make your own choices for that role," said Dominic.

"Would everyone leave except for Tessa? I don't know if Adam would answer me if I call to him," Hector said.

After everyone left the room Tessa said, "Just say it."

Hector paused for many moments then he said, "Angel Adam will you help me get my soul back and will you save my friend Clev who has followed me into this mess?" After a few moments Hector looked at Tessa, "I don't feel any different. Did anything happen?" She shrugged her shoulders. "Angel Adam will you save me and Clev from the Master?" Still nothing happened.

"He says you know the words," said Tessa.

"I'm getting out of bed for this," Hector said and stood up. "Tessa get behind me, I don't know what to expect." After she moved Hector said loudly, "Master, I denounce you and Clev denounces you. You have no power over us anymore. You have no power here. We have called to the Angels. We denounce you!" Hector collapsed on the floor.

"What the hell!" yelled Stephan as he was riding down a street with Clev, who passed out and fell off his horse.

Chapter XXIV
The Master

"I could use some help!" yelled Tessa.

Noah was the first to burst through the door, "Are you alright?" he asked.

"I am but I don't know about Hector. Adam had him denounce the Master then he passed out," Tessa explained as the men picked Hector up and put him on the bed.

"He's alive," said Shara. "Actually he should be doing better after this."

"I don't know," Tessa said solemnly. "Adam said that he owns his soul but he is still a dangerous person."

Stephan thought that Clev had been attacked and looked around for adversaries before he jumped off his horse. They were on a back street near the docks and people were looking at Stephan but no one came over to help.

Stephan rolled Clev onto his back and checked him for injuries. Adam's voice rang in Stephan's ear, "He will be awake in a moment get him back to the compound. Hector just denounced the Master and earned his soul and Clev's soul. The Master is enraged."

"The teams and everyone are in the city," Stephan said.

"They all have heard what I said although Hector's men have no idea how."

Dagger did not understand that an Angel had spoken to him although he instantly reacted. He almost picked Catherine up and put her in the boca. He yelled to his men and ordered everyone to return to the compound.

Claudius and Thaos were with Edward and Kate when they got the warning.

Angus rode around the city and yelled to the team members but they had already heard Adam's message.

Sorren ran into the house. "Miranda just said to prepare for an attack because the Master is pissed. What the hell happened?"

"Hector got his and Clev's soul back," Dominic said.

"Sorren, where do you want my men?" asked Showers and the two ran out of the house.

"I thought Adam was blocking it so the Master didn't know that Hector was here," Noah said.

"Adam what will we be fighting?" yelled Fennel. Then he ran out of the house yelling "Hutas!"

Clev was barely conscious when Stephan carried him into the mansion and laid him on the sofa in the parlor. Hector's men were running to the walkways on the top of the stone wall that surrounded the mansion. They had their bows as well as other weapons.

Catherine was almost crying when Dagger brought her into the house. They saw Stephan standing over Clev. "Stephan what has happened?" Catherine asked and ran to Clev.

"Well the good news is that Hector just got his soul back and Clev's. The bad news is that the monster who owned them is mad as hell."

"How did we hear that?" asked Dagger.

"The Angel Adam," Stephan said. "Where are the others?"

For two days the soldiers of Lentz and the Nordes Tribe fought Hutas. The City of Cadia had other matters. Huge waves and storms battered the coastal city.

The Master's rage was unrelenting. So focused was he on these areas that he failed to see that a small army of Patronus priests who were escorting three old priests entered the monastery at Malga. Nor did he see the Sanuri and Erebus nearing the castle of the King of Stordt.

"Get back in that damn bed!" yelled Mallory. "I can't fight and babysit you!" She was standing at one of Hector's bedroom windows. She released an arrow, then quickly released two more. Hector opened a chest on the floor of his room and grabbed several knives, a battle axe and a sword. He heard a sound and as he turned he threw a knife that landed in the chest of a Huta who was climbing through the second window of the room.

Hector quickly ran to the Huta soldier and cut his throat then pushed him out of the window. "What the hell is going on?"

"The Master is pissed that you took your soul back," Mallory yelled as she ducked because an arrow flew through the window and impaled the wall. "It's been like this for two days."

"What!" yelled Hector and ran into the parlor where Brock was fighting with a Huta soldier. Hector stabbed the Huta in the back then stabbed another who was coming through the window. He ran back into the bedroom and yelled when he saw Mallory lying on the floor in a pool of blood. He ran to her and cradled her head in his arms.

"Angel! Angel! These people shouldn't die because of me. Help them!"

"I agree," said Adam as he materialized.

"Help them. Save Mallory. Can't you stop this? What are you staring at? Please help her. What do you want from me?"

"Why now?" asked Adam. "For years you have seen the consequences of your actions. The destruction caused by your choices. Is this any different from all the other battles that you have caused?"

"These people are good. They don't deserve this. Why aren't you stopping this? Take me instead of her."

"You almost sound human," Adam said. "Her bleeding has stopped but her wound is serious."

"And the others?"

Hector and Adam heard loud cheers as thousands of Blue Hengers attacked the Huta army. "There is more power when you call to the Heavens than to the demons, you would be wise to remember that. Now give me your left forearm."

Hector wasn't wearing a shirt. He stood up and held his arm out. There were tattoos of a dagger with blood dripping from it and a rose next to it on this arm. Adam touched the rose and it disappeared exposing the sign of the Master. "This is how he has controlled you all of these years."

"Do you need a window?" Hector asked. Adam didn't answer. Hector took one of the knives out of his waistband and plunged it into his own arm at the site of the Master's sign. Adam disappeared. Hector picked Mallory up and laid her on the bed. He tore a pillowcase into strips which he used to bandage her wound as well as his own then he ran into the parlor. Brock had an arrow in his left shoulder.

"Sit down," said Hector and handed Brock a bottle of whiskey. Hector took the table cloth off from the dining room table and tore it into strips. He set the strips on the floor next to Brock's chair then he poured water into a small bowl and set that next to the chair also. "Drink more of that because this is going to hurt like hell."

Adam jumped through the window opened by Hector and Miranda followed him. Demons yelled and growled as they battled the intruders.

The storms in Cadia stopped as suddenly as they had started and at that same moment the Angel Ruth appeared in the parlor of the mansion.

Many of the people in that building were in the parlor at that time. Catherine screamed, Dagger jumped out of his chair and some of Hector's men stood motionless.

"She's an Angel," bellowed Claudius. "Ruth what is happening?"

"Clev come to me," Ruth said. He fearfully walked up to her. "Do you understand that the Master owned your soul and that Hector defied him to get it back?"

"Yes," Clev said in a whisper.

"The Master has branded you so there is still a connection. Hector destroyed that brand to open a window; Adam and Miranda are now in that domain fighting the demons." As Ruth spoke she gently took Clev's left arm and touched a tattoo he had of a sword. The tattoo disappeared and he gasped.

"Get that off from me. Get it off!"

"Clev, you need to understand that normally a person cannot get the soul back of another but Adam permitted it because Hector is the reason yours was taken. But this choice is yours. You have to denounce him."

"I denounce him, I denounce him," Clev said frantically.

"What do you mean that Hector opened a window?" asked Thaos.

"He impaled his knife in the brand and severed the connection. The window was only open for a moment and Adam and Miranda jumped through."

"Do they need some help?" Thaos asked.

"There are just two of them."

"Will you touch everyone with your holiness if they want to help?"

Ruth looked around the room then back at Thaos, "Yes."

"Clev are you going to sever that connection?" Thaos asked.

"Yes," Clev said as he pulled his knife from its sheath.

"Wait until we get everyone here," Thaos said as Stephan quickly left the room. "Dagger when they touch us with holiness we are strong enough to fight the demons and they are the best damn fights. Any of you are welcome to join us."

"Are you really an Angel?" Catherine asked as she walked up to Ruth.

"Yes."

"Will you pray with us?"

"Yes," Ruth said then she turned to Dagger. "I will stay with them."

"Let me get the boys," Dagger said and left the room. Within ten minutes the team members, the soldiers and Dagger's men were in the Great Hall because there wasn't room for them in the parlor.

"Clev do you denounce the Master?" Ruth asked.

"Yes," he said vehemently and thrust his knife into the brand. None of the warriors remembered leaving the mansion. They appeared next to the Angels.

"Where's the Master?" yelled Claudius.

"You aren't strong enough to destroy him," Adam said.

"But I can fight him," Claudius said and jumped up on a rock so he could see over the combatants. "Master get your ass out here and fight!" Stephan laughed loudly when he heard his father.

"Master show yourself!" Stephan yelled. Soon all of the warriors were yelling the same. A mantra that challenged the strongest evil in that world. The Master fled.

Two days earlier, well before Hector opened the window into the Master's domain, Miranda warned Mathas and Fahron that the Hutas would attack the Village of Tyger.

And starting the previous night, Cyril warned the other Nordes Villages of the impending attack on Sorren's Village.

The Huta army did not travel from another location they simply appeared. The Master was powerful enough to support the barbarians. They surrounded the village for miles but the soldiers and the responding Nordes warriors surrounded the hellish army. The Hutas were being attacked from the front and the rear. And Ruala warriors flew over the Hutas attacking them with arrows and explosives.

The Hutas that made it into the village itself went directly to the house that held Hector. The Master wanted to make an example of him. When Dominic's team realized this, they took Olin and Ryan out of that house and hid them. The team members, including Elexas surrounded the house and fought off the attackers. Mallory and Brock stayed inside to protect Hector and to protect others from him if there were still beasts inside of him.

Fortunately for Sorren's village only three or four hundred Hutas made it into the village over the two days. The real battle took place outside of the village.

Mallory did not wake until late that night. Jasmine was sitting next to the bed and immediately called to the others. Dominic, Fennel, Seth, Noah, Lawrence, Tessa, Elexas, Brock, Ryan, Hector and Olin filed into the room. Olin and Ryan were the only two who were not wearing bandages.

"You all look horrible but you're alive," Mallory said with relief as Jasmine helped her to sit up.

"We were really lucky," said Jasmine. "Miranda warned the soldiers and all the other villages and they fought the Hutas too."

"I finally get you in my bed and can't do anything about it," Hector said teasingly as he bent over and kissed Mallory on the forehead.

"Hector called to Adam to save you," Tessa said. "You were losing a lot of blood."

"You called to the Angels?" Mallory asked. "Does that mean you are good now?"

"I doubt it but I really don't know what it means," Hector said. "And when it was all over, Showers chewed my ass and quit."

"Quit? I thought you killed people who quit you," said Mallory.

"No, I pay them so much they don't want to quit but he's not going far," Hector said and grinned. "He asked Sorren if he could become a member of the tribe and Sorren took him in. But I talked him into taking care of the boys until Clev gets back."

"Why did he quit?"

"Everything with the demons but basically he likes all of you a lot better than me and my crew."

"Something isn't right about this," Mallory said. "What is going on here?"

"We've signed a permanent truce with Hector," said Dominic. "The teams, the tribe and Mathas. It doesn't mean that we are always going to be on the same side but we aren't going to try to kill each other."

"I don't believe it," Mallory said and the group laughed. Brock held out his right hand and people handed him money.

"You're a sure bet," Brock said to her and laughed.

"I should move to my room," Mallory said. "And I'm really thirsty."

"You can stay here," said Hector. "I'll sleep in your bed."

"There aren't any more demons in this room are there?" Mallory asked. "I never saw anything like that before. Hector did they tell you about it? The furniture and room were moving."

"We didn't have to," Dominic said. "Showers gave him all the details in living color and told him how he has been putting everyone in danger and that he doesn't appreciate any one."

"Something still doesn't seem right. Am I dreaming?" Mallory asked and everyone laughed.

"What are you talking about?" asked Brock. He was the only one who was not laughing.

"I don't know. I mean part of it is that Hector seems too nice about all of this but there is something else. I'm serious. Brock sit next to me and close your eyes."

"I am going to get her some soup," Tessa said and left the room.

"What are they doing?" asked Olin.

"Venatores are trained to sense things that others can't," Hector said and stopped smiling as he was watching Brock's body language.

"Get her out of this bed!" Brock yelled as he jumped up. Noah quickly grabbed Mallory.

Brock's left arm was in a sling. "Help me," he said and started to tear the blankets off the bed but that did not reveal anything unusual. Dominic and Fennel picked up the mattress.

"Don't touch it!" Hector said loudly.

"What is it?" asked Tessa as she returned to the room with a tray.

"There's a book under his mattress and it's moving," said Elexas.

"Angel!" yelled Hector. "Jasmine look at Mallory's back and see if there are any burns." Noah carried Mallory out of the bedroom and Jasmine followed.

"Interesting," Cyril said as he appeared in the room. "There is still so much darkness in you yet you won't touch that book."

"It has to be old magics or curses but how did it get there and is anyone hurt by it?" asked Hector.

307

"It is old magics. Hector who would benefit if you were filled with demons again?" Cyril asked.

"I have to think because it seems like that would be more of a curse to me then a benefit? Did the Master make it appear?"

Cyril smiled. "He is rather busy right now, running for his life. Your men in Cadia and the teams followed Adam and Miranda through that window you opened. They are fighting in the Master's domain. The humans are ridiculing and taunting him, which is about the worst thing that can happen to a demon; except maybe a visit from Angels."

"My parents," gasped Hector.

"They are more than protected. They asked the Angel who helped Clev to denounce the Master if she would stay and pray with them. It is their prayers that allowed Mallory to sense the evil in that book because it was blocked."

"And because you are free of demons, at least for the moment, your mother's prayers are affecting you. That too, Mallory sensed."

"Why her?" asked Hector.

"She has spent more time with you. She is so used to feeling the beast that she can feel the change of energy. Brock would have realized that too if he wasn't taking pain medication. The book is safe now and it is something you will be interested to read."

Seth picked the book up and opened the cover. "I can read the language. Cyril are you doing that?"

"Yes and I am serious, you should read it soon."

"Hector, I think this is about the Sisterhood," Seth said.

"Will Mallory be alright?" asked Brock.

"Neither of you were harmed by that book. Hector offered to exchange his life for Mallory's so Adam saved her but both of you must heal from your wounds."

"But he didn't take my life," Hector said.

"He didn't want your life, he wanted you to break a hole in that wall of darkness that surrounds you."

"Cyril," Tessa said. "Before you go, are you still working on that corner?" Cyril smiled and nodded. "Would you like something to eat and I will fix food for you to give others."

"You talked me into it," said Cyril.

"That's where I know you from," Olin said.

"Yes and I must say your attitude has greatly improved."

"You're an Angel pretending to be a street person? Why?" asked Olin.

"Why don't you join us in the kitchen," Cyril said and walked out of the room.

"Tessa, Mallory wanted to go back to her room," Noah said. "What did I miss?"

"We've got some reading to do," said Fennel.

"Cyril is it safe for Hector to stay in that room?" asked Dominic.

"It is now," Cyril said as he was looking at the books in the bookshelves. Cyril had his back to Hector. "Hector, say what you are thinking."

"I can't understand why the Angels keep helping me and why others are risking their lives to help me. Then Adam said I had a journey to take. Can you tell me, tell us what is going on?"

"I know the others have explained that we cannot tell you things which will affect your choices so there are some things that I will have the others explain to you after I leave. But I can tell you that life is so very much more complicated than humans realize. You come into these lives with purposes and things to learn but since you have freedom of choice you can change everything. Dominic tell him later what Angelina and Matthew did to save their son from becoming a monster."

"Has he been cursed like that?" Dominic asked.

"No but he has the same potential to affect this world in a good or bad way, which is why so many demons sought to own him. Hector you know how the dark worlds study the prophesies. Your energy was very different once. They could see the power in you. Otto paid Isabella a great deal of money to bring you to him and he scored the favor of the Master. You don't think that the Master gets that angry when he loses just anyone do you?"

"I cannot tell you what your journey is but the time is nearing which is why the Master and others have been throwing so much at you. Your friends here, and they are your friends, have risked their lives to give you the freedom to make choices. Good or bad, you now have the freedom. You, Hector are notorious for making the wrong choices and your friends cannot see the darkness in you that we can. I will tell you that if you continue to make the wrong choices that truce will not last."

"Will his choices affect what we are doing here," asked Lawrence. "I mean how it affects other worlds."

"That is another good story to tell him."

"Cyril, your food is ready," Tessa said and set several platters on the table. Cyril sat down at the table without looking again at Hector.

"So Isabella sold him out," said Jasmine. "I thought she was innocent."

"She spent her life being a traitor to everyone and everything including herself. You will learn more as you do your research."

"And Juleta?" asked Tessa.

"She was born a beast. She initially went after Hector as a power play but by that time the Master owned him and the beast in her was attracted to the beast in him."

"Will Sarah be protected from all of this?" asked Hector.

"That depends on you," Cyril said. "But she did not inherit any curses because of Selen's prayers."

"What aren't you telling me?" asked Hector.

"What I am not telling you could fill volumes."

"What did the Sisterhood create Juleta to do?" asked Ryan.

"Finally, I have been waiting for that question. The Sisters of Tameric believe that Lentz is a kingdom of great powers. She was supposed to take the throne and give it to them. Think of her as a vessel and the Sisters were filling it with all their darkness. The vessel couldn't hold all of that and her mind shattered. She was insane but she was unique. It was like her mind broke into pieces and each piece could separately control her body which is why her behavior was confusing to many. But it also allowed her to do incredible things like formulate multiple complex plans simultaneously."

"She boasted about these plans and she used them as threats and that is what the Sisterhood and others are after. She turned against them with the same passion that she did everyone who was close to her."

"Thank you, Tessa that was a wonderful meal. I will be going now," Cyril said and stood up. Tessa handed him two large baskets filled with food. "I will put this to good use."

"Wait," said Olin. "You didn't tell me what you were going to."

"You know my name," Cyril said and disappeared.

Chapter XXV
Risha

After Cyril left Hector's house, Dominic suggested that it would go faster if they read the book out loud as a group. Tessa and Jasmine brought food and beverages to the table. Although Mallory was very weak, she wanted to hear the readings so Noah brought her into the dining room. Dominic was the first to read. Elexas took notes and Hector had to explain a lot of what Dominic was reading. The text was very old but Cyril had translated it so the group could read it. But even with the translation it was wordy and confusing.

Other than Hector, no one spoke during the first hour that Dominic was reading. "I think we could all use a short break," Dominic said. "Does anyone have questions?"

"I thought that was a book of magics," said Lawrence. "It is more like a history."

"A horrible history," said Tessa. "I can't believe those women were treated like that."

"They thought they were witches," said Fennel. "I am not condoning it but I think the idea of witches brought more fear in those days."

"Most people just don't believe they exist anymore," Hector said. "The irony is that none of those women were witches but after being brutalized they became witches to protect themselves."

"That's what Hilgra did too," said Jasmine. "But that's changing the subject. Why didn't anyone protect those women?"

"I don't have an answer," said Hector. "Actually what I am wondering is who wrote that book. It sounded like a lot of those women were peasants and weren't educated. That style of writing is tedious to read but that was the writing of the wealthy and educated of that time."

"It sounds like they are trying to show off all the words they know instead of getting to the point," Seth said and everyone laughed.

The group only read for two more hours because everyone was exhausted. Most of the team members slept on the floor or doubled up in the beds. Hector gave his bed to Seth and Jasmine and slept on the sofa. Brock felt uneasy about leaving Hector unguarded and decided to sleep in a chair near the sofa. Elexas slept with Mallory and Ryan and Olin slept in Brock's bed.

"What are you doing?" Brock asked as he awoke.

"I can't sleep," said Hector. "Besides I was sleeping for two days. I am going to read; you can have the sofa."

"Hector, I have to ask; what are you going to do now?"

"I need to stay here until Shara and the others find cures for the curses but that is about all I know. I can't begin to explain how I feel. It's kind of like waking up from a dream and looking in the mirror and seeing a different face," he laughed. "Which has actually happened to me. I am always a step ahead of the game and right now I feel like a fish floundering on the shoreline."

"It's your business but after everything we have all been through I hope you don't sell yourself to demons again. Because then a lot of people got hurt for nothing. You can still be a criminal without doing that can't you?" Hector laughed.

It was another day before Claudius and the others returned from the Master's domain. Then it was another three days before Edward got his first shred of interesting information. After the Angel Ruth told Claudius and his sons that everyone was looking in the wrong places, they searched for underground cities like they found in Langer and Castor. The teams found a few tunnels but nothing else.

During his time in Cadia, Edward and been spending a great deal of money and making many inquiries. He was a personable man and Cadia was a rich city.

Edward was being introduced to the rich and powerful and he was being invited to many social functions. He was being offered a variety of investment opportunities but none of them sounded like anything that Otto and Juleta could have been involved with. But the real problem for Edward was that he had no idea of what types of business dealings those two dark lords had in that city.

He and Kate were finishing their dinner in an extravagant restaurant when a woman suddenly sat at their table. She was not dressed in the rich manner of the patrons in the restaurant. In fact, neither Edward nor Kate recognized her manner of clothing.

"You look like a man who would like to have his fortune read," the woman said and both Edward and Kate smiled.

"Be my guest," Edward said. "How much will it cost me?"

"The question should be what will it cost you if you don't," the seriousness of the woman's tone made Kate and Edward wonder if she was a member of the Sisterhood. He took a small pouch of gold coins out of his pocket and placed it on the table.

"Give me your hand," she said and proceeded to stare at the open palm of his left hand. "As you search for your answers, monsters are following you," the woman said without looking at anything besides his hand. "Your friends on the roofs and streets cannot see them because they are blocked but the Shadow Men can. You have a friend among them; can you tell me the name?"

"Risha," Edward said in a low voice. "Is she here? Can we speak with her?"

"That was the right answer," the woman said. "She is with the shadows now so communication is very different for her and that is where I come in."

"Are you a seer?" whispered Kate. The woman nodded.

"Can we talk here?" asked Edward

"No. My home is two miles south of the city. Stay on the main road; you will ride past it. It is a cottage surrounded by vast gardens. After breakfast tomorrow. Tonight return everyone to the compound and tell them what I have said."

"What is your name?" asked Edward. The woman smiled. "Do I know you?" he asked.

"Kate does, you were unconscious when I treated you."

"Are you Risha?" Kate asked in a whisper. "But how can that be?"

"Many things in this world are difficult to explain. Think of me as an extension."

"Are you here because of us?" Edward asked.

"There is more evil here than you realize. Tell Hector's men to stay within the compound tonight also. My people will be patrolling the streets tonight."

That same night in Lentz, Showers went to Hector's house. Although he was still working for Hector temporarily, Showers wasn't staying in the house. Everyone was up and sitting around the dining room table because they were still reading the book of the Sisterhood.

"Sorry to bother you," Showers said. "Looks like you are busy, I can come back."

"Is anything wrong?" asked Hector.

"No, I wanted to talk to Jasmine."

"We can certainly use a break; this book wears on you," Dominic said.

Jasmine stood up from the table and asked, "Can Seth come too?"

"Sure," Showers said with a huge grin. "I just have some questions to ask you. I don't care who hears."

"Then I am joining you," said Tessa. "I just have a feeling about the way you are smiling."

Showers, Tessa, Jasmine and Seth gathered in the parlor. "Jasmine, I met me a gal and I want to do things right so I need you to tell me how your tribe does things," said Showers.

"I knew it," Tessa said and smiled.

"Since I joined your tribe Norge and his misses have been inviting me over for dinner every night and his sister is staying with them. Jasmine, I'm not lying to you none. I can hardly talk around her. She is the prettiest thing and her two little boys are the cutest tykes I've ever seen. I want to get to know her better but I don't want to offend anyone so tell me what I need to do."

Jasmine was smiling. "Ruby is a very sweet person and you know she is a warrior too. Her husband was killed when Usman's men attacked our village so she hasn't been a widow all that long. I wonder if Norge is trying to push you together since he keeps inviting you over."

"Tomorrow go into the city and buy a really good bottle of whiskey. Give it to Norge and at the same time tell him what you told us. And ask him if you can see her. That would be the proper thing to do. Now, expect that he will ask you questions like, would you be good to her and the boys and would you take care of them so think about things like that before you go there. Talk to him alone."

"Then if you really want to score points do the same with Sorren. You know he is Ruby's cousin. We've had a lot of people marry into our tribe but you are the first person that I know of who asked to join us, so do it right. She likes wild irises, so when you plan to see her let me know and I will pick some for you."

"Should I get anyone else gifts?"

"Something nice but simple for the women and boys," Jasmine said.

"I don't know what that means," said Showers. "Will you come with me?"

"Dominic can we go into Langer tomorrow for a while?" Jasmine asked. "I'll pick up some more food while we are there."

"Sure," Dominic said with a grin since everyone sitting at the table could hear what Showers and Jasmine were saying.

"Mind if I ride along?" asked Hector.

"No, but are you up for it?" Showers asked.

"Yeah, I'd like to pick up a few things before my parents get here." Hector said then looked at Mallory. "Do you think you are up for a ride?"

"I think so but why?"

"Hector if she's not, she can borrow some of my clothes," Tessa said.

"No, I will buy her something and she's not the only one I need to buy for."

"If you are talking about me, will you tell me?" asked Mallory with confusion.

Hector smiled at her. "When my parents get here Rosa is going to have some functions and I would like you to go as my date."

Mallory looked so shocked that everyone started laughing. "I don't think it is even allowed," she said.

"You can go with him if you want," Dominic said. "We don't have any rules like that."

"Well, what do you mean by date?" Mallory asked Hector which made everyone grin.

"You know what a date is don't you?"

"I do but I don't know if you have the same meaning."

"Boy, you don't trust me at all do you? Just go with me to the functions."

Mallory looked at Brock who said, "Don't look at me for permission; go with him. What do you think is going to happen?"

317

"I don't know," she said. "I just feel strange because I have been guarding him and he has been the enemy and now to go out on a date."

"Well, if it makes you feel better pretend you are still guarding him," Fennel said and laughed.

"Hector, I hope you aren't doing this to try and make Madeline jealous because I don't want to be put in that position."

"I'm not but what would she be jealous of? She never had any feelings for me."

"Alright," Mallory said. "But it still feels strange."

Early the following morning all of Dominic's team escorted Hector and Showers into Langer. Dominic wasn't sure how much danger Hector was still in but he didn't want just a few team members to get ambushed on a shopping trip. Seth and Jasmine were driving a small boca while everyone else rode their horses.

No sooner had they left the village than Mallory asked, "Showers, so what does Hector do with all of his girl friends?" The group roared with laughter.

"I am not answering any questions. But I can tell you that I've never heard of him killing one," Showers said with a grin.

"Listen to you," Hector said. "Are you afraid of me?"

"No, this entire idea just feels awkward," Mallory said.

"He's just putting on a show for his parents," said Lawrence. "Do you think he would ask you out in front of us if he was going to hurt you?"

"I'm not afraid of getting hurt, I just feel strange about all of this," she said defensively then turned to Hector. "Really, is that what you are doing?"

"That certainly is part of it. But I like your company. I am just asking you to go with me, not to get married or something."

"It's not any of the things all of you are saying. I don't know why I feel so strange."

"It could be because you two are from incredibly different worlds and you don't know if he is a monster," said Noah.

"Actually that might be it," said Mallory. "Hector, I heard that your parents are really nice people. How did they get a son like you?"

Everyone laughed loudly. "Boy, you are really mean today," Brock said.

"I didn't mean it to sound like that. Sorry. I should have said how do they feel about all of this? I am asking because if I am your date are there things we can't talk about?"

"Yes and you will understand when you meet Mother," Hector said. "She kind of becomes everyone's mother and I am their only child. I was studying to become a priest and became a criminal instead. They are scared and confused by just about everything these days. They deserve a better son than me. Just follow my lead."

"Mallory, I know you only view yourself as a warrior," said Fennel. "But you are a really nice girl. Which is probably what his parents need to see since they are meeting the child he had with a monster."

"I didn't think about any of that," said Mallory. "It makes sense. Now I feel better about all of this."

"You don't have to act like you care about me, just be nice to my parents," Hector said then grinned. "Of course if we have sex that is just the icing on the cake." Everyone laughed again and Mallory blushed. "Brock has she had many boyfriends?"

"I am not getting involved with any of this," Brock said and laughed too. "But actually I can see both sides of this and I would have reservations if I was her too. Hector, you have been filled with demons and we are demon hunters. What if she really starts to like you then you call to demons again. You may put her in a position where she has to kill you or go against everything she is."

319

"Guess, I hadn't thought about that," Hector said solemnly.

Angus, Claudius, Thaos and Stephan rode with Edward and Kate to Risha's house early that morning. The Ruala warriors from both teams watched over the riders. It did not take them long to find the cottage she described.

"Is this real or an illusion?" asked Kate. "It is so beautiful here."

A picket fence surrounded the cottage and gardens. Herb gardens, flower gardens and a huge vegetable garden surrounded the home. A barn, a smoke house and a chicken coup were built in the rear of the cottage. There were numerous bird houses on the property and butterflies flew everywhere.

The group dismounted and walked towards the cottage but Kate stopped and surveyed the property. "Do you sense something?" Edward asked.

"Edward, we have never talked about anything really with our future. But if we were to ever have a home this is what I would want but with more animals and a couple of dogs and cats."

"Really," he said and now he looked around the property. "We work so many missions that we would have to hire men to care for the property but that is not a problem."

"But once we start having a family I will be home more at least when they are little," Kate said. "I love this place."

"It is pretty," Stephan said and looked at Thaos. "If they had a choice I'll bet our wives would prefer some place like this too."

"Edward what do you think? Well, we can talk about it later," said Kate.

"Honey, if this is what you want, this is what we will get. We can start looking for land as soon as we return to Wetpr."

"You won't mind being a farmer?" Thaos asked Edward.

"I was raised on a farm but it never looked this nice. Kate did I tell you that when I first went to work for Sudfad he offered me land but I preferred living in the castle at that time. I will write to him and tell him what we are looking for."

Kate ran up to Edward and kissed him while the other men smiled. When they turned back towards the cottage they saw the woman standing in the doorway smiling.

"I told Edward that I want to live in a place just like this," Kate said excitedly. "Is this real or an illusion?"

The woman laughed. "Please come in."

"Edward, she has a cat," Kate said excitedly and everyone laughed.

"Risha, I haven't seen Kate this happy in a long time," Edward said. "Wait, should I call you Risha? I really don't understand all of that."

"Come into the dining room and I will explain," the woman said and led them through the kitchen.

"Boy, something smells good," Thaos said.

The dining room table was set and had platters of freshly baked muffins, a pie, a pot of coffee and a pitcher of milk. "Risha, this is just the opposite of what your life was like in that cave isn't it?" asked Kate.

"Yes. I believe all of us have met before and I can tell how curious you are." The group sat down and Risha walked around the table pouring coffee as she spoke. "Edward, I am sure that the other's told you about me but everyone was so traumatized at the time that I will repeat my story because it will help you to understand."

"Hundreds of thousands of years ago, I was a healer who married a Venator and became a member of the Clan of Gesmal. We were only married for two years when word came to us of an evil so great that the demons were terrified and worshiped the monster."

"It was the Originator. He had opened a doorway in the lands near Marba. Our tribe traveled that great distance on foot."

"As today the Venatores are fearless but when we came to the opening of that cave everyone was struck with fear for the evil was inconceivable. The small army of Venatores were actually motionless. We all knew we would die. I was not a warrior as the others and my fear was great."

"Benza was our leader. He called to The Great Ruler. He did not ask to be spared or to be saved. With his courage, he asked that his people be allowed to continue their covenant with The Great Ruler even after death."

"I stood with my husband Sargei and we too said the same prayer as did all of the others. Then they ran into that doorway. The screams; never will I forget those screams for I have never heard anything like that in all my days. I turned and ran and I kept running until I came to the Safer Mountains. I too died that day but my body was not allowed to take rest because of my treason."

"I could no longer heal others because I was not healed myself, so I became a maker of potions. I rarely left the cave because it was a prison that I imposed upon myself. But Sargei would visit me often as would the others. At first I did not understand what they were and I thought I was being haunted for being a coward and a traitor. But my curse was that I could not die."

"I lived in a prison but I am not an ignorant woman. My prices were high and only the rich and powerful could afford me, which is against the creed that a healer takes. But most of the time I charged not money but information, scrolls and manuscripts. I have read the prophesies and when Sargei told me that some of my potions had been used to attack The Seven Sons I wept. Once again I was a traitor. My guilt had been so strong that I stopped calling to The Great Ruler but after I heard that, I had to atone for my deeds."

"I called to The Great Ruler and the Angel Ruth came to me. We talked for a very long time. She told me many things including the story of a small group of people who had the courage and faith to stand up to the demons, like the Shadow Men."

"After the attack on you, Prince Michael and Javier, I had a great increase in orders and I realized the dark worlds were going to attack everyone who they believed were The Seven Sons."

"I gave Ruth my fortune to help others. I set traps for the monsters who ordered my potions and I asked Ruth to take me to Lentz. I was there but a moment before I was pulled away from the casket and met your people. The Angel Adam came to me there. I had met him earlier. I heard about Samael and the worlds he tortured. I had to see for myself and I wept."

"You need to understand all of this to understand why I am before you. When I finally prayed to The Great Ruler after I heard about the attacks, I not only asked for forgiveness and the opportunity to live up to the covenant that I had once made with Him. But I asked to be able to make up for the darkness I had brought to the world. So here I am. I am still not sure what you would call me. I am more Shadow Man than ghost but yet too I am a person."

"Like all of you, I am sent to many places. There is an advantage to being as old as time and that is that you see and learn a great deal. And I promised Adam that I would do more if he would destroy Samael, which he has done."

Edward reached across the table and touched Risha's hand. "You feel real."

"I am. And Kate to answer the question you haven't asked; yes other Venatores become Shadow Men. It is a choice given at death."

"That is exciting," Kate said. "I need to tell the others."

"Risha, we were told that the Shadow Men traveled to Port Friada on ships is that true?" asked Claudius.

"No, the Shadow Men appeared because of the evil on those ships. But first I have a question for you. Why do you stay at the compound of Hector?"

"We came to save his parents. It turns out that we knew Hector before Juleta changed his appearance. But Adam and Miranda helped us to save him because a powerful demon was going to take over his body. He was dying because of all of the curses that Juleta set upon him."

"And his parents are at that compound?" Risha asked.

"Yes and they are innocents in all of this. And Hector is being protected by our teams as he heals," said Claudius.

"Let me tell you a little about him. But first I need to explain that everyone in the dark worlds is obsessed with power. They want to know who has it, how they get it and how they can keep it."

"Our friend Erebus told us those exact words," said Stephan.

"He is in a great deal of danger but I will get back to him. When humans are born into this world they have different levels of power even as infants. Most of you gain your power as you grow by the choices that you make. The demons in particular look for this because they believe that is how they will identify The Seven Sons and others of prophesies."

"Ruth now visits me often and I asked her about this. She told me that The Great Ruler has masked the power of The Seven Sons to protect them. Yes, I do know who they are and even without being the sons of prophesy they are incredibly powerful men; as are all of you which is why many eyes are watching you."

"But there are some who are born with such power that the worlds take notice. Jacob, the adopted son of Matthew and Angelina is one, as is a child that lives among your friends. His name is Christopher and I am told that he is part of your family too."

"He and my daughter have crushes on each other," said Thaos.

"You are all powerful men, guide him for your children will continue this fight after you are gone," Risha said.

"Well that is damn depressing," said Stephan.

"But there are others and isn't it strange how they are finding all of you," Risha continued. "Your new son Cassidy, Javier and Madeline. She is the only woman who I know of that was not an abomination like Juleta who was born with this power. And Hector was also. No one protected him. He was not born into a family of warriors nor did warriors adopt him. His parents are good and faithful people but they did not understand the things they saw and felt."

"He is an intelligent man but he had no idea of the worlds he now dwells in. He was courted and seduced by the demons and he loved every moment of it. Ruth told me that all of you are trying to help him fight for humanity. Let me explain what you are up against. Angus, I see one crumb on your plate. That is his humanity. Now compare that to this platter of muffins."

"If you are fighting for him do not expect to win that battle but don't give up because every crumb that ends up on that plate matters. It all makes a difference. Do not let the others be taken like he was."

"Are the people you named the only ones in this world who were born like that?" asked Claudius.

"Of course not. And I expect that others will find their ways to you but the demons can see this. They see these unusual power sources coming to you. Which makes them fear you even more. You should tell Javier and Madeline what I said because it will help them to understand many things. King Sudfad was wise to bring them into his family."

"Risha, the demons must be shitting their pants to know that Hector is with us," said Angus. "Are all our people in danger?"

"I believe that the Angels are blocking a great deal," said Risha. "So you now understand why Michael and Javier were attacked. But what about you Edward? Have you figured it out?"

"No," said Kate adamantly. "We thought he was attacked by mistake as a way to draw Erebus out."

"The demon Tobankto was aligned with Samael. He is the one who blew up that tavern and tried to take Erebus and Matthew and the others to his hell world. What a prize that would have been but he did not order the attacks on Javier and Edward. Ruth told me that Tobankto was aware of the bounties and just happened to be in the right place at the right time."

"Edward and Kate I want you to listen carefully because I hope that this helps you to heal. Kate had already given you of herself and lost your child in doing so, when I was taken to you. You had not improved the way you should have after such a sacrifice. I gave you potions and Shara, Angelina and I examined your body. You have many tattoos and I saw that the colors of one were very different from the rest. It was the one on the back of your right arm. When I examined it I found and Ipac seed. They are not found in this world so I took it."

"Ruth explained to me that the woman who shares Sorphat's bed was obsessed with you. Sorphat worked for Samael but Toni was listening to demons many, many years before she became his. Chaladrone is one of the Old Ones who came to this world with the first group of thirteen demons. He is very old and very powerful but he is considerably more in the shadows than his peers."

"Chaladrone spoke with Juleta, Toni and Fahron's son Timothy and he is one of the demons who the Sisters of Tameric are devoted to. You were attacked because Toni had a bounty on you. But she was already killing you with the Ipac seed which is very toxic. Kate, your baby never would have lived because of that. It was not the procedure that killed your baby it was that seed. It is found only in the World of Filsum."

"I am going to kill her!" Kate yelled.

"She is living a fate much worse than death, take solace in that. The Sisterhood was behind the attacks on Edward and Javier because it was believed that these men wronged women of that organization," explained Risha.

"Did Isabella put the bounty on Javier?" asked Kate. "Because Corsa thought she would."

"Yes, but I am not done. The web is still spun. Radnor put the bounty on Michael. The Warlord Zourlock had two separate bounties in the same area and thought he would use the same group of assassins to fulfill both. The Sisterhood asked Chaladrone to block the sight of the assassins because they wanted it to appear that the bounty was paid for by someone in Ryed; because powers in Ryed are trying to trick Erebus into going there."

"Oh my god, the Sisterhood is here? Will they put another bounty on Edward?" asked Kate.

"I would expect as much but there is no one to pay for a second attack," said Risha. "And they are after Hector because they believe he has things that belong to them."

"And Javier and Madeline are coming here," said Stephan.

"Let me see if I understand what you aren't saying," Claudius said. "We know that the Master and the Sisterhood are going to war. So they want us for revenge but also we are powerful and perhaps have powerful things which they need?"

"You are very good," Risha said. "And although Hector is free of the Master there is now no one to protect him from the Sisterhood in this realm."

"The Angels are protecting him for now," said Claudius. "They are practically pushing us to work together."

"Interesting," said Risha.

"What was the evil that you were talking about last night?" asked Edward.

"That too is associated with the Sisterhood. The Warlock Zane was extremely close to Juleta. It is my belief that he loved her. He is very powerful and his specialty is blocking things from sight. He is working with the Sisterhood. Those demons exist no more. The Shadow Men destroyed them all last night. They were looking for Hector."

327

Chapter XXVI
Spies and Conspiracies

As soon as the group with Showers entered the City of Langer Hector said, "Rosa sent me a letter telling me the plans she has for my parents. There will be at least one garden party because my mother loves them. There will be at least two small dinner parties and a ball. All of you are invited and since you never let me pay you for anything, I will buy your clothing. I don't want anyone not coming because you don't have the clothes. I am taking Mallory to Ashley's shop first. Anyone who wants clothes from there please join us."

"Are you serious?" Elexas asked excitedly.

"Yes and get as many outfits as you want. I need to get things for Shara, Angelina and Hilgra too so I hope you will help me." The men smiled at the excitement of the women.

"Are Brock and I the only two who have never been to a garden party?" Mallory asked.

"I will help you pick out your outfits," Hector said to her. "And that offer is for all of you."

"We have some nice things," Dominic said. "Because we go in disguise but Brock doesn't."

"Oh come in and shop," Tessa said. "This will be fun."

Moments later they were dismounting in front of Ashley's store. Hector tried to help Mallory off her horse but she gave him such a disapproving look that he laughed.

"Everyone wait up," Hector said as he unfastened one of his saddlebags. He took a large pouch of gold coins out and tossed it to Dominic. "You can be in charge of the money for the men. That does not include the clothing. But if you find something Sorren would like will you buy it, since I don't have any ideas."

"Are you sure?" Fennel asked.

"How many times have you risked your lives for me besides babysitting? If you don't spend it all just divide it up. Who wants to be in charge of the money for the women?" Hector asked as he took another pouch out of his saddlebags.

"I will," said Tessa and caught the pouch that he tossed to her.

"Showers this is a wedding gift," Hector said and tossed him a pouch.

"Thanks boss, but I don't know if she will marry me."

"You're thinking about it," Jasmine said with a huge smile. "Showers come in here and we can find some things."

As soon as the group entered the shop, Nikki, Ingr and Ashley walked up to them. Hector handed his saddlebags to Ashley. "These are full of money. All these people need outfits for all of the celebrations Rosa is having for my parents. Fix them up with whatever they want and that includes Ingr and Nikki since they took care of me too."

"Well, that is very generous of you Hector. Let me take all of you back to one of our private rooms," Ashley said.

"Hector since you are paying you have to help us decide," Elexas said. She was very excited.

"Is there any chance that you know what sizes Shara, Angelina and Hilgra wear because I owe them too," Hector asked Ashley.

"We do," said Ingr. "Thanks Hector. And you are looking a lot better."

After an hour the men in the group had purchased their items and left the shop. They were supposed to regroup at the White Rose Restaurant for lunch. Jasmine left when the men did so she could help Showers buy some gifts. She planned to return to Ashley's.

Hector was sitting in an elegant room. Tables of refreshments and luxurious furniture sat on top of thick richly designed rugs.

To one side of the room were changing areas that were separated by thick long drapes.

The women were trying on different outfits and walking out of the changing rooms so that Ashley and Hector could see them. He had initially explained to Ashley that Mallory would be spending more time with his parents than the other women and he preferred she didn't wear her warrior's outfit. Mallory felt self -conscious and awkward, which was evident to the group. The other women tried to get her to relax and enjoy the excursion.

"Hector what color does Clev like?" asked Elexas as she held an armful of dresses.

"Blue," Hector said and laughed.

Mallory walked out of the changing room in a light yellow gown and Ashley laughed when she saw the look on Hector's face. Mallory blushed. "You're embarrassing me," she said to Hector.

"Then you are going to be embarrassed a lot because you look beautiful." Nikki brought another armful of dresses into the private room and all of the women came out of the changing rooms to look at the clothing. At the same time Jasmine walked into the room and motioned for everyone to gather around the chair that Hector was sitting in.

"Don't turn now but has anyone noticed those two women who have been staring at Hector?" asked Jasmine.

"They haven't been looking at clothing," Ashley said. "And they carry themselves like warriors."

"I saw them too," said Ingr. "They aren't from our tribe."

"Hector, do you know who they are?" Tessa asked.

"I saw them. If I had to guess I would say the Sisterhood. They probably won't start anything."

"Well, wouldn't we like to know what they are up to?" asked Ingr. Then paused for a moment. "Mallory kiss Hector. If they are just admiring him we should be able to tell. If they are in the Sisterhood, we need to have a few words with them."

"Kiss him?" Mallory repeated as if she was confused by Ingr's words.

"It's obvious he likes you," Nikki said. "And the rest of us are married. We will move a little so they have a good view and we will watch them." Mallory didn't move. "Just do it!"

"You really are afraid of me," Hector taunted.

"No, I'm not," Mallory said.

"Then sit on my lap and kiss me."

Mallory gave Hector a defiant look. She sat on his lap and said dramatically, "Honey, thank you for all these wonderful gifts." As she spoke, she put her arms around his neck and kissed him. Hector put his arms around her and pulled her tightly against him. He kissed her passionately and the kiss lasted and lasted and lasted. When the embrace ended Mallory stared at him as a variety of emotions surged through her.

"Holy smoke," said Tessa. "I got hot just watching that."

"I almost left," said Nikki.

"But they didn't," Ingr said. "Hector, you are the one they are watching. Distract them for a few moments."

"Get up dear," Hector said to Mallory, who got off from his lap. He stood up and picked her up and walked towards the changing room. Mallory squealed. Nikki, Ingr, Tessa, Jasmine and Elexas walked towards the changing rooms then turned and walked around the curtains towards the front of the store. The two women walked into the private room when they lost sight of Hector. They were immediately surrounded by the female team members.

Ingr and Nikki were pressing knives into the backs of the women. "What's so interesting?" asked Ingr.

Jasmine and Tessa searched the women and took a knife off each of them. "Are you from the Sisterhood?" Tessa asked.

The women did not answer but the shocked looks on their faces confirmed to the others that they were members of that organization.

Hector and Mallory walked up to the group as Nikki was talking. "We know that Juleta turned against you and that you are looking for something of hers. But why are you watching Selen? She doesn't have any of Juleta's things and what do you want with Hector?"

The women did not answer but stared defiantly at the group. "Ashley, will you get some of the Nordes warriors from the arts room," Inger asked.

"We have ways to make you talk," Jasmine said to the women.

Hector had been staring at the two young women. He grabbed one of them and pulled her towards him. He stared into her eyes. The woman tried to fight him but he held her tight. "These women work for the Sisters but they aren't true members," Hector announced. "The true members have a small blue mark inserted into each eye; it looks similar to a lightning bolt. This one doesn't have it." Hector now grabbed the second woman and stared into her eyes.

Six Nordes warriors entered the room. "We need to tie these women up," said Ingr. "And get Dominic and the others."

"We will let you go if you just tell us what you want with us," said Tessa. The women didn't speak but stared angrily at her.

One woman had long black hair and the other long blonde hair. Elexas kept staring at both of them. "I am positive that I've seen these two at Otto's parties and that one with the dark hair has talked to Olin," Elexas said. "We need to get Abbott here. He will recognize them."

It wasn't long before Dominic and the others walked into the shop. The women had their wrists and legs tied and gags in their mouths. They were put into the small boca which was in the alley behind Ashley's shop. The entire group left the city to escort the women to the dungeons at Fort Langer.

Fennel had called to a flock of Enrops to escort them in case they were attacked by the Sisterhood. Dominic had previously sent Enrops to find Turner and tell him to bring some vials of the truth potion to the dungeons.

Olin and Ryan were working in the office in Mathas' castle when Elexas and Bart found them. "We need you to come with us," Elexas said. "We caught two women from the Sisterhood; they were following Hector. Olin, I have seen them at Otto's parties and I have seen you talking to at least one of them."

The women were being interrogated in separate cells. Dominic was leading one interrogation and Fennel the other. Turner's team and Abbott's team were divided between the two cells so they could observe the use of the truth potion.

Tessa was taking notes in Dominic's interrogation and Jasmine was taking notes in Fennel's. Hector walked back and forth between the two cells to listen to the information. The interrogations were well underway when Ryan, Olin, Elexas and Bart entered the dungeons.

Olin confirmed that he had seen both women at Otto's parties and long before Otto had sacrificed any of the members of the Sisterhood. Abbott too recognized the women and wondered why the Sisterhood was spying on Otto.

The interrogations lasted for hours. Mathas, Sorren, Gideon, Fahron and Matthew were in a meeting when they received word of the interrogations. This group went to the dungeons to observe the procedures. When they walked in, Noah motioned for them to go back into the hallway where he met them.

"These two women were spying on Hector and the girls caught them. They are foot soldiers for the Sisterhood. Apparently there is a lot involved to become a full member of that organization. Hector said the foot soldiers would not be told vital information."

"But so far we know that a war has been brewing between the Sisterhood and the Master for some time; neither were loyal to Samael but they used his antics, like the Gefrey Games, as diversions."

"They called Otto a child of the Master which makes us believe that Otto held more power than we originally thought. These gals say that the Master hates women and was responsible for atrocities committed against their members. And besides that, he has been sabotaging many of their plans."

"These women really don't know a lot of details but they know that the Sisterhood has established itself in most of the continents. The groups always settle in places where there is power; they are talking about some kind of energy. Apparently Lenz is considered very powerful and it is the kingdom where the Sisterhood came into existence so it is important to them."

"But the Master and others are interested in this kingdom because of its power too. We are confused by this but these two can't really explain it. As women work their way up the ladder in that organization they tattoo themselves. They somehow have small blue tattoos put in their eyes that look like lightning bolts. And they tattoo their arms with a series of symbols that denote their status and jobs. The foot soldiers aren't tattooed which is why they are sent into places like Otto's parties to spy."

"These two don't know anything about the prophesies of The Seven Sons. But there are prophesies that directly concern the Sisterhood. Tessa has them written down. They said there was a prophesy that told of a vessel that would bring the Sisters of Tameric to their true power and help them to avenge the wrongs done to them. Juleta was believed to be this vessel." Mathas shook his head with both sadness and disgust as he listened to Noah's briefing.

"Juleta had been given assignments to obtain things which she never turned over to the organization and they want these things before they go to war with the Master. Now, these two don't know specifically what these items are but they and others have been ordered to watch Selen, Hector, Stephan and Thaos."

"They can't get close to Selen because the Angels have surrounded all of the places she works and her home with holy energy. They have spies watching Hector's compound in Cadia and our teams there. Something happened last night and the leaders of this group said they felt a significant loss of energy in Cadia and they don't understand why."

"And apparently the Angels have been blocking Hector. These two just happened to see him and started to follow him. They didn't have time to send messages to their group."

"I'm confused," said Sorren. "Are you saying that Hector was in the city?"

"He was buying the team members and your family gifts for taking care of him and he is buying everyone clothes to wear at the celebrations that Rosa is planning for his parents. We were all surprised at how concerned he is with everything with his family. He asked Mallory to be his escort and to spend time with his parents. She's feeling uncomfortable but agreed to do it."

"This morning we were talking about his parents and he has a lot of guilt. It is a weakness as is Sarah. But I've got to tell you that he has been really decent since we got those demons out of him. But we know we can't let our guards down. What do you want us to do with the women?"

"I'll decide that after the interrogations are completed," said Mathas. "I am considering ransoming them back for information. Have they told us how they communicate?"

"Ravens."

"Well, we can't use them. Ask them how we would communicate with their leaders?"

Almost three hours later the interrogations ended. Everyone who had been conducting and observing them went to the Great Hall of Mathas' castle. That group included Hector and Showers.

Dominic and Turner went to the King's study while their teams sat in the Great Hall. Matthew, Sorren, Fahron and Gideon were with Mathas as they were all waiting for the interrogations to end.

"We have Hector and Showers with us," Dominic said. "Mathas, we couldn't very well leave them some place and besides they are useful in this."

"I know," Mathas said to Dominic then he turned to Matthew. "Tell your mother to bring Sarah here."

Ten minutes later all of the men who were in Mathas' study entered the Great Hall as staff were serving refreshments to the team members. A few moments later Rosa walked into the room holding Sarah. She stood in the doorway looking for Hector in the crowd. He stood up and she brought Sarah to him. "Hold your daughter," Rosa said and walked away.

This was the first time the team members had seen Hector with Sarah and they all smiled. The viciousness in him melted away when he saw his child. Showers too grinned at his boss.

Since Dominic and Fennel had led the interrogations they were standing in the front of the room briefing the ruling members.

"Noah told us that he told you some of the information," said Dominic. "As he told you, the two women we have are at the bottom of the totem pole. They didn't know much about Juleta, nothing about Isabella and little about Hector other than they were supposed to watch him and Selen. If they saw these two people or Stephan and Thaos do anything they considered suspicious they were supposed to contact the main group."

"But they know that Olin had somehow gone against Otto. They know about the bounties on Olin but as far as they are concerned he did them a favor. They also know that the Master is supporting Jack and has given him a great deal more powers than he had before. And they know that Jack has a new appearance."

"They said that Jack is traveling to Port Friada with a dozen men to meet with his brother-in-law's family. His brother-in-law was Andre Wilchess. Andre's father Chet and his older brother Philip are both powerful dark lords. His mother Darlene is a socialite who turns her head to these matters as long as Chet keeps giving her money."

"Olin also knew this information but nothing more. He said that the Wilchess family did not speak with his so he was surprised when Otto arranged a marriage between Joanna and Andre. Hector do you want to come up here?" Dominic asked.

Hector walked to the front of the room still holding Sarah. "Chet is a member of the Insidiae and gives a new meaning to paranoia," Hector explained. "In fact, his paranoia is so extreme that many consider him insane. And that worries some, and I am referring to other members of the Insidiae because he builds war ships and weapons. And he grows a lot of food that is sold all over. I have heard people say that if anyone is going to try and end the world it will be Chet."

"Apparently you already know about his businesses so I won't go into that. His wife is with him only for the money. She is out on the town every single night and is a big flirt but men are afraid to take her up on her offers because of Chet's reputation. If you have ever met Chet it is amazing that he hasn't killed the woman."

"Chet was always complaining to the Insidiae about Dieter because he thought that Dieter brought too much attention to the group. When a dark lord name Cisero set Dieter up a lot of the Insidiae thought it was Chet. While dark lords do this to each other all of the time, Cisero petitioned the Grand Masters to take Dieter's powers then sent an army of Rogetts against him."

"What Cisero did was unheard of and enraged a lot of the members who initially thought it was done by Chet. They chastised Chet which made him go deeper into the shadows. It is said that the oldest son Philp actually runs the businesses and keeps his father in line. There are a lot of members of the Insidiae who are afraid of Chet because of his extreme paranoia."

"Did you ever do business with him?" asked Mathas.

"Nope. He hated Juleta too and you know she was involved with Dieter so I was considered part of that group. Now, the really curious thing about all of this is Chet and Otto were practically enemies for a long time and I have never heard of Jack or Joanna socializing with that family. So what kind of arrangement did Chet and Otto make that they forced their children to marry to seal the deal? Joanna and Andre were powerful dark lords in their own rights and that is unheard of."

Chapter XXVII
Revelations

Although Risha gave Edward and the others a great deal of information, she could not tell them anything about the businesses of Juleta and Otto. But she did tell them to consider that the businesses might not be in Cadia.

When this group returned to the compound they briefed Clev and Dagger on their meeting although they would not tell the men the location of Risha's home. Claudius and Edward wrote letters to Mathas, Sudfad and Gabriel about their meeting with Risha. Then Claudius announced that the group escorting Hector's parents would leave the following morning.

By sunrise of the next day Claudius was leading the caravan to Lentz. They would be traveling considerably slower than the trip to Cadia because of the bocas and carriage. Catherine and Clarence were overwhelmed with excitement. They dearly wanted to return to the city they considered their home and they wanted to see their son and meet their granddaughter.

Claudius divided the group of soldiers who originally traveled to Cadia with him into two groups. One group remained in Cadia with the teams and the second were escorting Hector's parents to Langer.

Claudius felt uneasy about leaving the teams in Cadia although he knew they would work well with Hector's men. Risha's warning about there being much more evil in that city than any of them realized haunted Claudius. He was considering returning to Cadia.

Matthew, Gideon and Admiral Moraine made several trips to the City of Castor in preparation for the naval yard that was to be built there. The three men met with local business owners as well as the military commanders and citizens about the pending projects.

The business owners were more than enthusiastic about everything they were told. They could clearly understand how the naval yard would increase their business. The military commanders were more skeptical but they were relieved to learn that Admiral Moraine would be handling many responsibilities that they thought would fall to them.

Because the projects of building naval yards were so extensive, the naval yard at Silth would not be started until the ones in Langer and Castor were already underway. Part of the reason for this decision was determined by staffing. Another part was that this was the first time any of these men were building naval yards and they wanted to learn from their mistakes; so all three of the newly promoted admirals were working closely together.

The two women prisoners of the Sisterhood were kept in the dungeons because the ruling members hadn't decided what to do with them. Dominic's team members and Hector were still reading the book of the history of the Sisterhood and would periodically return to ask the prisoners new questions. These women were getting so ill from the truth potion that they decided to tell their captors the truth so they wouldn't be forced to take the potion. But this decision did not offer any great breakthrough of information.

The teams did learn that there were about twenty-five foot soldiers of the Sisterhood in the City of Langer. Being a foot soldier was the lowest level of that organization and all of the women had to earn their way to better positions. Unlike the true members of that organization, the foot soldiers did not have any identifying marks or tattoos. In fact, these women did not know how to identify each other. They worked in pairs and were only given the information for their specific assignments.

Gideon was anxious to get the new admirals set up in their projects. He was not happy that circumstances seemed to be delaying his marriage plans. Hector's involvement with the teams was so significant that Gideon had postponed his formal proposal to Ashley.

Now as he and Matthew rode back to Langer from Castor, Gideon could not stop talking about it.

"I've reserved one of the special dining rooms on the roof of the White Rose Restaurant for next week. I am going to propose there. The restaurant hired some musicians for me and the room will be filled with flowers." Matthew smiled at Gideon's excitement.

"Then I rented the best rooms at the Admiral's Gate Hotel. We will stay there for a few days and if there aren't any emergencies, we might stay a little longer," Gideon said.

"You have done nothing but work night and day since you came here," Matthew said. "Unless we are attacked, I will handle anything that comes up and if I need help I will go to one of the new admirals. Take some time off and enjoy yourselves."

"Thanks Matthew; I appreciate that."

"How do the boys feel about all of this?"

"They are really excited. Of course all those kids are going to be in the wedding. And it helps that we are still living at Claudius' castle because the kids are so at home there, it won't bother them that we are gone a few nights. In fact, Ashley and I are starting to worry about how they are going to take it when we move into our place."

"They're still going to training and school together so it shouldn't be that much of a transition for them."

"I hope not. It's so strange. Ashley and I rushed into things because of the circumstances we were in, in Port Friada. Then we barely knew each other and we adopt the boys. You would think all of that would be a recipe for disaster but it is really working." Matthew looked at his friend and smiled.

Mallory and Brock were still staying at Hector's house. He needed less care on their parts which was good since they were both healing from wounds.

Dominic had suggested that they move back to the team's house but neither of these Venatores believed that Hector was truly free of his demons.

Dominic and the core members of his team continued to go to Hector's house every day to work. Turner was in charge of the rest of the team and their responsibilities. He and his core members had been spending long hours training Abbott's men and briefing them on all that they needed to know for their new roles.

All of these men were hired by Mathas, so Turner and Abbott met with the King every day to brief him and to get assignments. Their current assignment was to locate more of the foot soldiers of the Sisterhood.

It was early morning and Mallory was changing Brock's bandage. Although injured, he liked to join the Nordes warriors for training in the mornings. Hector was still weak but he no longer needed help walking. He was sitting at the dining room table reading. When Brock left, Hector followed Mallory into the kitchen.

"So what is your relationship with Brock?" Hector asked as he filled his cup with coffee.

Mallory was slicing potatoes and looked up at him, "I'm not sure I understand your question."

"Do I need to be jealous of him?"

The shocked look on Mallory's face made Hector grin. "Brock is like my brother. Our families lived next to each other and all of us kids were raised together. And why would you get jealous of anyone? We don't have a relationship."

"And why is that?"

"What? Hector just say whatever you are getting at."

"I like you and you know it. And after that kiss, I'd say you aren't as resistant to me as you try to put on. We don't have a relationship yet because you are too scared."

"You keep saying that like it is some kind of power play," Mallory said angrily. "You want to know what I am afraid of? I'm afraid that if we let our guards down that you will call those demons back. I'm afraid that I am going to fall in love with you then have to kill you because you can't control the monsters. And Brock and I are both afraid that you will hurt our friends before we can stop you."

"I don't like your words but at least we got that in the open. You have been avoiding me since we kissed the other day and I needed to know why. I guess I don't really know what to say to you. I was attracted to you the moment I saw you and the more I am around you the more I care about you, even with the way you bust my chops," he said and smiled.

"I guess I don't know what to say to you either Hector. You are so confusing. Sometimes we can just see the evil in you and I am not talking about those demons and other times you are so nice and so much fun. Which is the real you?"

He didn't speak for a few moments. "I don't know, I think they both are."

"Hector maybe that is part of your problem. It's like you wear two faces which are totally opposite of each other. You were meant to wear one and at some point you are going to have to make a decision." Mallory looked back down at her cutting board. Neither of them spoke for several moments.

"So are you saying you won't have a relationship with me until I make that decision?"

"I don't know what I am saying," Mallory said and Hector heard the sadness in her voice.

He walked up to her and turned her around so she was facing him. He stared into her eyes. "You do have feelings for me," he said then bent down and kissed her gently.

She responded with more emotion than she wanted to believe. After a few moments they heard a sound and both looked at the front door.

"Sorry, I will come back," Showers said with a huge grin. "I didn't mean to interrupt."

"No, come in," said Hector.

"Breakfast isn't ready yet," Mallory said. "But there is coffee and the biscuits will be done in a moment."

"Are you two sure cuz, well, it looked like you were in the middle of something," Showers said and continued to grin.

"And we will continue it later," Hector said. "Is anything wrong? I got a message from Clev and he should be back in a couple of days if nothing goes wrong with them."

"No, I wanted to ask you something but now that I think about it, well it's kind of stupid."

Hector smiled "So ask."

Mallory handed Showers a cup of coffee. "Look how he's smiling," she said.

"Yeah, noticed that," said Hector.

"Yesterday I talked to Norge and Sorren about my interest in Ruby and they both gave me their blessings. So Norge invited me over for dinner again and Ruby and I took a walk. Turns out she is interested too so we are courting now. I'd like her and the boys to meet all of you."

"Why don't you bring them for dinner tonight," Mallory said. "I will go to the docks today and buy some special things. Did you want her to meet the entire team?"

"Yeah. Boss is that alright with you?"

"Yes and I would like to meet them too. Showers you aren't even the same man anymore. You're so damn happy; I don't recognize you."

"I know," Showers said and laughed.

Jasmine and Tessa were the first team members to enter Hector's house that morning. "Since we brought extra people we brought some food along," Jasmine said as they carried packages into the kitchen. Seth and Elexas followed with more packages.

"Turner's and Abbott's people are with us today," Seth announced. "What do you need me to do?"

"You can start slicing bread," Jasmine said.

Hector and Showers had been in Hector's bedroom talking now they both walked into the kitchen. "Heard what you said," Hector said to Seth. "Why are the others here? Is something going on?"

"Well, you're not getting attacked if that is what you are asking," Seth said and grinned. "They just want to talk about some stuff and they brought papers for you to look at that might be really important." Hector and Showers walked outside where most of the team members were.

"What is all this?" asked Hector as he saw the men unloading a boca.

"We decided it might be in all of our interest to have some more of the members join us. So we brought more tables and chairs and a lot more food," Dominic said. "The office is going to be crowded but Ryan made these tables and they fold up."

Dominic introduced everyone as the men moved the furniture and food into the house.

"Put some of those tables and chairs in the dining area," Tessa said. "Breakfast is almost ready because Mallory had most of it done."

"Before we talk business," Mallory said. "Everyone is invited for dinner. Showers is courting Ruby and bringing her to meet us. And I need to go to the docks to shop so if anyone wants to come with me you are welcome."

"We might all be going with you," said Turner. "But we will get to that later. Hector, you are a smart man and know that we can't give you all of our information as you can't us. But Dominic has spent more time with you and regards you as an asset, so we asked the Angels if we could show you something. Adam responded and merely said 'Yes.' And we will also get to that in a moment but that is one of the reasons we are all here."

"You know that my men and Abbott's men are all Elods and we have extensive knowledge of this city. Mathas has assigned us to try and find the foot soldiers of the Sisterhood. He is thinking about ransoming back the two we have for information. Damn, we've been working around the clock and can't figure out who they are. And no one out of the ordinary is going near Selen. So Abbott and I want to talk with you."

"If you want to use me for bait, that is fine," said Hector. "I was going to go into the city with Mallory anyways. But you should know that the Sisterhood probably doesn't care enough about the foot soldiers to compromise themselves. You need to find someone higher up in the organization."

"That's exactly what we were going to ask you," Turner said. "Got any suggestions?"

"Actually I was thinking about that last night. We've been reading a book that is about their history. It is wordy and boring so we haven't finished it. So far it tells about how all of these wronged women banned together for protection and turned to the Old Ones, Grand Masters and magics, also for protection."

"As the group developed they established duties and hierarchies. They have their warriors and their priestesses, not unlike Inferus. Now this book is old so the people the author is naming can't still be alive but already then there were power struggles. That is one thing that we can use to our advantage."

"I think we need to interrogate those prisoners again but ask questions about the makeup of their organization. And there is something that I have been questioning; which is how they could have so little control over Isabella and Juleta."

"Yes, they tricked Isabella but she went along enthusiastically like she did everything else in her life. She was not a leader or a strong person so how could they not have more control over her?"

"Of course Juleta was strong and a leader but they basically created her for themselves and from what I have read in those diaries it sounds like they lost control of her almost at the onset and she was a kid. None of that adds up unless there is internal struggles in the organization."

"They have powerful allies who seem to protect them from other threats but with internal problems the different factions would be making great promises to the Grand Masters and demons and they just love that shit."

"That book is over two thousand pages long and is so boring that we have to take frequent breaks just to stay awake. So we really haven't gotten that far into it. So what I am going to say is pure speculation. The curses against me are from Juleta but somehow aligned with the Sisterhood. Your healers are impressive and I believe that when Clev brings back all of the manuscripts that I have requested that those women will come up with cures to many things."

"Now depending on the magic's used, the sender would know if the curse suddenly stopped working for lack of a better word. And I believe they would want to find out why. So we might be able to draw them to us. They have to know that the curses they are sending against me are weaker than they were, unless the Angels are blocking things."

"So if they see you walking around the city looking fit as a fiddle they will get really curious," said Bart.

"I'm not close to being fit but I can put on an act for a while."

"If you don't mind, we will be joining your meetings," Turner said. "But we will bring out food since there are so many of us."

"That doesn't matter," said Hector. "But I want to be with you when you interrogate those women again."

347

"My impression of those two women is that they are relatively new to the spy game because they did an awful job. The real spies might have sent them forward to draw us out, which they did. Which means that everyone who was with us might be watched too."

"Mallory, he means you might be in danger," said Brock.

"Well, not just me."

"You were the one kissing him," Brock said and grinned.

"How do you know that?" Mallory asked and everyone started to grin.

"Mallory it wasn't that you kissed him," Tessa said with a sly smile. "But damn it was some kiss. I couldn't wait to get home to Noah." Everyone at the table laughed. Mallory blushed but she laughed also.

"Mallory it is your business who you see," Dominic said. "You have a great deal of integrity and none of us are worried that you are going to give away information that you shouldn't. But do understand you are going to be in more danger being with him because others will want to use you to get to him."

"So use me as bait too."

"You would have to be seen in public more for that to work," said Fennel. "And you would have to act like a couple. And secondly you are still healing from that wound."

"We always assume there are spies at every function anyone has," said Noah. "The two of you will be seen together at Rosa's celebrations so be aware of that."

"Now Ryan has something to show you," Dominic said to Hector.

"Before we go any farther let me bring some more food and coffee to the table," Mallory said and all of the women got up to help her.

"It's getting kind of like a big ole family here," Showers said kiddingly. "We've never done business like this before."

"What do you mean?" asked Seth.

"Well, we all eat together and socialize together. Most people that the boss does business with are so damn mean or strange we can't wait to be rid of them. And I can say this now since I won't be working for him as soon as Clev comes back."

"I can't argue with a word you said," Hector said. "This has been a whole new experience here but an enjoyable one."

As soon as the women sat down again, Turner explained to Hector about Sam Endleson, the investigator who Matilda Frankwich hired to find her husband. He explained how Endleson claimed that he was Frankwich while he was in Langer and how Otto had him killed.

"If you want more specifics about all of that Olin can tell you but you needed to know at least that much information before we showed you some things. Of course we searched all of Endleson's things after he was murdered and we found some papers he had hidden with notes of his investigation. He found the link between Frankwich and his half-brother Otto. Then he found a link between Otto and Juleta although he was just starting to look into that."

While Turner spoke, Ryan got up from the table and handed Hector three small maps. "Endleson had these hidden. As you can read those are the docks in Langer, Cadia and Port Friada. We are curious about those dots. Any ideas?"

Whenever Hector reviewed anything he stared at it with such intensity that the team members assumed he was memorizing the information. After a few moments he said, "No, but I would like to make copies of these so I can study them."

"Now for the rest," said Dominic. "Some of our team members searched one of Javier's homes because Corsa suspected that Isabella had hidden items there."

"They found an expensive, large leather wallet that contained a map and some papers they couldn't read. As it turns out, Abbott stole it from Otto's office and hid it in Javier's house because Otto's men were after him."

"He took it because Andre said that it seemed important but Otto, Joanna and Jack wouldn't let him in on their meetings about it. Now to go back to Endleson. We found a piece of paper with numbers which we assume are map coordinates. And there was a blank piece of paper. Tessa did something to it by putting it in tea and a map appeared. The same one that we found in that wallet. These are the things that we are going to show you."

Ryan handed these items to Hector and everyone stared at Hector's face as he looked at them. "Abbott, what exactly did Andre say about these and when did you steal them?"

"I befriended Andre because he needed someone to bitch to," Abbott explained. "He was a powerful dark lord but wasn't included in much of Otto's business or family meetings. He was telling me how Otto, Joanna and Jack were all recently paranoid about something."

"He was spying on one of their meetings and whatever they were afraid of had to do with that wallet. That was about six months ago."

"And that was around the time that Otto sacrificed those women from the Sisterhood," Hector said. "I will bet you anything that he got this off from them. Now, we know that the foot soldiers wouldn't be carrying anything important and that the regular members tattoo themselves. So old Otto knew exactly what he was doing when he gave those women to the Master."

"Hector, look at some of those sheets of paper," Jasmine said. "I am an artist and I have never seen paper like that before."

"This paper isn't old," Hector said as he examined it. "But I have never seen anything like it either." Hector moved his plates and spread all of the sheets of paper out on the table. "Didn't you ask your Angels what these were?"

"They usually want us to figure things out," said Dominic. "Any ideas?"

Once Hector had the papers perfectly placed on the table he examined the wallet. "This is very expensive. I would imagine these papers contain information that is being sent from a branch of the Sisterhood in another continent. And that would also explain the paper.

He carefully placed the wallet next to the papers. "I don't do a lot of magics because it's not my style. I do more research like all of you. But there are some things that I do use magics for. And I am going to do that now so any of you can leave if you want."

"What are you going to do?" asked several people in unison.

"I said a protection spell when you handed those papers to me. If they are as important as I think, they will probably have a spell attached to them. Now since none of you have been affected either your Angels stopped them or the spells take hold when you try to translate the information. I don't believe this is a language I think it is a code."

"I think we better stay in here with you," said Brock.

"Then I am going to ask all of you to move away from the table." Once everyone had moved Hector started to chant and as he did he moved his finger around the entire works as if he was drawing a circle around the papers and the wallet. Then he repeated the process around each individual item. He continued chanting as he touched each piece of paper and the wallet. His voice became louder and louder and smoke started to rise from the imaginary circle that he drew around all of the items. Loud popping sounds were heard.

The wallet itself started to move violently. It jumped several feet above the table and when it landed it had changed form. It was no longer a leather wallet but sheets of paper. The individual sheets too changed form. The paper that no one had seen before was thick because it encased other sheets of paper. When the smoke disappeared and the popping sounds stopped Hector looked at the items.

351

"The case was actually the code key," Hector explained. "And the real messages were hidden inside those thick pieces of paper."

"Can we translate it?" Ryan asked excitedly.

"Is it safe?" asked Dominic.

"I will say yes, but it wouldn't hurt for you to say a protection prayer," Hector said and smiled as Ryan, Elexas and Olin ran up to the table then stopped and prayed then they grabbed the papers and almost ran into the office. "They are very enthusiastic," he said.

"Look at me," Mallory said in a scolding tone as she turned Hector so she could stare into his eyes. "Brock come here in case I miss something."

"He's fine," Brock said after the two had been examining Hector.

"If you got another demon in you so help me I am going to slap you," Mallory said angrily.

Hector laughed and pulled her onto his lap. "You sound concerned," he said and laughed again at the angry look she gave him. Mallory tried to stand up but he pulled her back onto his lap. "Will you just sit still for a minute? I have been accepting of what all of you have been doing. This is the first time I have done any magics; you are going to have to accept me too. Especially if we are all going to be together for a while."

Before anyone else could speak Showers said, "Boss, I've spent a lot of time with these folks and they do accept you but when you were full of those demons it scared the shit out of all of us. If that girl cares for you, she is going to be scared. You know me, I've fought just about everything but I will admit that when those demons were coming out of you I almost pissed my pants."

Many people laughed at Showers' comment. "Showers, you know you don't have to quit," said Hector.

"I think I kinda do," Showers said. "If I play my cards right I will have a sweet little wife and two sons soon. Our life isn't the kind of life for no family man. I lost my first family; I would really like this one to work."

"I'm not arguing that but when Clev comes back he will be leading the men again. I'm thinking of something different for you. Kind of like a liaison position."

"I have no idea what that means."

"Well, we are going to be here a while and you're part of this tribe now and you get along well with the teams. I'm thinking you can be the person that makes sure things stay calm. I'm sure the boys are getting bored. Work with these guys. Have our boys go out on the streets and work with Turner and Abbott. I am sure there are things they can do in the village too."

"That's a good idea boss. Let me see what I can come up with."

Chapter XXVIII
Introductions

Brock and Lawrence stayed behind in Hector's house with Ryan, Olin and Elexas. The two men said they wanted to help with the translation but they really wanted to protect the three young people while the rest of their group went into Langer. Showers led a group of Hector's men into the city before Hector and the others arrived. The plan this morning was to use Hector as bait to lure some of the foot soldiers of the Sisterhood out of the shadows.

Once the group entered the city they split up. Hector and Mallory went shopping by themselves so they would seem like a more attainable target. They walked down the main street of the business district holding hands. They walked in and out of several shops before entering Ashley's store.

It was early and Ashley was still setting up the beverages and treats in the front of the shop. There were only a couple of customers in the store but about twenty Nordes warriors who were working.

"What happened with those women?" Ashley asked in a low voice as she approached Hector and Mallory.

"They were foot soldiers," Hector explained. "They are at the bottom of that organization and aren't privilege to a lot of information. Just to warn you I am acting as bait now."

"So you believe there are others?" Ashley asked.

"About twenty-five. We'd like to get them before Thaos and Stephan get back, since they are on the list too," Hector said to Ashley then turned to Mallory. "Look around and let me know if you see anything you like."

Hector told Ashley about the plans they had for capturing the members of the Sisterhood then he and Ashley walked over to Mallory who was looking admiringly at a gown.

"Do you like that?" Hector asked.

"It's so beautiful but look how thin it is. Ashley why would anyone make a dress out of such thin material?" Mallory asked and both Ashley and Hector smiled.

"Mallory that's not a dress it's a nightgown," Ashley said.

"A night gown! But look at it."

"We'll take it and any others you have," Hector said to Ashley as he tried not to laugh. Mallory gave him a confused look then her eyes widened. "That took you a little while to catch on," he said kiddingly. "Yes, they are for you and no they are not for you to wear in front of Brock."

Ashely left to get more nightgowns and Hector continued, "I don't like my girl sharing a bedroom with another guy. It's time you moved your things into my room. For the show you put on, I know you care about me. You aren't that good of an actress."

Mallory was lost for words for a few moments and when she started to speak Hector gently put his finger against her lips and said, "Dear, you may want to save that argument for later." Mallory knew from the tone of his voice that they were being watched.

Ashley walked up to them with six nightgowns. She held them up to show the couple and said in a low voice. "They are standing by the tables in front."

Hector nodded to Ashley and said, "We'll take them all and both of us will need robes. I expect that we will be spending at least one night with my parents."

"What!" gasped Mallory.

"Mallory, you will be just fine," Ashley said. "Do you want to stay here or walk to another area of the store?"

"I believe I could use a cup of coffee," said Hector and he and Mallory walked to the front of the store where two young women were standing. The women carried themselves like warriors but Hector and Mallory did not immediately see any weapons on them.

Neither Hector nor Mallory wanted to start a disturbance in Ashley's shop, they planned to lead the women outside. Hector poured two cups of coffee.

"Honey, you should probably get something for your parents," Mallory said.

"Actually, I planned for you and I to take them shopping. I couldn't even guess their sizes."

"Oh, but they have other things here too," Mallory said and took Hector's hand and led him to a display case.

"Those two look way too inexperienced," Hector whispered. "Someone sent them in and is watching us. We need to hold off on grabbing them."

Mallory took a ribbon out of her pocket and tied her hair in a ponytail. That act was the signal for the warriors who were watching the shop to remain in their positions. She kept talking, since the women had moved closer to them and were listening to their conversation.

"You should get a little something to hand your parents when we meet them," Mallory said. "Nikki told me that these jeweled combs are very popular and only made for Ashley." While Hector looked in the display case, Mallory positioned herself so she could look at the two foot soldiers who were not being discreet about staring at them.

Ashley walked up to Hector and Mallory with several robes, she too positioned herself so she could see the two soldiers. After they chose the ones they wanted, Hector said, "Ashley, I want some items in this case. Some will be for gifts so can you put them in something nice?"

"Certainly," Ashley said and walked behind the display case. Hector pointed out a number of items.

"You are buying so much," Mallory said. "Please don't tell me any of that is for me."

"Yes."

"But I don't wear fancy things like that," Mallory said.

"And is that because you don't have any?" asked Hector. "If you don't want them you can return them but I would like you to wear these things around my parents."

"There you are," said Jasmine as she and Tessa walked towards Mallory and Hector. They stared at the two foot soldiers and Hector shook his head from side to side.

"Girls, if you want something from in here pick it out and something for Elexas too," said Hector. "Then we will be going."

Hector's men and team members were lined along the streets and alleys. The city was bustling with activity so the men blended with the crowds. They saw Hector and the three women walk out of the store with two women following them. And they saw that Mallory had put her hair up. Now they looked through the crowds to see who was watching the foot soldiers.

Hector and the women walked down the street for two blocks then entered another shop and that was the move that exposed the spies. Two members of the Sisterhood who were dressed in clothing that blended in with the other citizens, stopped walking and watched the shop from across the street. Showers and three of his men walked up to the women and escorted them into an alley.

Hector was standing in the window of the shop and when he saw this he quickly walked out. He was concerned that the women would use magics against the men. As soon as he left, Tessa, Mallory and Jasmine grabbed the two foot soldiers who were going to follow Hector. Jasmine and Mallory each grabbed a woman and threw her to the ground while Tessa pulled rope from her pocket and tied the wrists and ankles of the women.

"These women are criminals," Jasmine yelled to the alarmed clerk. "We work for the King. We will have them out of here in a moment."

"But we may have to come back for our packages," Tessa said as she continuing tying the women.

"No you won't," said Seth as he, Bart, Noah and Turner entered the shop. The men grabbed the foot soldiers and the women grabbed their packages and they all left the shop and a very frazzled clerk.

Turner's team and Shower's and his men took the four women to the dungeons at Fort Langer. Dominic and Abbott's teams continued shopping. By the time Mallory finished buying everything she wanted for their dinner party, four more foot soldiers had been apprehended.

The entire group went to Fort Langer where they found Sorren, Gideon, Matthew and Turner interrogating the two women who were not foot soldiers. Showers and his men were watching the interrogations.

After a few minutes, Mallory, Tessa and Jasmine walked up to Dominic, Fennel and Hector. "We need to start working on the food for dinner," Mallory said. "Showers said he and his men will escort us back to the village. Is that alright?"

"Of course," said Dominic. "You know this is going to take hours. What time do you want us there?"

"Six, would be good," said Jasmine. "And tell Sorren too."

"Mallory put everything we bought in my room," Hector said, causing her to blush.

"What was that all about?" asked Tessa as they walked away from the group.

"He's jealous because I am sharing a room with Brock. He wants me to move into his room," Mallory said. "I don't know what to do."

"If you weren't a demon hunter and he didn't have demons would you like him?" asked Jasmine.

"I do like him. I like him a lot and that's the problem," Mallory said.

"He has changed a lot and you might be part of the reason," Tessa said. "To start with, why don't you think of him as a normal guy, then think of what you would do."

358

"And if I fall in love with him then have to kill him," Mallory said.

"One of us will do that for you," said Jasmine. "We've already talked about that. We understand your concerns and honestly we would feel the same way. But like Tessa said, you might be the reason he is changing and that would be a good thing for everyone."

"I can't believe how good it smells in here," Noah said as the teams were walking into Hector's house hours later.

"Look at this," said Turner. The women had rearranged the furniture and pushed tables together so there were three large tables in the dining area. They were decorated with fine cloths, flowers and candles. There were expensive dishes and wine and whiskey glasses at the settings. "This is really nice."

"Hector can I speak with you?" asked Mallory and the two walked into his bedroom and closed the door. Instantly the group heard their loud voices.

"Guess they're a couple now," Lawrence said kiddingly.

The bedroom door opened and Hector said loudly, "Brock, that room is all yours. Mallory is moving in with me. You are welcome to have house guests."

"Really? Thanks," Brock said with a big smile.

"I told you he wouldn't be mad," Hector said to Mallory.

"Mallory, you thought I would be mad?" Brock asked and laughed. "I know you are kind of naïve but it is different sharing a room with your sister and a real girl." Everyone laughed.

Mallory looked at Brock and said sarcastically, "I am going to slap you."

"Can some of you guys help me push those beds together and move Mallory's things?" Brock asked.

"What! You can't wait to get rid of me," Mallory said with surprise.

"No but now I am going to ask someone to this dinner party," Brock said.

"Brock go find her now because you aren't giving her much notice," said Tessa.

"First, tell us where you want things," said Fennel. Brock walked into the bedroom.

"Careful with all of those packages next to my bed," Mallory called out. "Actually, Sorren all those gifts are for your family and Hilgra. We invited them but I think only Shara and the boys are coming."

"Well, thanks but why did you buy us gifts?"

"They're from Hector. I just wrapped them," said Mallory.

"We bought some more today," Hector said to Mallory.

"Sorren, there are more that I haven't wrapped. I'll get them after dinner," Mallory said.

Brock walked out of the bedroom and towards the front door. Sorren asked, "Brock what is the girl's name?"

"Sabra," Brock said with a smile.

Sorren smiled and nodded. "She's a real nice girl and a beauty."

Brock took two more steps towards the door then stopped and said loudly. "So you know; she is pretty shy so don't scare her."

"Who are you talking to?" asked Tessa.

"You girls," Brock said with a mischievous grin.

"Brock, we are all going to slap you now get out of here," Tessa said and laughed.

"Sorren, we have a small pig and two turkeys on the fire pit," Jasmine said. "Olin and Ryan are watching them but I don't think they know what they are doing. Will you go out there?"

"My specialty," Sorren said with a big smile.

"Everything you will need is already out there," said Tessa.

"I'm going with Sorren," Turner said.

"Need help?" asked Bart.

"There's a case each of wine and whiskey. Can you open the bottles and put them on the tables," Tessa said. "We have a dozen pies cooling on a table next to the house; someone can bring them in. And Elexas is next door using their kitchen, someone can help her. We need bread sliced and more fruit cut up." The women laughed at how quickly all of the men went to work.

"I think they're hungry," Mallory said jokingly.

"We have all of your stuff moved into Hector's room," Noah said. "And the gifts are on the table in the office."

"Mallory did you give the girls their gifts?" Hector asked.

"No because they are from you. All of that stuff is on the table next to the window."

As soon as Hector walked into his room Tessa whispered to Mallory, "What were you yelling about?"

"I told him I would move in with him but I was embarrassed for all of you to know," Mallory said and laughed. "Guess that's not a problem anymore."

"Mallory, we don't care," said Jasmine. "We all like him. But if he turns back into his old self, don't put up with any crap."

"Here they are!" Fennel yelled so that everyone could hear.

"Oh my," gasped Ruby as she and Showers walked into the house. They were holding hands and each carrying a toddler.

Showers' face could not contain his smile when he saw how fancy the dining area was. "Ruby, I would like you to meet my friends," he said proudly and started introductions.

"Mallory where are the toys?" asked Tessa.

"In Hector's bedroom in that basket on the floor."

"Hector, I'm coming in," Tessa yelled and walked into the room. "I'm just getting teddy bears."

"Well, come here a second," Hector was standing next to the bed with his back to her. There were dozens of pieces of jewelry spread out on the bed.

"Oh my gosh; what is all of this?" asked Tessa.

"It's for all of you to wear for the functions for my parents but I don't know who wants what. And Mallory won't tell me what she likes but she picked out the gifts for my mother."

"Hector, why are you really doing all of this?"

"I never saw my mother cry until I made them go on the run. I chose that life not them and they have been suffering because of my choices for a long time."

"I just want them to have something normal again. They have been gracious and accepting of a lot of people that I knew really scared them or disgusted them. They are going to love all of you and it will feel like they have their old lives back."

"Wow, I am surprised to hear you say that. But I have to ask you. Do you really like Mallory or is she just a show for your parents?"

"That first day I thought she would be a great date to meet my parents but now I really care about her. And yes, I know how conflicted she is about us."

"I need to go out there," Tessa said.

"Well which of this do you want? Should I just let all of you choose?"

"No because Mallory won't take anything. She comes from a very poor family. Ok, give me a moment. So all of this stuff is for who exactly?"

"Most of it is for you, Jasmine, Mallory and Elexas but I bought a few extra things for Shara, Angelina and Hilgra."

"I just can't believe how much money you spend. You must be a very successful crook," Tessa said sarcastically and Hector laughed.

After a few moments Tessa had reorganized the jewelry into groups. That is for Mallory but don't give it to her until after dinner because she will be too embarrassed. That's for Jasmine," Tessa pointed at the groupings as she spoke. "Elexas, Shara, Angelina and Hilgra. This is mine and if I am wrong and someone wants something else I will trade with them. And thank you Hector."

"When should I give it to everyone?"

"After dinner," Tessa said and quickly left the room. "I have to tell you something later," she whispered into Mallory's ear then walked up to Showers and Ruby. "I'm Tessa, Noah's fiancé and look what I have." As Tessa spoke she had been holding two teddy bears behind her back and now showed them to the boys whose eyes lit up and they laughed. "Which one is Max?" Tessa asked.

"He is," Ruby said of the boy she was holding. Tessa handed him a teddy bear.

"And you must be Saul," Tessa said and handed the toy to the boy who Showers was holding.

"Thank you all so much," Ruby said. "I never expected anything like this."

"Well, we all wanted to meet the women who could make Showers so happy," Tessa said and winked at them. "I will talk to you later, I need to help with the food."

Brock walked into the house with a beautiful, young Nordes woman. She had long straight black hair that went to her knees and huge brown eyes. They were holding hands. Jasmine knew Sabra and walked up to her and hugged her.

"Brock is like our brother and he told us not to embarrass him," Jasmine said and both women laughed.

The dinner party was a success. Everyone laughed and talked for hours and not one person talked about work. After the dessert was eaten Tessa, Jasmine and Elexas quickly cleared the table. "Everyone stay right where you are," Tessa said and laughed.

Mallory walked out of Hector's bedroom carrying a laundry basket filled with gifts. "If you two don't get married we are going to feel really stupid," Dominic said as Mallory set the basket in front of Ruby and Showers. "Let's have a toast to them," said Dominic. Everyone raised their glasses to Showers and Ruby.

As they opened their gifts, Mallory and Tessa went into the office and each carried an armful of gifts to Sorren and Shara. "These are all from Hector and there are more that I didn't have time to wrap," Mallory said. "Some are for Angelina and Hilgra too. All of you are invited to the celebrations for his parents."

"Hector what is all of this?" asked Shara.

"It is nothing compared to what you have done for me," Hector said and stood up and walked into his bedroom. He returned to the table holding several pouches.

"Hector before you give those can I tell everyone what you told me in the bedroom?" Tessa asked. For the first time they saw Hector look embarrassed. "I really think they should know." He looked at Tessa and nodded.

"Hector has been buying all of us lavish gifts and clothing for the celebrations. I asked him why he was doing it. He told me he had never seen his mother cry until he made her go into hiding. He said he chose his life but they did not and they have suffered for his actions. He said they have been exposed to a lot of strange and scary people but he knows they will really like us. He wants to make them feel like they have their old lives back. He's not doing any of this because he wants something from us."

"Hector is that true?" asked Mallory. He nodded.

"Well, now I feel kind of embarrassed to hand these out," he said.

"Oh don't," Tessa said with a big smile.

"I got all of you dresses for the celebrations so here is the jewelry."

"What!" gasped Elexas and he laughed.

"Tessa help me hand these out," Hector said. "This is for Jasmine and this is for Elexas. Shara these are for you, Angelina and Hilgra. Tessa yours." He looked at Mallory and laughed. "Don't throw these at me," he said and handed her a pouch.

"Oh my god Hector, thank you," Elexas said and ran up to him and kissed him on the cheek.

"Hector, I can't take these," said Jasmine.

"Don't make me fight with you too," he said. "I can afford them."

"Well, thank you," said Jasmine and walked up to him and kissed him on the cheek, as did Tessa and Shara. Mallory didn't say a word but looked like she was going to cry. She walked up to Hector and kissed him on the lips.

Tessa pulled Brock away from the table and asked in a low voice, "Are you taking Sabra to those functions?"

"I would like to."

"Bring her to the team's house and between me and Jasmine we can loan her everything she will need."

"Thanks Tessa."

Several hours later Mallory walked out of Hector's bedroom wearing her robe. She laughed when she saw him and a group of the team members sitting at the dining room table.

"For weeks you have been saying you want me in your bed and now I am there and you aren't." Everyone laughed at her comment.

"Sorry," Dominic said. "We were just leaving when a flock of Enrops delivered letters. "We will leave soon."

"Don't leave on my account," she said.

Hector moved his chair back from the table. "Sit on my lap, you can read these too." He handed her several pages of the letter he was reading.

"There were actually two flocks that met up," Fennel said to Mallory. "We're handing the letters around. Claudius has started back with Hector's parents but he is worried about leaving the teams behind and may return."

"I would like to return with him," Hector said.

"You know you aren't up for that," Mallory said. "You're exhausted just from the dinner party."

"Hector did you get to the part yet about those monsters who got their strength from their armor?" Noah asked.

"Just reading that now."

"You might be more help trying to figure out the magic end of that. I doubt if that is the only time Jack is going to throw something like that at us," said Noah.

An hour later Mallory helped Hector into the bedroom. "Just sit down and I will take off your boots," she said. "You look like you are going to pass out."

"Honey, for all my big talk I might be too exhausted to make love tonight."

Mallory laughed and unbuttoned his shirt. "Are you sure that Juleta is the only one sending magics against you?" she asked. "Now stand up and I will get the pants."

"You mean because of what Jack did?"

"Yes. I'll be glad when Clev brings us those manuscripts. I think you've got more attacking you than Juleta's curses."

"Why do you say that?" he asked as she covered him up.

"I don't know, just a feeling." She slid under the covers and he put his arm around her.

"Tonight Tessa asked me if I really cared about you or if I just wanted window dressing for my parents. I hope you realize that I do care about you."

"I do Hector. I just hope it's enough."

Chapter XXIX
The Book of Tandum

"So how was it?" Tessa asked Mallory with a grin when she walked into the kitchen the following morning.

"Where did you come from?"

"Since it was so late, Sorren got housing for everyone. But Showers said we could use his room because he was going to stay with Ruby. Apparently she has a house but has been staying with her brother's family since her husband was killed."

"So you and Noah stayed in Shower's room?"

"Yeah. But you didn't answer my question."

"Yesterday was too much for him. I had to put him to bed and he is still sleeping."

"So you didn't have sex?" Tessa asked and smiled again.

"No," Mallory said and laughed. "Speaking of sex did Sabra spend the night?"

"No, I think they were in his room kissing for a while then Brock walked her home. He looks like he really likes her."

Within minutes Jasmine and Seth walked in. "We need coffee then put us to work," Seth said. "Elexas, Olin and Ryan are right behind us."

"Good because with the extra teams here it will take a little longer. We're having ham, scrambled eggs, blueberry pancakes, biscuits, bread and fruit," said Mallory.

The small group was busy preparing breakfast when Noah awoke about half an hour later. He walked into the kitchen and poured himself a cup of coffee. He turned to walk into the office and stopped. "Quiet everyone! Do you hear that?"

"What?" asked Olin.

Noah put his coffee cup down and ran into Hector's room; the others followed.

Hector was in bed thrashing around and talking incoherently. He was sweating profusely. "Someone get Shara!" yelled Noah as he was the first to see Hector.

Mallory threw the blankets off Hector so she could examine him. "Someone get me some cold water and a rag!" she yelled. "Wait," she said in a lower voice. "Does anyone feel that?" Everyone became quiet.

Jasmine and Seth pulled their knives from the sheaths then they quickly ran towards one of the windows. Jasmine threw her knife and a woman screamed. Seth and Noah ran out of the house. Hector stopped thrashing. Shara and Sorren ran into the room.

"Sorren, the men are chasing someone behind the house," Tessa said. "Wait, where is Elexas?" Without speaking, Sorren turned and ran out of the house.

"She ran out too," said Ryan as he carried a bowl of water into the room.

"Tessa watch the food so it doesn't burn," Mallory said. "I'll help Shara."

Minutes later Noah walked into the bedroom. "The Sisterhood found us," he announced. One is dead and Sorren is putting the other one in a cage. How is he doing?" Tessa had followed him back into the room.

"I don't know," said Shara. "Cyril will you help me?" Shara called out.

Cyril was not the only Angel to appear in the room; so did Adam.

"What did they do to him?" asked Mallory frantically. Neither Angel spoke. Cyril walked up to Hector and touched his forehead. "Are they trying to kill him or turn him into a monster or what?" Mallory asked. Still the Angels did not answer.

"Why aren't you saying anything?" asked Noah.

Cyril held up his hand for Noah to stop speaking. Hector shot up to a sitting position. He had a wild look in his eyes.

"Do you know where you were?" Cyril asked.

Hector looked at the Angels as he began to realize where he was. He took the hands of both Shara and Mallory and squeezed them. "I don't know where I was but now I know what they want; at least I think I do. I might have been dreaming."

"Here," Olin said and handed Hector a cup of coffee. Hector drank the coffee and it seemed to compose him. "It was like I was in a thick darkness and the only light I saw was illuminating the women who were interrogating me. They kept asking me where the Book of Tandum was and when I told them I didn't know they inflicted pain on me." Hector paused as he tried to recall his nightmare.

"Then, I am trying to remember who was talking..." Hector looked up at the Angels. "I read about the woman named Risha in the letters last night. Was she with me or did I dream that?"

"Was she interrogating you?" Shara gasped.

"No, she was whispering to me. She told me to call to Ruth. And somehow while she was saying this she showed me a book that I have seen before. Juleta had it. She said...I think she said it was a book of plagues."

"You heard her right," Cyril said. "When you called to Ruth then Mallory sensed the women outside of the window."

"Will you please tell us what is going on?" asked Mallory.

"You know that the Sisterhood and the Master have been on the brink of war for a long time," Cyril said. "They have been building up their arsenals in preparation. They are both powerful and could destroy each other. That is why they want areas of power so they can harness it to use in conjunction with magics."

"The Sisterhood used Juleta in many ways before she revolted against them. They had her use her power and wealth to procure items which they could not get. Juleta resented their intrusion into her life."

370

"One of the things they told her to find was the Book of Tandum. It originally belonged to the first high priestess of that group. She had once been a powerful healer and used her talents to create plagues of unimaginable destruction. The priestess was named Naomi and she was the older sister of Risha. They were both incredibly powerful healers but they led very separate lives. As you know Risha married into the Clan of Gesmal."

"But that is on the other side of the continent," said Shara.

"In those days the tribe was nomadic," Cyril said. "Risha had no idea how diabolical her sister was. Naomi always carried that book with her. One day as she was traveling with a group of warriors of the Sisterhood they were attacked and all of them killed. The book was taken but the demons who took it could not break the code."

"The Sisterhood tasked Juleta with finding it but after she learned what it was she had no intention of turning it over to them. Juleta spent many fortunes and killed many beings before she got her hands on it. But fortunately for this world she couldn't break the code either."

"So does Hector have it?" asked Tessa.

"No, but he will be the one who figures out where she hid her most valuable items. She was a highly intelligent, paranoid and rich woman. She anticipated powerful armies coming after her treasure," Adam said. "So what problem does that pose?"

"So that is why you wanted us to remind him what it was like to be human again," Dominic said. "If he died he would have become a demon and found it?"

"And if he lived he would have been the monster who found it," said Adam.

"Does he know the code?" asked Tessa.

"He is a very resourceful and intelligent man," Adam replied.

"Now just wait a damn minute. Did all of you befriend me because of some scam the Angels had?" Hector asked angrily.

Dominic started to speak but stopped when Mallory literally jumped onto Hector's lap so she was facing him. She grabbed his chin and made him look into her eyes. She was furious when she spoke.

"You listen here. They stopped us from killing you and sent us to help you which we did without question. But after a while we did wonder why the Angels have been protecting you as you did. They told us the demon in you was taking over and the thread of a human was barely existent. They said perhaps we could remind you that humanity was worth fighting for."

"We have protected you and worked hard to keep you a live. And along the way we all developed feelings even though we realize that someday you will kill us or we will kill you. This wasn't a big scheme. Stop acting like Juleta!"

"What do you mean?" asked Hector.

"Adam told you that she wanted to create the perfect husband but then she realized she made you in her image," Mallory said. "Did you really think about what he said? She made you to become her. Hector all she wanted was power and she was paranoid. Does any of that sound familiar to you? Were you like that before you let her change you? Is that how you wanted to change?" He stared at her without speaking.

"Hector, unfortunately I have feelings for you but in a way that makes you my responsibility. You are my rabid dog. So if you are going to kill anyone you better kill me first because I will put you down." Mallory jumped off from the bed and ran out of the room.

Hector started to get out of bed to follow her but Adam said, "We are not done here. Now do you realize there were no conspiracies here? Hector they showed you Mercy not a scam. Have you forgotten what that is too?"

"No," said Hector is a hoarse voice. "So are you telling me that I will find it and unleash it on the world?"

"It's all about choices," Adam said and the two Angels disappeared. It was then that Hector realized most of the team members were either in his room or in the hallway.

Tessa walked up to him angrily. "I just want to shake you. Has it been so long since you've had friends that you can't even remember what it is like? Hector, you are just an ass sometimes." Hector laughed at Tessa's last comment.

"I need to get up and I am naked, I don't care if you don't," he said.

Jasmine picked up his trousers from a chair and tossed them to him. "They are going to keep coming after you Hector. So how do we stop them?" she asked.

"I don't think it's your fight," Hector said. "I don't want any of you getting hurt."

"After what they just said, I think it's everybody's fight," said Turner. "Besides you can't even put your boots on much less fight. Are you going to work with us or send us away so there won't be anyone to stop you?"

"I don't see any reason in destroying this world but right now I need to talk to Mallory."

Mallory heard Hector walk into the kitchen but she kept her back to him. "We need to talk," he said.

"I am cooking now."

He gently turned her around so she would face him. She was crying. "I am sorry to put you through all of this," he said and kissed her on the forehead.

"I need to get back to this," she said.

"Mallory, you can move back into my room," said Brock.

"I want you to stay with me," Hector said to her.

"Seriously, we can talk about this later. I don't want to have to make breakfast all over."

The breakfast meal was in great contrast to the festivities from the previous night. The mood was somber and few spoke during the meal.

"Alright we're all disturbed by what the Angels said but really has anything changed?" Bart asked. "We knew that Hector had the potential to be a major threat but really all we learned was about that book."

Sorren and Shara were eating breakfast with the group. "If Risha was talking to him and telling him to call to the Angels there is hope," said Shara. "Bart is right. But we have to find a way to stop the Sisterhood from coming after Hector."

"Who exactly is Risha?" asked Hector.

"Now that is kind of hard to explain," Sorren said. "She is as old as time. She married into the Clan of Gesmal. She was a powerful healer. Her tribe was killed by the Originator but just prior to that they all asked The Great Ruler if they could carry on their covenant with Him even after death. She was not a warrior and while her tribe was being butchered she fled. She went to the Safer Mountains and hoped to die. She turned to magics and became a maker of potions. When she learned that some of her potions were used to kill Prince Michael she came to our side."

"I know of her. I know that Juleta tried to curse her because she would not cater to her," said Hector. "So she is a witch?"

"Have you ever heard of the Shadow Men?" asked Brock.

"Yes, actually they were mentioned in the letters," Hector said.

"That is what we become after death," Brock said with pride. "Risha helped Erebus out of the World of Illusions and died doing so. She became a Shadow Man but has somehow come back to help in another form."

"If she helped you like that, there has to be a very good reason," said Shara.

"Am I the only one here who doesn't understand what the hell is going on?" asked Tessa. "Is Hector supposed to find that book or are we supposed to keep him away from it? Is he the only one who will ever find it and if he does is he going to turn into a demon? And is he going to be attacked forever by the Sisterhood and who knows who else? Well, does anyone know?"

"Would any of the Angels care to join us?" asked Dominic.

Miranda appeared and Hector gasped. "I have seen you in my dreams. Wait, you were there that day that Samael was destroyed."

"Many of us have spoken to you but you usually do not listen," Miranda said. "You have many questions so what are your choices?"

"What they don't want to say is that if they let me die will the book be safe and will they get rid of a major pain in their butts," Hector said.

"Do you blame them?" asked Miranda.

"Not at all. I would not be so gracious in their place. But I too have the same questions as Tessa. I think we all do."

"Juleta hid the items well but they will be found; it is only a matter of time. Many know of individual pieces in her collection but no one knows of the arsenal she had accumulated. She too was considering waging a war. The temptation will be great for those driven by power."

"You aren't answering our questions?" said Hector.

"Did you ask me one?"

"Why did Risha come to me? I must know something that she didn't want me to tell the Sisterhood."

"You know considerably more than you remember."

"Did Juleta put a spell on me to forget things?"

"No but she drugged you considerably more than you realized. In the twilight of your mind you saw and heard many things."

"Why was she always drugging him?" asked Mallory.

"She never slept and often had visitors during the night."

"But, we only had an affair for a couple of weeks," Hector said. "Did she drug me other than that?"

"Hector, you read Claudius' letter about people who are born with certain powers and that is why the demons seduced you. Juleta sensed that power and was trying to figure out how to add it to her arsenal. Her big mistake was making you look like Thaos. For you that was a blatant act of betrayal. You would have gone along with much more of her wishes had she not done that."

"Did she experiment on him? Is that what you are saying?" Mallory asked fearfully.

"Yes and he was not the only one. Clev was another and there were others," Miranda said.

Hector stared at Miranda. "I know there is much more to this. What aren't you telling us?"

"What would be a better question?" asked Miranda.

"What?"

"Hector, you have to ask specific questions when it comes to information that can control your choices," said Dominic then he turned to Miranda. "Is Juleta still somehow controlling Hector or affecting his actions?"

"Yes."

"How is she doing this?" asked Hector.

"She planted a little of herself inside of you."

"What!" yelled Hector and jumped up from the table. "Can you get it out of me?"

"Why would you want it out? You enjoy your life?"

"I don't want any part of her in me!"

"Miranda, why did she do it and what will happen to him if you remove it?" Mallory asked.

"How is it controlling him?" asked Brock.

"Mallory reminded you that Juleta made you in her image. Your soul was already dark when you went into negotiations with her."

376

"You are a brilliant man and knew exactly what you were doing when you signed that contract. The problem for you is that you did not have the experience of a dark lord then. You didn't realize there was much more to that contract than you could see with your eyes," said Miranda.

"She wanted complete control over you. She took your soul but she wanted more. She put in you all of her desires and ambitions. In a way she was trying to make you into a vessel as she had been made into one by the Sisterhood. If you would have been a weaker man it might have worked but you are a power. So your power is always fighting with the magics she put inside of you. And that is how your insanity is beginning."

"Will you take it out of me? Please."

"What will happen if you don't?" asked Shara.

"He will become as insane as she was."

"And if you take it out?" Shara asked.

"He is very weak to remove it in his condition will make him worse; it could possibly kill him."

"What kind of man would he be afterwards?" Brock asked.

"That is up to him. But it would be his choice."

"Hector before you say anything else," Sorren said then turned to Miranda. "If you do this and he dies will he turn into a vessel for a demon?"

"No."

"Is the Sisterhood connected to him because of this?"

"Yes because Juleta was an extension of them."

"Besides dying what could be the down side of taking it out?" Sorren asked.

"Hector enjoys his life. He is addicted to power and the game as he calls it. While he will still be that man it will be like a drug addict being cut off from a main supply of the drug. He will have side effects."

"Can we care for those side effects?" asked Shara.

"Yes."

"If I live how long will I be sick? I don't want my parents to see me like that." Others could hear the fear in Hector's voice.

"Perhaps they would be pleased to have their son back."

"Miranda, do I have the medical supplies that I will need to take care of him?" asked Shara.

"I can do better than that," Miranda said and smiled as Cyril appeared in the room.

"Oh my god," said Shara. "She did that to more than Hector, didn't she?"

"Yes," Cyril said.

"If Hector does this; someone get Angelina. She will need to learn this also," Shara said.

"Can you give me a minute?" Hector asked Miranda and she nodded.

"Mallory, I need paper and a pen. Angels did she do this to Clev too?"

"Yes."

"Can you help him also?"

"Yes but he will need to be here so Shara can care for him. Call to us when he gets here."

"If I die, give this to Clev and if he dies give it to Showers," Hector said. "It is the distribution of my money. Clev will inherit my empire but if he doesn't want to stay in the business he has been directed to turn it over to Claudius to do as he pleases. I guess it would benefit all of you if I die."

"You still have a lifetime of choices to make," Cyril said. "And today you are actually making good ones."

"I am ready," said Hector. "Do you need me to lie down?"

"Yes," said Miranda.

Mallory kissed Hector and they walked into the bedroom holding hands. He laid down on the bed and closed his eyes.

Miranda and Cyril stood on either side of him with Shara and Mallory next to the bed. Turner's team left to get Angelina and the others filled the room and hallway.

The room began to warm and become filled with light. Hector started to twitch then convulse. Screams were heard but they did not come from his throat.

"Oh my god!" gasped Tessa. "What is happening to him?"

Chapter XXX
Cursed

Mathas was not holding a morning meeting but Fahron and Gideon were at the castle having breakfast with the Royal Family.

"I am really sorry to interrupt," Turner said as he hurried into the room. "But Shara wants Angelina at the village pronto."

"What's going on?" asked Matthew.

"It's a long story and we don't have a lot of time."

"Then give us a short version," Mathas said.

"Alright but I am telling you now you aren't going to like it," Turner said. "This morning some members of the Sisterhood came to the village and attacked Hector. We stopped them but then had to call to the Angels. This kind of gets complicated. Three Angels have visited us this morning."

"First, all the Angels said that Juleta was insane because the Sisterhood poured more evil in her than one person could hold. Turns out she was doing all kinds of experiments on people and that includes Hector and Clev. She drugged him and he didn't even know what she was doing. Miranda said because she wanted to control Hector that she put some of herself inside of him but the evil is causing him to go insane."

"She did it to others too, including Clev. Hector told the Angels to take it out but he is so weak it might kill him. Here," Turner said and walked around the table and handed a piece of paper to Mathas.

"What is this?" Mathas asked.

"His will. Ok, to finish. If Hector lives he is going to be in real bad shape for some time. The Angels are working on him now and it didn't sound good when we left." Angelina jumped out of her chair. "Wait. We found out why everyone is after him. Turns out that Juleta spent fortunes collecting the worst things in this world for her personal arsenal."

"Apparently when Hector was drugged up he heard and saw some things that he can't remember and everyone wants to get their hands on that arsenal."

"Mathas, I'm taking Sarah and going out there," Rosa said. "It was our daughter who was the monster; when are you going to realize that?"

"Rosa, the carriage is too slow," Angelina said. "I'm riding with Turner." Rosa nodded.

"Honey, just get what you need and I'll saddle our horses," Matthew said and he and Angelina ran out of the dining room.

As Rosa was leaving Mathas said, "I'm coming too. When you tell the soldiers to prepare your carriage; have them saddle my horse."

"Good," said Rosa and quickly left the room.

"Look at this," Mathas said and handed Hector's will to Fahron who read it then handed it to Gideon. "So if Clev doesn't want the empire, Claudius gets it to tear apart. I will say I am surprised."

"We'll come with you," said Gideon. "If he needs help remembering things perhaps I can help."

After the Angels removed Juleta's magics and poison from Hector's body, Cyril worked with Shara so she could care for Hector and others who would need the same procedure done.

Dominic wrote a letter to Claudius explaining everything that had happened and telling him to have Clev come to the village if he wanted Juleta's magics removed. He walked up to Miranda, "Would you help the Enrops deliver this? It's to Claudius' group. He should prepare Hector's parents and help Clev."

"Certainly," Miranda said. "What are you going to do with the members of the Sisterhood you have captured?"

"No idea. Any suggestions?"

"If you release them the Sisterhood will kill them because they will be viewed as traitors. If you kill them then you now have a war with the Sisterhood. If you want suggestions I would keep them in your prison. They still have information to give you."

"I can tell there is more," said Dominic.

"Yes, but for now tell Mathas and Sorren my words."

Turner's team, Matthew and Angelina had a twenty minute head start on Mathas and the others. When Matthew and Angelina ran into the house, Fennel and Noah stopped them.

"We have to tell you something before you go in there," Fennel said. "During whatever it was that the Angels did to him, Hector's face kept changing. He doesn't look like Thaos anymore. Matthew can you tell us if this is what he used to look like?"

"It was bad," Tessa said as she was making another pot of coffee. "I even cried."

Neither Matthew nor Angelina said a word as they followed Fennel and Noah into Hector's room. They immediately heard Mallory crying. Brock was standing next to her with his arm around her shoulders.

"The Angels left," Shara said to Angelina. "But we have a lot to do. Your father went into Langer to buy supplies for tonics and Jasmine and Seth are gathering other things that Cyril said we will need."

"This is what he looked like when he was Archer," Matthew said. "But he...is he going to live?"

"Cyril said he would but the poison that Juleta put in him was additive so he is going to have a lot of serious side effects. He was worried because he didn't want his parents to see him like this."

"Matthew, I am sorry but if Juleta was still alive I would kill her myself," said Mallory.

"You would have to stand in a very long line," said Angelina. "Did the Angels say how long he would be unconscious because Rosa is bringing Sarah out?"

"They didn't say," Shara said. "Monster or not this man has been through so much; I can't believe he is still alive."

Tessa walked into the room with a tray that held a pot of coffee and cups. "Mallory, you just concentrate on him. Elexas, Jasmine and I will take care of everything else. Abbott's team went into Langer with Sorren. They are buying all kinds of supplies. And Lawrence went out to find Showers."

"Last night they held a celebration here," Shara said to Angelina. "And Hector bought us all extravagant gifts for taking care of him. Yours are at the house."

"Turner said that you will need to do the same to Clev," Angelina said. "Is he staying in this house too? It would be easier for us that way."

"Yes, he has a bedroom here," Tessa said.

"Matthew, we should stay in the village for a while. When Rosa returns why don't you go with her and get the babies. The nurses can pack their things."

"I was just thinking that," Matthew said. "Shara..." Matthew did not finish his sentence because Lawrence and Showers walked into the room.

"He told me," Showers said as he walked up to the bed. "He's Archer again. But boy he looks awful." Showers stared at Hector for a few moments then said. "Let me know if you need anything and later can one of you help me call to the Angels and find out if she did that to any other of our boys besides Clev? I hope that witch rots in hell!"

"I am sure she is," said Mathas sternly.

"Mathas, it was horrible; I even cried," said Tessa. "And we have a lot to tell you."

Matthew moved so Rosa could get close to the bed. Tears were running down her cheeks. She was holding Sarah who held her hands out to Hector and said, "Daddy."

"How can she recognize him?" asked Mathew.

"I don't know," Rosa said in almost a whisper and set Sarah on the bed. The little girl played with Hector's hair then laid down beside him.

"Ok, I am going to cry again," Tessa said and walked out of the room.

"Why don't all of you come out here and we will explain everything," said Noah. All of the men left the room except for Brock. Rosa and Angelina remained in the bedroom with Shara and Mallory.

"Brock would you bring a couple more chairs in here?" Shara asked.

"What the hell!" yelled Claudius as a small flock of Enrops suddenly appeared in front of their faces. Thaos, Stephan and Clev were riding next to him.

"Miranda helped us," said one of the giant birds. "Dominic only had time to write one letter but it concerns many of you. Claudius, you are to read this now then tell the others."

Claudius stopped the caravan and remained on his horse as he read the long letter. He did not show it to anyone until he had finished it.

"I have to talk to Clarence and Catherine," Claudius said. "And I am going to let you boys read this now but Clev...well there is no easy way to say this. Juleta did experiments on you, Hector and others. She somehow put part of her into you and it's like a poison. Miranda told Hector he would become as insane as Juleta so he asked the Angels to take it out. He's so weak that it was hard on him but he is alive. One of the Angels told Shara all that she will need to take care of others who Juleta did this to."

"If you want to have it removed we need to get you straight to the village. They have a room ready for you. The decision is yours son but I would certainly get that shit out of me." Clev became pale as he listened to Claudius. Clev didn't speak but only nodded. Claudius handed Clev the letter then said to Stephan. "You boys stay with him."

Claudius rode to the middle of the caravan and climbed into the carriage with Catherine and Clarence. They cried as Claudius told them about what had been done to Hector by Juleta then by the Angels.

"Claudius say that last part again," said Catherine. "I'm so upset that I can't think right."

"He is very weak and will be sick for a long time but he will live. The Angels took all of the magics and poisons out of him. He doesn't look like Thaos anymore. You have your son back."

"I don't know whether to be happy or horrified," Catherine said.

"You should know that Hector told our team members how guilty he felt that he forced his life on the two of you. He had all these plans for when you got to Langer. He bought a lot of the team clothing and jewels because he wanted them to attend the celebrations in your honor. He didn't want you to see him sick."

"He is our son," said Clarence. "Nothing that he has done has changed that. Would it be possible for us to stay in that village also?"

"I don't know if there is room in the house that Hector is in but I am sure that Chief Sorren can make arrangements. I will send him a letter now. And we only live ten miles from that village; you are welcome to stay with us too."

"We may do that and thank you," said Clarence as he held his wife. "But, at first we want to be near him."

Clev read the letter and his hand was shaking when he handed it to Thaos. Stephan and Thaos read it together in silence.

"Clev, what are you going to do?" asked Stephan.

"Get that damn shit out of me," he said angrily. "I'll tell you Showers had the right idea. None of this is worth it anymore. Hector said that Showers is so happy now that he isn't the same man. The boss is like a brother to me but damn all of this. If Hector dies I don't want to take his place. Claudius can have everything." Clev laughed. "Boy that will be an explosion."

"You know he will tear it apart," said Thaos.

"I know but someone else will just take Hector's place."

All of the people who had witnessed the Angels healing Hector were shaken. Ryan, Olin and Elexas went into the office to work on the translations. They didn't speak about what they had witnessed; they focused on their work. The rest of the men in the house were in the dining area where Noah and Dominic were describing everything in detail that had taken place that morning.

"What are you doing?" Mathas asked as he walked into the office after being briefed about the morning.

"We're working on those papers that were hidden in Javier's house. Dominic asked the Angels if we could show them to Hector," Ryan explained. "There were sheets hidden inside the paper and he did some magic and the wallet turned into the code for the papers." As Ryan spoke, Olin handed Mathas some of the pages.

"This is from a group of the Sisterhood in Salszar. They sent representatives here and those were the women who Otto sacrificed to the Master. They are speculating on the locations of Juleta's hiding places. It sounds like there are groups of the Sisterhood all over just like the Insidiae and they are all preparing for war with the Master."

"Mathas, did the others tell you how bad the Book of Tandum is?" asked Elexas. He nodded. "We can't let any of these groups get it. We will all die."

"We haven't finished this yet," Ryan said. "But the Sisterhood knows that Juleta had a partner who she worked with obtaining the items for her arsenal. They suspected Dieter but since he is dead they have sent some of their members to locate men who might have been in high standing in that organization; obviously to get information."

"They also suspect Otto, Jack and Joanna. Since Jack is the only one alive they probably have people looking for him. They also suspect Zane and Hector. But interestingly, they don't think that Hector was her partner because she collected several items after she went to war with him."

"They are open to the idea that someone else could have been her partner but at the very least they believe that all the people I mentioned have information. We have to translate all of this one letter at a time so it is taking a while."

"The work you do is impressive," Mathas said. "I don't have any money on me now but when we return to the castle all of you will get a bonus."

"Mathas, thank you so much," said Elexas. "I haven't spoken with Ryan or Olin about this but I would like to stay here and help out. It's a lot of work just preparing meals and now with Hector as bad as he is and soon Clev will be here...well, we have all gotten so close I would like to help out. Of course I will still work on our things too."

"Elexas that is fine. In fact, if all three of you want to stay out here or come out here on a regular basis, I have no problem with that. I trust all of you but I worry for your safety so my only rule will be that none of you will be traveling without an escort of some kind. We just have too many enemies."

"That's fine with us," Ryan said. "I like working out here too because we have more resources, I mean with Hector and all the team members. But I will go back to the castle if Olin wants to work there."

"I like it here," Olin said. "And I think the three of us should stay together."

387

"I'll bet that Sorren could fix you up with a place out here if you asked him," Mathas said and turned as he heard the door to Hector's room open. Angelina and Matthew walked up to him.

"I am going to our workshop and start making some of these tonics," Angelina said.

"Father, I am going to get the children a little later and we will all be staying out here," said Matthew.

"I understand. Elexas, Ryan and Olin want to stay out here too and help. Perhaps they can go in with you and get some of their things," Mathas said then he looked at Angelina. "Do you think there is an extra cottage they can stay in?"

"Yes, we built a lot for the ceremonies," Angelina said to Mathas then looked in the dining room. "Showers can you come here?"

"What do you need?" asked Showers as he entered the office.

"All the houses close to this are filled with your men. Do you think we could move some of them farther away so that the people who will be helping with Hector's and Clev's care can stay near them?"

"You just let me know where you want them and I will get everyone moved."

"Let's go outside now," said Angelina and the two left.

"Father, did Dominic tell you what Miranda said about our prisoners?" Matthew asked. He did not want to admit it but he was shaken by Hector's appearance.

"Yes. Fahron and Gideon are going to do more interrogations when we return to the castle. And he did tell me about a different line of questioning that Hector suggested. We'll take that woman here back with us."

Chapter XXXI
The Monastery at Malga

The monastery at Malga was an ancient institution. The buildings and grounds had been added onto over the centuries turning the monastery into a sprawling complex. It was also the only monastery in Opots to be taken over by pure evil.

Several years earlier, Padre Thomas and Padre Bartholomew chanced upon information that led them to do an investigation which revealed that members of the Insidiae had taken over the monastery. These people called demons into the sacred areas. They sacrificed humans to them and committed a multitude of atrocities. The crimes flourished for centuries because no one would question the authority of the church.

Thomas and Bartholomew took meticulous notes of their findings and sent them to the Sanuri who sent the Patronus priests to Malga with orders to take back that monastery. High Priest Raphael was the leader of that army of Patronus priests. He personally did battle with the powerful King of Demons called Ahriman. After the Insidiae were kicked out of the monastery a group of Patronus priests were assigned there permanently to safeguard the institution.

The Patronus Headquarters were set up in the Building of Song which also housed the Hall of Antiquities. This hall held the valuables of the church and boasted the largest library in existence. The regular priests who were assigned to the monastery lived in the main building called the Building of Celebration.

A week earlier when High Priest Bernard led a small army of Patronus priests to that monastery they deliberately arrived under the cloak of darkness. High Priest Othnial, Padre Thomas and Padre Bartholomew were taken to the Building of Song as they did not want their presence known at the monastery.

These priests had learned that centuries earlier the Master was actually the Holy Lord of the monastery at Malga.

Holy Lord was the title given to the Highest Head Priest; the man who ran the monastery. But that term was abolished after the Master broke his covenant with The Great Ruler and worshipped the Originator. Since the Master was the first priest in that world to turn away from The Great Ruler he was rewarded richly by the demons. And the Originator himself gave the Master extraordinary powers.

Before Bernard's group left Langer, Olin gave Othnial a drawing of the areas underneath the monastery where the unholy altars were built. These were altars that High Priest Raphael had not found and they were altars which still gave the Master power. Olin was shown these locations in a dream.

Although Othnial did not tell Olin, he understood that if these altars were power sources for the Master that meant they were still being used. That someone in the monastery was worshipping the Master and offering him sacrifices.

Othnial, Thomas and Bartholomew intended to expose the priests who were worshipping the Master and calling his being into the monastery. Then they intended to destroy the Master. These three, wise and faithful men knew they had volunteered for a suicide mission. They did not fear death; they feared failure.

Hector did not regain consciousness during the four hours that Mathas, Rosa, Fahron and Gideon were at the house, so they returned to the castle. Matthew, Elexas, Olin and Ryan traveled with them to get their belongings so they could return to the Village of Tyger. Since Angelina would be occupied with medical issues, Matthew planned to bring two of the children's nurses to the village with his three children.

Once the entire group arrived at the castle they split up. Mathas, Fahron and Gideon went to the King's study. As soon as they entered the room there was a knock on the door. A sergeant of the Military of Lentz escorted an officer of the clandestine group known as the Guardians into the study.

"My Lord, this is Major Severson of the Military of Puntd. He has been waiting for your return to the castle."

"Thank you Sergeant Tyler that will be all," said Mathas.

As soon as the sergeant walked out of the room, Major Severson said, "You may call me Eli. I have been corresponding with General Fahron and Angus about Captain Josef."

"I am Fahron and this is Commanding Admiral Gideon." The men all shook hands.

"First, do you have time to discuss this matter now?" asked Eli.

"We will make time," said Mathas. "But before we get into that, how many men are with you."

"I came alone."

"I will have chambers prepared for you here," said Mathas and walked out of the study for a few moments. When he returned he was smiling. "My wife will have a feast prepared in your honor."

"She doesn't need to go to that trouble," said Eli. "But I will certainly welcome a hot bath and a bed." Eli was carrying a large leather pouch which he now opened. "Before we get down to business, I have personal letters for you from King Tobias, Queen Tasha and Captain Josef."

Fahron led the men to one of the large tables in the study, while Gideon poured four glasses of whiskey. "We had the books audited at Fort Castor," Mathas said. "And there were no discrepancies."

"I am not surprised," said Eli. "My team and I asked all of the questions that you sent us and more. Here are the written results. Perhaps you can find something that we did not. He told us that he took money from Otto Franks as a wedding gift. Josef said he didn't even open the pouch until sometime later and was shocked at the amount of money."

"He described it as one extremely large pouch with five smaller ones inside. Each of the smaller pouches contained gold coins. He said because of the size he never considered it could contain money. He said he spoke with Franks about it. Franks said it was a gift but he also had concerns about Isabella and wanted Josef to be aware of them."

"Josef said that Otto warned him about Juleta and speculated that she was a witch and had an axe to grind with Isabella. He told Josef to tell him if Isabella started to act strangely and perhaps he could help."

"Josef said that he didn't believe a word that Otto said but within a month of their wedding that Isabella was acting differently. He did tell Otto about it but Otto had no explanations. After a while Josef just accepted the changes in his wife."

"And what were the changes?" asked Mathas.

"She became distant and secretive. Then she, now I am using his words. She became obnoxious, argumentative and demanding," said Eli. "Honestly it sounded like he became so sick of her that he rather ignored her until he found her looking through his papers. He said he focused on his work and children instead of her."

"She was as he described her," Mathas said. "In fact, she was so obnoxious that we all sought to stay away from her but then we discovered it was all an act so we wouldn't find out about her activities, many of which were criminal. Eli, you are welcome to stay here as long as you like. I would ask that you stay until we have time to read all of this; in case we have questions."

"Certainly, I expected as much. By any chance are my former comrades here?"

"Angus and Edward are in Cadia working on a mission," Mathas said. "And at this point we have no idea when they might be back."

"Hopefully I will get a chance to see them before I return," said Eli.

"This is changing the subject but why did you travel alone?" asked Fahron. "We've heard of Huta attacks in your area."

"Actually all of the Guardians do. We don't want to draw attention."

"Interesting," said Gideon. "If you are going to be here a few days I will offer to give you a tour of at least one of the naval yards we are building. Mathas decided to create a navy after the last big attack on this kingdom."

"I would very much like that and I would like to hear about that attack in your words. I dare say that rumors about it spread throughout the continent."

"We can tell you now or wait until you freshen up," said Fahron. "But I have to warn you that you won't believe any of it."

Erebus and the Sanuri had been receiving regular correspondence from their friends in Wetpr, Lentz, Malga and Cadia. And each sender asked the Angels to help expedite the flight of the Enrops since they were all concerned for the safety of their comrades.

Traveling in a boca, especially in rugged terrain was considerably slower than riding a horse. The Sanuri and Erebus had been following the River Nebu north since they left Nora. The last two days they had been traveling east of the Rodite Forest, home of the Giant Gants. The screams of these wild animals on the hunt did not allow either man to get much sleep. This morning they stopped for an early lunch so they could read the letters they had received from three different flocks of Enrops.

As usual the Sanuri did the cooking while Erebus set up the campsite. As they ate they read their letters then exchanged them. "Perhaps you will get your chance to get to know Risha better," the Sanuri said after they read the letters written by Claudius. "I can't say that I understand exactly what she is but I would like to meet her also. Perhaps we should take a trip to Cadia."

Erebus laughed. "Two old men traveling the world together," he said jokingly. "But I would certainly be up for that. Although none of our letters have come right out and said that Malus is a ruse. I am beginning to believe more and more that he is."

"Although it would have to be a ruse created by someone who knows me well. Malus and I didn't exactly socialize in public. And I don't know who is aware of the guilt I feel for not trying to rescue my friends from hell."

"There is the possibility that one of the demons created an illusion to appear as your friend but I am sure that you have already taken that into consideration. What I question is why present Malus and not Cerephus? Weren't you and Cerephus much closer?"

"I have thought about that too. But would Cerephus create enough of a rumor to draw me into a trap? I don't have a good answer for any of my own questions."

"If all goes well; I expect to be at Roch's castle in two days. Tonight let's call to Miranda and see if she has any advice or information."

After High Priest Raphael was called to serve in Salar, High Priest Philetus took charge as the leader of the Patronus priests at the monastery at Malga. He was a pious man. Tall and thin with red hair and piercing blue eyes. His appearance did not disclose that he was a fierce and courageous warrior.

Under Philetus' leadership the Patronus priests developed a good working relationship with the priests at Malga while still managing to keep a professional distance. Initially the priests at Malga had been both suspicious and frightened of the Patronus but over the years they saw the warrior priests as their protectors.

Philetus knew that he would have to maintain a professional distance because he was convinced that more men were aware of the presence of the Insidiae and their crimes than were initially discovered. Also two Patronus priests had been murdered in the monastery the night that Sophie, sister of High Priest Meekos, escaped. The murderers had never been found.

High Priests Meekos, Tenebrae and Pravis had murdered their predecessors and literally taken over the monastery at Malga. They were members of the Insidiae and notorious dark lords.

They ruled that monastery for centuries and turned many of the priests into criminals. Padre Thomas and Padre Bartholomew exposed these dark lords.

Philetus and his men did not believe that of the thousands of priests at this monastery that only Thomas and Bartholomew had their suspicions. And as more and more of the crimes that were committed by the dark lords were exposed, Philetus was convinced that more priests had to have been involved with the cover-up.

Although most of the Patronus priests ate in the main dining hall of the monastery, Philetus had a smaller dining room built in the Building of Song and this is where Othnial, Thomas and Bartholomew ate their meals.

Neither Thomas nor Bartholomew were happy to hear Philetus' theories about more conspirators within the monastery but after reviewing his research they came to the same conclusions.

High Priest Bernard was tasked specifically with the protection of Othnial, Thomas and Bartholomew and he took his assignment very seriously. It was his decision that these three priests should not initially make their presence known at the monastery. Besides being dedicated to his job, Bernard both respected and liked these men. He was not going to let anything happen to them on his watch.

Out of courtesy for Catherine and Clarence, Claudius had not been pushing the caravan from Cadia to Langer hard. They took frequent and long breaks. But after receiving the letter about the experiments that Juleta had conducted on Hector and Clev, everyone was now anxious to get to Langer.

Claudius had sent letters to Mathas, Sorren and Bella, telling them that Hector's parents wanted to go directly to the Village of Tyger and stay there as well as Clev's desire to have the Angels heal him.

When Matthew, Ryan, Olin and Elexas returned to the village late that afternoon they had bocas with them. Prior to leaving the village, Elexas had gotten lists from all of the team members of the items they wanted brought out to them.

Olin and Ryan literally packed up their office to move to the village. Matthew had made arrangements with Sorren to give the three young people their own house to set up for their work.

Besides his family and their belongings, Matthew brought out a great deal of food and other supplies such as blankets and furniture. He had a feeling that the teams would be staying in the village considerably longer than originally anticipated.

The Sanuri and Erebus received another batch of letters before they made camp that night. They were far enough from the Rodite Forest that they did not hear the savage screams of the Gants. After their evening meal the Sanuri called to Miranda. But it was Ruth who appeared.

"Miranda will be here soon to answer your questions about the castle but first I would like to talk with you about several things," Ruth said. "You have received many letters because we have been expediting them. What are your thoughts?"

"The letters we received tonight about Juleta's arsenal, does that have anything to do with what we will be taking from Roch's castle?" asked the Sanuri.

"This mission is a little different than you might believe. There are many more people inside of that castle than the soldiers who work for Sorphat. Part of what you will be doing is a rescue mission. But before we go into that do you have other questions?"

"I was a warlock for many years and I never heard of the Book of Tandum," said Erebus. "How can that be?"

"Erebus, you know that the worlds of darkness exist in layers, so to speak. While you are familiar with many there are more than you ever imagined."

"Juleta understood this at a very early age and sought to conquer these layers. She did not but she visited many. Your teams in Cadia and Langer are dealing with many mysteries concerning magics. They could use your expertise."

"I will gladly go to either or both of those locations but you already told us to go to Ryed, has that changed?"

"For the time being," Ruth said. "As the two of you guessed, you have been watched and many traps are waiting for you in Ryed. You two will need to go there but first you are needed in Langer and Cadia. So tell me what are your thoughts about Hector?"

"He is considerably more of a victim than I would have imagined," said the Sanuri. "And Isabella was much more of a villain than I thought. Are we seeing the right things?"

"Every one of the players in this heinous play, wears or wore many faces. They were all victims and monsters. Some of them, as Hector, still have both of those sides to their personalities. The people in Lentz have done as we asked and made him respond to humanity again. They have performed their duties well and he is responding faster than some of us predicted he would. He now has friends whom he can trust, family and he is falling in love."

"The people in Langer are also responding to him. They genuinely like and respect him. They seek his counsel and they see him much more as a victim than a monster. They are warriors and intelligent people but there is one thing that none of them understand which Erebus does and that is addiction."

"Partly because of his own choices and partly because of Juleta's magics and treachery, Hector is as addicted to power as Erebus is to magics. That is why I am asking the two of you to go there. Erebus, you will understand him as the others do not."

"Because of the kindness and Mercy that has been shown to him, Hector wants to work with our teams. That is his current choice and is always subject to change. He is a brilliant man in his own right and will be very helpful to your cause. But he does not understand his own addiction. And he is going to help the teams find objects that possess great power."

"Do you want me to speak with him or stay until they find all of the objects?" Erebus asked.

"I believe you will know what you need to do as things play out but if you feel comfortable telling your story, there are many who would benefit from hearing it. Your close friends do not tell others of your addiction."

"The team members there have no idea of the struggles and pain you have gone through and you are a man of incredible strength. At the very least perhaps you could help them understand Hector and learn what to look for with him."

"And if I tell him?"

"As you say in this world, that would be the frosting on the cake," Ruth said and smiled. "Also, I spend a great deal of time with Risha these days. Now that she is out of her self-imposed prison she cannot offer her services enough to The Great Ruler. For the brief time the two of you were in the World of Illusions you bonded on a certain level. She is as curious to meet you again as you are her. She has a cottage two miles south of Cadia, a visit would benefit all of you."

"And is there a reason she is in that specific location?" asked the Sanuri.

"Of course," Ruth said and smiled. "And it is not just to protect your teams. Juleta's influence in that kingdom was considerably greater than anyone has imagined. Her poison was spread and like a plague it keeps spreading."

"Can you tell us where her arsenal is hidden?"

"That has not been revealed to any of us who are working directly with all of you. Which should let you know that many of you have significant roles to play in all of this. But we will certainly assist you as we can. Cyril is a very powerful Angel who begged The Great Ruler to work with us. We are happy to have his company and the two of you should learn to call upon him also. His expertise is healing and that has many forms."

398

Miranda appeared as soon as Ruth finished speaking. "Tomorrow you will pass the caves where the transformation between Roch and Omnibus was to take place. The trap that Ahriman set for the Sanuri is still there. Do not enter those caves," Miranda said.

"Why haven't you closed it up?" asked the Sanuri.

"We have our reasons," Miranda said and smiled. "Make your camp north of those caves and I will come to you tomorrow night. As Ruth told you there are many more beings in that castle than the soldiers. Sorphat was so intrigued with this world that he started to collect species for his own amusement. We will free them all. They are in a sort of stasis."

"As you know, many years ago Meekos sent the demon Demetries to watch over Roch. He paid Demetries to keep Roch from getting killed before he could fulfil his role as the vessel for Omnibus. Erebus, a few months before Cerephus asked you to come to the castle, Roch was on another of his obsessive journeys to find the Ruby Scroll. He attacked the cave of the Gants and lost."

"Demetries had Hutas attack Roch's castle and Taperia to force the King to return home and his plan worked. Unfortunately many innocent people died during those attacks. Demetries had an army of Hutas at his beckon call and they were led by a treacherous monster named Derlock. Sanuri, you saw Derlock on the night of the weddings of Raul and Simon. He was one of the few who escaped with his master Demetries."

"Demetries regularly sent Hutas into the secret tunnels of Roch's castle to steal his treasures. On one such assignment Derlock saw a ring that he liked and took it for himself. The ring is gold with a huge emerald stone. The ring was cursed by the Sisterhood. Roch's reputation for raping and brutalizing women was known far outside of the borders of Opots. The Sisterhood also knew of Roch's obsession for riches and gold."

399

"They had one of their members pose as a servant. She was allowed into the castle and placed the ring in Roch's chambers. Roch had a secret room in his chambers that he had filled with treasures as well as all of the rooms in the lower levels of the castle. Sophie found the ring and sensed the power in it. She put it into one of the rooms below the castle."

"The ring was meant to punish Roch for his crimes but instead it has been punishing Derlock. The ring is very powerful and the priestesses of the Sisterhood soon realized it was not worn by Roch but they did not know what had happened to it."

"Derlock lives but he looks like a crippled old man instead of the mighty warrior he once was."

"There are many members of the Sisterhood in Stordt because they are looking for Juleta's arsenal and they too wondered if it was in Roch's castle. You will be entering the castle before they get there. You will need to get that ring."

"And how do we find Derlock?" asked the Sanuri.

"That will be the easy part," said Miranda. "Besides the rooms filled with treasures, Roch had a room filled with items of power and importance. That is the room where we will go. Demetries sent Derlock to find it and he did. With his master destroyed, Derlock felt there was no one to protect him in his weakened condition so he lives in that room. He has not figured out that his coveted ring is what is cursing him."

"So I assume we will be transporting the items in the boca?" asked the Sanuri.

"Certainly Sorphat hasn't found that room yet," said Erebus.

"The answer is yes to both of your comments," said Miranda. "We will remove the items then release the beings."

"Can't we take some of that treasure and give it to the peasants in Ryed or others?" asked Erebus.

"We will not tell you to steal riches," said Ruth.

"Well, technically those riches are abandoned and they were stolen to begin with. If say, I was to claim the treasures that we found could I turn them over to you to feed the poor? Or whatever else you wanted to do with them?" asked Erebus.

"There is still one person who would have responsibility for those riches and that is Vitomas since she was Roch's Queen," said Miranda.

"So if we wrote a letter to her now, would you make sure it got to her before tomorrow night?" asked Erebus. "With her graciousness she would want that money to help the poor."

"We can do that," said Ruth. "How will you transport it?"

"I thought I would leave that up to you since there are many more riches than we could fit into the boca," Erebus said and the Angels disappeared. "They didn't wait for the letter. Do you think they will come back for it?"

"I think this will be a visit on their part," said the Sanuri and smiled.

Sudfad's family and guests were just finishing their dinner when Miranda and Ruth appeared in the dining room. The children squealed with delight, jumped out of their chairs and ran to the Angels.

"Our Angel!" screamed Nina and ran to Ruth as did her sisters.

"Is anything wrong?" asked Sudfad with great concern since the Angels usually did not appear in any rooms other than the study and the Great Hall.

"No," said Miranda. "We are delivering a message. The Sanuri and Erebus will free the hostages in Roch's castle tomorrow night. Also in that castle is a secret room which Sorphat has not yet found. It contains items of power and importance. They will be removing those items and bringing them here. Sudfad, not all of them can be put into the Holy Vault; you will need to find another place to lock them up within the castle."

"Are they a danger to our family?"

"We will prevent them from being a danger."

"Why not destroy them?" asked Javier.

"Because they will be needed some day," said Ruth. "Erebus asked if they could take all of the riches that Roch hoarded and give them to us to give to the needy. We could not give them permission to steal the riches but there is one person yet living who has a claim to them."

Raul and Simon looked at Vitomas and smiled. "Me?" she asked with surprise.

"You were his Queen when he obtained that treasure," Ruth said.

"Of course, take it. Take everything. I give it all to you. Do I need to put that in writing?" Vitomas asked then looked at Raul, then Sudfad. "I should have asked you if you wanted any of it."

"No," said Sudfad with a smile.

"We could use some," said Corsa.

"What!" said Javier and quickly turned and looked at her.

"No, not for us. Madeline and I want to build a lot of Adam's Homes. We want them in the entire kingdom and that will be expensive," Corsa said to Javier then looked at the Angels. "Of course if there are others who need it more, we will raise the money." The Angels smiled and disappeared.

"I'll bet some of the treasure finds you," Raul said to Corsa and grinned.

"Vitomas, you were Roch's Queen?" asked George. "I didn't know that. I heard he was a monster."

"He was and that is why we don't like to talk about it," Vitomas said. "Annabelle and I were both his prisoners."

"How did you escape?" asked Nina.

"Actually, I think we would all like to hear that story if you don't mind," said Javier.

"It might be too painful for them to talk about," said Madeline.

"Honey, they are all family," Raul said. "We should tell them some of the story."

"Alright but I don't want the little ones to hear."

"I'm not a little one," Nina said adamantly as she returned to her chair.

"We'll take the children to the playroom and have the nurses watch them," said Simon. "I think everyone should hear the entire story since it continues to haunt us."

"What do you mean?" asked Alex.

"Did you know that Roch was Father's brother?" Raul asked and grinned when Corsa and her brothers all turned and looked at Sudfad with amazement.

"Let's get some more wine," said Sudfad. "These are long stories."

Chapter XXXII
The Ring

The following night both Miranda and Ruth appeared in the campsite of the Sanuri and Erebus. The two men were in the back of the boca rearranging the cargo to make room for the items they would be taking from Roch's castle.

"We are waiting," Ruth said and both men peered out of the wagon.

"Sorry, we didn't hear you," said the Sanuri.

"Climb into the front seat," Miranda said.

"Are we going through the main or back gate?" Erebus asked and in that instant the men found themselves inside of the wall that surrounded the castle. The men looked around and did not see any sign of life.

"Miranda, are there any soldiers to stop us?" asked the Sanuri.

"They are under Sorphat's spell. That is why we will break the spell as soon as you have the items," Miranda said. "Erebus lead the way."

Although the actual entrances to the tunnels were outside of the wall, Sophie had once showed Erebus another way to enter the lower levels without being seen. He now directed the Sanuri to the back of the castle, near the kitchen door. There was just enough moonlight for them to see their way.

"Angels did you unlock this door?" Erebus asked.

"No," said Ruth.

"Well, this may not be a good sign," said Erebus and opened a door that led into as small warehouse. "This is where the deliveries are dropped off," Erebus whispered to the Sanuri as they entered the area.

Once inside of the warehouse it was total darkness. "Can we have some light?" whispered the Sanuri.

Suddenly a small ball of light appeared before the men. "You can control that with your mind or your voice," Ruth said in their ears.

"More light," said Erebus and the men stared at several dozen soldiers who were standing at attention and frozen in time. "Let's get out of here," Erebus whispered.

The men followed the ball of light down two dark hallways then the Sanuri said, "Take us to the room with the items of power." The ball of light started to move faster and the men followed it down three more hallways and a flight of stairs. They were now in an area that Erebus had never seen. The air was thick and dank. Rats scurried before the feet of the intruders.

The ball came to a stop several yards ahead of the men. The Sanuri grabbed Erebus' arm to stop him from walking forward. "We need more light," the Sanuri said and the ball grew in size until it illuminated the entire area they were in. They were no longer in a hallway but what appeared to be a cave.

"What did you sense?" Erebus asked in a whisper as he searched the area with his eyes.

"There aren't any rats in here. If Derlock isn't eating them then something else is."

"Miranda, is it safe for us to cross to the door?" asked the Sanuri.

"Yes. The monster you sense is inside."

"Well, that makes me feel better," Erebus said sarcastically.

The men approached the large wooden door with caution; they both carefully inspected it. The Sanuri said a silent prayer then extended his right hand towards the huge metal latch.

"Let me go in first and when he jumps me you get him," Erebus whispered and the Sanuri nodded.

The sound of metal on metal filled the air as Erebus opened the latch. The hinges groaned when he pushed the door open. The ball of light went into the room and illuminated it.

Erebus stood in the doorway and looked at piles of items that were on the floor and on old tables. He did not see Derlock. Erebus motioned to the Sanuri that Derlock was behind the door.

Erebus quickly threw his weight against the door so that it would slam back on anyone behind it then he and the Sanuri quickly entered the room. Erebus pulled the door back but Derlock was not behind it. They quickly turned as they heard movement. A being jumped up from behind a pile of things and ran towards the men.

The Sanuri quickly stepped to the side of the attacker and hit him in the stomach with a staff. Then the Sanuri hit the being behind the knees and pushed him forward. The being fell to the ground but quickly rolled onto his back. The Sanuri placed the tip of his staff against the being's throat.

"Are you Derlock?" the Sanuri demanded. The being stopped moving and stared at the Sanuri. "Are you Derlock the Huta?" This time the Sanuri asked his question in the language of the Hutas.

"Sanuri he is wearing the ring," said Erebus.

Derlock no longer resembled a human. He was emaciated and his body was gnarled like the branch of a tree. His face was twisted, his teeth rotted and his eyes were cloudy. He had little strength and he smelled of death.

"That ring is cursing you," the Sanuri said in Derlock's language. "You were once a mighty warrior and now you are an animal. Take if off!" Derlock understood his words. He looked at the ring on his hand then he looked back at the Sanuri and shook his head from side to side to indicate 'no'.

"Great Ruler destroy the power and evil of that ring," the Sanuri said loudly.

Derlock screamed in agony and rolled on the floor for several moments. He grasped his hand as if that was where the pain was originating from. He pulled the ring off and threw in on the floor. Erebus and the Sanuri stood in awe as they watched Derlock return to his old body and strength.

Derlock's mind had been as crippled as his body. He shook his head several times as his mind was now flooded with memories. He realized he was changing and stared at his own limbs in amazement. Then he touched his stomach, chest and head. He stood up and towered over Erebus, who expected Derlock to attack them.

"Tell him the truth," Ruth said as she now appeared next to the Sanuri but Derlock could not see her.

The Sanuri told Derlock that the Sisters of Tameric had cursed that ring and put it into Roch's chambers but it was moved and once Derlock slipped it on his finger the curse meant for Roch attacked him.

Derlock stared at the Sanuri as he spoke, then he said in his native language. "I know who you are. Who both of you are. Why would you help me?"

"Because you needed help," the Sanuri said. "Roch and Demetries are both dead. This castle has been owned by a series of demons. You are free to go or to attack us, the choice is yours."

"I will not fight you. Not ever again. I owe you my life," Derlock said.

"Don't go into the caves that you used to dwell in," said the Sanuri. "A demon opened a door and if you go in there you will be sucked into a hell world."

"Did you come here just to save me?"

"No. The Sisters of Tameric are attacking our friends and many others. Roch has things in here that will help us fight them. Derlock do you realize that you have been in here for years?"

"It seems like centuries," Derlock said. "I am remembering things now. I came in here because I wanted to be near the power because I had lost my own. I don't know what these things are but I can show you the most powerful ones. The Sisters of Tameric are now my enemies and when I find my tribe they will be the enemies of all Hutas."

Although Erebus could not speak the language of the Hutas, Ruth allowed him to understand what Derlock was saying. Derlock pushed things off from one of the tables then proceeded to sort through the piles of objects and place specific items on the table. Erebus bent down to pick something up and Ruth said, "Let him do it. Ask him what he knows about these things."

The Sanuri asked Derlock if he had any information about the items. Although Derlock did not understand what they were he did know where many of the things came from. He explained how Roch and Demetries would lead raiding parties and steal things from wealthy people, witches and dark lords.

He told of a time when he led an attack against a caravan traveling from Ryed. Demetries had ordered everyone killed. When the massacre was over the demon Demetries appeared on the battlefield and took the saddlebags off from one horse. Derlock now handed those saddlebags to the Sanuri. Then Derlock filled the table with small chests, scrolls, books, some jewels, a chalice and a sword.

"Tell him to leave the way he came in," Ruth said.

The Sanuri repeated Ruth's message then asked as an afterthought. "Have you ever heard of Juleta or Isabella?"

"Demetries spoke of a Juleta. He said she was our enemy. Is she a Sister of Tameric?"

"She was, she is dead now," the Sanuri said.

Suddenly Derlock turned and looked at Erebus. "You were friends with the witch that worked here. Demetries stole something of hers." Derlock turned and sorted through a few things. Moments later he handed Erebus a thick book.

Erebus nodded and thanked Derlock, who now turned and ran to his freedom. The Sanuri had picked the ring up from the floor and handed it to Ruth.

"Now you understand how powerful their magics are. The Sisterhood is a group driven by hatred. No one is safe from their wrath. They should be the focus of your energies now."

"Did you want anything else besides what he put on the table?" asked the Sanuri.

"The things that we need to retrieve are now in your boca," Ruth said. "Vitomas gave us everything here. Some of the money has been given to the hostages that Miranda released. The rest we will use for other purposes. The evil in this castle is overwhelming. Once all of you are gone the castle will cease to exist."

As Ruth spoke the three were returning to the warehouse. "There is also a chest in the back of your boca that contains items that belonged to Sudfad's parents and grandparents."

"Thank you," the Sanuri said. "He will very much appreciate that." Ruth smiled.

"Will Sorphat realize you've destroyed his castle," asked Erebus.

"Sorphat could feel the power here but he did not understand where it was coming from. He harnessed some of it to extend his spells. When this place is destroyed many beings will awaken again. He will feel the loss of power and will return."

"And then what?" asked the Sanuri.

"That is a choice for you," said Ruth as she tossed him the ring.

"The curse was never destroyed on this ring was it?" Erebus said. "And if the Sisterhood is in the area they will recognize the power and come for it. Do you want us to set a trap?"

"And if the wrong person puts this ring upon their hand?" asked the Sanuri. "No, we will not lower ourselves to fight as they do."

"I am glad to hear that," said Ruth. "But the curse was destroyed,"

"Then I don't understand," said Erebus. "Was this some kind of test?"

"Look at the back of the ring," Ruth said and disappeared.

Roch with love Isabella was inscribed in the back of the ring.

The Sanuri and Erebus quickly left the castle. Miranda had opened the gates to allow the hostages to flee. Both men wanted to get to Wetpr as soon as possible. They had no intentions of sleeping this night. They had only traveled a couple of miles when they heard an explosion that shook the earth. The horses were terrified by the noise and the Sanuri had to calm them.

"I think it is unlikely that Sorphat will miss that," Erebus said sarcastically. "Do you think that Ruth and Miranda are waiting for him? I for one would like to see that." The Sanuri laughed.

It was after midnight when Claudius entered Hector's house with Clev, Catherine and Clarence. Jasmine was in the kitchen making bread dough and grabbed a knife when the door opened.

"Jasmine, it's Claudius," he said quickly as he saw her movement. At the same time he moved in front of Hector's parents.

"I am sorry; there have just been so many attacks. Are those his parents?"

"Jasmine is a Nordes warrior and a member of one of our teams," Claudius said. "This is Catherine and Clarence. You know Clev."

"Hector hasn't woken up since the Angels healed him. Mallory is sitting with him now. Are any of you hungry?" Claudius nodded. Jasmine led them to the closed door of Hector's bedroom. She knocked before opening. "Hector's parents are here," she said to Mallory who stood up from her chair.

Catherine started to cry as soon as she saw her son. Neither of Hector's parents spoke. They both walked up to the bed and stared at him.

"I'll get another chair," Mallory said and left the room. Claudius and Clev followed her.

Seth had been sleeping in Mallory's bed. He and Brock both awoke when they heard voices. Now both men walked out of the bedroom.

"Clev; Shara and Angelina told us to wake them whenever you got here," said Jasmine. "Do you want us to get them now?"

"I don't know yet," he said. "I hate to wake them up."

"Well, I will fix you something to eat and you can think about it," said Jasmine. "Did you get all of the manuscripts?"

"Yes, they're in these saddlebags," Clev said of the two sets of saddlebags he had hanging over his shoulder.

"Shara will want us to wake them for that," said Seth. "I'll get them."

Mallory took a second chair into Hector's room. Then she returned with two blankets and put one around Catherine's shoulders and the other around Clarence's. She could see the pain in their faces. No one spoke.

Sorren and Matthew came to Hector's house with their wives. Matthew took them all into Hector's bedroom and introduced them to Clarence and Catherine who had many questions for the healers.

"We are fixing steaks and fried potatoes," Mallory said as she carried a tray filled with coffee cups into the room. "Does everyone want to eat?"

"I think so," said Sorren. In the few moments that he had spoken to Hector's parents his heart cried for them. Sorren couldn't imagine being in their place.

"We heard horses; is everything alright?" Elexas asked as she, Ryan and Olin walked into the house.

"Yes, his parents are here," said Claudius.

"You look exhausted," Ryan said to Claudius. "We are staying in the house next door. Why don't you get some sleep?"

"I might just take you up on that son, thanks," Claudius said.

Clev walked out of his bedroom when he heard Elexas' voice. The two stared at each other for a moment then she walked up to him and kissed him on the cheek. "I'm going to stay here and take care of you," she said and he hugged her.

"Claudius can have my room," Elexas said. "I am going to stay here and help."

After eating, Shara and Angelina immediately started to study the manuscripts that Clev had brought. They took all of the materials into the office because Mallory and Jasmine were already preparing breakfast for the team members. Ryan and Olin took Claudius to their house and showed him the office they had set up. Then they showed him Elexas' room. The young men decided they would try and get a few hours of sleep too.

Clev wanted to wait until morning to have the procedure done. He and Elexas sat on the front porch and talked for hours.

Sorren and Matthew took Catherine and Clarence to a house that was prepared for them next door. Once Hector's parents knew where the house was located they returned to their son's bedside. Sorren and Matthew moved the belongings into the house.

"I would not want to be them for all the money in the world," Sorren said. "Did you see their faces? Their hearts are broken."

"I know," Matthew said. "You haven't had a chance to get to know them yet but they are the nicest people. I keep wondering how Hector could have turned out like he did. It scares me for our children."

The members of the teams gathered at Hector's house for breakfast. Catherine and Clarence were surprised to see how many people were seated at the breakfast tables when they walked out of Hector's room. Claudius made the introductions.

As soon as everyone was seated Tessa said, "Mallory, you have to get some sleep today. Someone order her to sleep."

"I am fine," Mallory said.

"No you aren't," Brock said to her then looked at Hector's parents. "She's Hector's girl and she hasn't left his side until you came."

"Brock!" Mallory snapped.

"It's true," said Tessa then she grinned. "Brock and I will tie you to that bed if you don't try and get some sleep."

"We heard you did that to Hector," Clarence said and smiled. Mallory blushed deeply and others laughed.

"Honey, your friends are right," Catherine said to Mallory. "Now that we are here we will all work together and I mean with everything. There isn't any reason that Clarence and I can't help with the work around here because honestly you all look exhausted. You've been protecting our son from his enemies and taking care of him. We don't have the talents you do but he is our son."

"You two are just as exhausted as everyone else," said Shara. "You need to get some sleep too."

"We talked about that," Clarence said. "We want to be with Clev when he has that procedure done this morning."

"I don't know if that is a good idea," said Tessa.

"He doesn't have any family here so we will sit with him," Clarence said.

"Please don't get mad at me," said Jasmine. "We know you are very wealthy and probably have staff to do things for you. So when you say you are going to help what do you mean?"

Catherine and Clarence looked at each other and smiled. "You are right but my wife is a great cook and believe it or not I know how to do chores."

"The reason I ask is after Clev has the procedure we will be really busy with taking care of both of them and we would appreciate some help, especially in the kitchen," Jasmine said with embarrassment.

"Good," said Catherine and smiled. "Honestly we would rather help than sit around."

"I hear horses," Garvis said and got up from the table and looked out one of the windows. "It's Mathas and Rosa. Why are they here so early?" Garvis opened the door for the Royal Family to enter.

"Margarit say hello to Catherine and Clarence then go to your training," said Rosa. Hector's parents each hugged Margarit.

"I want to see Hector," Margarit said and ran into the bedroom. Mallory followed her.

Both Clarence and Catherine stood up and smiled as Rosa walked up to them with Sarah. "Meet your granddaughter," Rosa said emotionally and handed the girl to Catherine who hugged and kissed her.

"He looks like his old self," Margarit announced when she returned to the dining area. "I made a card for him. Shara, since I am going to start my studies to be a physician can I help with anything?"

"I would say yes but not today. You should go to training now," Shara said.

"Clev is your face going to change too," Margarit asked.

"Boy, I hope not," he said and grinned but everyone could hear the fear in his voice even Margarit.

She walked up to him and hugged him, "I'll make you a card too," she said then ran out of the house.

"Clev, we don't really know each other but it was our daughter who did this to you. Rosa and I came out early so we could be with you," said Mathas.

414

"I don't want to scare Clev but you might not be ready to see something like this," said Tessa and first looked at Mathas and Rosa then at Clarence and Catherine. "You realize it was like she put demons in them don't you? The Angels will make the demons leave Clev. You are going to see that. Of course, we all doubt that she put as many in him as she did in Hector but you should know what you are walking into."

Dominic and Fennel brought a couple more chairs to the table. Mathas and Rosa looked at each other, "Will someone keep Sarah out here while we are in that room?" Rosa asked.

"Of course," said Jasmine.

"We will be in there too," Clarence said as he cuddled his granddaughter.

The Sanuri and Erebus traveled all night because they didn't know if the items they carried could be detected by others. They crossed the border into Wetpr three hours after sunrise and made camp to give the horses rest.

Immediately after leaving Roch's castle the previous night, the Sanuri sent Enrops to King Sudfad telling him about the mission and asking for an escort. It did not take long for the birds to arrive in Wetpr. Now, in the early morning hours Raul, Simon, Alex, Javier, Kent and George were leading a company of soldiers south to meet their friends.

Chapter XXXIII
The Scream

Brock went to Sabra's house and asked her to take care of Sarah while the others were helping Clev. Sabra had not been present when the Angels healed Hector and now took the little girl to her home when she heard the screams coming from Clev's room.

Miranda and Cyril were healing Clev as the others watched and were prepared to do battle with any monsters that jumped out of him. Although Juleta had not changed Clev's appearance, different faces appeared as his during the healing process. Catherine, Rosa and Elexas cried.

When the process was done, Clev fell unconscious. "He will live but he needs a great deal of rest," said Miranda. "He was not as damaged as Hector. Mathas, I am glad you witnessed this. You give lip service to the monster that your daughter was; now perhaps it will sink in. Let go of your guilt. This certainly isn't her worst atrocity."

Sorphat was in the heat of battle when his castle in Stordt exploded. He now appeared to view the rubble. He was more confused than angry. He understood that only a powerful being could do such damage yet he had no idea why someone or something would do that.

He walked around the grounds trying to find some clue as to what had happened. He noticed there were no bodies and that only added to the mystery.

"Have you lost something?" asked an old woman who slowly walked up to the powerful demon.

"Woman do you know what happened here?" he demanded.

"I know all of your hostages were set free before the explosion."

Sorphat stared at Ruth. She was masking her holiness but he was not a fool. "How do you know this?" he asked suspiciously.

Ruth smiled and walked towards the rubble, "I know many things. You might say I am a seer of sorts."

"Do you know who did this?"

"Wouldn't a better question be why?"

Sorphat was watching Ruth closely and now backed away from her.

"Who are you?" he asked.

"I already told you."

"What are you?"

"Now, that would answer the question why."

Sorphat fell to the ground as the Angel's holy presence was over powering him. She was no longer in the guise of an old woman but in her glory and the light she emitted blinded the monster.

"You come to this world and treat The Great Ruler's children and creations as if they are toys for your amusement. This is no longer your playground. The Queen of Stordt gave this property to the Heavens. You are now lying on holy ground."

Sorphat jumped to his feet because his body felt as if it was on fire. He lost his guise as a human and the monster appeared. He lunged at Ruth but fell to the ground as his feet and legs were consumed by fire. He cursed the Angel and screamed with rage as his body burst into flames.

Raul and his men came upon the Sanuri and Erebus shortly after the two made camp.

The Sanuri was explaining what had happened at Sorphat's castle when Erebus suddenly grabbed his head and fell to the ground. Simon and Alex were the first to run to him.

"Ruth what is happening?" yelled Erebus.

"Are you sick?" asked Simon.

"No, there was just a major shift in power. I don't understand it," Erebus said.

Adam appeared and touched Erebus, who now was able to stand up. "All of you need to return to the castle. We will speak with you there. You and your horses will be refreshed."

"What has happened?" asked the Sanuri.

Adam smiled. "Because Vitomas gave Roch's property to the Heavens, Ruth was able to destroy Sorphat and lift his curses. And that has more significance for all of you than you can imagine. Letters just arrived at the castle. They were written by Claudius when he was in Cadia. Read them before we speak with you."

The hell worlds realized the demise of Sorphat before the citizens of Stordt did. Many demons were elated that another of their opponents had died. Only Toni felt grief for the loss of her lover but this emotion was fleeting. She had long ago given up her humanity. Sorphat's armies started to falter with the news that their leader was dead. Toni knew what she had to do and picked up her sword.

Enrops arrived at Gabriel's home as the family was finishing their breakfast. The great birds carried letters written by Thaos, Stephan and Claudius after they left Cadia. Natalie saw the look on Luca's face as he read his letter.

"Honey, what is it?" she asked.

He handed her the letter and showed her the passage where Christopher was named as one of the people born with special powers. "We need to have a meeting," Luca said.

"I agree. Everyone but the children and nurses in my study now," said Gabriel.

Archetenus, Jared and the team leaders had just arrived at Sudfad's castle when Enrops delivered the letters from Claudius and his sons. Before that flock left another entered and a single Enrop announced, "Because Vitomas gave Roch's belongings to the Angels, Ruth was able to destroy Sorphat. The Angels want to meet with all of you here. We think the Angel Adam is helping your sons and the Sanuri to return more quickly."

"Let's start the meeting now," said Sudfad.

"The Angels want you to read those letters first," said the same Enrop.

Raul and the group he led never realized anything was different on their return trip home until they reached the castle. "How the...what the...did Adam transport us?" Raul asked loudly.

"I think he affected time," said the Sanuri. "But I am not even sure about that."

"Well, how could everything seem so normal?" asked Kent.

"No idea," Simon said. "But we should unload those things before we meet with Father."

Raul dismissed the soldiers as they rode to the front of the castle.

"We'll move everything," said Alex.

"That large chest is for Sudfad," the Sanuri said. "Ruth said it was family things."

Javier knocked on the door to Sudfad's study then opened it. "Don't ask us how but we are back. We have a lot of stuff to unload if anyone wants to help."

All of the men in the study stood up to leave. "Javier let them do that; there is something you need to read," Sudfad said. Madeline walked up to her brother and handed him Claudius' letter.

Javier read in silence as others watched the look on his face. "This is incredible but it does explain a lot of things."

"That is what I said too" said Madeline.

The door to the study opened as Kent and George carried a large chest into the room. "The Angel said this was family things," said Kent. "Where do you want it?"

"Any place; it looks heavy," said Sudfad.

"The Angels want to talk to all of us; that's why they helped us back," said George with a big grin. "We think Adam changed time somehow."

Within twenty minutes all of the people had returned to the study. And before they sat down the room was filled with Angels. The Lion spoke first.

"The Queen of Stordt who suffered so much for others has had her prayers answered this day. You saved your people when you gave all of Roch's belongings to the Heavens."

Both Vitomas and Annabelle started to sob. Their husbands quickly went to them.

The Lion continued, "Ruth destroyed Sorphat this morning and broke all of his curses on this world. Stordt is without a king and for the first time in decades without demon rule. I hear your thoughts. Vitomas, you do not want Raul to be King of that dark kingdom. Annabelle, you are thinking the same thing of Simon."

"Perhaps it is time for you to adjust the way you look at things. Sudfad it is time for you to open that chest." Sudfad was shaken by the information and slowly walked to the chest as he was trying to compose himself. "Renya, you should help him," said The Lion.

When Sudfad opened the lid to the chest everyone in the room immediately saw two exquisite crowns. "Sudfad, your parents were kind and compassionate. It was their wish that you would free their people. But how do you take on such a great undertaking? They wanted you to be the King of Stordt. How do you rule two immense kingdoms? You combine them into one."

"You expand the borders of Wetpr and Stordt as it was, no longer exists. The kingdom belonged to Roch, it has been given to us and these are our wishes."

"You have enough family members and teams to accomplish this task. King Manu is already leading an army here to assist you and Thedes and Ibula have already been told it is time for them to share in the inheritance. You will get no resistance from the citizens but as Vitomas and Annabelle have told you many times; it was a dark place that called to dark men. The voices of darkness were real and they have been silenced."

"Ruth and Miranda destroyed the castle and released the hostages that Sorphat had captured for his amusement. There was too much evil there. But that land has been cleansed. This is the shift in power that Erebus felt. The chains fell off an entire kingdom."

"All of you look shocked and overwhelmed, as we expected. Of course we will be here to help you but all of you would be wise to establish forts and Patronus Headquarters quickly. When you go down to the basement. There are two rooms next to that in which you just stored the items of power. The room on the left has much of Roch's treasure to be used for the citizens of that kingdom. The storeroom on the right is riches to be used for the building of Adam's Homes as Corsa requested. And Ruth will use the remainder to help the peasants of Ryed as Erebus requested.

"Do you accept our terms?" asked The Lion.

"Yes, of course," stammered Sudfad. He recognized the crowns worn by his parents and this added to his emotions.

"Sanuri, will you please come up here and crown the new King and Queen of Stordt?" asked The Lion.

Renya too was overwhelmed and crying as the Sanuri officially put the crowns on them. Everyone in the room applauded. Then The Lion spoke again.

"This will change many of your assignments but ultimately you will have the same goals. Archetenus and Jared are men of Stordt, they know the area and the people."

"We would prefer that they go to Taperia immediately with their teams and set up order before the criminals take control again. While this may seem like a deterrent from the assignment that Miranda gave you, in reality it will be a short cut."

"All of the teams you have here should help in Stordt but we prefer that the teams in Lentz and Cadia stay on their missions and we would like the Sanuri and Erebus to join them."

"Because the Sanuri and Erebus showed Mercy to a monster, the Hutas are now the enemies of the Sisters of Tameric. This will actually save lives, although that is difficult for you to understand at this point."

"Benedict will you come forward please?" Benedict was shocked and bowed before the Angel. "We have saved your people from hell. Perhaps your people can help Sudfad's family save the people of Stordt from the hell they have been living in. Your worlds were very similar."

"Of course," said Benedict.

"Javier, Madeline, Corsa, Alex, Kent and George. All of you still do not feel a part of this family. I hope that by now you realize there are no coincidences. You are all here because you were meant to be."

"Sudfad and Renya have shown love and wisdom with all of the children they have brought into their home. Soon Ibula and Thedes will be here too. Every one of you has a role to play and a great deal of work to do."

Nina was sitting on Nyla's lap and now jumped to the floor. "What about us? We want to help too. We're part of the family."

The Angels smiled and the room warmed. "All of you will be part of this and do great things," said The Lion. "But the difference between you, Nyla and Saran is that you feel completely a part of this family."

Nina got a huge smile on her face. "Can I hug our Angel now?" she asked.

"You may hug us all," said The Lion. "Do you have any questions?" Nina immediately ran to the Angels; her sisters hesitated for a moment then they too ran to the Holy Messengers.

"I do," said Luca. "And if this is not the time please tell me; but today we received the letters that named some of our family members as having more power. Can you please explain that?"

"That includes all types of power, not just physical," said The Lion. "Power of their wills, their spirits not to be defeated, their connections within the universe are just examples. I can see you are confused. Think about the people she named. They all have strong, outgoing personalities and something else that you picked up on but could not explain. Risha was allowed to pass on that information as the teams in Langer and Cadia are learning a great deal about Hector and Clev. These men wear many faces are they the monster or the victim?"

"I am surely not saying they are innocents; they made their choices. But I promise you that whether your teams like or hate these men, they will never forget what they have seen. Several of your members have threatened to kill them yet wept for them. The lesson here is that nothing is black and white. Life is very complicated and that scares many so they would prefer to see things in a simple form but that is just putting on blinders."

"Catherine and Clarence are good and faithful people. Yet they failed to see so many things as they raised their son. He of course is responsible for his choices but he would have made different choices if he would have had more guidance. Do not make the same mistakes."

"Risha made it sound like the children and perhaps Madeline and Javier were meant to find us or us them," said Gabriel." The demons can somehow see or sense that power. I assume that since you are telling us about this that we will encounter more people like that. Can you help us to know what people have it so we can bring them in and protect them?"

"We have been waiting for that question," said The Lion. "Yes we will. But you do realize that all of the children that have been adopted idolize all of you and want to follow in your footsteps."

"All of you are doing things right but now you will know how to protect them better and that is not just the children with special power. All your children are doorways to you."

After the Angels left Raphael said, "I am getting our families and bringing them here. We should at least have a toast before we go to work."

"We're moving everything into the Great Hall," said Raul. "We should invite the priests from the Cicero Headquarters too."

"I will take care of that," said Simon. "Maddox, Ira, Vincente and Henrich your teams will be going to Stordt with Archetenus and Jared. Gather all of your members and bring them here for the planning. Although Annabelle and Vitomas had told us a hundred times about Stordt, I was not prepared for it. And I am sure that many of you will feel the same way."

"At this moment I am debating whether we should inform the citizens of Stordt that they are now citizens of Wetpr or wait until we have our men in place," said Sudfad. "Either way we need to notify Fort Nora and the Patronus Headquarters there. Raul and Gabriel will you write those letters now?"

"I need to make arrangements for our guests," said Renya. "I was so emotional; did The Lion say when the Rualas would arrive?"

"No," said Luca.

"Papa, there are a lot of papers and it looks like maps in this chest," said Saran. "I didn't touch any of them."

"Sudfad, look through that chest now," said the Sanuri. "Ruth put it in the boca so who knows what is in there."

Many of the people in the room were removing maps and charts from the walls to take to the Great Hall. "Everyone can I have your attention please," said Sudfad. "I don't think that I am alone when I say this has not really sunk in yet but let's not forget who made this possible. Vitomas, you freed an entire kingdom by one act of generosity."

Vitomas was still crying, "I only wish that I would have thought to do that before and even when I told the Angels to take everything I really didn't think of the entire kingdom. So I really didn't do anything extraordinary; it was all the Angels."

"Vitomas, most people would have wanted the power and wealth of that huge kingdom. You gave it all to charity; you just didn't realize how the Heavens would use your words," said Javier. "Personally I think that is extraordinary."

Chapter XXXIV
Gifts

Sudfad decided to wait until all the families and Patronus priests arrived at the castle before he held another meeting. In the meantime, the people who were still in the castle gathered again in the study to watch Sudfad and Renya open the chest of items that Ruth had sent from Roch's castle.

Although it was early, Simon had bottles of wine and glasses of grape juice brought into the study for a toast. The study was rearranged so that the items in the chest could be placed on a long table. Raul set chairs near the chest for his parents as well as Laurel and Alexander.

After the toast the children gathered closer to the chest as they watched Sudfad take out treasures from several generations. Immediately under the crowns was a layer of papers. Sudfad took out handfuls and handed them to all of his sons except for Petra and George.

Beneath the paperwork was a small chest. Sudfad opened it and first showed the contents to Laurel and Alexander who had been the personal attendants to his parents.

"Sudfad, those are your mother's jewels," said Laurel as tears came to her eyes. I can't believe Roch didn't take those."

"Maybe he did," said the Sanuri. "Like I said, Ruth simply told us the chest was in the boca."

Sudfad handed the chest to Renya who carefully placed each piece of jewelry on the table. "Sudfad, are these their wedding rings?" Renya asked and showed him a man's and a woman's ring set. Sudfad had been separated from his parents since early childhood and to see any of their belongings made him emotional.

He took clothing that belonged to his parents as well as his own baby clothing out of the chest. Sudfad picked up a book with his mother's name printed in gold lettering on the cover.

"That was her diary," Laurel said.

The King's hands shook as he paged through the book, reading various passages. Renya put her arm around her husband to comfort him. Many in the room were surprised at how emotional Sudfad was because he always concealed his feelings.

When the chest was empty the others in the room walked up to the table to look at the items. Olivia picked up a shawl when something fell out of it and landed on the floor. "I'm sorry," she said and picked up a stack of envelopes that were bound together by beautiful ribbon. She handed them to Sudfad without looking at the writing on them.

"The diary and these letters I would like Renya and I to read before we hand them to the rest of you," Sudfad said. "I am sure that you can understand."

Annabelle hugged Sudfad and said, "You don't have to show us a thing."

"I never had a chance to know my family and it tore me apart," Sudfad said. "All my life I wondered why my parents abandoned me. Now I want all of you to understand your roots and inheritance."

The group was scheduled to reconvene in the Great Hall late morning to give the Patronus priests from the Cicero Headquarters time to get to Sudfad's castle. Between Sudfad's meetings Benedict returned to the Elod community and held a meeting. He told his people about the Kingdom of Stordt, its history and now its freedom. He asked for volunteers to help the people in Stordt who had been victims as they had been in Inferus. Benedict was proud when he returned to the castle with hundreds of volunteers.

Archetenus and Jared returned to the castle with their wives. They wanted Delilah and Zoya to understand the new mission they would have.

In between meetings Sudfad and Renya read his mother's diary. They both wept and laughed at the passages. For the first time in his life, Sudfad had an understanding of the daily lives of his parents. He also learned how it tore them apart to send him away and for the first time he learned the details of Roch's childhood.

When the meeting resumed Raul and Simon told everyone about the relationship their wives had with King Roch as well as Sudfad's ties to him. The group needed to understand these details to understand the significance of what had recently happened in that kingdom. Neither Vitomas nor Annabelle wanted to speak to the group.

When the Princes were finished speaking about the history of Stordt, Sudfad told them to continue and they told of the recent events and the words of the Angels.

Raul turned to Delilah and Zoya. "We understand if you two are upset with your husbands being sent to Taperia but as you just learned it is the wishes of the Angels that they protect the people there."

"While Delilah and I are both very proud of our husbands, of course we don't like them being away from us or in danger. But I too am from Stordt and what a blessing this is," Zoya said. She was standing and now looked at the faces in the room. "To live in Stordt is to live in constant fear. My first husband was brutally murdered because he happened to walk out of a store when some beasts with horse whips were looking for some fun."

"It took me a long time to get used to a life were I didn't have to be afraid and I will never take that for granted. I believe that many of you in this room understand what I am talking about. For those who have never been in that position it is difficult to comprehend. We are proud that our husbands are going to help those people."

"Zoya, since you are from Taperia," said Simon. "Can you draw us maps of the city and perhaps write down what information you remember about the city and the people?"

"Of course. I will start that immediately."

"I can help her," said Natasha. "I spent a great deal of time in Taperia on a mission."

Sudfad and Renya walked to the front of the room holding hands. "As my sons told you, I never really knew my family and never understood why they sent me away until just a few years ago. In between meetings, Renya and I read my mother's diary. For the first time, I feel like I know them. But her description of the demon child that Roch was is by far worse than anything I had heard before."

"I want all of our children to read this book so they understand their inheritance. But the rest of you should read it too. One, so you understand what we are fighting for and two, it contains information that might be useful."

"Do you want us to read it right away?" asked Archetenus. "Since we are leaving first."

"It would be a good idea but even if only one of you reads it, that would be beneficial."

"Raul and I are going with them," said Simon. "I would like to read that tonight. And I am going to just jump into the meeting here. There are a lot of papers and maps that were in the chest that Ruth sent. Raul and Javier are forming a group to review those."

"Maxwell your family is responsible for the forts in Wetpr. We are going to extend that for Stordt too, at least for now. We would like you to gather together and review the maps and plan where we should build forts in Stordt. Father has building plans from the last two forts. Once you've run your decisions past us then you need to implement their construction immediately."

"Gabriel and Raphael, while we can use your expertise in many areas right now we need you to concentrate on the Patronus Headquarters and getting us more priests."

"Archetenus and Jared are going to Taperia first, but we don't expect this will be an easy transition because there will be a lot of criminals there. Conceivably we could be fighting our way throughout that kingdom."

"Once we get to an area we need to assess their needs, which I am sure are great. Once we get the forts established the soldiers can help with all of this but for now we may be moving from one city to village at a time."

"As Father will be telling you in a few moments he is going to be involved with all of the political work, which is a lot. Madeline you are very savvy about politics so we want you helping him to begin with. The work ahead of us is overwhelming and the groups I just named are just the bases of our work. We don't really know what all we need to do yet. Those people who I did not name are free to work in any groups they want. All of you have many talents."

Vitomas stood up and addressed the room. "Understand that I have not been in Stordt for a while but I doubt if the demons who replaced Roch did anything for the citizens. Roch destroyed all of the monasteries, schools and orphanages. While there are physicians, to my knowledge there are no hospitals. One of the things that Sudfad asked Annabelle and me to do was the paperwork for setting up some of these institutions and hiring workers for building them and running them. We need advice from all of you and we could use some help."

"In case no one realized it, the people who Simon named to specific groups are people who are very knowledgeable about Stordt," said Sudfad. "And those were ideas that we came up with on the spur of the moment. Of course, before everything is done, we all will be working in the different areas. Joshua, you are going to coordinate the day to day rescue efforts for the citizens. And at this point we have no idea what that might entail. Choose your team but I would also like Alex and Kent to work with you for the experience."

Sudfad laughed as Nyla, Saran, Olivia and George raised their hands. "Are you going to tell me that you want to help?"

"Yes," said Nyla.

"I think this is an invaluable experience for all of you but I don't want you to miss your studies. Raphael is there a way that we can combine some of this with their lessons?"

"Most definitely," said Raphael to Sudfad then turned to the young people. "Join whatever groups you are interested in for today and I will meet with you later this afternoon."

Hannah stood up and said, "We need to get Cicero College involved with this too."

"I agree, would you mind being the liaison?" asked Sudfad. "I know how busy your schedule is so feel free to say no."

"I would be happy to," Hannah said. "And to start with I want to work with Vitomas' group and Joshua's group."

"Sudfad can Zoya and I work with groups also?" asked Delilah.

"Oh my yes," said Renya. "We need everyone now."

"Before I cover the political work involved in all of this," said Sudfad. "We still have this kingdom to care for and defend. Any of you in here who are not on the payroll already and want to help, will be paid for your services. And all of you will be working long hours and wearing many hats and you will be paid additionally for that. My family cannot thank you enough."

The Sanuri and Erebus stayed in Salar two more days so they could attend all of the planning meetings for the acquisition of the Kingdom of Stordt. The meetings were long but in just a couple of days an enormous amount of work was accomplished.

The day after Erebus and the Sanuri left for Lentz, an army that consisted of team members, Patronus priests, soldiers from Fort Salar, Raul, Simon, Jared, Archetenus and Javier left for the City of Taperia.

Simultaneously troops from Fort Stanus crossed the western side of the Wetprian border into Stordt. And soldiers and Patronus priests from Nora covered the southwestern area of that kingdom. They all had the same mission, to declare the kingdom was now under the rule of King Sudfad of Wetpr.

Since everyone expected battles, the troops from Fort Salar and Fort Stanus would stay in the new lands permanently. After the fighting subsided Joshua and Benedict would bring in their teams to assess the needs of the citizens.

Generals Colter and Orlan were in charge of Fort Nora. The day before this mission was to start they held a meeting in the center of the City of Nora. This city had already been annexed as part of the Kingdom of Wetpr. The citizens wept and laughed at the news. The applause was so loud that many could not hear the words of the Generals.

The following morning as the Generals prepared to leave the fort they were met by a large group of citizens from the city. The citizens rode through the gates and dismounted. The governing body of Nora was made up of seven men who now walked forward. Each man carried a large pouch.

The members stopped and one man walked up to the Generals, his name was Peters. "We know you are leaving soon and we will only take up a moment of your time," Peters said. "For many of us the news is an answer to our prayers. Our kingdom has finally been liberated. So many of us had been hoping for this day that we made preparations for it. These pouches contain the flags of Wetpr; please take them and place them proudly in the areas you are going to. When you and your men return we will host a huge celebration."

Both Orlan and Colter were touched by the gifts. "Thank you," said Colter. "And we hope that other citizens are as enthusiastic about this as all of you have been."

"Oh they will be," said Peters. "But you know as well as I do that it's not the citizens who will stand against you. For far too long this has been a land of criminals and demons. You and the Patronus priests changed our lives. We no longer live in fear. We can never thank you enough."

It was still early morning and the team members had just sat down to breakfast in Hector's house. Catherine and Clarence had become part of the group and worked alongside of the team members.

"We forgot the honey," Mallory said and got out of her chair, as she turned towards the kitchen she gasped, "Oh my god!" and ran to Hector who was staggering out of his bedroom. Dominic was the closest and he too ran to Hector. "You shouldn't be up," said Mallory.

"I'm hungry," Hector said with a grin. He was weak and Dominic and Mallory helped him to the table. "When did you get here?" Hector asked his parents as Clarence held out a chair for him and Catherine stood up and cried.

"Four days ago," said Mallory.

"Four days!" Hector repeated. "I've been out that long?"

"You were out longer than that," Dominic said to Hector then to the group he said. "Hector is so weak, please wait until he is seated before you greet him."

Catherine hugged and kissed her son over and over. She was so emotional she could barely speak. Jasmine got up from the table to get Hector some dishes and Tessa ran out of the room.

Catherine did not want to let go of Hector but she knew that Clarence was waiting to hug him. When both of Hector's parents returned to their seats Tessa walked up to him with her arms behind her back and a big smile on her face.

"Why am I afraid to ask?" he said teasingly.

Tessa quickly brought the mirror from behind her back and held if for Hector to look at himself. "Of course you need a bath," she said and winked at him. "But do you notice anything different?"

Hector was speechless and took the mirror from her. Everyone was smiling as they watched him. After a few moments he asked, "Am I really seeing this?"

"You've got your face back," said Fennel. "Are you happy?"

"You can't believe how much," Hector said.

"I know you want to visit with everyone but you need to get some food in you," Mallory said. "If you don't think you can eat what Jasmine fixed for you, I will make something else."

"Mallory is right," said Catherine. "Everyone here has been taking such good care of you. They are good friends and I hope you appreciate that."

Hector laughed when Mallory set a large glass of milk in front of him. She looked at Catherine and said, "He was drinking whiskey for breakfast; we stopped that fast enough."

Clarence looked at Hector and said, "Your mother and I like Mallory. She might actually be able to keep you in line." Mallory blushed deeply while others laughed.

"The Angels healed Clev too but he hasn't woken up yet," said Elexas.

"I want to see him after breakfast," Hector said. "And I don't remember what happened to me. Someone fill me in."

"Let's have that conversation later," said Noah. "It wasn't pretty and it upset a lot of people. When the Angels get the demons or whatever out of you we see that in addition to a lot of changes your body goes through. Your parent's watched with Clev. I don't think they want to think about it again."

Hector was silent for a few moments as Noah's words scared him. "That bad?"

"Yeah," said Dominic. "But we can tell you about everything else. Rosa has been bringing Sarah out here every day so your parents can spend time with her."

"She recognized you right away even with your different looks," said Tessa. "She calls you daddy and a couple of times she laid down next to you." Hector looked touched by Tessa's words.

"Are you alright Honey?" Catherine asked Hector.

"I am starving but I am feeling a little sick eating. It's nothing."

"I'll get Shara," said Olin and left the house.

A few minutes later the door opened and Matthew said in a loud voice, "Now that you look like Archer again, which damn name are you going by?" Hector laughed.

Shara, Angelina and Sorren also walked into the room. "The food isn't sitting well with him," Mallory said to the healers. "I'll make him some soup."

Shara and Angelina went directly into the kitchen and started mixing ingredients they had brought. After a few minutes, Shara handed Hector a glass. "This will help you get your strength back so drink it all even if you don't like it." Matthew laughed when he saw the faces that Hector was making as he drank the tonic.

Angelina handed him a second glass. "This smells better," Hector said and drank it down. "Is something supposed to happen? The way everyone is looking at me."

"No," said Shara. "You have been unconscious so long, I'm surprised how well you are doing. We'll examine you after you finish eating."

"I really need to clean up and shave," Hector said.

"You might not be strong enough for all of that, but we can help you." said Shara. "Olin said that you needed help walking and honestly I am surprised you could get out of bed by yourself. We will get you up several times every day but don't overdo it. You stay in the house and no whiskey."

"You're no fun," Hector said kiddingly.

"How do you feel?" asked Angelina. "I mean do you feel different?"

"In a way but I feel so weak and groggy right now that I am not really sure. I do want to thank all of you for taking care of me."

"The good thing is that we haven't had any more attacks," said Sorren. "We still have those women in the dungeons and have gotten more information. Shara, Angelina and Hilgra have been pouring over those manuscripts you got."

435

"They still aren't sure what you might get for side effects. And I don't know if your parents told you that they are staying in the house next door."

"We really haven't gotten around to telling him much," said Clarence.

"Mallory did you give my parents their gifts," asked Hector.

"No, but I will get them," she said and left the room.

"Hector that girl has been really upset," Catherine said.

He looked at his mother and nodded. As Mallory walked up to the table Hector said, "I had planned on Mallory and I taking you shopping so these are just little things."

"You didn't have to get us anything Honey," said Catherine as Mallory handed out the gifts. Mallory was standing next to Hector's chair. He took her hand and squeezed it. She smiled and kissed him on top of his head.

Claudius and Bella planned to visit Hector and his parents after the morning meeting. Sorren had not been attending meetings since Hector and his men moved into the village because he considered the threat of attacks on Hector great. Every day someone brought Sorren the notes from the meetings so he could stay on top of things.

Eli was attending the meetings and was a source of information since he belonged to the Guardians. But even with his insight into privileged information he was not aware of the mission in Malga. The majority of this morning the ruling members were telling him about that mission, the Master and the prior missions at that monastery.

"I knew about Meekos and the others because after they were cleaned out of that monastery, King Tobias created our group and sent us all to High Priest Raphael for training," Eli said. "But it makes sense that they didn't eradicate all of the cancer."

"What do you mean?" asked Fahron.

"That monastery is huge but it is isolated and unlike other monasteries, the priests don't routinely open their doors to the citizens; or at least they didn't. It seems like every month we are hearing about a new crime that the Patronus uncovered there. Now, the crimes are attributed to Meekos and his gang but you tell me how that many priests could live in such close quarters and never suspect something is wrong?"

"My god, Meekos had the place filled with Hutas half the time. You can't tell me that no one ever saw one of those savages or heard the screams of the victims being dragged into the complex for sacrifice. That entire situation has always gotten under my skin. I am going to write to King Tobias and request that he let me assist on that mission."

As Eli was speaking a flock of Enrops flew into the study. The birds were excited and flew around the heads of the men. "Something is going on," said Claudius to the men.

"You must read these right away," said one of the birds that landed on Mathas' desk.

"Is anything wrong?" Mathas asked as he took one of the letters from a bird.

"The Kingdom of Stordt is no more, King Sudfad rules it all."

"What!" said Mathas and tore the first letter open. He read all of the letters out loud to the group who listened with amazement. "Fahron will you draft a letter to Sudfad immediately and tell him that our troops will be prepared to assist him if needed. In fact, we could enter Stordt from the east and help them clean that place out."

"Stephan and Thaos, get together with Matthew and work out some strategies for our troops. Besides freeing those poor people this is a real benefit for us."

"How do you mean?" asked Gideon.

"That is a kingdom rich in resources but Roch raped and stole from his own people. As you know, part of our kingdom borders Stordt and entering those lands was considered an act of war."

"So men would come across the border and commit crimes here and hide in Stordt and there wasn't a damn thing we could do about it. And besides that, we no longer have enemies at our backs. This will expand commerce and I am sure open other opportunities. Fahron in that letter tell Sudfad that we will offer anything that he needs."

Clev awoke as Clarence and Matthew were helping Hector to clean up and shave. He was weak but in considerably better shape than Hector although he had more difficulty stomaching the tonics that Shara gave him and immediately started to vomit.

Mallory and Tessa were changing Hector's bedding when he walked into the room with the help of his father.

"Well, you certainly look better," Tessa said.

"Feel a hell of a lot better. We stopped in Clev's room; the poor bastard is puking his guts out," Hector said and sat down on the side of the bed. "Tessa open that chest."

"I can't believe you still have this much money after all you've spent," Tessa said as she looked inside the chest that was filled with pouches of gold coins.

"Take whatever you need. Let's have a feast tonight," Hector said.

"Take Catherine shopping with you," said Clarence. "She has some special recipes that I am sure she will want to prepare."

"See Hector. I am taking two bags and will bring you the change," said Tessa.

Hector looked at his father, "It's like fighting with them to get them to take anything and they won't let me pay them."

"Your son has been a crook for so long he's forgotten what it is like to have friends," Tessa said kiddingly and winked at Clarence who laughed.

"If you don't mind, I would like to speak with Mallory alone," Hector said.

"Make her get some sleep," said Tessa as she and Clarence left the room.

Hector took Mallory's hand and gently pulled her towards him. She sat down on the side of the bed. "First, I want to thank you for everything you've done and secondly, if you don't get some sleep I will tie you to the bed," he said kiddingly and they both laughed. "I will be fine; you don't need to stay up around the clock."

"I did sleep now and then."

"And where did you sleep?"

"In my bed."

"In Brocks room?"

"Yes. Hector there is no reason in the world for you to be jealous of him. Brock is basically my brother."

"I know that, I just don't like the idea of you sharing a room with another guy. Move back in here."

"Not with your parents checking on you every ten minutes."

"That isn't necessary anymore and I will speak with them. Father said that Brock told them that you are my girl and they really like you." Hector paused then grinned. "I probably shouldn't tell you this but Father said it's about time I dated a nice girl."

"Actually I am not sure how I feel about that," Mallory said and smiled.

"Well, you know that two of the women I dated were Juleta and Isabella so that should tell you something."

"Didn't you date Joanna Franks too?"

"Yes, but she was pretty normal," Hector said and laughed. "So, I have to ask. How do you feel about seeing my real face? Does that change anything?"

"It is kind of strange to get used to but I like it. You are a handsome man, in fact, I think you look better this way. I just don't understand why you let her do that to you in the first place."

"Didn't I tell you that I faked my death to protect my family? And honestly I should have asked more questions, I never though the transformation was going to be so drastic and I certainly didn't think she would make me look like someone she had feelings for."

"You are getting really pale."

"I know, I need to lie down but are we alright?"

"Yes. I will move my things back in here."

"I have to tell you that I was surprised when my parents told me how upset you were."

"Why?"

"Why?" Hector repeated with emphasis. "Because you wouldn't let me know that you had feelings for me. Tell me, if I wouldn't have gone through all this would you have ever have let me know?"

"I really don't have an answer for you. Hector this isn't...I mean we aren't two normal people and this isn't a normal relationship; certainly you see that."

He grinned and pulled her towards him and kissed her passionately. They became lost in their desires. He gently laid her on the bed and moved on top of her.

Stephan knocked on the door three times before he opened it. "Sorry," he said and laughed. "I thought you were too sick for that."

Both Hector and Malloy stood up. They laughed as they straightened up their clothing. "I probably am too weak," Hector said. "But what a way to go." Mallory blushed and slapped his arm and both men laughed again.

"A bunch of us are here," Stephan explained. "We just came from Mathas' morning meeting and we have a lot to tell everyone; thought you might want to join us."

Chapter XXXV
The Proposal

Claudius, Gideon, Stephan, Thaos, Rosa and Sarah went to the Village of Tyger to brief the teams and Sorren's family about all of the letters they had received from Wetpr. Hilgra was also invited to the meeting since she had lived in the Kingdom of Stordt for most of her life. Showers and Clev attended although Clev could barely sit up in his chair.

The meeting was held in Hector's house which was filled to capacity. The group sat spellbound as Claudius read the letters detailing the encounter with Derlock, the demise of Sorphat and Wetpr's acquisition of Stordt. He saved one of the letters from the Sanuri for last. "Hector, there is a part in here that concerns you," Claudius said. "You might want to read this yourself."

"Go ahead and read it," Hector said. "It can't be worse than what everyone here already knows about me."

"The Angel Ruth told the Sanuri and Erebus that our people here have had a learning experience working with you," Claudius said.

"You can say that again," Tessa said sarcastically and everyone laughed.

"She said that we all had ideas set in our minds of what you and Clev were like but since we've been working with you we are learning that nothing is black and white. And while many of us saw you as monsters we now see you as victims of Juleta's. She said that most of the players here, like Isabella, are both victims and criminals and that is a good learning experience for us," Claudius continued.

"Then she asked the Sanuri and Erebus to come here for two reasons. One, is the complicated magics that we are dealing with and the second is that you, Hector, are as addicted to power as Erebus is to magics and you don't realize it. Erebus has learned a great deal about his addiction and besides possibly helping you he can help us to understand addictions, which is also a learning experience."

"Are you mad?" Mallory asked Hector when she saw the look on his face.

"I'm not sure. I will have to think about that. The Angels have said that before but I didn't think that someone could really be addicted to power."

"Juleta was," said Claudius. "And I don't want to get into your business but you might want to think if you were like that before her or if that is something else that she did to you."

"Interesting," said Hector thoughtfully.

"We are passing the letters around," said Claudius and most of us will be out here for a while if anyone else has questions."

"I just want to make sure that I understand," said Dominic. "The teams here and in Cadia are to remain on these assignments and everyone else is going to Stordt?"

"At least for now, that is what the Angels want," said Claudius and grinned. "Now we have an announcement before Gideon pops his buttons."

Gideon walked to the front of the room with a smile that his face couldn't contain. "As many of you know, Ashley and I have... well hell... I'll just start at the beginning. Ashley and I met in Port Friada when Hector was our enemy. We agreed to marry but I didn't want to propose when we were on the brink of war. Then we adopted our sons and between missions and our work we haven't done much about our wedding plans."

"So as soon as I leave here, I am taking a week off. Tonight, I have a romantic evening planned and am finally proposing. Then we are going to have some fun and get our wedding preparations done so she won't be at the shop either."

"In two weeks Bella and Claudius are giving us an engagement party which all of you are invited to. We haven't set the date for the wedding but now that the Sanuri is coming we will want it soon and all of you are invited to that too. The only problem is that a few of the gals she asked to be in the wedding aren't in Lentz now but as I said we have a lot to work out."

443

Everyone in the room applauded and some yelled war cries. Stephan walked next to Gideon. "There is one more thing," Stephan said. "Because I am sure someone is going to ask. Gideon and Ashley both have money and well, basically everything they want. So they have asked that instead of gifts they would like people to donate to the Adam's Home projects. Thaos and I and our wives will be taking care of all that while Gideon and Ashley are busy with their wedding."

"What is that project?" asked Clarence and an awkward silence fell over the room.

"The Angel Adam saved the boys that Gideon and Ashley adopted," said Stephan. "Gideon wanted to repay Adam who asked for homes to protect children so they wouldn't be preyed upon. So they are setting up homes all over Langer and now homes like that are being built in Wetpr too. So if there aren't any more questions..."

"I am afraid to ask," said Clarence. "Although everyone's reactions spoke volumes. What exactly were those children saved from?" Once again the room fell silent.

Catherine was sitting in a chair holding Sarah when she suddenly jumped up and yelled, "Oh my god! Oh my god! We read all those stories. Thaos we read about you. Hector were you behind that?"

"Yes," he said solemnly.

"How could you do something that disgusting? That is worse than anything we could have imagined. Hector we know of some of the things you have been involved with but...but...I don't ..." Catherine started crying and quickly walked out of the house. Hector and Clarence followed her.

Since Archetenus was more familiar with the City of Taperia than the other leaders of his group he was put in charge of the takeover of that city which was not initially done as a direct military attack. Simon and Raul stayed hidden with the army as Jared, Javier and Archetenus led groups of team members and Patronus priests into the city.

Before this group of fighters left Salar, Zoya convinced them that innocent people might be in precarious situations and need to be rescued; and that these people might become victims if a battle erupted. The groups that entered the city were disguised as travelers; they wanted to get a sense of what was going on in that city before the Princes claimed Taperia for Wetpr.

Some of the Ruala warriors from Gabriel's team joined this army since they had been on previous missions in this city. Simon and Raul were happy to find the abandoned hotel where they hid with Gabriel's team on a prior mission. The hotel was far enough outside of Taperia that few people paid any attention to it. Although the building was in worse shape than it had been several years earlier, it was huge and a suitable hideout for their army.

Javier had only been to Taperia once before and that had been many years earlier but his strength was in reading people so he was leading one of the groups. No one believed it was a good idea for either Simon or Raul to enter the city as they might be recognized.

Maddox, Ira, Henrich and Vincente were team leaders. Of these four men only Vincente had experience working in clandestine operations so it was decided he would stay in Wetpr and work with Joshua's group thus giving the other team leaders some experience.

While all of the team members were well trained warriors they lacked experience working in disguise, so this mission was a training exercise for many.

Archetenus knew well how dangerous it was for women in that city so the first two days he only wanted the men working in Taperia. This decision angered all of the female team members but he argued that if one of them was attacked the situation would cause the other members to expose themselves.

"Good thing you're a big guy," Jared said kiddingly as he and Archetenus rode down the main business street of Taperia. "Cuz those gals are gonna kick your butt." Both men laughed.

445

"Yeah, I know they are all pissed at me but I know this city. Look at when Natasha was here. What? Was she in the city a couple of hours before a group of men tried to rape her. No, I want to check things out before we get into a mess."

Most of the men who were assigned to go into Taperia had entered the city during the night and early morning hours. As Archetenus and Jared rode down the street they saw many of their men on the streets. Javier was in the restaurant of the New Moon Hotel eating breakfast. This hotel was built after the Taperia Imperial Hotel was destroyed in the battle between Gabriel's team and the demon Ahriman.

The New Moon Hotel was now the most exclusive hotel in the city. Javier was seated by himself at a table near the large front window and watched Archetenus and Jared riding down the street. The dining room was filled even at this early hour and Javier was listening to conversations. To his surprise he did not hear anyone mention the destruction of Roch's castle.

It was a couple of hours after sunrise. The streets were bustling but quiet. After Archetenus and Jared rode through the business district they decided to see other areas of the city, which were more residential.

"People must have just picked up and left after those Huta attacks," said Jared as they saw dozens of homes that had been burned and damaged.

"I heard a hell of a lot of people died here," Archetenus said. "Something just seems different around here; can't put my finger on it."

They rode through the entire city then returned to the business district. "I promised Zoya I would check on her friend. Do you want to do that now?" Jared asked. Archetenus nodded. Jared led him down one of the side streets where the smaller shops were located. Jared saw the distinctive sign which had a crescent moon and an eye painted on it but no store name.

They dismounted and Jared looked up and down the street. "I followed Sophie back here," he explained. "That's how I found this place. The owner of that tobacco store across the street was always spying on this place and said it was a shop for witches."

The two men entered the shop which was empty except for the owner who was cleaning shelves. She looked frightened when she saw them.

"We mean you no harm," Jared said. "Do you remember Zoya?"

"Yes, do you know her?" the woman asked as she started to relax.

"I'm married to her," Jared said and smiled. "We have a son. My name is Jared and this is my friend Archetenus. Are you Norma?"

"Yes," the woman was drying her hands with her apron as she walked towards the men.

"Here, she sent you a letter," Jared said.

"Please come into the back and have some coffee," Norma said and led the men into the room where Zoya used to do her readings. Archetenus and Jared sat down as Norma carried a pot of coffee and cups to the table. She put a plate of biscuits on the table with a jar of honey.

"I am just so excited to read this. I miss her," Norma said.

"I came in here for a reading and that is when I met her," Jared said as he looked around the room. "Everything still looks the same here."

"In the store yes but not in the city," said Norma as she got back up from her chair and carried a dish of butter to the table.

"What do you mean?" asked Archetenus.

"This has always been a dangerous place," Norma said. "But after the Huta attacks, King Roch disappeared then there were rumors that there was a King named Zieman but no one ever saw him. Some people said that he didn't exist and others said he was a demon."

"Then he disappears and another man named Sorphat declares himself King and everyone saw him. Sorphat was in the city all of the time. He was a very handsome man and was always flirting with women but after a while we realized those women would disappear. Then it was said that men were disappearing too but it has always been like that in Taperia so who knows what is real and what is rumor."

"So how has anything changed?" Archetenus asked. "I lived here a long time ago and it sounds the same as I remembered."

"Well, in a lot of ways it has gotten worse," Norma explained. "Roch was the devil himself and was horrible to everyone but he had such a bad reputation that in a way he protected us. When he disappeared, all kinds of really bad criminals came here and not like the ones before; these were strong men who fought to control the city. So there were huge wars in the streets between these rival gangs and a lot of innocent people were killed."

"When Roch was here, everyone knew he ran the city so the criminals were more like hired men. But now that I think of it, Jared, Zoya told me she was leaving to visit a sick aunt and that she would write. I never heard from her so I feared the worst. But almost right after she left a man came in here looking for her. I had seen him in here before but at that time I didn't realize he was the leader of one of those gangs. I don't think Zoya knew that either. His name is Addison and the reason I am bringing this up is because he acted so strangely after she left."

"What do you mean he acted strangely?" asked Jared.

"He had been in here before and was never a problem but when I told him she was gone he got so angry that I just stared at him. He demanded to know where she went. Now, Jared I had seen you in here that same day that she left but I never put it together. I told him what she told me. He stomped into this room and looked around like he was looking for a note or something. Then he said he was going to her home and ran out. He never came back in here again."

"Can you describe him?" Jared asked.

"Big man, not as big as either of you but big. He has brown wavy hair. Real clean cut and nice looking, actually he is kind of fancy. He wears suits, which I thought was unusual when I found out he was a criminal."

"Norma, read that letter then we have some things to tell you," Jared said. "Do you mind if I look around because I am confused about what Addison could have been looking for."

"By all means," said Norma. She looked excited as she took the letter out of the envelope. Neither of the men spoke while she was reading. They knew that Zoya had written about her life in Salar and explained that they worked for King Sudfad.

"She sounds so happy," Norma said and smiled warmly. "But if you work for the King of Wetpr why are you here?"

"You know that King Sudfad is the brother of King Roch, don't you?" asked Jared.

"I had heard that but I didn't think it was true."

"It's true and it is a long story but basically he knows that Roch is dead and let's say a friend of his just killed Sorphat, who was a demon. We are here because Sudfad is claiming all of Stordt as part of Wetpr. All of you are free people now but since Taperia has such a bad reputation we wanted to find out what was going on around here before we brought the troops in. Zoya was afraid that innocent people could get hurt."

"Innocent people get hurt here every day," Norma said. "Are you telling the truth? Are we really citizens of Wetpr now?"

"You sure are and you are invited to come and stay with us," Jared said. "But can you tell us where these gangs are so we can round them up before anyone else gets hurt?"

"Addison lives in the New Moon Hotel. Another one named Willart is always in Walt's Tavern. His gang is in there too. And there is a third named Bastine; he spends most of his time in the Back Door Tavern. Those are the only three that I know of."

449

"If you aren't familiar with the city, those three places are in different areas so I don't know if that means those are the territories of those gangs."

"Thanks, you are a lot of help," said Archetenus. "Do you know what Willart and Bastine look like?"

"I can't really tell you about Willart. If I've seen him I didn't realize it but Bastine is a really handsome man. He has short black curly hair and a thin mustache. He is really tan and has a little bit of an accent but I don't know where he is from. All three of these men are dangerous so be careful."

"Norma, we are going to be here a while, so I'll come back and check on you as I can. If you decide that you want to move to Salar, I will help you," Jared said.

"This is all just so exciting. I can't wrap my mind around it. But don't worry I won't tell anyone."

After Jared and Archetenus left Norma, they found some of their men and told them about the gangs, these men were to spread the word. One of the men was told to ride to the abandoned hotel to brief Raul and Simon. In the meantime Jared and Archetenus went to the New Moon Hotel to speak with Javier.

Javier had not seen anyone who matched Addison's description so he decided to get chambers at the New Moon so he could learn more about this crime boss. Javier was forming a plan to make contact with Addison.

Now that they had information about the main criminals in the city, Archetenus and Jared divided their men into groups. Each team leader was responsible for gathering information about one of the gangs. Archetenus wanted the gang leaders watched around the clock.

After the assignments were made, Archetenus and Jared rode out of the city to the abandoned hotel to meet with Raul and Simon. All four men were in agreement that they needed to learn more about these gangs before they stormed the city.

After Hector spoke with his parents, they decided to move out of the Village of Tyger and into the cottage on the royal grounds. Catherine was distraught after learning that Hector had been running a child trafficking business.

Hector cancelled the feast that he wanted to have that evening. This was the first time that he had really talked about his criminal life with his parents and it was the first time they had turned their backs on him. While Hector took responsibility for his actions he was consumed with a variety of emotions and spent the rest of the day alone in his room.

After the meeting Raul and Simon rode into Taperia with Archetenus and Jared. The soldiers who had been at the abandoned hotel with the Princes also rode into the city but none of them were wearing their uniforms. They were dressed in the manner of the citizens of Taperia and entered the city in small groups.

Prior to meeting with Simon and Raul, Archetenus had ordered the team members and Patronus priests who were already in Taperia to concentrate on the three locations that the gangs frequented. The soldiers were now given the same orders.

One of the Royal Carriages stopped in front of the White Rose Restaurant. Gideon got out and helped Ashley out of the carriage. They both looked at the restaurant which sat on the shore of the Sea of Grevdt. "The view will be beautiful when the sun sets," Ashley said.

"Not as beautiful as you, My Dear," Gideon said and kissed her on the cheek.

She took his arm and they walked inside of the restaurant. Neither of them could stop smiling. They found the host immediately.

"Admiral Gideon, your room is prepared but since this is such a special occasion we would like to present you with some tokens of our appreciation." As the host spoke two waiters walked up to them, one presented a dozen white roses to Ashley and the other handed Gideon a box of fine cigars.

"Thank you; these are lovely," Ashley said as she smelled the flowers.

The host led the couple up several flights of stairs before they came out on the roof of the restaurant. The roof was decorated with statues and fine plants including small trees. There were four private dining rooms and Gideon and Ashley were led to the one that had a small balcony which overlooked the ocean.

"Carlos will be your private waiter this evening," said the host and left the room. Within moments four waiters walked into the room each carrying a floral arrangement which they set on pedestals. Three of the men left the room and the fourth walked up to Ashley and Gideon and handed them four cards.

"My name is Carlos. The young lady I spoke with said that the flowers were sent from your friends. She handed me these cards."

As Carlos spoke the three waiters returned, one was carrying a small table with a white cloth. He set it down and the other two men filled it with gifts they had been carrying on trays. Gideon and Ashley laughed happily.

"I take it you have many friends," Carlos said with a warm smile.

The three waiters returned to the room. One was carrying a tray with a bottle of fine wine and two glasses. The second waiter was carrying a tray of rare and expensive delicacies and the third waiter walked up to Carlos. This man was carrying a small tray with two small boxes on it and an envelope. Musicians started to play outside of the door of the dining room and Ashley giggled.

"The woman who brought these gifts had very specific instructions," Carlos said as he handed one gift to Ashley and the second to Gideon. "You are to open the gifts first then read the note."

"Thank you Carlos," Gideon said. After Carlos left the room Gideon said to Ashley. "I have a feeling we should open these gifts right away."

"Open yours then I will open mine," Ashley said and watched as Gideon opened a box which contained a golden pocket watch. The watch itself was ornately decorated. The chain had large golden links and attached to four of the links were small golden disks. Each disk contained one name. The names were Logan, Marty, Cassidy and Amy. The inscription inside of the watch read, *With all our love.*

"I like this very much," Gideon said with emotion and handed the watch to Ashley.

"This is so beautiful and thoughtful," she said.

"Open yours dear," said Gideon.

Ashley gasped and took a long golden chain out of the box. The chain was braided. Tiny white pearls and four small lockets were attached to the chain and each locket had the name of a child inscribed on it. Tears came to her eyes as she showed it to Gideon.

"This is beautiful," he said. "But I am going to add another locket with my name and I want another disk on my watch with your name." Ashley kissed him.

"Honey read the note," she said.

Gideon opened the envelope and laughed then handed the note to Ashley. *Sorry, Amy and Cassidy demanded that their names be on everything too. Have a wonderful evening. Nikki.*

Ashley laughed and reread the note while Gideon poured two glasses of wine. "To our future," he said and they both sipped from their glasses.

"Honey, I had planned to wait until the end of the evening but I just feel like now is the right time," Gideon said as he set his glass on the table and got down on one knee. He took a small velvet box out of his pocket and held it out to Ashley.

"Gideon, another ring?"

"Open it. It's to wear under the large diamond."

Ashley cried as she looked at a silver band with diamonds. She took it out of the box and removed her large diamond then put the smaller ring on her finger with the large diamond above it. "They fit perfectly but how did you do that? We got them in different cities."

"I had that made in Port Friada," he said then took her hand. "Ashley, I never knew I could love anyone the way I love you. You have changed my life and filled my heart with happiness. I promise to always love you and care for you. Will you marry me?"

The tears were flowing down Ashley's face as she said, "Yes."

Chapter XXXVI
Sharing

"Do you want some company?" Mallory asked as she walked into Hector's room. She was carrying a tray of food. "You didn't come out for dinner. Are you alright?"

Hector was sitting up in bed reading. "Come in but close the door. I don't feel up to a lot of people." He turned and sat on the side of the bed as she placed the tray on a small table and sat down next to him. "Thanks. Did my parents say anything to you before they left?"

"Your mother was too upset but your father thanked us all and invited us to their house."

"Well, that is more than I got."

"Hector, what did you expect? You're a notorious criminal. Did you really think you could keep it from your parents forever?"

"I guess in a way I did."

"I think you really underestimate them. They want to see you as their little boy but they aren't stupid. They see and hear a lot of things. I think they could pretend that some of the things you did were alright until they found out about the children."

"None of my men actually grabbed those kids, I just bank rolled the operation. And the kids in Ganz, I wasn't letting them sell them because I figured that Thaos and the others would try to save them. Thaos had some things that I wanted and I thought..."

"No Hector the problem is that you don't think. There isn't anything you can say that can justify what you did. Your hands aren't clean because you 'just bank rolled the operation.' That entire thing was disgusting and evil. How can you be so loving to Sarah and do that to other children? It's like everything is a game to you and you don't care about the consequences as long as you win. I think that is what the Angel meant when she said you were addicted to power."

Hector didn't say anything; he continued to eat. "I have a question that you should think about because it might be important. Your desire for power; do you remember when that started?"

"What do you mean?"

"Well, was that always part of your personality or did Juleta do something to you to make you that way?"

"I really will have to think about that because I don't know off the top of my head. Claudius asked that too. I just don't know yet."

"Well everything Juleta did to you was poison. So you should try to remember."

"Did you come in here to tell me you are going to leave me too?"

"I am not sure why you asked that. But I will tell you that I don't know what to think and that has been the problem since I met you. Hector, knowing the one side of your personality makes it almost impossible to believe you do such horrible things; yet you do. It's like there are two of you. I've told you that before. How can anyone have such drastic sides to their personality? I've met people who were crazy who were like that but you aren't crazy; you choose all of this. It is very difficult for me to understand you."

"I am sorry that I am putting you through this but I don't have any answers."

"What! You are an incredibly intelligent man. You don't have any answers because you don't want to. You spend all of your time strategizing what others will do and you don't even understand yourself; I don't believe that. And here you are feeling sorry for yourself because your parents are horrified by your actions..."

"I am not feeling sorry for myself but I am feeling guilty, which is something that I am not used to. You know; my life was going just fine until I got involved with all of you."

"Yeah, you were dying and full of demons, that was a wonderful life! What you really mean is that you get so caught up playing the game that you forget what it's like to be a person and when you remember then you see yourself as we do and you don't like that."

"Maybe your right. Mallory, do you see me as a monster?"

"Most of the time no. But I have seen that in you and it scares me. Did you know that Juleta left a letter for Stephan and Thaos and she told them about Sarah? She said she was hiding her from the monster in you. Now, who knows if she was telling the truth but coming from her... well if the monster in you scared her then maybe you should look in the mirror."

"I didn't know that. I would never hurt Sarah."

"Hector, we saw the demons in you. How can you say for sure what you would do?" Neither of them spoke for several moments. "Would you like some more food?"

"Yes. Mallory, I don't want to scare you."

"Hector, I am not afraid that you will hurt me. I am afraid of what you might do to others. What I am really afraid of is that you will force me to hurt you and I don't want to."

Mallory stood up and picked up the tray. As she walked towards the door he said, "Mallory, don't leave me. We will work something out." She left the room.

Mallory returned to Hector's room a few minutes later. But this time she also had a glass of whiskey and a glass of wine on the tray with the plates of food. Hector saw the glasses and said, "Well, I hope that is a good sign."

Mallory set the tray on the table and Hector took her hand and kissed it. "You are probably right about everything you said but I am not lying to you. I don't have answers for you right now and I have a lot to think about; that's why I've been in here. When I saw the looks on my parent's faces my heart broke."

"So did you tell them the truth?"

"I answered their questions truthfully and offered some information but I didn't go into detail about my life. I really love them; I never intended to hurt them like that."

"I just don't understand how you thought they would never find out. Hector that is either being naïve or in denial and you don't strike me as having either of those characteristics. There are just so many things about you that confuse me."

"I probably shouldn't tell you this, but one night Catherine and I were up late working in the kitchen. She was telling me all about your childhood. She sounded so happy and proud then she got sad and said she didn't know where they went wrong with you. She said they never saw it coming; that one day you were their sweet boy and the next you had changed so. She said that they didn't recognize you at times. Well, I didn't know what to say to her so I just listened."

"She knows you run a criminal organization and she has heard about some of your crimes but I don't think that she or Clarence wanted to believe the stories. But after you put them in hiding they realized that what they had heard must be true. She was telling me about the men who you had taking care of them. Your men scared them at first because they look like criminals. But after a while she and your father really liked them."

"She told me that you had sex with a lot of women but you didn't have relationships and she didn't understand that. She said that she was happy that we have a relationship but she told me that she hoped I knew what I was getting into. She also said that I had to be patient with you because you probably didn't know how to act in a relationship."

"Hector, your parents are very intelligent people. You do them a disservice by acting like they are naïve fools."

"I don't think of them as fools but I guess I do think of them as being more naïve than they are. Mother was right with what she said but does that change anything between us?"

458

"I read Isabella's diaries and other things. I knew you were a slut," she said sarcastically. He laughed. "And that is another thing that confuses me. You screw anything but you are jealous because Brock is like my brother?"

"Now that I am going to correct you on. I have had sex with a lot of women but I don't screw anything...although that is not much of an argument when it comes to Juleta. And I am not jealous of Brock; I just don't like you sharing a bedroom with him."

"I didn't grow up in a big fancy house. Us kids all shared bedrooms and with a lot of others. He would be the safest guy for me to share a room with."

"I need to know, why do you like me?"

"The good part of you is very easy to like. You have a lot of good qualities. You are smart and funny. You are courageous and a fighter. And you can be so kind and generous that it amazes me."

"Hector, you have seemed really happy here. You've made a lot of friends, you have your baby and now your parents. Is it really that easy for you to give all of this up again?"

Like any large city, Taperia was always bustling with activity. But in the evening is when its true lawless nature was exposed.

"Norma said the real crooks sleep all day and come out at night," Jared said as he, Archetenus, Simon and Raul rode down the main business street together.

Men were fighting in the streets, others were yelling war cries and throwing bottles of whiskey at people who walked past them. "Archetenus are there any dungeons here for us to throw these guys in?" asked Simon.

"The only ones that I knew about were in the castle and that is gone now."

"I think we will need a fort here," said Raul. "We're going to have to hang the gang members because there's no place to put them."

The men all stopped their horses when they heard a woman scream. "There!" yelled Simon and rode towards an alley. The others followed him. Three men were dragging a woman into the alley. Simon never stopped his horse. He jumped from it and landed on top of one of the men. This action momentarily distracted the other two. One of them continued to hold onto the woman while his partner pulled a knife and lunged at Simon who was wrestling on the ground with one of the men.

"Simon stay down!" yelled Raul and threw one of his knives which impaled the heart of the man brandishing a knife.

Archetenus and Jared had ridden around the block and were entering the alley from the other side. Simon killed the man he had been fighting with and stood up. The man holding the woman now put a knife to her throat and said. "Stay back or I'll kill her."

Raul didn't speak to the man but looked at the woman. "When I tell you to duck you do it," he said. Raul's words distracted the assailant who thought until that moment that he was in control of the situation. Now he looked behind him and saw Archetenus and Jared in the alley.

"I'll give you the woman; just let me go."

"We're freeing her," said Raul. "Now your life is another matter. We want information. Think you know enough about this city to save your life?"

"Hell yah. What are you a new gang?"

"You might just say that," said Raul. "Now let her go."

As Raul was talking to the man, Simon was walking closer to him and now grabbed the arm of the woman. "I won't fight you," said the man and dropped his knife on the ground. The woman was crying and flew into Simon's arms.

"Where do you live?" Simon asked the woman.

"On Elm Street."

460

"I'll take you home," Simon said. "Do you know of any empty buildings where we can talk to this guy?"

"Hey, I thought you were going to let me go!"

"We might just do that but do you want the gang members seeing you talking with us?" asked Raul.

"You've got a point there," said the man. "The block behind us there are a couple of empty buildings. I'll show you." The man was clearly intimidated by Raul, Simon, Jared and Archetenus who were all huge men and looked like professional fighters. The man turned to walk towards the back of the alley.

"You try running and you're dead," said Jared.

"Figured as much," said the man.

The entire group walked to the back of the alley which opened onto a street containing small shops. The man pointed at three buildings that were abandoned.

"He's telling the truth," said the woman. "Everyone started leaving after the Huta attacks. If you let him go, what will stop him from coming after me again?"

"We can be very persuasive," Simon said and smiled.

"We'll take him to the blue building," Archetenus said. "Raul go with Simon."

Archetenus and Jared looked up and down the street before they walked towards the abandoned building. They were leading their horses. "I don't recognize that brand," said the man nervously.

"You an expert on brands?" Jared asked sarcastically.

"Hell yah, I'm a horse theft," the man said with pride and both Archetenus and Jared laughed.

The three men walked around to the back of the building where they tethered the horses. The building was unlocked and appeared to have been a store. Archetenus searched it while Jared and the man found some candles.

"So horse thief, you got a name?" Jared asked.

"Willy."

"Willy, we are gonna kind of play a game," said Jared. "Me and my partners are pretty damn good at reading people. If we feel that you are lying to us, well...guess I'll have to start removing body parts. You understand?"

"Yeah, you got a spot for a horse thief in your gang?"

"Horse thief is one thing, rapist is another," said Jared. "None of us hold much with rapists. But we also pay well so you give us good information and we might be able to work something out. Now sit."

The woman sat in front of Simon on his horse. He and Raul rode two city blocks before she pointed at a house. "Do you live by yourself?" Raul asked.

"No," she said suspiciously.

"Don't be afraid," said Raul. "I was going to offer to check your house before you went in."

"Oh, sorry. I live with my father. Why don't you come in and meet him. My name is Penny what are yours?"

"I'm Simon and that's my brother Raul. How long have you lived here?"

"In Taperia? Not long. My father heard there was work in the mines so we moved here from Tpra, that's in the Kingdom of Gandt. We used to have a farm there but there has been a bad drought that has lasted for years so Father thought we had a better chance here. We heard rumors but we never realized how awful this place really is."

Penny talked as the three dismounted. The men tied their horses to a hitching post in front of the small house. An old man came onto the front porch. He had a crutch under his left arm and he was holding a huge butcher knife in his right hand.

"Penny what is going on? Are you alright?"

"Yes Papa, these men saved me. I told them to come in and meet you."

"Saved you from what?" asked the old man and Raul and Simon could hear the fear in his voice.

"I'm Simon," Simon said and held out his hand to shake with the old man who placed the knife on a rocking chair on the porch and shook hands. "And this is my brother Raul." Raul and the man shook hands.

"Well come in. Our place ain't fancy none, but I was just making some stew if you are hungry," the man said and led the group inside of the house. "My name is Milt."

"Milt, we've already eaten," said Raul. "But mind if we talk with you for a few minutes?"

"No come on in and take a seat," Milt said.

"Papa, I was coming home from work and three men grabbed me," Penny said as tears came to her eyes. "Simon, Raul and their two friends killed two of them and took the third to ask him questions."

"Questions?" Milt said suspiciously.

"And that is why we want to talk to you," said Raul. "Penny said that you are from Gandt. So you may not know the history here." As Raul spoke Milt motioned for the men to sit down. King Roch who was the King here for a long time has a brother who is the King of Wetpr."

"King Sudfad, yes we have heard about him," Milt said.

"Well, we are his sons..." Raul did not finish speaking because Penny gasped.

"You're Princes! I was saved by Princes!" Penny said and Milt looked shocked.

463

"Milt and Penny, we are going to tell you some things that we don't want public yet," said Simon. "Now that we know that Roch is dead and not in hiding, Father is claiming the entire Kingdom of Stordt as part of Wetpr."

"Our flags are being raised in other areas of the kingdom but we heard that Taperia was filled with gangs and there might be a war if we do that here. So we want to get rid of the gangs first so innocent people don't get hurt."

"Are you telling the truth?" Milt asked in obvious disbelief.

"Wait here," said Raul and walked outside.

"We just got here," said Simon. "And we've got a lot of questions. If you could give us some answers we would pay you."

"If you are who you say you are, I'm not taking your money. This is the most wonderful news I've ever heard. Penny do you understand what they are saying? Wetpr is a free kingdom. The people are free and they don't have to live in fear."

"Really?" asked Penny as if the concept was inconceivable to her.

Raul walked back into the house with the folded flag of Wetpr which he now unfolded and showed Milt.

"By The Great Ruler, this is the most wonderful thing I have ever heard," Milt said and looked like he might cry.

"Milt, we are telling the truth," said Simon. "We want to protect the people here while we clean this place up. So our first question is are there dungeons or a jail of any kind around here?"

"Penny run next door and get the neighbors," said Milt. "Bring them all here." Penny ran out the door and Milt stood up and walked into the kitchen. He took some cups from a cupboard and carried them into the parlor. He set them down and returned to the cupboard and brought a bottle of whiskey into the room. "We haven't been here all that long," Milt explained. "My neighbors are good people and will be able to answer more of your questions."

Within moments excited people entered the house. Some of them carried bottles of wine and others brought food. Within thirty minutes the entire house was filled with people who were all looking at the flag. Everyone was smiling and many were crying.

"We really didn't expect such a reception," said Raul as he and Simon now stood in front of the group. "We are sure that you have many questions as do we. First, we will tell you what we told Milt and Penny."

"Thought you got lost," Archetenus said sarcastically when Raul and Simon walked into the abandoned building two hours later.

"We just had our first meeting with the citizens," Simon said. "Did you get any good information?"

"Willy here is a horse thief and wants to join our gang," Jared said with a grin. "He's an independent but says you pretty much need to be part of a gang here just for the protection. He drew us maps of the territories owned by the gangs and gave us approximate numbers of the men in each."

"All of Addison's men wear the blue bandanas around their necks," Archetenus explained. "Bastine likes red. And from what Willy says he has a strange fixation for that color. His men wear red shirts like their boss and he even made the owner of the Back Door Tavern decorate the place in red."

"That could be more than liking a color," said Simon. "That might be some magic or power thing." Then he looked at Willy. "Is Bastine a dark lord?"

"I don't know but he ain't from around here so he might have different magics where he comes from."

"And Willart's men wear black bandanas," continued Archetenus. "There isn't a jail house but the gangs themselves have built dungeons and the buildings on this map show where they are." Archetenus kept talking as Raul and Simon looked at the rough map that Willy had drawn.

"Willy says that emotions are running high around here between the gangs and it doesn't take much to get them fighting, they all want to run this place but at this point they are pretty evenly matched with about one hundred and forty men each."

"So what makes Taperia so important?" asked Raul. "Seems to me that the kings stole everything the people had."

"It's the mines," said Willy.

"There aren't any mines around here," said Raul.

"There sure as hell are," Willy said. "And it sounds like they were found by accident. The story that I heard said that some people were running from the Hutas and hid in one of the caves and found gold."

"You mean the caves by the River Nebu?" asked Raul.

"No, there are small caves near the Lake of the Pors between here and Cana. The caves look small from the outside but they are deep. Bastine's gang took over Cana and has them working some of the mines. Addison and Willart are doing the same thing here in Taperia."

"Willy, you are on the payroll," said Simon and handed him a small pouch of gold coins. "But if we even hear that you looked sideways at another woman I will cut your throat."

"Thanks boss," Willy said with a smile. "Where you all staying?"

"I'm thinking we take over these abandoned buildings for now," said Archetenus. "Willy do I need to tell you what will happen if you betray us? We've got a shit load of men in the city and they will be watching you."

"Hey, this is good money," Willy said. "But if you didn't know about the mines why are you here?"

"We've got our reasons," Jared said and the look on his face stopped Willy from asking anymore questions.

Hector and Mallory talked long into the night. She brought a bottle of whiskey and a bottle of wine into the room because she wanted to take advantage of the fact that Hector was willing to open up about his life and his feelings.

The conversation was not casual and both were upset at times by what the other one said. They decided to stop the discussion because they were exhausted and emotionally drained; not because they had worked through all of the issues.

"Hector, it is final. Tomorrow we are going to visit your parents and you are going to apologize. I don't think any of us expect big changes but you need to reach out to them and heal all of this. And you're not giving gifts; you are talking and I mean really talking. Your parents feel they are responsible for your choices; at least free them of that guilt."

"You know for someone so young you..."

"I what?" asked Mallory as she stood up and walked towards the closet.

"You just seem older than you are."

"Why do I have a feeling that's not what you were going to say first?" she said and laughed.

"You know I am not going to tell them everything," he said loudly since she was now in the closet.

"I don't expect you to but you have to stop treating them like fools."

"Why are you in the closet?"

Mallory didn't answer but walked towards the bed wearing a sheer, silver colored nightgown. The cut of the gown was both revealing and flattering.

Hector stared at her as if he was shocked. "You are so incredibly beautiful. You bust my chops all night then you walk out here dressed like that and you say I am confusing," Hector said with a grin and stood up and quickly tore off his clothing.

"Well, you didn't buy me any ugly nightgowns," she said coquettishly and slid under the blankets.

"You do know that you drive me crazy," he said as he got under the covers and gently pulled her close to him.

"You were crazy long before you met me," she said and laughed then stopped talking because Hector was staring at her so intently. He didn't speak, he stared at her face as he stroked her hair, then he took her into his arms and kissed her. As soon as their lips touched they forgot their anger and worries. They forgot they were from separate worlds. In that moment they forgot they were separate people.

Chapter XXXVII
Ruse

After Willy left the abandoned building Jared went to find some of their men while Archetenus, Raul and Simon searched the other two buildings.

Jared returned with Ira, Maddox and Henrich. Since it was now dark the Ruala warriors had also entered the city. Dagon, Joao and Dack joined the men.

"We're going to take over these three buildings," Archetenus said. "So that we have something in the city. Ira, Maddox and Henrich you should bring your healers here and have them set up medical stations. Tomorrow start stocking these buildings up with food, beds and whatever else in case we need to hold up here. We got a lot of information but before I cover that, Raul and Simon met with a bunch of citizens."

"We found three men dragging a young woman off the street," Simon said. "We killed two of the guys and Archetenus and Jared questioned the third. Her name is Penny and we took her home and met her father Milt. We told them why we were here and the whole damn neighborhood joined us. Those people are so happy they were crying. But they understand the need for secrecy now."

"This is just like it was in Nora, the people can't do enough to help us. They are going to spread the word. Now, none of them are warriors but they want to know how they can help. We told them information would be the best way, so we want all of you to go back there with us tomorrow so we can introduce you."

"These people live in terror so it might be a matter of them handing us notes or telling us to go into certain stores and such. We didn't have time to hear all of their stories but it just pissed us off the way they have been treated. Then one of them..." Raul stopped talking for a moment because he became emotional.

"One of them was telling us about Roch and said that Queen Vitomas would stand up for the people and things got considerably worse after she was killed."

"I told them she was alive and my wife and not only did some cry but they want to send her letters."

"Some gold mines were discovered near the Lake of the Pors and the three gangs that own this city are forcing the people to work those mines. Archetenus will fill you in on the rest. I want to go to the New Moon and check on Javier."

The New Moon Hotel had a tavern area besides the dining room. This tavern was open to the public but the high stakes poker games that were held in the back rooms were by invitation only. Javier was sitting at a table in the front end of the tavern playing solitary and watching the back rooms when Simon and Raul sat down at his table.

"If you've got any money I can play something more interesting," he said loudly.

Both Raul and Simon put gold coins on the table and Javier dealt the cards. Unlike most of the taverns in the city this bar room had servers and they were all young women. Simon motioned one over to the table. When the woman was at the table Javier said, "Marly, these are my friends Simon and Raul and they are interested in getting in those big games too."

"Now Javier, you know I don't have no say over that. I already told Snapper that you wanted in."

"Who's Snapper?" asked Raul with a grin.

"The bartender." When Marly said this all three men glanced at the giant of a man behind the bar. "Can you guess how he got that nick name?"

"Snapping necks," Simon said and grinned.

"Just bones in general," said Marly.

"How much money do we have to give him to get in?" asked Raul.

"Well, it's like I told Javier. Snapper is the gatekeeper, it's Addison who really runs those games."

"Well how do we get his attention?" asked Raul. "Because a friend of ours has a message for him."

"I'll bring you some paper and you can write it down. I'll give it to him but I'm not making any promises."

"That will work for us," said Simon. "Can we have a bottle and two more glasses?"

Marly brought the glasses, whiskey and paper to the table. She waited as Raul wrote several lines on the paper then folded it and handed it to her. Simon paid for the drinks then gave her a tip for bringing them and a separate tip for taking the note to Addison. When she left the table Javier asked, "What did you tell him?"

"That a seer in Salar named Zoya said he was in a lot of danger. She kept seeing a dark haired woman and the color red," Raul said with a grin.

"When we are done here we should all take a walk," Simon said as he looked at his cards.

It was almost twenty minutes later when Marly returned to the table. "He made me wait to give it to him," she said with disgust. "Here," Marly handed Raul a note.

Stakes are too high, can't break away but want to talk to you. Meet you in front in two hours.

Marly left the table while Raul was reading the note. He handed it to Simon who handed it to Javier. "Let's finish this hand then take that walk," Javier said and motioned for Marly to come to the table.

"Marly, my friends here are new in town so I am going to show them a few sights then we're coming back," as Javier spoke he put a fistful of gold coins into her hand.

"What is this for, you already paid your bill?" she asked.

"That's to give that information to anyone who asks," Javier replied.

Marly stared at all three men as if she was trying to read them. Then she leaned forward and picked up their glasses and said in a low voice. "All of you are new here. This ain't the kind of city where you flash around money without someone jumping you."

"What about the back room?" asked Simon.

"Same thing," she said.

"Marly, you're my favorite girl," Javier said with a grin.

"Yeah, and just how many women have you said that to tonight," she said sarcastically and all the men laughed.

After they finished their hand of cards the three men walked out of the hotel. They walked around the streets to determine if they were being followed before they walked to the abandoned buildings which now held more team members.

"We're already setting up," Ira said. "The Rualas are flying a lot of things in."

"Good," said Simon. "We just showed Javier the buildings and we have an appointment with Addison in a couple of hours. Where are Jared and Archetenus?"

"Checking on some of the crew. They should be back shortly," said Ira.

"Well, we can start catching you up now," Raul said to Javier and proceeded to tell him the information they had uncovered.

Archetenus and Jared walked into the building fifteen minutes later. They both had blood on them.

"What did you two get into?" asked Maddox.

"You might say we was adjusting attitudes," Jared said with a grin.

"Well, you might get mad at me," Raul said. "I sent Addison a note that said Zoya had a warning for him. It got his attention and he's meeting us later."

472

"Smart thinking," Jared said and laughed. "Of course, I'm gonna beat the hell out of him before this is over. Here." As he spoke, Jared took a dried flower from his pocket and handed it to Raul. "Zoya loves these blue Iris's. She always had a vase full in her shop. If he watched her at all he will recognize this."

"Thanks," said Raul. "We got warned tonight about flashing too much money around."

"No shit," said Archetenus. "Hell, they'll steal the gold fillings out of your teeth around here. That's why I have Rualas practically perched on Javier's balcony."

Raul, Simon and Javier returned to the tavern in the New Moon Hotel an hour later. They acted like they were somewhat intoxicated since they didn't know who might be watching them. As soon as they sat at a table Marly came up to them. "Been having fun?" she asked with a smile.

"Just seeing the sights," Simon said with a slight slur. "Can we have a bottle and three glasses?"

"Addison's game got done early; he's waiting for you in the back room. Follow me."

They entered a room in the rear of the tavern. It was elegantly furnished with crystal candelabras and expensive furniture. Two huge men were standing behind a man who was seated at the table.

"Addison, this is Javier, Raul and Simon," Marly said. "Raul wrote the note."

"Bring us another bottle and more glasses," Addison said and Marly left the room. "Have a seat gentlemen. Now tell me why you are here? Did Zoya send you?"

"No," said Raul. "Simon and I are brothers and business partners. We heard about some mines around here and wanted to check them out. Our wives are regular customers of Zoya's; when she heard we were coming here she sent along a message."

As Raul spoke he took the dried Iris out of his shirt pocket and handed it to Addison. "Now don't ask me what that means but she sent it so you would know the message was from her."

"She always had bouquets of these in her shop," Addison said as he looked at the flower. "Before we get to the message how are the two of you connected with Javier?"

"Cards," Simon said and laughed. "We've played with him in Salar."

"Why are you interested in checking out the mines?" asked Addison.

"Investments," said Simon. "It's kind of what we do."

"Have you been to them yet?" Addison asked.

"No, we just got here and decided to have a drink and found Javier," said Raul.

Addison stared at the three men as he was trying to read them. "Ok, let's hear the message."

"Understand she told our wives and they told us," said Raul. "So we didn't get it directly from her but she said she has been having a lot of visions about you for the last few weeks. She said they are pretty much the same and she is taking them as a warning. She sees weapons, a dark haired woman and the color red and feels that you are in great danger. Hope that means something to you."

"More than you realize," Addison said then stopped talking when Marly walked into the room carrying a tray containing glasses. Simon handed her several gold coins.

"So do you own this place?" asked Raul.

"In a way," Addison said and smirked. "I also own one of the mines. There are three and each has a different owner. I want to get my hands on the other two. The three of you are all built like fighters but you sound like noblemen what are you?"

"We were fighters," said Simon. "But you kind of have to give that shit up when you start having babies so we are businessmen now."

"I see," said Addison with a grin. "And Javier?"

"I am a jack of many trades," Javier said. "For example; I couldn't help but notice that from the positions that your men stand in they can see the reflections of other's cards in those mirrors. I assume you always sit in the same position."

Addison laughed, "You are actually the first person to realize that. The three of you seem more like fighters to me and very intelligent ones to boot. I can always use good men."

"Looks to me like you have enough men," Javier said. "Unless you are going to war."

"On the brink. This city is split into thirds as a treaty between our three gangs but we all want the entire pie and not just a piece. That is why Zoya's message has significance for me. I'm not looking for investors but I would be damn interested in hearing what my competition says. How about I pay you to give them the same pitch. And I pay well."

"If there are three gangs in this city you know you are being watched," said Javier. "Won't they think we are your spies?"

"I'll take you around tomorrow," said Addison. "We can go to the Land Office, a few other places and the mines. We'll make it look like a business meeting. Where are you staying?"

"We haven't got rooms yet," said Raul. "We thought about getting them here but it would look like we do work for you if that is the case."

"Not necessarily but it will look like you have money to spend if you stay here," said Addison.

"Ok, what aren't you telling us?" asked Simon. "Your face is screaming that there is more to all of this."

Addison laughed again. "I like you guys. The treaty is hanging on by a thread. All our gangs know each other's men. You are fresh faces and you certainly look like you can handle yourselves if things get rough."

"So you're sending us in the lion's den to see if we get our butts kicked," said Simon.

"No. If my competitors are interested in investors I will be the one investing but you will be the faces."

"Sounds like you better pay pretty well," Raul said as he took a sip of his whiskey. "I'm interested but we need to talk this over. What time do you want to meet tomorrow?"

"How about nine in the front lobby," said Addison. "By chance would you have a trade card?"

Raul took one from his pocket and handed it to Addison who said, "I am surprised. You might actually be businessmen." Raul smiled.

Jasmine and Tessa kept looking at each other and smiling as they prepared breakfast with Mallory. "Mallory, you sure are happy this morning, did you have a good night," Tessa asked and giggled.

Mallory laughed. "We talked through a lot of things last night."

"And that is why you are smiling?" Jasmine asked with a grin.

"No, we..."

Mallory did not finish her sentence because Hector walked up behind her, turned her around, bent her backwards and kissed her. Both Tessa and Jasmine laughed. Mallory too laughed when the embrace was over.

"We made love last night," Hector said. "I think it is just what the doctor ordered."

"We wouldn't have guessed," Tessa teased. "Was it that obvious the first time that Noah and I made love?"

"Oh yeah!" said Jasmine and laughed. "The guys were laying bets."

"Bets on what?" asked Tessa.

"You should ask them," Jasmine said and laughed again.

"We're going to the castle to talk to Hector's parents this morning if you want to come along," said Mallory.

"Some of us should just in case you get attacked," said Jasmine.

"Do you know what you are going to say?" Tessa asked. "I'm serious; I wouldn't want to be you today. You know you can't tell them everything."

"Oh, believe me I am thinking about that," said Hector. "But Mallory said they feel guilty because they think they are responsible for my life. She's right, I can't let them feel like that."

"If nothing works tell them you are crazy," Tessa said kiddingly and laughed.

"You are joking but I actually thought about that. Everyone thinks that Juleta is responsible for everything and yes she screwed me over a lot but I was a crook before I got involved with her. I met her at the orgies and when she heard that I had a crew and we did high end robberies she hired me."

"Do your parents know that?" asked Tessa.

"They will after today."

"Yeah but you were still...well your personality changed totally after Juleta got her hands on you," Clev said. Everyone turned and smiled when they saw him and Elexas walk out of his bedroom holding hands.

"We never killed anyone and we robbed from the rich bastards," Clev continued. "We had a hell of a lot of fun and then it all changed. And Hector, I don't know if you even realize how much you changed."

"So you became a crook for fun?" asked Jasmine.

"That and boredom," Hector said.

"Do you want me to go with you?" Clev asked. "Because I don't know if you remember everything right."

"Maybe we should talk first," Hector said seriously. "So why didn't you say any of this before?"

"Tried to but you always got pissed off. I almost never saw you pissed before Juleta. And now that I am healing, my head seems clearer."

"Let's grab some coffee and go for a walk," said Hector.

"Clev, last night I asked Hector if he was addicted to power before he met Juleta or if that was something she did to him. He doesn't know. Do you?" asked Mallory.

"I'd have to think about that," Clev said. "Partly because I am not sure I understand how someone can be addicted to power but if the Angels said it, I am sure it is right. Hector was always a powerful man and a leader but after Juleta poisoned him it was like all of his negative traits became really exaggerated and I now wonder if the same happened with me. Don't get me wrong, we were both crooks and did some really bad things but we weren't monsters and that's what we both became."

Clev paused. "Hector, did I become addicted too? I look back and it's like I don't recognize myself. I don't even want to tell you girls some of the things we done."

"But you both still chose to do them," Mallory said. "We've sat with both of you while demons jumped out of you and you were being healed from Juleta's poisons. I think you both need to seriously think if any part of you now is because of Juleta because if it is...well then she still has her claws in you."

Hours earlier Raul and Simon had gotten chambers in the New Moon Hotel that had the balcony facing the back of the building so the Ruala warriors and Enrops could enter without being seen. They were one floor above Javier's chambers. Three hours before sunrise Dack flew into their room and woke them up.

"I've got your clothes and things," said Dack as he emptied the huge pack that he had been carrying on his back. "And we have warriors near the mines. We'll be watching you but it's harder for us Rualas in the daylight."

"Thanks," said Raul. "We want to get an idea of how many hired fighters are at the mines and if they are forcing the people to stay some place or if they let them go home and if so what times. We're just afraid that a lot of innocent people are going to get hurt."

"We all agree," said Dack. "Dagon and Joao are already at the mines drawing maps and Joao is going to maybe draw some of the people and whatever."

"It's the middle of the night. How can they see to draw maps?" asked Raul.

"Our eyes are different from yours," said Dack. "Seriously, we are like birds, we can fly and see at night."

"Good to know," said Simon. "And we are glad you three volunteered. We just don't know the new members well enough to know how they will react."

"We know. The whole household wanted to come but most of them have to work on the plans for the new forts and Patronus Headquarters." Dack laughed. "Even Natasha wanted to come and you know how that went over with Calen."

"I can't say a word," said Raul. "I am much worse than he is."

"Did Joao tell you that Olivia wanted to come along? She thought that if there were people kept in prisons that she would be able to hear them. I think that was their first fight."

"It is too dangerous for her here," said Simon. "Although she did have a good idea. Isn't she getting off those crutches soon?"

"Hannah said she will be off before we get back, so Joao wants to take her dancing."

"It's none of my business and tell me that if you want but you and Joao were inseparable before Olivia; how is that working out?" asked Raul.

479

"It's really fine. You know there always was that group of us; that's how we grew up. It changed when we got here and Fala was killed then Melinda. Olivia just fits in with all of us. I wouldn't say this to the others but she reminds me of Fala, its nice having her around."

Moments later there was a knock on the door, Simon opened it and Javier walked in.

"Thought you would be up," Javier said. "I couldn't sleep. Is anything wrong that Dack is here?"

"I just brought their clothes," Dack said.

"I couldn't sleep because I had a nagging feeling all night," Javier said. "We all expect this to be a trap but I feel like there is more to it. Like we have to be looking more carefully for something."

"Most of us have learned the hard way that when you get those overpowering feelings, sometimes it's the Angels sending them to you," Simon said.

"Should I call to them?" asked Javier.

"I would," Raul said.

"But, I don't know which one."

"Just ask if someone is trying to talk to you," said Dack. "Or just ask if anyone wants to talk to you. Sometimes they do this to train you to contact them."

Miranda and Cyril appeared in the room and they were both laughing. "Dack, we enjoyed how you said that," Miranda said. "And that is exactly what we were doing. So tell us why you are going with Addison today."

"We have learned that the three gangs that control the city are forcing people to work in the mines. We want to see how the setups are in case we need to rescue those people from the mines or find out if they are being kept some place else," said Simon.

"Do you think that Addison recognizes who you are?" Miranda asked.

480

"We didn't think about that," said Raul. "He didn't act like it last night."

"But he has had time to check into your story," said Cyril. "I go in disguise myself," he said and smiled. "Using your real names and saying that you are brothers and friends of Zoya's wasn't smart."

"He now suspects who you are but he doesn't know why you are here or want to speak with him. Your situation has changed greatly in the last few hours."

"Did any of the citizens that we told, tell who we are?" asked Raul.

"No but they have prayed for you," said Miranda. "Javier, you are the expert in disguises what would you suggest?"

"First, am I compromised too?"

"For now by association only," Miranda said. "He hasn't learned that you are their brother."

"We need to get out of here and our best bet would be the Rualas. I suspect that Addison wants information from us then he wants to ransom us to Sudfad. But he is probably really suspicious that we asked about the mines so he might change procedures. If we can do it without getting innocent people hurt we should make it look like one of the other gangs grabbed us during the night."

"Very good," said Miranda. "I am impressed. You got it all right. Now tell me how you would do this?"

"It's short notice and you will probably say you started sending me feelings hours ago so it is my fault," Javier said. "But we need to have some of the other gang members seen in or around this building. Let me think about this."

"First, you are learning to listen to us," said Miranda. "But you must also learn to work with us. How could we prevent innocent people from being hurt?"

481

"A storm or something else that would keep them off the streets," said Dack. "And perhaps powerful enough to keep the people out of the mines. A Rogett attack! Not a real one but a rumor."

Miranda and Cyril both smiled at Dack's suggestions. "We will comment on those in a moment but why would you want Addison to think that another gang grabbed you?"

"To get them to fight each other instead of us and to expose who they are," said Raul then he smiled. "I've got a red shirt with me. I could tear a piece off and make it look like it was torn during a fight."

Dagon and Joao landed on the balcony. "Ruth just told us to come here," Dagon said. "It's quiet at the mines, they don't work night crews."

"How do we best protect the citizens?" asked Raul.

"Where are your horses?" Cyril asked.

"At a livery stable down the street," said Raul. "We don't have a lot of time and we don't want the citizens hurt so I am asking for suggestions here."

"Javier has good ideas about making all the rooms look like a fight took place, said Miranda. " But your friends should fly you to your horses. Go to the home of Milt and Penny and tell them to get the word out for people to stay off the streets. These people live in danger every day they have systems in place."

"Your men outnumber the gangs. Tensions are high so it won't take much to start a fight. And if you would have asked, we would have told you that Roch's dungeons are intact. They were underground and on the Taperia side of the castle. The keys hang from pegs near the front door."

"Of course, these are just suggestions," said Miranda. "But whatever you decide you will have to move quickly."

"Are we going to be fighting any demons?" Simon asked.

"No," said Cyril.

"Will you protect the citizens while we deal with the gangs?" Raul asked.

"Yes," said Miranda. "But, what did Javier tell you about his feelings?"

"That there was more to all of this. More than what we are seeing," Javier said. "We haven't had time to really check out this city."

"Derlock, the Huta Captain who the Sanuri and Erebus saved has returned with an enormous army," explained Miranda. "And this will actually benefit you. While the gangs did not recognize you the members of the Sisterhood did. They have been following you. They do not realize what you are planning and if they did, it wouldn't matter to them."

"They came here looking for the items of power that Roch had hidden in his castle. They know that the castle has been destroyed and that has them concerned because they know they have rivals seeking those items. They called for reinforcements and their army far outnumbers the gang members here."

"They also know that Roch was your uncle and believe you might know where these items are. Derlock also knows Raul and Simon but his hatred is fixated on the Sisterhood. For perhaps the only times in your lives, the Hutas have your backs."

"But how do we keep them all out of the city?" asked Raul.

"That will not be a problem," said Cyril. "The Hutas have found the camp of the Sisterhood, which is south of here. They are surrounding it as we speak. That is what will keep the people out of the mines."

"But what stops them from entering the city?" asked Javier. "And is the army of the Sisterhood all women?"

"You will not be fighting against demons this day but the Hutas will. The battle will consume their resources. The city will be of no concern to them."

"Are you saying both armies will be destroyed?" asked Raul.

"No," Cyril said. "Both of those armies have sold their souls to demons who have vested interests in the outcome of the battle. And some of the demons may not want those groups fighting each other. We are saying they will be too distracted and exhausted to pay attention to anything else."

Chapter XXXVIII
Deliverance

After Dagon, Joao and Dack left the Princes at the livery stable they went first to the abandoned buildings to tell Archetenus, Jared and the team leaders what the Angels said.

"So what should we say to stir up the gangs?" asked Maddox.

"I think we tell Bastine that Addison grabbed the Princes of Wetpr and is pinning it on his gang," said Joao.

"I like that," said Archetenus. "But you know whoever says those words is gonna get grabbed by Bastine's men. Let me and Jared do that. And what about Willart?"

"Tell him the other two are conspiring to take his mine," said Ira. "That ought to get his goat."

"Before we do that, I am going to warn Norma," Jared said.

Although the mines did not have operations at night they did have guards. Ruala warriors sat in the trees near the mines. The Angel Ruth had already warned them about the pending battle between the Hutas and the Sisterhood and told them not to get involved.

Tate and Moxy, two of the Ruala warriors on Ira's team had been spying on the armies and now returned to their comrades to brief them. "There must be two thousand Hutas surrounding that camp," Moxy said to Shey, a Ruala warrior on Henrich's team. "And that camp is lit up like you can't believe which I don't understand because the Hutas can see everything going on. They..." Moxy did not finish her statement because loud explosions came from the location of the camp.

The Ruala warriors saw strange burning objects propel through the night sky then explode. But the explosions seemed to release demons and monsters.

Two thousand Hutas screamed their war cries and all of the hired killers who were guarding the mines ran out into the night. The guards expected to fight with Hutas; they were not prepared for an aerial attack by the Rualas. The battles were brief, the guards were taken by surprise and killed. The Rualas picked up the men and dumped their bodies in front of the stronghold of each of their gang leaders. The Rualas remained in the city so they could join the battle that would soon be taking place there.

Jared and Archetenus were playing cards in the Back Door Tavern, which was open all night. Bastine wasn't in the front end of the tavern but most of his gang was.

"I've never seen so damn much red in my life," Jared said under his breath. "It's starting to hurt my eyes."

A man wearing a red shirt ran into the tavern yelling, "Boss! Boss!" He ran through the front end of the tavern and into a back room.

"Show time," Archetenus said with a grin as he dealt cards.

Bastine and three other men ran out of the back room following the first man. All the gang members jumped out of their chairs and ran out of the building.

Ten minutes later Bastine and a dozen men walked back into the tavern.

"What's going on?" yelled Jared.

Bastine gave Jared an angry look but did not speak. "There's a bunch of bodies out front," one of the other men said.

"Damn, I guess they were telling the truth," Archetenus said and dealt another card to Jared. "I thought they were full of bull."

Bastine stopped walking when he heard Archetenus' words. He turned and walked up to the table. "What are you talking about?" demanded Bastine.

Both Jared and Archetenus looked at him with annoyance. "Who are you?" asked Jared.

"Bastine and this is my place and my territory."

Both Archetenus and Jared laughed. "Damn, we're in the wrong place," Archetenus said and poured more whiskey into their glasses.

"I demand to know what you are talking about," yelled Bastine.

"Listen buddy, you may own the bar but you don't own us so stop with the demanding crap!" snapped Archetenus and Bastine's men now surrounded the table.

"Do you just want to split them down the middle, six and six?" Jared asked Archetenus as he looked at his hand of cards.

"What the hell," Archetenus replied and in that instant he threw a knife that landed between Bastine's eyes.

Jared had three throwing stars up his sleeve and threw them with lightning speed; they all hit their marks. As soon as Archetenus threw his knife he knocked the table over and stood up. He grabbed his chair, broke it, took one of the legs and thrust it into the chest of the man closest to him.

Jared was wielding two large knives. Both Archetenus and Jared were fast on their feet and agile. A man jumped onto Jared's back and Archetenus grabbed the man and broke his neck while Jared stabbed the man in front of him.

Archetenus quickly turned and punched the man behind him then used him as a shield as two of Bastine's men tried to stab him. There was no loyalty in this crew and Bastine's killers stabbed their own comrade to death. Archetenus threw the body at his attackers then ducked as a chair flew over his head. Six Patronus priests ran into the tavern and attacked the men fighting with Jared and Archetenus.

"Thanks but we really didn't need any help," Jared said and wiped blood from his mouth.

"It worked, the streets are exploding," said one of the priests.

"Good," said Archetenus as he pulled his knives out of bodies. After the men retrieved their weapons they ran outside. "Let them fight each other first!" yelled Archetenus.

The streets were filled with gang members who were fighting with each other. Team members and priests were forming an inner perimeter to keep the gang members away from the citizens. Raul and Simon were surrounding the city with Wetprian soldiers.

Javier and Maddox led a group of warriors into the New Moon Hotel. Addison was watching the fighting from the large window in the tavern. Javier and the team members entered through the front lobby and walked into the tavern so they were behind Addison.

"Boss!" yelled Snapper and grabbed a bat that was behind the bar.

Torrance, one of the Nordes warriors on Maddox's team threw a knife that landed between Snapper's eyes. When the giant of the man went down he tore part of the bar off its frame.

Addison quickly turned and Javier punched him in the jaw then punched him in the stomach. When Addison bent over from the blow, Javier grabbed his head and pounded it on a table until the table broke.

Maddox and his team fought with Addison's men who were trying to save their boss. Addison was barely conscious when Javier threw him against the wall.

"Who are you?" snorted Addison.

"The sons of King Sudfad," Javier said with pride. "We've taken the kingdom and you're going to hang."

An hour earlier, Raul and Simon pounded on the door of Milt's house and yelled his name. Lights started turning on in the surrounding houses. "Milt, it's Raul and Simon," Raul yelled and Penny quickly opened the door.

"Penny do you have some way of warning everyone not to leave their homes?" Raul yelled loudly as he knew that neighbors were getting up and coming out of their houses.

"We have a signal," yelled Thronson, a neighbor of Milt's.

"Do whatever you have to do," said Simon. "We're taking out the gangs. Don't anyone go into the streets."

"How much time do we have?" yelled Milt as he hobbled onto his front porch.

"An hour maybe more," Raul yelled. "And no one goes to the mines today."

People came out of their homes carrying clubs and candles. They were still in their night clothes and they ran down the streets warning people. Thronson and four other men ran to an abandoned building that long ago had been a church. They ran up the dilapidated stairs to the roof and rang the old church bell. The bell was massive and took two men to pull the rope that moved the bell.

Some citizens cried out of fear for the bell was a warning for them to hide. Other's cried at hearing the bell which so long had been silent. Some people grabbed weapons, some people prayed but the entire city was alerted to danger. The irony of the situation was that while the citizens listened to the bell, the gang members ignored it. There were no churches and a bell was ringing in the middle of the night yet the gangs felt secure in their positions and did not question the unusual occurrence. A few surmised that drunks were ringing the bell.

Ira and Henrich were already in Walt's Tavern before the Rualas dropped the bodies of the mine guards in front of it. They had no idea what Willart looked like so they carefully watched the people in the crowded room. A man opened the door and yelled, "Get the boss now!" Several men ran outside while others ran up a staircase that was to the side of the bar.

Minutes later a large man with gray hair and a gray beard charged down the stairs with his men behind him. He ran out the front door of the tavern and immediately started cursing. He marched back into the tavern and yelled, "The war's begun. Everyone in the damn streets now!" As the hired men ran out of the tavern, Willart ran up the stairs to his chambers and Ira and Henrich followed him. Willart quickly turned when he heard the men. He released the knife in his hand which grazed Ira's shoulder.

Henrich dove down and grabbed Willart's knees. The gang leader fell forward and broke his nose when he hit the steps. He quickly rolled onto his back and punched Henrich who punched him back. The two men exchanged several blows before Ira was able to get around them and grab Willart.

Ira and Henrich pulled Willart to his feet. Willart threw his weight backwards to free himself from their grasps but in so doing he broke through the railing of the staircase and fell to the floor below. The fall might not have killed him had he not broken his neck when he hit the side of the bar.

The majority of the fighting was taking place in the streets of the main business district. Raul and Simon had the city surrounded and entered it from the outskirts. They killed gang members as they found them. They saw no signs of Hutas or the Sisterhood as they worked their way through the streets.

The business district was filled with bodies when Raul and Simon reached that area. The fighting was between the gang members who were so distracted they failed to notice they were surrounded and being watched.

The team members had stopped the gangs from burning buildings or dragging innocent people into their battle. As Raul and Simon watched the scene from opposite sides of the area they realized that the bodies of the gang leaders were hanging from trees. The leaders had been executed. Only a couple of dozen men were still fighting in the streets. Simon ordered his men to attack. The battle ended quickly.

"This was too easy," Raul said to Simon as they walked through the streets. "Miranda, what did we miss?"

"This morning nothing," Miranda's voice rang in their ears. "But this is not an area where you can let your guard down. You planned to leave some of your soldiers here. Send for reinforcements before you leave the city."

"We found a spot," Javier said as he walked up to Raul and Simon. "It isn't great but it will do for now."

Raul returned to his horse and took the Wetprian flag from his saddlebag. He joined Javier, Simon and Maddox as they walked down the street. "Archetenus found it," Javier explained. "Apparently there used to be a statue of Sudfad's father there."

The men stopped at an area that once was a small park. Archetenus had men clearing the brush away which exposed an old stone fountain and stone pathways. Citizens started to enter the streets. Many now gathered around Archetenus and his crew. Raul climbed a tree and hung the flag from a sturdy branch. Citizens, soldiers and team members yelled and applauded.

Simon stood on top of a large rock and announced, "We are the sons of King Sudfad and we have taken the Kingdom of Stordt. All of you are now citizens of Wetpr. You are free men and women!"

The screams of the people were deafening. They hugged each other and cried. Many ran to get their neighbors; others hugged the soldiers and team members and some danced in the streets.

Norma found Jared in the crowd and jumped into his arms and hugged him. "You did it, you really did it," she kept repeating.

Chapter XXXIX
Confessions

"Hector, that is a two hour ride each way; you aren't ready for that," scolded Shara.

"I really need to speak with my parents. If I get too weak I am sure that Mathas will let me use a bedroom for a while," Hector said.

"Mallory, I don't trust that Hector would even tell Mathas that he was too weak to travel," Shara said. "I hope you are planning on going with him."

"Yes."

"Then let me make you up some tonics and take some extra clothing in case you need to spend the night there."

"I feel bad now," Mallory said. "I'm the one who is forcing him to do this."

"You aren't forcing me and you are right," said Hector. "If we need to stay there we need to stay."

"Well, you aren't going by yourself," said Dominic. "After we get you to the castle I am going to the dungeons. Am I the only one who feels uneasy that we haven't heard from the Sisterhood since we locked up some of their people? I would have expected some of them to try and breakout our prisoners."

"I was thinking about that too," said Hector. "Don't dismiss them because they are women. They are cunning and savage warriors. And in a way it all seemed just too easy when we captured them. I have been wondering about that."

"Now bear with me because I am not myself yet and sometimes things seem fuzzy. But that letter that Claudius read; didn't he say they locked all of the items of power they took from Roch's castle in Sudfad's? The Sanuri isn't traveling with any of those things is he?"

"Are you thinking that the Sisterhood can detect the power of those things?" asked Noah.

"I wouldn't put it past them," Hector said. "Does Sudfad and the others know the Sisterhood might come for those things? If they don't you better warn them."

Fennel was walking out of the house before Hector finished speaking. He called to a small flock of Enrops and gave them messages for both Sudfad and the Sanuri.

As soon as the Wetprian flag was raised in Taperia, Simon sent a message to Sudfad telling him the news. Simon said that the city was safe enough for Joshua's team to come and start working with the citizens. Simon also said that he and Raul decided a fort should be built near the city so he was requesting more soldiers to that area.

The few gang members who were alive were taken to the dungeons at Roch's castle. "The Angels must have done this deliberately," Simon said as he and others were examining the old prison. "All of the rubble is away from the dungeons. I don't know if you realize it but the dungeons were under the castle. There is absolutely no way that could have happened by nature."

Raul was listening to his brother but not talking. He left the dungeons and walked around the rubble of the castle. "Miranda or any Angel can I ask a question?"

"Certainly," said Ruth as she and Miranda appeared.

"Thank you for coming," Raul said. "You may have already told us this but with everything that went on is the land around here safe for building? I mean is it cursed or anything?"

"It is safe now," said Ruth.

"I'm thinking this might be the perfect site for the fort. And the way you broke up the castle, well, we can use the rocks for building. But there is that cave with the trap not far from here. What are your thoughts on that?"

"We agree with your choice," said Miranda. "And it would be beneficial to have the soldiers close to that cave. Sudfad has been interviewing generals for the positions here. He has asked for our guidance and as we speak The Lion is meeting with him. While you believe that taking Taperia was easy, this kingdom will be a challenge for all of you for a very long time."

"Do you know how the other groups are doing?" Raul asked.

"Colter and Orlan have met with no resistance so far. They had already established themselves in that area and have the full support of the citizens."

"It has been more challenging for the troops from Fort Stanus but nothing they have not been able to handle. But you do realize that many of the criminals will not expose themselves as easily as the gangs did here. So while there is no resistance when your armies ride through an area, there are still criminals and demons here."

"But now that the citizens of Stordt have hope again. They will find their courage and eventually they too will stand up to those who had been victimizing them."

After the flag was raised in Taperia, the team members and the soldiers went from building to building searching for gang members. They also explained to the citizens that they had a new King and encouraged them to attend one of the public meetings that Raul and Simon would be holding over the next two days.

Archetenus found a large building in the business district for them to use as a temporary headquarters. Javier was meeting with the local business people to set up provisions for the soldiers and team members who would remain in Taperia while Jared was having the bodies removed from the city streets.

In the very first meeting that Raul and Simon had with Milt, Thronson and their neighbors, they asked the people to provide lists of the things they wanted and needed. These people now contacted the other citizens of the city for their input.

Not since Sudfad's father was King had the citizens been asked for input about anything; to them this mere act was incomprehensible.

Hector did not send advanced notice of his arrival. His parents were unpacking their belongings and arranging their new home when Hector, Clev and Mallory walked onto their porch.

Clarence came to the door but didn't speak. "Father, don't slam the door on me. I came to apologize and to explain a few things," Hector said.

"I would never slam the door on you son," Clarence said and stepped aside so the three could enter.

Catherine walked out of the kitchen. "Mother..." Hector started to say.

"I heard," Catherine said. "The dining room is full of crates. Come into the kitchen. I just baked a morning cake."

Mallory hugged both Clarence and Catherine as everyone walked into the kitchen.

"I came along to help tell the story," Clev said. "Because I don't think that Hector always remembers everything and after we talked this morning, I now wonder if I always have it straight."

"What do you mean?" asked Clarence.

Mallory was sitting and now stood up. "Hector and Clev are both intelligent and powerful men and they made many choices that were not at all influenced by either of you. But, and I am saying this because I think they are embarrassed. As our teams have been working with them we have all discovered that many times along the way they were also victims and they are trying to sort all of that out."

"Victims of Juleta?" asked Catherine with astonishment.

"Mother it might be easier for me to just start at the beginning," Hector said. "You are going to hear a lot of things that you won't like."

495

"I want you to know that I never wanted to hurt either of you and I am very sorry that I have. Mallory thinks I underestimate you because I thought I could keep my life from you. But you have to understand that the choices that I made, whether they were totally under my power or not, were my choices. You are wonderful parents and are not responsible for what I have done. So stop feeling guilty," Hector said and smiled but he was the only one in the room who was smiling.

The first meeting with the citizens of Taperia was scheduled for just before noon. Simon and the others wanted to remove the signs of battle before families came to the area. The meeting was being held in the small park where the Wetprian flag was flying.

As the soldiers and team members were cleaning up the streets they were surprised to see citizens gathering near the park more than an hour before the meeting was to start. Javier walked up to some of the people. "Is there a problem? The meeting isn't for another hour?"

"No problem what so ever young man," one of the women said. She was so happy that she was almost singing the words. "We don't know how we will ever repay you for freeing us but the very least we can do is fix you a feast." The old woman then kissed Javier on the cheek. "You saved us from hell. All of you are our heroes."

"You are answers to our prayers," said another woman. "The Great Ruler forgive me but I had almost lost all hope of ever being saved and I know I wasn't alone."

The words of the women touched Javier. He did not speak because for a moment he felt that he couldn't. He bowed and walked away.

By time the meeting started the streets surrounding the park were filled with tables and chairs. And the tables were filled with food and beverages. Musicians were playing in the streets and the atmosphere was festive.

Some of the citizens built a small platform in the park for the Princes to stand on when they addressed the crowds. Raul and Simon introduced themselves then the leaders of their groups. They explained again, that the Kingdom of Stordt was now part of the Kingdom of Wetpr and would exist under that name.

The Princes explained that a fort would be built in the location where Roch's castle once stood and that other groups were already traveling to Taperia to help the citizens in reestablishing their lives. Simon was telling the people that they should vote for leaders in their group to form a governing body for the city.

As Simon was talking a group of Enrops flew around the Princes. Raul took the notes from the birds and read them then handed them to Javier. "These are from Father," Raul announced. "Two generals are being assigned to Fort Taperia, they are General Cook and General Ortist. These generals are already traveling here with five thousand troops."

"When we built Fort Nora, the citizens quickly learned that having a fort near their city was good for business. We will be purchasing all of the building supplies from you and the supplies necessary to sustain the army. I am telling you this now so you can prepare. When the troops get here they will have lists of items that they will need. We know that in some cases your businesses were ravished so if you need things to get your businesses started again meet with me, Simon or Javier."

"Additionally," continued Raul. "The fort will be an employer. Anyone interested in signing up to be a soldier, to help with the building of the fort or to work at the fort please meet with Maddox and Henrich after the meeting."

"You mean we can be soldiers in your army?" yelled a man.

"You sure can," Simon said. "And we are going to need more soldiers."

"Some of us will leave when the generals arrive," explained Raul. "Our mission is to claim the lands for Wetpr. One of our ruling members named Joshua is already traveling here with a team to help all of you figure out your needs. At the very least, you need a school and a hospital here."

"My wife wants to know if we can have a monastery," yelled another man.

"Most definitely," said Raul. "As you can imagine taking over this entire kingdom is a huge project so we need your help. We will finance the building projects but this is your city. You determine where you want them. We will hire all of you to build these sites."

As Raul spoke an elderly woman slowly worked her way through the crowd until she reached the platform. Ira stepped down to speak with her then helped her up on the platform. "Emily has something she wants to say," Ira announced with a warm smile.

"Some of us found out yesterday that our beloved Queen Vitomas was not murdered by Roch as we imagined but escaped and lives in Salar with her husband Prince Raul and their children. If anyone is interested in sending her a letter or gift we have a basket on the table with the pink cloth."

Raul kissed Emily on the cheek and said, "My wife would appreciate hearing from you. She has always worried about the citizens here."

"Perhaps now would be the time to tell you that Annabelle, daughter of Alexander and Laurel is my wife," said Simon. "Some of you may remember that Alexander and Laurel were the personal attendants to our grandfather and grandmother. They all live in Salar as does Gala the healer from Cana. If any of you want to send letters to them, you are welcome to."

The crowd chattered excitedly then applauded. Raul looked at Javier and said, "The next place you are giving the speech. Are you ready for that?"

"Giving the speech is no problem it's seeing these people. Earlier this morning when I was checking the buildings for gangs, people were coming up to me and shaking my hand and kissing me. Some of them tried to give me gifts. I will say that I didn't expect this. I thought we would be fighting every step of the way."

The emotional drain of confessing to his parents wore on Hector. By noon his fatigue was apparent to everyone in the room. Clev also was not physically ready to spend an entire day out of bed.

Catherine was crying and it had been years since Clarence yelled at his son. Everyone's emotions were raw. "The worse part of all of this is that we know you have only told us the parts that you thought we could handle," Clarence said. "My son, how could you have come from us?"

Clarence's words cut Hector like a knife. When Mallory saw the look on Hector's face she stood up. "Shara was against them coming here because neither of them should be out of bed much less riding. I think it is best for everyone if we go now."

"Surely they can't ride all that way now," Catherine said. "Stay here and I will fix some food."

"Honestly, as emotional as everyone is that may not be the best thing right now," Mallory said. "Our team's house is not far from here; they can rest there. Catherine and Clarence, I will not make excuses for Hector or Clev. I too think that much of what they have done is despicable but they came here to explain all of this to you so you would not carry the guilt that you have. They came here because they care about you. I know that you are upset but I hope you don't close the door on them. I really can't see how that would benefit anyone."

"While I agree with what you say," Clarence said. "I think all of you will understand that we need a little time."

Hector nodded and stood up, he, Mallory and Clev left the house. "Do you think you can ride about a mile?" she asked.

"Yeah," Hector said solemnly. "But I am sure that Mathas would let us rest in the castle."

"We can certainly ask, but I think you would feel more comfortable with the team," Mallory said. "But once I show you our headquarters you can't come back and attack us."

"You didn't even sound like you were joking when you said that," Clev said.

"She wasn't," said Hector.

No one spoke as they rode to the other side of the royal grounds. "I know this place," Hector said as they approached the mansion. "We used to play around here when we were kids."

"Mathas had it remodeled for us," Mallory said. "It is beautiful. I am going to get the two of you inside then take care of the horses."

"We can do that," said Clev.

"The two of you don't look like you could hold each other up," Mallory said as they dismounted and tied their horses to a post. "Just leave the saddlebags," Mallory said to Hector. "I'll bring everything in."

"Is anyone here?" yelled Mallory as they entered the mansion.

"In the dining room," Abbott yelled.

"Hector and Clev need to eat then lie down," Mallory announced to the team members. "They aren't supposed to be out of bed but he wanted to apologize to Catherine and Clarence."

"Grab a seat," Louis said. "There's plenty of food. I'll get some more plates."

"Do we still have some empty rooms or I can put them into mine?" Mallory asked.

"There's room," said Turner. "Are you going to eat?"

"I'm going to take care of the horses first."

"Hector are you going to make it?" asked Garvis. "You look like you could pass out."

"It's been a long day. I think we just need to eat something. Thanks."

"And don't worry, we are never going to attack your place here," Clev said. "I can't believe that Mallory even said that."

Mallory smiled and winked at her team members then walked out of the building.

"After you two rest we can give you the tour," said Turner.

A few minutes later Mallory walked into the room and put a bottle in front of Hector and another in front of Clev. "That is Shara's tonic. You need to drink that. I'll be back."

As soon as Mallory left the room Bart walked to a cupboard, poured two glasses of whiskey and gave them to Clev and Hector. "That's to wash that crap down. I can't even stand the smell; I don't know how you can drink it."

Both Hector and Clev laughed. "It tastes like shit," Hector said. "But it does make you feel better."

"She's back, hide the glasses," Bart said kiddingly.

"I heard that," Mallory said and laughed as she walked up the stairs with the saddlebags.

When Mallory returned to the table she said to Hector and Clev, "The horses are taken care of; they are in the pasture in back and your things are upstairs."

"Thanks," said Hector and kissed her on the cheek.

"I am sorry about this morning," Mallory said. "I knew it would be rough but I didn't think it would be that bad."

"I didn't either but you were right; it needed to be done," Hector said to her then looked at the others at the table who were looking at him. "I know a lot of you have spent time with my parents. I really thought that I could keep my life from them. Mallory told me they knew more than I thought they did and they thought that everything I did was their fault. That's why we came this morning."

"I'm glad to hear you say that," said Quinn. "I mean that Mallory told you. Your parents talked to all of us like they thought we were your best friends."

501

"I for one didn't have the heart to tell them that I barely knew you because then I would have to explain why I was there. And Mallory was right. They are really nice people."

"Yeah and I am sure that I broke their hearts today," Hector said.

"It's not my business but I am still learning about how everyone is connected here," said Spencer. "Did Clev talk to them too?"

"Clev and I have been friends for years and he has spent a lot of time with my family," Hector said.

"That and he doesn't remember everything so I was filling in the blanks," Clev said. "They aren't even my parents and I feel like shit."

"But when things settle down a little they will appreciate that you told them the truth," said Turner.

"Of course I couldn't tell them everything and Father realized that," said Hector.

No one spoke for a few moments then Mallory said to Turner, "Hector said that he used to play around here when he was a kid. If he's up to it maybe we should ask him."

"Ask me what?"

"Don't get pissed," Mallory said. "But remember you were our enemy for a long time so the group was deciding if we should bring you out here. I'll let Turner tell you the rest because he knows more about it than I do."

"First of all," Hector said angrily. "We were enemies and who knows maybe we will have differences again but things will never be like they were. I owe all of you so much as does Clev. You've saved every member of my family, I'm not going to attack you or yours. If you don't believe me that's your problem but we need to get that on the table."

"No kidding," said Clev. "I can't believe you think we would do that after all that we have been through. Hell, that is why Showers quit. He likes all of you so damn much he would never go against you."

"Well, that is good to hear," said Turner. "But you are both shrewd men so I know you can understand our concerns. We will speak of this no more but we do have some questions if you are up to it."

"Ask them," said Hector.

"Dominic's team is busy right now but they were the ones who were here when...well, let me start at the beginning. When Mathas and the others first started to suspect that Isabella was a traitor they interrogated her. She was so difficult that they used the truth potion and during one session she said the reason she made her family move out of this castle was because she saw Juleta hide a body on this land."

"They figured that Juleta was about fifteen at the time which of course devastated Mathas. Isabella took them to that pond near here and they found the body of a little girl that was wrapped in a rug and stuck between some rocks. The description fit with what Isabella had said. The little girl had been stabbed so everyone figured she was a sacrifice."

"How do you know that she was stabbed?" asked Hector.

"The marks on her bones," Turner said. "There is a lot of land around here and we wondered if you knew of any hiding places she may have had."

"Let me think about that," Hector said. "When we were kids, I used to play with Matthew, Stephan and Timothy. We hated Juleta and wouldn't let her into our group. Then after Matthew said that she had crushes on me and Stephan we really didn't want her around. I didn't really talk to her until years later when I met her at Otto's orgies. By that time I had my own crew and she approached me because she wanted to hire us."

Hector looked at Mallory and asked, "You aren't going to get mad if I talk about this are you?"

"I certainly don't want to hear the details," she said and smiled.

"We do but you can tell us later," Bart said and everyone laughed.

"Juleta was always a loner. I don't think she had any friends as a kid. If she did, well I didn't know about them and like I said we didn't want her around us so I may not be much help. But later we can walk around here and I can show you some of the places where we used to play and explore, if you think it will help."

"It couldn't hurt," said Turner. "Both of you are starting to look better but you probably need some rest first."

"This is my room," Mallory said and opened the door. "Hector your things are on the desk. Clev, I put you next door."

"Thanks," Clev said and walked into his room.

Hector sat on the side of the bed and took off his boots, "Are you going to take a nap with me? You didn't get any sleep last night either."

"I was thinking about it. "I really am sorry about this morning."

"You don't have anything to be sorry about," Hector said and took her hand. She sat down next to him. "I like it that you care enough about all of us to want us to work things out. And you were right, I don't know why I thought they would never find out."

"This morning was awful but I would think it is easier not to have to keep all of those lies, I would never be able to keep them straight."

"Well, you are going to have to work on that if you are going to work in disguise and I am serious. When you enter my world you have to know what you are doing or you won't last long."

Chapter XXXL
Perceptions

The Sanuri and Erebus entered the royal grounds of Mathas' castle without fanfare because they did not send prior word of their arrival time. "Rosa will be mad," the Sanuri said to Erebus. "But they always go to such extremes to welcome me that sometimes...I mean it is very thoughtful but it can be tiring."

"Your secret is safe with me," Erebus said and chuckled. "And I know exactly how you feel."

By time the Sanuri stopped the boca in front of the main entrance of the castle Mathas and Rosa were running down the front steps to greet them. A soldier had gone into the castle and announced the arrival of the two men.

"Why didn't you let us know you were coming?" asked Rosa. "I would have prepared a feast."

Both the Sanuri and Erebus laughed as they climbed down from the boca. "That is exactly why I didn't let you know. You always go to such trouble," the Sanuri said.

"It's never any trouble," said Rosa and hugged both of the men. Mathas shook hands with his friends.

"Besides gifts, I have a crate full of study items for Margarit," the Sanuri said. "Is she here?"

"Yes and she will be so excited," said Rosa.

"We have much to catch up on," Mathas said and called to two soldiers to help carry items from the boca.

"We didn't get any sleep," Hector said as he lay on top of Mallory. "But I sure feel better. Making love with you is like a tonic."

She laughed loudly, "You tell that to Shara when she gets mad because you aren't getting your rest."

"I want to see Sarah while we are here," Hector said as he got out of bed.

"I thought as much. Did you want to walk around the grounds too? Because if so, some of the others want to come with us."

"I understand but we can do that later. We could just spend the night here too."

"Should we ask Clev if he wants to come along?"

Hector and Mallory dressed and walked out of her room. He knocked on the door to Clev's room and called, "We're going to the castle if you want to come."

"Yeah, just wait a minute," Clev shouted. A few minutes later he opened the door. "Boy, you two are noisy," he said with feigned agitation. Mallory blushed deeply while Hector and Clev laughed.

"My Lady, you have more visitors," one of the housekeepers said to Rosa who was in the family parlor.

"Please show them in," Rosa said.

A few moments later Hector, Clev and Mallory walked into the room. Hector was going to speak but stopped when he saw his parents sitting with Mathas, Rosa, Erebus and the Sanuri.

"I am sorry to bother you," Hector said. "I was wondering if I could visit with Sarah for a few moments."

"It is not a bother," Rosa said. "Please come in. Mathas make introductions while I get Sarah."

"It is good to see your old face back," the Sanuri said with a grin and shook hands with Hector. "I hear we have a truce now."

"Yes but apparently no one believes it," Clev said and glanced at Mallory.

"Clev, I didn't say that to make you mad," Mallory said.

Clev didn't respond to Mallory but focused on Erebus when he was introduced. "We need to talk to you," Clev said.

"Certainly, about what?" asked Erebus.

"Claudius read us your letter. You said that Hector was addicted, can you tell if I am?"

"Clev, what are you talking about?" asked Catherine.

"An Angel told Erebus that Hector was addicted to power and that he should explain addictions to us," Clev said.

"Hector, you didn't tell us that," said Catherine with concern.

"Would it really have made any difference?" Hector asked. "Besides I don't understand it."

"Honey, we were there when Claudius read that letter," Clarence said to his wife.

Catherine gave him a blank look. "I've been so upset about things that I guess I am not thinking straight," Catherine said.

"This may not be my business," said the Sanuri. "But there is certainly a great deal of tension in this room. Is there any way that I can help?"

"Catherine and Clarence have been filled with guilt because of Hectors' life choices," explained Mallory. "So this morning he and Clev came here against Shara's wishes and told his parents about their lives. They hoped that Catherine and Clarence would understand that they were not responsible but it got ugly and every one of them was hurt during that conversation."

Rosa was standing in the doorway with Sarah. "Mathas and I are still filled with guilt over Juleta but we would have loved for her to have talked to us just once."

"Daddy," Sarah squealed and held out her arms to Hector who took her and kissed her. Both the Sanuri and Erebus watched the interaction.

"We would like to hear what you have to say too," Clarence said to Erebus.

"I think it is better if Clev and I talk to him first," said Hector.

507

"We can meet in any form you want," Erebus said. "Honestly, I am surprised you are eager to talk about this."

"We've been through a lot lately," said Clev. "And we aren't making excuses but we don't understand some of it and we don't remember other parts. Mallory keeps asking us if we are the same as we were before Juleta and hell...sorry. I mean we aren't even sure."

"We certainly were anything but innocent but we weren't monsters and that is what we became. Do you think you can help us figure some of this out?"

"Hector, does Clev speak for you too?" asked the Sanuri.

Hector nodded but did not speak. "Hector!" Mallory said in a scolding tone.

"I don't want to talk about any of this in front of my parents. Right now I just want to spend a little time with my baby." Hector was holding Sarah and walked out of the room.

"What the hell is wrong with him?" Clev asked. "Sorry ladies I have to stop saying that around you."

"Don't you know?" asked Mallory.

"No, do you?" Clev asked.

"I'll tell you later."

"Actually, I would like to know too," said Clarence.

Mallory glanced at the open door. Rosa was standing and now looked out into the hallway then closed the pocket doors to the parlor. "He's gone," she said.

"Clev, I don't know how to explain this without you possibly getting mad," said Mallory.

"Just say it," Clev said.

Mallory turned to Hector's parents. "Hector and Clev are both strong and powerful men and from what I have seen they seem pretty fearless."

"They are not used to being victims but they were and all the things they have been through lately have scared them more than they want to admit."

"I'll admit it," Clev said. "This is more than I bargained for when I signed up for this crew."

Mallory didn't say anything to Clev but looked back at Catherine and Clarence. "It tore Hector apart to have to admit all those things to you but he would rather take responsibility for, I think things he didn't even do than to admit he wasn't in control. If he does have an addiction I don't believe he will admit it."

"Actually that is pretty typical," said Erebus. "I was a very powerful sorcerer. I never sold my soul; I did it all on my own. But I am addicted to magic and the power it brings. I am trying to live a life without it and I am and I might say very happy but I wouldn't be able to do this without my friends."

"I have so much more to explain but Clev if either of you have an addiction you will not be able to conquer it and return to your old life and both of you must realize that."

"I've already been thinking about that," Clev said. "One of our lieutenants named Showers just up and quit. No one has ever quit Hector. Showers did it because he likes everyone here so much he refused to fight against them. He asked Sorren to become a member of his tribe. Now he has a girl that he wants to marry and he is so happy, he's not the same guy anymore."

"Now what I am telling you doesn't go farther than this room but I have been thinking about the same thing. But I have been with Hector so long that I don't want to leave him. Honestly he needs me. And Mallory is right about what she said."

"Mallory, I am saying this as a father," Clarence said. "Now that we know more about our son's life I don't know if it is a good thing for you that you are dating him. But it is a great thing for him. You are very good for him. He respects you and your opinion. Now saying that, know that Catherine and I will always be here for you."

"Thank you, that is very sweet and believe me; I have had the same thoughts," said Mallory.

"I don't know if I understand the effects an addiction has," said Catherine. "Are you saying that Hector wouldn't have done any of those things if he wasn't addicted?"

"No," said Erebus. "Actually, Clev said it very well. He said they did bad things but they weren't monsters before. The addiction would bring out the monster. But this situation with Clev and Hector is a lot more complicated than that, which is why I need to speak with them. They have been attacked by extremely powerful magics and survived things most people would not have. I want to figure out the effects of those magics."

"They wouldn't have survived without the Angels," Mallory said. "And they both realize that. I am going to look for him."

"They are probably in back in the play yard," said Rosa. "She likes to be pushed on the swing."

Mallory found Hector in the back of the castle. He was pushing Sarah in a swing and she was laughing loudly.

"You know your parents don't hate you," she said. "It will just take them a while to understand all of this."

"I really don't think they will be able to. I mean they might accept it but they won't understand it."

"Do you always understand it?"

Hector didn't answer the question.

"Do you ever think about having Sarah live with you?"

"She is much better off with Rosa and Mathas."

"And what if I get pregnant. I'm not going to abandon the baby and you will have hell to pay if you do."

Hector stopped pushing the swing and looked at Mallory with a huge grin on his face. He took Sarah off the swing and set her in the sandbox which was filled with toys. Then he returned to Mallory.

"So just where did that come from?" he asked as he was still grinning.

"I am just being responsible. You act like everything is a game, even being a father."

"If you believe that then we need to talk more. In fact, we haven't talked about that subject at all. Now I have a question for you. I know your concerns about our relationship and I know you are taking it a day at a time which is smart from your point of view. But that comment sounds like you are thinking about us long term. Is that true?"

"Yes and maybe I am over thinking it because everything is so complicated. Does that scare you?"

"Not at all. It pleases me. Every day I expect you to tell me we are over because you can't deal with all of this."

"Every day I probably do think about it. I hope you know that I wouldn't be sleeping with you if I didn't really care about you. I'm not like most of the girls you date."

"Oh believe me, I know that," he said and pulled her close to him. "So since we're talking about it. How do you feel about me having Sarah?"

"I'm not sure I understand what you are asking."

"Just the entire situation."

"Well to start with, I can't believe you made love to Juleta but that is water under the bridge. And it is just a blessing that Sarah wasn't affected by everything. But she is a precious little girl and you are her father. I am glad you want to spend time with her but personally I think you should be more involved with her life. Before you know it she will be grown up. Hector, you really need to think about these things."

"I was afraid that you resented her because of Juleta."

"How in the world did you come up with that?"

"Because we never talk about her."

"Hector, it's like your life is in a crisis. There is a lot that we haven't talked about. I will be honest, when we saw those demons coming out of you, I wasn't sure if it was safe for her to be with you."

"I was wondering the same thing. Just because we haven't talked about things doesn't mean that I am not thinking about them."

"Well then, maybe we should start talking."

"I agree. Now is as good a time as any."

An hour later Hector and Mallory returned to the King's parlor. They were holding hands and he was holding Sarah.

"You look like you are in a better mood," the Sanuri said to Hector.

"I'm with my two girls," he said as he looked at the faces in the room. "None of you look happy. What is going on?"

"Erebus used to be a sorcerer and he has been explaining magics to us, the kind that were used against you and Clev," Clarence said. "Actually it is horrifying."

"I can understand why you look upset but Mathas why do you?" Hector asked.

"It is very difficult for me to understand the monster that Juleta was. Hector, one minute I was holding her like you are Sarah and the next...well, all this. It is like someone stole our little girl and substituted her with a monster."

"Hector, I am going to tell you the same that I told them," said Erebus. "I am a very direct person and some people find that insulting so just bear with me."

"You do understand that the Angels sent us here? I know you are a dark lord but Clev has been telling us that you rarely use magics is that true?"

"Yep, I still do things the old fashion way. I do research like the teams do and I don't sacrifice anything. In fact, neither Clev or I do those stinking altar things. If I need to speak with someone I pay for an audience."

"You did that one spell," Mallory said to Hector then looked at the others. "All of those papers that were found in Javier's home were disguised and Hector did a spell and the real pages appeared and the wallet turned into a list with the codes."

"That's basically the one I do," said Hector. "That and a few little ones. Magic just never has had much of an appeal for me. But I have heard about you too. Your power was notorious and you may be the only person I have heard of that became that strong on your own. I heard about what you did in Ryed. I'll tell you, I didn't even think anything like that was possible. If you haven't told my parents that story you should."

"I'm not sure they are ready for that yet," said Erebus. "But I want to spend some time with you later and I want to read those manuscripts that Clev said you bought. Hector, I suspect that magics as old as time were used on you and I don't think anyone these days really understand the effects or powers of them."

"I am addicted to magics so I can't, I mean I won't do any reversal spells if they need to be done but we can call to the Angels."

"You think they are still a threat to him don't you?" asked Mallory.

"Yes," said Erebus. "While I don't use magic anymore I still have some, I guess you can say gifts. For example, I can feel and see the energies around people."

"You mean auras?" asked Hector.

"That is what some people call them. Everything is made up of energy and when I look at a person I usually see what looks like an extension of them. It is like a silhouette of energy around their bodies. Of course it can change colors, for example if someone is enraged but for the most part it is calm and steady."

"For example, the Sanuri's is a bright white light. Sometimes it is difficult to look at him. A demons' is thick, black and I usually see images. Sorren for example; when I first met him, his aura told me he was a courageous and passionate man and I think we all agree those are his strong characteristics."

"You are going to tell us that Clev and I don't have normal auras, aren't you?" asked Hector.

"Yes and we can talk about this in private if you want."

"No, there have been enough secrets, just say it."

"While both of you appear calm your auras are in utter chaos and I honestly don't understand what I am seeing. As you know, we have received many letters from the people here who have explained about their encounters with both of you and what you have gone through. Yet, I was not prepared to see how normal both of you seem. I would never believe who you are if I had not been introduced so I understand why our people are so confused."

"A few moments ago Mathas said it was like Juleta was two different people. That is kind of what I am seeing with the two of you but..."

"There aren't more demons in us are there?" asked Clev and everyone could hear the fear in his voice.

"No but something isn't right. I came here to help but of course the choice is yours as to whether you will allow me." Erebus now turned to the Sanuri. "Can you see what I am seeing?"

"No but in a way I can hear it."

"Tell us what you are seeing," said Catherine as tears filled her eyes.

"Their auras are alive with images. It is like watching dozens of plays at the same time. But I don't know if these are things of their past, their future or unrelated."

"How could they be unrelated?" asked Clarence.

"Because old magics are alive, like a living person and what Erebus is seeing could be something that was attached to them," said Hector. "I too have never heard of what you describe. But I will tell you other than feeling weak and exhausted I feel fine. Erebus do you see anything that would make me a threat to Sarah?"

"Not directly and I will tell you if I do but I am being honest, I don't understand what I am seeing."

"Did you know that Dominic assigned Mallory and Brock to babysit me because they are demon hunters?"

"Yes and we read about them being able to see the demons inside of you," Erebus said to Hector then turned to Mallory. "Have you seen anything strange lately?"

"No and I am a little concerned that my feelings for him might be clouding my perceptions."

"Are you staying here?" asked Erebus. "Perhaps we could talk later."

"We are staying at the team's house," said Hector. "We were originally just going to take a short rest but they asked me to walk the property with them and since it is getting late we will spend the night."

"Why do they want you to do that?" Mathas asked.

"Because I used to play here when I was a kid and they are wondering if I can remember any places that Juleta might have used to hide things. Turner said they asked Matthew and Stephan but they thought she might have been more inclined to tell me things. I told them that we all hated her and hid from her when we were kids but who knows, maybe I will remember something."

"Know you are welcome to stay here also," said Mathas. "And you certainly can join us for dinner."

"If we do we may have to stay," said Mallory. "They are both exhausted although they won't admit it."

"That is fine," said Rosa. "I will have rooms prepared. How many?"

Hector smiled at Mallory as she blushed, "Two," he said. "Mallory is my girl now. We aren't seeing other people."

"Well, that makes your father and me very happy," said Catherine and walked up to Hector and Mallory and hugged them both.

Javier worked tirelessly in Taperia. Raul and Simon thought that he was trying to prove himself but that was not the case. Javier was a confident man who understood himself well. He worked night and day because he was proud to be part of Sudfad's family and proud of the work he was doing.

In many ways the people of Taperia reminded him of the people of his homeland. Javier wondered if all oppressed people were the same. This thought made him wonder if the oppressors perhaps had some type of guidelines on how to demoralize huge groups of people. It always amazed him how a handful of people could control a large populace.

Javier was a thoughtful man who was intrigued by people. As he questioned the ideas of power, he also saw a birth of sorts in the eyes and hearts of the Taperians. In the few days his group was in the city, the people of Taperia seemed to come alive as if their spirits had been returned to them.

Major Hampton was leading the troops from Fort Stanus into Stordt. They initially followed the River Cheban so that they could bypass the Caves of Muldun. Hampton knew that if there were any terrorists near the caves that they would not long be alive since that was the territory of the Giant Gants.

The first community they entered was the large Village of Fargo. Hampton's army greatly outnumbered the inhabitants of this village. He led his troops into Fargo and raised the flag of Wetpr. The villagers gathered around him as he explained that they were now free citizens of Wetpr. No sooner had he uttered these words than one of the soldiers fell from his horse with an arrow in his chest.

Villagers scattered as arrows rained upon the soldiers. Fortunately for Hampton only a portion of his army was in the center of the village. Those on the outskirts surrounded the village and advanced. The arrows were being launched from the rooftops of buildings. Hampton did not have any Ruala warriors with his troops.

The soldiers who were in the center of the village charged into buildings, running up the staircases and in some buildings the soldiers were fighting their way to the roofs. The soldiers who had surrounded the village were climbing up outside stairs and ladders to reach the attackers.

When the battle was over, Major Hampton had lost thirty-two men. All of the hired killers employed by the notorious Monroe family were dead or in custody. Once Hampton learned who had ordered the attack he had the hired killers hanged and he led his men to the Monroe compound.

The Village of Fargo was east of the River Cheban which separated the kingdoms of Stordt and Ryed. The Monroe compound was west of the village and built on the shore of the river.

Hampton and his men did not have difficulty finding the compound since a road led from the village to the front gate of the wall that surrounded the complex. From the roadway, the compound looked like a small version of a fort. Hampton ordered his men to surround the wall, which they could only do on three sides. There was not a wall on the back of the compound which was on the shore of the river.

As the soldiers were taking positions some of them saw huge barges on the river. The barges were filled with men and horses who were traveling west towards Ryed.

Hampton was alerted and when he saw the barges he led his men inside of the compound using the shore entrance. The compound was deserted. As the soldiers searched the buildings it was apparent that the people had left quickly. There was still food cooking on the hearth in the kitchen of the home. Chairs were overturned and doors were left open.

"I know there is more to all of this," Hampton growled. "Tear this place apart and search everything!" Hampton was furious that the Monroe Clan had escaped.

Chapter XLI
Voices

Hector, Mallory and Clev ate dinner with Mathas' family and guests but both men were so exhausted that they went to bed immediately after the meal so they didn't speak with Erebus. After Mallory gave the men their tonics she returned to the dining room where the others were talking and drinking wine.

"Erebus, they aren't avoiding you," Mallory explained. "They aren't supposed to be out of bed. They only came here to speak with Clarence and Catherine and Shara had a fit that they were going to travel."

"We can all see they are weak," Erebus said. "I didn't think they were avoiding me. You have become quite the caretaker of them. In a way that surprises me."

"Me too," Mallory said and laughed. "Hector wasn't taking care of himself or following the healers' directions. Dominic knew the Angels wanted to keep him alive and was getting so frustrated that he reassigned me and Brock to take care of him. Dominic is sending double pay to our families for us doing this."

"At first it was easy because we clearly saw him as our enemy and we were following orders but as...well...all of us got to know them, and I am talking about Showers and some of the others too...well everything got murky."

"What do you mean?" asked Catherine.

"The village was attacked a couple of times because of Hector and we all fought together and basically live together and started to like and depend on each other. Showers just changed his life around and joined our side. He's...oh Sanuri I forgot to tell you. Showers and Ruby want to meet with you when you have time. They would like you to marry them."

"I guess he did turn his life around," the Sanuri said and smiled.

"Showers is a tough man with a bad reputation," Mallory said. "But I think part of that was because he lost his wife and baby to the Hutas and he was just filled with hate. He refers to us as his family now and you should see him. Ruby is a young widow with a one year old and a three year old. Showers rocks those kids to sleep every night. I don't know if I have ever seen a happier man."

"Well, I am getting off the subject but the more all of us got to know each other our perceptions got blurred because they like us too. It's been very confusing for all of us especially when the Angels healed them and we saw the demons. I'm a demon hunter and I am in love with a man who calls to demons. Sorry, Catherine and Clarence, I don't know if you knew that."

"Actually, I think all of this is rather amazing," said the Sanuri. "And Mallory instead of feeling guilty, you should realize you are the perfect woman for him." The Sanuri now turned to Hector's parents. "I don't know how much you know about all of this but basically Hector was so lost in the darkness that he was close to losing his humanity. The Angels wanted our teams to help him and remind him that humanity was worth fighting for."

"From the letters it sounds like everyone was just themselves but the interactions were...I am not sure of a good word so I will say amazing."

"Oh, we all fought a lot and told each other off," said Mallory. "In fact the children ganged up on Hector when he was really sick and they made him feel so guilty that..." Mallory glanced at Hector's parents. "He is like a king in his world. He doesn't always get his hands dirty so he justifies his actions by saying that he just bankrolled things. All of us have gotten on him a lot and he has to take it because we are taking care of him."

"Let me stop you there," said the Sanuri. "He is like a king and he has an army in the village as well as in this city and many others. He could have left Tyger anytime he wanted. Obviously that would not have been wise but he certainly could afford to pay other healers. No, he's been staying with all of you for probably many reasons that he doesn't even understand."

"Mathas, you have been so quiet all day. That is not like you. What is on your mind?"

"Lots of things and some of it is confusion and some guilt. Just listening to Clarence and Catherine as they are faced with the monster in their child is bringing back so many memories. I see so much of us in them. Then today when Hector walked in with Sarah and Mallory, for just a moment he reminded me of me."

"Clarence, Catherine, you have to know that he is a notorious criminal and I am sure that he did not tell you about all of his crimes; yet I have tried to blame him for many things which our child is responsible for. Mallory, you and the teams aren't the only ones feeling confused."

It was getting dark and Hampton planned to have his troops make camp at the compound. While many of the villagers looked poor and thin, Monroe's compound was filled with riches. Hampton planned to take all of the livestock, food and some of the moveable property to the village the following day.

He also wanted to spend some time with the villagers and find out more about the Monroe Clan and how they knew the soldiers were coming to the village.

It was almost midnight when one of the soldiers literally stumbled onto something. Private Shuester was taking his turn at guard duty and walking around the compound. Shuester was a young man who had grown up on a farm. While he did not miss the work, he very much missed his menagerie of pets. As he was walking past a hay pile near one of the barns, Shuester thought he heard a puppy whimpering; he followed the sound.

Because they were in a hostile environment, Hampton had huge bond fires lit in the compound and he had lit torches attached to many things. As Shuester walked he heard the sound getting louder but couldn't find the animal. He walked to the barn and grabbed one of the torches that was attached to the outside wall.

He returned to the hay pile and tripped over the handle of a pitch fork. Shuester fell forward and the torch started the hay on fire. He quickly grabbed the torch and threw it onto the dirt. Then he picked up the pitch fork and removed the burning hay, which he also threw on the dirt and stomped it out. As Shuester was checking the hay pile for smoke he heard the whimpering again and it was growing louder. He quickly started to remove the hay. He wasn't sure why but he felt a sense of urgency.

Shuester never understood why he said it. In fact, he almost didn't recognize his own voice. He was not a person who believed in The Great Ruler or any other deity. But as he was shoveling the hay he heard himself say, "God, help me save them." And in that instant he heard voices.

Shuester started to yell for help as he shoveled the hay rapidly. "What are you doing?" yelled Private Thompson as he ran to Shuester.

"Listen, don't you hear the voices?" Shuester asked.

"Holy shit!" yelled Thompson. "Help! We need help by the barn!" He started to grab the hay with his hands and throw piles of it behind him. Soon several more men joined them. Then Sergeant Carson ran up to them.

"Sarge, we hear people," Shuester yelled as he continued to shovel hay.

"What!" yelled the Sergeant.

"I found something," yelled Corporal Jackson. The hay mound was huge and now the men all ran to where Jackson was pulling at a rope. The men tore away the hay in that area and found a huge wooded door that the rope was attached to.

"Get that torch!" yelled Carson as the men pulled open the heavy door.

"Help us! Help us!" were the frantic screams coming from the darkness.

Thompson ran to the group with a lit torch. The light exposed the faces of dozens of terrified people. "We'll get you out," yelled Carson. "Is there a ladder?"

"No," yelled a man.

"We'll find something. We aren't leaving you," Carson yelled as Shuester ran into the barn to look for a ladder. "Someone get the Major!"

"Where have you been?" Hector asked as Mallory walked into the bedroom.

"Did I wake you? I am sorry. I was taking with your parents. Clev got back up and he's down there talking to Erebus now. How are you feeling? You really over did it today."

Hector sat up in bed and watched Mallory undress. "I was going to say I am too exhausted to make love but that may be changing by the minute," he said with a grin. She laughed and crawled under the covers next to him.

Mallory kissed Hector then said, "Your parents are doing much better. They aren't as mad anymore."

"I don't think they were ever really mad. They were hurt and disappointed and that was worse. But they really like you. I like it that you take the time to talk with them."

"I really like them; they are sweet people."

"You know when I was listening to you tell my folks about your village I thought that I should do something for your family."

"Why?"

"You have been working hard to get my family to heal. I have men in Ryed. Do you think they would get killed if they rode into your village to give your family some money?"

Mallory sat up straighter and stared at him. "Well, first that would be a little awkward. You know even they have heard of you."

"So, you haven't told them about us?"

"Hector! Telling my family that I am in love with a notorious criminal isn't something you do in a letter."

"In love. Are you in love with me?" Hector was smiling as Mallory stared at him. "Boy, it's like pulling teeth trying to get you to talk about your feelings."

"That is because everything is so complicated."

"Well then, I guess you are just going to have to take me home to meet the family. But you might want to write at least a little about us so it isn't such a shock."

"Are you serious?"

"Why wouldn't I be?"

"Hector do you even know what you are going to be doing in the next few months? Going back to running your gang or staying here?"

"First of all, I am running my organization from here. I send and receive messages. And secondly, no I don't know what I am going to be doing. Listen, I am falling in love with you and you feel the same so unless you kill me we are probably going to be together for a long time." The shocked look on Mallory's face made him laugh loudly.

"So you are still running your organization?"

"Of course I am. I couldn't take this much time away. But I don't need to be in any one place to do that unless something comes up. Mallory the look on your face. What did you think?"

"I don't know. Really I don't. But for some reason it surprises me and I guess it shouldn't." She paused then looked angry. "You aren't stealing anymore children are you?"

"No and I never will again. I have most of my men tracking down information. When Jack Franks got to Port Friada he vanished."

"Are you sure that he got there?"

"Yes, some of my men saw him. Then I have men gathering information on the Sisterhood and others tracking down more manuscripts."

"So none of them are committing crimes?"

"Now, I didn't say that."

"Hector, I don't know what to think."

"Honey, you know what I do. Perhaps that will change some day but it hasn't yet. And honestly I don't know why you would think it did."

Mallory was upset but she didn't understand why. She wanted to change the subject. "So have your men in Cadia found anything?"

"No and they are working hard with your teams there. There have been two more attacks on them and they caught spies both from the Sisterhood and Franks organization; which makes them believe they are close to finding something."

"Why didn't you tell us this before?"

"Clev handed me the note this morning before we left and with the way the day went, I forgot about it. I wasn't keeping information from you. You are looking at me like you don't trust me again."

"I want to. You can't believe how much I want to."

By time Major Hampton got to the barn at the compound, his soldiers had helped fourteen people out of the underground prison and they were still rescuing others. Many soldiers were awake now and bringing blankets and water to the people.

"Major, some of the guys are making food," announced a soldier as Hampton joined them.

"What is going on here?" asked Hampton.

"We are from Fargo," said a man. "Monroe took us and forced us to work for him. Then this morning he had us put in there. We thought we were gonna die. How did you find us anyways?"

"That's a good question," said Hampton then he asked loudly, "How did you find these people?"

"It was Shuester, Sir," said a private who was helping a woman out of the prison.

"Shuester!" yelled Hampton.

The young private ran up to his commanding officer. "Yes Sir."

"How did you find these people?"

"I was patrolling and I heard a pup whimpering. I was looking for it, then I really can't explain it but I just knew something was wrong. You see I tripped and dropped a torch on the hay and when I was putting the fire out I started to hear their voices. I never did find the pup so it must have been them that I heard."

"It wasn't us," said the astonished man. "We didn't know you were here. We had resigned ourselves to the idea that we would die down there."

Mallory was sitting in bed thinking. She hadn't spoken for several minutes.

"So are you mad at me now?" asked Hector.

"I think that I am always mad at you on some level," she said sarcastically. "But something is bothering me. Something that you said and I am not even sure why. Hector, how do you get these messages since I have never seen a raven around you?"

"I'm not that kind of dark lord," he said and chuckled. "The dark lords who use ravens control them with magic." He paused then added, "Well, actually I have used them on occasion but rarely."

"I have men in the city and several designated places where messages can be dropped off for me. When I send one out, I have my men deliver it. Why?"

"I don't know, just bear with me a moment. So I suppose all of your men stand out in a crowd?"

"Not really but they spend a lot of time in the taverns."

"How did the Sisterhood track you down?"

"I don't know but they too are good at what they do."

"When you first came here, when the Angels fought those demons, did any escape?"

"I was so damn sick that I wouldn't know. Mallory, I have men in many cities so just the sight of them doesn't mean that I am in the area. And remember we went into the city a couple of times."

"I know," she paused. "Can I see that note?"

"It's in my shirt pocket," he said and started to get out of bed.

"No, you stay, I'll get it," Mallory said and jumped out of the bed and picked up Hector's shirt that was lying on the floor. She found an envelope in the left front pocket. She took the envelope out of the pocket but did not take the letter out of the envelope.

"Angels, is there something wrong or dangerous about this message? If there is can you let us know?" Mallory asked then quickly jumped and dropped the letter that had burst into flames. As she stomped out the flames they heard voices coming from the fire. "Hector is that supposed to happen?"

"No. Call to the Angels again."

"Wait until I put some clothes on and you get dressed too."

"Do you think they care that we are naked?"

"I'm never going to find out; now get dressed!"

They both dressed quickly then Mallory asked, "Angels, will someone tell us why that happened?"

Miranda was smiling when she appeared in the room. "That message was not from your men in Cadia it was a trap to draw you to Cadia."

"Why and why are you always helping me?" asked Hector.

Miranda did not answer his question. "Hector, the team members have told you several times that we rarely appear to people and when we do it is important. While you question why we help you, you dismiss the question as soon as it enters your mind. Why is that?"

Hector didn't answer right away. "Fear, I suppose."

"I am surprised that you admit that," said Miranda. "You are a thoughtful man. You would be wise to ponder all of this."

"Do you need me...?" Hector started to ask.

"We don't need you," Miranda interrupted.

"Ok, do you want me to find Juleta's arsenal?" Miranda didn't answer.

"Hector, they can't tell you things that will affect your choices so keep asking questions," said Mallory.

"Do you need me to do something to find the arsenal?"

"Now that is a much better question. But I have one for you. You know how cunning Juleta was. Do you think she would hide everything in one place?"

"No and there will be traps. And probably false sightings."

"Risha..." Mallory started to say.

Miranda held up her hand for Mallory to stop talking. "Let Hector answer the questions."

"Risha told the teams that there was a lot of danger in Cadia but they can't find anything," Hector paused as he was thinking out loud. "Wait, one of you told us that the Sisterhood thinks I heard things."

"You did hear things when you were drugged."

"The Sanuri can help you remember," Mallory said. "Let him look into your mind."

"I'm not sure he is ready for that," Hector was trying to sound like he was joking but there was fear in his voice.

"Do you really think he will see anything new?" asked Miranda.

"I don't know."

"Wait," said Mallory. "If Hector is addicted to power is he trying to hide that information for himself or how can we trust him around those things?"

"And that is what Hector is afraid to think about," Miranda said then stared into Hector's eyes. "For all of your courage, you are afraid of your own fears. You need to look in a mirror because soon everyone you love will need you to make a decision. Including that baby that is growing inside of Mallory."

"What!" yelled Mallory. "We can't; not yet."

"Why do you think you have been thinking so much about a baby? You sense the one within you. Hector, as always the choice is yours but you need to stop thinking about how to keep things from everyone and start thinking about how to protect them. All those who have been caring for you will soon need you. Tell me, which face will they see?" Miranda disappeared.

"Hector, I don't know what you are going to decide but I am going downstairs and tell the Sanuri about this."

"Just give me a moment."

Mallory started towards the door then stopped. "Oh my god! I am pregnant. Hector what are we going to do?"

"We'll get married."

"I don't know if I am ready for that."

"Honey, you are in shock. Wait, I will go down with you but I don't want my parents in there if he looks in my head."

"Are you two alright?" asked Rosa as Mallory and Hector walked into the parlor where everyone was sitting and talking.

"No," said Mallory. "We just talked to Miranda."

"Who is Miranda?" asked Clarence.

"An Angel," Mathas said to Clarence then spoke to Hector and Mallory. "You both look like you've seen a ghost. What did she say?"

Mallory looked at Hector who put his arm around her. "Well, the good news is that we are having a baby. And the bad news is that I have information in my head that the Sanuri needs to find. Information about Juleta's arsenal. But...she said I was afraid to face my own fears and that I would need to make some decisions soon because I need to protect everyone who has been protecting me."

"You both look so scared," said Catherine. "Is it about the baby or whatever else you are talking about? Because I am really happy about the baby."

"I think we are both in shock and both scared about everything," Mallory said. "Obviously Hector is afraid for the Sanuri to look in his mind. But those items in the arsenal are things of great power and if he is addicted to power..."

Hector was looking at the faces in the room as Mallory was speaking. "Mallory, you stay here with my parents. Sanuri, Clev and Erebus can we go into another room?"

"Use my study," said Mathas.

"I want to go with you," Mallory said.

"No, stay here," Hector said then looked at Catherine. "Mother talk her into marrying me." He said with a smile. The four men left the parlor and walked into the King's study.

"Mind if I have a drink?" Hector asked as he poured himself a glass of whiskey. "I have to admit that I am a little nervous."

"What are you really afraid of?" asked Erebus.

"Miranda said that I needed to protect everyone I love and everyone who has been caring for me. But is it me they need protection from? Sanuri can you tell?"

"I don't know yet and I do have to tell you that most of the time when I see things it is in fragments, like broken pieces of glass."

"She said that I overheard things when Juleta had me drugged, if that helps you to know what you are looking for," Hector said and gulped down his whiskey.

"Then maybe you should look into my head too," Clev said to the Sanuri. "But you aren't going to like most of what you see."

"Hector, you are so pale; why don't you sit down," said the Sanuri and pulled up a chair next to him. "This isn't going to hurt and I can't tell you how long it will take."

"Do you need me to do anything?" asked Hector.

"No, just don't talk."

Clev poured himself and Erebus each drinks as they watched in silence. Hector started sweating. He didn't know if it was from weakness or fear. He did not want to hear that he was the threat to those he cared about.

"Sanuri, his aura is changing," said Erebus.

"I am not surprised," replied the Sanuri. "I am trying to heal him. Juleta did a lot more than drug him. Hector don't speak."

Another ten minutes passed before the Sanuri spoke again. "I am continually amazed at Juleta's depravity. Clev, I am sure that I will need to heal you too."

"Well, what did you see?" asked Hector anxiously.

"This is kind of difficult to explain. I saw several instances where you were drugged and lying on a table of sorts and Juleta was torturing you. In each of these instances women entered the room. Women from the Sisterhood."

"Even though you were unconscious Juleta feared that your mind would hold memories so she put a sort of magical lock on part of it. I was able to unlock it but I couldn't see the memories. I think you need to call them forward."

It was another thirty minutes before the men reentered the parlor. "Where is everyone?" asked Hector.

"In the other room praying that the demons in you don't harm the baby," Mathas said as he stood up and poured drinks. "All of you look like you could use this. So what did you discover?"

"You tell him," Clev said to the Sanuri as he gulped down his whiskey.

"Juleta drugged and tortured these men," the Sanuri said. "But she was brilliant enough to realize that their subconscious minds might remember things that they heard. It appears that members of the Sisterhood visited her on a regular basis. I can't explain it better than to say she put a sort of lock on parts of their memories. I healed them and opened the locks but it is their choice if they will call the memories forward."

"Now that I don't understand," said Mathas.

"None of us do," said Clev and poured more whiskey into his glass. "It sounds logical but I tried to remember and I can't."

"We'll get Gideon to help," Mathas said. "Hector, you haven't said anything and you look like hell. Are you alright?"

"I don't know," Hector said wearily. "I am having memories filling my head but I don't think they are the right ones. Which room is Mallory in?"

"We're here," said Clarence as he, Catherine, Rosa and Mallory entered the parlor. Mallory looked like she had been crying.

"What did you learn?" Mallory asked.

"I'll tell you later," Hector said and put his arm around her.

"Actually, I would like to hear now. I need something else to think about."

"She tortured us." Catherine gasped when Hector said this. "Then she put some types of locks in our heads so we wouldn't remember what we heard when we were drugged. The Sanuri opened the locks but we can't remember, at least the right things. I really need to go to bed. Are you coming with me?"

"Yes," Mallory said as she realized how pale Hector was. She put her arm around his waist and the two left the parlor. They didn't speak until they entered their chambers.

As they were undressing Hector walked up behind Mallory, put his hands on her waist and kissed her neck. "Honey, everything will be alright." She started to cry and turned around and leaned against him. Hector put his arms around her.

"I just don't understand how I can be pregnant."

"Seriously?"

"No, I mean...we haven't made love that much."

"Well, we must be pretty powerful. Guess that means we are going to have lots of kids." Mallory laughed and playfully punched Hector's chest. "Honey, I am going to take care of you. I'll take care of everything," he said.

Chapter XLII
Tropaion

All of the Wetprian groups within Stordt were sending continuous messages between each other, Sudfad's castle and the forts in Wetpr. The messages were being delivered by Enrops so they were quickly arriving at their destinations.

Everyone in Sudfad's and Gabriel's households were intrigued by what they were reading. Maxwell's family was relieved that they already had two requests for locations of forts; one in Taperia and the second near Fargo and the border between the kingdoms of Stordt and Ryed.

As a ruling family, Maxwell's family was responsible for the forts in Wetpr and now in Stordt. This responsibility was so enormous that all of Maxwell's sons and Elan worked on the assignment besides Maxwell and Emeral. Sudfad provided them with reports and statistics concerning the existing forts to aid them in their planning. And Maxwell was in constant communication with the commanding generals of the forts in Wetpr to get ideas and advice.

Calen had already drawn up multiple copies of the basic plans for the installations, which of course would need to be altered depending on the topography of the locations.

Elan and Koby were determining the basic supply needs for each fort while Emeral and Misha were determining the number of troops and their breakdowns by rank for each fort.

Luca and Maxwell were determining the supplies needed to actually build the forts and Dagon was already in Stordt working with Raul and Simon.

While Maxwell's family had grasps on their assignments, they knew little about the Kingdom of Stordt and had initially felt overwhelmed by the idea of choosing the locations for building sites.

Gabriel and Raphael had been working diligently on determining possible locations for headquarters for the Patronus priests. After they made their preliminary determinations and had them approved by Sudfad, they sent copies to the leaders of that organization.

King Sudfad was a realistic man and knew there would be staffing issues so he offered to pay for the educations for all new students who wanted to go through the rigorous training of becoming a Patronus priest. This information was included in the letters sent to the Patronus leaders and within the week posters were being circulated throughout the Kingdom of Wetpr with plans on circulating them throughout the continent.

After this initial work was completed for the Patronus Headquarters, Gabriel and Raphael joined Joshua's group and Vincente's team. They were traveling to Taperia to assess the needs of the citizens. Benedict and his people would follow as a second wave after the situation was stabilized. Each group or wave as they called themselves would be accompanied by soldiers.

Joshua's team consisted of his sons Micha and Thomas and their wives Bianca and Sasha, Thor, Tanya, Kent, Alex, and Batina. This was the first assignment that Sudfad had sent Alex and Kent on and they both wanted to prove themselves.

All of the wives of men working on assignments in Stordt were working on their own assignments in Wetpr.

In a last minute change of plans, Maxwell, Emeral, Elan, Luca, Koby, Calen, Ratri and Misha joined Joshua's group traveling to Taperia. The entire caravan arrived in Taperia the morning of the third day after the flag of Wetpr had been raised.

The soldiers leading the caravan were wearing the uniforms of their kingdom and carried the flag of Wetpr. The citizens of Taperia gathered in the streets to welcome them. People were applauding, crying and throwing flowers. All of this fanfare took everyone in the caravan by surprise.

Raul, Simon and Javier stopped the caravan at the small park where the Wetprian flag flew. "We stopped you here because the people are fixing a feast for all of you," Raul said as he greeted his friends. "Everyone else will be here soon. Archetenus and Jared are working at the site where we want the fort; they are with Generals Cook and Ortist."

"The main body of soldiers are camped there but several companies are patrolling the area and have already encountered problems."

"Henrich and Maddox have picked out a couple of sites for the Patronus Headquarters and want to take Gabriel and Raphael on tours and Ira is working on housing for everyone."

After Simon greeted the new arrivals he motioned for some men in the crowd to come to them. "This is the new governing body of the city," Simon said proudly. "They have never had these positions before so everyone is learning here. This is Bill, Victor, Harry, Donald and Red." Simon took these new members of the city board through the group and made introductions.

Alex and Kent immediately sought out Javier. "You two are staying with me," Javier said. "I'll tell you this has been one hell of an experience. I wouldn't have missed it for the world. In fact, it is like recreating a world. I've got a lot to tell you. Let's take care of your horses and I'll take you on a tour."

Calen found his parents in the crowd. "After we get settled in, some of us are going to that abandoned hotel. I want to show it to you. You know that is where Natasha and I got married. As awful as that assignment was we had some really good times."

"We would love to see it," said Emeral. "Perhaps you can find a little something there to take back to Natasha as a remembrance." Calen laughed loudly and nodded.

Within minutes of the caravan stopping in the city, musicians started to play their music as citizens set up tables for their visitors.

"They are setting everything up in the middle of the streets," Emeral said with surprise.

"That's what they've been doing," said Raul. "These people are so happy it's like every day is a celebration."

As Raul was speaking a boy ran up to him. "My Lord, Pa wants you to come with me."

"Is something wrong?" Raul asked.

"Oh no, but I'm not supposed to spoil the surprise. All of you can come."

Most of the team members followed the boy as he crossed the street then walked north two blocks. They were now in the primary area of the business district.

"Weren't we just talking to you?" Simon asked with a grin as they saw the city board members standing on the sidewalk smiling at them.

"Pa, I didn't tell them," said the boy and ran up to Donald.

"Mind you, we haven't had a lot of time," said Bill. "But...well follow us." The board members turned and walked about one hundred feet then entered a building. "This is the Morning Glory Hotel or at least it was. The owner and his family left because the gangs were extorting so much money from them. The building is in good shape and we've been really cleaning it out. We thought this could be your headquarters at least until you find something better."

"There are thirty-six rooms, a big kitchen, dining room and tavern. We've already got people willing to work here if you want them and we know how busy you are so we can change anything around for you."

"This is great," said Raul as he walked around the huge front lobby.

"This is a lovely place," Emeral said as she walked into the dining room. "It's a shame the owners left it."

"We're glad you like it," said Victor. "There is something else that we want to show you." The group followed him as he spoke. "Of course all of the rooms lock but the owners lived here too. And their chambers were fixed up more like a home. There is an office in here." Victor opened a door and the group walked inside of the chambers. "Now, that office is kind of small but really you could use these entire chambers for your office."

"This is a lot nicer than those abandoned buildings we have been using," said Javier. "I'm moving my things in here."

"I think we all are," said Simon. "We'll hire the people who want to work here. I assume there are cooks?"

"Well actually there is the entire staff that used to work here. Can't say you will need them all but who knows," Bill said.

"Thank you," said Raul.

"We have a favor to ask," said Red. "We heard there are a couple of priests here?"

"High Priest Gabriel and High Priest Raphael," Simon said and moved so the two men could move to the front of the group.

"We haven't had any churches or anything here in a real long time," Red said. "Some of us are wondering if you would be willing to do some services. And I wouldn't be surprised if you are asked to do some christenings and maybe a wedding or two. If you're willing; we can fix up a building."

"We would be honored to," said Gabriel.

"I don't know why we can't hold the services in that park that you are already fixing up. It is beautiful and there is plenty of room there," Raphael said.

"Oh, thank you," said Red. "People are gonna be so excited."

"Let's do our first service tomorrow morning, say eight," said Gabriel. "Red, do you think you can get the word out?"

"You betcha."

Mathas scheduled his morning meeting for dawn. Since Hector was at the castle all of the team members who were staying in the village and Sorren attended the meeting.

As the people entered the Great Hall they saw that tables were set up for the breakfast meal. The Sanuri and Erebus were already in the room greeting people as they entered.

Mallory was waiting in the foyer and when she saw Brock she led him outside. "Is something wrong?" he asked. But before Mallory could answer Brock said, "Mallory, you look like you have been crying. Did Hector hurt you? I'll break him in two."

"No it's nothing like that," she said and smiled. "Last night we talked to Miranda and all of that will be covered in the meeting but she told me I am pregnant and... well... I didn't handle it well." Brock stared at her without speaking. "I wanted to tell you in person before you heard it from someone else."

"I want to congratulate you but I can tell there is so much more to this. How is Hector taking the news?"

"Oh, he is really happy and wants to get married right away. And his parents are just so excited."

"And you?"

"I love him but I love one part of him. Who knows if he will call the demons back and I don't want to leave the team. I'm going to talk to Dominic when he gets here."

"I don't see any reason you should have to leave the team unless Hector wants to move. But with his parents and Sarah here don't you think he will want to stay?"

"He says so but did you know he is still running his business from here?"

"Yeah."

"How did I miss that?"

"He's still running things but Showers told me that Hector is getting out of some of the areas he was in before and that is because of us."

"Mallory, in case you haven't noticed Hector is a proud man. I don't get the idea that he likes to admit that he isn't in total control of everything. And yet, he has changed a lot since he has been with us but he may not admit to that. And have you considered that might scare him?"

"No. I am glad that you are telling me this. I've been so focused on and confused about my feelings for him. Never in a million years...I mean I just start my new life and I fall for a dark lord...I don't know what is wrong with me."

"He's a likable guy. And he isn't a normal dark lord. He's more of a criminal who knows a little magic. We all like him but I do understand why you are worried. You know, even if things don't work out between you two I'll bet his parents will help you with the baby. You know, watch it while you are on missions."

"Oh, I know they will. And I just love them. But if Hector goes back to his old ways I can't stay with him and having a baby just complicates things so much."

Hector walked into the Great Hall and found Jasmine. "I need to talk to you girls. Where are Tessa and Elexas?"

"They stopped at our team's house. They should be here soon. Is something wrong?"

"Last night Miranda told us that Mallory was pregnant and she is in shock. I think she could use some time with her girlfriends."

"Should I say congratulations?"

"Oh, I am really happy about it. But you know how torn she is because of all the things with me."

"Why would an Angel tell you she was pregnant? I mean is the baby special or something?"

"I don't think so," Hector said and laughed. "You'll hear about it during the meeting but basically I am going to be in a position where I need to protect all of you and I have decisions to make. That's how the subject came up."

"Well, I am happy for you. I hope things work out."

Brock went with Mallory when she told Dominic she was pregnant. To her surprise Dominic hugged her. "Dominic, I don't want to leave the team. I will work something out."

"I'm not going to make you leave. It will be nice to have a baby around. And there is always so much work to do that we can change your assignments. But how does Hector feel about it?"

"Well, if he isn't going to stop being a criminal, I am not going to stop working on the team."

"This isn't sounding like a good start to me," said Dominic. "You two really need to talk about this."

"I know. We have a lot to talk about."

Mathas stood in the front of the Great Hall. There was a head table behind him and all of the ruling members, the Sanuri, Erebus and Gideon were seated at that table.

"First, I want to thank Gideon for giving up a day of his long overdue holiday," said Mathas and smiled then looked at Gideon. "So I am adding two days to your time off to make up for this."

"Last night some things came up. Hector and Clev came here against Shara's orders to work some things out with his parents. Both men were too weak to ride back to the village so they stayed the night. Hector and Mallory were in their chambers when she became suspicious of a message he had received from his men in Cadia. She called to the Angels and the message burst into flames then Miranda appeared."

"She told them that the message was a trap and when Hector kept asking her why the Angels were helping him she said he had decisions to make. She said very soon he would be in a position where he had to save everyone he loved and everyone who had been caring for him. Which of course is all of you."

"Miranda was not directly answering some of his questions but it became apparent that her warnings were related to things he overheard when Juleta had him drugged. Both Hector and Clev asked the Sanuri to look into their minds. What he saw was that my daughter had tortured both men and also had frequent visitors from the Sisterhood. At some point Juleta feared that the men might remember things they overheard when they were drugged and she put some kind of magical locks in their minds."

"The Sanuri was able to open the locks and although memories are returning to both men, they don't remember anything they consider significant. That is why I asked Gideon to come here today."

"This morning after Hector and Clev talked with the Sanuri and Erebus they decided to let Gideon put them into a trance in front of all of you. The reasoning is that one of you might hear something and realize the significance when others do not. Now as you can imagine, this could be an embarrassing situation for them so I ask you to keep that in mind. You have probably noticed there is paper and pens on each table for you to take notes."

"If any of you do not want to witness this you may leave. And on the other hand if any of you want to sit up here with one of the men, you may do that also."

As soon as Mathas finished speaking, Gideon stood up and rearranged some of the furniture in front of the room.

"I'll go first," Hector said and he and Mallory walked to the front of the room holding hands. "Before we start I want to say that although I don't care that you guys see this I don't want my parents here. So please don't tell them the ugly stuff afterwards."

"And last night Miranda told Mallory and me that we are having a baby. Needless to say that was a shock. So I need all of you to talk Mallory into marrying me," Hector said and laughed as did the people in the room. Mallory blushed deeply and gave Hector a disapproving look which caused another round of laughter.

"We think that is great," Dominic said loudly. "We need some babies around here." When he said these words all of his team members looked at Noah and Tessa and everyone laughed again.

Elexas got out of her seat and sat down next to Clev and held his hand. "Thanks," he said.

Hector and Mallory sat down in two chairs that faced the one Gideon was sitting on.

"Hector and Clev, since this information is so important and since I really don't know what questions to ask I am going to ask the Angels for guidance. Which means one of them may appear," said Gideon.

"That is fine," said Hector. "Perhaps you could ask them how I need to protect everyone."

Stephan was taking notes and moved closer to Gideon who was saying a silent prayer. Gideon started to move his watch back and forth then stopped. "Mallory, don't you stare at it or you will be asleep too."

"It's hard not to," she said and laughed. Then she abruptly stopped. "Gideon, don't ask me why but put me to sleep with him. In fact, Miranda is saying that Clev and Brock should come up here too."

"Can I?" asked Elexas.

"Miranda said that you can but they are sending us on a journey so if you want to come with us you have to let Gideon put you into a trance."

"In that case, everyone needs to have a weapon," Matthew said and stood up. "Hector, you take my sword."

"Do we need more than knives?" asked Mallory.

"Probably," said Thaos and handed her his sword. Everyone who was going on the journey now had a knife and a sword.

"Miranda, do they need more of us to go with them?" asked Matthew.

Miranda appeared in the room. "There are many more worlds than all of you are aware of. Juleta was powerful enough to have traveled to some. When Hector and Clev remember the words they heard, they still will not understand the meaning so they will be experiencing the meaning."

"I believe that Erebus and I need to go to. Because if I understand what you haven't said. Juleta hid her arsenal in other worlds and that is why we can't find them," said the Sanuri.

Miranda smiled. "There really is no limit as to who can go but remember that Hector and Clev are leading this."

"Miranda, I would like to go," said Mathas. She nodded.

"I believe we all would," said Claudius. "How many need to stay here?"

"Just Gideon but your bodies aren't going on this journey although to you it will seem like it," said Miranda. "But you must remember that you are accompanying Hector and Clev on their journey. No one tries to take charge of them on this."

"Miranda will Mallory and the baby be alright?" asked Hector.

"Yes. Gideon do as you normally would and I will allow everyone to go into a trance."

"Miranda are you coming with us?" asked Tessa.

"I am now," she said and in that instant everyone including Gideon was transported from the room. No one remembered how they got into the darkness but they all felt dizzy and sick. The light emitting from Miranda allowed them to see. "Asking me to accompany you has greatly changed things. You are now here in your bodies, which you will find advantageous."

"Everyone, you are feeling sick because we are in another dimension," Erebus explained. "Miranda, would I be right in guessing that this world is near Cadia?"

"You really are a brilliant man," Miranda said. "Continue explaining."

"I have read that different worlds or realities are very close together. As was the case when I was in the World of Illusions. Think of walking through a mirror and coming out in a different world. Risha told our teams that there was great evil in Cadia but no one could find it. This is why I suspect the entrance to this world is somehow connected to the ocean there."

Hector suddenly grabbed his head and looked as if he was in great pain. His knees started to buckle so Stephan and Thaos grabbed him.

"Do you smell that?" Clev asked. "I remember that smell." No one else in the group smelled what he was sensing. Clev bent over and vomited several times. The rest of the group watched in silence.

"Hector are you alright?" Mallory whispered.

"Let him go," Miranda said and Hector fell to his knees. He was rocking back and forth and whimpering as he clutched his head. Hector was visibly shaking. He took his right hand away from his head and started to draw in the dirt with his finger. The others watched as he appeared to have difficulty doing this task.

"Erebus," Hector whispered.

"Erebus he wants you," said Brock.

"Miranda can we have more light?" Erebus asked as he was trying to see what Hector had drawn in the dirt.

"It appears to be a mask but I don't recognize it," Erebus said.

"Oh my god!" said Mallory. "Brock come closer and look at this. Hector is that who is hurting you?"

"Yes," he said through clenched teeth. As Hector spoke, Clev fell to his knees and clutched his head.

"I'll do this one," Mallory said. "Brock have Clev draw his attacker."

Elexas was kneeling down and holding Clev who was rocking back and forth. "Clev, I can stop it but you have to draw the mask," Brock said.

"Miranda, do we need to do this differently here?" asked Mallory.

"No."

Mallory took a knife from its sheath and held it into the air. "Great Ruler use me as the instrument to stop Baal's power," Mallory said loudly then she thrust her knife into the drawing and started to chant. "Baal be gone, you have no power here." She repeated her chant and soon Brock was saying the same chant.

"Should we join them?" asked Sorren.

"No," Miranda said. "Watch."

The ground under the drawings started to shake. Slowly at first then with increased intensity. When the shaking became violent Mallory pulled her knife from the drawing and wrapped Hector's fingers around it. She held his hand onto the knife and thrust it back into the drawing. "Hector say the words with me."

"Baal be gone, you have no power here," they chanted in unison. A moment later Clev and Brock were also chanting. Hector and Clev were in such pain they could barely speak but they continued chanting. The ground shook with more intensity. Mallory jumped and pulled Hector away from the drawing as the ground split open. Elexas and Brock pulled Clev away from his drawing.

The people watching were now having difficulty standing. As the ground opened a putrid smell filled the cavern they were in and several people vomited. Screams were heard as the drawings literally sunk into the ground.

"I remember now," said Hector and stood up. He pulled Mallory to a standing position with him. "Honey, are you alright?"

"I am but that was the demon Baal."

"But he was destroyed," said Sorren. "How can that be?"

"Hector and Clev are experiencing their past," said Miranda. "Hector tell us."

"I was tied on an altar and Juleta was wearing that mask and nothing else. She was dancing around me and three women walked into the room and started to yell at her. She turned and threw the knife in her hand and it killed one of the women. The other two started to curse her. Juleta left the altar and she was sending curses at the women."

"Then I heard a scream that I think came from upstairs because moments later a lot more women ran into the room and they all had weapons. One of the women yelled at Juleta and said, 'You are giving your boyfriend to Baal so he will cloak things for you. What is so important?' Then one of the other women yelled. 'It's the book, she has our book.' Then I don't remember, I must have passed out."

"For those of you who went on the mission to the Kingdom of Ryed, you know that Baal was the creator of the Kingdom of Ogg and we defeated them there. And you know that Juleta had put bounties on your teams. She paid the King of Ogg to carry them out," Miranda explained.

"Did she pay the Valdees to hide her arsenal?" asked Claudius. "Because if that is the case it is under water."

"It's more than that," said Clev loudly. "I remember...that smell. She had me tied up. I was barely conscious but this awful smell woke me up. I saw something that looked like it was part man and part fish talking with Juleta. He was telling her that the army was there."

"The Valdees are fish men," said Sorren.

"Well, she hired an army of them to guard something," Clev said.

"And thus the evil which Risha spoke of," said Miranda. "Thaos can you add anything?"

"I was gone a lot but the guys were telling me that she had ordered huge shipments of building supplies. But I never saw any new buildings on her land."

547

"As shrewd as she was, certainly she would not have hidden all of her things in one location," said the Sanuri. "Are they all underwater and guarded by the Valdees?"

"You are right. There are others that are under the oceans and guarded by the Valdees but still others are hidden differently," said Miranda.

"Miranda, can you let our teams in Cadia know that Valdees are in that area?" asked Claudius. She nodded.

"We have been believing that whatever Juleta had in Cadia she was sharing or working with Otto Franks," said Turner. "Is that true?"

"Otto helped her finance the vault and the army of Valdees because he fully intended to use it but before he put anything into it he caught her in a number of lies and dissolved their partnership. Jack does not know about the vault but he knows that his father gave Juleta chests of gold and he wants the family money back."

"Miranda, why are we here, in this place?" asked Hector. "This has to be significant. And can the Valdees still survive without Baal?"

"They have survived because they now worship Baal's first lieutenant. The demon Matraxt. Do you not recognize this place?"

Both Hector and Clev slowly walked forward and touched the walls of the cavern. "Miranda, can we have more light?" asked Hector. Miranda did not speak nor did she provide more light. They were slowly running their hands over the dark walls when Hector jumped back. "I know what this place is. I thought it was a nightmare. Matthew and Mathas shouldn't be here. Send them back."

"They are precisely the ones who should be here," said Miranda.

"No!" Hector said.

"What is this place?" demanded Mathas.

"Hector, is this her Tropaion?" Erebus asked.

"Yes. Miranda are Clev and I in here?" asked Hector.

"Not anymore."

"Will someone please tell us what this is?" Matthew asked with a sense of dread.

"As you know many civilizations take trophies of war and display them. Sometimes they are offerings to gods and sometimes the story of the battle is attached to them," Erebus said. "I would imagine this area is filled with images of the souls that Juleta took."

"Miranda let me look upon this," said Mathas as his knees weakened.

"Wait," said the Sanuri. "Are these images of people who are still living?"

"Both," Miranda said.

"Miranda please let us see this," said Mathas.

The room filled with light. The floor was no longer made of dirt but marble. It was a long marble hallway. The walls held hundreds of what looked like windows and behind each pane of glass was the full image of a person."

"This is like the spookiest museum I have ever seen," said Tessa as she walked up to a window.

Mathas wept as he slowly walked down the hallway and looked at the faces of his daughter's trophies. Many he recognized.

"Is this that little girl whose body we found in the rug?" asked Sorren.

"Yes," replied Miranda.

Mathas stopped walking and stared in a window. "Miranda please, is this our son, the one who died so Juleta could become a monster?"

"Yes."

"Now just wait a minute," Mallory said loudly. "If these people didn't freely give up their souls, can't we help them, at least give them some peace?"

"Can Juleta still own their souls if she is in the Abyss?" asked Jasmine.

"Hector, Juleta gave you much of her powers," said Miranda.

"I don't own these souls," he gasped with horror.

"No but you can release them."

"How? Tell me!"

"You once studied to become a priest," Miranda said.

"Ask The Great Ruler to take them," said Dominic.

Mallory took hold of Hector's hand. "Do you want me to help you?" she asked.

"I remember," he said. Hector got down on his knees, closed his eyes and prayed, "Great Ruler please take these souls, save them from their horror, free them from their prison." When Hector opened his eyes they were back in the Great Hall of Mathas' castle.

Chapter XLIII
Removing Veils

Juleta screamed with rage in the thick blackness of her prison in the Abyss. "No! No! You can't!" she screamed over and over as she felt herself weakening. Every soul that The Great Ruler healed took from her power and strength. "If I ever get out of here I will kill you all!"

"I have as many questions now as I did before," Thaos said as he materialized in the Great Hall. "Miranda, are you still here? Miranda." She did not answer.

"Well did I miss it? Did we find out the location of the vault outside of Cadia? Or how many Valdees we are going to have to fight?"

"No and I am confused too," said Sorren as he watched Mallory help Hector to a chair. "Maybe those two are too weak to do anything else right now."

"So what was all of that with Baal?" asked Matthew. "Sanuri, do you know?"

"You are all so frustrated but we learned a great deal besides saving all of those poor souls. And we will start by talking about them. How many did you recognize because those were your spies?" explained the Sanuri.

"But they aren't now?" Matthew asked.

"No but they can always sell their souls to someone else. We now know about her system of vaults and her relationship with both Otto and King Douma. And we know who is spying on our people in Cadia."

"But when they destroyed those images of Baal did that unlock anything else in Hector's and Clev's minds?" asked Noah.

"That I don't know," replied the Sanuri. "But you learned yet another way to destroy the power of demons."

"Sanuri that was our past. So did all that change anything that occurred after that?" asked Hector.

"That was the question that I was waiting for and again I do not know the answer. But I cannot see how it could not."

"Hector and Clev, do you feel any different?" asked Brock.

"I just feel sicker and weaker," said Clev.

"Me too," Hector said as he nodded his head.

"Neither of you are in any shape to travel. Stay here," said Mathas. "And I am so very sorry for what Juleta did to you."

"Mathas, I have to believe there is a reason that Miranda had you see that," said the Sanuri.

As the Sanuri was speaking Gideon walked up to one of the walls and was looking at maps. "The look on your face. What is it?" asked Fahron.

"For centuries ships disappeared from the waters around the Kingdom of Ogg. Well, that isn't the only area. Now mind you that sailing the seas is a dangerous life and besides the dangers of nature there are things that can affect a man's mind. Sailors sometimes think they see things in the water that aren't there. And sometimes, and I too have experienced this; sometimes you are in an area that seems eerie. Like you are in a different time. I am now wondering if there is an explanation for these occurrences; like Juleta's magics."

Edward was leading the morning meeting of the teams in Cadia when Enrops simply appeared in the room. "Damn! I just never get used to this," yelled Angus as he jumped and spilled his coffee.

"The Angel Miranda was on a journey with Hector, Clev and the teams in Langer," announced one of the birds.

"Hector and Clev were freed from some of their bonds and are trying to remember things that they overheard when Juleta had them drugged and was torturing them. They are trying to figure out where her arsenal is. There are several locations but one is in the sea here by Cadia. It is a vault in the ocean that is guarded by an army of Valdees. That is the evil here. That is the evil that watches you."

Hector and Clev had to be helped to their chambers. Mallory and Elexas gave them their medicines then returned to the meeting. As soon as they entered the Great Hall the Sanuri spoke.

"Mallory, I hope by now you realize that you were meant to be in Hector's life. For how long is up to the two of you but I believe your impact on him is important right now. I am not telling you to marry him or to stay with him for any length of time but we can all see the panic in you. Now would not be a good time to leave."

"I'm that obvious?" she asked and sat down.

"She has legitimate concerns," said Brock defensively.

"On that we all agree," said the Sanuri. "And Elexas, your impact on Clev is no small thing either. While everyone here has heard of their deeds, none of you have really spent time with them until after Hector was weakened. All of you have had positive effects on them. I don't claim to understand why but many Angels are working on keeping them in our company right now. Mallory, if you go home now that may upset whatever the Angels have in motion."

"Trust me, I have been thinking about that. I do love him and at the same time I hate myself for caring about him. I still don't know if he is a man or a monster and honestly I don't think he does either."

"I can raise a baby on my own of that I am sure. But during all of this I have wondered if someday I would have to kill him and having his child just makes everything more complicated."

"First of all, we will help you," said Jasmine. "All of us are a family now. You won't be alone and if he becomes such a monster again that we are forced to put him down, well, you shouldn't be the one to do it."

"We all agree with what Jasmine said," Fennel said. "And I agree with the Sanuri too. Honestly, I would not want to be in your position Mallory but the guy does seem to love you and you love him. Just give it a little time."

Olin stood up and looked sheepish. "I haven't spoken about any of this because honestly it scares me. You see I can understand things on both sides. And now that I know that a great deal of what happened to Hector and Clev was done without their knowing it...well, it just makes me wonder. But look how I've changed since I got my soul back. I think you should stop thinking about killing him and think about making your relationship work."

"That didn't come out the way that I meant. But think about it. Mallory and Elexas even if you don't marry the guys they are valuable resources for us. Everyone says that we are at war; wouldn't you rather have them on our side?"

As soon as the Enrops delivered their message, Edward called to Miranda but it was Adam who appeared. "Adam, how do we find that vault?" asked Edward.

"That task I would leave to the members in Langer for now. But know that the Valdees walk these streets to kill and take victims. That is where you should focus your energies for one. Now tell me, what were the reasons that you came here?"

"To find out what Juleta and Otto were doing here and to find out if King Fahra is a terrorist," Edward replied.

"Otto gave Juleta a fortune to build the vault because he thought he would be using it too. But they had a falling out before it was completed. Jack knows how much money his father gave to Juleta but he doesn't know what it was used for."

"He desperately is trying to get his family money back so he can raise an army. He has many spies in this city and they are hoping that you will lead them to the money. He does not know about the Valdees."

"Now that you have that question answered you can turn your focus to the King. War many times makes unlikely allies. You are now at a point where you should include Hector's leaders here in your meetings. Hector has many choices to make yet. But for this moment in time he is trying to keep his fears and addictions under control. You would be wise to take advantage of the situation as they are doing in Langer. If nothing else you will understand them better if you become enemies again."

When Mallory returned to Hector's room she found him sitting up in bed and talking with his parents. "Do you want to be alone?" she asked.

"Oh no child, come in," said Catherine. "We came here to talk with both of you. Clarence..."

"We understand, well, at least we think we do all of the things the two of you are going through," Clarence said. "But the bottom line is you are having a baby and Catherine and I couldn't be happier. If you decide not to marry; Mallory, you will always have a home with us. We will certainly support you and the baby in any way we can." Mallory smiled warmly.

"And if you do decide to marry, well, Hector wanted us to have a jeweler come out here but Catherine thinks you are a sentimental girl so we brought you the rings of both of Hector's grandmothers and if you like one you should have it."

As Clarence spoke, Catherine took a silk handkerchief from her skirt pocket, placed it on the bed and unfolded it, exposing four rings. "These are the engagement and the wedding rings," she said.

Mallory walked up to the bed. "I haven't seen these in ages," Hector said as he picked up one of the rings and looked at it. "Mallory, I know that right now you are scared to death but we can have a long engagement if that will make you feel better."

"I love you and want to marry you. I am not sure if you are ready to think about this now but if you don't want these rings we will find something you like."

Mallory hugged Catherine then Clarence. "I will admit that I am panicking right now. I just wasn't ready for this but you are both so sweet and I appreciate everything you said." She sat down on the side of the bed and said, "So tell me the stories behind these rings."

After Adam left, Edward sent Sol to find Dagger and bring him to the meeting. Up to this point, Edward and Angus had briefed Dagger on most of the information they got since he ran the Cadia compound but they had not invited him to their meetings. Dagger was not insulted since he did not invite the teams to his meetings with his men.

"Dagger, one of the Angels just left here and we have a lot to tell you and I will go into details momentarily but the danger we were warned about here turns out to be Valdees soldiers. I don't know if you have seen or fought those bastards before but they are savage. We will need to work together on this and I think you should be a regular member of our meetings unless you feel otherwise," Edward said.

"I have heard that word before but can't rightly say I remember where or why," Dagger said as he looked at the faces in the room. "All of you look so serious and in my opinion you're all tougher than shit so these Valdees must be real bad asses. I have no problem combining forces."

"Here," said Angus and handed Dagger a cup of coffee. "Just a warning, you probably aren't going to believe some of this."

After Catherine and Clarence left Hector's room, Mallory stayed. "You look exhausted but can we talk for a few minutes?" she asked.

"Only if you promise not to yell at me," he said and smiled weakly. "All that stuff with the rings was their idea. I had nothing to do with it."

"I'm not going to yell," she said and took his hand. "And honestly I just love your parents. And I know how excited they are about us and the baby."

"And your mother is right, I will probably choose one of the rings that they brought but we..."

"Wait. So you are going to marry me?"

"Probably, unless you call to more demons. I have been doing a lot of thinking and I just want to tell you, well, my thoughts. The other night when I was crying you looked so guilty and you have no reason to feel like that. And then when you told me that I tell Catherine and Clarence more about my life than I do you; I realized you are right."

"My village is small compared to Sorren's Tribe but we are all close and fierce warriors. As you know we start to train as children so our entire lives we are told that we have a purpose in this world. Almost two years ago now the Angels told us to stop hunting demons for a variety of reasons and one is that they don't want us to get involved with the civil war. Another is that they bring people to our village for us to protect."

"We are a poor village and when we can't hunt demons there isn't a lot else to keep us busy and between that and not feeling like we have a purpose any more...well Brock and I jumped at the chance to get on the teams. It's the first time either of us have been out of Ryed. And you can't believe how hard we worked to get accepted and that was when we didn't even realize we were getting paid."

"Brock and I make good money and we send most of it home. Our families have been able to help others in our village with the money we send them." She paused. "Hector, this was my chance to have adventures and to start a new life. I came here believing you were not just an enemy but a formidable one. Then as I got to know you; actually as all of us got to know each other things really changed. But I am and will always be a Venator."

"I was not ready to have my opinion of you change much less fall in love with you. And I really wasn't ready for getting pregnant. So all of these things...it was like getting hit over the head. It's like my head was spinning and I didn't know which end was up."

"I am going to tell you something that will probably make you mad but I was feeling very angry at myself for having feelings for you."

"Trust me, I could tell that. And I am glad that you are telling me this."

"Olin said something this morning that, ok let me back up. When he first joined us he was our prisoner and the guy never stopped talking which we found odd. But it turns out he really didn't have any friends and was glad to have our company. You know he was a dark lord and did some really bad stuff but he didn't know that the Master owned his soul and that little guy defied the Master. Did anyone tell you what he did?"

"No and I would like to hear it."

"I'll tell you when I am done with what I have to say. But that little guy was braver than a lot of warriors. Then afterwards he was so lost. He really had no one and he had bounties on him so we kind of took him in and he has proved himself over and over. Well, I didn't realize it because I have been so focused on you but he doesn't talk that much anymore. He said it was because watching everything that was going on with you and Clev was scaring him because he had kind of been in your shoes in a way."

"He said that I should stop worrying so much about what will happen if you call to demons again and look at our relationship which surprised me coming from him. But he also said that everyone keeps saying we are at war and that even if things didn't work out between us we should still want to be allies. I can tell from your face that you don't like hearing some of this but I thought it only fair to tell you what I have been thinking."

"Like I said I am glad you are telling me this and I had already guessed a great deal of it. Mallory, you want me to tell you that I am going to give up my life and join your teams don't you?"

"I would love that but I don't expect it."

"I can't make any promises at least not yet and even if I did it wouldn't be for a while. I too have a lot of irons in the fire. You were right when you said that we all changed as we got to know each other; hell look at Showers and Clev is thinking about leaving me too. We have a truce so we are allies now and I don't plan on breaking that truce. But none of us can predict the future."

"Mallory, you have seen sides of me that I didn't know existed. The sides where I was basically victimized but I am not a victim and I liked my life. You have to understand that. Now I certainly wasn't planning on falling in love or having another child either. Our lives have changed greatly but they are still our lives. You are worried that you will have to kill me if I become a demon and I am worried about how I can keep my life and keep all of you safe."

"Everything has changed now. I want to spend my time with you and my children and my parents. This is a good life but I haven't let go of the old one yet and maybe I never will. You don't like hearing this yet you don't look surprised. I know that you are embarrassed by the fact that I am a criminal and I am sorry for that. In many areas my status commands respect. In some ways it is like you and I are as different as day and night and yet, it's like what my parents say; you are the perfect woman for me."

"This isn't an easy transition for either of us but I believe we can make it work. Are you still willing to try?"

"Yes and I don't think it will suddenly get easier for us. Hector, I plan to stay on my team. I'm trying to think how to say this. We share a lot with you but there are so many more things I would like to tell you but I don't know if you will use that information to hurt someone. And you have so much going on that I don't know about and maybe I shouldn't but if we are going to be married we can't be afraid to talk to each other. At some point we have to trust each other and how are we going to do that?"

"I have been thinking about that too."

"Well, we have to figure something out. You know we don't have to get married because I am pregnant. I can raise the baby. Is that the only reason you asked me?"

"I was waiting for that question to come up. No, I have been thinking about it but I was so sure that you would bust my chops that I didn't say anything. Then when we found out about the baby it just seemed right."

"I know exactly what you are saying. I never would have told you my feelings. See we can't talk about anything that is important, how can a marriage work?"

"Before I address that I want to go back to your comment about raising the baby by yourself. It is my child too and I want to be part of its life whether we marry or not. And my parents like you more than me right now. Do you think they would let you do that alone? Besides that they love you and want grandchildren, this is the closest they have been to having a normal life in a while. They thought I was dead then they find out that I am a criminal then we go on the run. It has all been very difficult for them."

"They are used to living in a mansion with staff and here they are living in that little cottage and they couldn't be happier. And I am glad because they are safe here with all of you."

"Mallory, you keep worrying about my choices and well, you are being realistic but don't blind yourself to the fact that being associated with me is dangerous. I would prefer that you stay on the team because they can protect you if I can't."

Mallory was staring intently at Hector. "We need to get a few things straight now. Neither of us are perfect and now that we are starting to talk I believe that both of us are seeing the issues more clearly. But it is what you aren't saying that is disturbing. You stayed away from Sarah and your parents to protect them. Don't think you are going to do that with me. We are a family now and I don't believe that either of us run from demons."

"I know your heart was in the right place but I think that your choices hurt the ones you love more than it helped them. This is why we need to talk if for no other reason so we know who our enemies are but I have a question."

"For the sake of argument, if you were to get out of your business would you still be in danger?"

"Yes for one, because of what I know about people. There is always revenge and people and demons want things that I have and that they think I have. Then there is all the crap that Juleta did that others think I was part of. Honey, right now it is safer for all of us that I stay in the business."

"I had a feeling that is what you were going to say. Hector, I just can't see how a marriage could work with so many secrets. In my tribe husbands and wives share many roles, they fight and hunt together; they are partners. That is what I would want also. I will not become a criminal but after what you just said I think I need to learn more about your business." She paused. "Perhaps you and I should talk with the Sanuri or Claudius or someone to get more perspective on this."

"I like you saying that we are a family," he said and kissed her hand. "And it is a new thing to have my girl say she will fight at my side."

"According to your mother it's a new thing for you to say you have a girl," Mallory said teasingly.

"You know with the two of you getting so close I am not going to get away with much," Hector said and laughed.

"Actually, I think your parents have already figured that out," she said and smiled. "You know there might be times when they have to take care of the baby so we can fight or go on missions."

"They aren't naïve. I think they are already planning on it."

"I am surprised that I am feeling better just talking this little bit. So we need to talk about getting married."

Hector laughed loudly, "You are full of surprises."

"Well, Catherine keeps asking me questions. Hector, I am a warrior who grew up poor. I don't understand some of the things she is talking about. In my tribe when people marry they exchange their lamsmans which is the most important thing they own. In your world it is the rings."

"I know your family is wealthy but I do not think it is wise to have a huge open wedding unless we wait for a long time. I think that is what your mother wants. You are her only child."

"Did you tell her how you feel?"

"No, I wanted to talk with you about it first. And if that is what we end up having then I want to have my family here also. The Rualas will get them. Now, if you do want a wedding that has hundreds of people invited to it and you want it soon then we need to plan for an attack so we should keep that in mind. Your mother certainly won't think about that."

Hector laughed loudly again and pulled Mallory closer to him. They kissed for several moments. "We could have a wedding with just our friends and family or we could have one with just you and me."

"You are a fool," she said and smiled. "This ceremony will be more for your parents. Perhaps after we have children I will understand the importance but right now I don't."

"But I feel the same way; that your parents have been through a lot and we can do this for them. I caught Catherine and Rosa talking about invitations which is why I bring this up. You might want to have a talk with her."

"And I will. So what did you think about those rings?"

"I like the history to them. Starting a marriage is like a new plant and history gives it roots. What I would like to do is wear one ring from each set so we have both sides of your family represented."

"So you are saying the engagement ring from one set and the wedding ring from the other?"

"Yes, do you think it will be alright with them?"

"I think that if you explain it to them exactly like you did to me they will be very happy. But you know I will buy you a ring too."

"No, I like the idea of wearing the family rings and they are beautiful. I am not sure which of them I would want."

"Why don't you ask my parents to help you decide?"

"Hector, I am feeling so much better now that we are talking. And I can't really explain it but I want to talk with someone else for guidance before I give you my lamsman or take your ring."

"You're talking the Sanuri or Claudius?"

"Someone wise that understands everything that is going on. I mean we may be missing something altogether. It doesn't have to be just one person. But I think Clev or Brock are too close to us to perhaps see some things."

"So you think we need help seeing things from all angles?"

"Yes. And I am saying this because this is a very complicated relationship that affects more than just us."

"If you want every angle then I would suggest Bella too. Or just Claudius' family and the Sanuri. They are all level headed people with lots of insight and experience. Is Claudius still downstairs?"

"He was when I left."

Hector started to get out of bed. "No, you stay here," Mallory scolded. "I will go down and see if he is still here. But you do realize that you may have to open up more about your businesses."

"That is exactly what I am thinking about. I left them to Claudius if I died."

"What! You know he would tear them apart."

"And that is why I did it. Clev would follow me into hell and he has but he doesn't want this life anymore. I offered him my business and he wanted nothing to do with it. I am going to need a lot of paper and a pen."

Claudius was mounting his horse when Mallory found him. After she explained to him that she and Hector wanted to speak with the entire family, Claudius sent soldiers to get Bella, Ingr and Nikki who were in Langer.

Then he went into the office to get Stephan and Thaos. Mallory found the Sanuri who suggested that Erebus be included in the meeting.

Thirty minutes later, Mallory, Tessa and Jasmine walked into Hector's room. Each woman was carrying a tray with coffee, cups and sweet rolls. "We aren't staying," said Tessa.

"Actually I don't care," Hector said. "Can someone get me more paper?"

"The others will be here soon," Mallory said and handed Hector a cup of coffee while Tessa left the room to get paper.

"I'm not really sure that we should be a part of this," said Jasmine. "But holler if you need us for anything."

"Chairs," said Mallory and the three women left the room. As they were returning to the room they met Stephan and Thaos in the hallway who took the chairs they were carrying and set them in Hector's room.

"We'll be back," Stephan said. Five minutes later, the Sanuri, Erebus, Mallory, Claudius, Bella, Ingr, Stephan, Thaos and Nikki were seated in the room.

Stephan and Hector were grinning at each other. "Are you really going to ask us for marriage advice?" Stephan asked.

"It's more complicated than that," Hector said. "But basically yes. Ok so I am just going to cut to the chase. You know that Mallory and I love each other and are expecting a baby. You also know that with all of the events we haven't gotten to talk about a lot and we are, let's just say from different worlds. She is afraid of my choices and what she may have to do about them."

"This morning we started talking and this is where we need your help. I am still running my business from here and have no intention of giving it up at the moment and that is for a variety of reasons that include the safety of my family. Mallory intends to keep working on the teams. I intend to keep our truce but how do we have a marriage when we have to keep so many secrets from each other? And do we have to keep those secrets?"

"You can't have a marriage when you keep such secrets," said Nikki passionately. "That was a big issue for me and Thaos. But the two of you are in a different situation and honestly I give you credit for asking for advice. I say we start with the bottom line being you either don't marry or marry and don't keep secrets and work from there."

"And I think this is where I come in," said Erebus. "The next person to speak was going to say that a lot has to do with your choices Hector. But you are a brilliant man and already know that. So I have to ask why are we really here. Before you answer that, we haven't talked about your addiction which greatly influences your choices. The Angels said you have an addiction. You have not acknowledged that. Even if you deny it, I think you are afraid that you do and that is why you called us here."

"I can't disagree with anything yet," said Hector. "I am a decisive person and although many of you want to believe that I am a victim, I am not. Alright, a little but that is the part that makes me question things. As all of you, I like being in control and all of the things that have been happening and I mean everything even the Angels make me question how much control I or any of us have."

"I don't know if I have an addiction to power but if I do, I agree it will influence my decisions. This is a good life here and I am happy with many things but this is one part of my life. While I know that all of you disapprove of many things I did, I enjoy the cat and mouse game of my life. I enjoy the strategizing and planning. Mallory asked me earlier if I just gave up my business if I would be safe. Thaos, you more than anyone else should realize that staying in my business is keeping many safe."

"I love Mallory and want to be a father but I can't tell you what the future holds at this point. I respect your opinions and I know none of you mince words so have at it." No one said anything for several moments.

"I think we are quiet because we are trying to figure out what you are really asking us," said Claudius. "First, tell us what you have written on that stack of papers."

"This is my business. Unless something changes greatly, Clev is going to stay here and follow in Shower's example and I can't blame him. Claudius, I am leaving the business to you so you should be aware of what it is."

Mallory stared at Hector. "Have there been threats against you?"

"Honey, there are always threats against me. My men in Salszar are waging a war against the Discedo group and I should be there. I have compounds in other continents too and most of that is because of Juleta. She had built an empire that was hard to turn down. Now that we know about her arsenal, you need to be aware of those locations. I will tell you that even if I have the addiction I am not interested in setting loose plagues that will destroy this world."

"Are you thinking of taking off because your enemies will look for you here?" asked Thaos.

"The thought has crossed my mind as have many others. If I wasn't so incapacitated I would have left already. Mallory, don't give me that look you know you would do the same thing." Mallory stared angrily at him but did not speak.

"Claudius, here are my businesses," Hector said and held out a handful of papers. "I have put J's by everything that I inherited from Juleta."

Claudius took the papers and quickly reviewed them. "This is incredible," he said.

"That may answer some of your questions," said Hector.

"Why is this sounding like a will?" Stephan asked.

"How many times have I almost died just since we have been reunited? I have a family now to think of. I put two stars by the businesses or areas where I consider my strongest threats come from. So if something happens to me, my family will still need to be protected."

"Something isn't right here," said Bella as she stared at both Hector and Mallory.

"I think we all agree with that," Ingr said. "But remember, the Angels wanted us to save you and they tell us what information that we can share with you. Hector, your tone of voice, you really are sounding like you expect the worst."

"I always do but it was easier when it was just me. I included the locations of my money. Claudius make sure that Mallory and her people are taken care of and the rest do with as you see fit."

"Now you are scaring me," Mallory said. "Hector, this isn't why we asked them here."

"Actually it is. We have been two opposing armies for a long time. And all of you are afraid that our truce is temporary and that is why you are afraid to share things with me and that is smart on your part. I don't know anymore which choices were mine but I was a criminal long before I met Juleta."

"You were a robber not a murderer or a monster," Nikki said. "While I am not condoning robbery there is a big difference there."

Bella had been staring intently at Hector and now stood up and walked close to the bed. "I helped raise you so don't try to pull one over on us. Hector, you saw or heard something on that journey that you aren't telling us. What was it?"

Chapter XLIV
Agony

Gabriel and Raphael were both excited about and intrigued with their new roles in helping the Kingdom of Wetpr assimilate the lands and people of the kingdom formally known as Stordt. They found these roles rewarding because the people had lived in such terror and poverty that they were grateful for every act the team members performed.

These two priests held their first service on the morning after their arrival in Taperia. All forms of religion had been banned for decades in Stordt. All of the churches, temples and monasteries had been destroyed by King Roch. Gabriel and Raphael held the service in the park where the Wetprian flag was flying. They hastily built a small altar and purchased a few candles.

The service was to start at eight. By seven the park was filled with citizens who brought their own chairs or blankets to sit on. By seven thirty the streets surrounding the park were filled and by eight o'clock people were standing on the walkways of the businesses across from the park.

The priests were amazed at the attendance. And even more amazed at the groups of people who stayed to speak with them after the service. Before that day was through, Raphael and Gabriel conducted two more services and three christenings. Before dusk that evening, they met with the newly elected Taperian board members. The men walked around the city and chose the locations for their new religious buildings.

Early the following morning, before they were to perform another service; Gabriel and Raphael met with the Patronus priests who had accompanied the Princes to the city. Two dozen of these priests volunteered to be reassigned. They would stay in Taperia and help the citizens with their religious needs and with the construction of the buildings. The enthusiasm of the citizens did not fade as the days went by.

The elation that Gabriel and Raphael felt in their new roles was tempered only by their concern for the priests who were working on the mission in Malga. Those priests were looking for the terrorists in that monastery who were calling in the presence of demons. Such charges were not to be made lightly so High Priest Othnial and his group were meticulous in their research.

Because the investigation was so daunting Othnial's group would go days and weeks without sending messages to King Sudfad, Raphael or Gabriel. This lack of communication was causing a great deal of anxiety for Gabriel and Raphael, who now were contemplating taking a trip to Malga.

Claudius' family, Erebus and the Sanuri left Hector's room without him answering Bella's question. And Hector's silence made them all realize that he had experienced more on his journey than they were aware of.

Mallory remained in the room with Hector. "There are so many things that I want to talk about but you look awful and need to sleep," she said and gave him a glass of tonic. "I will need to make sure that Clev takes his medicine then I will come back."

"We didn't get your questions answered," he said weakly as he lay back against his pillows.

"I know but I think we made a lot of headway. Actually, I was shocked when you gave Claudius all of that information about your business. Do you mind if I look at it?"

"No, I was going to suggest it. But I can always write it down again for you."

"I may just make a copy of what you gave him. I want to stay with you but you don't sleep when I am here. Do you think you will be alright if I am gone for a little while?"

"Of course I will be. Perhaps you should talk to Mother before she invites the entire kingdom to our wedding."

Mallory kissed Hector on the forehead then turned towards the door. She stopped and looked around the room. She took two more steps then stopped again. She turned and returned to Hector's bed.

"Change your mind?" he asked groggily.

Mallory didn't answer his question. She took off her necklace which held a pendant of a holy crystal from the Ice Caves of Mordv and fastened it around Hector's neck. "What are you doing?" he asked.

"Just giving you a gift," she said. "Hector, I know you are barely awake so I will explain this later. She removed her lamsman from her ankle and pulled the sheet up that was covering Hector's feet. She fastened the lamsman around his right ankle. "Hector, I take you for my husband and I ask the Heavens to bless our marriage." Hector was asleep and did not respond.

Mallory walked over to the chair where Hector's clothing was piled. She removed two knives from his belt and stuck them in hers. She was wearing her warriors outfit. "Miranda, I am ready," Mallory said and disappeared from the room.

After learning about the Valdees in the area, Edward, Angus and Dagger decided to assign teams of warriors to monitor the docks and shoreline. The teams were instructed to watch the Valdees soldiers and kill them only if necessary; Edward wanted them captured. All of the Ruala warriors were assigned to this mission as were Angus and Dagger who were going to rotate shifts supervising these plans.

Edward was turning his focus to King Fahra. Although none of the team members had seen the King or any member of the Royal Family since their arrival in Cadia, they certainly heard a great deal about them.

King Fahra was a middle aged man. His wife Queen Sitha was a few years his junior. These two were married at very young ages because of arrangements made between their families. Sitha was the daughter of Malcom and Renault. Malcom owned most of the mineral rights in Zorta although he lived in Port Friada.

Fahra and Sitha were basically children when they married. They grew up together and viewed each other more as brother and sister than husband and wife. They had very separate lives. They were educated separately and each had their own circle of friends. Of course they maintained an appearance of unity and performed their required functions but everything was a show for them.

The only thing that remotely united these two was parenthood. They had been ordered by their fathers to produce heirs to the thrown and as everything else they followed their orders. Fahra and Sitha were not in love but they did love their three sons, Shon, Corwin and Dagon.

Shon was the oldest at thirteen, Corwin was ten and Dagon was nine. Although these boys were loved and pampered they realized the rift between their parents and they heard the rumors.

Fahra was known as a man who enjoyed the company of women. His family lived in the royal castle but he had a separate mansion where he entertained his guests. Sitha was not jealous of his affairs, in fact they brought her relief because then she did not have to endure her husband.

While this information about the Royal Family was known throughout the Kingdom of Zorta, it did not pass the borders. As Edward was compiling an understanding of the Royal Family he changed the plans of his team.

Jasmine walked into Hector's bedroom a little after noon with a tray of food. Hector awoke when he heard her enter. As he was sitting up in bed he laughed. "There is enough food there for an army. Just how hungry did you think I would be?"

"I thought Mallory was with you so I brought lunch for her too."

"She was going to check on Clev then talk to Mother," Hector said and took a sip of his coffee.

"When was this?" asked Jasmine. "Because Tessa and I were at your parent's cottage helping them to unpack. We stayed here because after you rest we want you to walk around the grounds."

Hector was now sitting on the side of the bed. He was wearing little and had the blanket covering his lap. "You must be really healing because that crystal hasn't burned you," Jasmine said.

"Sit down and eat with me," Hector said and handed her one of the plates of food. "What are you talking about?"

"Your crystal necklace is made from the crystals of the Ice Caves. They have been blessed by The Great Ruler Himself. The holiness in them will heal you and will smoke if it comes in contact with darkness."

Hector took off the necklace and looked at it. "Mallory must have put this on me while I was sleeping. I wonder why." He refastened the necklace around his neck. "I wonder where she is."

"There is a lot going on, I am sure she is around here someplace." Jasmine walked across the room and picked up a small chair and carried it to the table that she had previously pushed up to Hector's bed. "You ass! Why didn't you tell us!"

"Tell you what? About the necklace?"

"That you got married."

"Jasmine, it may be the medicine but I don't know what the hell you are talking about."

"Don't lie to me. I can see the lamsman on your ankle. So why didn't you tell us?"

Hector pushed the small table away and turned so his legs were again on the bed. "Jasmine, I wasn't wearing this before. I have a really bad feeling. We need to find her."

The members of Edward's and Angus' teams were still staying at Hector's compound in Cadia. After the first couple of days in the city, Edward made many of the team members stay inside of the compound until he figured out what roles he wanted them to play.

Edward had five women on his team: Kate, Nana, Risa, Audrey and Marta. Kate was a Venator, Risa and Nana were Ruala warriors and Audrey and Marta were Nordes warriors. There were only three women on Angus' team and they were all Nordes warriors, Blanche, Celine and Lorna.

Edward did not want the presence of the Ruala warriors known in Cadia because dark lords and demons knew that race worked on behalf of The Great Ruler. He assigned Nana and Risa to work with the men who were searching for the Valdees.

Edward called a meeting with the six remaining women. "First, the good news. You are coming out of hiding and will be going to work," Edward said with a big grin. "But you may not like your assignment. I am still gathering information about King Fahra but I have learned that he and his wife do not love each other and he plays around a lot. All of you are going to be decoys."

"What do you mean, decoys?" asked Marta.

"We have to flirt with him and get close to him or his inner circle," Kate explained.

"Kate, you are in charge of that part of the mission," explained Edward. "Which means you need to work with the others to make sure they are prepared. I am still working on your cover stories but I plan to move all of you to one of the finest hotels."

"To get invited to the King's private celebrations all of you will need to look and act as if you are from money. Kate can help you with that. We have brought with us an extensive wardrobe of disguises and jewels but once all of you are ready you will need to be seen around the city. Which means lots of shopping."

"We've had so much down time that I have already been working with them," Kate said. "We're ready."

"Good because I want everything perfect; I don't have a good feeling about this. I have just heard too many inconsistencies, it is certainly possible that our presence is known here and you will be walking into a trap."

"You might want to turn around, I'm naked," Hector said to Jasmine.

"Aren't you always," she said jokingly and walked over to the chair where his clothing was piled. She picked everything up including his boots and carried them to the bed. Then she turned her back. "I don't know what you think you are going to do," she said. "You really look like hell. I think I will send someone to get Shara."

"There's a problem," Hector said and Jasmine turned around and faced him. "She took my knives. What the hell is she doing?"

"Hector, seriously you stay here, I'll be right back," Jasmine said, turned and ran out of the room.

Hector quickly finished dressing then he searched the room, thinking that Mallory might have left a note for him. Brock ran into the room so quickly that he inadvertently kicked the chair that Jasmine had been sitting in. "Tell me what happened?" he demanded.

"I'm not sure. She gave me my medicine which made me tired. She was going to give Clev his medicine then she was going to talk to Mother about our wedding. That is the last thing I remember. Jasmine woke me up and Mallory put her necklace and lamsman on me and took my knives. Do you have any idea what she is doing? I've been looking for a note."

Brock ran to the door and yelled, "Someone bring the Sanuri here now!" Then he turned to Hector. "Jasmine has everyone searching for her but they aren't going to find her."

"What are you saying?"

"Hector, I need you to listen to me and do as I tell you. You stay in this room and I will be right back and I will explain. In fact sit back down on the bed."

"What the hell are you talking about? I can't stay here."

"Look at the floor! Stay within that circle!" Brock yelled and ran out of the room.

For the first time Hector looked down at the floor and saw that a circle was drawn around his bed. He now was on the outside of that circle and walked up to it. He bent down and examined the thin line which was made of a finely ground powder. Hector picked some of it up and smelled it; he had no idea what it was.

Tessa and Noah ran into the room. "Get inside of that circle," yelled Noah. "I'll pick you up if I have to." Both he and Tessa had weapons drawn.

"What the hell is going on? Do you know where Mallory is?" Hector asked as he stepped inside of the circle.

"No, we have to wait for Brock," Noah said. As he spoke Tessa was searching the room. "Venatores are a very different lot. They are the ancient demon hunters of this world and they have always surrendered themselves to The Great Ruler. They have practices that are very spiritual and they can sense things that other humans can't."

Hector stared at Noah and the color drained from his face. "Angel!" yelled Hector. "Angel!" Others now ran into the room but no Angels appeared.

"Brock, she is trying to protect me somehow isn't she? Tell me!" demanded Hector.

"Stay inside of that circle," Brock snapped. "And let me work! And I need everyone to be quiet." Brock closed his eyes then slowly walked around the crowded room.

Everyone was amazed that he did not bump into a person or object. He maneuvered around the room as if he had sight. At certain spots he would hold up one or both of his hands in such a manner that it appeared that he was touching something.

Brock turned and walked to the bed. His eyes remained closed as he stepped over the circle and walked around the bed. He walked up to Hector and held up his hands then he crossed the circle and held up his hands then crossed it again and stood next to Hector.

"Erebus do you see anything?" Brock asked.

"No but there are different energy levels in this room. Do you mind if I step inside of the circle?"

"No, I was going to suggest that. Sanuri, what do you see?"

"Perhaps you should explain what you are seeing as everyone here is very anxious," said the Sanuri.

"In a way we are a people of the Spirit," Brock said. "It is difficult to explain but understand that is how the Shadow Men can exist. We train ourselves in many ways so that we are worthy of things that others do not believe in. It is obvious that Mallory sensed a great danger against Hector. She gave him her crystal and her lamsman and both acts are significant."

"The crystal is of the Spirit and the lamsman of this world. By giving him her lamsman they became one which allows her to work on his behalf. You might say it gives her rights that she would not otherwise have. And she took his weapons so she is going into battle."

"What is that stuff on the floor?" asked Tessa.

"It is soil from our burial grounds. She has asked that the spirits of our people which are the Shadow Men stand guard over Hector."

"Oh my god!" said Hector and quickly sat down on the bed. And just as quickly he stood up. "Angel! Angel!" he yelled. "Sanuri, look into my mind! Angel!"

Claudius had been standing in the doorway of the room. "Perhaps now would be the time to tell us what you saw on your journey."

Hector hesitated for a moment. "I saw the face of the Master then I saw a great battle. I think it was between the Master and the Sisterhood. Then, actually I am not sure if it was this world that I saw but everything was destroyed. It looked like a forest after a fire and I knew there was no life. That's it."

"That doesn't make sense," said Claudius. "You gave us your will. Did you think the threat was against you?"

"No," Hector said wearily and shook his head from side to side. "I was going to stop it. But I hadn't figured out how to yet. Brock, could Mallory have seen inside of my head?"

"She could if an Angel helped her," said Risha who appeared in the room.

"Risha?" asked Erebus. "You look so different. Is that you?"

"Yes, it is amazing how one transforms when they let go of their guilt. I am here because Mallory called to the Shadow Men. Hector when you saw that vision so did Mallory only she saw more of it. You can't go where she is but she is not alone."

"What do you mean I can't go?"

"You aren't worthy to go on a journey like this. Mallory understood that, although she was proud of you for wanting to. She has been given a great gift. Miranda is letting her hear the voices in your head. You have had them so long you don't distinguish them anymore."

"I am worthy for such a journey," Brock said. "Take me."

"I agree but that is not my decision," said Risha and looked at the Sanuri.

"Hector what are you going to do?" the Sanuri asked. "Your pregnant wife is fighting your battles."

"I know that," yelled Hector and everyone saw the rage within him.

"You have been at a crossroads for a long time," continued the Sanuri. "It is like you have one foot on either side of that circle. At some point you have to make a decision. The world will not wait for you; I think you understand that now."

"Did the Angels set this up to force me to decide?" Hector screamed.

"No," replied the Sanuri. "They have kept you alive to give you the chance to make a decision. Like all Venatores, Mallory is strong and fearless. She will do what you cannot but how will that change her views of you? What is really crippling you? All of these people have been caring for you and carrying you for some time now yet you get worse. You have powerful healers working on you, yet you get worse."

"Why do you think that Mallory has been so conflicted? She knows the darkness in you is killing you. You have such potential and yet you lie here in this bed as your body and soul dies. Why? Is it because you can't make a decision or you can't let go? Or is it because you do remember what you overheard and you know where the objects of power are hidden and the darkness in you desires them?"

"Hector is that true?" asked Seth. Hector didn't answer.

"You're disgusting," Tessa said. "After all of this...I just don't know what to say. I hope she takes back her lamsman when she returns."

"If she returns," said Dominic. "We need an Angel here!"

"Any particular one?" asked Cyril as he appeared. "My friends are rather busy."

"This is not Mallory's battle to fight. Let us help her," said Dominic. "Take us too."

"Some battles are earned," said Cyril.

"Then I have earned such a journey," said Brock boldly. "I will not let my sister walk that path alone." Cyril nodded and in that instant Brock disappeared from the room.

"Take us too," said Jasmine. Cyril, Risha, the Sanuri and Erebus disappeared. Jasmine jumped over the circle and punched Hector in the stomach then in the jaw. "I hate you! You are nothing but a coward. And if Mallory dies I will kill you!"

"You are going to have to stand in line," said Claudius. "Everyone leave us. Now!"

When the last person left the room, Claudius slammed the door shut then walked towards Hector. "You can't believe how badly I want to beat the crap out of you."

"Actually I can and I deserve it," said Hector.

Claudius stopped and took a couple of deep breaths as he suddenly remembered words that Miranda had once said to him. "Hector sit down." Claudius walked to a small table and poured two glasses of whiskey. He handed one to Hector. "Now son, you are going to do some explaining. And don't tell me you don't understand yourself, you are a brilliant man."

"I know you love Mallory and I know you are a courageous man but it is as if I am seeing you become more crippled before my eyes. Now you explain to me what it happening."

Hector sat down without speaking.

"What is worth allowing your pregnant wife to die?"

"Nothing!" Hector screamed then started to cry. "I don't know what is wrong with me. I feel like I am going crazy."

"Are you afraid of dying?"

"You know better than that."

"Actually, I don't know anything. You have been nothing but inconsistencies since we saved you. A lot of people have been hurt keeping you safe and...and what Hector? You tell me what the hell is going on and you tell me now!"

"Look at me," Hector said and held out his hand which was shaking. "I've been like this since I joined all of you. I thought it was the sicknesses at first. I'm in pain and I too thought that was the sicknesses."

"But when I went on that journey this morning and had that vision I suddenly felt whole again and that horrified me. I don't want to see the world destroyed."

"Was it the power to do that destruction that made you feel like that?"

"Yes. And when I realized that it made me sick. This morning is the first time that I realized I had an addiction. How else could the most horrible act in the world make me feel complete? Either that or I have more demons within me. I didn't tell you because I was ashamed."

"Then what is holding you back?"

"It's like my feet are nailed to the floor...no that doesn't explain it. That feeling I had was like euphoria. Do you understand what I am saying? I was in ecstasy at seeing something powerful enough to destroy the world. All of you have seen me as a monster; now I see myself that way. And the worst part is that I want that feeling back."

"I guess the real question is do you want it more than your wife and child."

"The Great Ruler forgive me but apparently I do because I know what I have to do to change this."

Claudius stared at Hector for he was lost for words. Hector was crying and Claudius sat down on a chair and continued to stare at him. Claudius gulped down his drink and said under his breath, "Miranda, I don't know how I can help him."

Chapter XLV
Shame

Brock was not surprised that Cyril transported him but he was surprised at where he found himself. He was standing in a jungle. There was nothing to be seen but foliage. He squatted so that his head would not be visible above the plants and looked at his surroundings. It was very humid and he started to sweat.

A moment later he felt a presence behind him. Brock quickly turned and pulled a knife from a sheath on his belt at the same time. "Sanuri," he whispered as he stopped himself from releasing the weapon. The Sanuri and Erebus both knelt down next to him. "Do you know where we are?" Brock asked.

"Inferus," whispered the Sanuri.

"Inferus?" repeated Brock. "Do you know if Mallory is here?"

"We weren't told anything," Erebus whispered. "I have been here before and something feels very different."

"We may not be in present time," the Sanuri whispered then held his hand up for the others to be silent.

The ground began to shake and the men lowered themselves in the foliage for concealment. A small army of Elod soldiers riding Stratas soon came into view. The soldiers of this kingdom were genetically bred to be huge men, considerably larger than a normal Elod.

"Telsor, you are finally going to get that promotion," one of the men said then laughed.

"I guess that depends on what is in that damn box," Telsor replied. "But Baruk won't be happy when he learns that so many of our men were killed. And you know the ones on top are going to find the bodies."

"Doesn't Andrac usually clean up those messes?" asked a third soldier.

"That was before," Telsor said. "After that Angel cursed him he spends all of his time in his work room."

"Well, I heard that he's the one who funded this mission," said the first soldier. "So you would think he would go to Langer and clean that mess up..." the soldiers were moving slowly because Stratas did not have the speed of horses. The Sanuri, Erebus and Brock did not hear the last of the conversation between the soldiers and they didn't want to move and possibly expose their locations.

After the soldiers were well out of sight Brock said, "I know who Andrac is but who is Baruk?"

"He is the leader of the Abuckto," explained the Sanuri. "The Abuckto were once the spiritual leaders of these people but they became corrupted by power and greed. They are the rulers of Inferus. Madeline said that many people feared the Abuckto were working with some of the sorcerers although they all profess to hate each other. I guess we know now."

"Well, you know the Angels wouldn't have dropped us here to overhear about that box if they didn't want us to go after it," said Erebus. "I just don't know if this is present time or last year when that Strata washed up on shore in Langer."

"Those men are giants and those creatures are huge, how could they ride around Langer without being seen?" asked Brock. "Can they breathe underwater? Maybe they fought the Valdees."

"They might have been cloaked by magic," said Erebus.

"Well then wouldn't you think their dead would be too?" asked Brock. "Sanuri, what are you doing?"

"I am trying to call to the birds with my mind but I am not connecting. I believe we are in present time or close to it. When the Angels saved the Elods they also saved the creatures. They left the monsters here and those who choose to serve them."

"The Angels sealed off the passageways to our world but if those soldiers were just in Langer we have some problems. The Sisterhood and Hector are near the city. And who knows if there are Valdees there too. This isn't a coincidence. Erebus do you think that some of the items in Juleta's arsenal can be sensed by others?"

"That is a real possibility and that would explain why all these groups seem to be converging on that area. We need to get that box. But first, do either of you sense the energy here?"

"The air seems thicker here," said Brock.

"That was the same as before," said Erebus. "This is different. This is very different."

Mallory had been returned to the area where Hector freed the souls of Juleta's victims. Earlier in the morning when all of the team members were there with Hector and Clev, Mallory realized she was hearing things that the others were not. And at that time she wondered if she was hearing what Hector heard.

Both Brock and Mallory had sensed a strange energy when they were with Hector and Clev and after the group was returned to Mathas' castle, Mallory sensed that energy again in Hector's bedroom. Because she did not know if something could hear her she spoke to Miranda with her mind.

Mallory did love Hector but she would not allow herself to get caught up in her feelings because she sensed the conflict within him and the danger that surrounded him. Mallory protected Hector the best that she could and called to Miranda to take her where his beasts dwelled.

"Miranda why is this so complicated?" asked Mallory as the two walked down the corridor that once held Juleta's trophies. "It is like we are working our way through the layers of Hector's life."

"That is exactly what we are doing," Miranda said. "Venatores tend to see things from different views than most people. But even your training does not prepare you for how incredibly complex humanity is. Hector started out as a very good man. He has exceptional intelligence which caused him to become bored with many things in his life."

"He is a talented man who tended to excel at whatever he put his mind to and this inflated his ego greatly. His ego became so inflated that it blinded him to many things."

"He knew on some level that he was different from others but at the time he knew so little of the world that he didn't realize what that really meant."

"You know he once studied to become a priest. A part of him never took it seriously although he excelled at his studies. He still does not know this but it was Otto, working for the Master who led Hector away from the priesthood. Otto had sold the souls of his children at their birth and he used them to entice Hector and put doubts in his mind. Joanna was the first woman he had sex with although they were both very young. Joanna was subtle as were Jack and Otto but they groomed Hector and graduation was the orgies."

"Hector was excited about his new sexual adventures but the real trap were the people in attendance. Hector was very popular at these gatherings because many of the players wanted the powerful young man. I tell you this because Hector was not only seduced by darkness but deceived by it long before he realizes."

"I don't understand. Was he a victim?"

"And that is a very gray area. In many ways he was. Yet he knew how to protect himself spiritually and physically. His ego did not let him realize the danger he was in. At any time he could have prayed for help and he knew that. In some ways he was a victim of himself."

"So is it that we have to deal with demons at every layer?"

"In a way. Every human is a product of their lives to that point in time. Their choices, fears, desires and so much more all build upon each other. I know this is confusing you. You use the word layers and that is a good analogy. Using that concept, let's just say there were seeds planted on every layer."

"But even if we can clean out all those seeds, will he make the right choices?"

"I cannot give you an answer."

"You won't or you can't."

"I don't know that answer yet. You are already planning a life for you and your baby without him yet you gave him your lamsman, why?"

"I wanted to protect him. I do love him and I have told him that we will marry but I just can't understand how it will work."

"Why don't you think it will work?"

"I am afraid that he will choose the demons and darkness again."

"He has changed a great deal and he loves you."

"Miranda, I am not a fool. It is like I see him dying before my eyes. I know this has been difficult for both him and Clev but I sense there is more. I think the darkness is sabotaging his healing."

"And what darkness would that be?"

Mallory thought about the question for a few moments. "I don't really know. It seems that most of the demons would want him to be strong except for Juleta who was trying to destroy him."

"The darkness you are talking about is guilt and fear and you are right. We are here now."

Miranda stopped before a door in the marble corridor. Mallory pulled two knives from their sheaths. The door opened. Mallory only saw darkness then the interior of the room lit up and she heard voices.

"It is not what you think," said Miranda. "You may enter."

Mallory stood in awe as she watched a scene from another time. "I know that place," she gasped as she watched four little boys playing. The boys had fastened a rope to a large tree limb and they were using it to swing over a pond. They would jump from the rope into the water below. They were having fun and laughing loudly.

"Who are they?" asked Mallory.

585

"Matthew, Stephan, Timothy and Hector."

"What is making the shadow? I don't see anything that could make that."

"Keep watching."

Mallory was distracted from the shadow by a movement. She turned her gaze and saw a little girl hiding in the brush watching the boys. After a few moments the girl came out of hiding and walked up to the pond. "I want to play too," she said.

"Juleta get out of here, we don't want you here," yelled one of the boys.

"Girls aren't allowed," yelled another.

"I hate you!" Juleta yelled.

"Good because we all hate you," a boy yelled.

The boys continued to swing over the water as Juleta stood on the edge of the pond and mumbled.

"What is she saying?" asked Mallory.

Juleta's voice grew louder so that Mallory could hear it; the boys in the scene did not. "I curse you! I curse you!" she kept repeating.

"She's just a little..."Mallory stopped talking and watched as one of the boys started to scream for help and acted like something was pulling him down in the water. The other boys did not hesitate and jumped in to save Timothy. When they pulled him to shore he had claw marks on his ankles. Timothy was crying as Juleta laughed.

"She's a witch," screamed Timothy.

Stephan jumped up and grabbed a handful of small rocks and threw them at Juleta.

"Leave her alone," yelled Matthew and stared at the water.

"Oh my god!" said Mallory. "She didn't hide that little girl's body by the pond, she took it there as an offering. What is in that water?"

"That is where the beasts began. Five children whose lives will greatly affect your world. Matthew is one of The Seven Sons and a Keeper of the Scrolls. Stephan chose to work with Matthew and Stephan is a powerful man in his own right. Timothy who listened to the voices of demons until they destroyed him. Hector who has consistently made the wrong choices. And a little girl who is so evil that her body can't contain it."

"Was she born a dark lord?"

"She was born a monster."

"How did Mathas and Rosa not see that?"

"Mathas was away at war. Rosa grieved the loss of her first baby for a very long time. Juleta was the first born to them who lived. They saw her through eyes of love and attributed much of her behavior to being a child."

"Miranda, are you showing me this to warn me about the child that I carry?"

"No. We have heard your prayers and those of Rosa, Catherine and Clarence. Your son will be born a normal child. Of course like everyone else he will have his choices to make."

"Thank you. So if this is where it began then all of them were cursed and there is something in that water. Hector said he hasn't been here for a long time. Is whatever is in that water affecting him?"

"It affects them all and they don't realize it."

"Wait! Is this the place of her beginning too?

"It is the first time she really understood the power she had."

"So then that is a place of great importance to her. Some of her arsenal is down there isn't it?" Miranda did not answer. "Thank you, I will get it."

587

"No, it should be the boys who get it. They have to face their shadows. But…"

"But what?" Mallory fearfully. "Has something else happened to Hector?"

"We have spoken of him yet you do not mention his addiction. Why is that?"

"I don't really understand it and that makes me fear it."

"It is his shadow. He is losing the war to it."

"Miranda, I really don't understand. That scene, they were all cursed and what…they became filled with fear? And they have to face those fears?"

"They were touched by pure evil. As a child you were trained to identify it and resist it. These children were not. They will not want to admit that is where their nightmares began. When you return, others will want to get what is down there but it must be Matthew, Stephan and Hector."

"But Hector isn't strong enough to do that."

"You have no idea how right you are."

"Miranda, please it is like you are talking in riddles. Can just Matthew and Stephan get it?"

"It should be all three."

"Will you heal him enough to get it?"

"Return and tell the others what you saw."

"What is going on?" yelled Mallory as she appeared in Hector's bedroom.

"Mallory are you alright?" Hector asked as he rushed to her. He hugged and kissed her over and again.

"Yes but I have much to tell all of you but why are you bleeding?"

"Your husband was having a temper tantrum," said Claudius who was still sitting in a chair. Mallory looked around the room and saw that all of the mirrors were broken and had blood on them.

"I don't understand," she said.

"He can explain later," said Claudius. "Where have you been?"

"Miranda showed me a scene when Matthew, Stephan, Hector and Timothy were boys. That is when the curses began. Claudius we need to get Matthew and Stephan here because the three of them have to do something together. It is very important but it might be dangerous. Are they in the castle?"

"I don't think so," Claudius said as he stood up.

"Get them and call everyone for a meeting and I will explain. Mathas should be there too," Mallory said then she turned to Hector. "And you better pull yourself together because you are needed to do this thing and if you can't then you pray for help. Don't you give me that look! We are having a son and it would be nice if his father lived long enough to meet him."

Claudius laughed. "Hector listen to your wife; she makes more sense than you do." Claudius started for the door then turned to Mallory. "Did the Sanuri and others come back with you?"

"What are you talking about?" asked Mallory.

"Brock wanted to go on your journey with you and called to the Angels. Cyril took him, Erebus and the Sanuri."

"And Risha," said Hector.

"I haven't seen any of them. I've been with Miranda."

After Claudius left, Hector said to Mallory, "I have somethings to confess to you."

"Perhaps we should wait on that. Hector, what you are about to do is very important and it might be terrifying for you. Now let me clean up your hands. I suspect you will need to fight. I asked if I could go in your place but Miranda said it had to be you."

"And that is the last time you will ask that," Hector said sternly.

"Then you start taking the responsibility. You are letting the darkness in you slowly kill you. You have a child and another on the way aren't they worth living for? You are notorious as a fighter yet you fold to your inner fears. Our training teaches us to destroy them first because they are more dangerous than the demons we hunt. Whatever you need to do to get control of yourself do it now! I mean it Hector because if you don't Matthew and Stephan might die."

"Cyril," whispered Brock. "Is Mallory here?"

"No," said Risha as she appeared next to the three men. "She is safe and on another very important mission. I have requested to help you."

"Is your sister's book in that box?" asked the Sanuri.

"No, something much worse. Juleta was experimenting with the potions that Naomi developed. The vials from her experimentations are in that box. They were hidden in the ocean near Langer. Andrac spends much of his time with demons these days. He learned that a group of Valdees soldiers were guarding a box near Langer. The Elods and the Valdees fought. Andrac used powerful old magics to assist the Elods in that battle. He does not know what is in that box but as deranged as he is he will use the chemicals to kill."

"We heard the soldiers say they are taking the box to Baruk," said Erebus. "He was the one who sent the soldiers."

"Then we must hurry," Risha said.

Thirty minutes later the teams and others were in the Great Hall of Mathas' castle. Mallory walked to the front of the room. "I am going to keep this brief because I feel there is an urgency here."

"When we went on that journey this morning with Hector and Clev, I was hearing some of the voices in Hector's head and I felt a strange energy which I again felt later in his bedroom. I protected him and asked Miranda to take me to his beasts."

"I expected a battle but instead she showed me something from the past. Matthew, Stephan, Hector and Timothy were playing at that pond near the castle. They had tied a rope to a tree and were swinging over the water then they would jump in. While the boys played I saw a huge shadow watching them. I saw nothing that could make that shadow."

"Then I saw a little girl in the bushes. It was Juleta and she was watching the boys. She walked to the pond and told them she wanted to play. All of the boys yelled for her to leave and ridiculed her. She started to curse them and suddenly something in the water grabbed Timothy and started to pull him under. The other boys saved him. That was the moment when Juleta realized her powers and that was the moment when the curses against them began."

"There is something powerful in that pond because that little girl that Juleta killed was placed in those rocks as an offering; Juleta wasn't just hiding that body. That was a spot of great importance to her. Miranda said that Matthew, Stephan and Hector have to go into that pond. I asked to go in Hector's place and she said it should be those three. I didn't ask her but I felt that this is going to be very dangerous."

"I don't remember that," said Matthew.

"Neither do I," said Stephan.

"Me neither," Hector said.

"When all of you saved Timothy his ankles had claw marks on them and were bleeding," Mallory added.

"I remember that," said Fahron as he stood up. "He came home crying and wouldn't tell us what had happened. Mallory are you saying that is why he ended up as he did?"

"Fahron, that I don't know. But that moment in time was significant to them all."

"I want to understand this," said Thaos. "Miranda said that no one could go in their place but did she say that no one could join them?"

"We didn't talk about that. I don't know."

"We'll Juleta has cursed me more than most so I think I've earned the right to join them," Thaos said.

"Are you going because you're afraid I can't hold up my end?" asked Hector.

"No but now that you mention it you do look like hell."

"Mallory said that Miranda will give me what I need and I am going to ask her. I'm not putting my friends in danger."

"Good to hear but I am still going."

"Guys, I can't tell you why but I think we need to do this soon," said Mallory. "So no fighting and everyone do what you need to do."

"The rest of us can be there can't we?" asked Mathas.

"She didn't say that you couldn't," Mallory said. "And when this is done I am going after Brock."

"We all are," said Hector and walked out of the room.

"Miranda, I know I don't deserve it but will you make me whole again so I can do this?"

"You are right, you don't deserve it," Miranda said as she appeared in the small room. "And what do you want me to do?"

Hector looked surprised by her question. "I'm not sure. I need my strength back." The two stared at each other for a few moments.

"You can do better than that," she said.

"Mallory said the darkness in me is killing me."

"We don't have all day. Stop playing with words. Why did you break those mirrors?"

"Because I was ashamed," Hector said in a low voice.

"Now that is an honest answer. Keep going."

"I was ashamed because I think I desire power more than protecting my family. More than anything."

"So why did you break the mirrors?"

"Because I hate myself and I," he paused and looked at the floor. "I wanted to kill the me I saw."

"Now we are getting somewhere. So I ask you again what do you want me to do to help you?"

"Stop my desire for power."

"And what else?"

"Help me to rise above my fears."

"We will talk again."

Chapter XLVI
Pandora's Box

"Are you ready?" Stephan yelled when Hector returned to the Great Hall.

"Yes," he said as the tears ran down his cheeks.

Everyone had been saddling horses while Hector spoke with Miranda. The group now left the castle.

"Hector is Miranda coming with us?" asked Tessa.

"I don't know."

"Miranda," called Claudius. "You are welcome to join us."

"You are learning," her voice was heard by all the people riding to the pond.

"Miranda, after this is over I want to know how those curses affected our sons," said Claudius.

"That will come," she replied.

Claudius motioned for the group to surround the pond. Stephan, Thaos, Matthew and Hector dismounted. They all had knives in various sheaths on their bodies.

"Miranda, will you help us remember?" asked Matthew. And in that instant they all saw the scene that Miranda had shown to Mallory. Only now Miranda showed them more of the past. They saw images of Juleta as a little girl of different ages standing by the pond and talking. They could not see who she was speaking to nor could they hear her words.

They watched as she brought dead animals to the pond as offerings then murdered children. Mathas wept. "Miranda, let us hear the words she is saying," he said as the tears ran down his face. "Who is she talking to?"

"What did she say?" asked Fahron.

"She called it Nimbi. Is that right?" asked Stephan. "Did I hear that right?"

"Be quiet," scolded Jasmine.

They watched as Juleta stood next to the pond and carried on conversations as if she was talking with a friend. They could hear no voice besides hers but they all saw the gigantic shadow that Mallory had seen.

"The demon casting that is powerful," Mallory commented.

"She's not saying Nimbi," said Angelina. "She's saying Naomi, Risha's sister, the high priestess of the Sisterhood. But she died centuries ago?"

"That shadow is a demon," said Mallory. "It may be tricking Juleta."

The images disappeared. Matthew, Stephan, Hector and Thaos all took off their boots as they prepared to go into the water.

"If you are to reenact this, I will play Timothy's role," said Fahron. He took off his military jacket which was heavy with medals and his boots. Dominic handed him an additional knife which Fahron stuck in his belt.

As the men walked towards the shoreline Mallory said loudly, "Miranda protect them!"

The men lined up. Matthew gave the command and they all jumped into the water simultaneously. They all disappeared and the water started to churn. Giant bubbles covered the surface then waves. Mallory started to run towards the water but Turner grabbed her and held her tightly. He ended up lifting her feet off the ground as she sought to get out of his grasp.

The clear blue water turned black and none of the men had come up for air. A wind started to blow. Debris from the ground started to swirl. Branches and leaves fell from the trees. The ground trembled and the horses became agitated.

"Miranda do they need help?" Seth asked. She did not answer. Seth started to take off his boots.

"No," said Claudius. "I think they need to break the spell."

"Well, if we don't see them soon, we are all going in," said Dominic and pulled off his boots.

"Get back!" yelled Garvis as a large box flew into the air and landed on the shore.

"Don't touch it yet," Mathas yelled.

"What is going on?" yelled Sorren as he and Shara rode up to the group.

"Another!" yelled Bart. A second box flew out of the water and landed on shore.

"We can't explain now," Claudius yelled to Sorren. "But glad you are here."

A third box then a fourth flew out of the water. After the fourth box landed on the ground screams were heard coming from the water. The shaking of the ground became more and more violent. Horses were rearing on their hind legs and screaming.

"Mother did you bring your medical bag?" Angelina yelled fearfully.

"Yes," Shara said and dismounted.

"Oh my god!" yelled Tessa as she watched Matthew fly into the air and fall to the ground. Fahron was next. The people on the shore ran to these men. Stephan, Hector and Thaos all flew out of the water at the same time and landed on the shore.

Stephan laughed loudly, "Now that was a good fight."

"What threw you out?" asked Fennel as he helped the men stand up. "Are there more demons down there?"

"It wasn't a demon that tossed us," Thaos said with a grin. "It was Adam. Guess we opened a door to a hell world."

"They're fine," Shara announced of Matthew and Fahron.

"What's in the boxes?" asked Bart.

"Don't know but these huge creatures were guarding them," Matthew said. "Miranda can we open them?"

"Set them side by side," said Miranda as she appeared among them. "Hector."

Hector and Mallory were hugging and kissing each other. He now looked up. "Honey, I have to go," he said to Mallory and walked to one of the boxes which he picked up. "Where do you want it?"

"There," said Miranda and pointed at an area on the ground.

The boxes were identical. They were all made of a light weight metal that had a green patina. Each box was about a foot square. There were no obvious markings on them.

Hector took three steps and started to sweat profusely then he started to shake. At first it was just his hands but by time he moved the box to the location that Miranda had indicated his entire body was exhibiting erratic movements. The people stared at him but no one spoke and neither did Hector. He set the box near the feet of the Angel.

"Have you had those reactions before?" Miranda asked. Hector nodded. "Speak so that the others may hear you."

"Yes," he said in a hoarse voice.

"When have you had them?" Miranda asked. Hector did not speak. "Answer the question."

"When I am near something of great power or well, it's power."

"Has anyone here seen these reactions before?" asked Miranda.

"That is what Erebus gets like when he touches magic things," Sorren said. "And that is because of his addiction."

"Hector do you question now that you have an addiction?" asked Miranda.

"I've known."

"Do you know when it started?"

Hector was surprised at Miranda's question. "I've never thought about that. Let me try and think."

"While he is trying to remember," said Miranda. "Fahron pick up a box and set it next to this one."

Fahron grabbed a box and didn't complete the first step before he stopped in his tracks. "Miranda, what is happening?"

"Just carry the box over here then tell us what you see."

As Fahron walked his eyes grew wide at the images that were running through his mind. He set the box to the left of Hector's. "I saw faces of demons and heard voices, it sounded like hundreds of voices."

"Both of you stand by those boxes. Stephan, it is your turn," said Miranda.

Stephan was not smiling anymore as he picked up a box and walked towards Miranda. He did not speak and looked confused. He set the box to the left of Fahron's. "Miranda, I don't know if I understand what I saw," Stephan said. "I expected to see monsters but I saw my, well my dating life."

Miranda did not speak to Stephan. "No Matthew not you. Mathas, you pick up the next box."

Mathas picked it up then immediately dropped it on the ground. "Sorry, it burned my hands," he said and picked it up again. "I see monsters," he said as he set the box to the left of Stephan's.

"Mallory please come up here," Miranda said. "Do not touch any of the boxes." Miranda looked at the faces in the crowd. "When Mallory explained the journey we took she did not go into great detail. She told you the points that she considered the most important but she did not understand what she saw."

"Mallory stand next to me so that you are facing everyone. The boy Timothy what was he yelling at Juleta?"

Mallory paused for a moment before she spoke. "He said they all hated her. He repeated that several times. He called her a witch and after he was attacked he said he was going to tell his father what she did."

"He said something else," Miranda said.

"That witches are bad and she was going to burn in hell," Mallory said. "Oh my god! You said this is where their nightmares started. He turned into a monster that served the demons."

"Fahron, from that day Timothy was haunted by those images and voices that you saw and heard," Miranda said. "Many of us came to him and told him to pray and to allow us to help him and every time he refused," Miranda explained then turned back to Mallory. "What did Hector say?"

"He was telling Timothy that she was too stupid to have power. He said she was crazy and he told her they didn't want her around them. She did this to him didn't she?"

Miranda did not answer the question but asked, "What happened concerning Stephan?"

"Timothy said that she was there spying on Stephan because she liked him. Then Hector started to tease Stephan and he said that he could never like her and that he hated her."

"Stephan, you thought that your conflict over Ingr was because you didn't want to give up your lifestyle which had basically separated you from everyone you cared about. Juleta wanted to curse you with a loveless life. She wanted you and if she couldn't have you she was not going to allow someone else to. That is why she became enraged when she learned of your relationship with Ingr. The Sanuri did not understand the entire situation but he saw the lock on your heart and healed you in many ways."

"Mallory, what did Matthew say?" asked Miranda.

"Nothing bad. He told the other boys to leave her alone."

"Matthew always stood up for his sister. He did not like her but he loved her and sought to protect her. And for a very long time Juleta felt a bond with him but as the darkness grew in her it broke all of her bonds. But as much as she once cared for Matthew she was always jealous of him. He was well liked and had many friends. He excelled at almost everything he did and he would someday sit on the throne of Lentz. Mathas did you and Juleta ever speak about her assuming the throne?"

"All of the time. Even as a small child she wanted to be...Miranda her curse was on me wasn't it?" Miranda nodded. "Is that why I can't see her as she really was?"

"She hated you the most," Miranda explained. "And yet at the same time she greatly desired your attention and approval. She wanted you to look upon her as you did Matthew. And she realized that your biggest weakness was your love for your family. That was how she would cripple you. Those monsters you saw were the faces of your daughter."

"Miranda free me, free us all of these curses," begged Mathas. "And how do I atone for what she did to Timothy?"

"First, let me explain a few things," said Miranda. "I asked Mallory what she saw in that scene. We discussed the shadow. And the fact that every one of those children was considerably more powerful than most and would make incredible choices someday. That shadow represented the demons and the groups who have been watching all of you for a very long time."

"Fahron, you will not like to hear this but Timothy did not become a monster because of Juleta, she opened a door for him. He was already listening to the voices that the other boys dismissed. But you have more children now and you must protect them. Now you know what to do."

"Mathas you can only ask for your own healing. Each of you will have to tell me what you want."

Mallory walked away from Miranda and stood next to Hector and held his hand. He started to laugh. "I am sorry but she is breaking my fingers. Miranda, I want to be healed."

"You understand it will cause you great discomfort?"

"It can't be worse than what I have already gone through. And don't let me slide back."

Miranda did not speak but looked at Fahron. "I want healing and protection for my family."

"I want healing," Stephan said. "But I will admit that I am a little confused by this. I want healing and protection for all of our families."

"I ask for healing," Mathas said. "And forgiveness. I should have seen through this. Miranda, I don't know exactly how to say this but can you give me clear sight?"

The boxes disappeared. "Now you are ready to go to war," Miranda said.

I stumbled through the darkness
The thickness of the wall
That I had built to bind me
To perpetuate the fall

I fell and no one listened
No one heard me call
Because the boundaries that we built
Perpetuated the fall

As I lay there dying
I was touched with Holy Grace
By an Angel who heard me crying
In the darkness of this place

By Sandra J Yearman
As Angels Hover Over ©2008

Glossary of Characters

Aaron: an escaped prisoner from Wetpr

Aaryan: a male Grand Master of the Insidiae

Abaddon: an ancient demon/one of the Old Ones

Abbott: an Elod/a member of the Charto/

Abekk: the ancient leader of the Clan of Elods, author of the Prophesy of Isto

Abella: daughter of Prince Lakin and Princess Zada/Ruala

Abigail: sister of Marie/ nurse for grandchildren of King Sudfad

Abigale: a waitress in Langer

Abrass: a demon from the World of Planteen

Abraxas: the demon that Hector sold his soul to

Ackley: hired fighter for Mayor Deckor of Langer

Ackly: an arms dealer in Ryed

Ada: demon midwife to Nada

Ada: neighbor of Milt and Penny/wife of Thronson

Adam James: a notorious pirate

Adam: an emissary of The Great Ruler who takes on the disguise of a human man

Adam: Nordes child/brother of Celia

Addison: one of three notorious gang leaders in Taperia

Adi: son of Elen and Batya/ Ruala

Adin: male Ruala warrior

Adler: a male Nordes warrior

Adrone: youngest son of Joshua and Iris/younger brother of Vivian/Clan of Gesmal

Adwell: Prince/ son of King Zachariah and Queen Noella of New Samona/husband of Nada/father of Misha/ Adwell was killed in battle leaving Nada to raise ten children/Ruala/

Ael: an ancient demon/ one of the Old Ones

Aetes: Shettee warrior

Agnes: owner of the Midnight Tavern in Stoba Lentz/wife of Bert

Agnus: a captain in the covert organization The Guardians

Ahriman: an ancient demon/ one of the Old Ones

Aiden: five year old Ruala boy/son of Artis and Jenna/nephew of Ratri

Akasha: former king of Ryed/grandfather of Nehmota

Alex: Nordes warrior/brother of Corsa, Kent and George

Alexander: former servant of King Roch's parents/ father of Annabelle

Alexander: one of the twin sons of Simon and Annabelle

Alexandras: King of Wetpr/brother of Jaretta/uncle of Sudfad and Roch

Alexas Rose: daughter of Matthew and Angelina

Alexis: son of Usman, the leader of the Valdore Tribe

Alice: and her husband find Jorge near death in Nora

Alicia: a female Nordes warrior

Aloeus: Shettee warrior

Amelia: baby Ruala girl

Amiee: sister of Marie/ nurse for grandchildren of King Sudfad

Amper: a Florine

Amundsen: Commanding General of Fort Friada in the Kingdom of Ganz

Amy: a young girl who was kidnapped by Sal

Ana: eleven year old Nordes girl/daughter of Edgar and Cora/younger sister of Batina

Ana: Princess/daughter of Zeman and Oda/niece of King Manu of New Samona/Ruala

Anda: one of Chief Romogi's three wives/Huta

Andrac: a powerful sorcerer and seer in the Kingdom of Inferus/Elod

Andre Wilchess: son of Chet and Darlene/ husband of Joanna Franks/ brother of Philip

Andrea: female Ruala warrior/ sister of Bekka

Andres: Princess of Ryed/daughter of Oren and Astrel/ has twin sister Jorga

Andrew: jeweler in Salar

Andrus: father of Rabi/Ruala

Angelina: daughter of Sorren, Chief of the Nordes Tribe/female warrior

Anka: Elod child

Annabar: daughter of King Sharonne

Annabelle: handmaid and best friend to Queen Vitomas of the Kingdom of Stordt

Annie: female Nordes warrior/ girlfriend of Terrance

Anthony: one of the twin sons of Simon and Annabelle

April: a young girl who was kidnapped by Sal

Arca: Enrop leader who protects King Mathas' family

Archer: Hector's true identity

Arches: a Patronus priest

Archetenus The Brave: Captain in the Taperian Army

Argail: a homeless mother

Arianna: daughter of Simon and Annabelle

Ariel: daughter of Raul and Vitomas

Arland: male Nordes Warrior

Arlene: housekeeper and cook for Erebus/wife of Theodore

Arlene: wife of Dixon/friend of Olivia

Armstrong: soldier and scout in the army of Wetpr

Arthur Marcus: father of Hannah

Artis: an old sailor from the Navy of Ganz

Artis: male Ruala warrior/oldest brother of Ratri/husband of Jenna

Asgar: an Old One on the planet Filsum

Asher: male Ruala warrior

Asher: youngest of three brothers who formed the Libertas in Ryed

Ashlee: young female Nordes warrior

Asmodeus: an ancient demon/ one of the Old Ones

Astar: General in the Military of Ryed who tries to take over the kingdom after the fall of Teivel

Astrel: former princess of Ryed/daughter of Akasha and Norah

Atomos: Elder of the Centras and Keeper of the Box of Itifer

Audrey: a female Nordes warrior on Edward's team

Augustus Endleson: a wealthy businessman who owned part of the City of Nora

Ava: twin of Benjamin/daughter of Archetenus and Delilah

Axel Sam: a notorious pirate

Azu: a Florine

Baal: an ancient demon/ one of the Old Ones

Babu: Enrop

Bac: male Ruala warrior

Bachnenus: warrior guarding refugees/Shettee

Baird: an Elod/a member of the Charto/

Bali: Enrop leader of the flock that does battle at Juleta's castle

Balin: Prince of Norkv/son of Thaddius and Omara/grandson of Benjeman and Esther

Balius: Shettee warrior/brother of King Neputa

Banacus: General in the army of King Tobias of Puntd

Banaka: a female Grand Master of the Insidiae

Barak: Prince of Norkv/grandson of Benjeman and Esther

Barak: Prince/son of King Neputa and Queen Tiara/Shettee

Barid: Prince of Ogg

Barid: Prince of Ryed/son of Nehmota and Vasart

Barnabas: a member of the wealthy and elite in Ryed

Bart: male Elod/member of Javier's and Madeline's team

Bart: male Ruala warrior/ married to Bekka's sister Andrea

Bartholomew: alias used by Raphael in Ryed

Baruk: the leader of the Abuckto Sect in the Kingdom of Inferus/Elod

Barush: a major in the Military of Ryed

Bastine: one of three notorious gang leaders in Taperia

Bastra: Huta captain

Batina: young female Nordes warrior

Batya: wife of Elen/Ruala

Beatrice Endleson: wife of Augustus

Beatrice: an Elod healer

Becca: Princess of Norkv/daughter of Thaddius and Omara/granddaughter of Benjeman and Esther

Behtay: Princess/daughter of Segal and Cahina/niece of King Manu of New Samona/Ruala

Bekka: female Ruala warrior

Bella: wife of Claudius and mother of Stephan

Benedict: leader of the Credo in Inferus/father of Anka, Santi and Linus/husband of Cyrene/ Elod

Benedict: Prince of Norkv/son of Benjeman and Esther

Benix: boss of Ivan/ from the Kingdom of Inferus

Benjamin: twin of Ava/son of Archetenus and Delilah

Benjeman: vicious rebel leader who overthrew the government of Samona

Benny: adopted son of Fahron and Isadore

Benson: a Private in the Wetprian military

Bentra: an ancient demon/ one of the Old Ones

Benza: ancient chief of the Venatores

Bert: owner of the Midnight Tavern in Stoba Lentz/husband of Agnes

Berta: cook at Racing Horse Tavern

Berta: Queen of Stordt/wife of Micha/grandmother of Roch and Sudfad

Bertha: an elderly woman from Nora

Bertuck: the demon who Usman sold his soul

Bethany: female Ruala healer

Betsy Sarbush: wealthy socialite in the City of Langer in the Kingdom of Lentz

Betty: a woman from Nora

Betu: male Ruala warrior

Bianca: young female Nordes warrior

Bill: a member of the Taperian City Board

Bill: owner of a butcher shop in Stoba Lentz

Bishop: General in the Army of Lentz

Black Jack: a regular patron at the Ghost Ship Tavern in Port Friada

Blackjack: works for Hector

Blanche: a female Nordes warrior on Angus' team

Bode: Shettee warrior

Boris: a general in the Military of Ryed

Botis: a demon

Brandon: Nordes child/son of Marsha and Kyle/nephew of Jasmine

Bremmer: an arms dealer in Ryed

Brent: a soldier from Lentz who fights in the Gefrey Games in Ryed

Brik: son of Prince Lakin and Princess Zada /Ruala

Brina: Princess of Norkv/daughter of Valor and Cai/granddaughter of Benjeman and Esther

Brinkman: Admiral of naval yard at Silth

Brit: male Nordes warrior

Brock: male Venator

Bruce: male Nordes warrior/eldest son of Edgar and Cora/older brother of Batina

Bryce: male Ruala warrior

Burto: high priest of the Abuckto in the Kingdom of Inferus

Cabal: son of Karzman and Nadia

Cabot: an Elod/a member of the Charto/

Cacu: Enrop leader that joined Raul and Simon on a mission

Cade: son of King Pergo and Queen Vinus/ Kingdom of Gandt

Cadi: daughter of Prince Hadar and Princess Paj/ granddaughter of Manu/Ruala

Cadmus: the demon that the Dura Tribe worships

Cael: Shettee boy who is adopted by Thedes and Ibula

Cage: male Ruala warrior

Cahina: Princess/ married to Segal son of King Zachariah and Queen Noella of New Samona/Ruala

Cai: Princess of Norkv/wife of Valor who was the son of Benjeman and Esther

Cal: male Nordes warrior

Caleb: son of Luca and Natalie

Calen: male Ruala warrior/cousin of Luca/son of Maxwell and Emeral/

Calla: female Ruala warrior

Callie: Nordes child/younger sister of Bianca/daughter of Tyler and Dora

Calus: a dark lord/member of the Insidiae

Calvin: a desk clerk at The Captain's Retreat Hotel in Port Friada

Campbell: one of the spies at the Castle at Wetpr

Canton: Cisero's second in command

Captain Morgan: Wetprian Military/Fort Serpha

Cara: Princess of Ogg

Carl: a drifter/travels with Zeke, Sam and Johnny

Carlsman: a Lieutenant in the Army of Lentz

Carlson: Sergeant in the Wetprian Army

Carlton: alias used by Archetenus in Ryed

Carson Dormors: a wealthy landowner in the Kingdom of Ganz

Carson: male Nordes warrior/ husband of Marlas/ father of Lana, Tanya, Norris, Terrance, Dalton, Lola and Curtis

Carson: Sergeant in the Wetprian Army

Carston: member of the governing body of Nora

Casey: male Ruala warrior/father of Melanie/husband of Tasha

Cass: one of Hectors' men

Cassandra: female Ruala warrior

Cassidy: homeless boy

Cates: alias used by Sorren in Ryed

Catherine: second wife of Clarence/ stepmother of Archer

Cedrick Teivel: a ruthless, powerful man in the Kingdom of Ryed

Celia: Nordes child/sister of Adam

Celine: a female Nordes warrior on Angus' team

Celo: Prince of Ryed/son of Oren and Astrel

Cere: daughter of Tristt/Shettee

Cerephus: General in the Taperian Army

Cerey: orphan girl/sister of Nicholas/adopted daughter of Gabriel and Hannah

Ceria: Princess/daughter of Gunnel and Uma/niece of King Manu of New Samona/ sister of Elan/Ruala

Chaez: son of Fahron

Chaladrone: an ancient demon/ one of the Old Ones

Chalice: hired fighter for Dieter

Chalta: daughter of King Pergo and Queen Vinus/ Kingdom of Gandt

Chance: works with the Patronus

Chara: three year old Ruala girl/ daughter of Orin and Rene/niece of Ratri

Charlene: a woman from Nora

Charles Moses: a violent and abusive man

Charles: Father of Cassandra, Joao and Melinda

Charles: hired farmhand of Arthur Marcus

Charter: Colonel in the Military of Ryed

Chasity: missing sister of Joey and Tommy

Chet Wilchess: husband of Darlene/ father of Philip and Andre/rich businessman in Port Friada

Chet: owns a company of barges in the Village of New Flounder in the Kingdom of Zorta

Chief Romogi: leader of the Hutas/ Kingdom of Marba

Christopher: six year old boy who Luca saves from the Hutas/brother of Lila

Ciao: female Ruala warrior

Cicely: adopted daughter of Elan and Cassandra

Cisero: a member of the Insidiae

Clair: a woman from Nora

Clair: female Ruala warrior/mother of Ratri/wife of Joseph

Clarence: Father of Archer/ wealthy nobleman/ husband of Matilda then Catherine

Claudius: General in the Army of Lentz

Clay: the manager of the Teivel Manor Hotel in Ryed

Clem: a drunk who works odd jobs

Cleo: a man who works for Cicero/a vessel

Cleta: female Ruala warrior who fought in Ryed

Clev: Hector's head lieutenant

Clifford: a general in the Military of Ryed

Cobren: Prince of Norkv/son of Grace and Makalo/Grandson of Benjeman and Esther

Cody: orphan boy

Collins: Lieutenant in the Army of Ganz

Compro: Taperian soldier injured at Wall of Dorath

Conrad: father of Jasmine/husband of Leta/Nordes Tribe

Conway: nickname Connie/homeless barber from Castor

Cook: General in the Military of Wetpr

Cora: mother of Batina/wife of Edgar/Nordes warrior

Corina: young female Nordes warrior

Corsa: female Nordes warrior/healer

Corwin: son of King Fahra and Queen Sitha of Zorta

Crater: a Sergeant in the Wetprian army

Crater: a soldier in the army of Wetpr

Crispus: a guard at King Roch's castle

Crocell: a demon

Cronn: a demon

Cronos: Shettee warrior

Crowley: Admiral of naval yard at Langer

Crystal Jillian: daughter of Raphael and Vivian/ sister of Robert

Curtis: male Ruala warrior who fought in Ryed

Curtis: Nordes child/youngest brother of Lana and Tanya

Cyrene: wife of Benedict/mother of Anka, Santi and Linus/Elod

Cyril: a street preacher

Daceron: a demon from the world of Balterak in the Mensor Galaxy

Dack: male Ruala warrior

Dacron: former prince of Ryed/is murdered by his younger brother Nehmota for the throne

Dael: an ancient demon/ one of the Old Ones

Dafney: a witch

Dagger: one of Hector's lieutenants/in charge of compound in Cadia

Dagon: a male Ruala warrior

Dagor: son of King Fahra and Queen Sitha of Zorta

Dai: son of Gael, grandson of Manu/Ruala

Daisy: a young woman from Langer

Daisy: nine year old Nordes girl/ daughter of Edgar and Cora/younger sister of Batina

Dalton: male Nordes warrior/brother of Lana and Tanya

Damas: an ancient demon/ one of the Old Ones

Danar: a man created to be a vessel for demons

Daniel: an emissary of The Great Ruler who takes on the disguise of a human man

Danilla: mother of King Mathas

Dano: seven year old Nordes boy/son of Edgar and Cora/youngest brother of Batina

Darius: Prince of Samona/son of Thomas and Rewel/brother of Varden

Darla: young female Nordes warrior

Darlah: sister of Marie/ nurse for grandchildren of King Sudfad

Darlene Wilchess: wife of Chet/mother of Philip and Andre/ socialite

Dax: a male Nordes warrior

Dea: Nordes warrior/mother of Adam and Celia/wife of Vilem

Deborah: a servant of Charles Moses

Deckor: mayor of Langer, the capital city of the Kingdom of Lentz

Delilah: wife of Dieter

Delilia: Queen of New Samona/mother of Ibula, Lakin, Gael and Hadar/ wife of King Manu/Ruala

Demanko: a demon

Demetries: a demon

Denise Froush: wife of Martin who is a wealthy ship builder in Port Friada

Denks: a soldier in the army of Wetpr

Denton: one of the spies at the Castle in Wetpr

Derek: friend of Thaos

Derlock: Huta warrior

Desavo: the demon who leads the Armada of the dead

Diana: a Venator/sister of Thor

Dieter: member of the Insidiae

Dillion: hired killer who works for Otto Franks

Dillion: one of Karzman's hired fighters

Dion: Princess of Samona/wife of Yorggi who was the son of Thomas and Rewel/brother of Varden

Dirk: Nordes Tribe/father of Corsa, Alex, Kent and George/fisherman

Dixon: a Taperian soldier

Dixon: Chief Seaman of the Falcon

Dixon: husband of Arlene/friend of Olivia

Dominic Petlov: was the senior High Priest at the monastery at Malga before he was murdered

Dominic: oldest of three brothers who formed the Libertas in Ryed

Donald: a member of the Taperian City Board

Dora: Nordes warrior/mother of Bianca/wife of Tyler

Dorack: an Elod man

Dorme: Prince of Ogg

Doros: works for High Priest Meekos

Douma: King of Ogg

Dr. Theodore Jackson: head of the medical school at Cicero College in Salar

Drake: worked for Karzman

Dresden: a Sergeant in the Wetprian army

Duncan: Chief of the Clan of Gesmal in Ryed/ husband of Liza

Duran: father of Nikki/Nordes Tribe

Durst: Colonel in the Military of Wetpr

Dymas: Shettee warrior

Eachann: Shettee warrior

Edgar: father of Batina/husband of Cora/Nordes warrior

Edith: wife of Lloyd a banker in Nora

Edna: a Nordes healer

Eilig: male Ruala warrior

Elan: male Ruala warrior/son of Gunnel and Uma/

Eldridge: works with the Patronus

Elen: son of Andrus and Naomi/ brother of Rabi/ Ruala

Elexas: a female Nordes warrior

Eli: Major Severson of the Military of Puntd/ also a member of the Guardians

Elizabeth: wife of Wickfield

Ella: female Ruala warrior/mother of Bekka/wife of Sam

Elliot: a hired fighter who works for King Friada of the Kingdom of Ganz

Eloise: a store clerk in Salar

Eloise: female Ruala warrior/oldest sister of Bekka/wife of Tony

Elsa: female Ruala warrior/mother of Mia/wife of Tyron

Emeral: mother of Calen/Ruala

Emeric: a male Grand Master of the Insidiae

Emily: an old woman in Taperia

Emily: sister of Angus

Emma: daughter of Luca and Lila

Emmet: worker for Gabriel

Emon: a male Grand Master of the Insidiae

Enzo: male Ruala warrior

Erebus: sorcerer from Ryed

Eric: a male Nordes warrior

Erwat: a member of the Half-Man's Tribe who helps the Clan of Gesmal

Esser: Prince/son of Segal and Cahina/nephew of King Manu of New Samona/Ruala

Esteban: a member of the Insidiae

Esther: Queen of New Norkv/wife of rebel leader Benjeman

Ethan: a male Ruala warrior

Everite: a Major in the Wetprian Army

Fabron: Prince of Ogg

Fadil: a male Grand Master of the Insidiae

Fahra: King of Zorta

Fahron: General in the Army of Lentz

Fairoot: demon/ lieutenant for Salzar

Fala: female Ruala warrior

Farnsworth: General in charge of building Fort Serpha in Wetpr

Fatima: Prince of Ryed/ son of Oren and Astrel

Fatronas: an ancient demon/one of the Old Ones

Felistine: a member of the wealthy and elite in Ryed

Fengu: Enrop leader who helps Gabriel and his group against Omnibus

Fennel: one of three brothers who formed the Libertas in Ryed

Ferguson: a Sergeant in the Army of Lentz

Fiona: mother of Nadia/grandmother of Michael

Flores: Captain in the Military of Lentz/stationed at Fort Castor

Fraisier: a businessman and member of the Insidiae in Nora

Frank: a villager in Telmark

Frankie: Nordes child/younger brother of Jasmine/son of Conrad and Leta

Frankwich: husband of Matilda/father of Olin/warlock

Fred Stapleton: a farmer in Wetpr

Fred: a bartender at The Treasure Chest Tavern in Port Friada

Friada: King of the Kingdom of Ganz

Gabi: an Enrop

Gabriella: sister of Marie/nurse to grandchildren of King Sudfad

Gad: male Ruala warrior

Gael: Prince/son of King Manu and Queen Delilia/Ruala

Gala: a healer from the Kingdom of Stordt

Galen: male Nordes warrior

Garvis: male Elod/member of Javier's and Madeline's team

Geobel: General in the Military of Ryed who tries to take over the kingdom after the fall of Teivel

Geof Thurstand: ship owner/husband of Linda

Geoff: Prince of Lentz/son of Princess Isabella and Captain Josef

Geoff: Prince of Norkv/son of Benedict and Sasaha/grandson of Benjeman and Esther

Georganson: an arms dealer in Ryed

George: an advisor for King Fahra of Zorta

George: middle son of Chief Duncan and Liza of the Clan of Gesmal in Ryed

George: Nordes warrior/brother of Corsa, Kent and Alex

Gideon: Admiral in the Navy of Ganz

Gilder: a dark lord from the Kingdom of Inferus

Giles: hired fighter for Mayor Deckor of Langer

Gilmore: a Wetprian soldier

Giovani: Rachel's older half-brother

Gita: wife of Hadi/ Ruala

Gladys: member of Nordes Tribe/ mother of Nikki

Glenda: great, great, great grandmother of Gala/ a healer from the Kingdom of Stordt

Grace: Princess of New Norkv/daughter of Benjeman and Esther

Gracie: cook for the Arthur Marcus family

Grady: worker for Gabriel

Grant: a male Nordes warrior

Great Ruler: God

Gregory Bancar: a wealthy landowner in the Kingdom of Wetpr and member of the Insidiae

Greta: older Ruala woman/friend of Emeral's

Greta: wife of Hugo/mother of Sasha/ sister-in-law of Sorren

Gunnel: Prince/ son of King Zachariah and Queen Noella of New Samona/husband of Uma/father of Elan/Ruala

Gunter: Seaman in the Navy of Lentz

Gus: husband of Penelope/ killed for trying to help Nadia and Michael escape from Karzman

Gus: owner of Racing Horse Tavern

Haas: a Lieutenant in the Wetprian military

Hadar: Prince/son of King Manu and Queen Delilia/Ruala

Hadi: son of Andrus and Naomi/ brother of Rabi/ Ruala

Hadi: son of Andrus and Naomi/brother of Rabi/Ruala

Hadu: female Ruala warrior

Halsal: Sergeant in the Military of Lentz

Hamon: one of the members of the Nordes Tribe who was injured in an attack at Snakes Crossing

Hamond: General of the Taperian Army who declares himself king

Hampton: Major in Wetprian Army

Hanger: one of the spies at the Castle at Wetpr

Hangered: Wetprian soldier

Hank: low level criminal

Hannah: physician in Nora/ Roch murdered her sister

Haris: an assassin

Harlow: an investigative reporter for The Port Friada Gazette

Harold: husband of Berta/part owner of the Racing Horse Tavern

Harold: owner of the general store in Nora

Harriet Marcus: mother of Hannah and Laurabelle/wife of Arthur

Harris: male Ruala warrior who fought in Ryed

Harrison: Lieutenant in the Military of Lentz

Harry: a member of the Taperian City Board

Harvard: President of the Port Friada Bank

Hatus: General in the Army of Lentz/on loan to Sudfad

Hazel: housekeeper at Erebus' mansion in Salar

Hector: fighter hired by Juleta

Hector: Prince of Samona/son of Varden

Henry: and his wife Alice find Jorge in Nora

Henry: husband of Noreen/father of Jacob

Hermanas: second in command to Archetenus at Wall of Dorath

High Priest Aaron: member of the Patronus

High Priest Alfonso: a member of the Patronus

High Priest Amos: a member of the Patronus

High Priest Barnabas: most Senior High Priest of the monastery at Leven

High Priest Bernard: a member of the Patronus

High Priest Caleb: member of the Patronus

High Priest Ephraim: a member of the Patronus

High Priest Felix: senior HP at the Patronus Headquarters in Langer

High Priest Frederick: a member of the Patronus

High Priest Gabriel: member of the Patronus/demon hunter

High Priest Gideon: a member of the Patronus

High Priest Gregory: member of the Patronus

High Priest Henrich: a member of the Patronus Priests

High Priest Ira: a member of the Patronus Priests

High Priest Joseph: member of the Patronus, in charge of the Cicero Headquarters

High Priest Josiah: member of the Patronus

High Priest Maddox: a member of the Patronus Priests

High Priest Meekos: priest at the monastery at Malga

High Priest Nicholas: most Senior High Priest of the monastery at Philiste and most Senior High Priest of the Patronus

High Priest Norbert: Senior High Priest at the monastery at Casum in NW Wetpr

High Priest Othnial: Senior High Priest of the monastery in Rubar in the Kingdom of Ryed

High Priest Paulas: member of the Patronus

High Priest Phanuel: member of the Patronus

High Priest Philetus: member of the Patronus in charge of Malga Headquarters

High Priest Pravis: priest at the monastery at Malga

High Priest Raphael: a leader of the Patronus

High Priest Rueben: member of the Patronus in charge of Nora Headquarters

High Priest Silas: a member of the Patronus

High Priest Tenebrae: priest at the monastery at Malga

High Priest Timothy: was murdered by Meekos, Pravis and Tenebrae

High Priest Tyrus: a member of the Patronus

High Priest Uriel: member of the Patronus

High Priest Vincent: assigned to the monastery at Malga before he was murdered

High Priest Zophar: priest at monastery at Malga/ trained as a healer

Hilgra: a witch

Hobart: a man who works for demons

Horace: father of Rachel and Zach/husband of Zelda/freedom fighter in Ryed

Hores: son of Chief Romogi and Anda, Kingdom of Marba/Huta

Hors: a clerk at The Rooster

Horta: Prince/son of Gunnel and Uma/nephew of King Manu of New Samona/brother of Elan/Ruala

Howie: one of Deckor's hired fighters

Hugh: Manager of The Rooster

Hugo: younger brother of Sorren/father of Sasha/husband of Greta

Hunter: Prince of Samona/son of Varden

Hunter: son of Natalie and Troy/Clan of Gesmal

Ian Maxwell Luca: son of Koby and Bekka

Ian: husband of Mia/ brother in law of Calen/ Ruala

Ibula: warrior princess and healer of the Ruala Tribe/daughter of King Manu and Queen Delilia/

Iden: warrior guarding refugees/Shettee

Igor: brother of King Sharonne

Ike Ferguson: elderly neighbor of Gabriel and Hannah

Imad: a male Grand Master of the Insidiae

Ina: daughter of Mia and Ian/ Ruala

Ingr: female warrior of Nordes Tribe

Inon: one of Cisero's men/a vessel

Ipos: an ancient demon/ one of the Old Ones

Iris: mother of Vivian/wife of Joshua/Clan of Gesmal in Ryed

Irit: daughter of Hadi and Gita/ Ruala

Isabella: Princes of Lentz, sister of Mathas, Renya and Tasha, married to Captain Josef

Isadore: wife of Fahron

Isla: daughter of Prince Lakin and Princess Zada/Ruala

Isla: female warrior of Nordes Tribe

Ivan: boss of Javier and Madeline/from the Kingdom of Inferus

Ivan: youngest son of Chief Duncan and Liza of the Clan of Gesmal in Ryed

Iverson: hired killer/foreman

Jace: husband of Oda/ brother in law of Calen/Ruala

Jack Franks: son of Otto and Ruthie/old money in Langer

Jack: member of governing body of Nora

Jackson: a private in the Army of Lentz

Jackson: an escaped prisoner from Wetpr

Jackson: Corporal in the Army of Lentz

Jackson: Corporal in the Wetprian Army

Jackson: one of Deckor's hired fighters

Jackwitz: Sergeant in the Military of Lentz

Jacob: boy who Angelina found in the woods

Jacot: son of Prince Lakin and Princess Zada/ grandson of King Manu/Ruala

Jaden: Sergeant in the Army of Lentz

Jago: son of Elen and Batya/ Ruala

Jake: hired fighter for Mayor Deckor of Langer

Jake: works for Talverson Transport Company in Port Friada

Jakiv: Prince/son of Segal and Cahina/nephew of King Manu of New Samona/Ruala

Jama: Enrop leader who protects Chief Sorren's family

James: Taperian soldier

Jana: female Ruala warrior

Janja: Princess/daughter of Gunnel and Uma/niece of King Manu of New Samona/ sister of Elan/Ruala

Janson: Wetprian soldier

Jared: hired fighter

Jaretta: King of Stordt/husband of Queen Lillian/ father of Roch and Sudfad

Jarrod: works for Pravis/leads attack on castle in Wetpr

Jarvis: a farmer who is killed by escaped prisoners

Jasmine: young female Nordes warrior

Jason: male Nordes warrior

Jasper: a large white dog that Gabriel brings home

Jasper: Prince of Lentz/son of Princess Isabella and Captain Josef

Jatu: Enrop leader who protects Fahron's family

Javier: a spy from the Kingdom of Inferus/brother of Madeline

Jeb: friend of Thaos

Jeb: one of Cisero's men

Jela: Queen of Samona/wife of Varden

Jenna: female Ruala warrior/married to Ratri's oldest brother Artis

Jenny: secretary of Mayor Deckor

Jeremy: cousin of Andrew the jeweler in Salar

Jerik: a male Grand Master of the Insidiae

Jess: a soldier of Wetpr

Jillian: Queen of Ogg/wife of King Douma

Jinn: an ancient demon/ one of the Old Ones

Joanna Franks: daughter of Otto and Ruthie/old money in Langer

Joao: male Ruala warrior

Joe: works for Hector

Joey: adopted son of Elan and Cassandra

Johnny: a drifter/travels with Zeke, Sam and Carl

Jonas: Captain in the Taperian Army

Jonathan Gabriel Maxwell: son of Calen and Natasha

Jonathon Blackmoore: a physician who attended college with Hannah

Jonathon: a waiter at the Calla Lily Restaurant in Teivel Ryed

Jordy: male Nordes warrior

Jorga: Princess of Ryed/daughter of Oren and Astrel/ has twin sister Andres

Jorge: a cook who is kidnapped from Endleson Hotel in Nora

Josef: Captain in the Lentz military/ married to Princess Isabella, sister of King Mathas

Joseph: male Ruala warrior/father of Ratri/husband of Clair

Joseph: nine year old Ruala boy/son of Artis and Jenna/nephew of Ratri

Josh: Nordes warrior/husband of Stella

Joshua: father of Vivian/husband of Iris/Clan of Gesmal in Ryed

Josie: an escaped prisoner from Wetpr

Juleta: cousin to Raul and Simon/daughter and oldest child of King Mathas and Queen Rosa

Julie: a young woman from Langer

Kadin: a member of Valdore Tribe

Kagen: a man who kidnaps and exploits children

Kalee: female Ruala warrior/married to Ratri's older brother Quinn

Kane: a thug who lives in Castor

Kantof: hired killer/foreman

Karin: wife of Mayor Deckor of Langer

Karl: two year old Ruala boy/son of Artis and Jenna/nephew of Ratri

Karta: male Ruala warrior

Karzman: leader of Kozach Tribe/ stepfather of Michael

Kasper: Prince/son of Zeman and Oda/nephew of King Manu of New Samona/Ruala

Kata: Princess/daughter of Gunnel and Uma/niece of King Manu of New Samona/ sister of Elan/Ruala

Kate: a Venator from the Clan of Gesmal

Keith: an enforcer for Hector

Kent: Nordes warrior/brother of Corsa, Alex and George

Khryriss: an ancient demon/ one of the Old Ones

Kiana: Princess/daughter of Gunnel and Uma/niece of King Manu of New Samona/ sister of Elan/Ruala

Kinsman: a warrior from the Valdore Tribe

Klass: Lieutenant in the Wetprian Army

Koby: male Ruala warrior

Koh: son of Prince Gael and Princess Mada/grandson of King Manu/Ruala

Kora: Princess/ married to Raphael son of King Zachariah and Queen Noella of New Samona/ mother of Luca/ Raphael and Kora were killed in battle when Luca was a small boy/Ruala

Korbin: one of Teivel's lieutenants

Korth: son of Tristt/Shettee

Kraus: hired fighter and intended vessel, works for Dieter

Kretcher: Commanding General of Fort Polta in Wetpr

Krister: Princess of Samoan/daughter of Thomas and Rewel

Kyle: Nordes warrior/older brother of Jasmine/son of Conrad and Leta/husband of Marsha/father of Brandon

Kyra: young sister of Marie/ friend of Petra

Laban: Prince of Samona/son of Yorggi and Dion/grandson of Thomas and Rewel

Lael: daughter of Nina and Rhea/ Ruala

Lakin: Prince/son of King Manu and Queen Delilia/husband of Zada/Ruala

Lala: Princess/daughter of Adwell and Nada/niece of King Manu of New Samona/ sister of Misha/Ruala

Lana: female Nordes warrior/older sister of Tanya/

Lana: female warrior of the Nordes Tribe

Lana: Princess/daughter of Segal and Cahina/niece of King Manu of New Samona/Ruala

Lance: a gang leader in Langer

Lance: Nordes warrior/older brother of Jasmine/son of Conrad and Leta

Lani: daughter of Mia and Ian/Ruala

Lara: one of Usman's wives

Larry: one of Hector's men

Larson: a fighter hired by Juleta

Laurabelle: Hannah's sister who was murdered by Roch

Laurel: Annabelle's mother and former servant of King Roch's parents

Lawrence: a member of the Libertas

Lawrence: father of Dack/husband of Rose/Ruala

Lazo: fighter hired by Juleta

Lea: Princess/daughter of Adwell and Nada/niece of King Manu of New Samona/ sister of Misha/Ruala

Leith: four year old Ruala boy/son of Quin and Kalee/nephew of Ratri

Leo: Prince of Samona/son of Darius and Rebek/grandson of Thomas and Rewel

Leon: Captain in the Military of Ryed/ a member of Teivel's inner circle

Leta: mother of Jasmine/wife of Conrad/Nordes Tribe

Lieutenant Strater: Wetprian Military/Fort Serpha

Lieutenant Tarp: Lieutenant in the Wetprian Army

Lila: seventeen year old girl who Luca saves from the Hutas/sister of Christopher

Lilian: female warrior of the Nordes Tribe

Lillian: Queen of Stordt/wife of Jaretta/ mother of Roch and Sudfad

Lily: daughter of Calen and Natasha/Ruala and human

Linda Thurstand: wife of Geof/lover of Mayor Deckor

Linus: Elod child

Liza: wife of Duncan the Chief of the Clan of Gesmal in Ryed

Lloyd: banker in Nora

Loftus: Commanding General of Fort Styls

Logan: boy stolen by Hector's human trafficking ring

Lola: female Nordes warrior/sister of Lana and Tanya

Lordes: Seaman in the Navy of Lentz

Lorna: a female Nordes warrior on Angus' team

Louie: works for Talverson Transport Company in Port Friada

Louis: male Elod/member of Javier's and Madeline's team

Luca: male Ruala warrior

Lucene: male Nordes warrior/oldest son of Hugo and Greta/older brother of Sasha

Lucifer: an ancient demon/ one of the Old Ones

Lucile: a member of the wealthy and elite in Ryed

Lucky: Sally's puppy

Lucy: one of the housekeepers in King Mathas' castle

Lulu: female dog adopted by Gabriel's household

Luque: Prince/son of Segal and Cahina/nephew of King Manu of New Samona/Ruala

Mab: a female Grand Master of the Insidiae

Mable: a servant in the castle of King Nehmota of Ryed

Mabon: warrior guarding refugees/Shettee

Mada: Princess /wife of Prince Gael/Ruala

Madam Bular: owner of a dress shop in Port Friada

Madeline: a friend of Princess Isabella

Madix: General in the Army of Ryed/member of Teivel's first inner circle

Maggie: elderly store owner in Salar

Maggie: Mayer Tetly's wife

Mahon: son of King Neputa

Makalo: Prince of Norkv/husband of Grace who was the daughter of Benjeman and Esther

Malana: daughter of King Neputa

Malard: Captain in the military of Wetpr

Malcom: father of Queen Sitha of Zorta/husband of Renault

Mali: Princess of Norkv/daughter of Makalo and Grace/granddaughter of Benjeman and Esther

Maligma: an ancient demon/ one of the Old Ones

Malik: member of the Insidiae

Mallory: female Venator

Malus: sorcerer from Ryed

Mandrake: Taperian soldier

Manhure: Sergeant in the Army of Lentz

Manu: King of New Samona/The Chief of the Grand Council made up of Rualas and Shettees/ father of Ibula, Lakin, Gael and Hadar/husband of Delilia

Manutu: King of the Gants

Marcia: friend of Hannah's/ Roch's men murdered her family

Marcus Stephan: son of Stephan and Ingr

Margarit: daughter of King Mathas and Queen Rosa of the Kingdom of Lentz/ cousin of Raul and Simon

Margerie: female cook of King Mathas and Queen Rosa

Margo: a young girl who was kidnapped by Sal

Margolia: girl from Nora who was sacrificed to a demon

Marie: a cook for King Sudfad and Queen Renya

Marina: female Ruala healer

Markus: a soldier in the Army of Wetpr

Marla: High Priest Meekos' housekeeper

Marlas: female Nordes warrior/ wife of Carson/ mother of Lana, Tanya, Norris, Terrance, Dalton, Lola and Curtis

Marly: a cocktail waitress at the New Moon Hotel in Taperia

Marsha Jarvis: a sixteen year old girl who is raped and killed by Timothy

Marsha: wife of Charles Moses

Marsha: Nordes warrior/wife of Kyle/mother of Brandon/sister-in-law of Jasmine

Marshal: Captain in the Military of Lenz

Marshal: Major in Army of Lentz

Marta: a female Nordes warrior on Edward's team

Martha: a cook for Cerephus

Martha: hotel owner in Telmark

Martin Froush: wealthy ship builder in Port Friada/husband of Denise

Martin: a member of the Libertas

Martiz: a ghost

Marty: boy stolen by Hector's human trafficking ring

Mary: Jared's young wife who was brutally murdered by Hutas

Mata: Igor's wife

Mateo: Chief Healer of the Ruala Tribe

Mathas Sorren: son of Matthew and Angelina

Mathas: King of Lentz/ brother to Queen Renya

Matilda Frankwich: wife of Frankwich/mother of Olin

Matilda: first wife of Clarence/ mother of Archer

Matilda: one of Usman's wives

Matraxt: a demon/first lieutenant of Baal

Mattel: hired killer/foreman

Matthew: son of King Mathas and Queen Rosa of the Kingdom of Lentz/ cousin of Raul and Simon

Matty T: son of Stephan and Ingr

Max: one of Hector's men

Max: young Nordes boy/son of Ruby/brother of Saul

Maximus Bartholomew Joshua: twin son of Misha and Diana/brother of Thor Adwell Gabriel

Maxwell: father of Calen/ Ruala

Maxwell: infant son of Nina and Rhea/grandson of elder Maxwell/Ruala

Maynard: an Elod healer

McAvoy: Sergeant in the Army of Wetpr/stationed at Fort Serpha

Melanie: female Ruala warrior/daughter of Casey and Tasha

Melina: mother of Thaos

Melinda: grandmother of Misha

Melinda: older sister of Cassandra and Joao

Mia: daughter of Maxwell and Emeral/ Ruala

Mia: female Ruala warrior/daughter of Tyron and Elsa

Mica: Princess of Norkv/daughter of Benedict and Sasaha/granddaughter of Benjeman and Esther

Micha: oldest son of Joshua and Iris/older brother of Vivian/Clan of Gesmal

Micha: son of King Sharonne/ grandfather of Sudfad and Roch

Michael: ancient king of Wetpr/father of Queen Sumona

Michael: son of Sudfad and Nadia

Milo: abused monkey

Milo: male Ruala warrior

Milt: an old man who lives in Taperia/ father of Penny

Miranda: daughter of Raul and Vitomas

Miranda: emissary of The Great Ruler who takes on the disguise of a human seer

Miriam: a friend of Hannah's/works at Endleson Hotel in Nora

Misha: male Ruala warrior/lieutenant

Mister Harper: an elderly man who lives next to one of the Adam's Homes in Langer

Molach: a member of the Insidiae

Moloch: an ancient demon/one of the Old Ones

Monroe Family: a family of criminals who lived in the Kingdom of Stordt

Moraine: Admiral of naval yard at Castor

Morgan: Sergeant in the Wetprian Army

Morris: member of governing body of Nora

Morton: Cedrick Teivel's original name

Moxy: female Ruala warrior

Muhar: Shettee warrior

Murdock: Major in the Wetprian Army

Murphy: Lieutenant in the Army of Wetpr/stationed at Fort Serpha

Myla: wife of Rex, the owner of the Dragons Inn in Salar

Myrtle: homeless teacher from Castor

Naal: warrior guarding refugees/Shettee

Nabi: male Ruala warrior

Nada: Princess/ married to Adwell son of King Zachariah and Queen Noella of New Samona/ mother of Misha/ Adwell was killed in battle leaving Nada to raise ten children/Ruala

Nadene: a member of the wealthy and elite in Ryed

Nadia: wife of Karzman/mother of Michael

Nami: mother of Frankwich/ a witch

Nana: female Ruala warrior

Naomi: an ancient priestess of the Sisterhood

Naomi: mother of Corsa, Alex, Kent and George/wife of Dirk/Nordes Tribe

Naomi: mother of Rabi/ Ruala

Napo: Enrop leader who protects Claudius' family

Nash: a soldier of Lentz

Natalie: female Venator/wife of Troy/mother of Hunter

Natasha: sister of High Priest Gabriel

Nathaniel: Sorren's oldest son/ Nordes Tribe

Nebula: son of Chief Romogi and Anda/ Kingdom of Marba/Huta

Ned: Patronus priest

Negal: a demon

Nehmota: King of Ryed

Nelpus: Shettee warrior

Neputa: leader of the Shettee Tribe when it was conquered by the Hutas

Nestor: a demon that specializes in procuring things for a price

Nethers: one of Karzman's hired killers

Nica: Enrop leader who protects Sudfad's family

Nicholas: orphan boy /brother of Cerey

Nicolas: Prince of Puntd/son of King Tobias and Queen Tasha

Nieatzae: an ancient demon/ one of the Old Ones

Nigel: Chief Seaman in the Navy of Lentz

Nikki: female warrior of Nordes Tribe

Nina: daughter of Maxwell and Emeral/Ruala

Nina: youngest daughter of Karzman and Nadia

Nita: Princess/daughter of Adwell and Nada/niece of King Manu of New Samona/ sister of Misha/has twin brother Waed/Ruala

Noah: a member of the Libertas

Nobel: former prince of Ryed/son of Akasha and Norah/father of Nehmota

Noel: a cook at the Teivel Manor Hotel

Noella: the first Queen of New Samona/wife of King Zachariah/mother of seven sons/Ruala

Norah: former queen of Ryed/grandmother of Nehmota

Norbert Franks: father of Otto and Frankwich/husband of Tomina/old money in Langer

Noreen: mother of Jacob/ wife of Henry

Norge: male Nordes warrior/cousin of Sorren/godfather of Angelina

Norge: Private in the Wetprian Army

Norma: owner of a shop in Taperia where Zoya used to work

Norris: hired fighter and intended vessel, works for Dieter

Norris: male Nordes warrior/ oldest brother of Lana and Tanya

Novack: Corporal in the Wetprian Army

Nyla: oldest daughter of Karzman and Nadia

Oda: daughter of Maxwell and Emeral/ Ruala

Oda: Princess/ married to Zeman son of King Zachariah and Queen Noella of New Samona/Ruala

Odam: male Ruala warrior

Odell: one of the spies at the Castle at Wetpr

Olin Frankwich: son of Frankwich and Matilda/dark lord

Olin: Patronus priest

Oliver: a member of the Libertas

Oliver: homeless teacher from Castor

Olivia: young girl who can hear people's thoughts

Omar: Prince/son of Zeman and Oda/nephew of King Manu of New Samona/Ruala

Omara: Queen of Norkv/wife of Thaddius who was son of Benjeman and Esther

Omnibus: an ancient demon/ one of the Old Ones

Omoria: former queen of Ryed/wife of Nobel/mother of Nehmota

Opago: an ancient demon/ one of the Old Ones

Oran: son of Visterle and Nada/twin brother of Verto

Orcus: Shettee warrior/brother of King Neputa

Oren: former prince of Gandt who marries princess Astrel of Ryed

Oriah: name used by the Grand Master Banaka

Orin: male Ruala warrior/older brother of Ratri/husband of Rene

Ortist: General in the Military of Wetpr

Otis: Nordes Warrior/first adopted father of Benny

Ottillia: Princess of Lenz/daughter of Princess Isabella and Captain Josef

Otto Franks: husband of Ruthie/father of Jack and Joanna/old money in Langer

Otu: son of Hecate and Sampson

Padre Augustus: a member of the Patronus

Padre Bartholomew: survives the massacre at the monastery at Avaide

Padre Bishop: assigned to the monastery at Leven

Padre Cornelius: a member of the Patronus

Padre Darius: a member of the Patronus

Padre Dibon: a priest at the monastery at Malga

Padre Dominick: priest at monastery at Malga

Padre Edgar: member of the Patronus

Padre Edward: a member of the Patronus

Padre Finn: Patronus priest assigned to the Cicero HQ

Padre Francis: priest at monastery at Malga

Padre Joram: member of the Patronus

Padre Lucas: a member of the Patronus

Padre Markle: a Patronus priest

Padre Nebat: alias for Dominic leader of the Libertas

Padre Octavos: runs orphanage in Salar

Padre Philip: a member of the Patronus

Padre Philip: a priest at the monastery at Malga

Padre Simpson: priest at the monastery at Malga

Padre Sorben: a member of the Patronus

Padre Sornce: Patronus priest assigned to the Cicero HQ

Padre Stephens: priest at monastery at Malga

Padre Thomas: priest at the monastery at Malga

Padre Tobias: a member of the Patronus

Padre Xavier: priest at monastery at Malga

Paj: Princess/wife of Prince Hadar/Ruala

Pallas: Shettee warrior

Parker: a banker in Port Friada

Pata: daughter of Chief Romogi and Trina/Huta

Paterson: a Private in the Wetprian military

Patrick: owns a company of mercenaries/ a member of the wealthy and elite in Ryed

Patris: six year old Nordes girl/daughter of Hugo and Greta/younger sister of Sasha

Paul: third son of Joshua and Iris/younger brother of Vivian/Clan of Gesmal

Paulas: a man who works for Cicero/a vessel

Paulas: Sergeant under Archetenus in Taperian Army

Paullo: works for High Priest Meekos

Paxel: Major in the Military of Lentz

Pearl: eldest daughter of King Tobias and Queen Tasha of Puntd

Penelope: wife of Gus/ killed for trying to help Nadia and Michael escape from Karzman

Penny: young woman who lives in Taperia/ daughter of Milt

Pergo: King of the Kingdom of Gandt

Peter: Sorren's second son/Nordes Tribe

Peters: member of the governing body of Nora

Petorus: an ancient demon/one of the Old Ones

Petra: peasant boy from Ort who saves Padre Bartholomew

Phifer: nine year old Nordes boy/ son of Hugo and Greta/younger brother of Sasha

Philip Wilchess: son of Chet and Darlene/ brother of Andre

Philip: Prince of Puntd/ son of King Tobias and Queen Tasha

Phillip: Court Physician to the Royal Family of Wetpr

Polgate: one of the men who kidnapped Petra

Potomas: warrior guarding refugees/Shettee

Powell: a lieutenant in the Military of Lentz/stationed at Fahron's castle.

Prescott: a hired killer

Quin: male Ruala warrior/older brother of Ratri/husband of Kalee

Quinn: an Elod/a member of the Charto/

Rabi: male Ruala warrior

Rachel: member of the freedom fighters in Ryed

Radnor: a male Grand Master of the Insidiae

Rael: Prince of old Samona/husband of Krister who was the daughter of Thomas and Rewel

Rafa: an Enrop

Rahi: a female Grand Master of the Insidiae

Rakio: Prince/son of Adwell and Nada/nephew of King Manu of New Samona/brother of Misha/Ruala

Rako: a male Ruala warrior

Ralf: male Ruala warrior

Ralph: an old sailor from the Navy of Ganz

Randolph: a manager of The Rooster

Raphael: Prince/ son of King Zachariah and Queen Noella of New Samona/husband of Kora/Ruala/father of Luca/ Raphael and Kora were killed in battle when Luca was a small boy/Ruala

Ratri: male Ruala warrior

Raul: Prince/son of King Sudfad and Queen Renya of the Kingdom of Wetpr

Raum: an ancient demon/ one of the Old Ones

Raven: female Nordes warrior/healer

Rebek: Princess of Samona/wife of Darius, who was the son of Thomas and Rewel

Rebke: six year old Ruala girl/ daughter of Orin and Rene/niece of Ratri

Red: a member of the Taperian City Board

Red: a spy

Reed: male Nordes warrior

Reese: a male Ruala warrior

Reid: foreman for Jack Franks

Remi: an Enrop

Renault: Mother of Queen Sitha of Zorta/wife of Malcom

Rene: female Ruala warrior/married to Ratri's older brother Orin

Renya: Queen of Wetpr/ wife of Sudfad

Rewel: Queen of Samona/wife of Thomas/mother of Varden

Rex: a notorious pick pocket in Port Friada

Rex: owner of the Dragons Inn in Salar/husband of Myla

Rhea: husband of Nina/ brother in law of Calen/ Ruala

Richard: third husband of Madeline

Ridon: General in the military of Wetpr

Riftca: male Ruala warrior

Riker: a scout in the Wetprian military

Riley: an abused dog that Luca saves

Risa: female Ruala warrior

Risha: a witch who deals with potions

River: one of Karzman's soldiers who he murdered

Roch: King of the Kingdom of Stordt/brother of King Sudfad

Rogers: one of the men who kidnapped Petra

Rolif: son of Chief Romogi and Silva/ Kingdom of Marba/Huta

Romale: member of the Insidiae

Romos: an elder of the Centras

Rosa: Queen of Lentz/wife of King Mathas

Rosalie: a dressmaker in Nora/wife of Peters

Rose: mother of Dack/wife of Lawrence/Ruala

Roy: owner of the Pirates Flag Tavern in Langer

Ruby: young Nordes widow with two small sons Max and Saul

Rudy: a criminal in Castor

Ruth: emissary of The Great Ruler who takes on the guise of a frail old woman

Ruthie Franks: wife of Otto/mother of Jack and Joanna/old money in Langer

Ryan: grandson of Jeb/friend of Thaos

Rybkin: Warlock who worked for the dictator Teivel

Sabot: member of the Insidiae

Sabra: female Nordes warrior

Sahil: a male Ruala warrior

Sal: a murderous pedophile/also goes by the name Tyrone

Sally: a young girl who was kidnapped by Sal

Salzar: powerful demon on Sidus

Sam Endleson: an investigator

Sam: a drifter/travels with Zeke, Carl and Johnny

Sam: male Ruala warrior/father of Bekka/husband of Ella

Sam: Patronus priest

Samael: a demon as powerful as Ahriman who rules the hell world Xibalba

Samara: wife of Tristt/Shettee

Samat: son of Chief Romogi and Silva/ Kingdom of Marba/Huta

Samos: Prince of Norkv/son of Thaddius

Sampson: oldest son of Chief Duncan and Liza of the Clan of Gesmal in Ryed

Sampson: Sergeant in the Taperian Army

Samuel: a high priest at the monastery at Malga who was murdered

Samuel: Prince of the original Samona/grandson of Thomas and Rewel

Samuel: second son of Raul and Vitomas

Santi: Elod child

Sanuri: a holy man/emissary of The Great Ruler/warrior

Sar: an Enrop

Sar: male Ruala warrior

Sara: daughter of Usman

Sara: female Nordes warrior/ girlfriend of Norris

Sarah: baby granddaughter of Mathas and Rosa

Sarah: housekeeper for Claudius and Bella

Saran: daughter of Karzman and Nadia

Sargei: a Venator/ husband of Risha

Sasaha: Princess of the original Samona/granddaughter of Thomas and Rewel

Sasha: young female Nordes warrior

Sasha: female warrior of the Nordes Tribe/wife of Galen

Satan: an ancient demon/ one of the Old Ones

Satter: male Ruala warrior

Sattleman: a Sergeant in the Wetprian army

Sauer: male Ruala warrior

Sauer: Nordes warrior/older brother of Bianca/son of Tyler and Dora

Saul: young Nordes boy/son of Ruby/brother of Max

Saunders: a Taperian soldier

Saxton: powerful lieutenant who works for Teivel the dictator of Ryed

Schroeder: man who works for Insidiae leader Dieter

Schuester: Commander of a special unit of Teivel's government/identifies betrayers

Sean: one of Karzman's hired killers

Segal: Prince/ son of King Zachariah and Queen Noella of New Samona/husband of Cahina/Ruala

Seguna: former princess of Ryed/daughter of Akasha and Norah/ committed suicide

Selen: house keeper for Juleta

Seth: a member of the Libertas

Sez: male Ruala warrior

Shadow Men: a spirit army of Venatores

Shanksaw: mercenary

Shara: wife of Sorren/Nordes Tribe

Shard: Captain in the Military of Ryed/ a member of Teivel's inner circle

Sharon: one of Mayor Deckor's lovers

Sharonne: King of Stordt; great, great, grandfather of King Roch and King Sudfad

Shaun: one of Hector's men

Sheba: a female Nordes warrior

Shey: male Ruala warrior

Shon: son of King Fahra and Queen Sitha

Shone: Princess/daughter of Zeman and Oda/niece of King Manu of New Samona/Ruala

Showers: one of Hector's foremen

Shuester: Private in the Wetprian Army

Sicily Bella: daughter of Stephan and Ingr

Sila: Princess of Ogg

Silva: one of Chief Romogi's three wives/Huta

Simmons: Commanding General of Fort Nir

Simon: adopted son of King Sudfad and Queen Renya of the Kingdom of Wetpr

Sinclair: King of Lentz/father of King Mathas

Sirius: works for High Priest Meekos

Sisterhood: another name for the Sisters of Tameric

Sisters of Tameric: clandestine organization/ancient/brutal

Sitha: Queen of Zorta

Smoking Joe: a regular patron at the Ghost Ship Tavern

Snapper: a hired thug that was a member of Addison's gang

Sol: male Ruala warrior

Sonja: female warrior of the Nordes Tribe

Sophie: cook and servant of King Roch

Sorphat: demon/ a lieutenant of Samael's

Sorren: leader of the Nordes Tribe

Soto: male Ruala warrior who leads first death squad for criminals

Spencer: an Elod/a member of the Charto/

Spooner: an architect in Lentz

Sporos: priest turned demon

Stafus: a powerful sorcerer who first broke the code to one of the demonic languages

Steele: an elusive crime boss

Stella: Nordes warrior/wife of Josh

Stephan: Captain in Army of Lentz/son of Claudius and Bella

Stiller: a fighter hired by Juleta

Stolas: an ancient demon/one of the Old Ones

Stone: an alias used by Dominic during the mission in Ryed with Gabriel's team

Stone: hired fighter and intended vessel, works for Dieter

Strait: Lieutenant in the Army of Ganz

Stranton: Colonel in the Military of Wetpr

Strauss: Lieutenant in the Military of Lentz

Sudfad: King of the Kingdom of Wetpr and brother to King Roch of Stordt

Sudfad: little Sudfad is grandson of King Sudfad

Sumona: Queen of Wetpr/wife of Alexandras/aunt of Roch and Sudfad

Suzette: a clerk at The Chicken and The Egg

Sven: male Nordes warrior

Swenson: one of Shanksaw's hired men

Syrius: a Bakken hired by Juleta

Tabeth: daughter of Fahron

Tabith: son of Tristt/Shettee

Tabitha: Princess of Lentz/daughter of Princess Isabella and Captain Josef of Lentz

Tadeo: Prince/son of Adwell and Nada/nephew of King Manu of New Samona/brother of Misha/Ruala

Tafer: a warlord who drove the Hutas out of the Kingdom of Norkv after years of wars and rebellions

Tahira: a female Grand Master of the Insidiae

Tahira: Princess of Samona/granddaughter of Thomas and Rewel

Taj: a Florine

Tal: son of Oda and Jace/ Ruala

Tally: worked for Karzman

Talmai: Shettee boy who Thedes and Ibula adopt

Talon: a male Ruala warrior

Tambor: male Ruala warrior

Tamour: General in the Army of Lentz/on loan to Sudfad

Tanner: a Lieutenant in the Wetprian army

Tanner: a Sergeant in the Army of Lentz

Tanner: one of Deckor's hired fighters

Tanya: a female Nordes warrior/younger sister of Lana

Tapster: a demon who works for Meekos

Tarig: a lieutenant in the Huta army

Tarin: son of King Neputa and Queen Tiara/Shettee

Tarla Grey: wealthy socialite in the City of Langer in the Kingdom of Lentz

Taron: Prince/son of Adwell and Nada/nephew of King Manu of New Samona/brother of Misha/Ruala

Tasha: female Ruala warrior/mother of Melanie/wife of Casey

Tasha: Queen of Puntd/ married to Tobias/ sister of Renya and Mathas

Tate: a Lieutenant in the Wetprian Army

Tate: male Ruala warrior

Tatterd: a Sergeant in the Wetprian military

Tavin: son of Prince Lakin and Princess Zada/Ruala

Ted: one of Juleta's hired men

Ted: one of Karzman's hired fighters

Teddy: male Nordes warrior/son of Edgar and Cora/ older brother of Batina

Teddy: owner of a general store in Stoba Lentz

Teddy: works for Hector

Tega: housekeeper for the cabins of the captains of the Taperian Army

Tegman: soldier of Wetpr

Tehtfote: a Lieutenant for Dieter

Telsor: an Elod soldier

Temark: villager of Neva

Teresa: the manager at The Chicken and The Egg

Terrance: male Nordes warrior/ older brother of Lana and Tanya

Teshmer Brothers: four highwaymen in Ryed

Tessa Demat: a con artist

Tetly: a mayoral candidate in Langer/ Kingdom of Lentz

Tetro: Huta warrior who was a captive in Ogg

Thadddius: Prince of the new Kingdom of Norkv/son of Benjeman

Thaddies: member of Nordes Tribe/ father of Ingr

Thanatoes: an ancient demon/ one of the Old Ones

Thaos: a hired fighter

Thatcher: Prince/son of Zeman and Oda/nephew of King Manu of New Samona/Ruala

Thatus: Taperian soldier

The Lion: emissary of The Great Ruler who takes on the appearance of a lion when he is in the world of man

The Master: a monster beyond comprehension

The Originator: the original darkness/father of demons

Thedes: warrior guarding refugees/Shettee

Theodore: handyman for Erebus/husband of Arlene

Theodore: the physician at Fort Stanus in the Kingdom of Wetpr

Thomas: King of the original Kingdom of Samona/father of Varden

Thomas: second son of Joshua and Iris/older brother of Vivian/Clan of Gesmal

Thomas: the young husband of Zoya who was murdered in Taperia

Thompson: Private in the Wetprian Army

Thompson: Wetprian soldier

Thor Adwell Gabriel: twin son of Misha and Diana/brother of Maximus Bartholomew Joshua

Thor: a Venator/brother of Diana

Thot: an emissary of The Great Ruler

Thronson: neighbor of Milt and Penny/husband of Ada

Thronson: one of Meekos hired killers

Tiara: Queen of Shettee Tribe when it was conquered by Hutas/wife of Neputa

Timothy: son of Fahron

Tina: Mother of Cassandra, Joao and Melinda

Tito: member of Valdore Tribe

Titus Derek: son of Thaos and Nikki

Titus: a lieutenant in the Taperian Army

Tobankto: an Old One from the World of Filsum

Tobart: a member of the Nordes Tribe

Tobey: a carriage driver in Ryed who helps Gabriel's team

Tobias: King of Puntd.

Tom: a homeless family man

Tomas: works for High Priest Pravis

Tome: a businessman and member of the Insidiae in Nora

Tomi: son of Usman the leader of the Valdore Tribe

Tomina Franks: wife of Norbert/mother of Otto/old money in Langer

Tommy: adopted son of Elan and Cassandra

Toni: young female Nordes warrior

Tony: a male Ruala warrior

Tony: male Ruala warrior/ married to Bekka's oldest sister Eloise

Toomback: Huta warrior

Torance: father of Thaos

Torin: oldest son of Karzman and Nadia

Torrance: male Nordes warrior

Trace: male Ruala warrior

Trace: one of Karzman's hired fighters

Tratz: one of the men who kidnapped Petra

Travor: Taperian warrior who was injured at the Wall of Dorath

Tresdor: nephew of Usman

Tresdore: son of King Sharonne

Trevor: Prince/son of Zeman and Oda/nephew of King Manu of New Samona/Ruala

Tria: daughter of Oda and Jace/Ruala

Trina: an Elod healer

Trina: one of Chief Romogi's three wives/Huta

Trina: Princess/daughter of Zeman and Oda/niece of King Manu of New Samona/Ruala

Trist: a male Ruala warrior

Tristt the Horrible: Shettee warrior

Tritor: a powerful demon of Sidus and ex-lover of Hecate

Troy: male Venator/husband of Natalie/father of Hunter

Tye: Prince of Norkv/son of Princess Grace and Prince Makalo

Tyler: Nordes warrior/father of Bianca/husband of Dora

Tyler: Sergeant in the Military of Lentz

Tyron: male Ruala warrior/father of Mia/husband of Elsa

Tyson: Wetprian soldier

Ulger: a demon

Uma: Princess/ married to Gunnel son of King Zachariah and Queen Noella of New Samona/mother of Elan/Ruala

Umar: Prince/son of Adwell and Nada/nephew of King Manu of New Samona/brother of Misha/Ruala

Uri: an Enrop

Uri: son of Nina and Rhea/ Ruala

Usman: leader of the Valdore Tribe

Valdus: name used by the Grand Master Emeric

Valerie: young female Nordes warrior

Valor: Prince of the new Kingdom of Norkv/son of Benjeman and Esther

Vandrew: Petra's male tutor

Vania: Princess of Samona/daughter of Yorggi and Dion/granddaughter of Thomas and Rewel

Varden: last king of Samona/he and his family were murdered by rebels

Vardin: one of the men who kidnapped Petra

Vasart: Queen of Ryed/ wife of Nehmota

Verto: son of Visterle and Nada/twin brother of Oran

Victor: a member of the Taperian City Board

Viktor: an ancient priest in Ryed who tried to stop the Insidiae

Vilem: Nordes warrior/father of Adam and Celia/husband of Dea

Vinca: Queen of Stordt, wife of Sharonne

Vincent: Prince of Ryed/son of Nehmota and Vasart

Vincente: a captain in the covert organization The Guardians

Vinus: Queen of the Kingdom of Gandt

Violet: homeless teacher from Castor

Visterle: a powerful demon

Vitomas: Queen of Stordt

Vivian: a demon hunter from the Clan of Gesmal

Voltar: Prince of Samona/son of Darius and Rebek/grandson of Thomas and Rewel/later becomes King of Wetpr

Voss: one of Karzman's hired killers

Vuall: a demon

Waed: Prince/son of Adwell and Nada/nephew of King Manu of New Samona/brother of Misha/has twin sister Nita/Ruala

Wainburst: Commanding Admiral of the Navy of the Kingdom of Ganz

Wallis: member of governing body of Nora

Wanda Ferguson: elderly neighbor of Gabriel and Hannah

Watkin: an Elod/a member of the Charto/

Wickfield: editor of the most powerful newspaper in the Kingdom of Lentz

Wicksom: Sergeant in the Military of Lentz/ stationed at Fort Castor

Wilard: Captain at Fort Polta

Willart: one of three notorious gang leaders in Taperia

William: son of Jared and Zoya

Willis: son of King Pergo and Queen Vinus/ Kingdom of Gandt

Willy: a horse thief

Xeni: a female Grand Master of the Insidiae

Yara: daughter of Nina and Rhea/Ruala

Yorggi: Prince of Samona/son of Thomas and Rewel/brother of Varden

Yori: son of Usman the leader of the Valdore Tribe

Yuri: Prince/son of Adwell and Nada/nephew of King Manu of New Samona/brother of Misha/Ruala

Zac: one of the men who kidnapped Petra

Zachariah: first King of New Samona/husband of Queen Noella/father of seven sons/Ruala

Zack: eight year old brother of Rachel

Zada: Princess/wife of Prince Lakin/Ruala

Zadok: a male Grand Master of the Insidiae

Zander: a male Nordes warrior

Zane: one of Juleta's husbands

Zede: an ancient demon/ one of the Old Ones

Zehmann: an ancient demon/ one of the Old Ones

Zeke: a drifter/travels with Sam, Carl and Johnny

Zelda: mother of Rachel and Zack

Zeman: Prince/ son of King Zachariah and Queen Noella of New Samona/husband of Oda/Ruala

Zieman: a demon

Zorda: Taperian soldier injured in battle at the Wall of Dorath

Zortus: demon/lieutenant of Visterle

Zourlock: a notorious warlord from the Continent of Salszar

Zoya: a seer from Taperia

Glossary of Terms

Aboultis: the calling cards of demons

Abrax: the planet that orbits closest to the three suns/ uninhabited

Abuckto: a sub race of superior intelligence in the Kingdom of Inferus

Abyss: a vast void used to imprison demons

Acura: the whispering shadows/are in the inner circle of demons that directly serve the Old Ones

Adros: one of five solar systems in the Mensor Galaxy

Alferto: a type of grain that is common in Opots

Altar of Kenar: the special altar mandated for the Blood Moon Ceremonies

Amark: ancient language of The Great Ruler

Amper Tree: special wood/forests of these trees are found in the lands of the Valdore Tribe

Amulth: means filth in the language of demons/these monsters are made out of the waste of tortured souls from the hell dimensions

Anewa: one of seven continents in the World of Nunc

Aplewort: an herb when mixed with water purges poisons from a body

Asherane: ancient tribe that lived in the northern regions of the Kingdom of Lentz

Ashta: a common herb/when the dried leaves are boiled they give off a pleasant scent

Astras: the ancient underground city of the Centras

Astrum: the solar system that consists of three suns that form a triangle and seven planets

Backor: one of the eight worlds in the Naz Solar System in the Mensor Galaxy

Balterak: one of the eight worlds in the Naz Solar System in the Mensor Galaxy

Beltrad: a species of lower level demons

Blood rings: Large red rubies set in silver with markings of the Old Ones

Boca: a covered wagon pulled by horses

Book of Tandum: an ancient book of plagues created by the Sisterhood

Box of Itifer: a gift to the world of man from The Great Ruler; this gift affects the balance of creation

Bozie: a game of skill played by the Nordes Tribe

Calphy: an ancient art form from Ryed

Cava plant: a poisonous plant that grows freely near bodies of water

Centras: ancient race of creatures who have the responsibility of protecting the Holy Box of Itifer

Cerfic: an ancient language widely spoken among many kingdoms/a language of the masses not royalty

Chalice of Ascension: a gift from The Great Ruler, this gift contains unimaginable powers

Charto: the most radical political faction in the Kingdom of Inferus

Cheyweg: the ancient language of the Village of Tameric in the Kingdom of Marba

Cicero College: in Wetpr, outside of Salar, where Raul, Simon and Hannah attended college

Clan of Gesmal: a tribe of demon hunters who live in the southern region of the Kingdom of Ryed

Code of Denark: the ancient code hidden within the Cerfic language

Credo: a secret group in Inferus who worship The Great Ruler

Crystal pillars: in the Ice Caves of Mordv/are blessed by The Great Ruler and filled with spiritual life force

Cyrus cloth: an ancient cloth made in Ryed

Czarsta: one of seven continents in the World of Nunc

Daliosis Demons: an ancient species of demon that lives underground in lairs

Danger Card: Elod slang for a person's trigger

Demalogs: an inferior species of demons

Demosa: a slow acting poison from the cava plant

Diamond of Cazo: a gift from The Great Ruler, this gift can unleash powers from the center of the world

Dirtx: one of the eight worlds in the Naz Solar System in the Mensor Galaxy

Discedo Sect: a radical sect of the Insidiae

Durisks: large demonic birds/their elongated beaks contain rows of fangs

Ekel Beast: similar to a deer

Elods: a race of people who live in the center of the World of Nunc in the Kingdom of Inferus

Engas: a wild cat that inhabits the Vandrew Mountains

Engor: a small pack animal that lives in trees

Enot: a demonic unit of measurement comparable to 1.5 inches

Enrop: a large species of bird that can speak many human languages

Epocos: one of the original tribes in the Kingdom of Ryed

Eto: a sub race of beings in the Kingdom of Inferus. They are all seductresses

Farduth: a Shettee necklace that symbolizes a male has completed his rite of passage to become a warrior

Filsum: the sixth planet in the Astrum Solar System/ two moons

Florines: a brightly colored species of bird that lives in the Kingdom of Inferus

Frebre: one of five solar systems in the Mensor Galaxy

Fuln: one of the eight worlds in the Naz Solar System in the Mensor Galaxy

Gafet: an ancient Shettee weapon

Gafferd: a type of demon created by the dark lord Gilder of the Kingdom of Inferus

Gamay: an ancient language that was once popular in the lower kingdoms of Opots

Gants: large apelike creatures/Watchers of the Caves of Muldun

Gartose: demons that resemble huge cats but with wings and protruding teeth

Gate of Isula: the only opening in the great Wall of Dorath

Gefrey Games: games of sport where men fight each other and great beasts to the death

Grand Masters: the first people to call to the demons and invite them into this world

Great Ruler: God

Half-Mans: a tribe of creatures that are partially human and partially nature. They are three feet tall and walk on two legs but can change their coloring to match their environment.

Hall of Antiquities: a giant hall located in the monastery at Malga/ a sanctuary for holy items and manuscripts

Hall of Light: the Great Hall in the Ice Caves of Mordv

Halrut: an herb commonly found in the Kingdom of Stordt/used to help people sleep/

Hells Wrath: the ship that Tessa Demat travels in from Port Friada to Langer

Hengers: giant blue eagles/ birds of war

Highland Pass: the only passage through the Rosu Mountain Range

Holy Scrolls: gifts given to each kingdom by The Great Ruler, these gifts contain powers, wisdom and immortality

Holy Vault: a secret vault under the King's study in the castle in Wetpr designed to protect holy objects

Horn of Asher: a horn used by the Patronus warrior priests to signal each other

Horn of Cass: a horn used by the Wetprian soldiers to signal each other

Horn of Cornwell: a horn used by Dieter's men to signal each other

Horn of Eel: a horn used by the Ruala warriors to communicate with each other

Horn of Esker: a horn used by the Valdore Tribe to communicate with each other

Horn of Ire: a horn carried by the Taperian soldiers to communicate with each other

Horn of Shana: a horn carried by the soldiers of Lentz to communicate with each other

Horn of Tula: a horn used by the members of the Nordes Tribe for communication

Horn of Vamont: a horn used by the Kozach Tribe for communication

Horn of Xepoltr: a horn used by the Shettee warriors to communicate

Huta: a race of humans that is driven by hatred and ideas of racial superiority who live in the Kingdom of Marba

Insidiae: means conspirators/a highly organized secret group of humans who have sold their souls to demons

Ipac seed: a highly poisonous seed not found in the World of Nunc

Irtma: one of the eight worlds in the Naz Solar System in the Mensor Galaxy

Jacar: giant leech-like creatures

Jacept Plant: a plant that a powerful poison is made from

Jaze: one of the eight worlds in the Naz Solar System in the Mensor Galaxy

Juntos: Talismans of black magic that Karzman would use to terrorize and weaken his opponents

Kafer: a small crescent shaped knife carried by the Beltrad

Keepers of the Scrolls: the Royal Family of the Kingdom of Wetpr entered into a covenant with The Great Ruler to protect his gifts until a time when they can be safely given back to the world of man

Keno: a demonic unit of measurement comparable to 13 inches

Kier: one of five solar systems in the Mensor Galaxy

Kinsman: the capital city of the planet Sidus

Kozach: a tribe that lives in the far north central regions of the Kingdom of Wetpr

Lafz: one of five solar systems in the Mensor Galaxy

Lamsman: an ankle bracelet worn by Venatores/stones in the bracelet signify great feats they had to accomplish to become a demon hunter

Learning Center: the first of its kind/a complex educational facility that is open to multiple peoples and guards the students and staff from terrorists

Leaves of the Talamar plant: used for food and medicine but also used in black magics to alter people's senses and to create illusions of the mind-in small quantities/ in large quantities can effect time/

Libertas: the name of a group of freedom fighters in northern Ryed

Linges plant: a plant that grows in damp, swampy regions in Opots/the white berries are used to make the drug Melanwhop

Lithanize: an ancient language common to the southern kingdoms of Opots.

Lynswood: an herb that reveals tracks that are concealed by black magic

Mark of Satan: a coiled red snake with green eyes and a yellow tongue

Matu potage: a food staple of the Shettee Tribe

Mayka: one of seven continents in the World of Nunc

Melanwhop: a drug made from the linges plant, causes lethargy and apathy

Mensor Galaxy: is 20,000 light years from the Astrum Solar System/this galaxy contains five solar systems: Adros, Kier, Lafz, Frebre and Naz

Menzine: a species of giant snake in the Kingdom of Inferus

Mordov: the special place in hell for hypocrites

Motfer: the land of the dead

Muysack: a huge flying beast from hell

Naz: one of five solar systems in the Mensor Galaxy/this solar system has eight worlds: Balterak, Nords, Jaze, Fuln, Backor, Dirtx, Irtma, Puner

Nefandus: a secret sect within the Insidiae

Nordes: a tribe of fiercely trained warriors who live in the northern region of the Kingdom of Lentz

Nords: one of the eight worlds in the Naz Solar System in the Mensor Galaxy

Nuberry Nuts: common to Ryed/used for medicinal purposed like poultices for snake bites/

Nunc: the world where this story takes place/third planet from the three suns

Old Ones: the original demons that came to the World of Nunc

Opatu bread: a food staple of the Shettee Tribe

Opots: one of seven continents in the World of Nunc/the continent where this story takes place

Oran: a tobisk that is filled with a mixture of ramni oil, buruto powder and meno salts, designed to explode on impact

Orantho: the seventh planet in the Astrum Solar System/inhabited/four moons/ large planet/many hell worlds

Patronus: an elite group of men who serve as the protectors of the church

Pfison screen: a type of demonic cloaking devise/it is sensitive and has to be calibrated for the specific individuals it is intended for

Planteen: the fourth planet in the Astrum Solar System/inhabited/two moons

Plyogram: a drawing containing pictures within pictures to hide secret messages.

Porto: one of seven continents in the World of Nunc

Prophesy of Isto: an ancient prophesy of the Elods

Prophesy of Izera: Predicts the downfall of the Teivel regime

Prophesy of the Blood Moon: a demonic prophesy that predicts the doors to hell being opened.

Propilatry: a powerful form of demonic curse

Prostras: an ancient tribe that once inhabited the Ice Caves of Mordv

Puner: one of the eight worlds in the Naz Solar System in the Mensor Galaxy

Raftifa: ancient bat-like creatures that devour human flesh

Rappal demon: a lower level demon with slimy skin and an unusual smell

Ravens: messengers used by the dark lords

Recupero: a sect within the Insidiae that worships the demon Omnibus

Rites of Purification: an ancient ritual to close the windows of the demons

Rogetts: a tribe of humans that have digressed into murderous mutant monsters

Rualas: an ancient tribe of warriors said to be half human and half bird

Ryisone: a sedative

Salszar: one of seven continents in the World of Nunc

Salts of Envoy: a sleeping potion

Schumack roots: used for food and medicine but also used in black magics to alter people's senses and to create illusions of the mind-in small quantities/ in large quantities can effect time/

Scio: a crystal ball

Scroll of Imari: a gift of The Great Ruler, a scroll that unleashes the power of The Box of Itifer

Seal of Natun: a gift from The Holy Ruler that can open doors to other worlds

Second Sons: men bred to become vessels for demons

Serpents of Satan: can only be called forth by dark lords and demons, large red snakes with green eyes and yellow tongues

Seven Sons Prophesy: an ancient prophesy about seven sons who stand up against the demons and dark lords

Shadow Men: creature that can only be seen when illuminated at night

Shaker Winds: incredible storms that form when the currents and winds of three oceans converge

Shamac: the most commonly spoken language in the Continent of Opots

Shesone: an ancient fighting style of the Shettee Tribe

Shettee: an ancient tribe of warriors said to be half human and half lion

Sidus: the fifth planet in the Astrum Solar System/inhabited/red fog surrounds the planet

Solv: a specific prison within the Abyss

Song of the Second Son: an ancient prophesy about an evil that is passed between second son's of a family resulting in a monster that brings terror and darkness to the world of man

Stratas: Creatures bred by the Elods

Sundra Templer: a gift from The Great Ruler that was stolen by dark lords/an orb with extraordinary powers that can be used in multiple ways such as transporting humans through other worlds

Tabutu: an ancient form of fighting developed by the Asherane Tribe of the Kingdom of Lentz

Tagnit Trilogy: a group of three spell books that are so powerful they have living powers

Talisman: an object with magical or supernatural meaning

Talmuth: giant red dragon-like creatures

Talus paper: a strong but almost transparent paper

Taluth: a light weight metal used to make the ancient Shettee weapons called the Gafets

Tameric: the place where Karzman claims he came from although it does not exist on any map of Opots/also the name of the collective hell worlds of Nunc

Tangers: large wild, grazing animals that travel in herds

Tansof: one of seven continents in the World of Nunc

Tarus demon: huge, power creatures that walk on two legs but have the head, neck and shoulders of an ox

Telgras: a hell beast that looks like it is half wolf and half panther

Teragon: death terror/a monster created as a result of diabolical acts

Terbot bear: a bear that roams in the northern regions of the continent of Opots

Tervator: fourteen foot monster that walks like a man with long dark hair over its entire body and bull-like horns protruding from its head

Texts of Semalia: ancient texts about demonic language and rituals

The Boldface: Admiral Gideon's ship

The Book of Horror: a book that is worshipped by demons/contains prophesies

The Celebration of Days: an annual celebration of the Centras

The Dead Runner: ship of the notorious pirate Axel Sam

The Hall of Knowledge: the primary meeting room in the Temple of the Abuckto in the Kingdom of Inferus

The Hall of Understanding: the building in Astras where the history of the Centras is documented in drawings

The Hunters: another name for the Shettee Tribe

The Lion: a very powerful messenger of The Great Ruler assumes the form of a lion when he walks in the worlds of man

The Tempest: a clandestine organization made up of witches and warlocks

The Thirteenth Color: not seen in the world of man it is the color of horror/hell

Thresiose: a knife used in demonic ceremonies

Timbar: ghost dragons/ demons that can fly

Tinchure water: an herbal pain remedy used by the Nordes Tribe

Tincture of the Redeti Plant: Hutas dip the tips of their weapons in this insect infested liquid. The insects lay eggs inside of the victim. When the eggs are mature and hatch, two inch worm-like creatures are produced and will eat the organs of the victim causing a long and painful death

Tobisks: sphere shaped objects, metal and hollow inside that are designed to be launched from a Trebuchet

Tramor: a flying monster in the Kingdom of Inferus

Traxsor: the second planet in the Astrum Solar System

Trebuchets: wooden machines used to catapult objects

Trimoth: a game of skill, strength and speed

Triolie: a Nordes gambling game

Tropaion: a grouping of trophies

Twanize: a language common to the Continent of Porto

Tygrus: a ship that docked in Port Friada

Unholy altar: altar used to worship demons

Valdees: the tribe that lives in the underwater Kingdom of Ogg

Valdore: a tribe of merciless separatists who live in the extreme northern regions of the Kingdom of Lentz

Velvadera: purgatory

Venator: means hunter in the old language

Venom of the Atha serpent: one of the poisons that Hutas put on their arrows

Vessel of Darkness: a human created from darkness to hold the essence of a powerful demon

Vue: a flute-like instrument used in the Kingdom of Inferus

Wall of Dorath: a giant wall that separates the Kingdoms of Norkv and Xepoltr from the Kingdom of Marba

Willimonns: small furry creatures that are hunted for food and sport

Xelope: the oneness of spirit with all that lives

Yellow head snake: a very poisonous snake found in the swamps of Ryed

Yellow Jay: a bird native to Opots

Yellow Mandeze: a song bird common to Opots

Zehno demon: thin, creature with long red and blue plumes on the back of its head with large eyes and round mouths

Zendoti: demons that are distinguished by the geometrically shaped tuffs of hair that protrude from their heads

Glossary of Maps

The maps are displayed in order of relevance

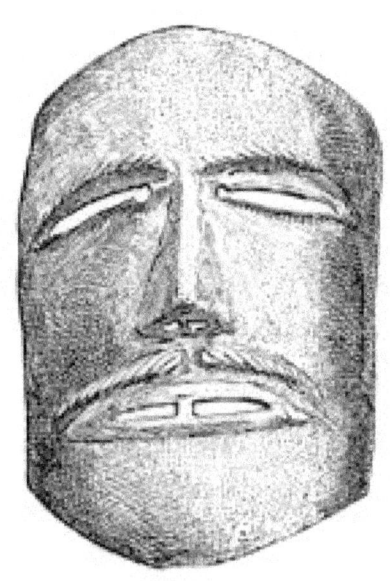

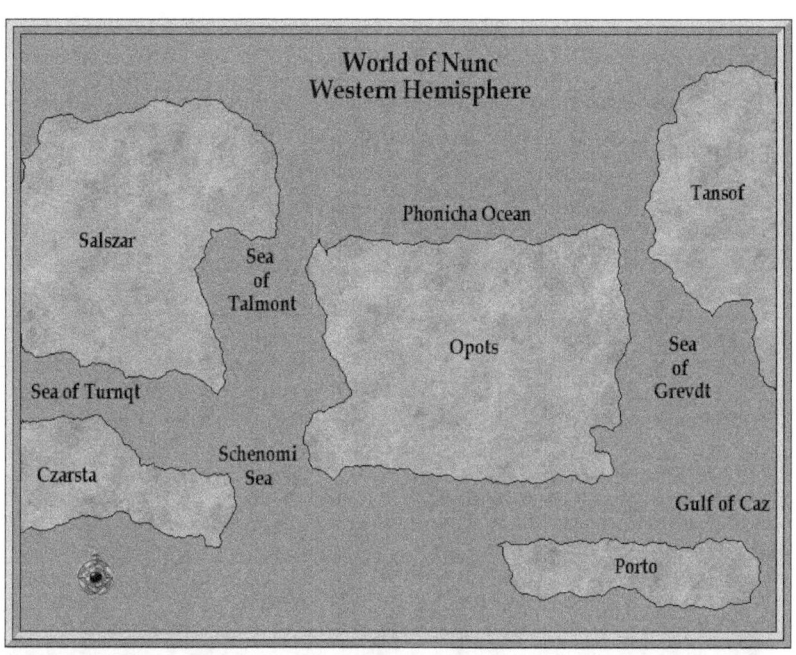

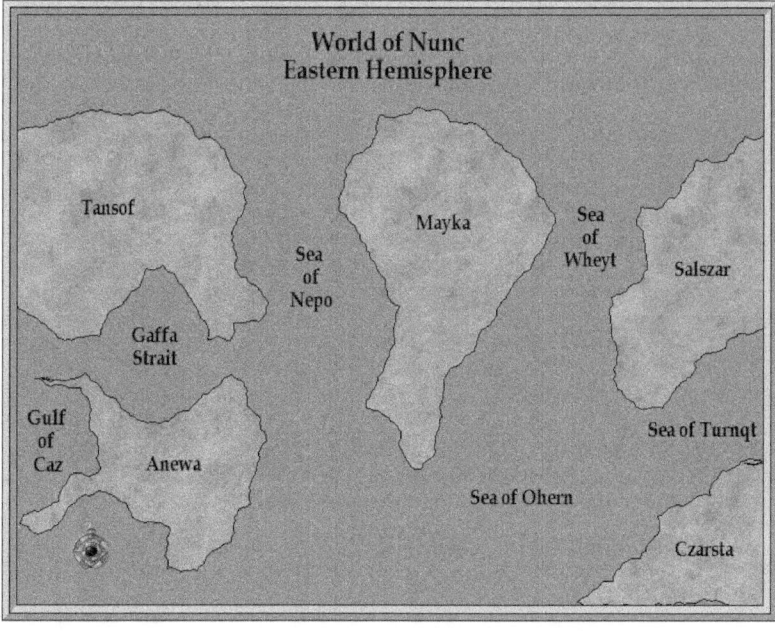

Continent of Opots
With new forts

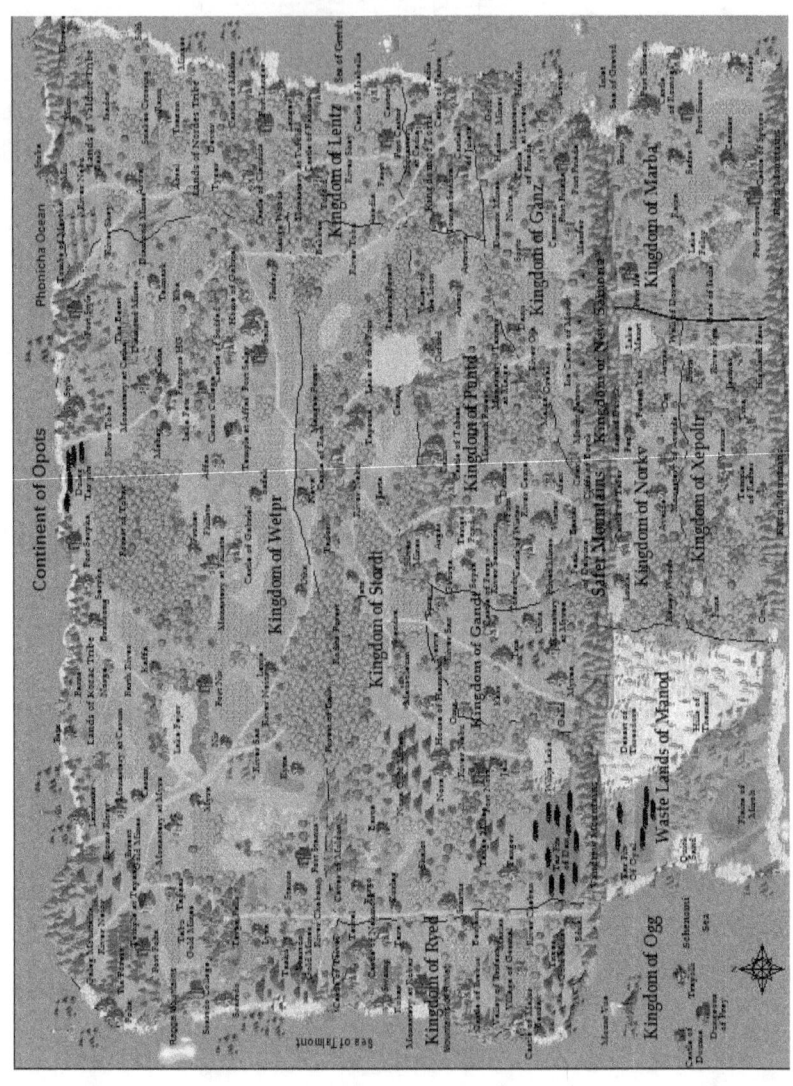

666

Western Stordt
With Fort Nora

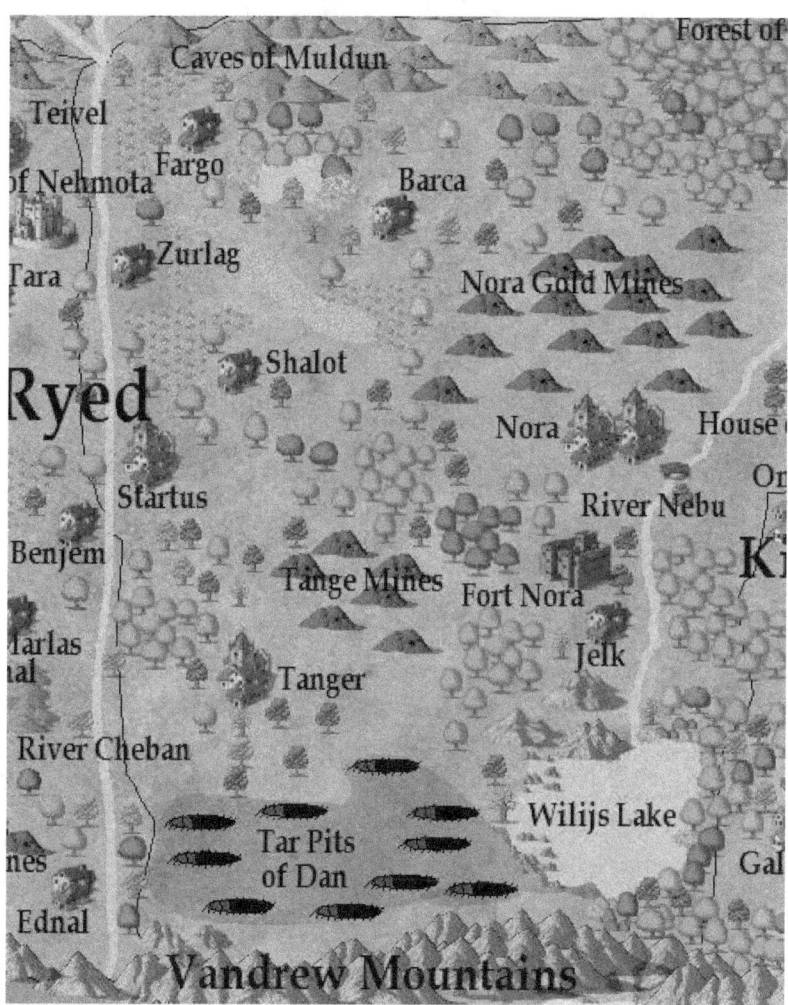

Northern Stordt

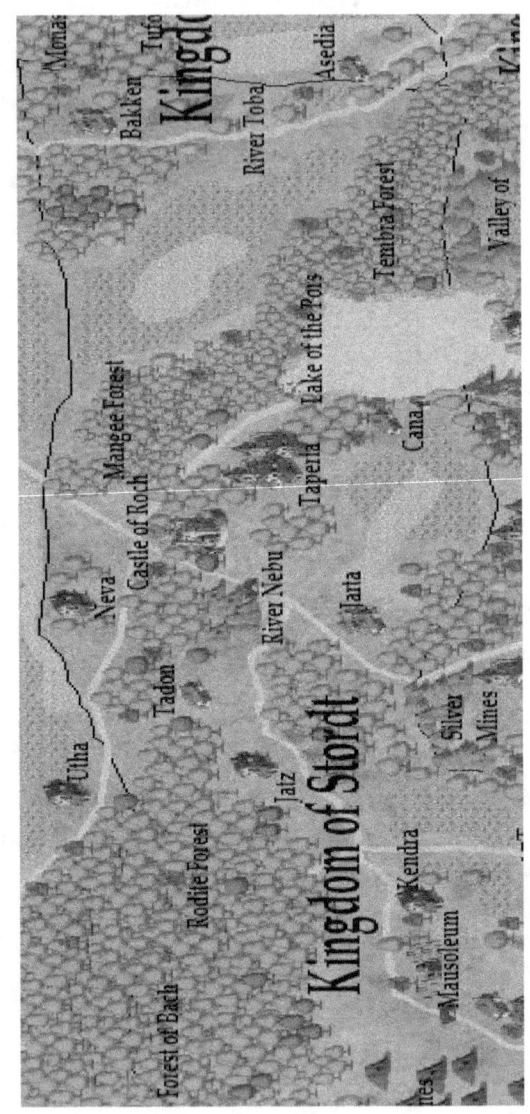

Western Wetpr
With Fort Stanus

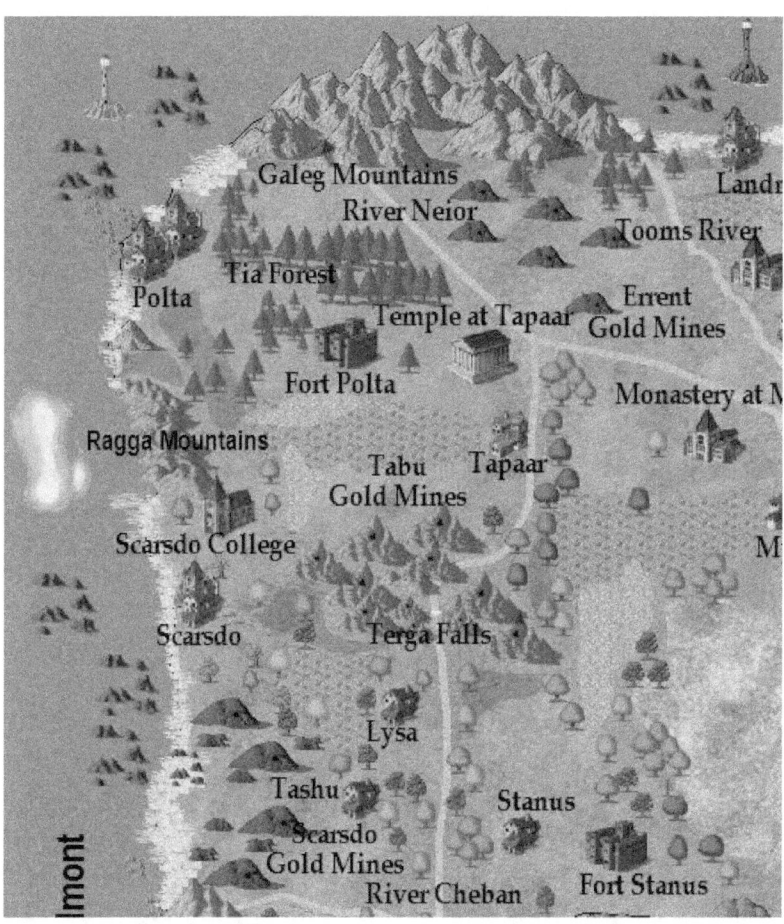

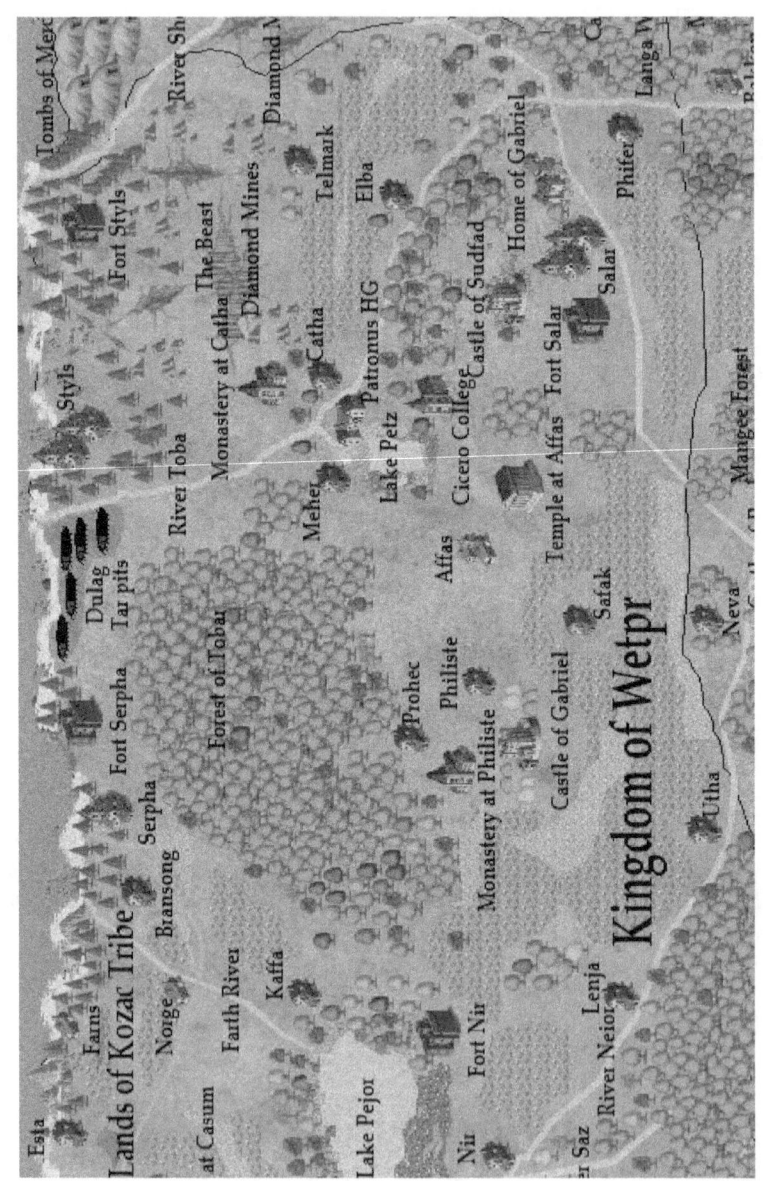

Northern Lentz

Marba

Safer Mountains
Peak of Delpine
Czar
Cliffs of Borck
Mount Petrov
Kingdom of New Sa
Pass of Duvuk
Lake Manrt
Astras
Wall of D
Gate
River Kya
Highland Pass
Forest Yar
Ort
Zorts
Jasmer
Castle of Tafer
Paz
Uma
Kingdom of Norkv
Avaide
Monastery of Avaide
Kingdom of Xepoltr
Vamur
Temple of Rafter
Lomai
Keiser Woods
Rosu Mountains
Puna
Ott

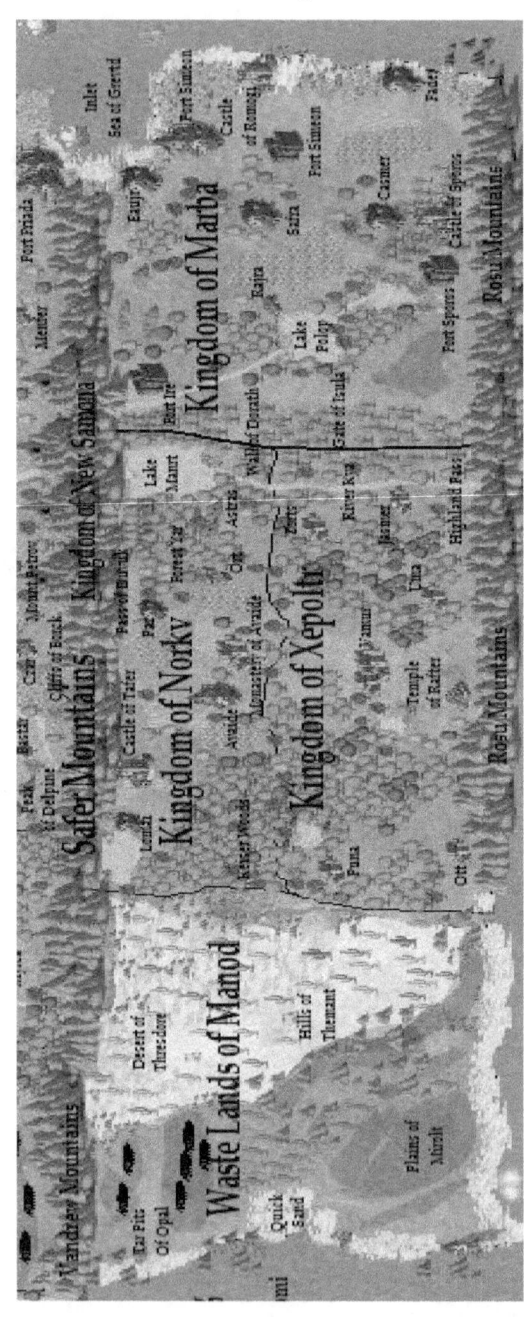

New Samona
Ice Caves of Mordv

678

Astrum Solar System

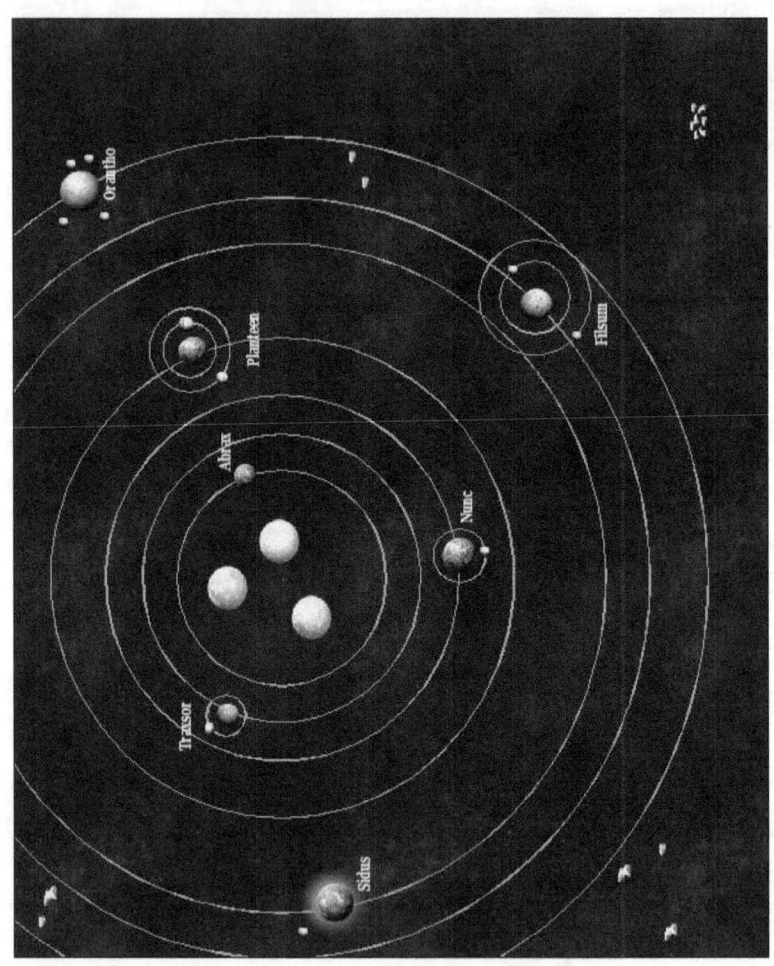

www.ingramcontent.com/pod-product-compliance
Lightning Source LLC
Chambersburg PA
CBHW052339020726
47503CB00001B/24